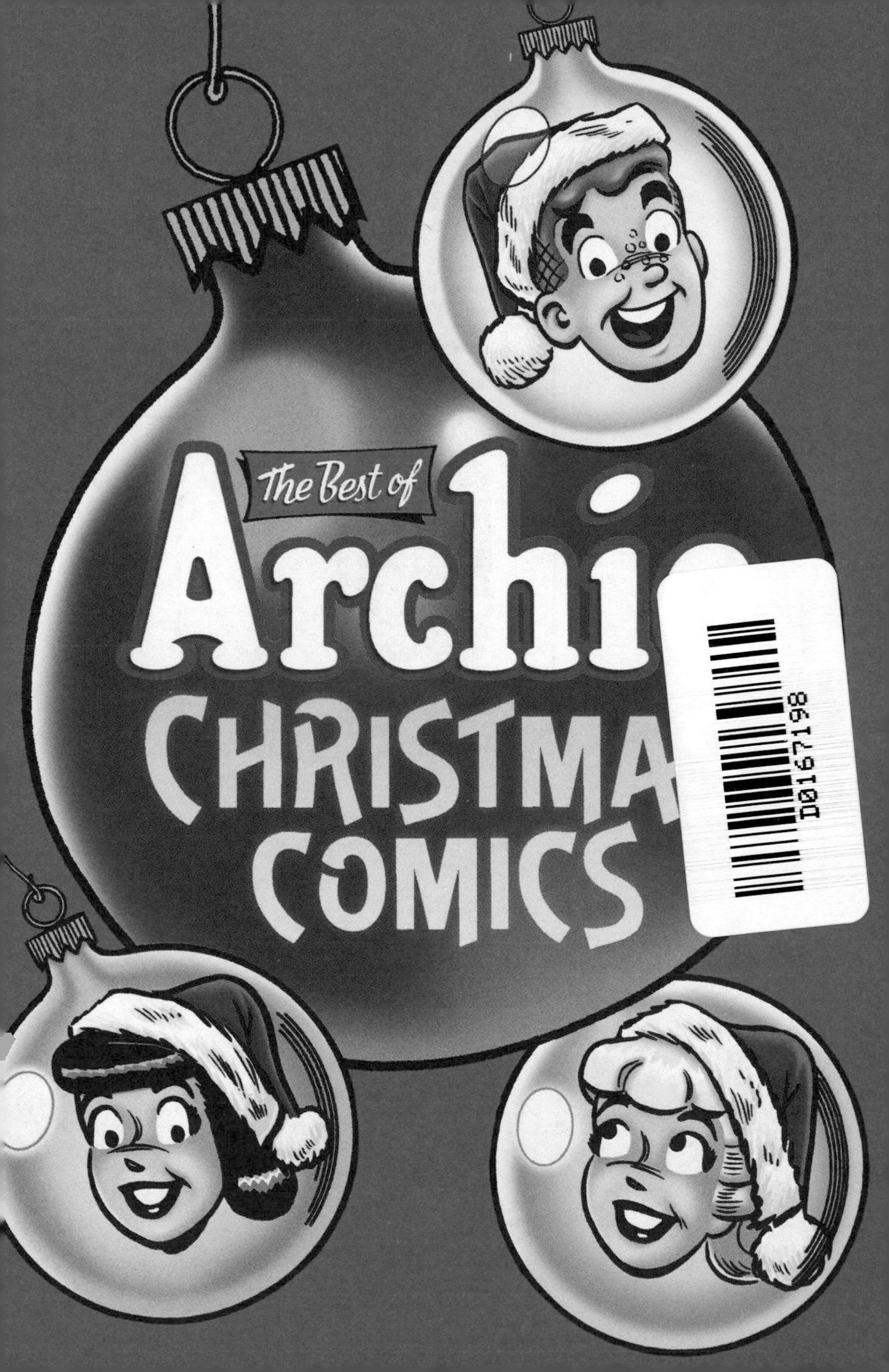
The Best of
Archie
CHRISTMAS
COMICS

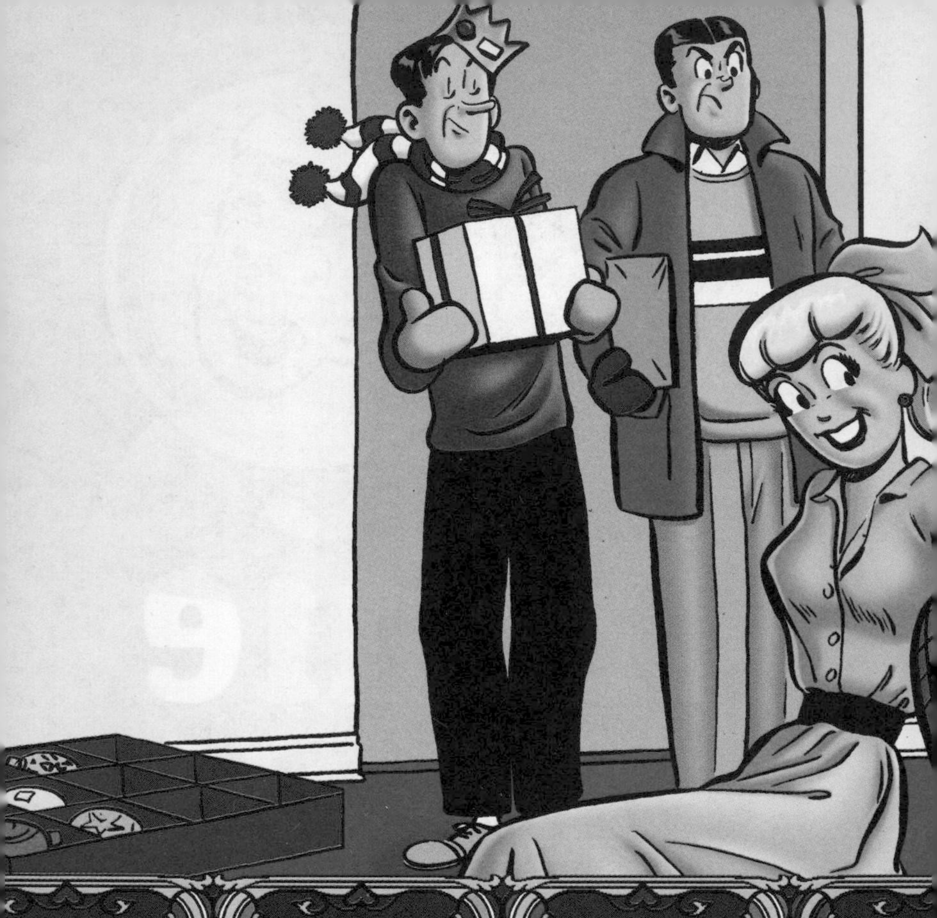

FEATURING THE TALENTS OF:

Frank Doyle, Bob White, Bill Vigoda, Terry Szenics, Barry Grossman, Dan DeCarlo, Rudy Lapick, Vince DeCarlo, George Gladir, Samm Schwartz, Jon D'Agostino, Bill Yoshida, Harry Lucey, Marty Epp, Jimmy DeCarlo, Stan Goldberg, Dick Malmgren, Bob Bolling, Dan DeCarlo Jr., Kathleen Webb, Hy Eisman, Hal Smith, Henry Scarpelli, Jeff Shultz, Mike Pellowski, Dan Parent, Bill Galvan, Bob Smith, Glenn Whitmore, Jack Morelli, Angelo DeCesare, Pat & Tim Kennedy, Rosario "Tito" Peña

Published by Archie Comic Publications, Inc. 629 Fifth Avenue, Suite 100, Pelham, NY 10803-1242.

Printed in Canada. First Printing. ISBN: 978-1-64576-954-5

Jon Goldwater Publisher / Co-CEO

Victor Gorelick Co-President / Editor-In-Chief

Mike Pellerito Co-President

Alex Segura Co-President

Roberto Aguirre-Sacasa Chief Creative Officer

William Mooar Chief Operating Officer

Robert Wintle Chief Financial Officer

Jonathan Betancourt Director

Stephen Oswald Production Manager

Kari McLachlan Lead Designer

Jamie Lee Rotante Editor

Carlos Antunes Associate Editor

Nancy Silberkleit Co-CEO

THE HOLIDAYS COME TO RIVERDALE!

Tis the season to be jolly—and who could be anything but jolly with Archie, Betty, Veronica, Jughead, and all the pals 'n' gals from Riverdale?

The holidays are a time of giving, togetherness, and cheer—but when Archie gets thrown into the mix, get ready for some festive foul-ups and merry mayhem on top of the Christmas tree! This collection of the best and brightest holiday stories has been lovingly hand-picked and restored for this chronological collection that's sure to get you into the Christmas spirit!

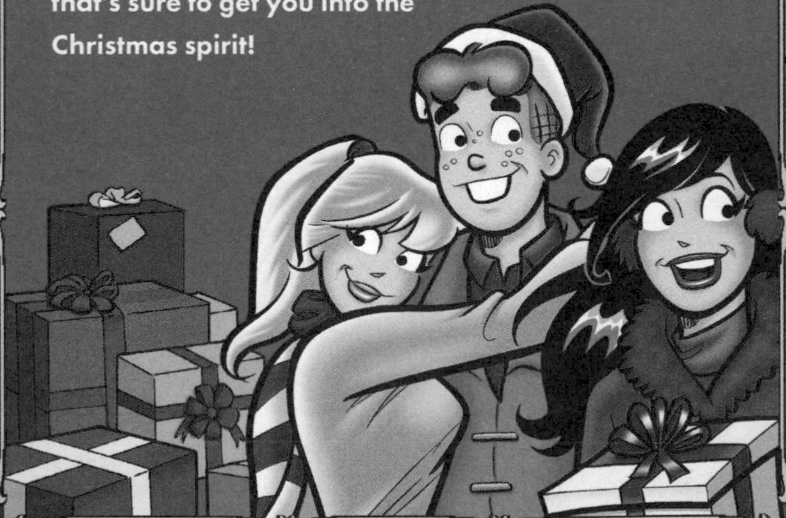

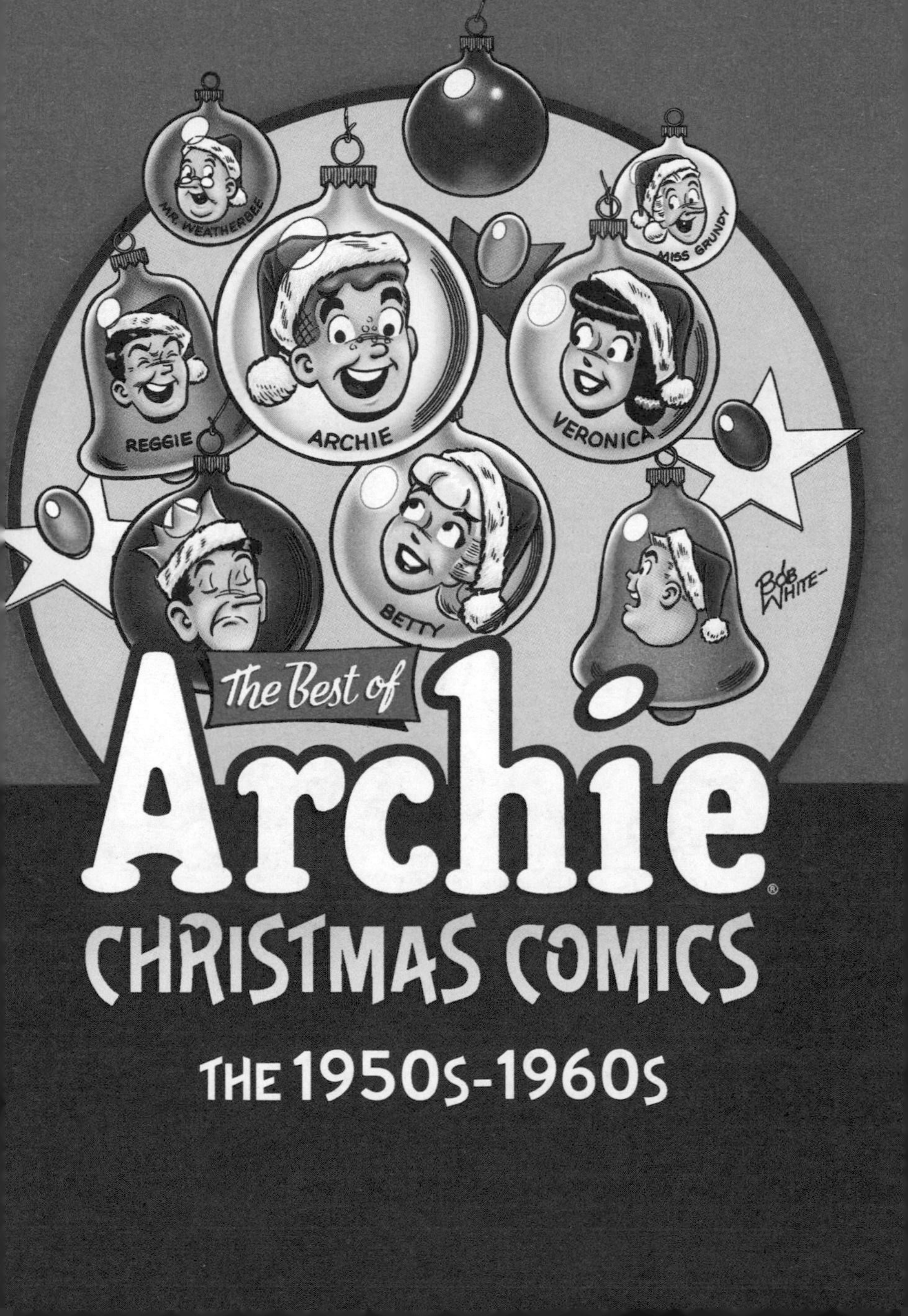
MR. WEATHERBEE
MISS GRUNDY
REGGIE
ARCHIE
VERONICA
BETTY
BOB WHITE

The Best of Archie® Christmas Comics

The 1950s–1960s

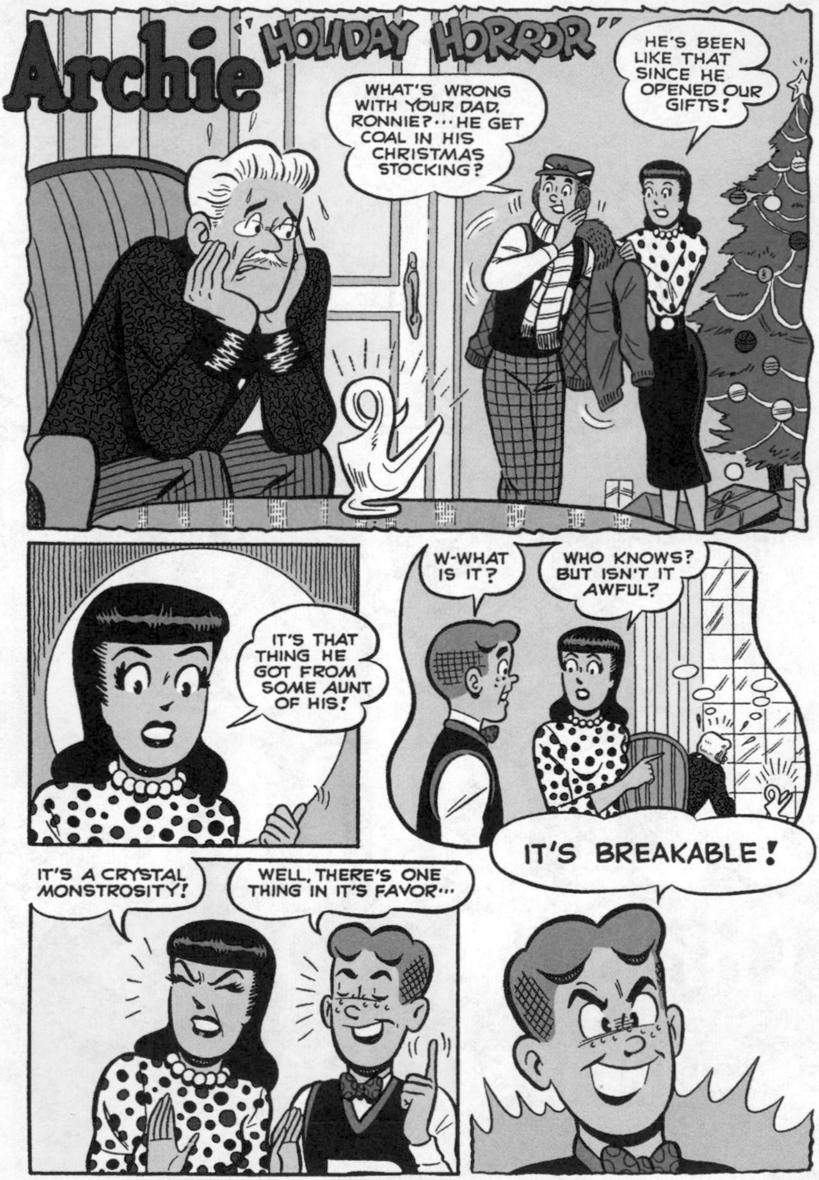
Archie
"HOLIDAY HORROR"
WHAT'S WRONG WITH YOUR DAD, RONNIE?... HE GET COAL IN HIS CHRISTMAS STOCKING?
HE'S BEEN LIKE THAT SINCE HE OPENED OUR GIFTS!
IT'S THAT THING HE GOT FROM SOME AUNT OF HIS!
W-WHAT IS IT?
WHO KNOWS? BUT ISN'T IT AWFUL?
IT'S A CRYSTAL MONSTROSITY!
WELL, THERE'S ONE THING IN IT'S FAVOR...
IT'S BREAKABLE!

• **From Archie #98, Feb 1959** •

Frank Doyle • Bob White

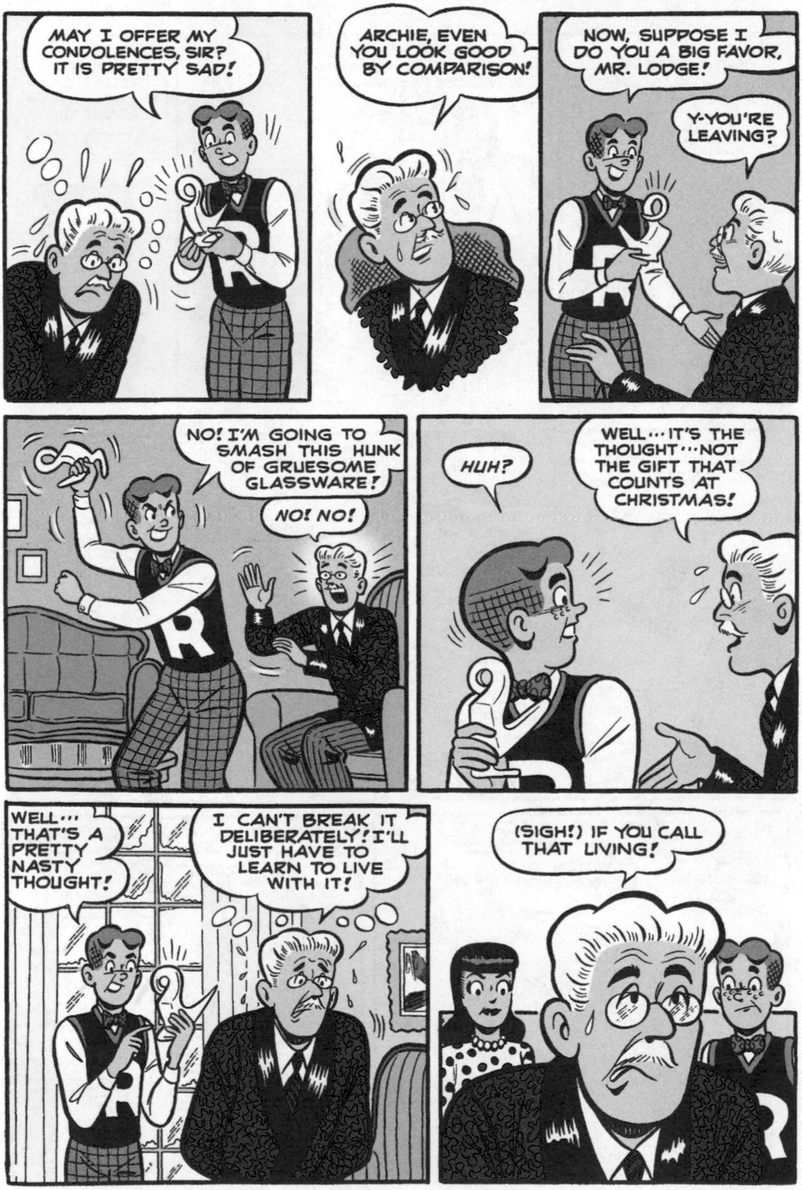
MAY I OFFER MY CONDOLENCES, SIR? IT IS PRETTY SAD!
ARCHIE, EVEN YOU LOOK GOOD BY COMPARISON!
NOW, SUPPOSE I DO YOU A BIG FAVOR, MR. LODGE!
Y-YOU'RE LEAVING?
NO! I'M GOING TO SMASH THIS HUNK OF GRUESOME GLASSWARE!
NO! NO!
HUH?
WELL... IT'S THE THOUGHT... NOT THE GIFT THAT COUNTS AT CHRISTMAS!
WELL... THAT'S A PRETTY NASTY THOUGHT!
I CAN'T BREAK IT DELIBERATELY! I'LL JUST HAVE TO LEARN TO LIVE WITH IT!
(SIGH!) IF YOU CALL THAT LIVING!

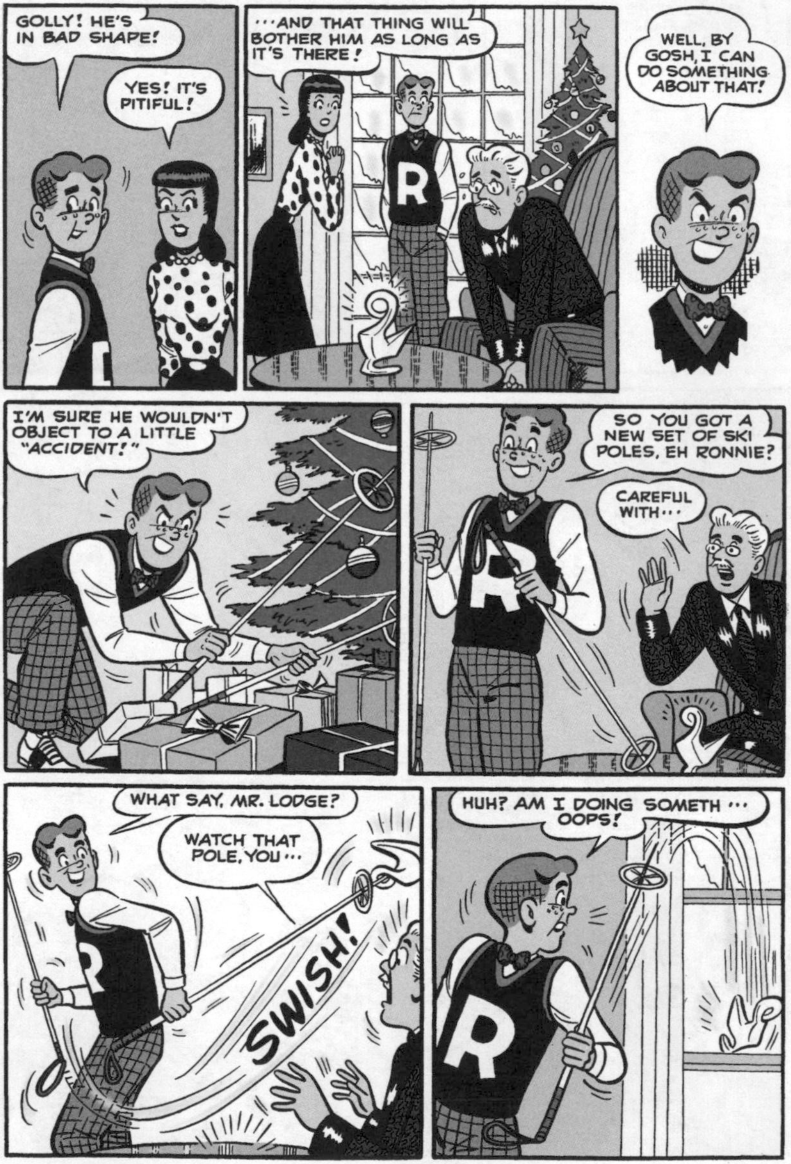
GOLLY! HE'S IN BAD SHAPE!
YES! IT'S PITIFUL!
...AND THAT THING WILL BOTHER HIM AS LONG AS IT'S THERE!
WELL, BY GOSH, I CAN DO SOMETHING ABOUT THAT!
I'M SURE HE WOULDN'T OBJECT TO A LITTLE "ACCIDENT!"
SO YOU GOT A NEW SET OF SKI POLES, EH RONNIE?
CAREFUL WITH...
WHAT SAY, MR. LODGE?
WATCH THAT POLE, YOU...
SWISH!
HUH? AM I DOING SOMETH... OOPS!

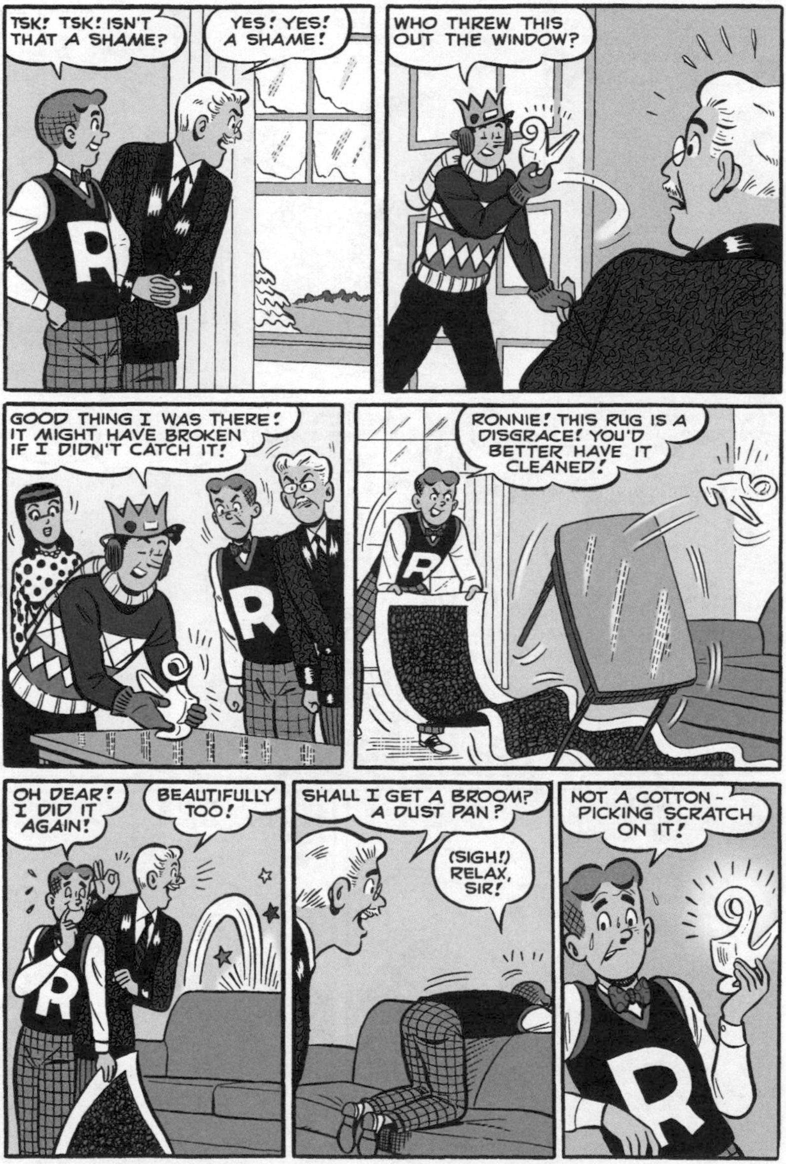
TSK! TSK! ISN'T THAT A SHAME?
YES! YES! A SHAME!
WHO THREW THIS OUT THE WINDOW?
GOOD THING I WAS THERE! IT MIGHT HAVE BROKEN IF I DIDN'T CATCH IT!
RONNIE! THIS RUG IS A DISGRACE! YOU'D BETTER HAVE IT CLEANED!
OH DEAR! I DID IT AGAIN!
BEAUTIFULLY TOO!
SHALL I GET A BROOM? A DUST PAN?
(SIGH!) RELAX, SIR!
NOT A COTTON-PICKING SCRATCH ON IT!

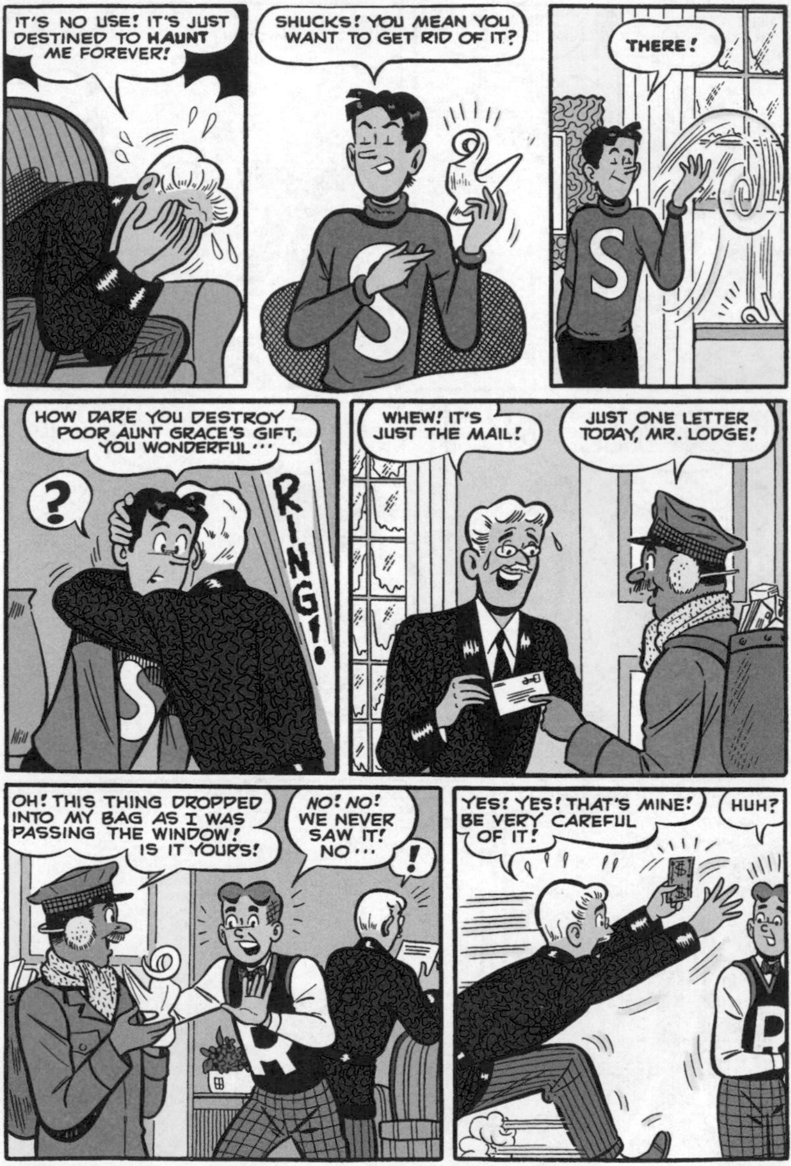
IT'S NO USE! IT'S JUST DESTINED TO HAUNT ME FOREVER!
SHUCKS! YOU MEAN YOU WANT TO GET RID OF IT?
THERE!
HOW DARE YOU DESTROY POOR AUNT GRACE'S GIFT, YOU WONDERFUL···
?
RING!!
WHEW! IT'S JUST THE MAIL!
JUST ONE LETTER TODAY, MR. LODGE!
OH! THIS THING DROPPED INTO MY BAG AS I WAS PASSING THE WINDOW! IS IT YOURS!
NO! NO! WE NEVER SAW IT! NO···
!
YES! YES! THAT'S MINE! BE VERY CAREFUL OF IT!
HUH?

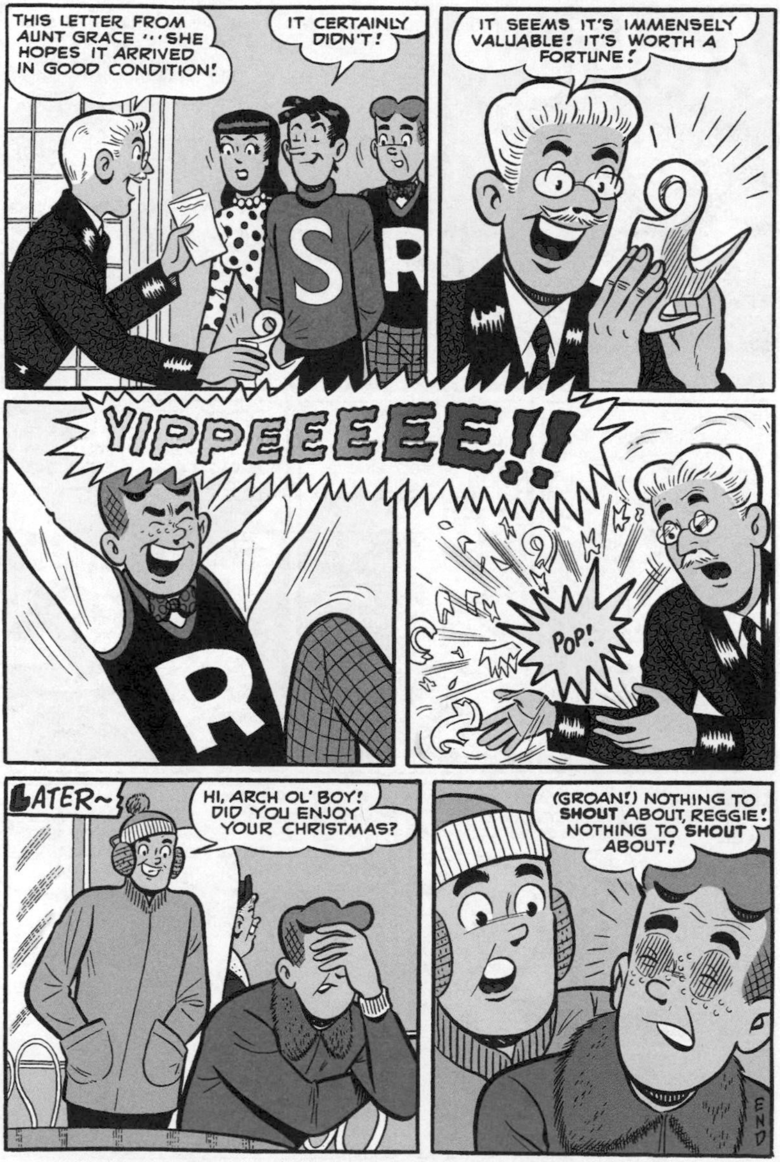
THIS LETTER FROM AUNT GRACE ··· SHE HOPES IT ARRIVED IN GOOD CONDITION!
IT CERTAINLY DIDN'T!
IT SEEMS IT'S IMMENSELY VALUABLE! IT'S WORTH A FORTUNE!
YIPPEEEEEE!!
POP!
LATER~
HI, ARCH OL' BOY! DID YOU ENJOY YOUR CHRISTMAS?
(GROAN!) NOTHING TO SHOUT ABOUT, REGGIE! NOTHING TO SHOUT ABOUT!
END

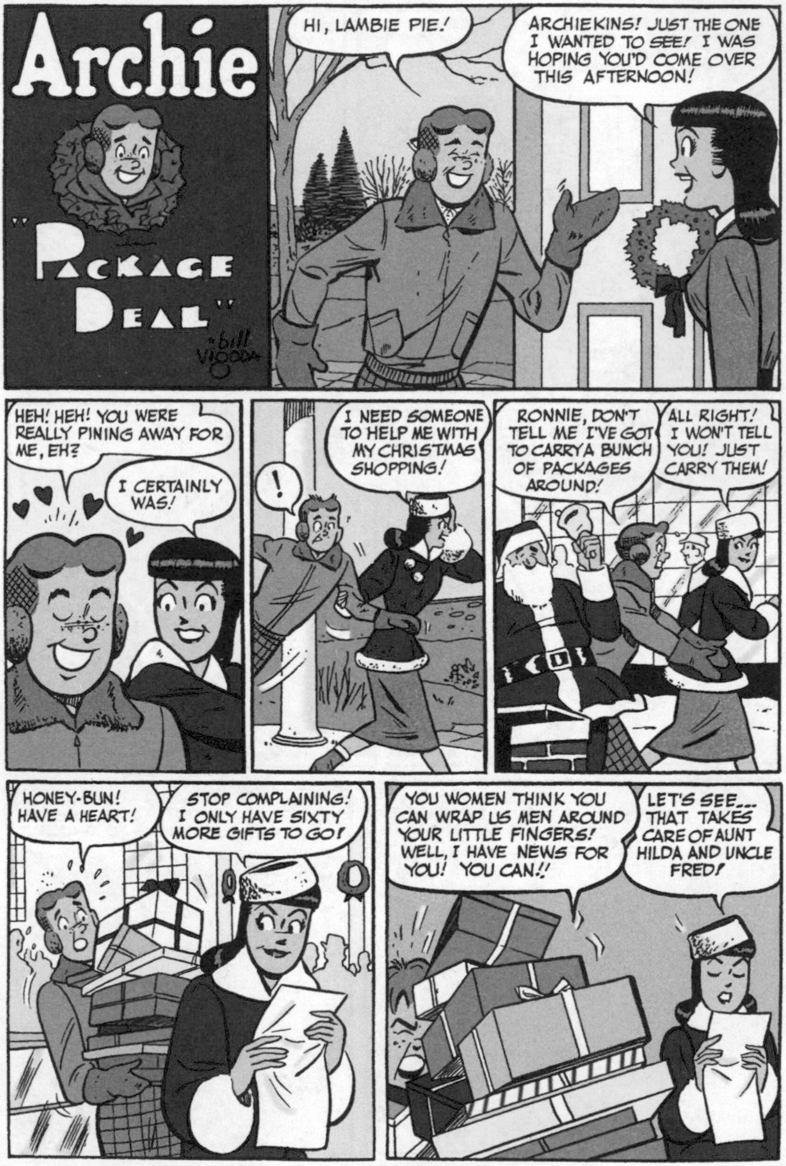
Archie
"Package Deal"
bill Vigoda
HI, LAMBIE PIE!
ARCHIEKINS! JUST THE ONE I WANTED TO SEE! I WAS HOPING YOU'D COME OVER THIS AFTERNOON!
HEH! HEH! YOU WERE REALLY PINING AWAY FOR ME, EH?
I CERTAINLY WAS!
I NEED SOMEONE TO HELP ME WITH MY CHRISTMAS SHOPPING!
!
RONNIE, DON'T TELL ME I'VE GOT TO CARRY A BUNCH OF PACKAGES AROUND!
ALL RIGHT! I WON'T TELL YOU! JUST CARRY THEM!
HONEY-BUN! HAVE A HEART!
STOP COMPLAINING! I ONLY HAVE SIXTY MORE GIFTS TO GO!
YOU WOMEN THINK YOU CAN WRAP US MEN AROUND YOUR LITTLE FINGERS! WELL, I HAVE NEWS FOR YOU! YOU CAN!!
LET'S SEE... THAT TAKES CARE OF AUNT HILDA AND UNCLE FRED!

• From Archie #98, Feb 1959 •

Bill Vigoda

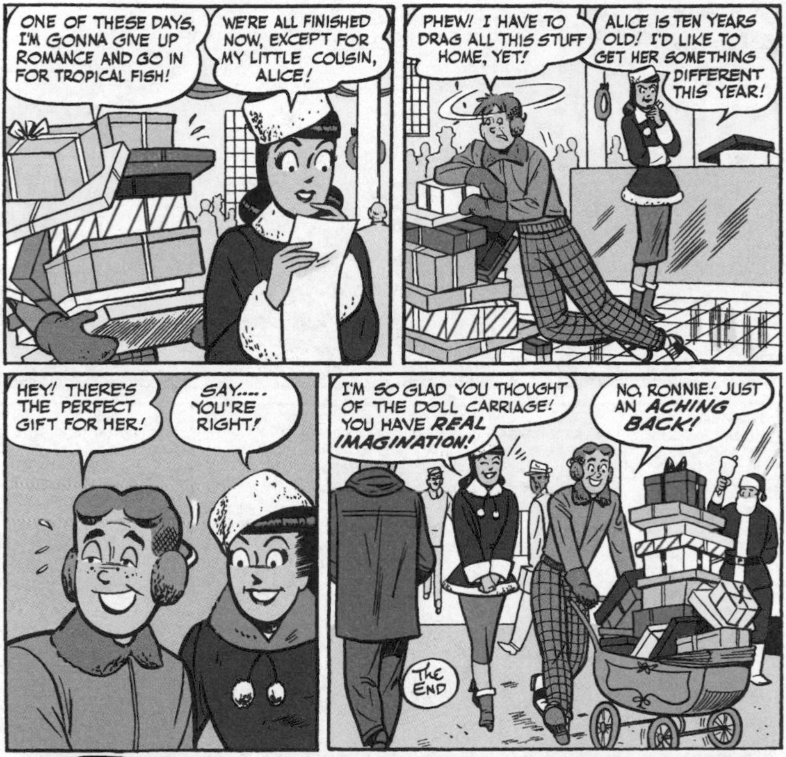
ONE OF THESE DAYS, I'M GONNA GIVE UP ROMANCE AND GO IN FOR TROPICAL FISH!
WE'RE ALL FINISHED NOW, EXCEPT FOR MY LITTLE COUSIN, ALICE!
PHEW! I HAVE TO DRAG ALL THIS STUFF HOME, YET!
ALICE IS TEN YEARS OLD! I'D LIKE TO GET HER SOMETHING DIFFERENT THIS YEAR!
HEY! THERE'S THE PERFECT GIFT FOR HER!
SAY..... YOU'RE RIGHT!
I'M SO GLAD YOU THOUGHT OF THE DOLL CARRIAGE! YOU HAVE *REAL IMAGINATION!*
NO, RONNIE! JUST AN *ACHING BACK!*
THE END

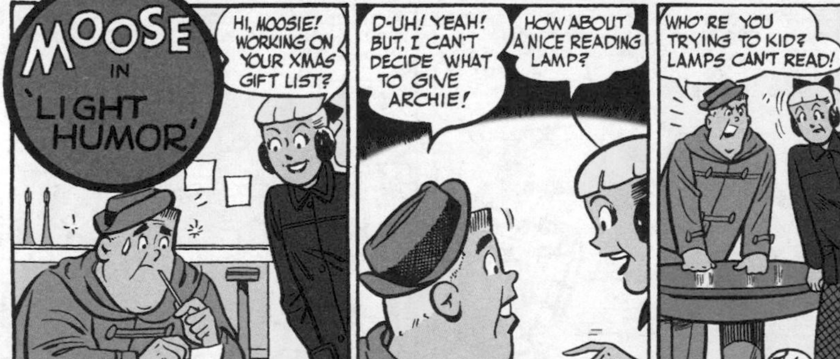
MOOSE IN 'LIGHT HUMOR'
HI, MOOSIE! WORKING ON YOUR XMAS GIFT LIST?
D-UH! YEAH! BUT, I CAN'T DECIDE WHAT TO GIVE ARCHIE!
HOW ABOUT A NICE READING LAMP?
WHO'RE YOU TRYING TO KID? LAMPS CAN'T READ!
THE END
2.

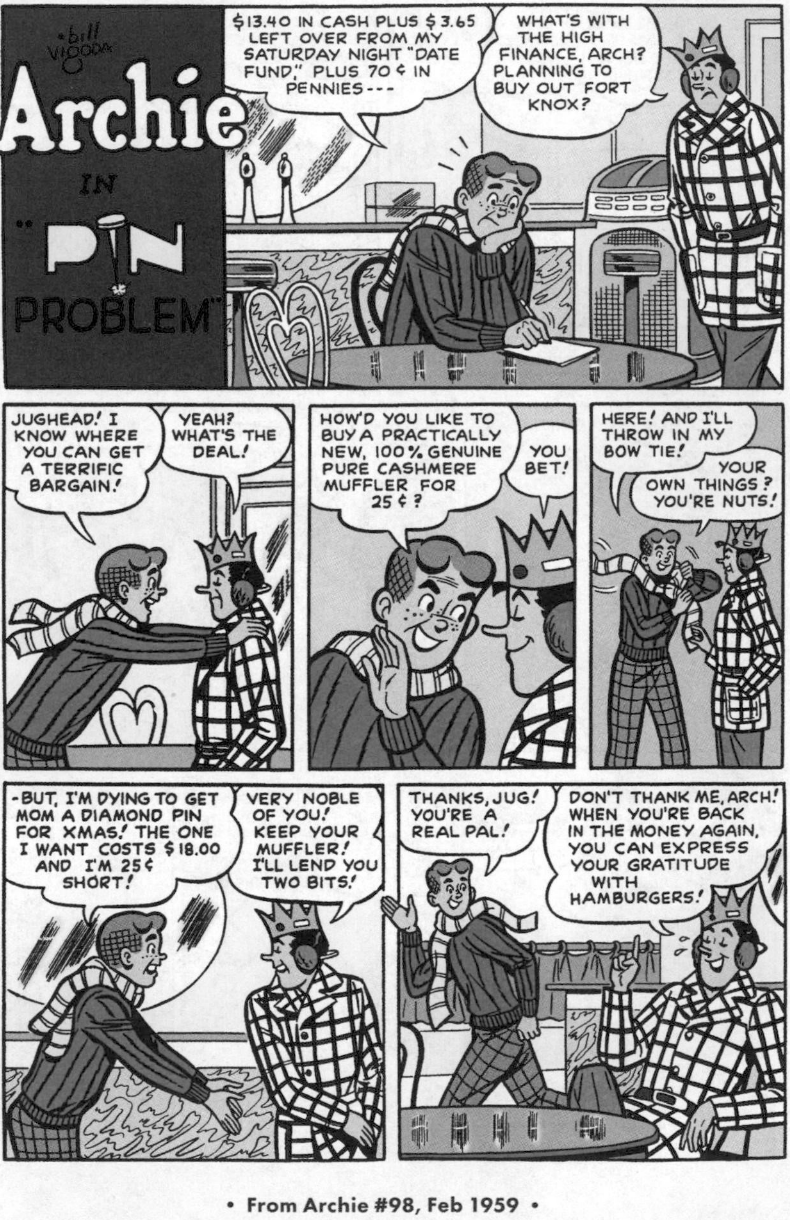
bill Vigoda
Archie
IN
"PIN PROBLEM"
$13.40 IN CASH PLUS $3.65 LEFT OVER FROM MY SATURDAY NIGHT "DATE FUND," PLUS 70¢ IN PENNIES---
WHAT'S WITH THE HIGH FINANCE, ARCH? PLANNING TO BUY OUT FORT KNOX?
JUGHEAD! I KNOW WHERE YOU CAN GET A TERRIFIC BARGAIN!
YEAH? WHAT'S THE DEAL!
HOW'D YOU LIKE TO BUY A PRACTICALLY NEW, 100% GENUINE PURE CASHMERE MUFFLER FOR 25¢?
YOU BET!
HERE! AND I'LL THROW IN MY BOW TIE!
YOUR OWN THINGS? YOU'RE NUTS!
-BUT, I'M DYING TO GET MOM A DIAMOND PIN FOR XMAS! THE ONE I WANT COSTS $18.00 AND I'M 25¢ SHORT!
VERY NOBLE OF YOU! KEEP YOUR MUFFLER! I'LL LEND YOU TWO BITS!
THANKS, JUG! YOU'RE A REAL PAL!
DON'T THANK ME, ARCH! WHEN YOU'RE BACK IN THE MONEY AGAIN, YOU CAN EXPRESS YOUR GRATITUDE WITH HAMBURGERS!

• From Archie #98, Feb 1959 •

Bill Vigoda

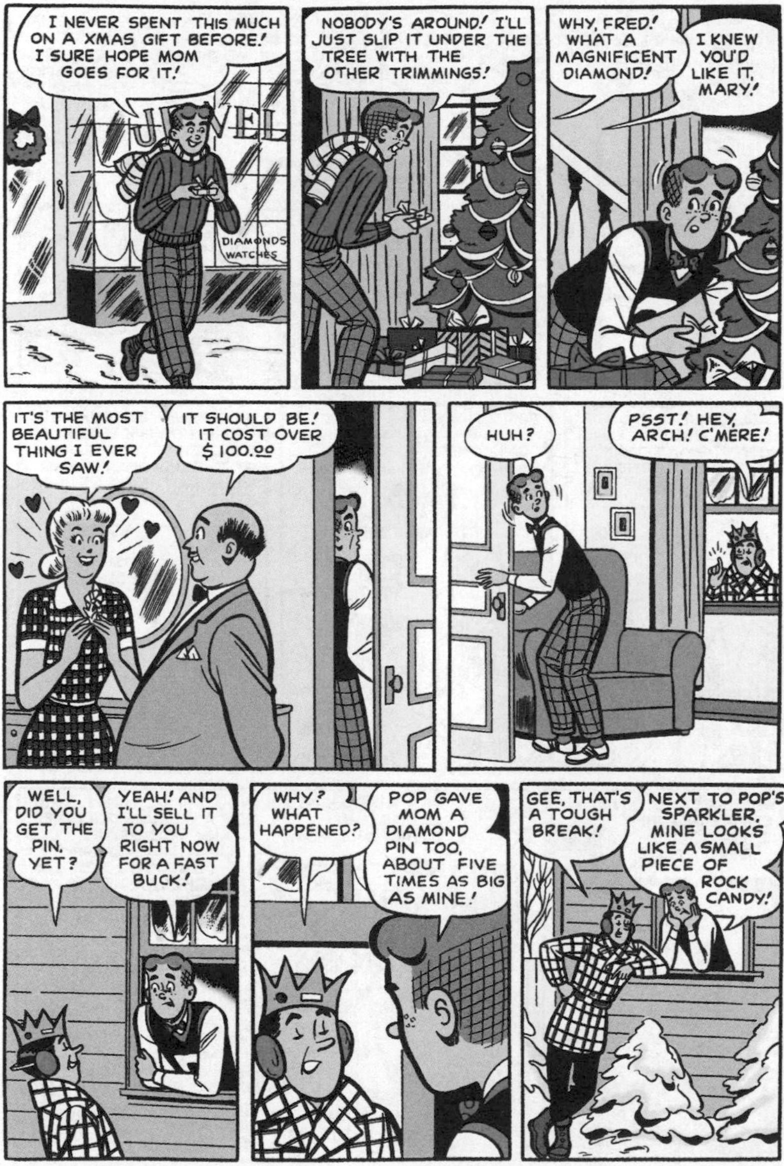
I NEVER SPENT THIS MUCH ON A XMAS GIFT BEFORE! I SURE HOPE MOM GOES FOR IT!
JEWEL
DIAMONDS WATCHES
NOBODY'S AROUND! I'LL JUST SLIP IT UNDER THE TREE WITH THE OTHER TRIMMINGS!
WHY, FRED! WHAT A MAGNIFICENT DIAMOND!
I KNEW YOU'D LIKE IT, MARY!
IT'S THE MOST BEAUTIFUL THING I EVER SAW!
IT SHOULD BE! IT COST OVER $100.00
HUH?
PSST! HEY, ARCH! C'MERE!
WELL, DID YOU GET THE PIN, YET?
YEAH! AND I'LL SELL IT TO YOU RIGHT NOW FOR A FAST BUCK!
WHY? WHAT HAPPENED?
POP GAVE MOM A DIAMOND PIN TOO, ABOUT FIVE TIMES AS BIG AS MINE!
GEE, THAT'S A TOUGH BREAK!
NEXT TO POP'S SPARKLER, MINE LOOKS LIKE A SMALL PIECE OF ROCK CANDY!

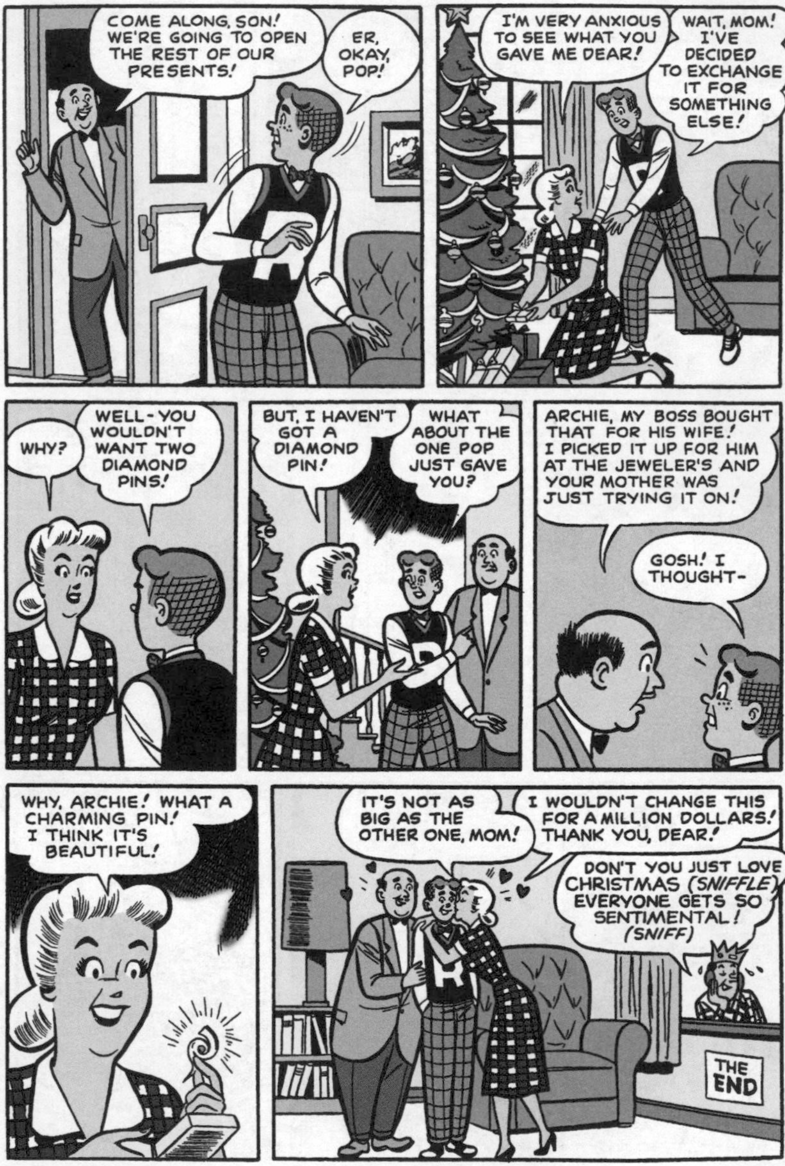
COME ALONG, SON! WE'RE GOING TO OPEN THE REST OF OUR PRESENTS!
ER, OKAY, POP!
I'M VERY ANXIOUS TO SEE WHAT YOU GAVE ME DEAR!
WAIT, MOM! I'VE DECIDED TO EXCHANGE IT FOR SOMETHING ELSE!
WHY?
WELL- YOU WOULDN'T WANT TWO DIAMOND PINS!
BUT, I HAVEN'T GOT A DIAMOND PIN!
WHAT ABOUT THE ONE POP JUST GAVE YOU?
ARCHIE, MY BOSS BOUGHT THAT FOR HIS WIFE! I PICKED IT UP FOR HIM AT THE JEWELER'S AND YOUR MOTHER WAS JUST TRYING IT ON!
GOSH! I THOUGHT-
WHY, ARCHIE! WHAT A CHARMING PIN! I THINK IT'S BEAUTIFUL!
IT'S NOT AS BIG AS THE OTHER ONE, MOM!
I WOULDN'T CHANGE THIS FOR A MILLION DOLLARS! THANK YOU, DEAR!
DON'T YOU JUST LOVE CHRISTMAS (SNIFFLE) EVERYONE GETS SO SENTIMENTAL! (SNIFF)
THE END

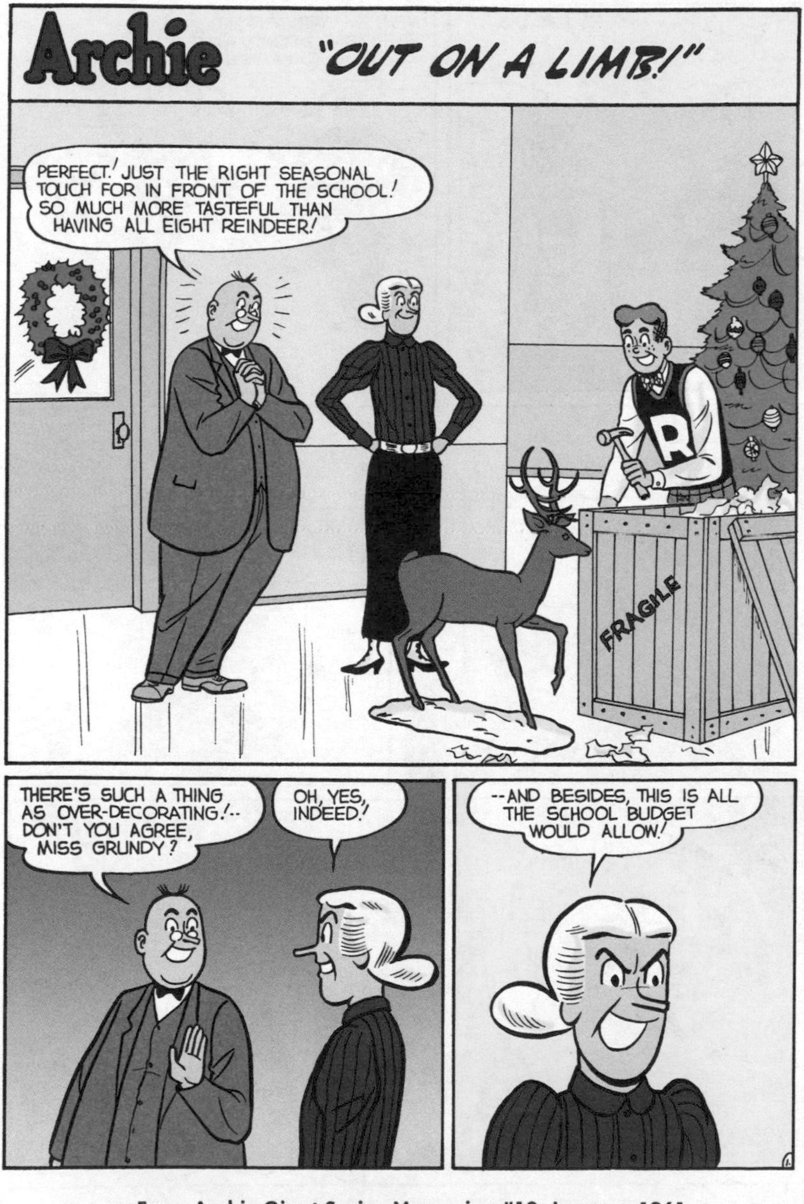
Archie
"OUT ON A LIMB!"
PERFECT! JUST THE RIGHT SEASONAL TOUCH FOR IN FRONT OF THE SCHOOL! SO MUCH MORE TASTEFUL THAN HAVING ALL EIGHT REINDEER!
FRAGILE
THERE'S SUCH A THING AS OVER-DECORATING!-- DON'T YOU AGREE, MISS GRUNDY?
OH, YES, INDEED!
--AND BESIDES, THIS IS ALL THE SCHOOL BUDGET WOULD ALLOW!

• **From Archie Giant Series Magazine #10, January 1961** •

Frank Doyle • Bill Vigoda

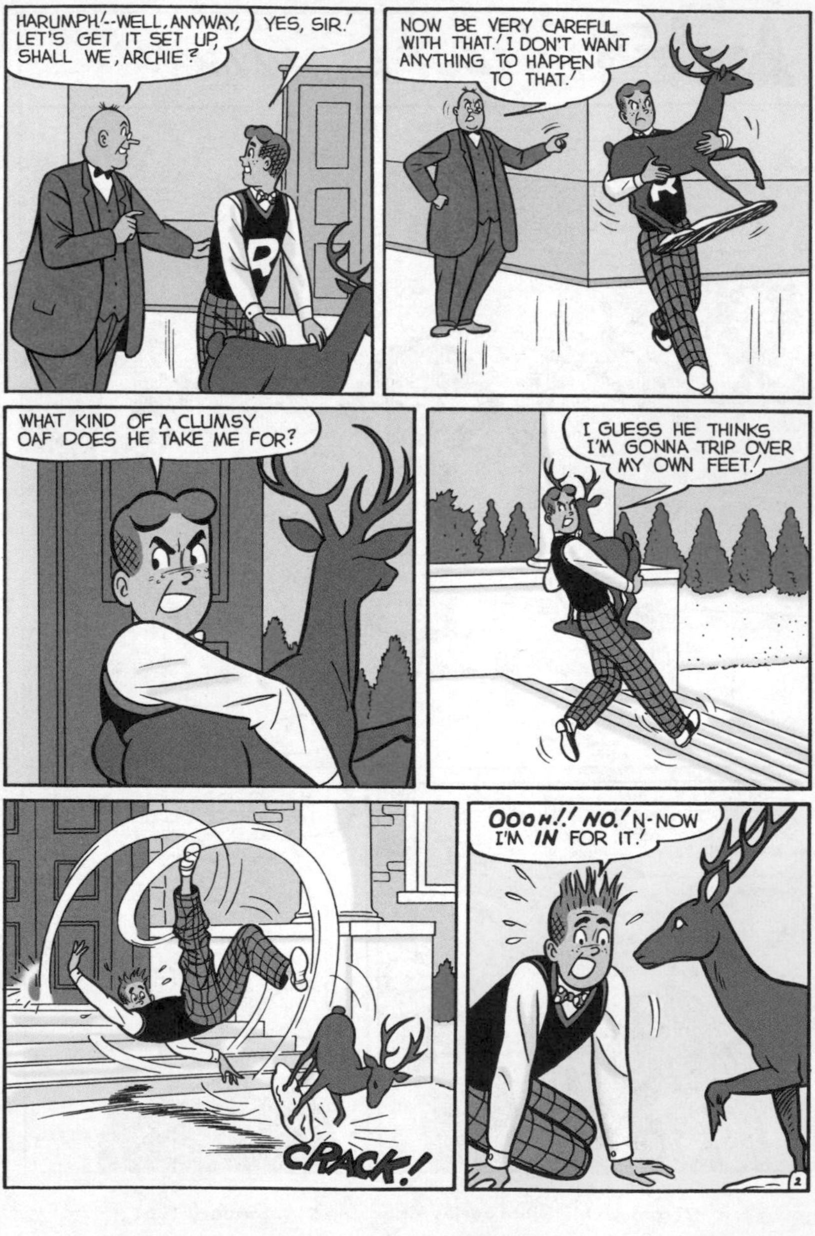
HARUMPH!--WELL, ANYWAY, LET'S GET IT SET UP, SHALL WE, ARCHIE?
YES, SIR!
NOW BE VERY CAREFUL WITH THAT! I DON'T WANT ANYTHING TO HAPPEN TO THAT!
WHAT KIND OF A CLUMSY OAF DOES HE TAKE ME FOR?
I GUESS HE THINKS I'M GONNA TRIP OVER MY OWN FEET!
CRACK!
OOOH!! NO! N-NOW I'M IN FOR IT!
2

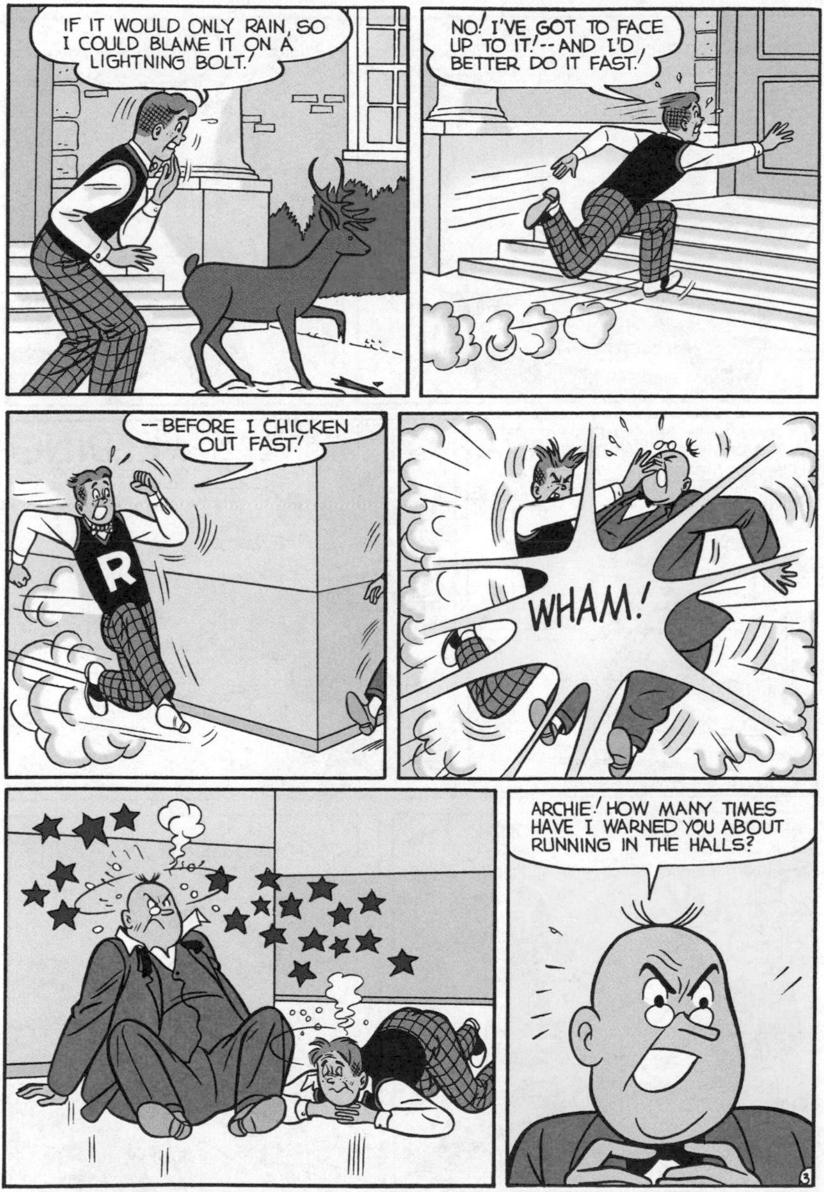
IF IT WOULD ONLY RAIN, SO I COULD BLAME IT ON A LIGHTNING BOLT!
NO! I'VE GOT TO FACE UP TO IT!--AND I'D BETTER DO IT FAST!
--BEFORE I CHICKEN OUT FAST!
WHAM!
ARCHIE! HOW MANY TIMES HAVE I WARNED YOU ABOUT RUNNING IN THE HALLS?
3

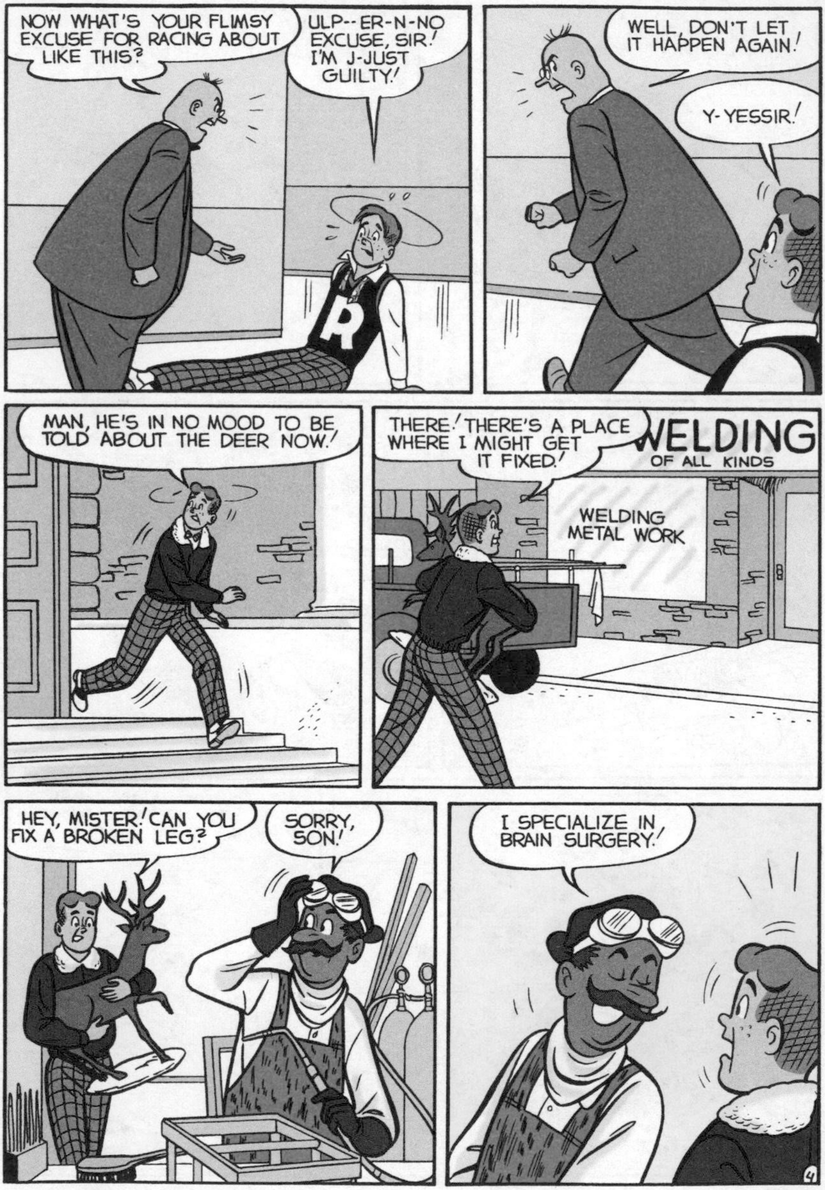
NOW WHAT'S YOUR FLIMSY EXCUSE FOR RACING ABOUT LIKE THIS?
ULP--ER-N-NO EXCUSE, SIR! I'M J-JUST GUILTY!
WELL, DON'T LET IT HAPPEN AGAIN!
Y-YESSIR!
MAN, HE'S IN NO MOOD TO BE TOLD ABOUT THE DEER NOW!
THERE! THERE'S A PLACE WHERE I MIGHT GET IT FIXED!
WELDING
OF ALL KINDS
WELDING
METAL WORK
HEY, MISTER! CAN YOU FIX A BROKEN LEG?
SORRY, SON!
I SPECIALIZE IN BRAIN SURGERY!
4

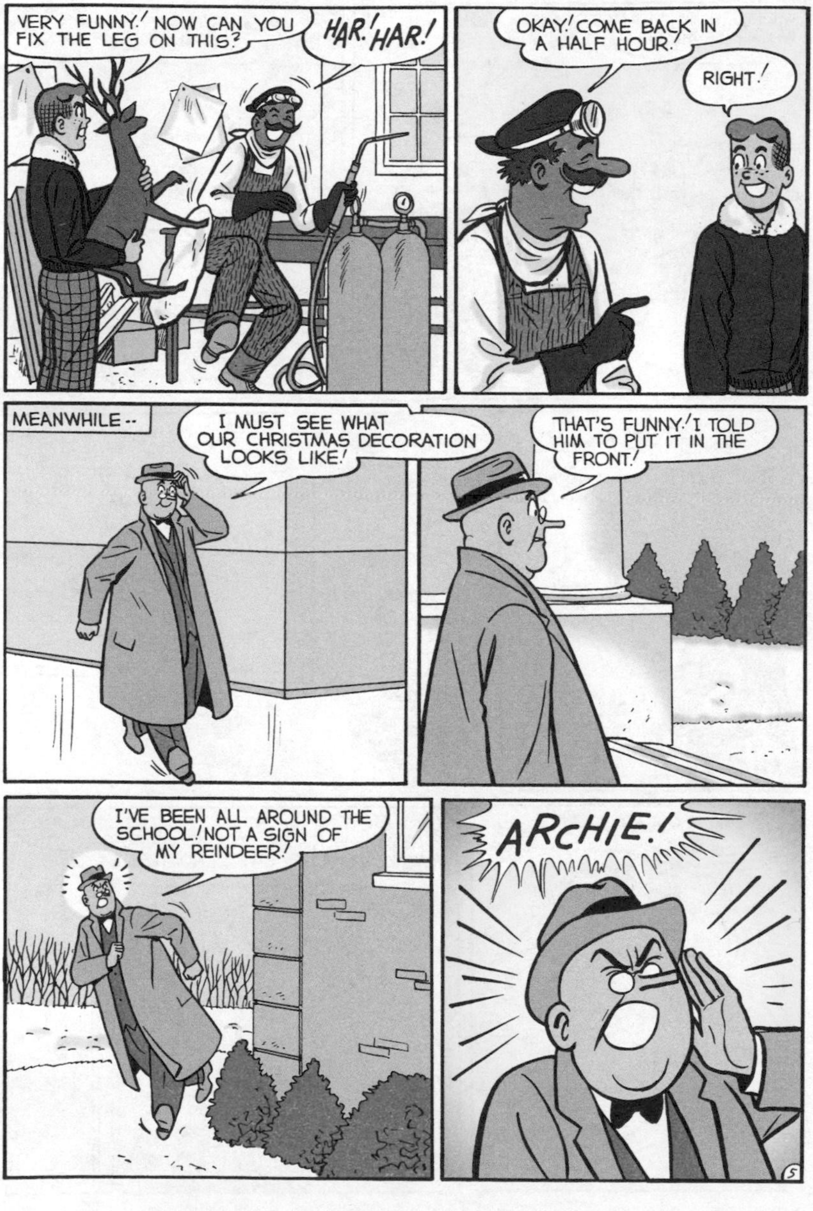
VERY FUNNY! NOW CAN YOU FIX THE LEG ON THIS?
HAR! HAR!
OKAY! COME BACK IN A HALF HOUR!
RIGHT!
MEANWHILE --
I MUST SEE WHAT OUR CHRISTMAS DECORATION LOOKS LIKE!
THAT'S FUNNY! I TOLD HIM TO PUT IT IN THE FRONT!
I'VE BEEN ALL AROUND THE SCHOOL! NOT A SIGN OF MY REINDEER!
ARCHIE!
5

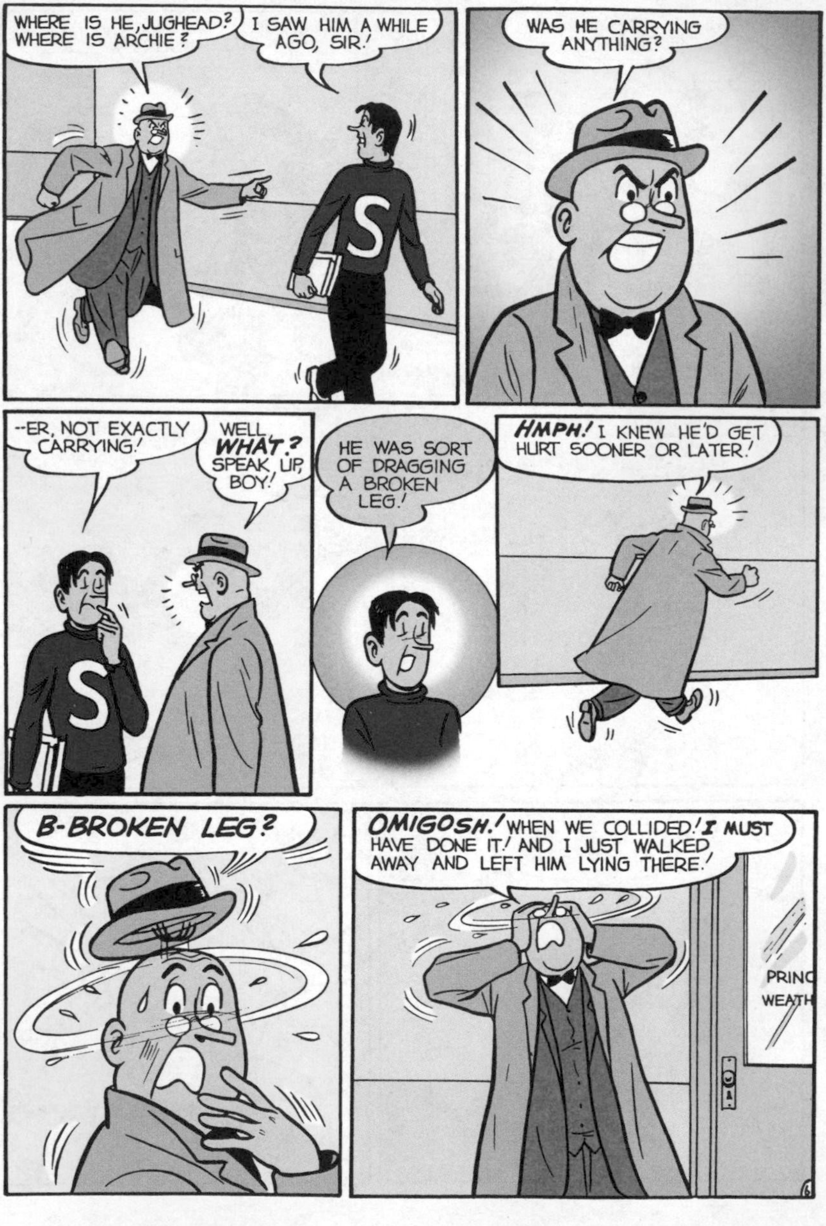
WHERE IS HE, JUGHEAD? WHERE IS ARCHIE?
I SAW HIM A WHILE AGO, SIR!
WAS HE CARRYING ANYTHING?
--ER, NOT EXACTLY CARRYING!
WELL WHAT? SPEAK UP, BOY!
HE WAS SORT OF DRAGGING A BROKEN LEG!
HMPH! I KNEW HE'D GET HURT SOONER OR LATER!
B-BROKEN LEG?
OMIGOSH! WHEN WE COLLIDED! I MUST HAVE DONE IT! AND I JUST WALKED AWAY AND LEFT HIM LYING THERE!
PRINC
WEATH

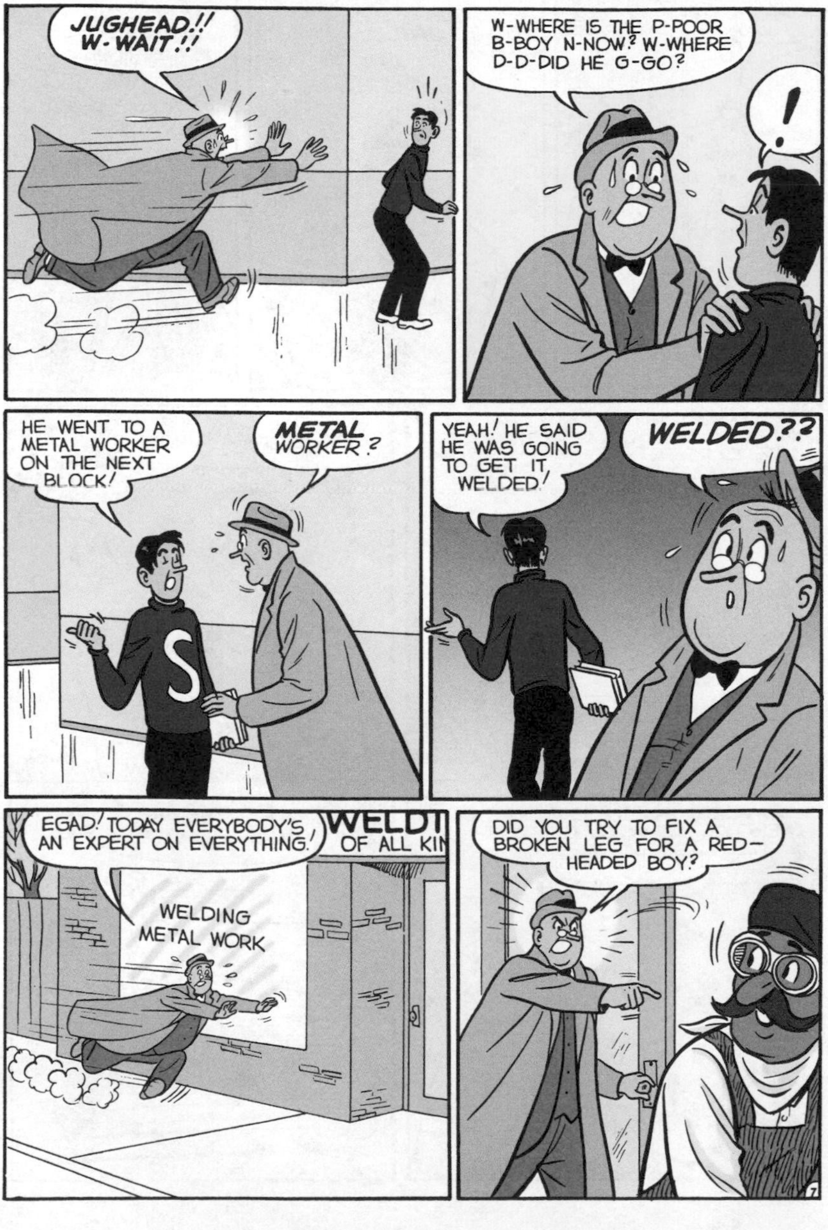
JUGHEAD!! W-WAIT!!
W-WHERE IS THE P-POOR B-BOY N-NOW? W-WHERE D-D-DID HE G-GO?
!
HE WENT TO A METAL WORKER ON THE NEXT BLOCK!
METAL WORKER?
YEAH! HE SAID HE WAS GOING TO GET IT WELDED!
WELDED??
EGAD! TODAY EVERYBODY'S AN EXPERT ON EVERYTHING!
WELDI
OF ALL KI
WELDING
METAL WORK
DID YOU TRY TO FIX A BROKEN LEG FOR A RED-HEADED BOY?
7

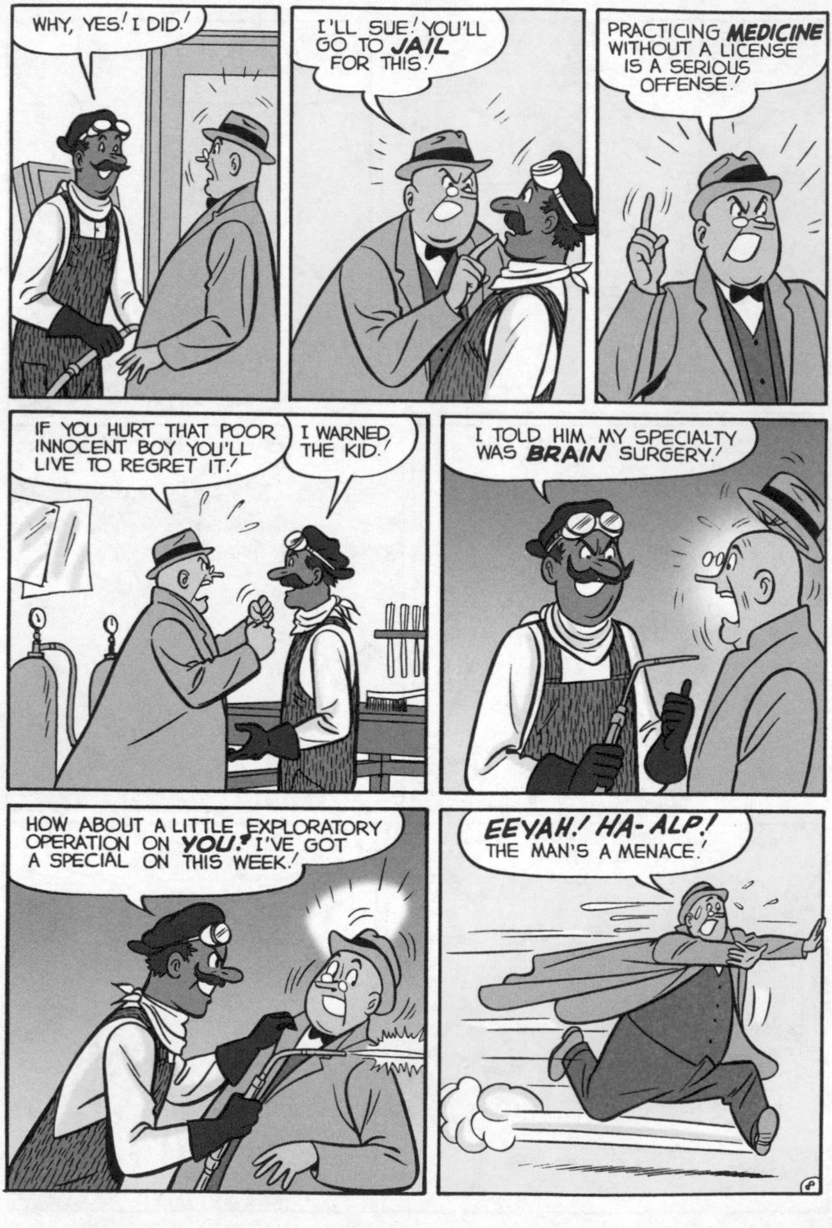
WHY, YES! I DID!
I'LL SUE! YOU'LL GO TO JAIL FOR THIS!
PRACTICING MEDICINE WITHOUT A LICENSE IS A SERIOUS OFFENSE!
IF YOU HURT THAT POOR INNOCENT BOY YOU'LL LIVE TO REGRET IT!
I WARNED THE KID!
I TOLD HIM MY SPECIALTY WAS BRAIN SURGERY!
HOW ABOUT A LITTLE EXPLORATORY OPERATION ON YOU? I'VE GOT A SPECIAL ON THIS WEEK!
EEYAH! HA-ALP! THE MAN'S A MENACE!

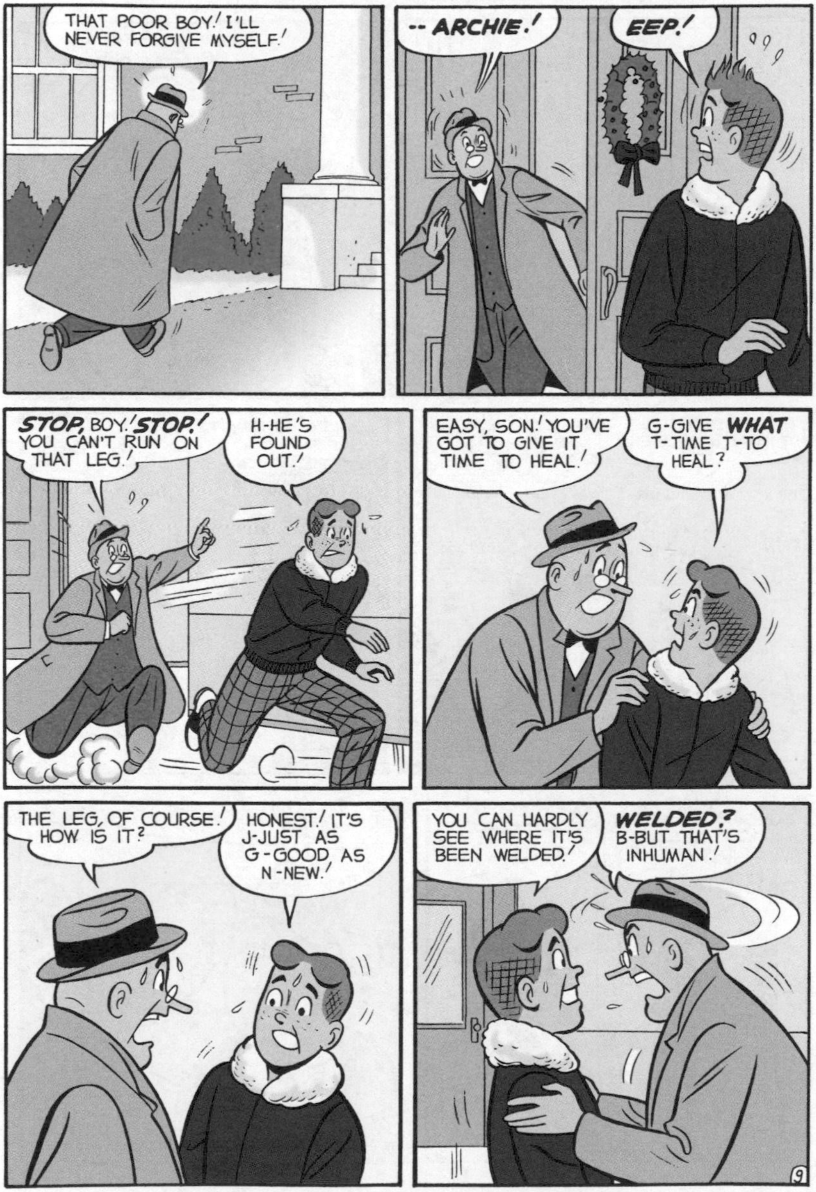
THAT POOR BOY! I'LL NEVER FORGIVE MYSELF!
-- ARCHIE!
EEP!
STOP, BOY! STOP! YOU CAN'T RUN ON THAT LEG!
H-HE'S FOUND OUT!
EASY, SON! YOU'VE GOT TO GIVE IT TIME TO HEAL!
G-GIVE WHAT T-TIME T-TO HEAL?
THE LEG, OF COURSE! HOW IS IT?
HONEST! IT'S J-JUST AS G-GOOD AS N-NEW!
YOU CAN HARDLY SEE WHERE IT'S BEEN WELDED!
WELDED? B-BUT THAT'S INHUMAN!
9

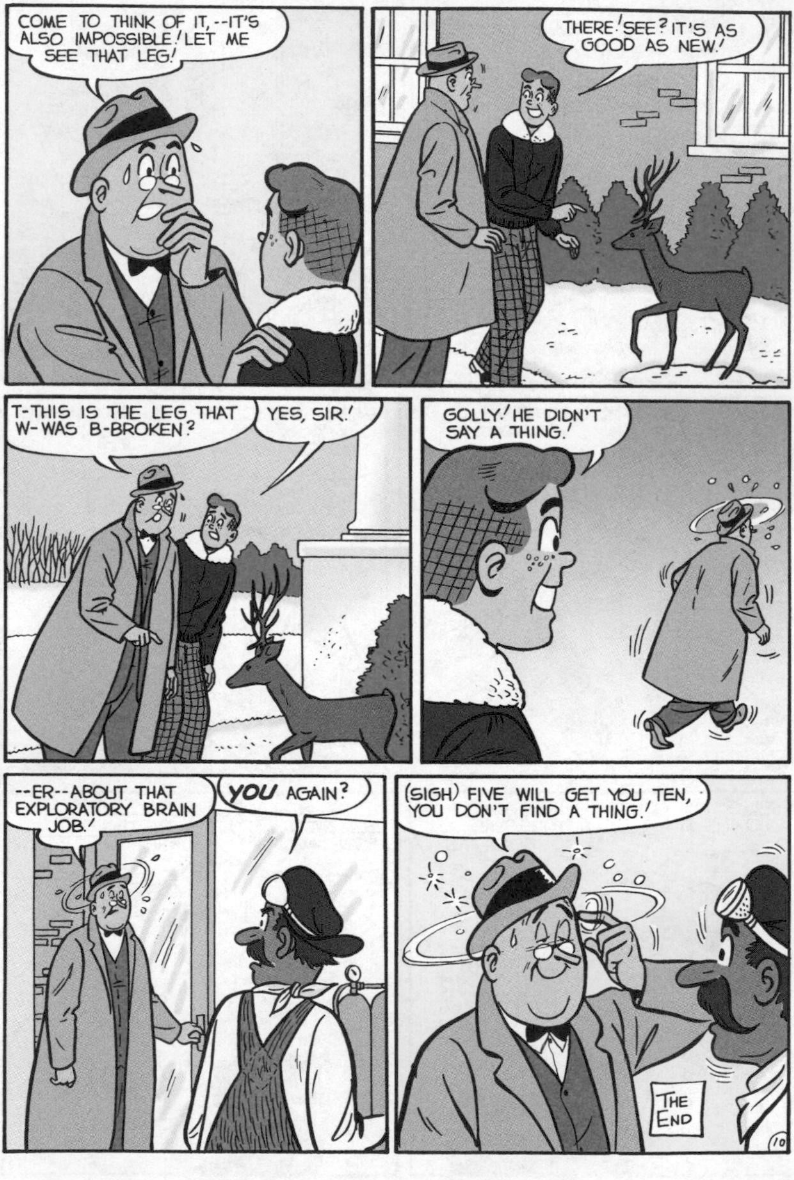
COME TO THINK OF IT, --IT'S ALSO IMPOSSIBLE! LET ME SEE THAT LEG!
THERE! SEE? IT'S AS GOOD AS NEW!
T-THIS IS THE LEG THAT W-WAS B-BROKEN?
YES, SIR!
GOLLY! HE DIDN'T SAY A THING!
--ER--ABOUT THAT EXPLORATORY BRAIN JOB!
YOU AGAIN?
(SIGH) FIVE WILL GET YOU TEN, YOU DON'T FIND A THING!
THE END
10

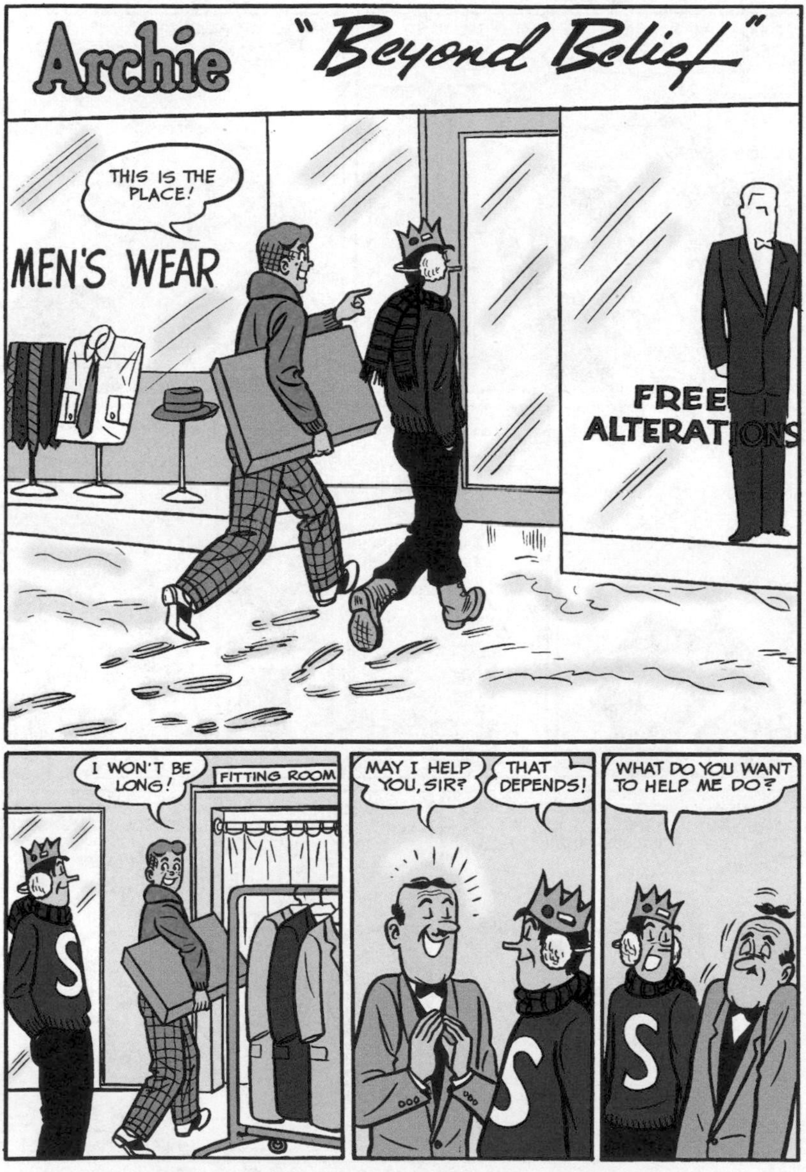
Archie
"Beyond Belief"
THIS IS THE PLACE!
MEN'S WEAR
FREE ALTERATIONS
I WON'T BE LONG!
FITTING ROOM
MAY I HELP YOU, SIR?
THAT DEPENDS!
WHAT DO YOU WANT TO HELP ME DO?

• **From Archie Giant Series Magazine #10, January 1961** •

Bill Vigoda • Terry Szenics • Barry Grossman

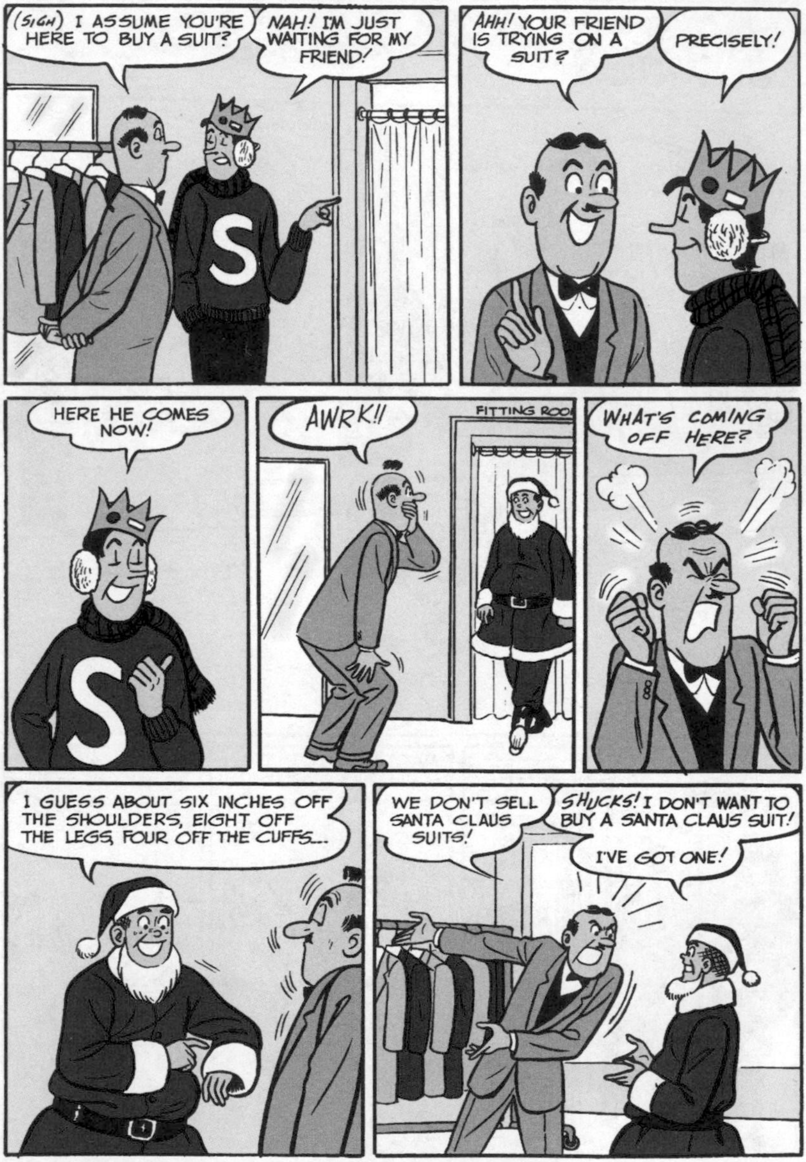
(SIGH) I ASSUME YOU'RE HERE TO BUY A SUIT?
NAH! I'M JUST WAITING FOR MY FRIEND!
AHH! YOUR FRIEND IS TRYING ON A SUIT?
PRECISELY!
HERE HE COMES NOW!
AWRK!!
FITTING ROO
WHAT'S COMING OFF HERE?
I GUESS ABOUT SIX INCHES OFF THE SHOULDERS, EIGHT OFF THE LEGS, FOUR OFF THE CUFFS...
WE DON'T SELL SANTA CLAUS SUITS!
SHUCKS! I DON'T WANT TO BUY A SANTA CLAUS SUIT!
I'VE GOT ONE!

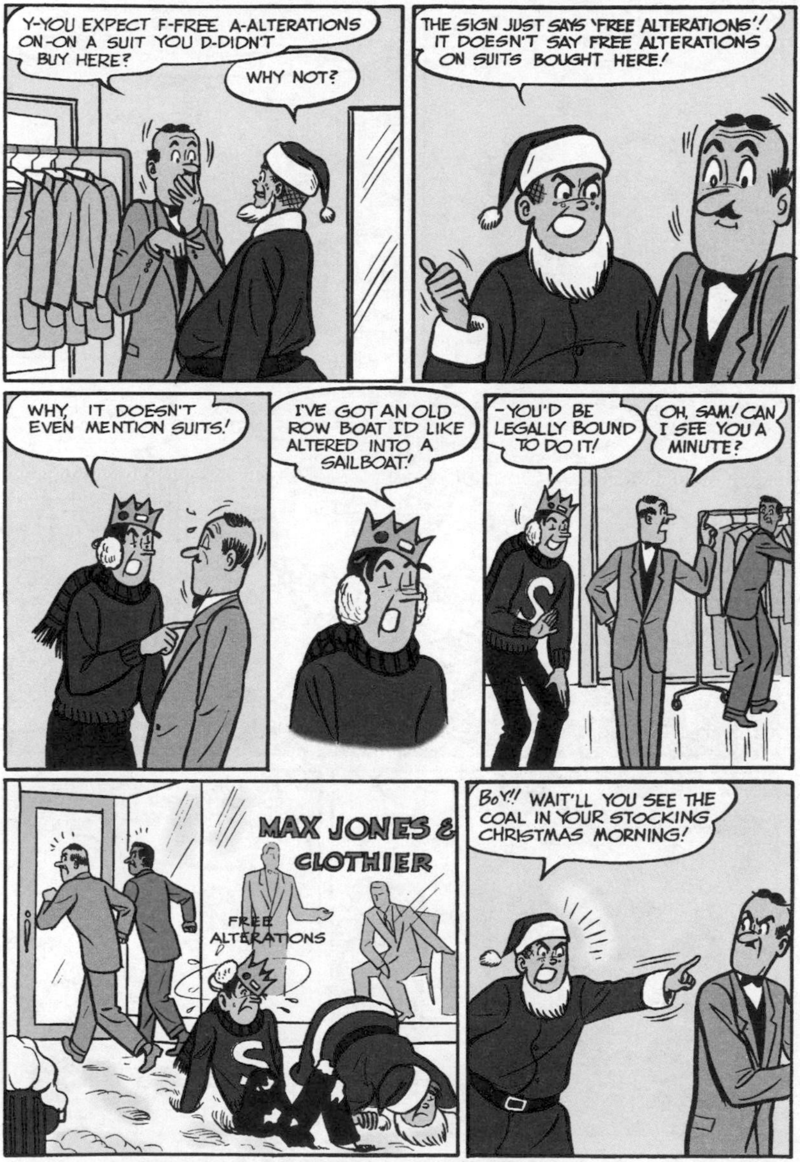
Y-YOU EXPECT F-FREE A-ALTERATIONS ON-ON A SUIT YOU D-DIDN'T BUY HERE?
WHY NOT?
THE SIGN JUST SAYS 'FREE ALTERATIONS'! IT DOESN'T SAY FREE ALTERATIONS ON SUITS BOUGHT HERE!
WHY, IT DOESN'T EVEN MENTION SUITS!
I'VE GOT AN OLD ROW BOAT I'D LIKE ALTERED INTO A SAILBOAT!
-YOU'D BE LEGALLY BOUND TO DO IT!
OH, SAM! CAN I SEE YOU A MINUTE?
MAX JONES & CLOTHIER
FREE ALTERATIONS
BOY!! WAIT'LL YOU SEE THE COAL IN YOUR STOCKING CHRISTMAS MORNING!

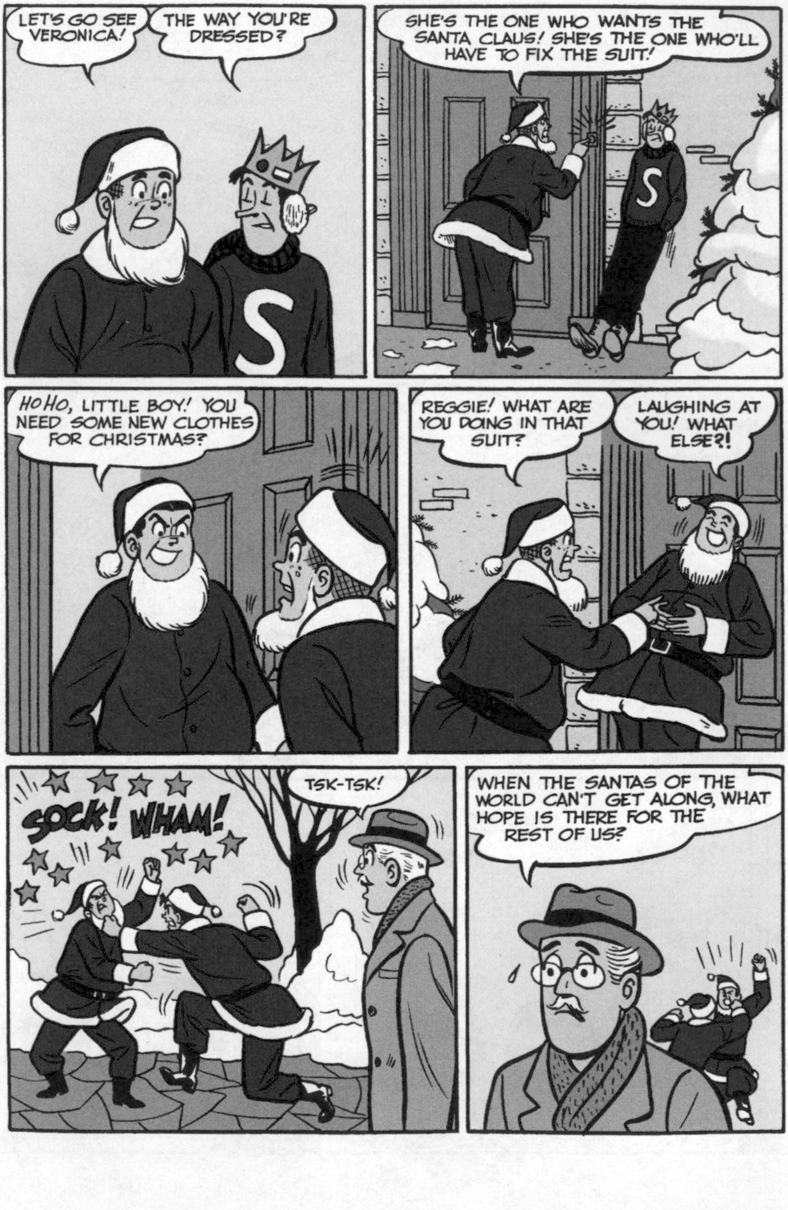
LET'S GO SEE VERONICA!
THE WAY YOU'RE DRESSED?
SHE'S THE ONE WHO WANTS THE SANTA CLAUS! SHE'S THE ONE WHO'LL HAVE TO FIX THE SUIT!
S
S
HO HO, LITTLE BOY! YOU NEED SOME NEW CLOTHES FOR CHRISTMAS?
REGGIE! WHAT ARE YOU DOING IN THAT SUIT?
LAUGHING AT YOU! WHAT ELSE?!
SOCK! WHAM!
TSK-TSK!
WHEN THE SANTAS OF THE WORLD CAN'T GET ALONG, WHAT HOPE IS THERE FOR THE REST OF US?

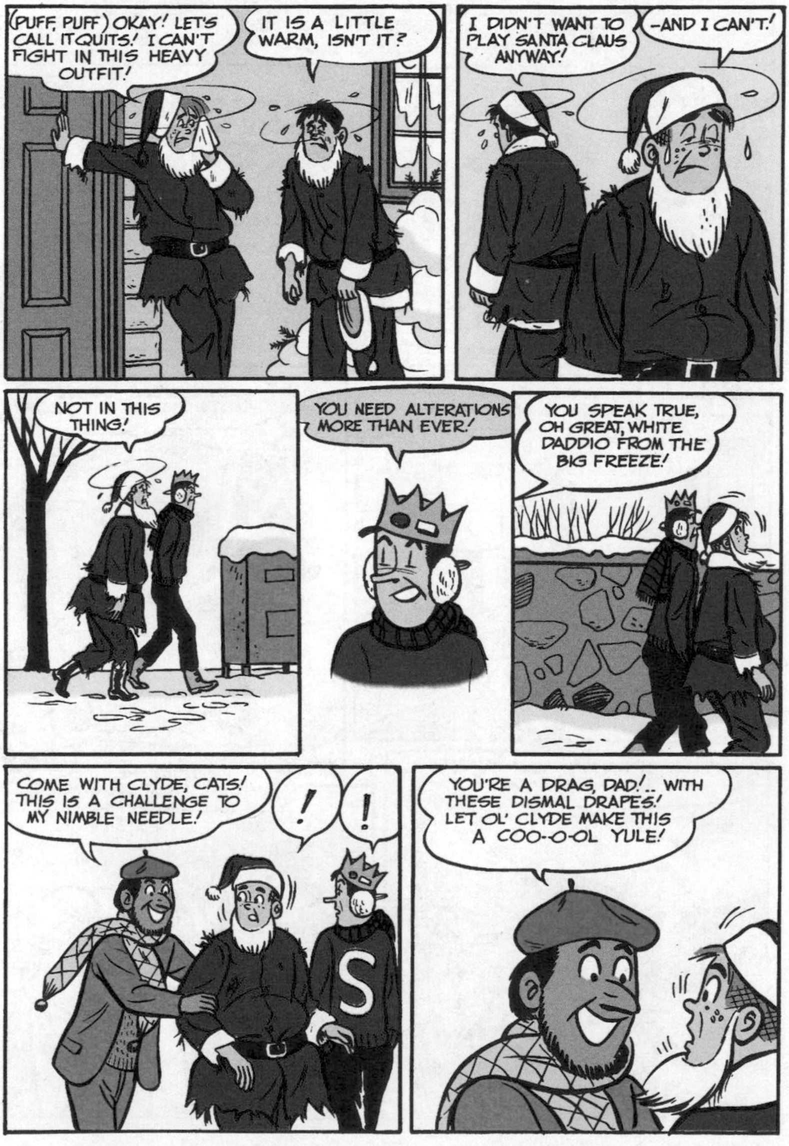
(PUFF, PUFF) OKAY! LET'S CALL IT QUITS! I CAN'T FIGHT IN THIS HEAVY OUTFIT!
IT IS A LITTLE WARM, ISN'T IT?
I DIDN'T WANT TO PLAY SANTA CLAUS ANYWAY!
-AND I CAN'T!
NOT IN THIS THING!
YOU NEED ALTERATIONS MORE THAN EVER!
YOU SPEAK TRUE, OH GREAT, WHITE DADDIO FROM THE BIG FREEZE!
COME WITH CLYDE, CATS! THIS IS A CHALLENGE TO MY NIMBLE NEEDLE!
!
!
YOU'RE A DRAG, DAD!.. WITH THESE DISMAL DRAPES! LET OL' CLYDE MAKE THIS A COO-O-OL YULE!
S

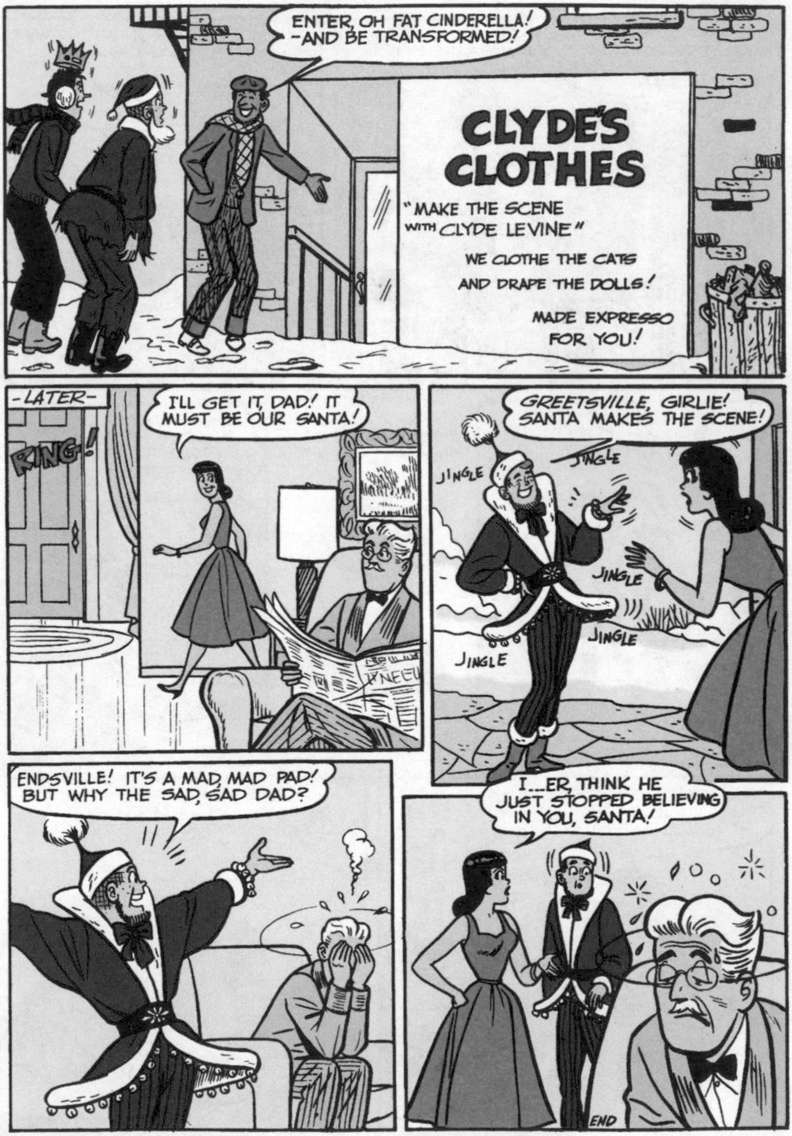
ENTER, OH FAT CINDERELLA! -AND BE TRANSFORMED!
CLYDE'S CLOTHES
"MAKE THE SCENE WITH CLYDE LEVINE"
WE CLOTHE THE CATS AND DRAPE THE DOLLS!
MADE EXPRESSO FOR YOU!
-LATER-
RING!
I'LL GET IT, DAD! IT MUST BE OUR SANTA!
GREETSVILLE, GIRLIE! SANTA MAKES THE SCENE!
JINGLE
JINGLE
JINGLE
JINGLE
JINGLE
ENDSVILLE! IT'S A MAD, MAD PAD! BUT WHY THE SAD, SAD DAD?
I...ER, THINK HE JUST STOPPED BELIEVING IN YOU, SANTA!
END

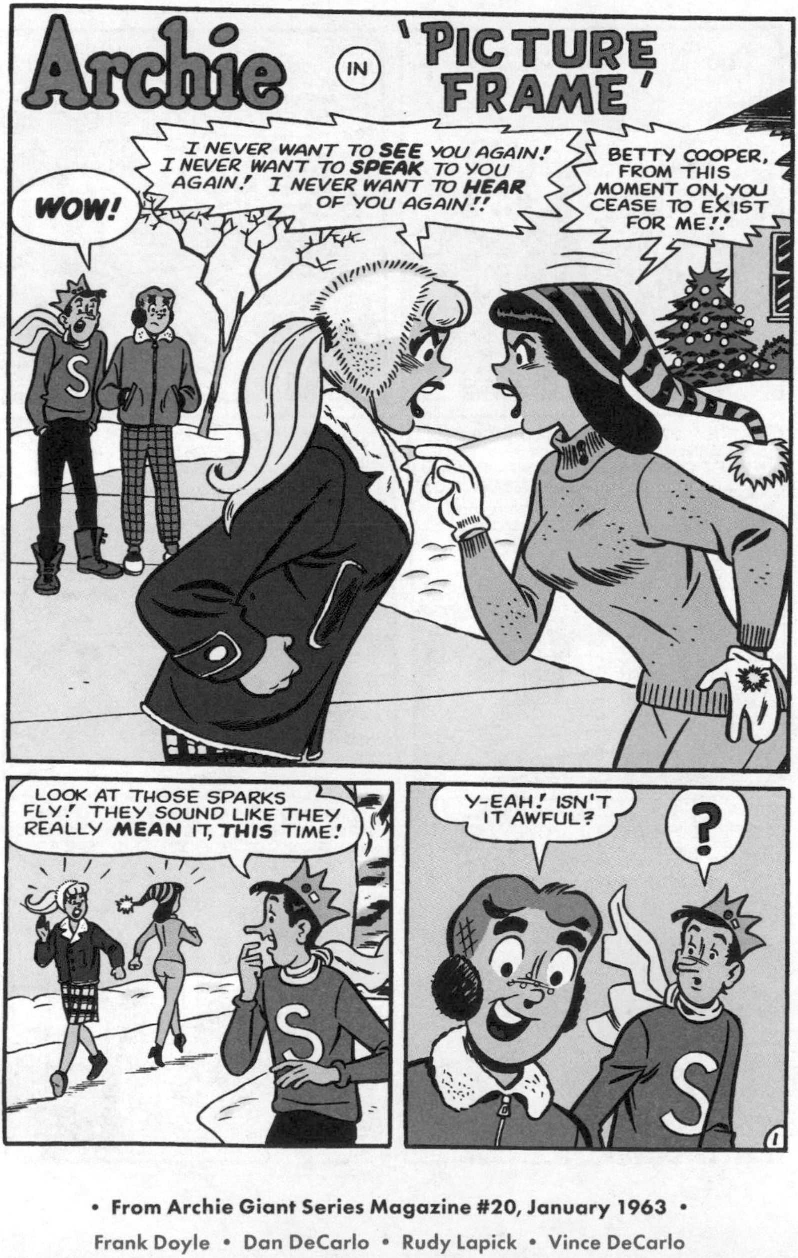
Archie IN 'PICTURE FRAME'
I NEVER WANT TO SEE YOU AGAIN! I NEVER WANT TO SPEAK TO YOU AGAIN! I NEVER WANT TO HEAR OF YOU AGAIN!!
BETTY COOPER, FROM THIS MOMENT ON, YOU CEASE TO EXIST FOR ME!!
WOW!
LOOK AT THOSE SPARKS FLY! THEY SOUND LIKE THEY REALLY MEAN IT, THIS TIME!
Y-EAH! ISN'T IT AWFUL?
?
1

• **From Archie Giant Series Magazine #20, January 1963** •

Frank Doyle • Dan DeCarlo • Rudy Lapick • Vince DeCarlo

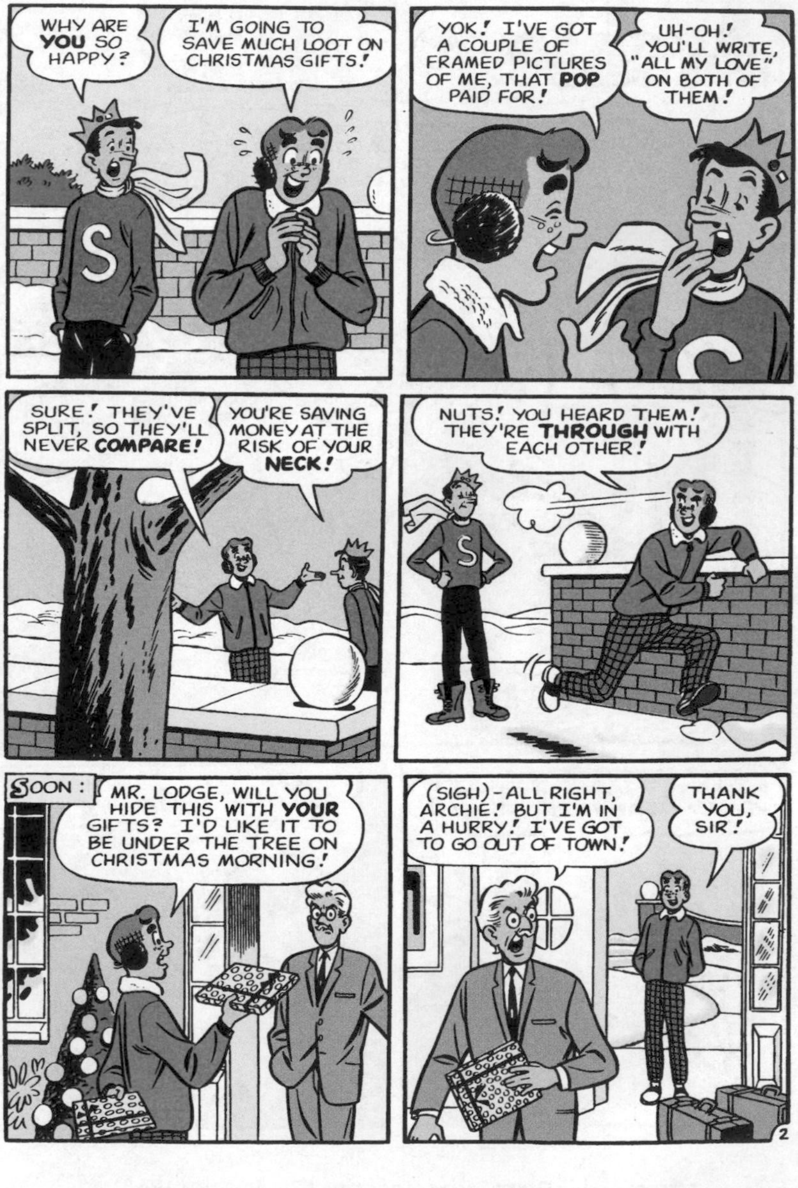
WHY ARE YOU SO HAPPY?
I'M GOING TO SAVE MUCH LOOT ON CHRISTMAS GIFTS!
YOK! I'VE GOT A COUPLE OF FRAMED PICTURES OF ME, THAT POP PAID FOR!
UH-OH! YOU'LL WRITE, "ALL MY LOVE" ON BOTH OF THEM!
SURE! THEY'VE SPLIT, SO THEY'LL NEVER COMPARE!
YOU'RE SAVING MONEY AT THE RISK OF YOUR NECK!
NUTS! YOU HEARD THEM! THEY'RE THROUGH WITH EACH OTHER!
SOON:
MR. LODGE, WILL YOU HIDE THIS WITH YOUR GIFTS? I'D LIKE IT TO BE UNDER THE TREE ON CHRISTMAS MORNING!
(SIGH)-ALL RIGHT, ARCHIE! BUT I'M IN A HURRY! I'VE GOT TO GO OUT OF TOWN!
THANK YOU, SIR!
2

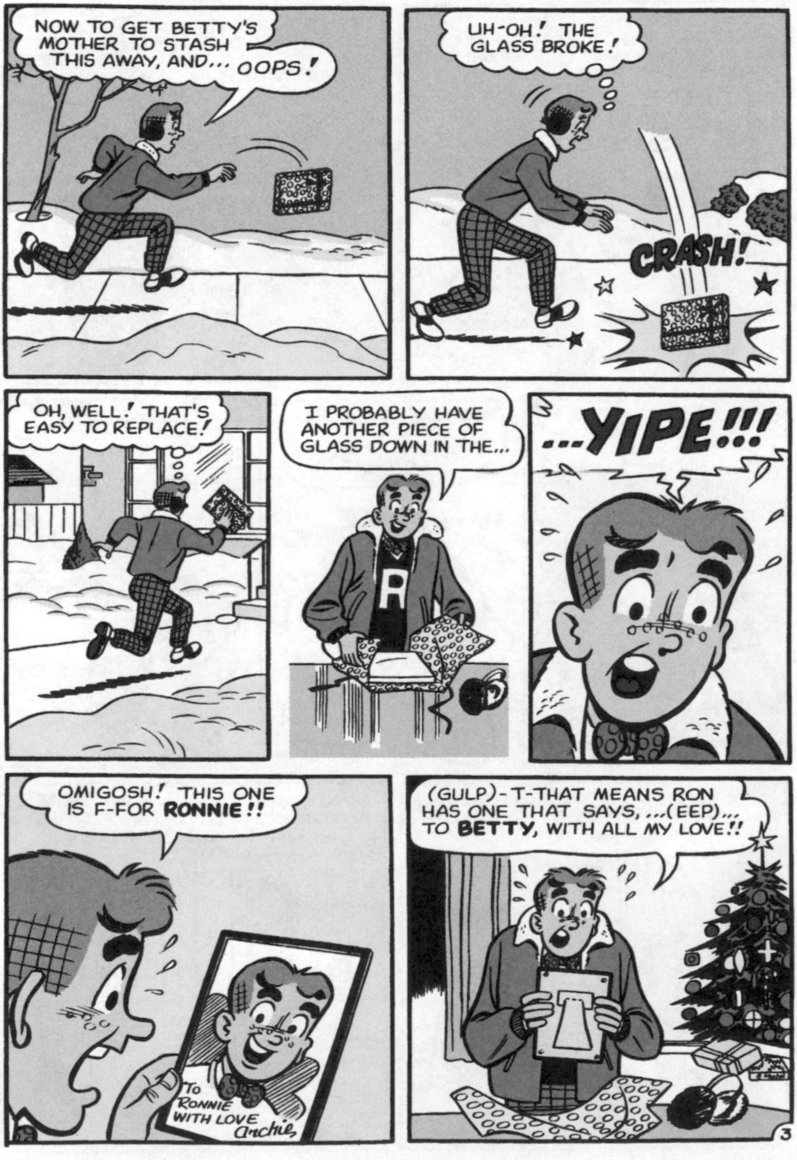
NOW TO GET BETTY'S MOTHER TO STASH THIS AWAY, AND... OOPS!
UH-OH! THE GLASS BROKE!
CRASH!
OH, WELL! THAT'S EASY TO REPLACE!
I PROBABLY HAVE ANOTHER PIECE OF GLASS DOWN IN THE...
...YIPE!!!
OMIGOSH! THIS ONE IS F-FOR RONNIE!!
TO RONNIE WITH LOVE Archie
(GULP)-T-THAT MEANS RON HAS ONE THAT SAYS, ...(EEP)... TO BETTY, WITH ALL MY LOVE!!
3

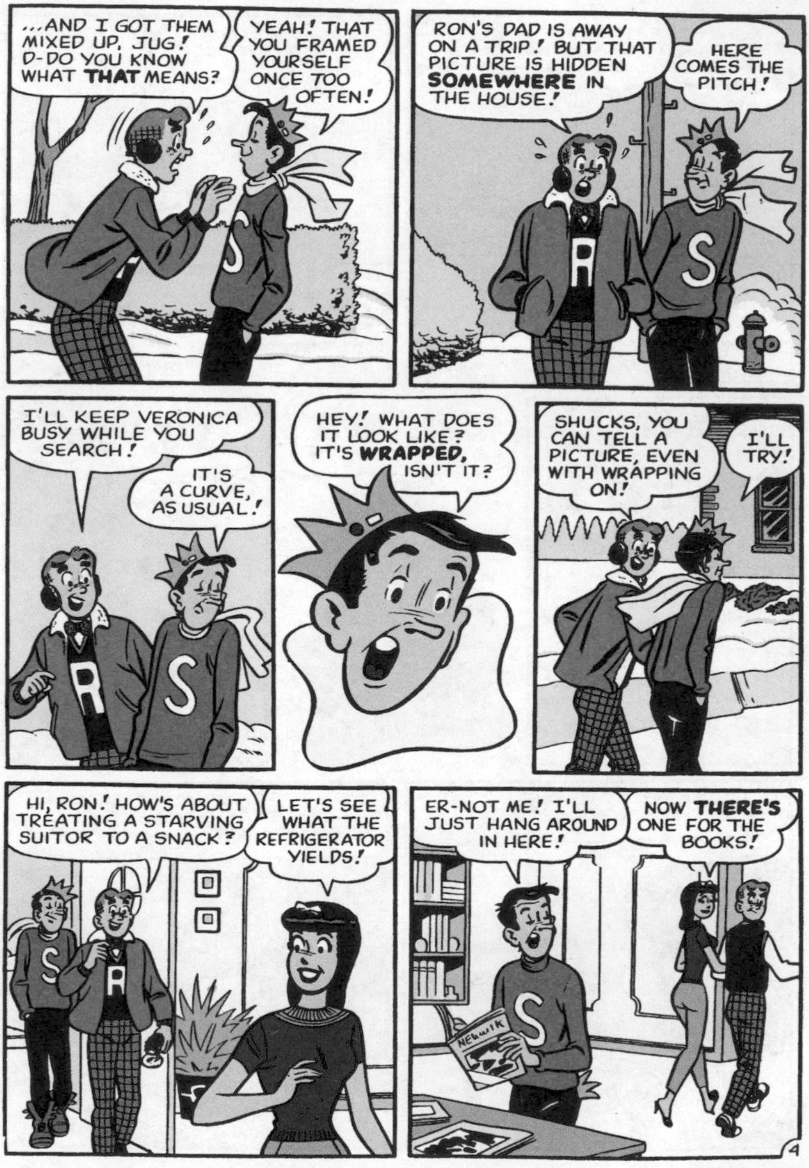
...AND I GOT THEM MIXED UP, JUG! D-DO YOU KNOW WHAT **THAT** MEANS?
YEAH! THAT YOU FRAMED YOURSELF ONCE TOO OFTEN!
RON'S DAD IS AWAY ON A TRIP! BUT THAT PICTURE IS HIDDEN **SOMEWHERE** IN THE HOUSE!
HERE COMES THE PITCH!
I'LL KEEP VERONICA BUSY WHILE YOU SEARCH!
IT'S A CURVE, AS USUAL!
HEY! WHAT DOES IT LOOK LIKE? IT'S **WRAPPED,** ISN'T IT?
SHUCKS, YOU CAN TELL A PICTURE, EVEN WITH WRAPPING ON!
I'LL TRY!
HI, RON! HOW'S ABOUT TREATING A STARVING SUITOR TO A SNACK?
LET'S SEE WHAT THE REFRIGERATOR YIELDS!
ER-NOT ME! I'LL JUST HANG AROUND IN HERE!
NOW **THERE'S** ONE FOR THE BOOKS!
NEWWIK
4

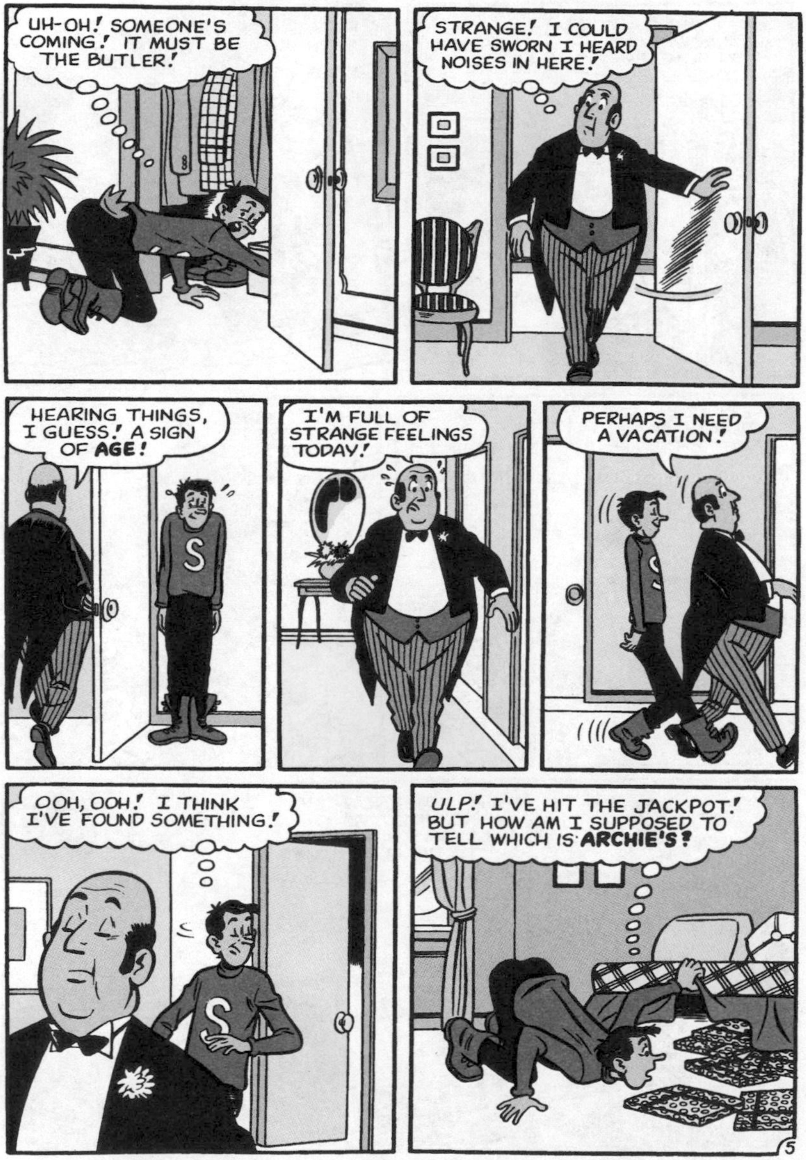
UH-OH! SOMEONE'S COMING! IT MUST BE THE BUTLER!
STRANGE! I COULD HAVE SWORN I HEARD NOISES IN HERE!
HEARING THINGS, I GUESS! A SIGN OF **AGE**!
I'M FULL OF STRANGE FEELINGS TODAY!
PERHAPS I NEED A VACATION!
OOH, OOH! I THINK I'VE FOUND SOMETHING!
ULP! I'VE HIT THE JACKPOT! BUT HOW AM I SUPPOSED TO TELL WHICH IS **ARCHIE'S**?
5

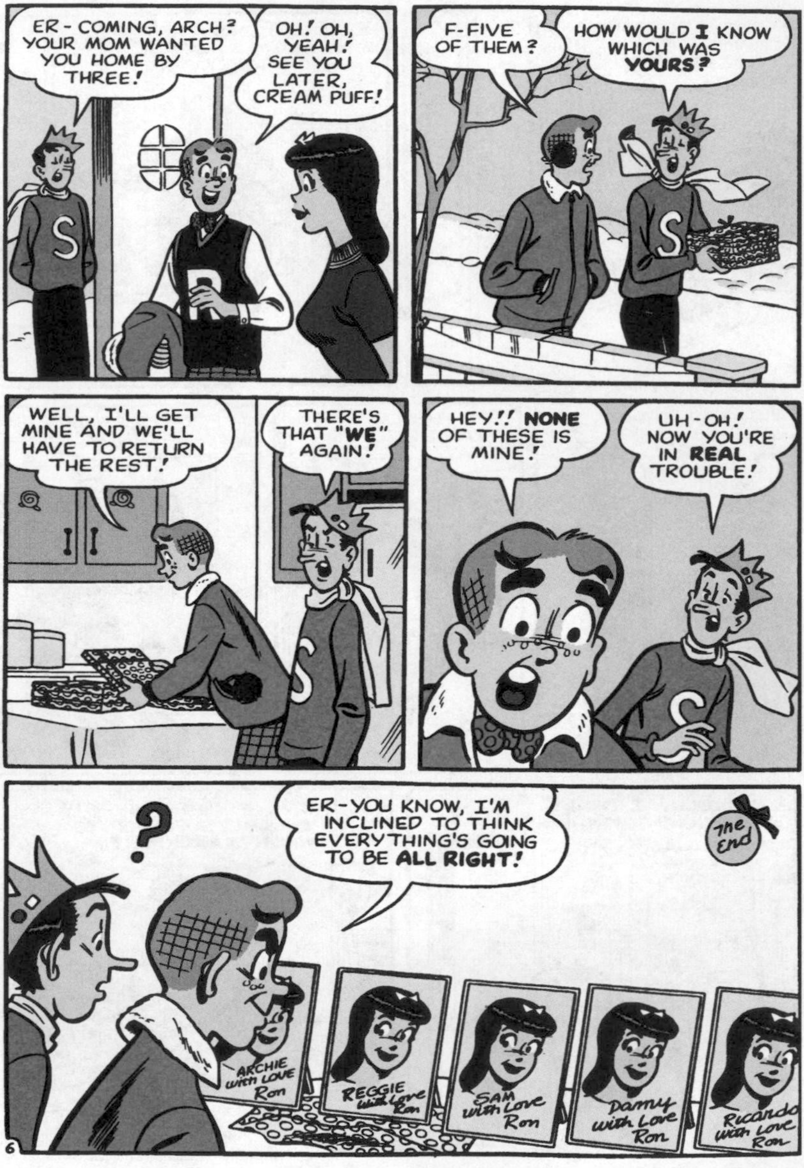
ER-COMING, ARCH? YOUR MOM WANTED YOU HOME BY THREE!
OH! OH, YEAH! SEE YOU LATER, CREAM PUFF!
F-FIVE OF THEM?
HOW WOULD I KNOW WHICH WAS YOURS?
WELL, I'LL GET MINE AND WE'LL HAVE TO RETURN THE REST!
THERE'S THAT "WE" AGAIN!
HEY!! NONE OF THESE IS MINE!
UH-OH! NOW YOU'RE IN REAL TROUBLE!
?
ER-YOU KNOW, I'M INCLINED TO THINK EVERYTHING'S GOING TO BE ALL RIGHT!
The End
ARCHIE with LOVE Ron
REGGIE with Love Ron
SAM with Love Ron
Danny with Love Ron
Ricardo with Love Ron
6

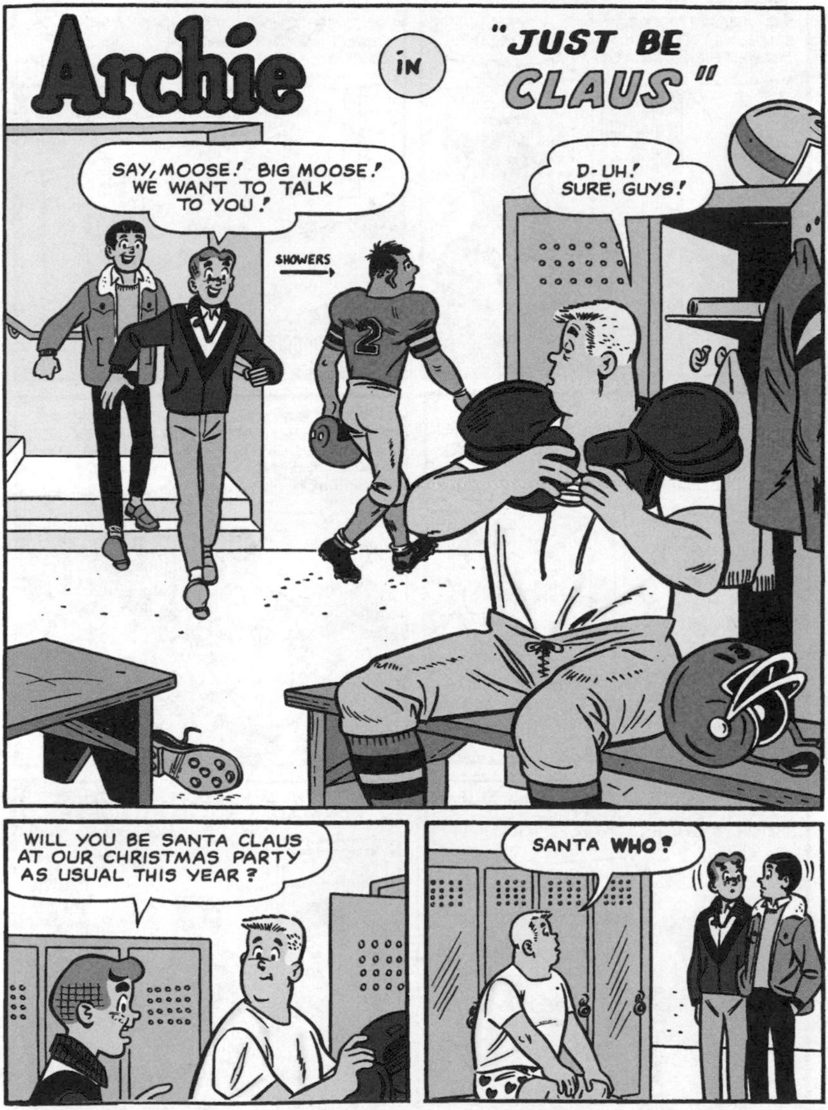
Archie
IN
"JUST BE CLAUS"
SAY, MOOSE! BIG MOOSE! WE WANT TO TALK TO YOU!
SHOWERS
D-UH! SURE, GUYS!
WILL YOU BE SANTA CLAUS AT OUR CHRISTMAS PARTY AS USUAL THIS YEAR?
SANTA WHO?

• From Archie Giant Series Magazine #31, January 1965 •

Frank Doyle • Dan DeCarlo • Rudy Lapick • Vince DeCarlo • Barry Grossman

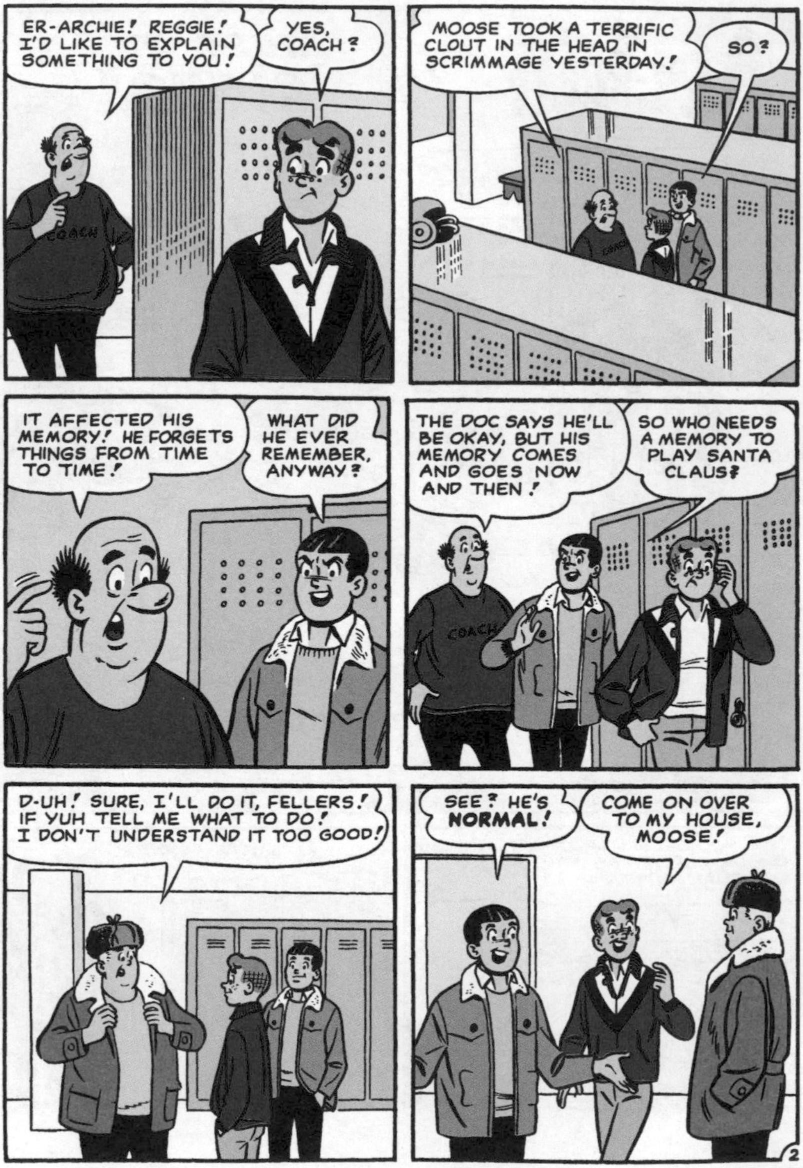
ER-ARCHIE! REGGIE! I'D LIKE TO EXPLAIN SOMETHING TO YOU!
YES, COACH?
COACH
MOOSE TOOK A TERRIFIC CLOUT IN THE HEAD IN SCRIMMAGE YESTERDAY!
SO?
IT AFFECTED HIS MEMORY! HE FORGETS THINGS FROM TIME TO TIME!
WHAT DID HE EVER REMEMBER, ANYWAY?
THE DOC SAYS HE'LL BE OKAY, BUT HIS MEMORY COMES AND GOES NOW AND THEN!
SO WHO NEEDS A MEMORY TO PLAY SANTA CLAUS?
COACH
D-UH! SURE, I'LL DO IT, FELLERS! IF YUH TELL ME WHAT TO DO! I DON'T UNDERSTAND IT TOO GOOD!
SEE? HE'S **NORMAL**!
COME ON OVER TO MY HOUSE, MOOSE!
2

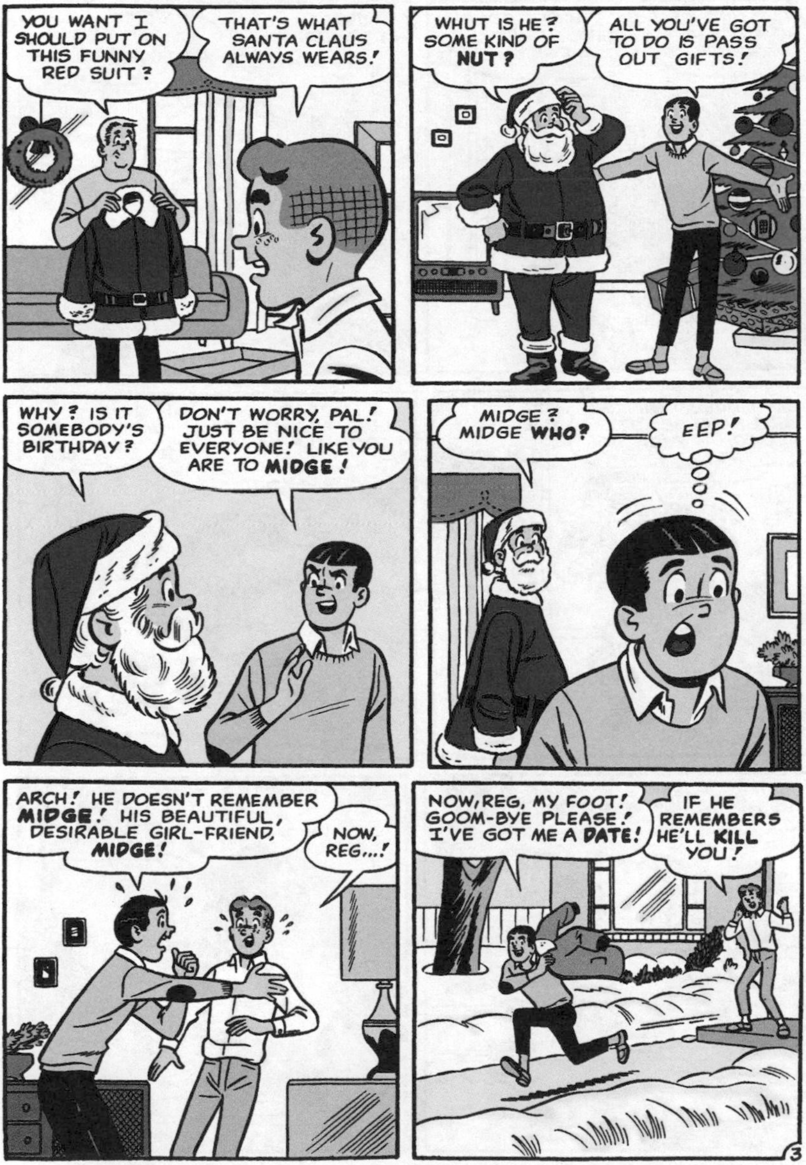
YOU WANT I SHOULD PUT ON THIS FUNNY RED SUIT ?
THAT'S WHAT SANTA CLAUS ALWAYS WEARS!
WHUT IS HE ? SOME KIND OF NUT ?
ALL YOU'VE GOT TO DO IS PASS OUT GIFTS!
WHY ? IS IT SOMEBODY'S BIRTHDAY ?
DON'T WORRY, PAL! JUST BE NICE TO EVERYONE! LIKE YOU ARE TO MIDGE!
MIDGE ? MIDGE WHO?
EEP!
ARCH! HE DOESN'T REMEMBER MIDGE! HIS BEAUTIFUL, DESIRABLE GIRL-FRIEND, MIDGE!
NOW, REG...!
NOW, REG, MY FOOT! GOOM-BYE PLEASE! I'VE GOT ME A DATE!
IF HE REMEMBERS HE'LL KILL YOU!
3

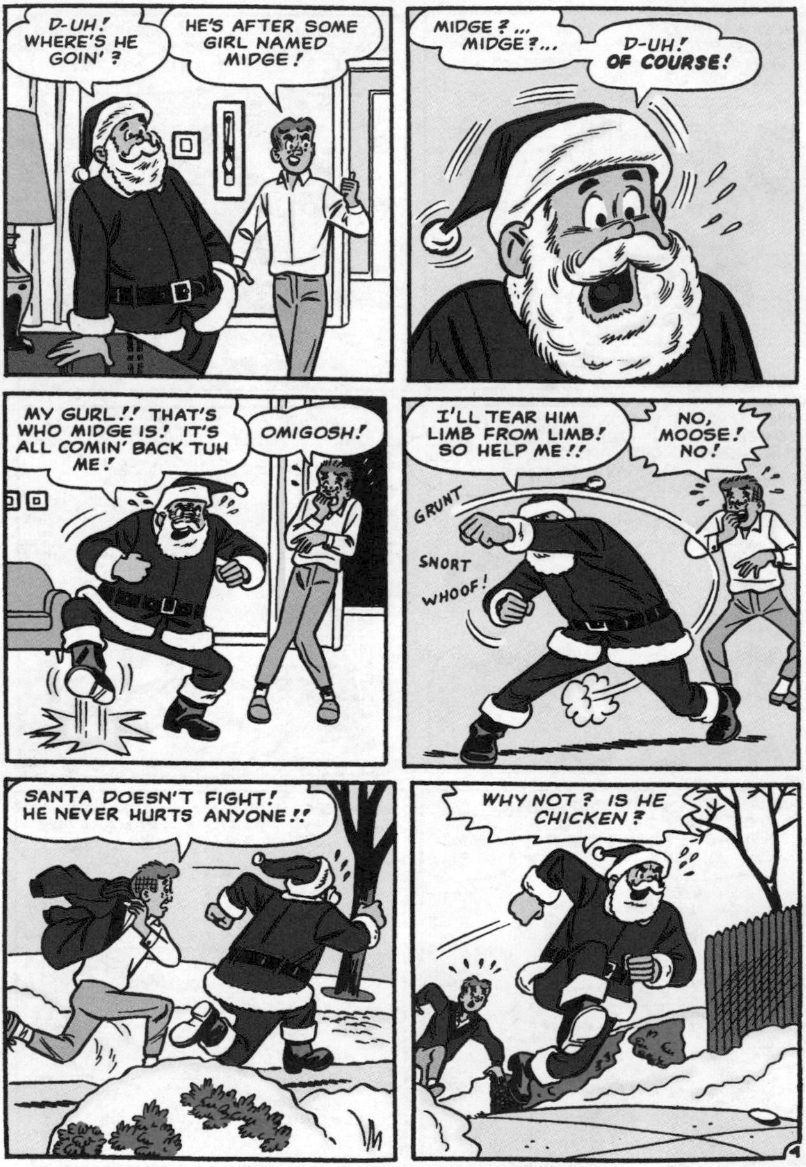
D-UH! WHERE'S HE GOIN'?
HE'S AFTER SOME GIRL NAMED MIDGE!
MIDGE?... MIDGE?...
D-UH! OF COURSE!
MY GURL!! THAT'S WHO MIDGE IS! IT'S ALL COMIN' BACK TUH ME!
OMIGOSH!
I'LL TEAR HIM LIMB FROM LIMB! SO HELP ME!!
NO, MOOSE! NO!
GRUNT
SNORT
WHOOF!
SANTA DOESN'T FIGHT! HE NEVER HURTS ANYONE!!
WHY NOT? IS HE CHICKEN?
4

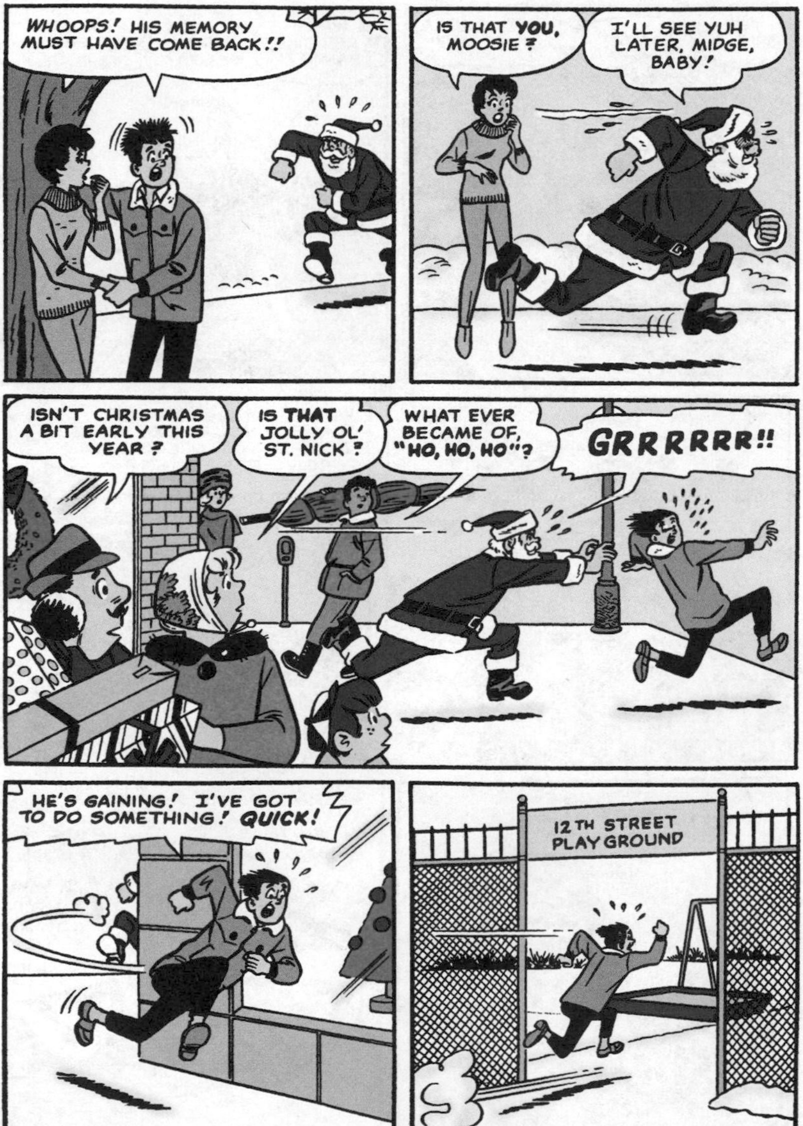
WHOOPS! HIS MEMORY MUST HAVE COME BACK!!
IS THAT YOU, MOOSIE?
I'LL SEE YUH LATER, MIDGE, BABY!
ISN'T CHRISTMAS A BIT EARLY THIS YEAR?
IS THAT JOLLY OL' ST. NICK?
WHAT EVER BECAME OF, "HO, HO, HO"?
GRRRRRR!!
HE'S GAINING! I'VE GOT TO DO SOMETHING! QUICK!
12TH STREET PLAYGROUND
5.

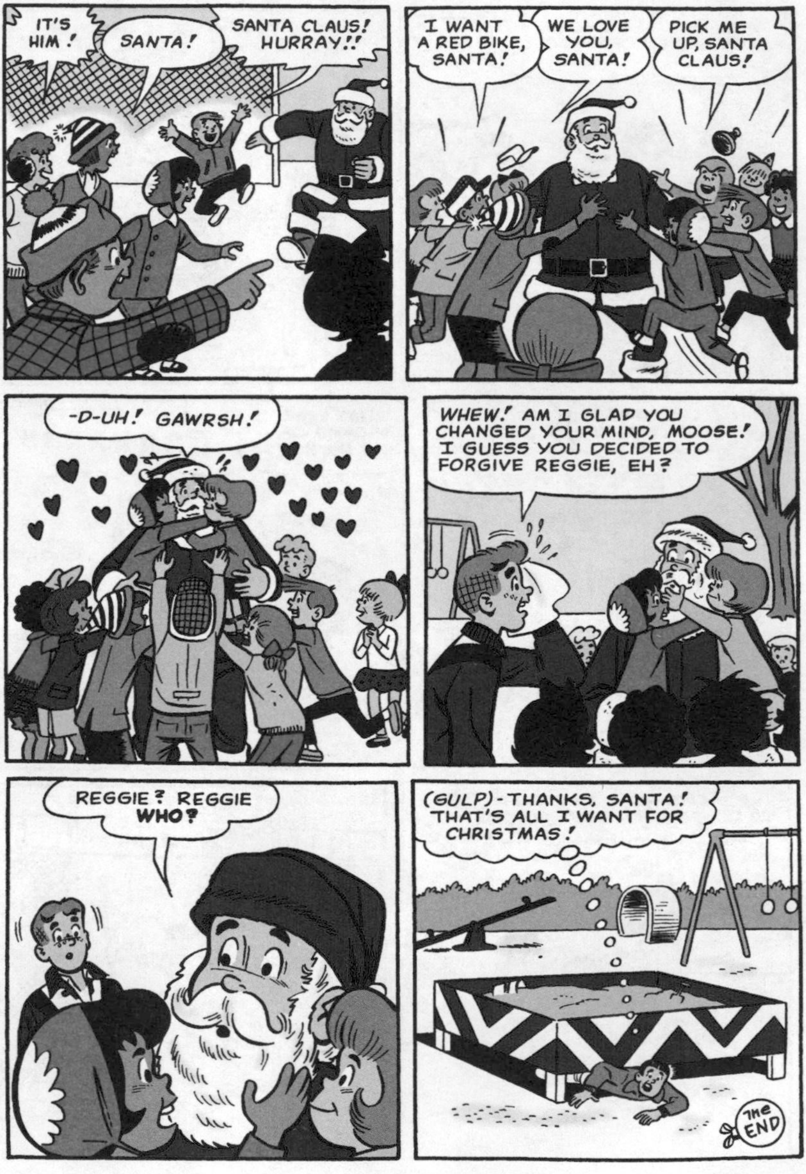
IT'S HIM!
SANTA!
SANTA CLAUS! HURRAY!!
I WANT A RED BIKE, SANTA!
WE LOVE YOU, SANTA!
PICK ME UP, SANTA CLAUS!
-D-UH! GAWRSH!
WHEW! AM I GLAD YOU CHANGED YOUR MIND, MOOSE! I GUESS YOU DECIDED TO FORGIVE REGGIE, EH?
REGGIE? REGGIE WHO?
(GULP)-THANKS, SANTA! THAT'S ALL I WANT FOR CHRISTMAS!
THE END

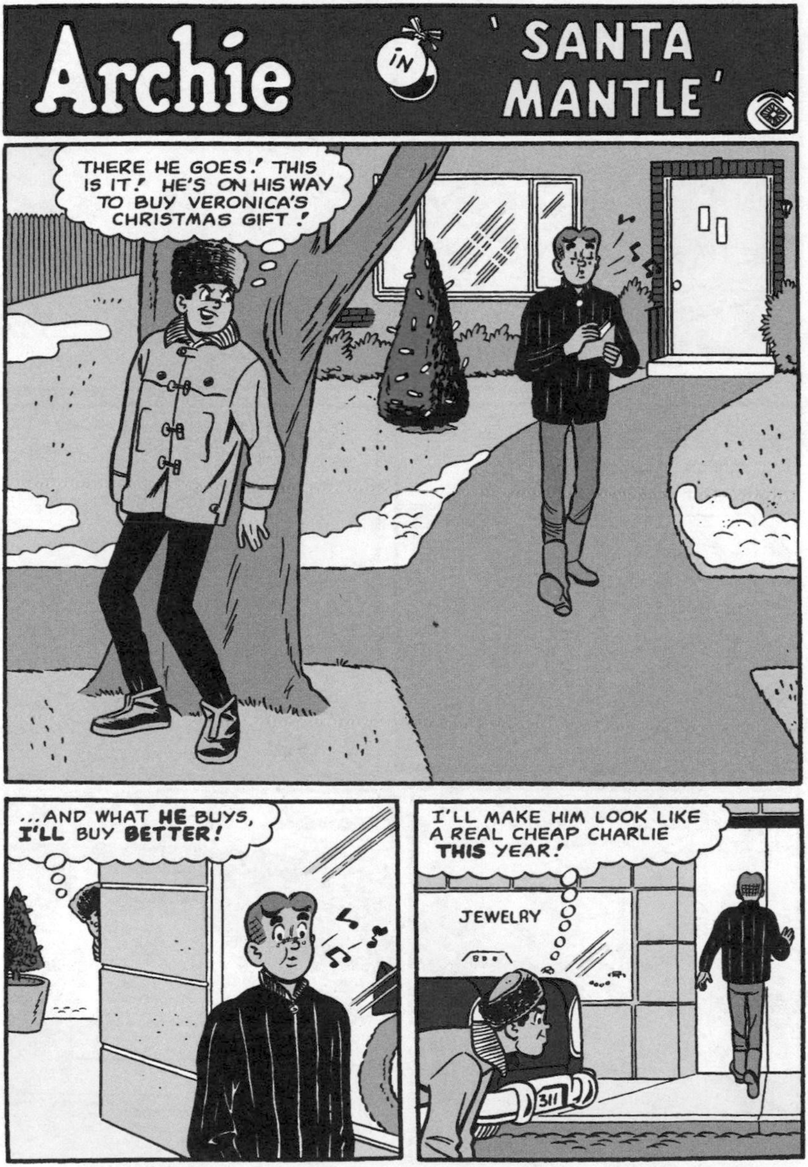
Archie
IN
'SANTA MANTLE'
THERE HE GOES! THIS IS IT! HE'S ON HIS WAY TO BUY VERONICA'S CHRISTMAS GIFT!
...AND WHAT HE BUYS, I'LL BUY BETTER!
I'LL MAKE HIM LOOK LIKE A REAL CHEAP CHARLIE THIS YEAR!
JEWELRY
311

• From Archie Giant Series Magazine #31, January 1965 •

Frank Doyle • Dan DeCarlo • Rudy Lapick • Vince DeCarlo • Barry Grossman

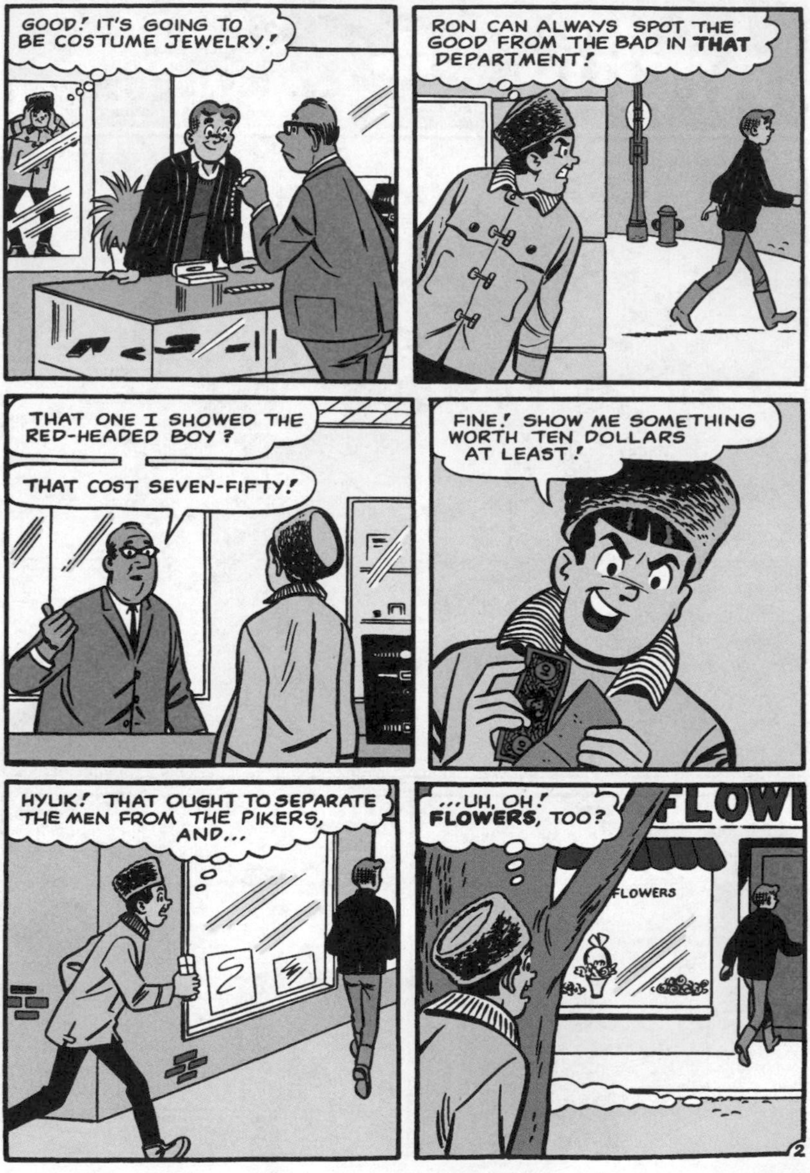
GOOD! IT'S GOING TO BE COSTUME JEWELRY!
RON CAN ALWAYS SPOT THE GOOD FROM THE BAD IN THAT DEPARTMENT!
THAT ONE I SHOWED THE RED-HEADED BOY?
THAT COST SEVEN-FIFTY!
FINE! SHOW ME SOMETHING WORTH TEN DOLLARS AT LEAST!
HYUK! THAT OUGHT TO SEPARATE THE MEN FROM THE PIKERS, AND...
...UH, OH! FLOWERS, TOO?
FLOW
FLOWERS
2

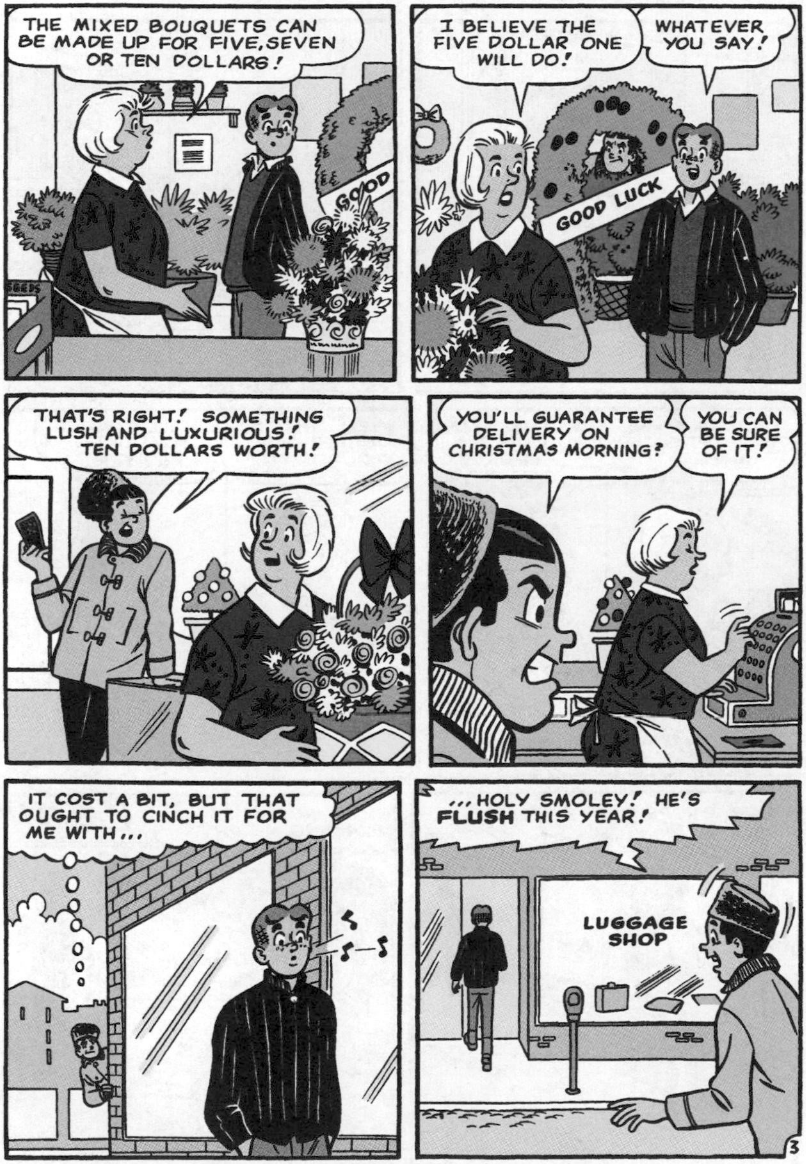
THE MIXED BOUQUETS CAN BE MADE UP FOR FIVE, SEVEN OR TEN DOLLARS!
GOOD
I BELIEVE THE FIVE DOLLAR ONE WILL DO!
WHATEVER YOU SAY!
GOOD LUCK
THAT'S RIGHT! SOMETHING LUSH AND LUXURIOUS! TEN DOLLARS WORTH!
YOU'LL GUARANTEE DELIVERY ON CHRISTMAS MORNING?
YOU CAN BE SURE OF IT!
IT COST A BIT, BUT THAT OUGHT TO CINCH IT FOR ME WITH...
...HOLY SMOLEY! HE'S FLUSH THIS YEAR!
LUGGAGE SHOP
3

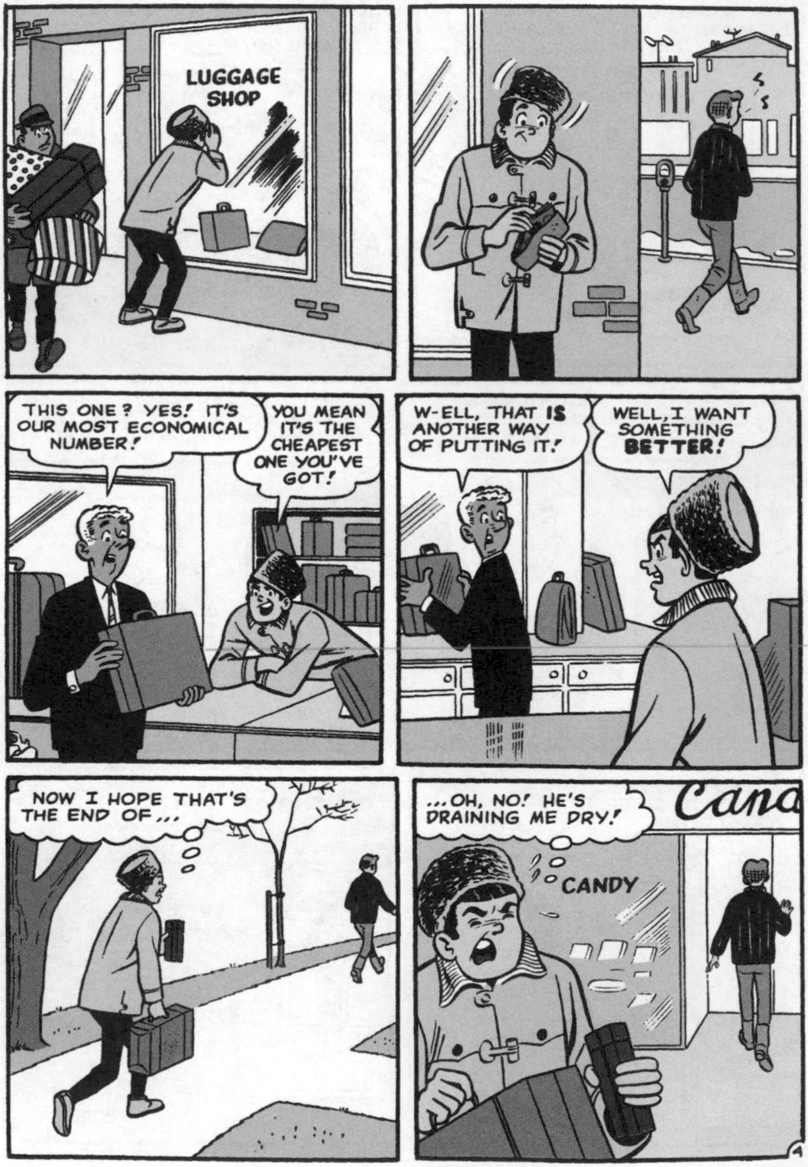
LUGGAGE
SHOP
THIS ONE? YES! IT'S OUR MOST ECONOMICAL NUMBER!
YOU MEAN IT'S THE CHEAPEST ONE YOU'VE GOT!
W-ELL, THAT IS ANOTHER WAY OF PUTTING IT!
WELL, I WANT SOMETHING BETTER!
NOW I HOPE THAT'S THE END OF...
...OH, NO! HE'S DRAINING ME DRY!
Cand
CANDY
4

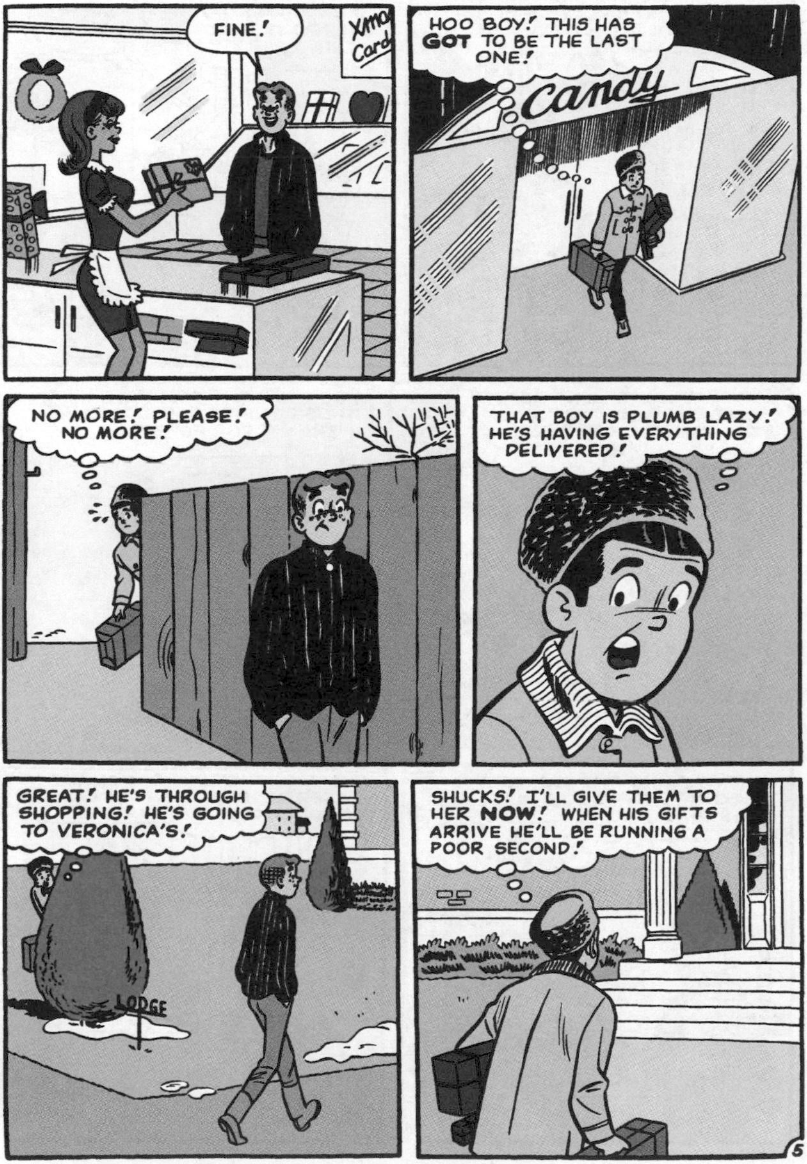
FINE!
Xmas Cards
HOO BOY! THIS HAS GOT TO BE THE LAST ONE!
Candy
NO MORE! PLEASE! NO MORE!
THAT BOY IS PLUMB LAZY! HE'S HAVING EVERYTHING DELIVERED!
GREAT! HE'S THROUGH SHOPPING! HE'S GOING TO VERONICA'S!
LODGE
SHUCKS! I'LL GIVE THEM TO HER NOW! WHEN HIS GIFTS ARRIVE HE'LL BE RUNNING A POOR SECOND!
5

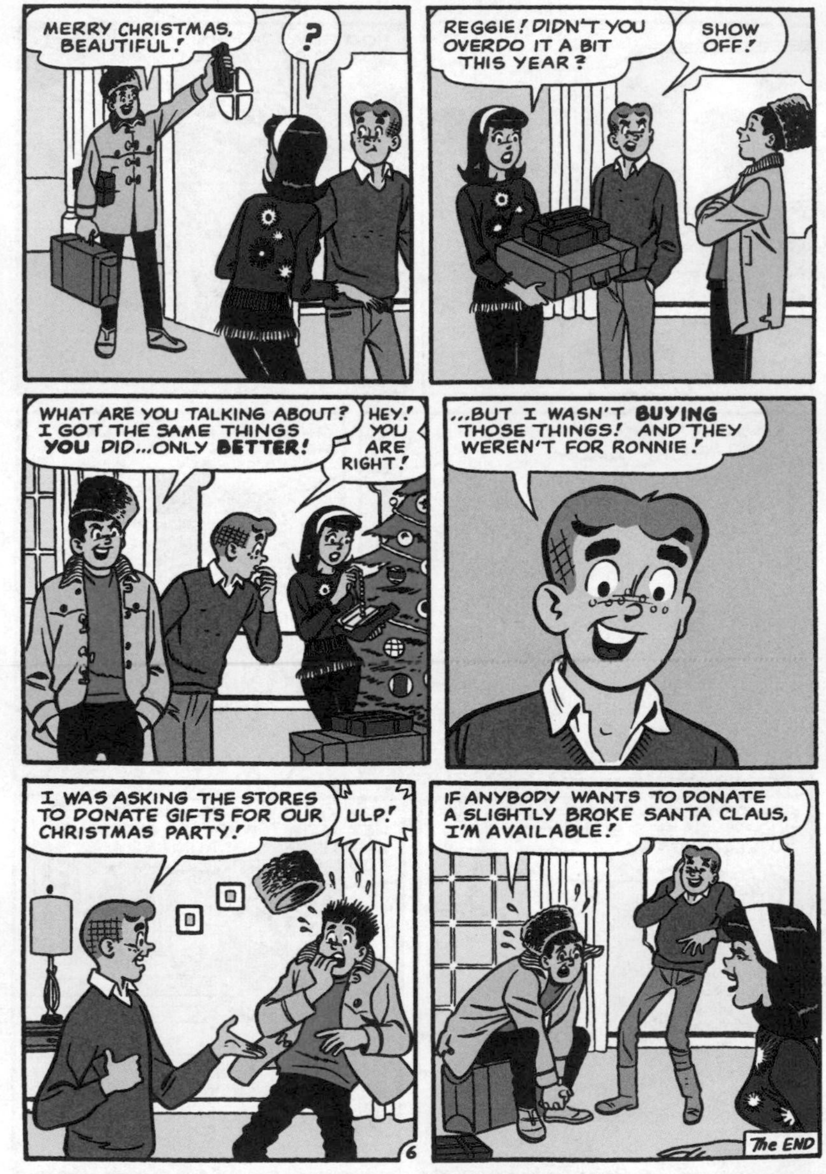
MERRY CHRISTMAS, BEAUTIFUL!
?
REGGIE! DIDN'T YOU OVERDO IT A BIT THIS YEAR?
SHOW OFF!
WHAT ARE YOU TALKING ABOUT? I GOT THE SAME THINGS YOU DID...ONLY BETTER!
HEY! YOU ARE RIGHT!
...BUT I WASN'T BUYING THOSE THINGS! AND THEY WEREN'T FOR RONNIE!
I WAS ASKING THE STORES TO DONATE GIFTS FOR OUR CHRISTMAS PARTY!
ULP!
6
IF ANYBODY WANTS TO DONATE A SLIGHTLY BROKE SANTA CLAUS, I'M AVAILABLE!
The END

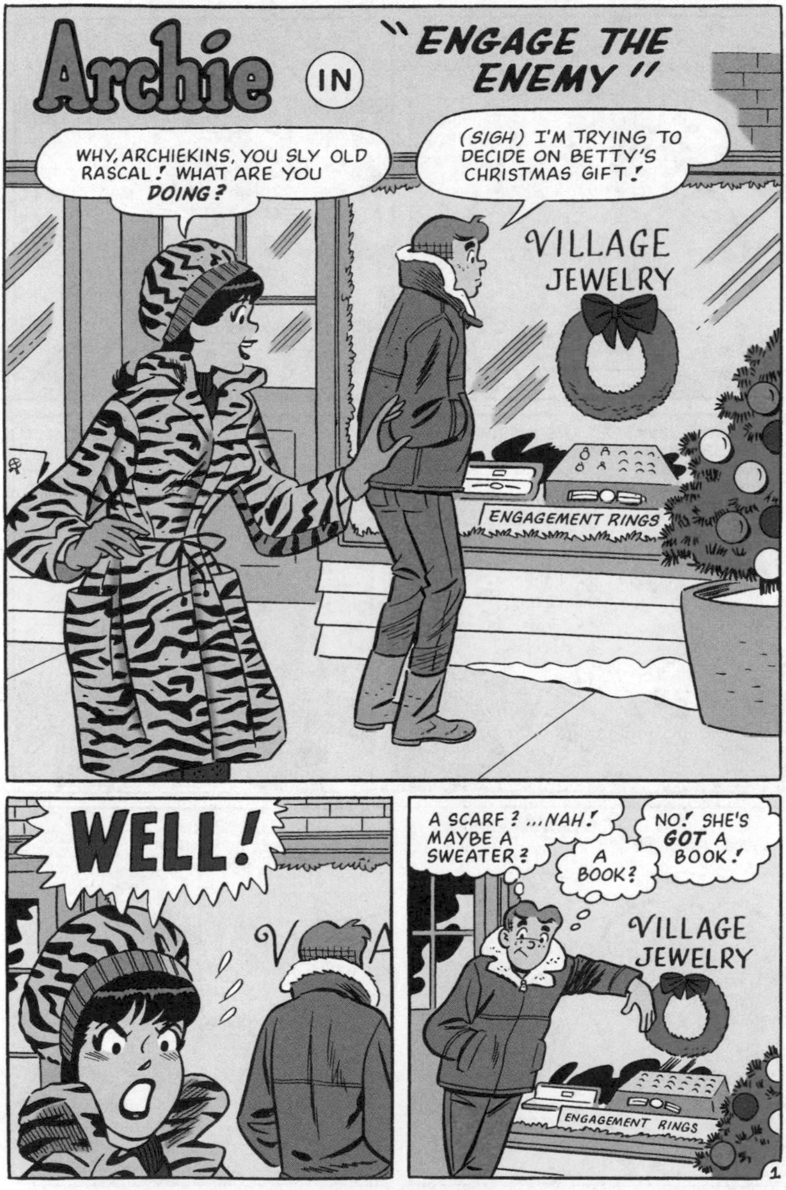
Archie IN "ENGAGE THE ENEMY"
WHY, ARCHIEKINS, YOU SLY OLD RASCAL! WHAT ARE YOU DOING?
(SIGH) I'M TRYING TO DECIDE ON BETTY'S CHRISTMAS GIFT!
VILLAGE JEWELRY
ENGAGEMENT RINGS
WELL!
A SCARF? ...NAH! MAYBE A SWEATER?
A BOOK?
NO! SHE'S GOT A BOOK!
VILLAGE JEWELRY
ENGAGEMENT RINGS
1

• **From Pep #202, February 1967** •

Frank Doyle • Dan DeCarlo • Rudy Lapick • Vince DeCarlo

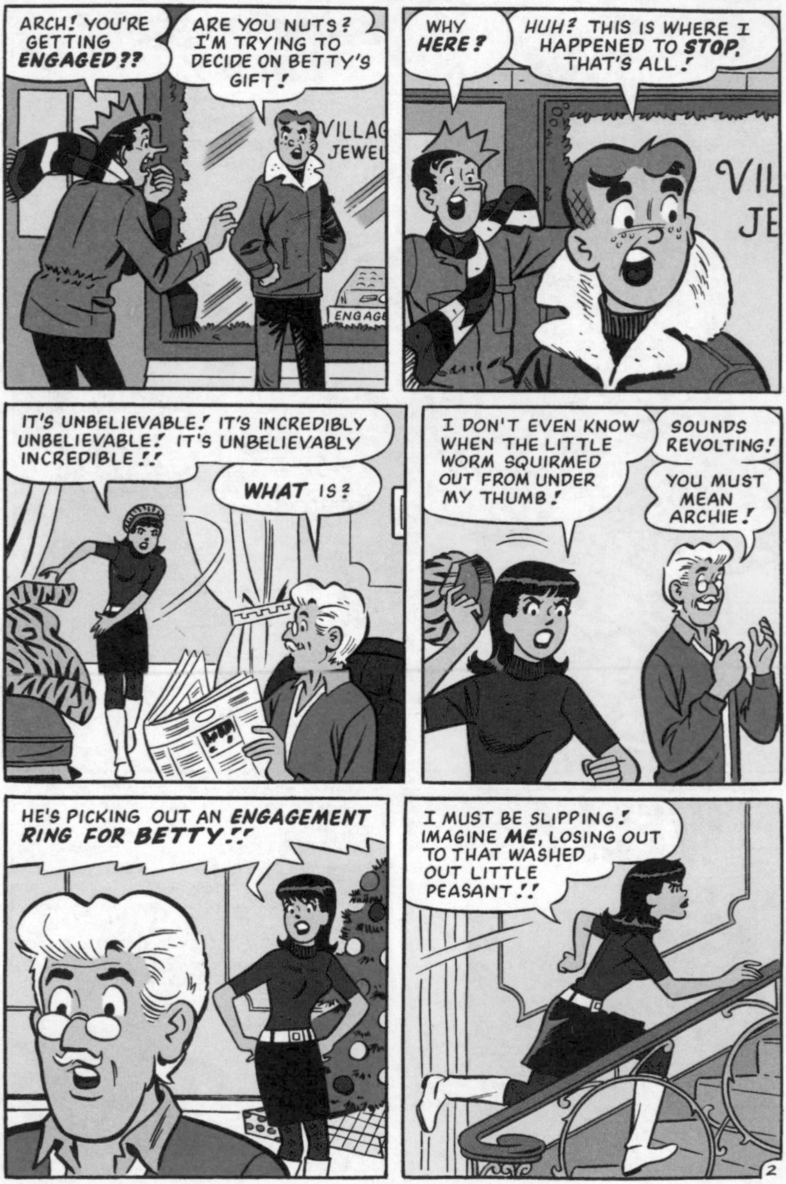
ARCH! YOU'RE GETTING ENGAGED??
ARE YOU NUTS? I'M TRYING TO DECIDE ON BETTY'S GIFT!
VILLAG JEWEL
ENGAGE
WHY HERE?
HUH? THIS IS WHERE I HAPPENED TO STOP, THAT'S ALL!
VIL JE
IT'S UNBELIEVABLE! IT'S INCREDIBLY UNBELIEVABLE! IT'S UNBELIEVABLY INCREDIBLE!!
WHAT IS?
I DON'T EVEN KNOW WHEN THE LITTLE WORM SQUIRMED OUT FROM UNDER MY THUMB!
SOUNDS REVOLTING!
YOU MUST MEAN ARCHIE!
HE'S PICKING OUT AN ENGAGEMENT RING FOR BETTY!!
I MUST BE SLIPPING! IMAGINE ME, LOSING OUT TO THAT WASHED OUT LITTLE PEASANT!!
2

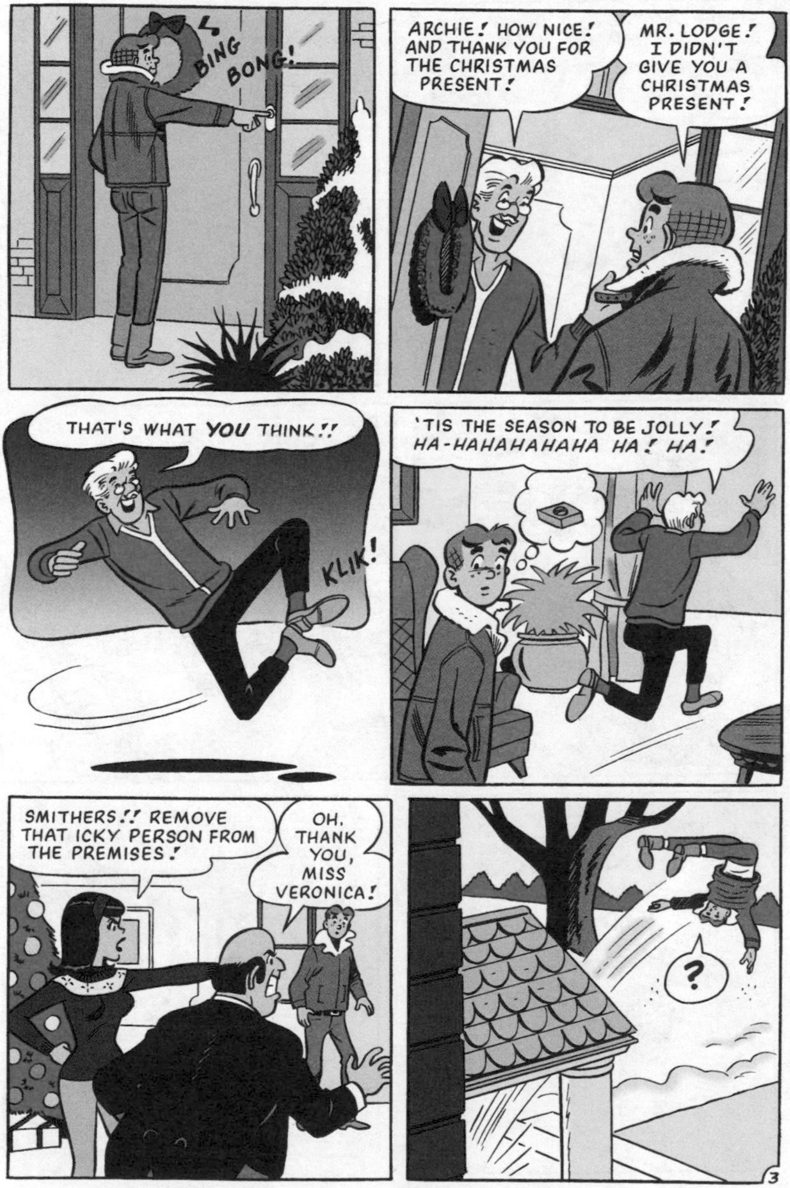
BING BONG!
ARCHIE! HOW NICE! AND THANK YOU FOR THE CHRISTMAS PRESENT!
MR. LODGE! I DIDN'T GIVE YOU A CHRISTMAS PRESENT!
THAT'S WHAT YOU THINK!!
KLIK!
'TIS THE SEASON TO BE JOLLY! HA-HAHAHAHAHA HA! HA!
SMITHERS!! REMOVE THAT ICKY PERSON FROM THE PREMISES!
OH. THANK YOU, MISS VERONICA!
?
3

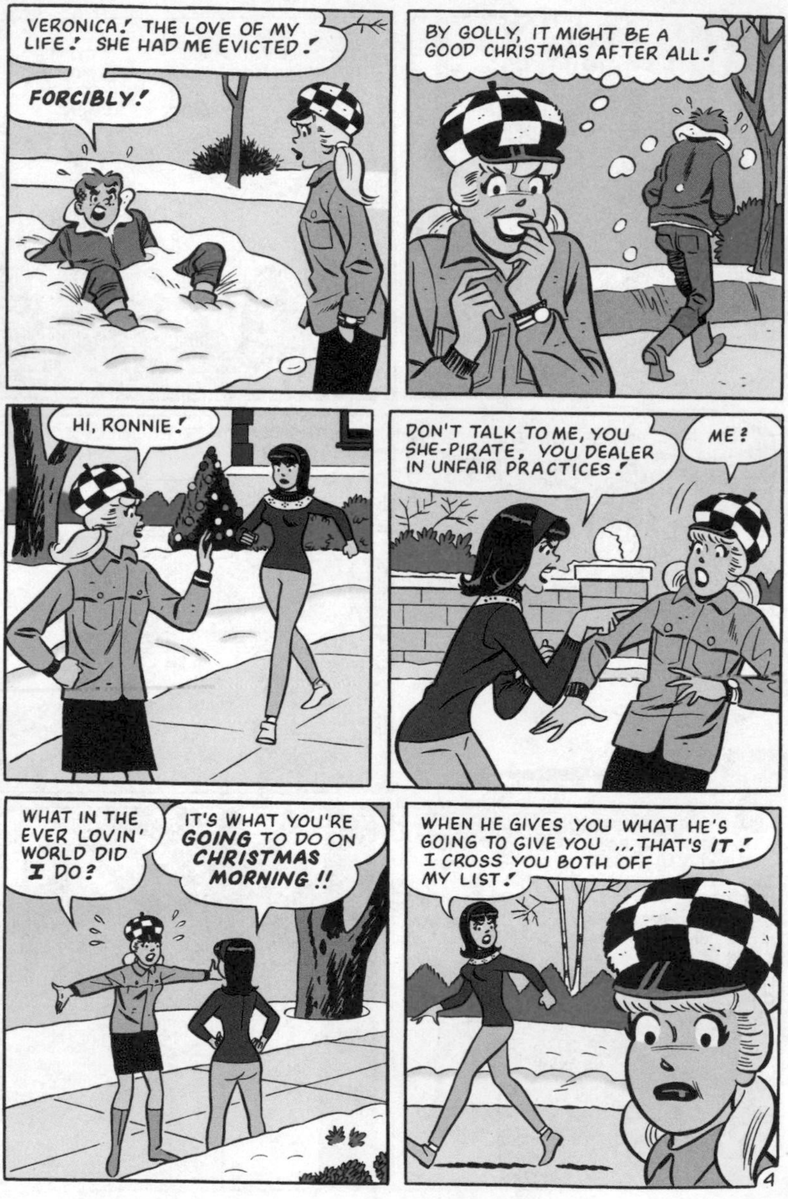
VERONICA! THE LOVE OF MY LIFE! SHE HAD ME EVICTED!
FORCIBLY!
BY GOLLY, IT MIGHT BE A GOOD CHRISTMAS AFTER ALL!
HI, RONNIE!
DON'T TALK TO ME, YOU SHE-PIRATE, YOU DEALER IN UNFAIR PRACTICES!
ME?
WHAT IN THE EVER LOVIN' WORLD DID I DO?
IT'S WHAT YOU'RE GOING TO DO ON CHRISTMAS MORNING!!
WHEN HE GIVES YOU WHAT HE'S GOING TO GIVE YOU ...THAT'S IT! I CROSS YOU BOTH OFF MY LIST!
4

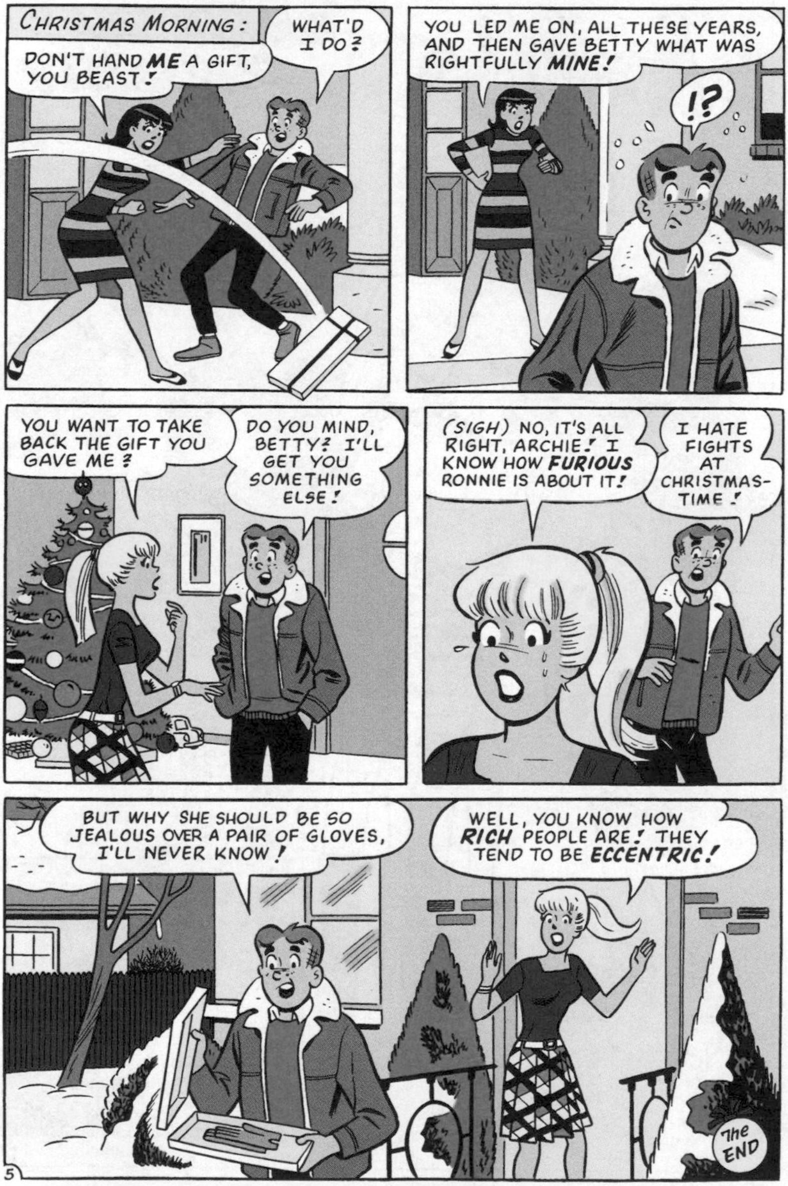
CHRISTMAS MORNING:
DON'T HAND ME A GIFT, YOU BEAST!
WHAT'D I DO?
YOU LED ME ON, ALL THESE YEARS, AND THEN GAVE BETTY WHAT WAS RIGHTFULLY MINE!
!?
YOU WANT TO TAKE BACK THE GIFT YOU GAVE ME?
DO YOU MIND, BETTY? I'LL GET YOU SOMETHING ELSE!
(SIGH) NO, IT'S ALL RIGHT, ARCHIE! I KNOW HOW FURIOUS RONNIE IS ABOUT IT!
I HATE FIGHTS AT CHRISTMAS-TIME!
BUT WHY SHE SHOULD BE SO JEALOUS OVER A PAIR OF GLOVES, I'LL NEVER KNOW!
WELL, YOU KNOW HOW RICH PEOPLE ARE! THEY TEND TO BE ECCENTRIC!
5
The END

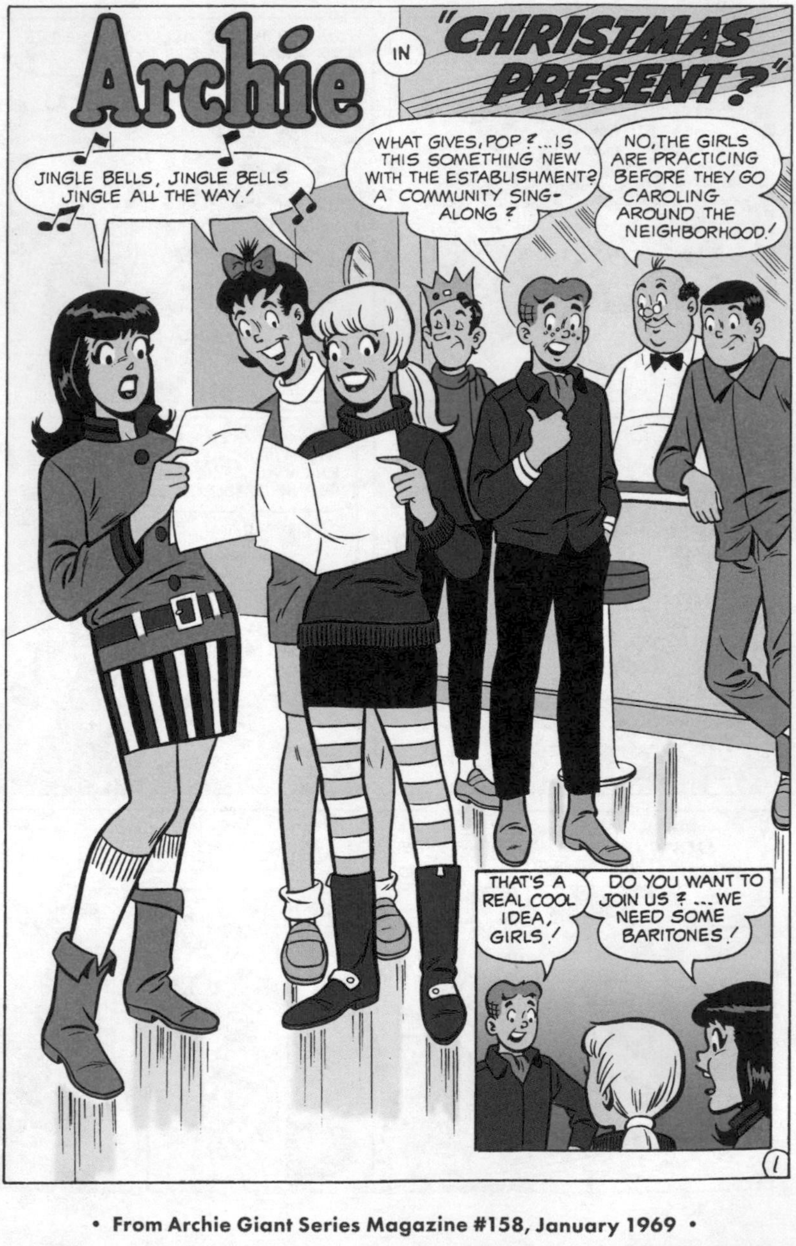
Archie
IN
"CHRISTMAS PRESENT?"
JINGLE BELLS, JINGLE BELLS JINGLE ALL THE WAY!
WHAT GIVES, POP ?...IS THIS SOMETHING NEW WITH THE ESTABLISHMENT? A COMMUNITY SING-ALONG ?
NO, THE GIRLS ARE PRACTICING BEFORE THEY GO CAROLING AROUND THE NEIGHBORHOOD!
THAT'S A REAL COOL IDEA, GIRLS!
DO YOU WANT TO JOIN US ? ... WE NEED SOME BARITONES!
1

• **From Archie Giant Series Magazine #158, January 1969** •

George Gladir • Samm Schwartz • Jon D'Agostino • Bill Yoshida • Barry Grossman

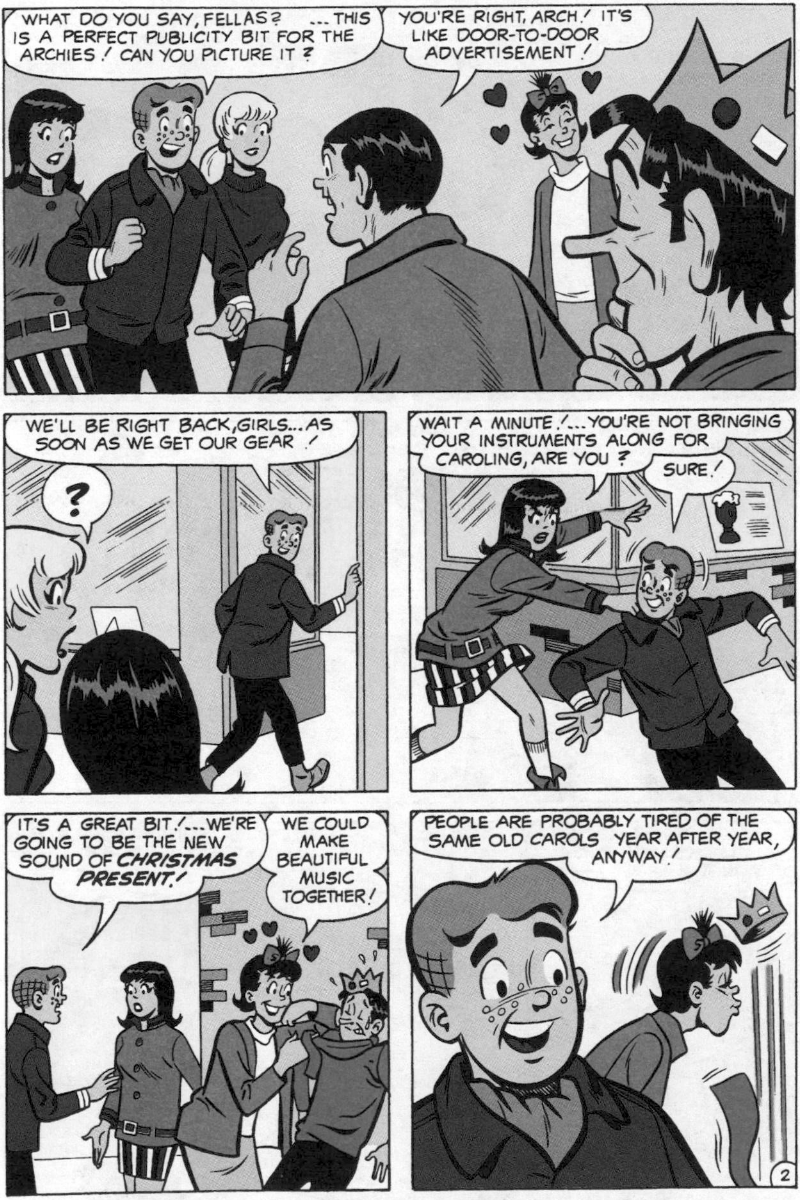
WHAT DO YOU SAY, FELLAS? ... THIS IS A PERFECT PUBLICITY BIT FOR THE ARCHIES! CAN YOU PICTURE IT?
YOU'RE RIGHT, ARCH! IT'S LIKE DOOR-TO-DOOR ADVERTISEMENT!
WE'LL BE RIGHT BACK, GIRLS... AS SOON AS WE GET OUR GEAR!
?
WAIT A MINUTE!... YOU'RE NOT BRINGING YOUR INSTRUMENTS ALONG FOR CAROLING, ARE YOU?
SURE!
IT'S A GREAT BIT!... WE'RE GOING TO BE THE NEW SOUND OF CHRISTMAS PRESENT!
WE COULD MAKE BEAUTIFUL MUSIC TOGETHER!
PEOPLE ARE PROBABLY TIRED OF THE SAME OLD CAROLS YEAR AFTER YEAR, ANYWAY!
2

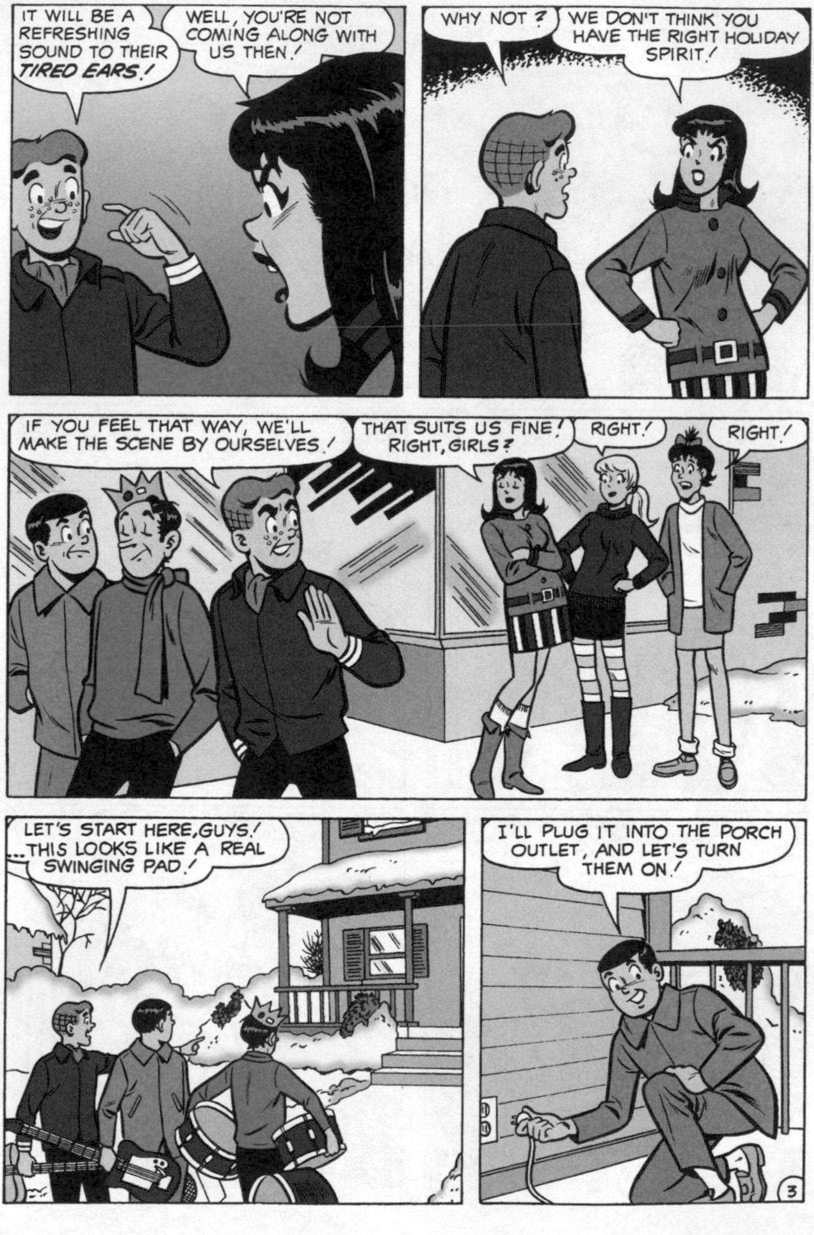
IT WILL BE A REFRESHING SOUND TO THEIR *TIRED EARS*!
WELL, YOU'RE NOT COMING ALONG WITH US THEN!
WHY NOT?
WE DON'T THINK YOU HAVE THE RIGHT HOLIDAY SPIRIT!
IF YOU FEEL THAT WAY, WE'LL MAKE THE SCENE BY OURSELVES!
THAT SUITS US FINE! RIGHT, GIRLS?
RIGHT!
RIGHT!
LET'S START HERE, GUYS! ...THIS LOOKS LIKE A REAL SWINGING PAD!
I'LL PLUG IT INTO THE PORCH OUTLET, AND LET'S TURN THEM ON!
3

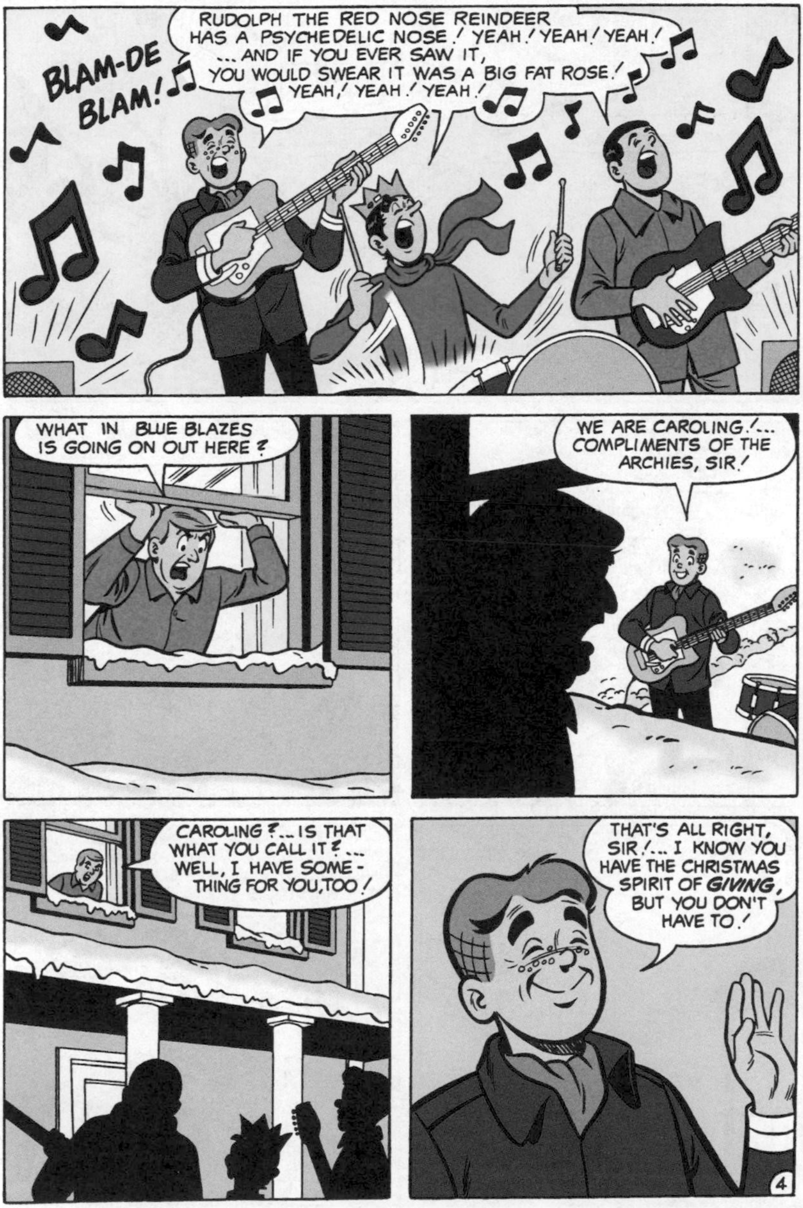
BLAM-DE BLAM!
RUDOLPH THE RED NOSE REINDEER HAS A PSYCHEDELIC NOSE! YEAH! YEAH! YEAH! ...AND IF YOU EVER SAW IT, YOU WOULD SWEAR IT WAS A BIG FAT ROSE! YEAH! YEAH! YEAH!
WHAT IN BLUE BLAZES IS GOING ON OUT HERE?
WE ARE CAROLING!... COMPLIMENTS OF THE ARCHIES, SIR!
CAROLING?...IS THAT WHAT YOU CALL IT?... WELL, I HAVE SOME-THING FOR YOU, TOO!
THAT'S ALL RIGHT, SIR!... I KNOW YOU HAVE THE CHRISTMAS SPIRIT OF *GIVING*, BUT YOU DON'T HAVE TO!
4

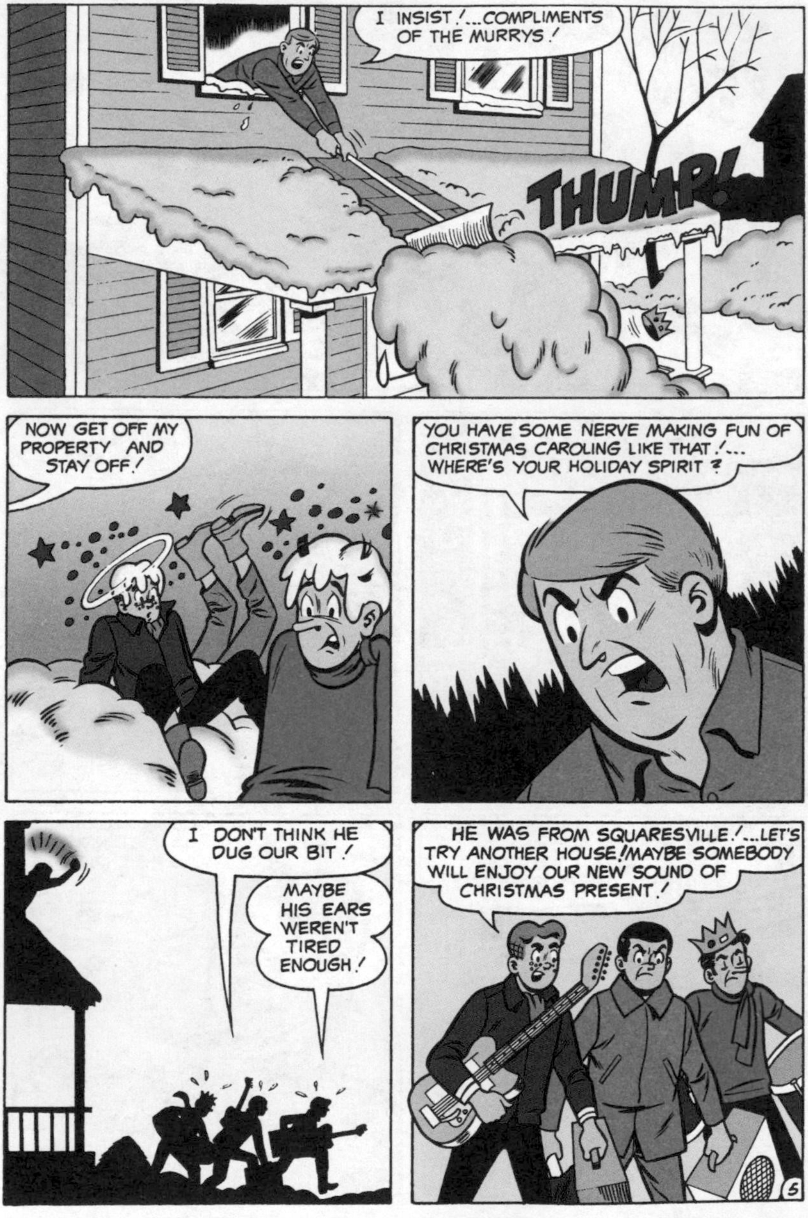
I INSIST!...COMPLIMENTS OF THE MURRYS!
THUMP!
NOW GET OFF MY PROPERTY AND STAY OFF!
YOU HAVE SOME NERVE MAKING FUN OF CHRISTMAS CAROLING LIKE THAT!... WHERE'S YOUR HOLIDAY SPIRIT?
I DON'T THINK HE DUG OUR BIT!
MAYBE HIS EARS WEREN'T TIRED ENOUGH!
HE WAS FROM SQUARESVILLE!...LET'S TRY ANOTHER HOUSE! MAYBE SOMEBODY WILL ENJOY OUR NEW SOUND OF CHRISTMAS PRESENT!
5

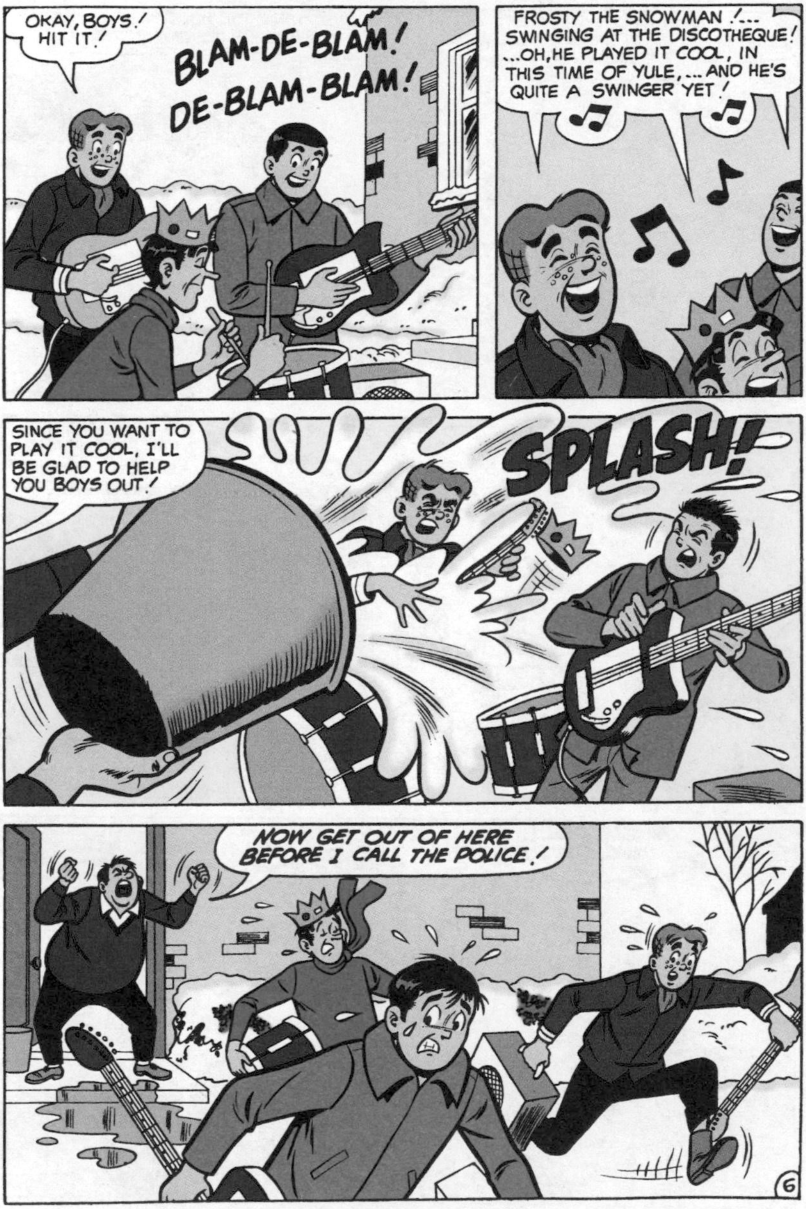
OKAY, BOYS! HIT IT!
BLAM-DE-BLAM! DE-BLAM-BLAM!
FROSTY THE SNOWMAN!... SWINGING AT THE DISCOTHEQUE! ...OH, HE PLAYED IT COOL, IN THIS TIME OF YULE, ... AND HE'S QUITE A SWINGER YET!
SINCE YOU WANT TO PLAY IT COOL, I'LL BE GLAD TO HELP YOU BOYS OUT!
SPLASH!
NOW GET OUT OF HERE BEFORE I CALL THE POLICE!
6

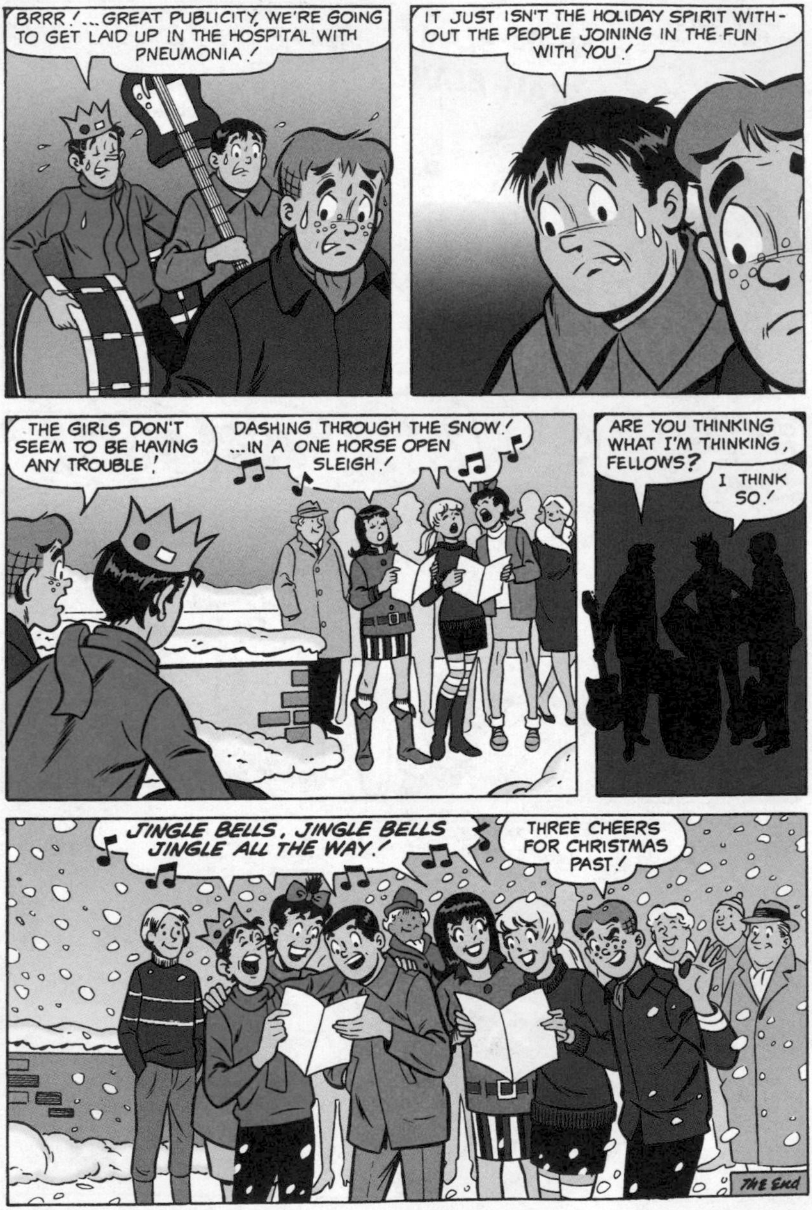
BRRR!...GREAT PUBLICITY, WE'RE GOING TO GET LAID UP IN THE HOSPITAL WITH PNEUMONIA!
IT JUST ISN'T THE HOLIDAY SPIRIT WITHOUT THE PEOPLE JOINING IN THE FUN WITH YOU!
THE GIRLS DON'T SEEM TO BE HAVING ANY TROUBLE!
DASHING THROUGH THE SNOW! ...IN A ONE HORSE OPEN SLEIGH!
ARE YOU THINKING WHAT I'M THINKING, FELLOWS?
I THINK SO!
JINGLE BELLS, JINGLE BELLS JINGLE ALL THE WAY!
THREE CHEERS FOR CHRISTMAS PAST!
THE END

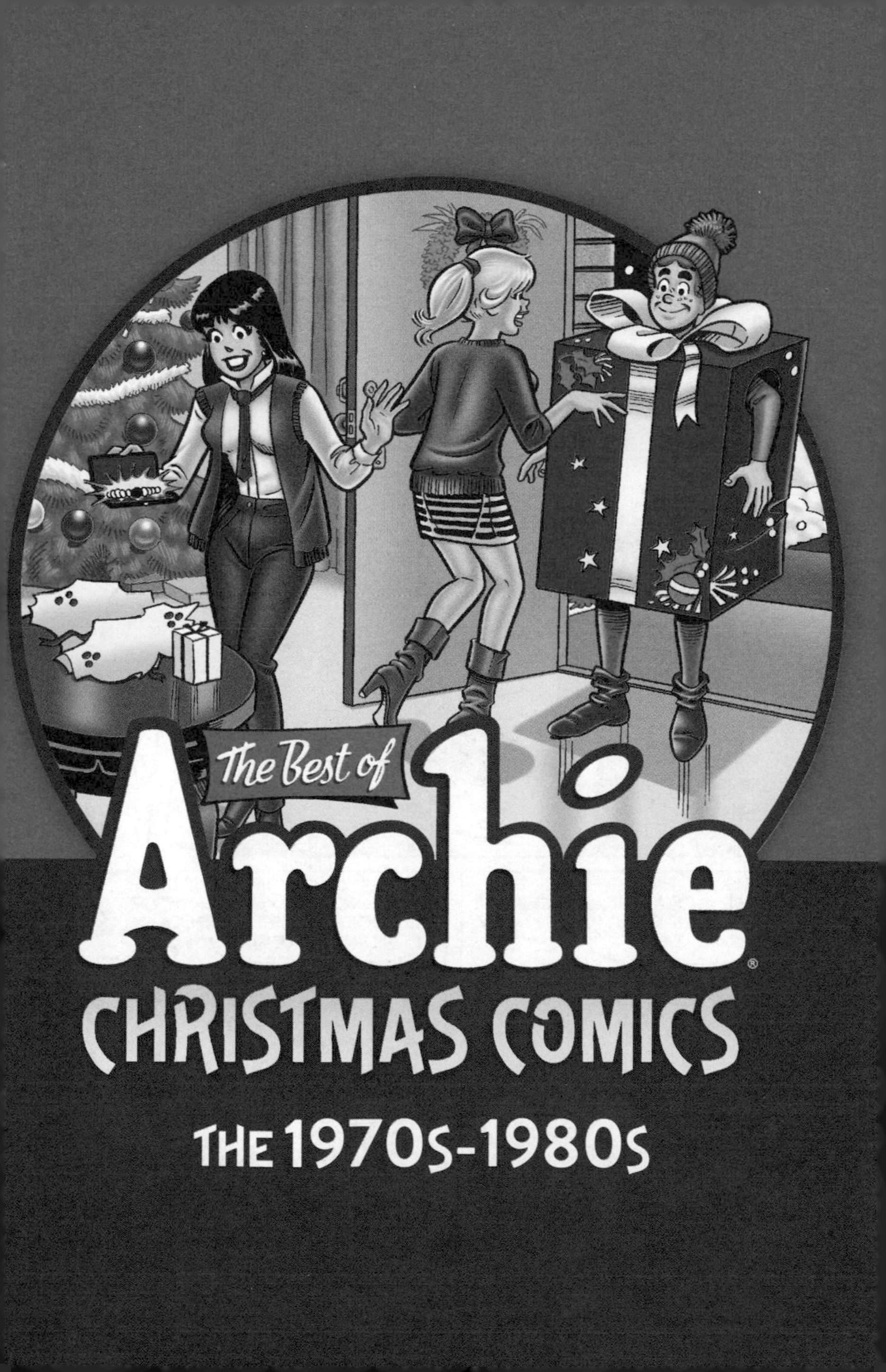

The Best of

Archie®

CHRISTMAS COMICS

THE 1970s-1980s

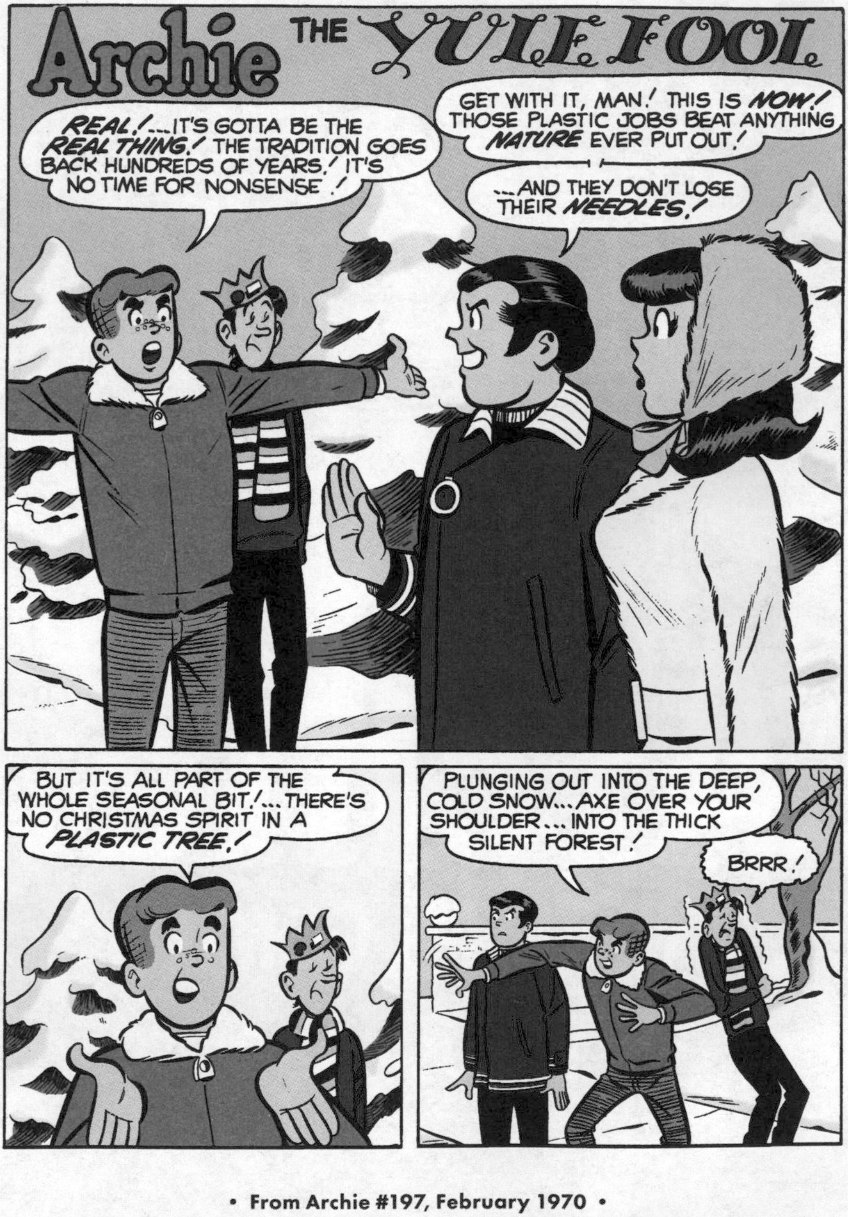
Archie THE YULE FOOL
REAL!...IT'S GOTTA BE THE REAL THING! THE TRADITION GOES BACK HUNDREDS OF YEARS! IT'S NO TIME FOR NONSENSE!
GET WITH IT, MAN! THIS IS NOW! THOSE PLASTIC JOBS BEAT ANYTHING NATURE EVER PUT OUT!
...AND THEY DON'T LOSE THEIR NEEDLES!
BUT IT'S ALL PART OF THE WHOLE SEASONAL BIT!...THERE'S NO CHRISTMAS SPIRIT IN A PLASTIC TREE!
PLUNGING OUT INTO THE DEEP, COLD SNOW...AXE OVER YOUR SHOULDER...INTO THE THICK SILENT FOREST!
BRRR!

• **From Archie #197, February 1970** •

Frank Doyle • Harry Lucey • Marty Epp • Bill Yoshida

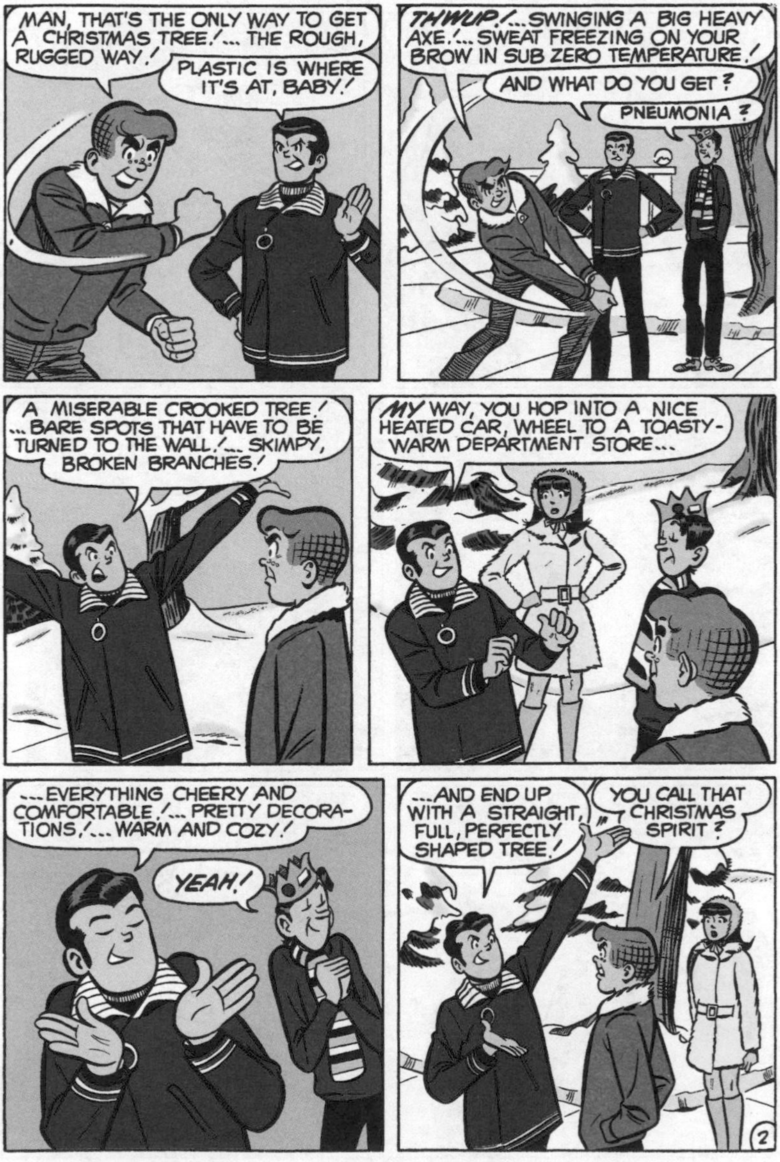
MAN, THAT'S THE ONLY WAY TO GET A CHRISTMAS TREE!... THE ROUGH, RUGGED WAY!
PLASTIC IS WHERE IT'S AT, BABY!
THWUP!... SWINGING A BIG HEAVY AXE!... SWEAT FREEZING ON YOUR BROW IN SUB ZERO TEMPERATURE!
AND WHAT DO YOU GET ?
PNEUMONIA ?
A MISERABLE CROOKED TREE!... BARE SPOTS THAT HAVE TO BE TURNED TO THE WALL!... SKIMPY, BROKEN BRANCHES!
MY WAY, YOU HOP INTO A NICE HEATED CAR, WHEEL TO A TOASTY-WARM DEPARTMENT STORE...
...EVERYTHING CHEERY AND COMFORTABLE!... PRETTY DECORATIONS!... WARM AND COZY!
YEAH!
...AND END UP WITH A STRAIGHT, FULL, PERFECTLY SHAPED TREE!
YOU CALL THAT CHRISTMAS SPIRIT ?
2

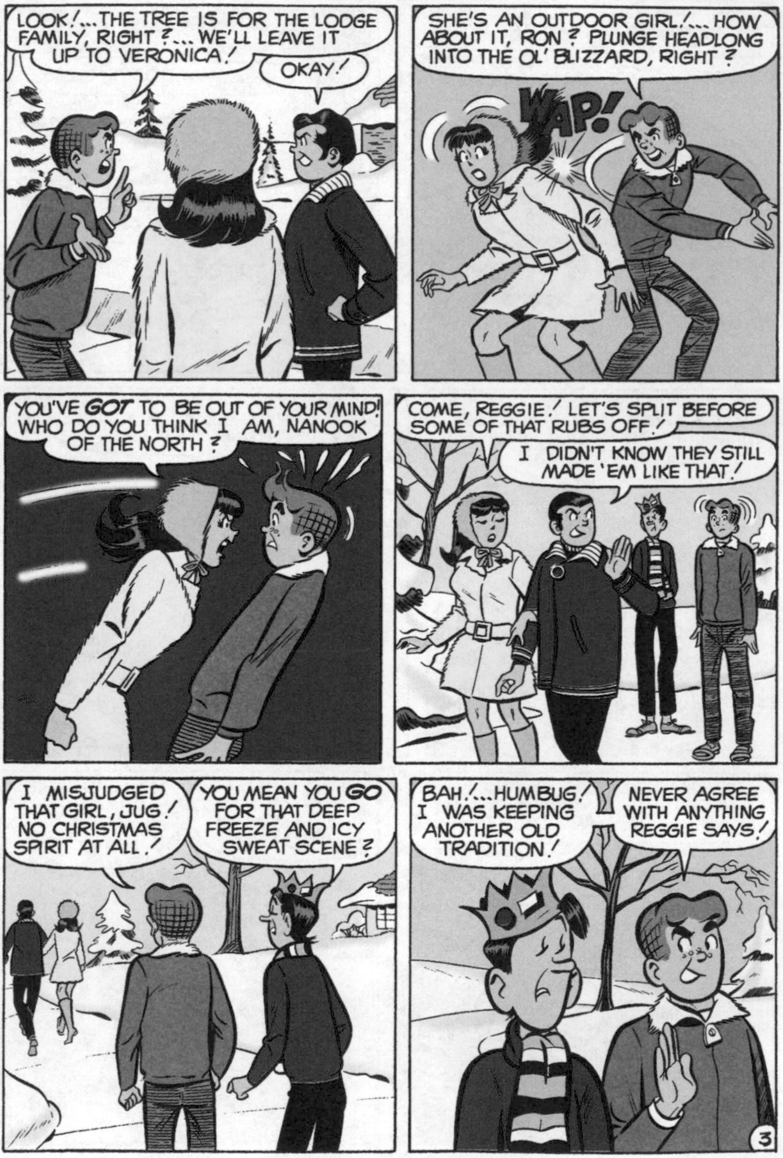
LOOK!... THE TREE IS FOR THE LODGE FAMILY, RIGHT?... WE'LL LEAVE IT UP TO VERONICA!
OKAY!
SHE'S AN OUTDOOR GIRL!... HOW ABOUT IT, RON? PLUNGE HEADLONG INTO THE OL' BLIZZARD, RIGHT?
WAP!
YOU'VE GOT TO BE OUT OF YOUR MIND! WHO DO YOU THINK I AM, NANOOK OF THE NORTH?
COME, REGGIE! LET'S SPLIT BEFORE SOME OF THAT RUBS OFF!
I DIDN'T KNOW THEY STILL MADE 'EM LIKE THAT!
I MISJUDGED THAT GIRL, JUG! NO CHRISTMAS SPIRIT AT ALL!
YOU MEAN YOU GO FOR THAT DEEP FREEZE AND ICY SWEAT SCENE?
BAH!... HUMBUG! I WAS KEEPING ANOTHER OLD TRADITION!
NEVER AGREE WITH ANYTHING REGGIE SAYS!
3

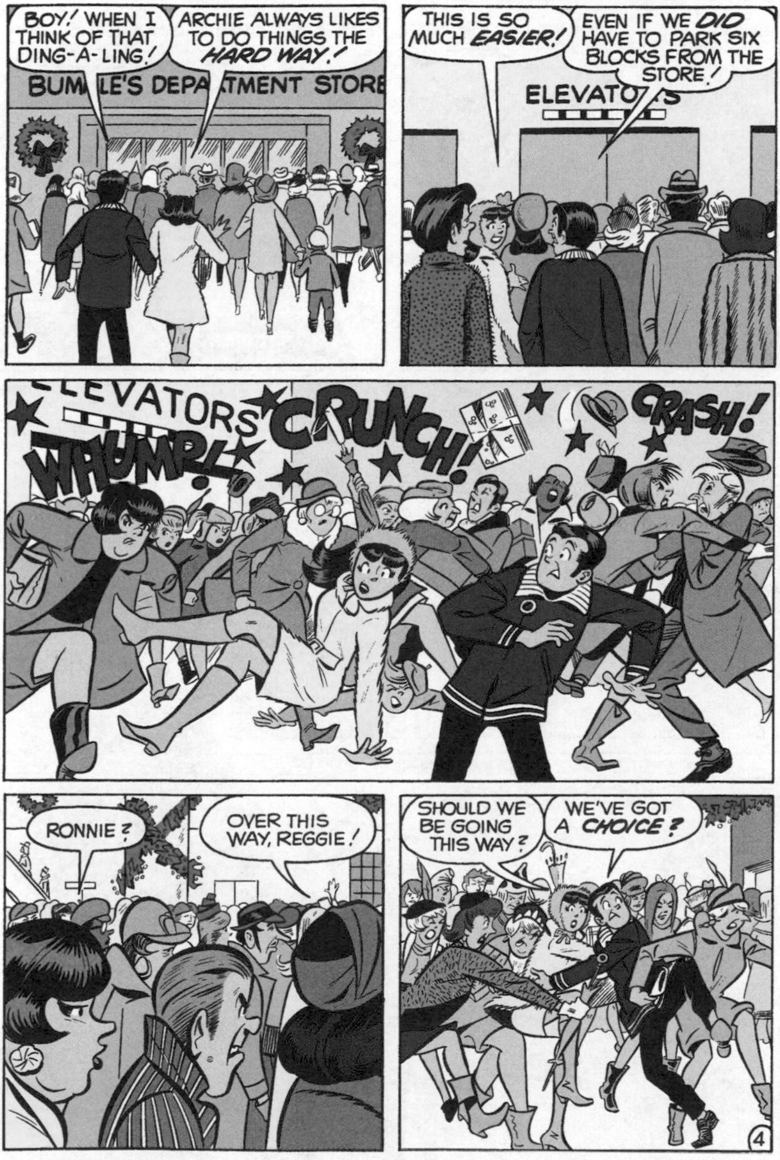
BOY! WHEN I THINK OF THAT DING-A-LING!
ARCHIE ALWAYS LIKES TO DO THINGS THE HARD WAY!
BUM LE'S DEPA TMENT STORE
THIS IS SO MUCH EASIER!
EVEN IF WE DID HAVE TO PARK SIX BLOCKS FROM THE STORE!
ELEVATO S
ELEVATORS
WHUMP!
CRUNCH!
CRASH!
RONNIE?
OVER THIS WAY, REGGIE!
SHOULD WE BE GOING THIS WAY?
WE'VE GOT A CHOICE?
4

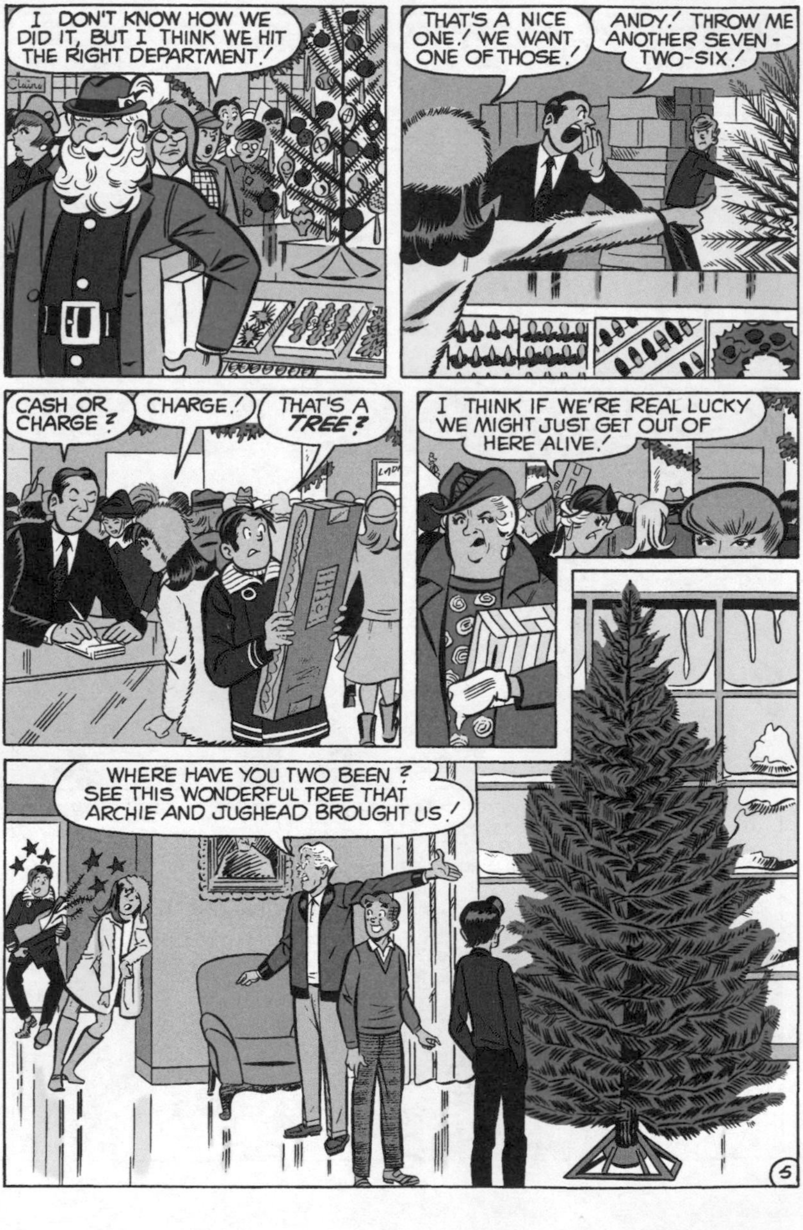
I DON'T KNOW HOW WE DID IT, BUT I THINK WE HIT THE RIGHT DEPARTMENT!
THAT'S A NICE ONE! WE WANT ONE OF THOSE!
ANDY! THROW ME ANOTHER SEVEN-TWO-SIX!
CASH OR CHARGE?
CHARGE!
THAT'S A TREE?
I THINK IF WE'RE REAL LUCKY WE MIGHT JUST GET OUT OF HERE ALIVE!
WHERE HAVE YOU TWO BEEN? SEE THIS WONDERFUL TREE THAT ARCHIE AND JUGHEAD BROUGHT US!
5

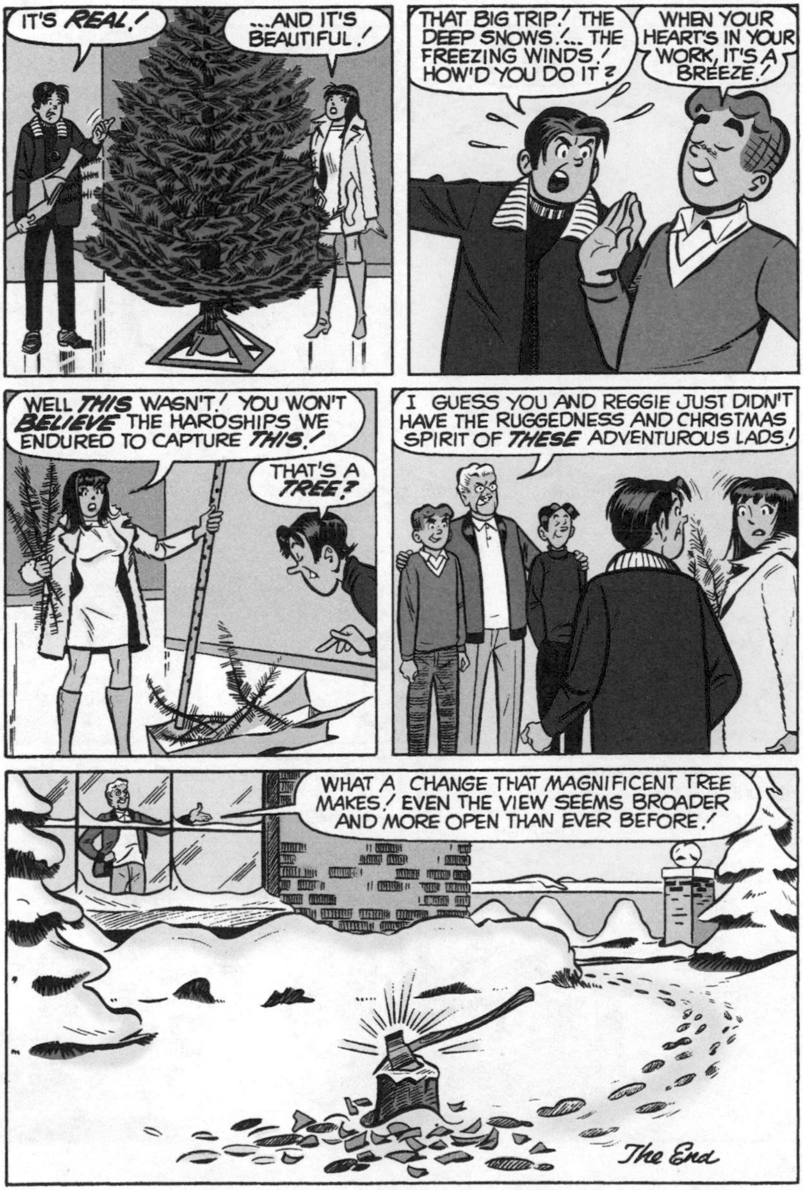
IT'S REAL!
...AND IT'S BEAUTIFUL!
THAT BIG TRIP! THE DEEP SNOWS!... THE FREEZING WINDS! HOW'D YOU DO IT?
WHEN YOUR HEART'S IN YOUR WORK, IT'S A BREEZE!
WELL THIS WASN'T! YOU WON'T BELIEVE THE HARDSHIPS WE ENDURED TO CAPTURE THIS!
THAT'S A TREE?
I GUESS YOU AND REGGIE JUST DIDN'T HAVE THE RUGGEDNESS AND CHRISTMAS SPIRIT OF THESE ADVENTUROUS LADS!
WHAT A CHANGE THAT MAGNIFICENT TREE MAKES! EVEN THE VIEW SEEMS BROADER AND MORE OPEN THAN EVER BEFORE!
The End

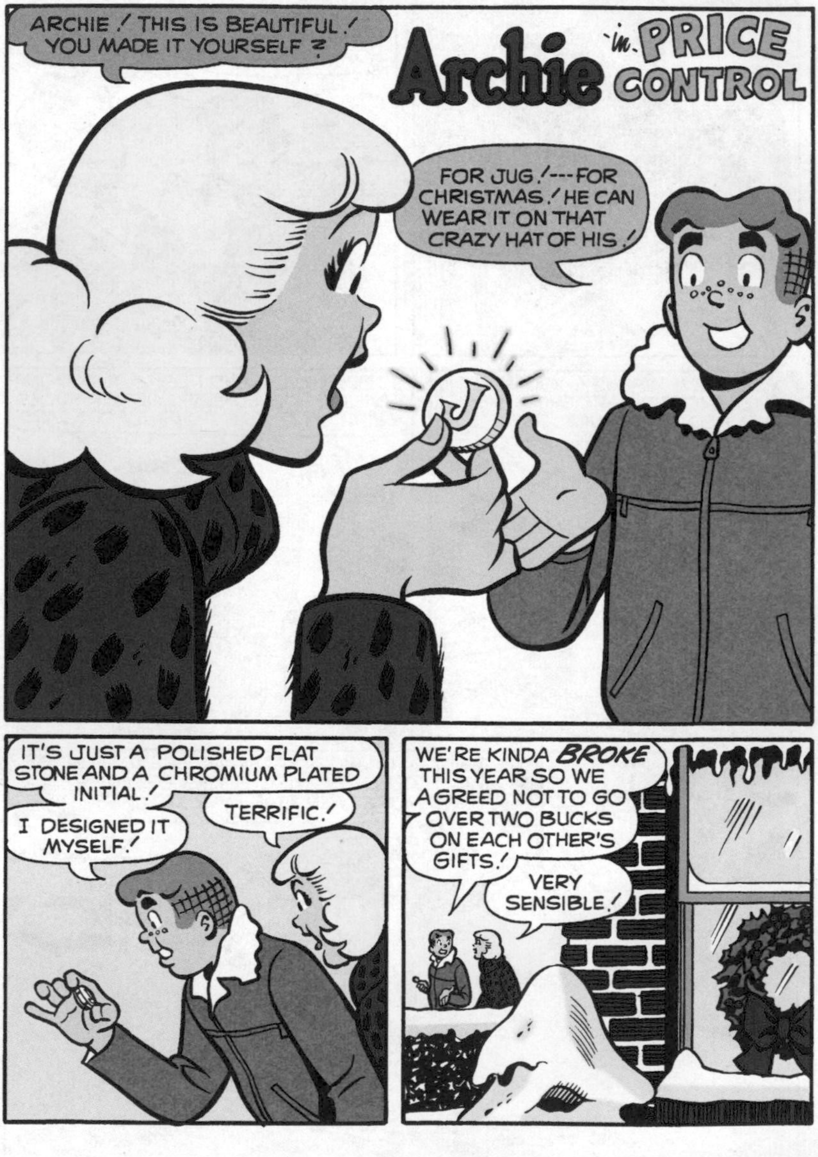
ARCHIE! THIS IS BEAUTIFUL! YOU MADE IT YOURSELF?
Archie in PRICE CONTROL
FOR JUG!---FOR CHRISTMAS! HE CAN WEAR IT ON THAT CRAZY HAT OF HIS!
IT'S JUST A POLISHED FLAT STONE AND A CHROMIUM PLATED INITIAL!
I DESIGNED IT MYSELF!
TERRIFIC!
WE'RE KINDA BROKE THIS YEAR SO WE AGREED NOT TO GO OVER TWO BUCKS ON EACH OTHER'S GIFTS!
VERY SENSIBLE!

• From Archie Giant Series Magazine #240, December 1975 •

George Gladir • Harry Lucey • Bill Yoshida

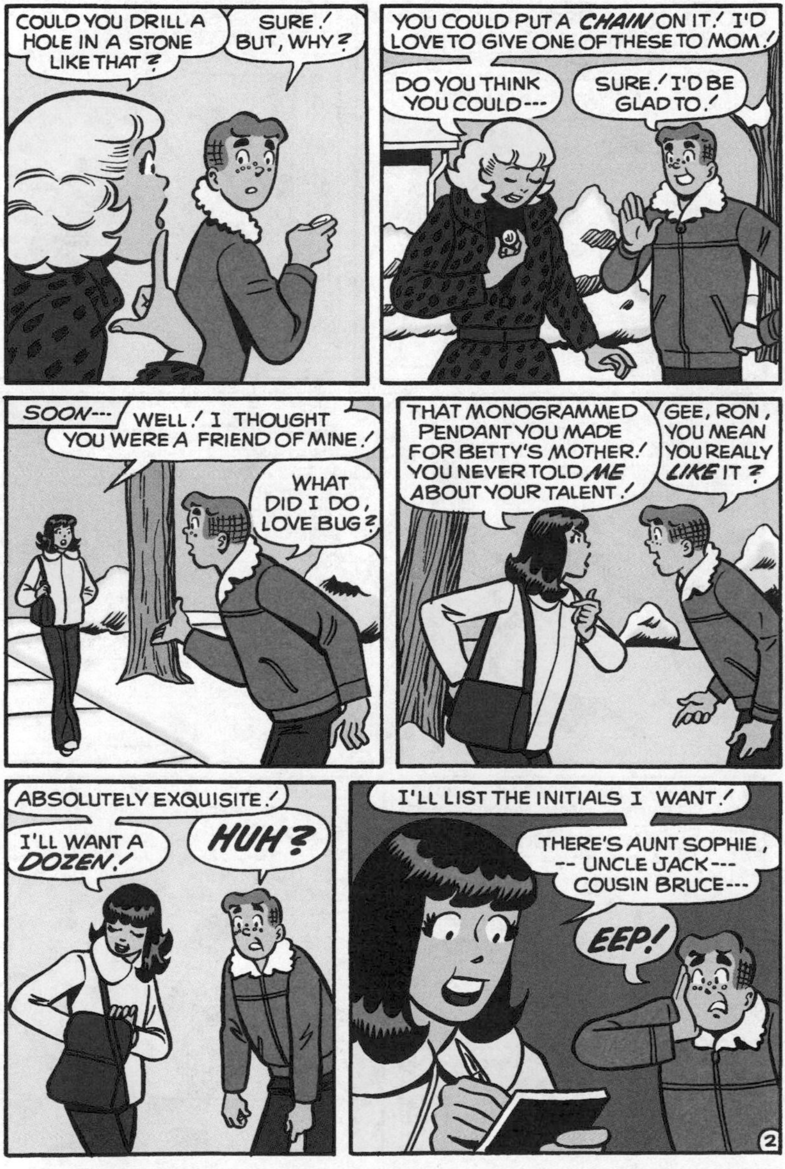
COULD YOU DRILL A HOLE IN A STONE LIKE THAT?
SURE! BUT, WHY?
YOU COULD PUT A CHAIN ON IT! I'D LOVE TO GIVE ONE OF THESE TO MOM!
DO YOU THINK YOU COULD---
SURE! I'D BE GLAD TO!
SOON---
WELL! I THOUGHT YOU WERE A FRIEND OF MINE!
WHAT DID I DO, LOVE BUG?
THAT MONOGRAMMED PENDANT YOU MADE FOR BETTY'S MOTHER! YOU NEVER TOLD ME ABOUT YOUR TALENT!
GEE, RON, YOU MEAN YOU REALLY LIKE IT?
ABSOLUTELY EXQUISITE!
I'LL WANT A DOZEN!
HUH?
I'LL LIST THE INITIALS I WANT!
THERE'S AUNT SOPHIE, -- UNCLE JACK--- COUSIN BRUCE---
EEP!
2

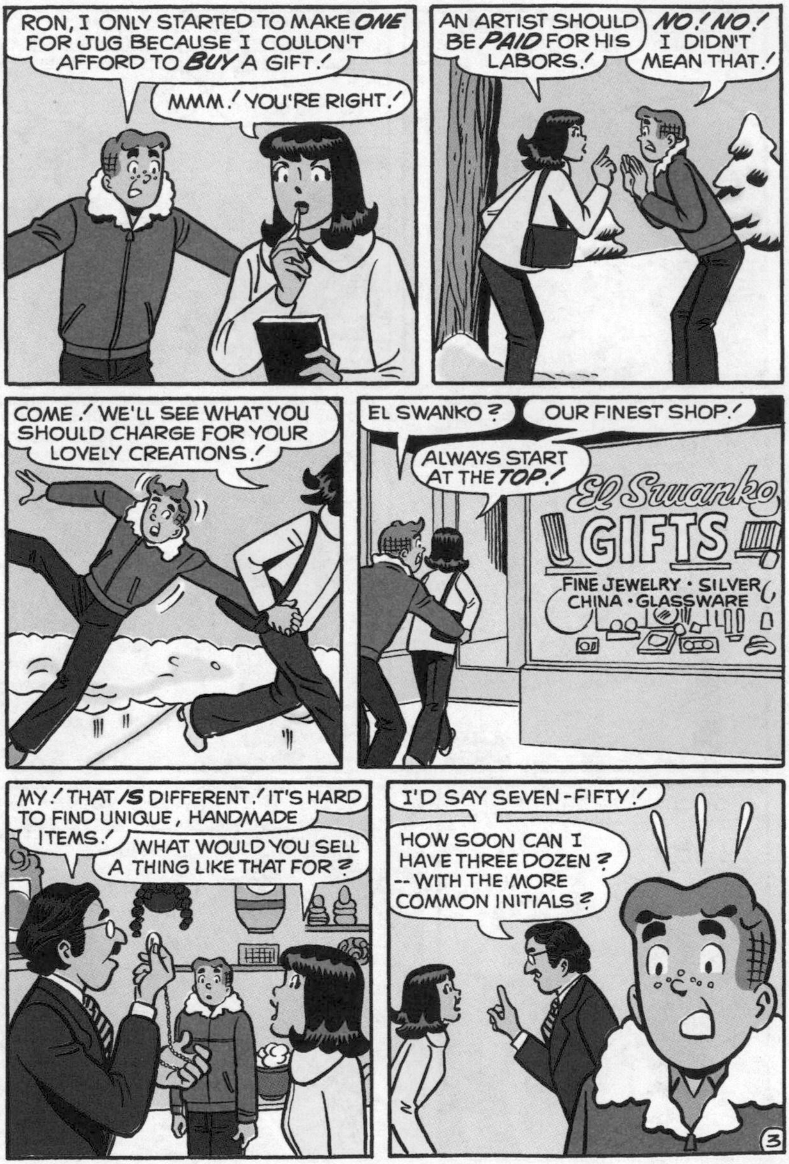
RON, I ONLY STARTED TO MAKE ONE FOR JUG BECAUSE I COULDN'T AFFORD TO BUY A GIFT!
MMM! YOU'RE RIGHT!
AN ARTIST SHOULD BE PAID FOR HIS LABORS!
NO! NO! I DIDN'T MEAN THAT!
COME! WE'LL SEE WHAT YOU SHOULD CHARGE FOR YOUR LOVELY CREATIONS!
EL SWANKO?
OUR FINEST SHOP!
ALWAYS START AT THE TOP!
El Swanko
GIFTS
FINE JEWELRY • SILVER
CHINA • GLASSWARE
MY! THAT IS DIFFERENT! IT'S HARD TO FIND UNIQUE, HANDMADE ITEMS!
WHAT WOULD YOU SELL A THING LIKE THAT FOR?
I'D SAY SEVEN-FIFTY!
HOW SOON CAN I HAVE THREE DOZEN? -- WITH THE MORE COMMON INITIALS?
3

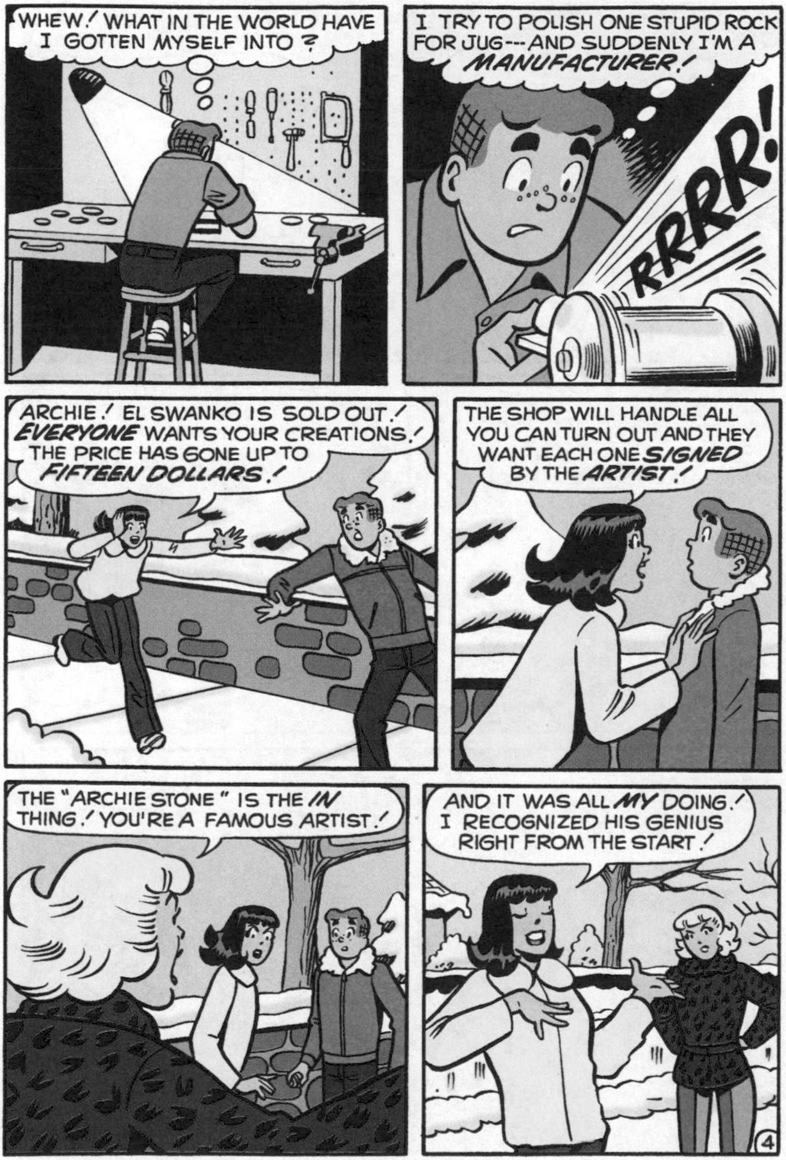
WHEW! WHAT IN THE WORLD HAVE I GOTTEN MYSELF INTO?
I TRY TO POLISH ONE STUPID ROCK FOR JUG---AND SUDDENLY I'M A MANUFACTURER!
RRRR!
ARCHIE! EL SWANKO IS SOLD OUT! EVERYONE WANTS YOUR CREATIONS! THE PRICE HAS GONE UP TO FIFTEEN DOLLARS!
THE SHOP WILL HANDLE ALL YOU CAN TURN OUT AND THEY WANT EACH ONE SIGNED BY THE ARTIST!
THE "ARCHIE STONE" IS THE IN THING! YOU'RE A FAMOUS ARTIST!
AND IT WAS ALL MY DOING! I RECOGNIZED HIS GENIUS RIGHT FROM THE START!
4

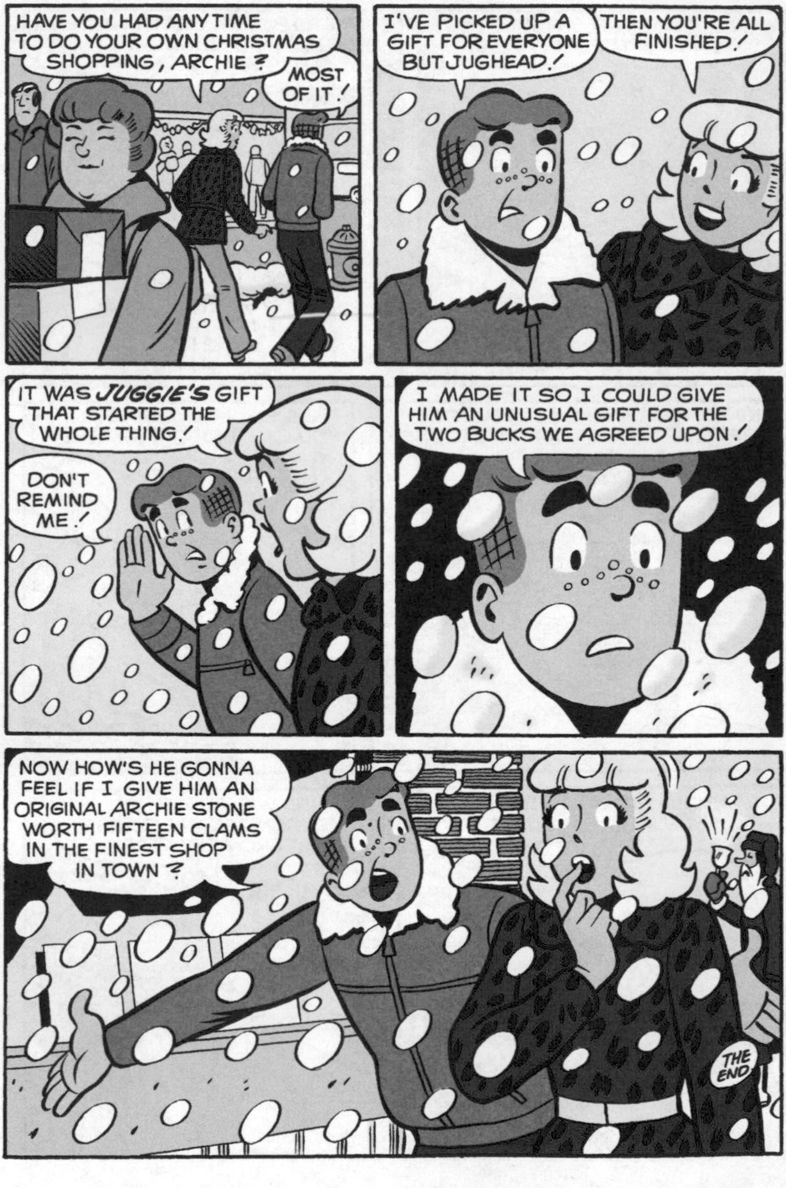
HAVE YOU HAD ANY TIME TO DO YOUR OWN CHRISTMAS SHOPPING, ARCHIE ?
MOST OF IT!
I'VE PICKED UP A GIFT FOR EVERYONE BUT JUGHEAD!
THEN YOU'RE ALL FINISHED!
IT WAS JUGGIE'S GIFT THAT STARTED THE WHOLE THING!
DON'T REMIND ME!
I MADE IT SO I COULD GIVE HIM AN UNUSUAL GIFT FOR THE TWO BUCKS WE AGREED UPON!
NOW HOW'S HE GONNA FEEL IF I GIVE HIM AN ORIGINAL ARCHIE STONE WORTH FIFTEEN CLAMS IN THE FINEST SHOP IN TOWN ?
THE END

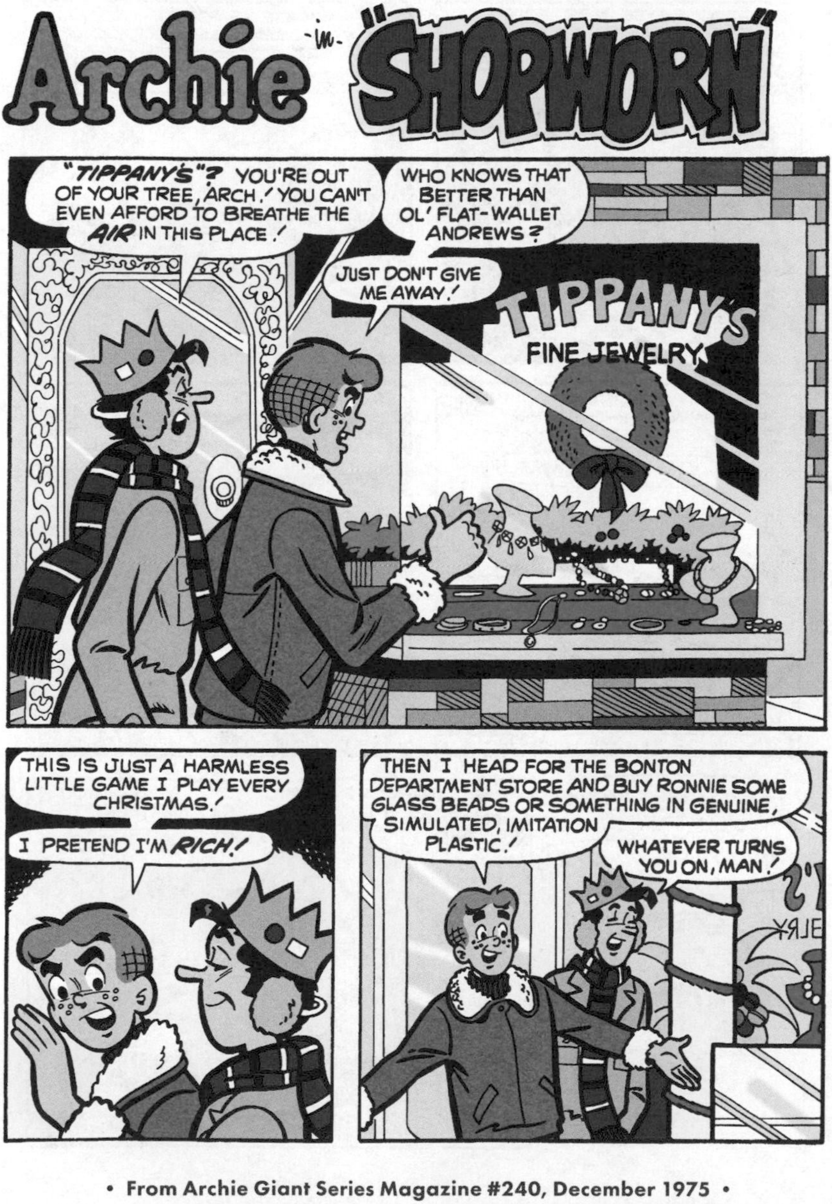
Archie -in- "SHOPWORN"
"TIPPANY'S"? YOU'RE OUT OF YOUR TREE, ARCH.! YOU CAN'T EVEN AFFORD TO BREATHE THE AIR IN THIS PLACE.!
WHO KNOWS THAT BETTER THAN OL' FLAT-WALLET ANDREWS?
JUST DON'T GIVE ME AWAY.!
TIPPANY'S
FINE JEWELRY
THIS IS JUST A HARMLESS LITTLE GAME I PLAY EVERY CHRISTMAS.!
I PRETEND I'M RICH!
THEN I HEAD FOR THE BONTON DEPARTMENT STORE AND BUY RONNIE SOME GLASS BEADS OR SOMETHING IN GENUINE, SIMULATED, IMITATION PLASTIC.!
WHATEVER TURNS YOU ON, MAN.!

• **From Archie Giant Series Magazine #240, December 1975** •

George Gladir • Stan Goldberg • Rudy Lapick • Bill Yoshida

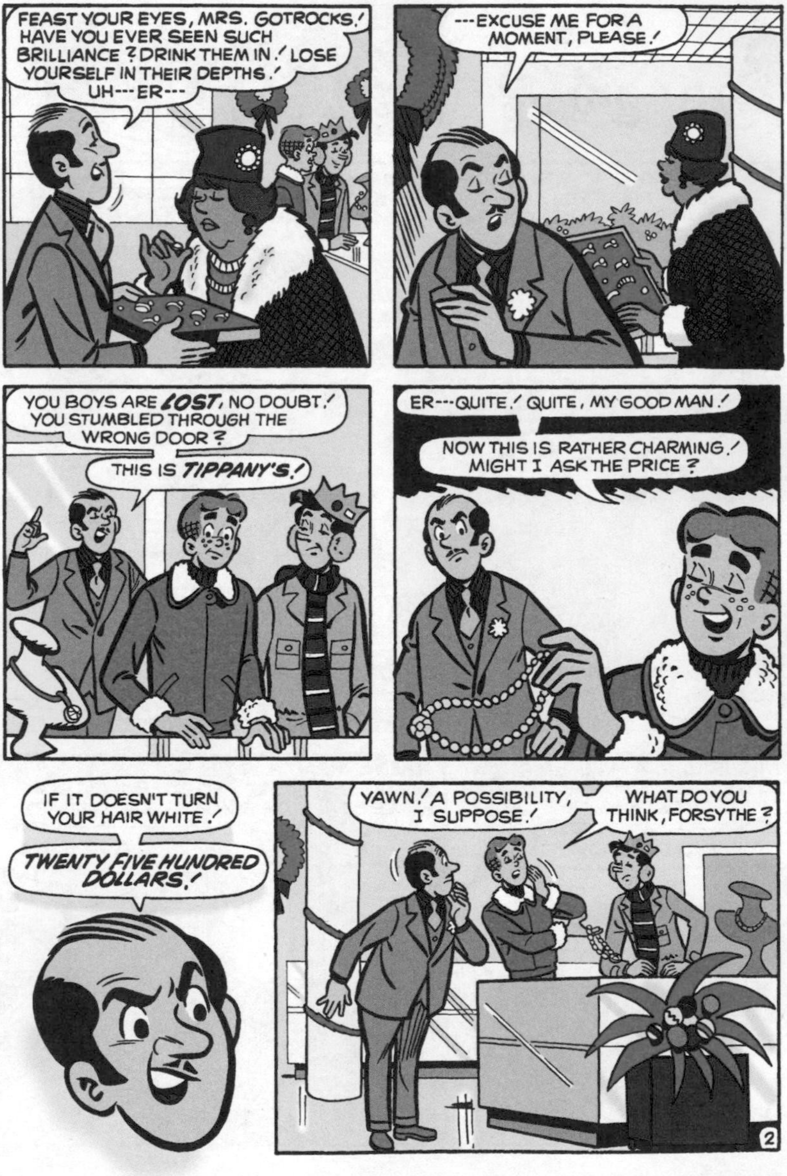
FEAST YOUR EYES, MRS. GOTROCKS! HAVE YOU EVER SEEN SUCH BRILLIANCE? DRINK THEM IN! LOSE YOURSELF IN THEIR DEPTHS!
UH---ER---
---EXCUSE ME FOR A MOMENT, PLEASE!
YOU BOYS ARE LOST, NO DOUBT! YOU STUMBLED THROUGH THE WRONG DOOR?
THIS IS TIPPANY'S!
ER---QUITE! QUITE, MY GOOD MAN!
NOW THIS IS RATHER CHARMING! MIGHT I ASK THE PRICE?
IF IT DOESN'T TURN YOUR HAIR WHITE!
TWENTY FIVE HUNDRED DOLLARS!
YAWN! A POSSIBILITY, I SUPPOSE!
WHAT DO YOU THINK, FORSYTHE?
2

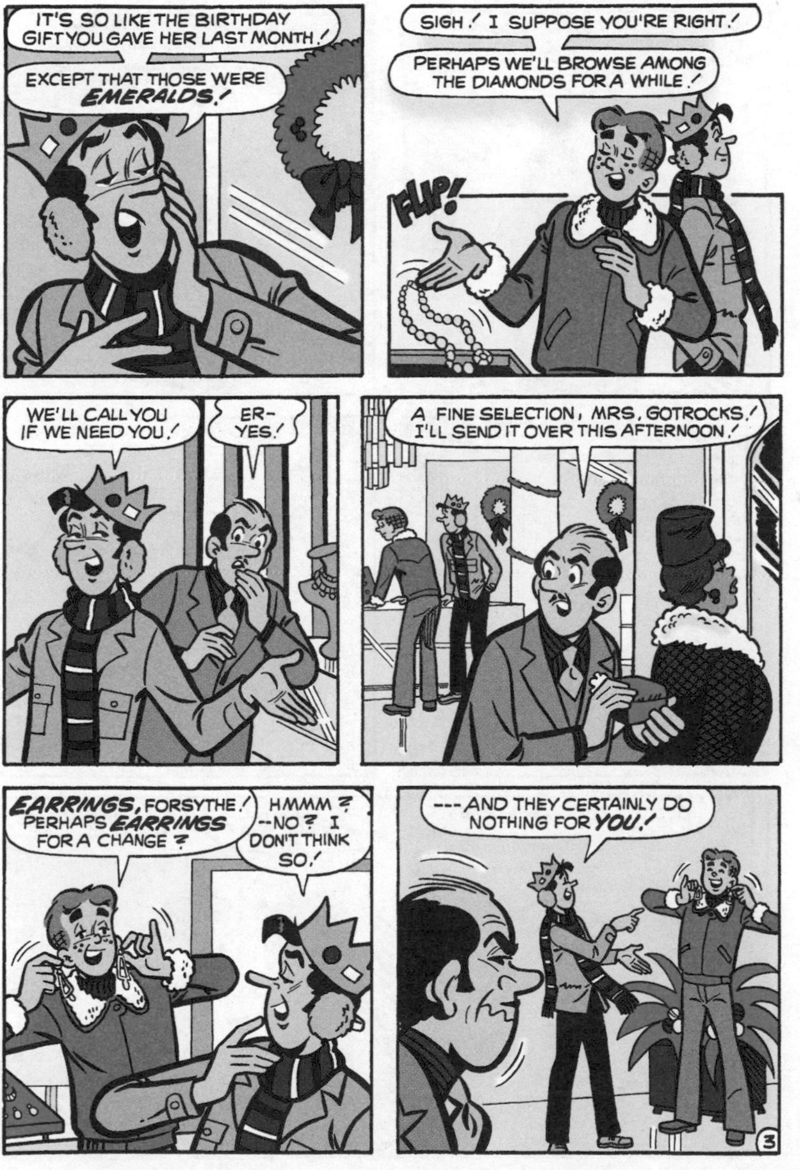
IT'S SO LIKE THE BIRTHDAY GIFT YOU GAVE HER LAST MONTH!
EXCEPT THAT THOSE WERE EMERALDS!
SIGH! I SUPPOSE YOU'RE RIGHT!
PERHAPS WE'LL BROWSE AMONG THE DIAMONDS FOR A WHILE!
FLIP!
WE'LL CALL YOU IF WE NEED YOU!
ER- YES!
A FINE SELECTION, MRS, GOTROCKS! I'LL SEND IT OVER THIS AFTERNOON!
EARRINGS, FORSYTHE! PERHAPS EARRINGS FOR A CHANGE?
HMMM? --NO? I DON'T THINK SO!
---AND THEY CERTAINLY DO NOTHING FOR YOU!
3

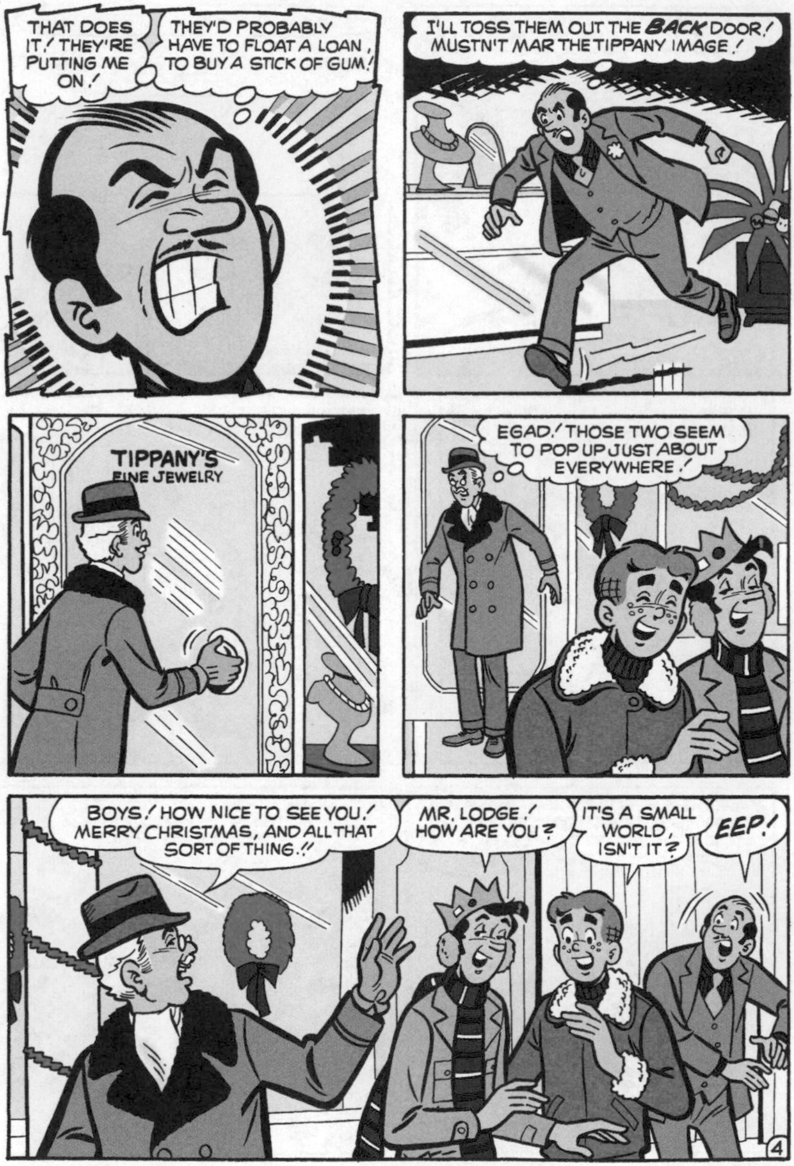
THAT DOES IT! THEY'RE PUTTING ME ON!
THEY'D PROBABLY HAVE TO FLOAT A LOAN, TO BUY A STICK OF GUM!
I'LL TOSS THEM OUT THE BACK DOOR! MUSTN'T MAR THE TIPPANY IMAGE!
TIPPANY'S FINE JEWELRY
EGAD! THOSE TWO SEEM TO POP UP JUST ABOUT EVERYWHERE!
BOYS! HOW NICE TO SEE YOU! MERRY CHRISTMAS, AND ALL THAT SORT OF THING.!!
MR. LODGE! HOW ARE YOU?
IT'S A SMALL WORLD, ISN'T IT?
EEP!
4

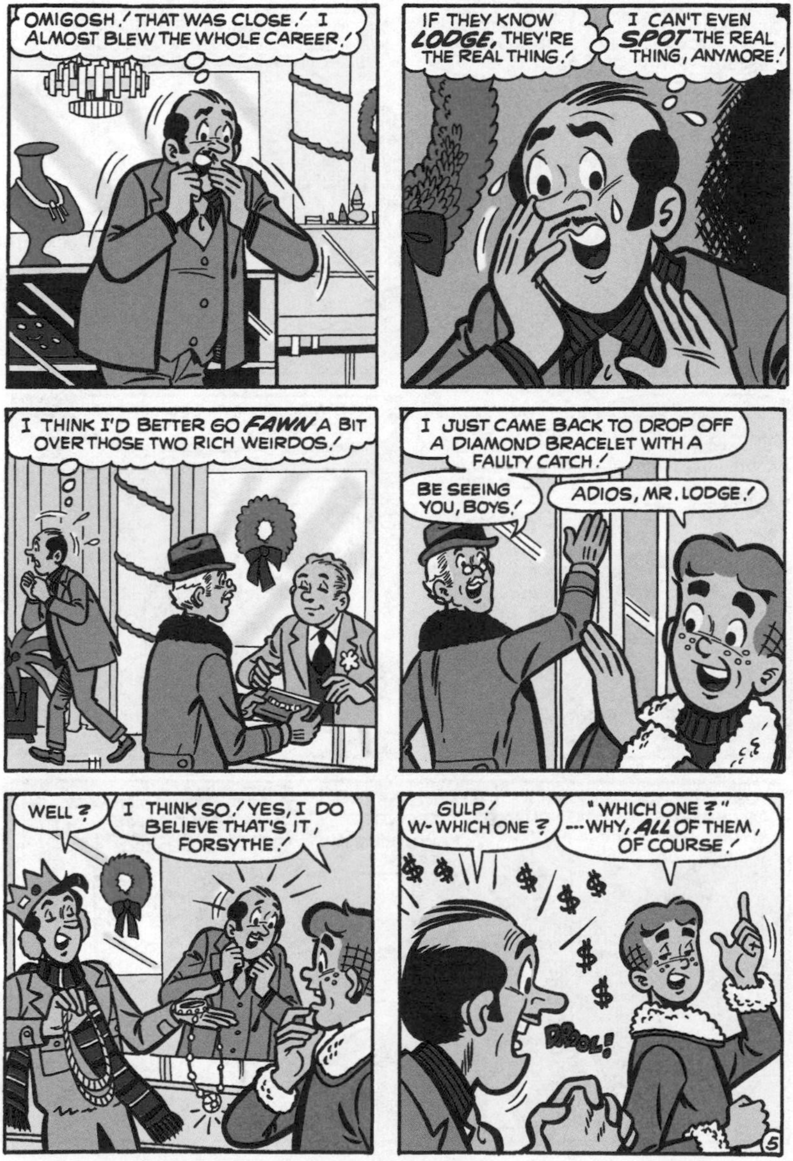
OMIGOSH! THAT WAS CLOSE! I ALMOST BLEW THE WHOLE CAREER!
IF THEY KNOW LODGE, THEY'RE THE REAL THING!
I CAN'T EVEN SPOT THE REAL THING, ANYMORE!
I THINK I'D BETTER GO FAWN A BIT OVER THOSE TWO RICH WEIRDOS!
I JUST CAME BACK TO DROP OFF A DIAMOND BRACELET WITH A FAULTY CATCH!
BE SEEING YOU, BOYS!
ADIOS, MR. LODGE!
WELL?
I THINK SO! YES, I DO BELIEVE THAT'S IT, FORSYTHE!
GULP! W-WHICH ONE?
"WHICH ONE?" ---WHY, ALL OF THEM, OF COURSE!
DROOL!
5

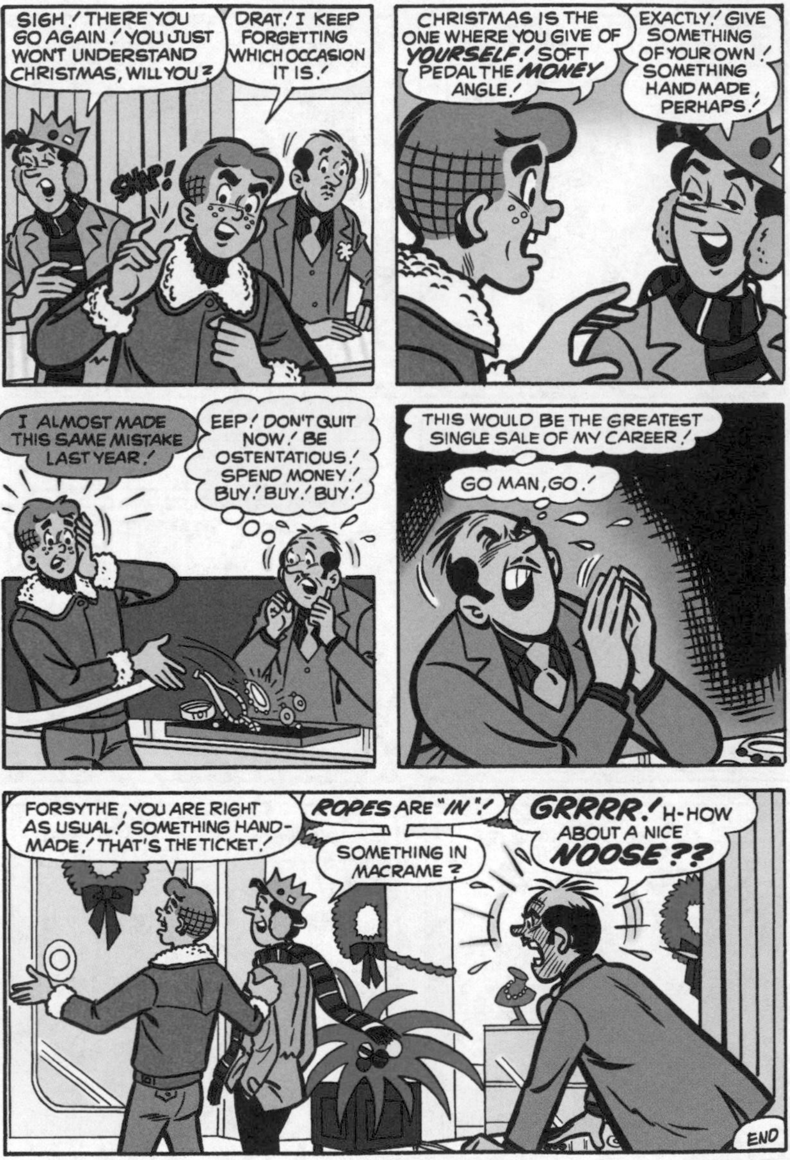
SIGH! THERE YOU GO AGAIN! YOU JUST WON'T UNDERSTAND CHRISTMAS, WILL YOU?
SNAP!
DRAT! I KEEP FORGETTING WHICH OCCASION IT IS!
CHRISTMAS IS THE ONE WHERE YOU GIVE OF YOURSELF! SOFT PEDAL THE MONEY ANGLE!
EXACTLY! GIVE SOMETHING OF YOUR OWN! SOMETHING HAND MADE, PERHAPS!
I ALMOST MADE THIS SAME MISTAKE LAST YEAR!
EEP! DON'T QUIT NOW! BE OSTENTATIOUS! SPEND MONEY! BUY! BUY! BUY!
THIS WOULD BE THE GREATEST SINGLE SALE OF MY CAREER!
GO MAN, GO!
FORSYTHE, YOU ARE RIGHT AS USUAL! SOMETHING HAND-MADE! THAT'S THE TICKET!
ROPES ARE "IN"!
SOMETHING IN MACRAME?
GRRRR! H-HOW ABOUT A NICE NOOSE??
END

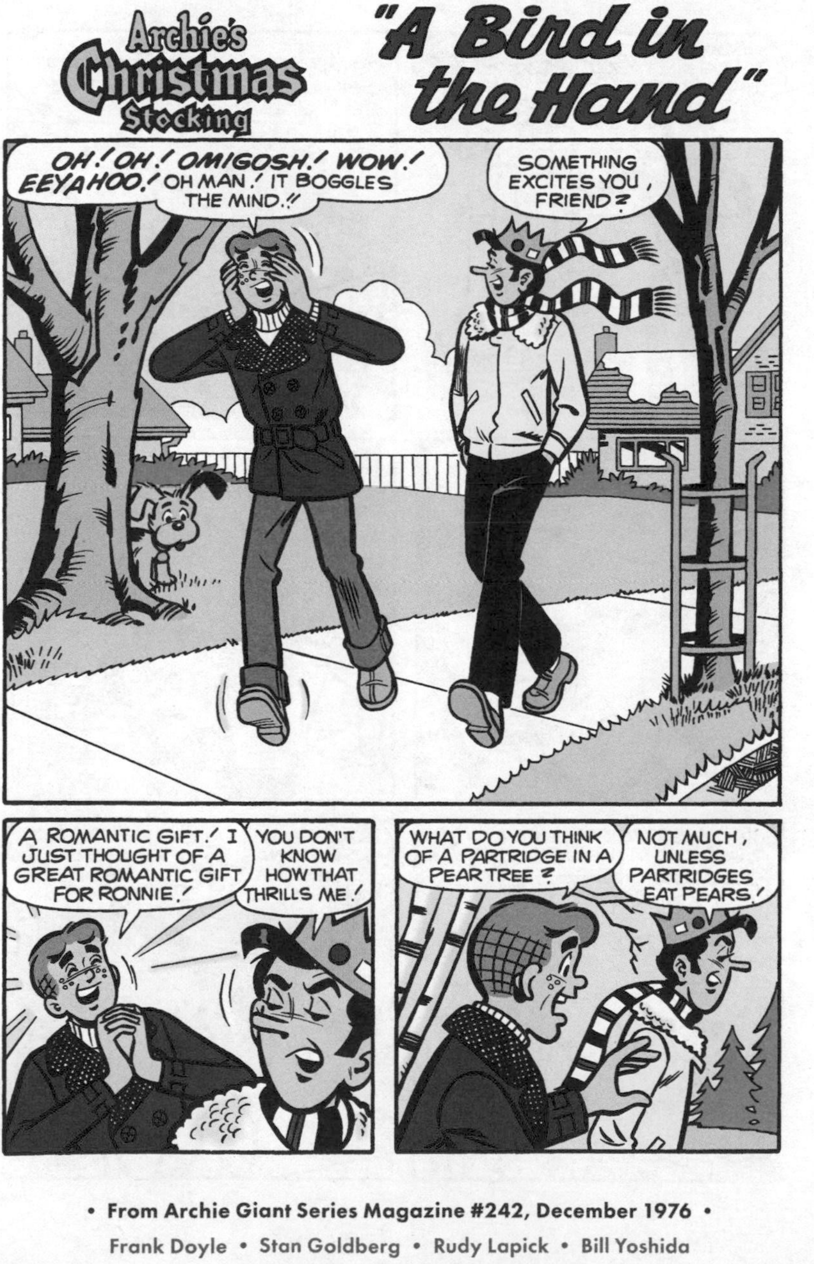
Archie's Christmas Stocking
"A Bird in the Hand"
OH! OH! OMIGOSH! WOW! EEYAHOO! OH MAN! IT BOGGLES THE MIND!!
SOMETHING EXCITES YOU, FRIEND?
A ROMANTIC GIFT! I JUST THOUGHT OF A GREAT ROMANTIC GIFT FOR RONNIE!
YOU DON'T KNOW HOW THAT THRILLS ME!
WHAT DO YOU THINK OF A PARTRIDGE IN A PEAR TREE?
NOT MUCH, UNLESS PARTRIDGES EAT PEARS!

• From Archie Giant Series Magazine #242, December 1976 •

Frank Doyle • Stan Goldberg • Rudy Lapick • Bill Yoshida

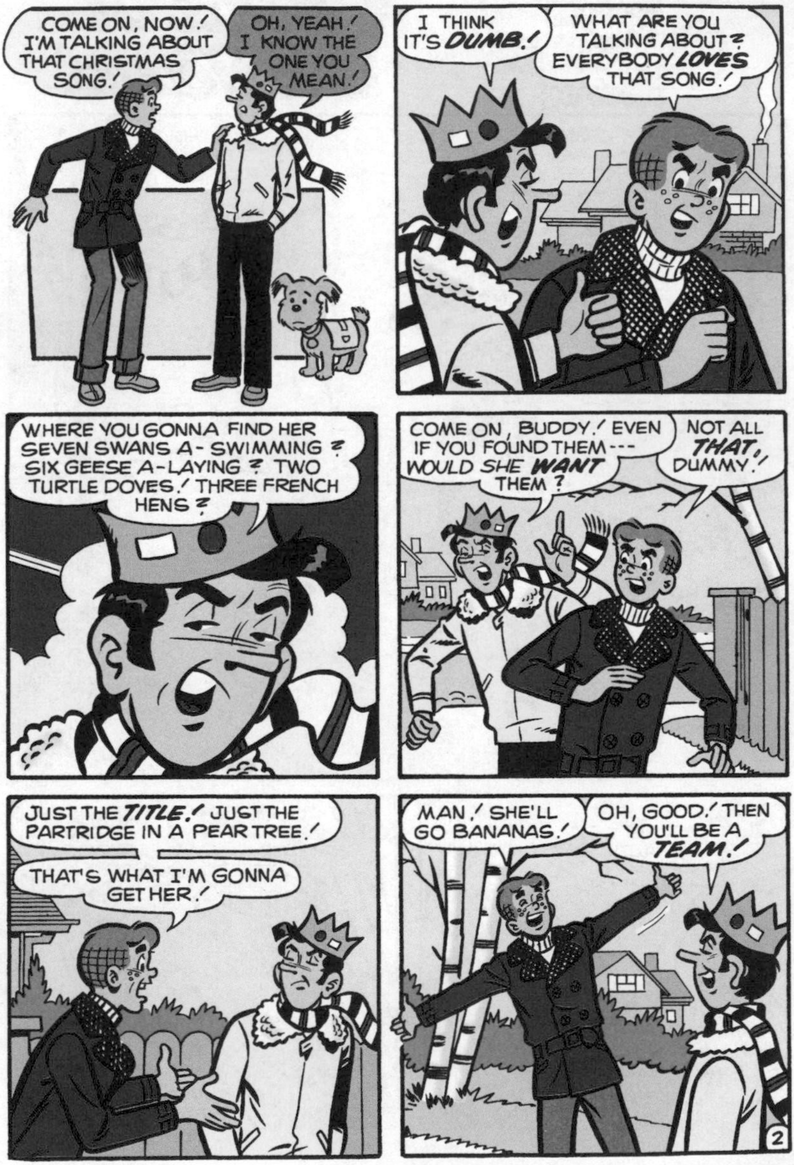
COME ON, NOW! I'M TALKING ABOUT THAT CHRISTMAS SONG!
OH, YEAH! I KNOW THE ONE YOU MEAN!
I THINK IT'S DUMB!
WHAT ARE YOU TALKING ABOUT? EVERYBODY LOVES THAT SONG!
WHERE YOU GONNA FIND HER SEVEN SWANS A-SWIMMING? SIX GEESE A-LAYING? TWO TURTLE DOVES! THREE FRENCH HENS?
COME ON, BUDDY! EVEN IF YOU FOUND THEM--- WOULD SHE WANT THEM?
NOT ALL THAT, DUMMY!
JUST THE TITLE! JUST THE PARTRIDGE IN A PEAR TREE!
THAT'S WHAT I'M GONNA GET HER!
MAN! SHE'LL GO BANANAS!
OH, GOOD! THEN YOU'LL BE A TEAM!
2

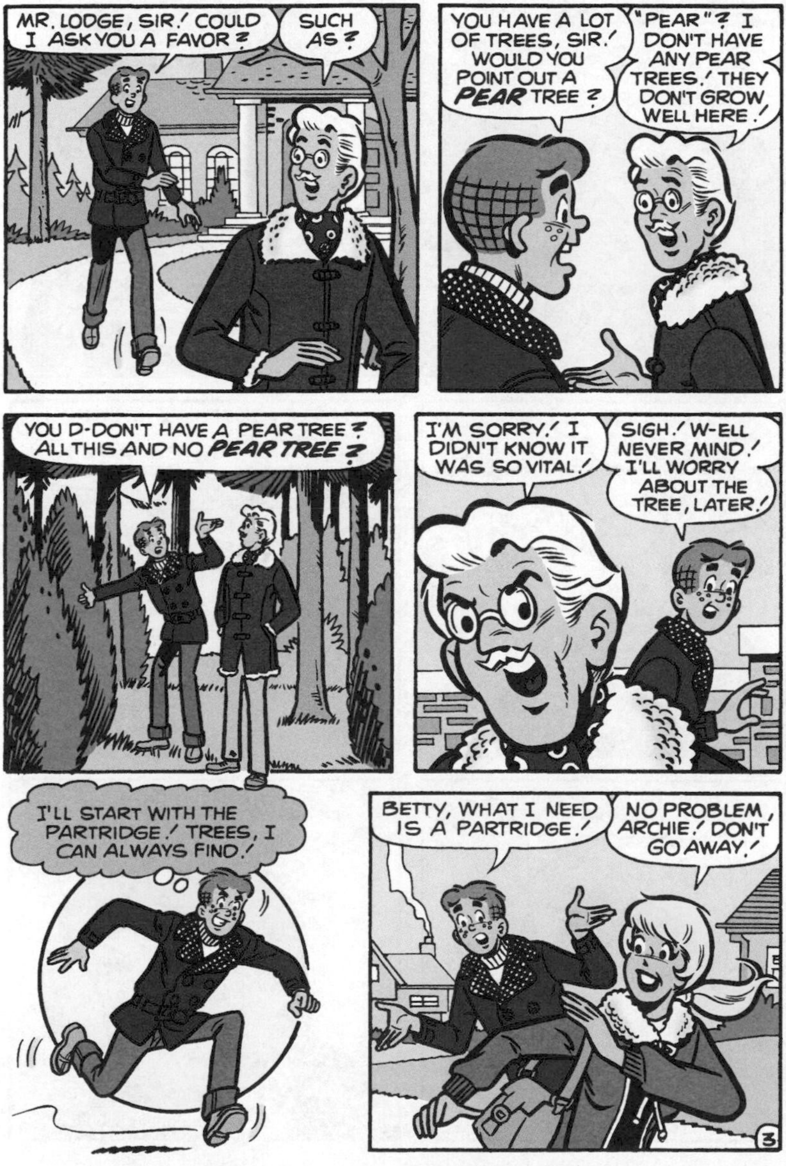
MR. LODGE, SIR! COULD I ASK YOU A FAVOR?
SUCH AS?
YOU HAVE A LOT OF TREES, SIR! WOULD YOU POINT OUT A PEAR TREE?
"PEAR"? I DON'T HAVE ANY PEAR TREES! THEY DON'T GROW WELL HERE!
YOU D-DON'T HAVE A PEAR TREE? ALL THIS AND NO PEAR TREE?
I'M SORRY! I DIDN'T KNOW IT WAS SO VITAL!
SIGH! W-ELL NEVER MIND! I'LL WORRY ABOUT THE TREE, LATER!
I'LL START WITH THE PARTRIDGE! TREES, I CAN ALWAYS FIND!
BETTY, WHAT I NEED IS A PARTRIDGE!
NO PROBLEM, ARCHIE! DON'T GO AWAY!
3

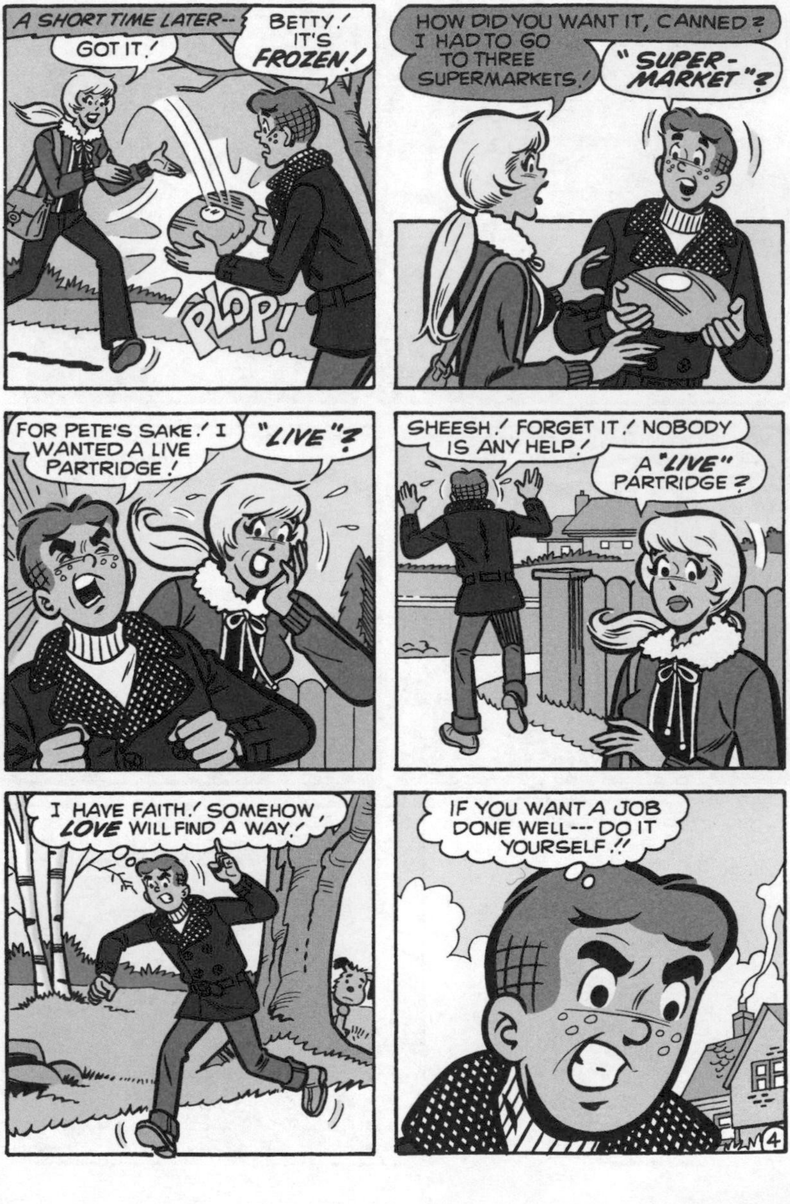
A SHORT TIME LATER--
GOT IT!
BETTY! IT'S FROZEN!
PLOP!
HOW DID YOU WANT IT, CANNED? I HAD TO GO TO THREE SUPERMARKETS!
"SUPER-MARKET"?
FOR PETE'S SAKE! I WANTED A LIVE PARTRIDGE!
"LIVE"?
SHEESH! FORGET IT! NOBODY IS ANY HELP!
A "LIVE" PARTRIDGE?
I HAVE FAITH! SOMEHOW LOVE WILL FIND A WAY!
IF YOU WANT A JOB DONE WELL--- DO IT YOURSELF!!
4

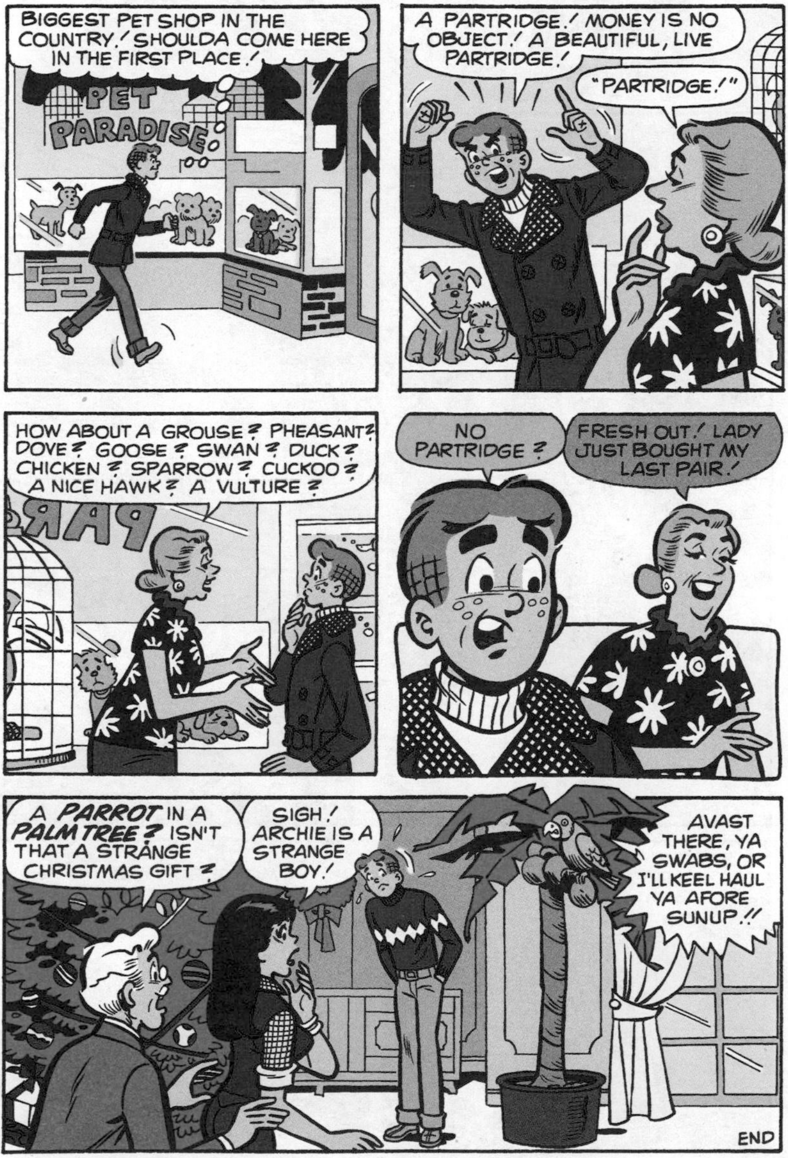
BIGGEST PET SHOP IN THE COUNTRY! SHOULDA COME HERE IN THE FIRST PLACE!
PET PARADISE
A PARTRIDGE! MONEY IS NO OBJECT! A BEAUTIFUL, LIVE PARTRIDGE!
"PARTRIDGE!"
HOW ABOUT A GROUSE? PHEASANT? DOVE? GOOSE? SWAN? DUCK? CHICKEN? SPARROW? CUCKOO? A NICE HAWK? A VULTURE?
NO PARTRIDGE?
FRESH OUT! LADY JUST BOUGHT MY LAST PAIR!
A *PARROT* IN A *PALM TREE*? ISN'T THAT A STRANGE CHRISTMAS GIFT?
SIGH! ARCHIE IS A STRANGE BOY!
AVAST THERE, YA SWABS, OR I'LL KEEL HAUL YA AFORE SUNUP!!
END

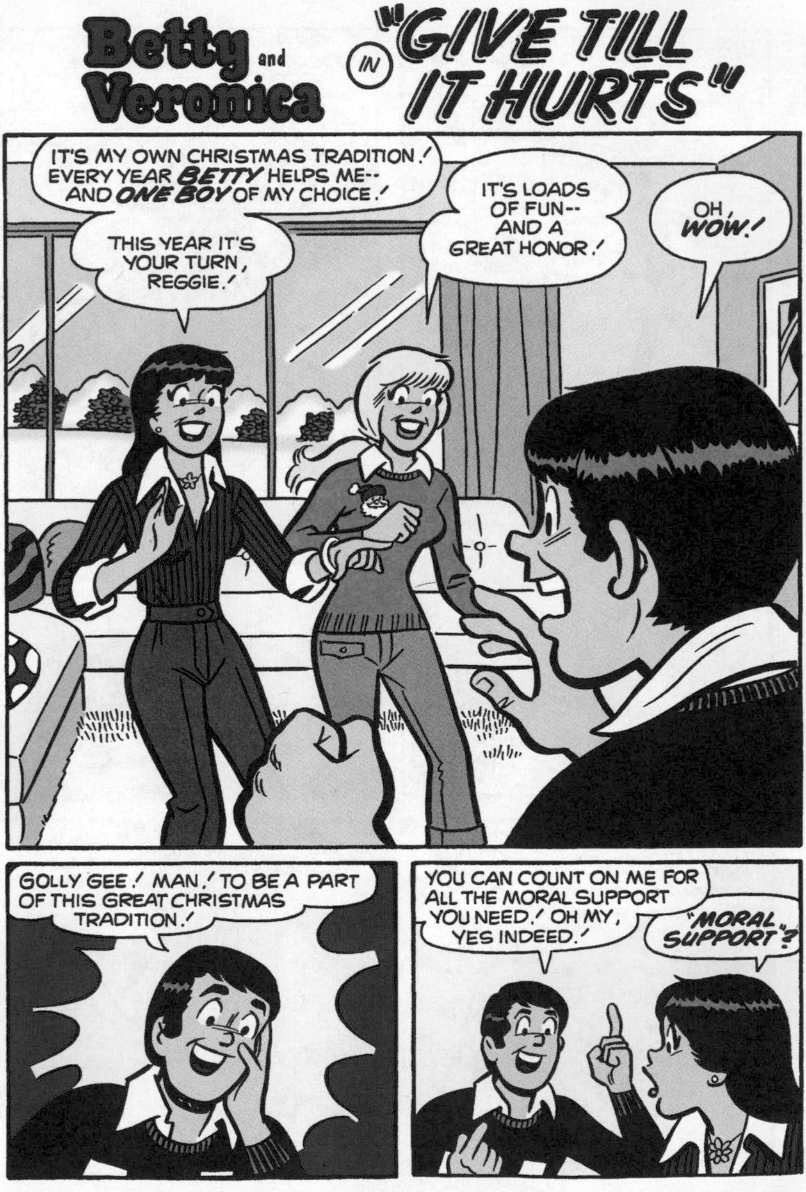
Betty and Veronica
IN "GIVE TILL IT HURTS"
IT'S MY OWN CHRISTMAS TRADITION! EVERY YEAR BETTY HELPS ME-- AND ONE BOY OF MY CHOICE!
THIS YEAR IT'S YOUR TURN, REGGIE!
IT'S LOADS OF FUN-- AND A GREAT HONOR!
OH, WOW!
GOLLY GEE! MAN! TO BE A PART OF THIS GREAT CHRISTMAS TRADITION!
YOU CAN COUNT ON ME FOR ALL THE MORAL SUPPORT YOU NEED! OH MY, YES INDEED!
"MORAL SUPPORT"?

• **From Archie Giant Series Magazine #453, December 1976** •

Frank Doyle • Dan DeCarlo • Jimmy DeCarlo • Bill Yoshida

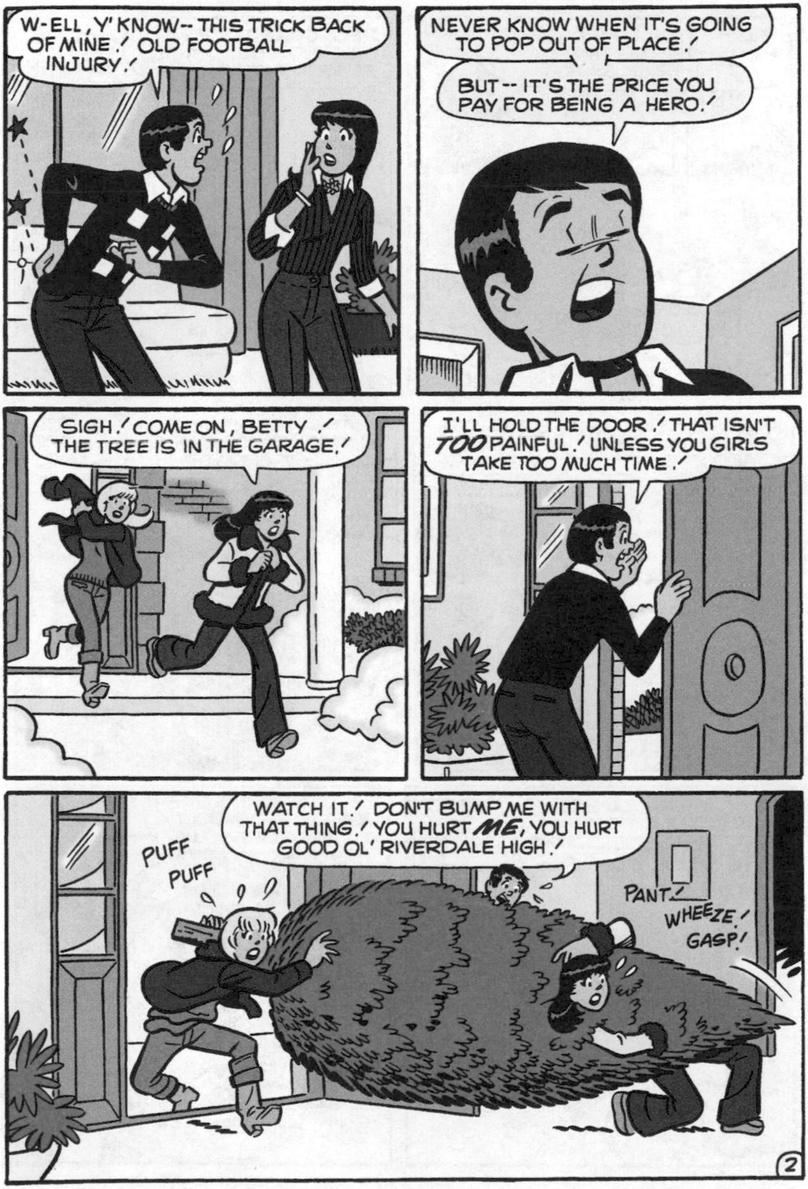
W-ELL, Y' KNOW-- THIS TRICK BACK OF MINE! OLD FOOTBALL INJURY!
NEVER KNOW WHEN IT'S GOING TO POP OUT OF PLACE!
BUT -- IT'S THE PRICE YOU PAY FOR BEING A HERO!
SIGH! COME ON, BETTY! THE TREE IS IN THE GARAGE!
I'LL HOLD THE DOOR! THAT ISN'T TOO PAINFUL! UNLESS YOU GIRLS TAKE TOO MUCH TIME!
WATCH IT! DON'T BUMP ME WITH THAT THING! YOU HURT ME, YOU HURT GOOD OL' RIVERDALE HIGH!
PUFF
PUFF
PANT!
WHEEZE!
GASP!
2

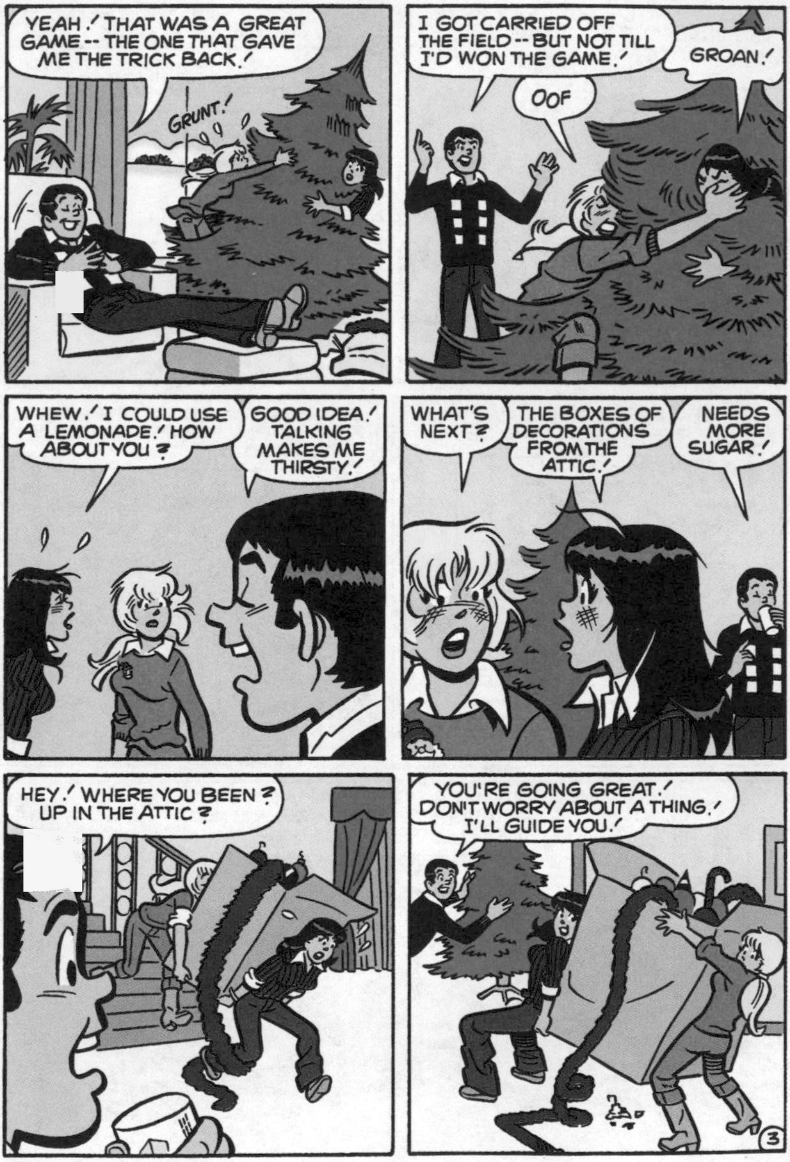
YEAH! THAT WAS A GREAT GAME -- THE ONE THAT GAVE ME THE TRICK BACK!
GRUNT!
I GOT CARRIED OFF THE FIELD -- BUT NOT TILL I'D WON THE GAME!
OOF
GROAN!
WHEW! I COULD USE A LEMONADE! HOW ABOUT YOU?
GOOD IDEA! TALKING MAKES ME THIRSTY!
WHAT'S NEXT?
THE BOXES OF DECORATIONS FROM THE ATTIC!
NEEDS MORE SUGAR!
HEY! WHERE YOU BEEN? UP IN THE ATTIC?
YOU'RE GOING GREAT! DON'T WORRY ABOUT A THING! I'LL GUIDE YOU!
3

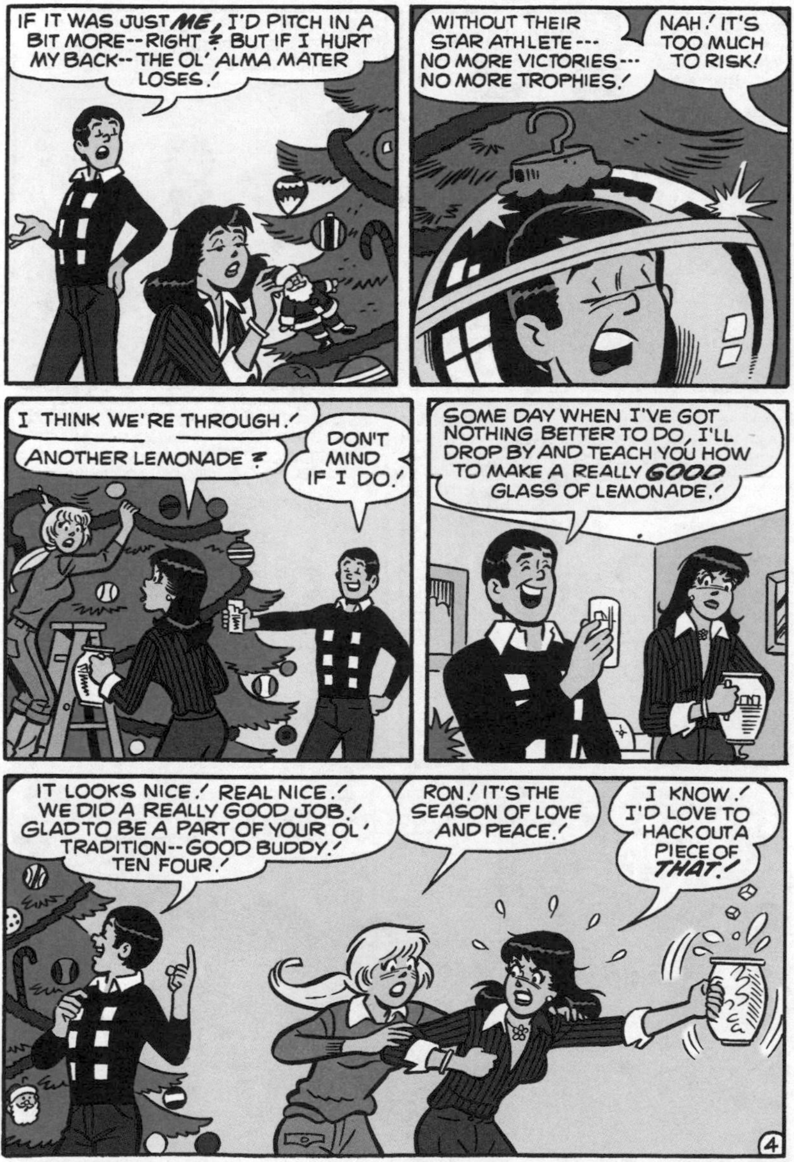
IF IT WAS JUST ME, I'D PITCH IN A BIT MORE--RIGHT? BUT IF I HURT MY BACK--THE OL' ALMA MATER LOSES!
WITHOUT THEIR STAR ATHLETE--- NO MORE VICTORIES--- NO MORE TROPHIES!
NAH! IT'S TOO MUCH TO RISK!
I THINK WE'RE THROUGH!
ANOTHER LEMONADE?
DON'T MIND IF I DO!
SOME DAY WHEN I'VE GOT NOTHING BETTER TO DO, I'LL DROP BY AND TEACH YOU HOW TO MAKE A REALLY GOOD GLASS OF LEMONADE!
IT LOOKS NICE! REAL NICE! WE DID A REALLY GOOD JOB! GLAD TO BE A PART OF YOUR OL' TRADITION--GOOD BUDDY! TEN FOUR!
RON! IT'S THE SEASON OF LOVE AND PEACE!
I KNOW! I'D LOVE TO HACK OUT A PIECE OF THAT!
4

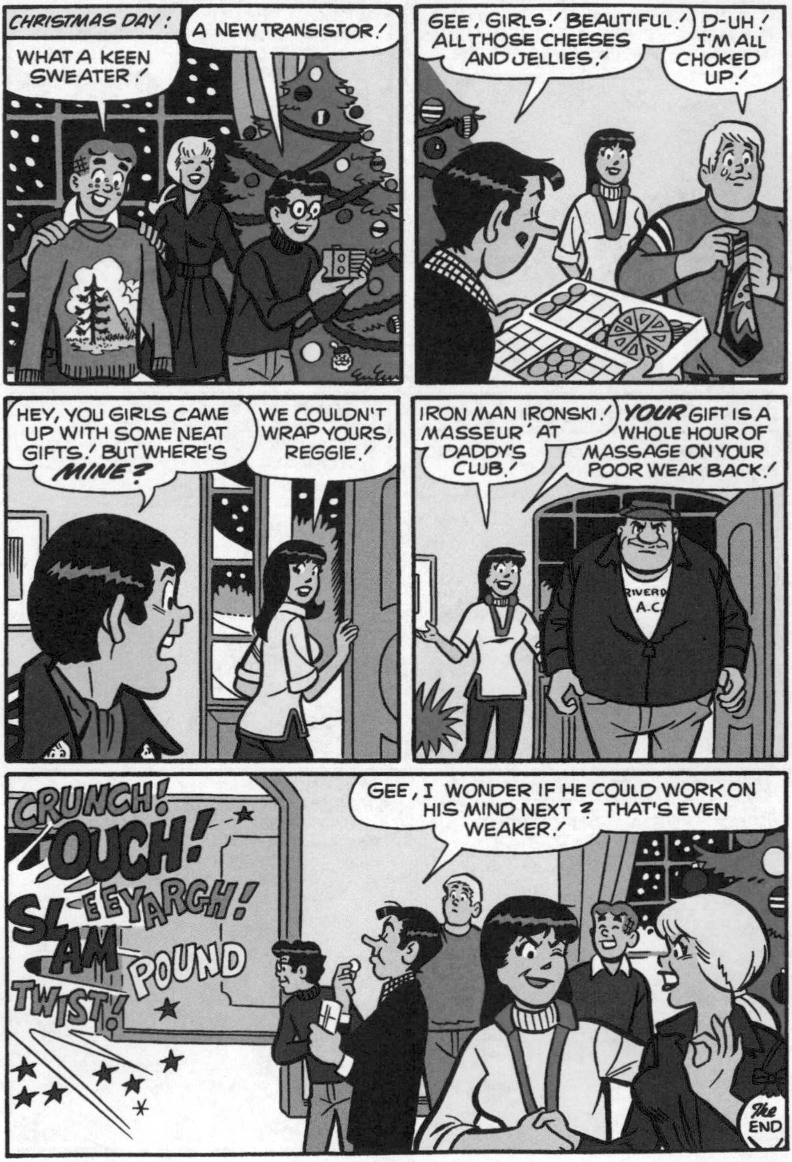
CHRISTMAS DAY :
WHAT A KEEN SWEATER !
A NEW TRANSISTOR !
GEE, GIRLS ! BEAUTIFUL ! ALL THOSE CHEESES AND JELLIES !
D-UH ! I'M ALL CHOKED UP !
HEY, YOU GIRLS CAME UP WITH SOME NEAT GIFTS ! BUT WHERE'S MINE ?
WE COULDN'T WRAP YOURS, REGGIE !
IRON MAN IRONSKI ! MASSEUR AT DADDY'S CLUB !
YOUR GIFT IS A WHOLE HOUR OF MASSAGE ON YOUR POOR WEAK BACK !
RIVERD A.C.
CRUNCH! OUCH! EEYARGH! SLAM POUND TWIST!
GEE, I WONDER IF HE COULD WORK ON HIS MIND NEXT ? THAT'S EVEN WEAKER !
The END

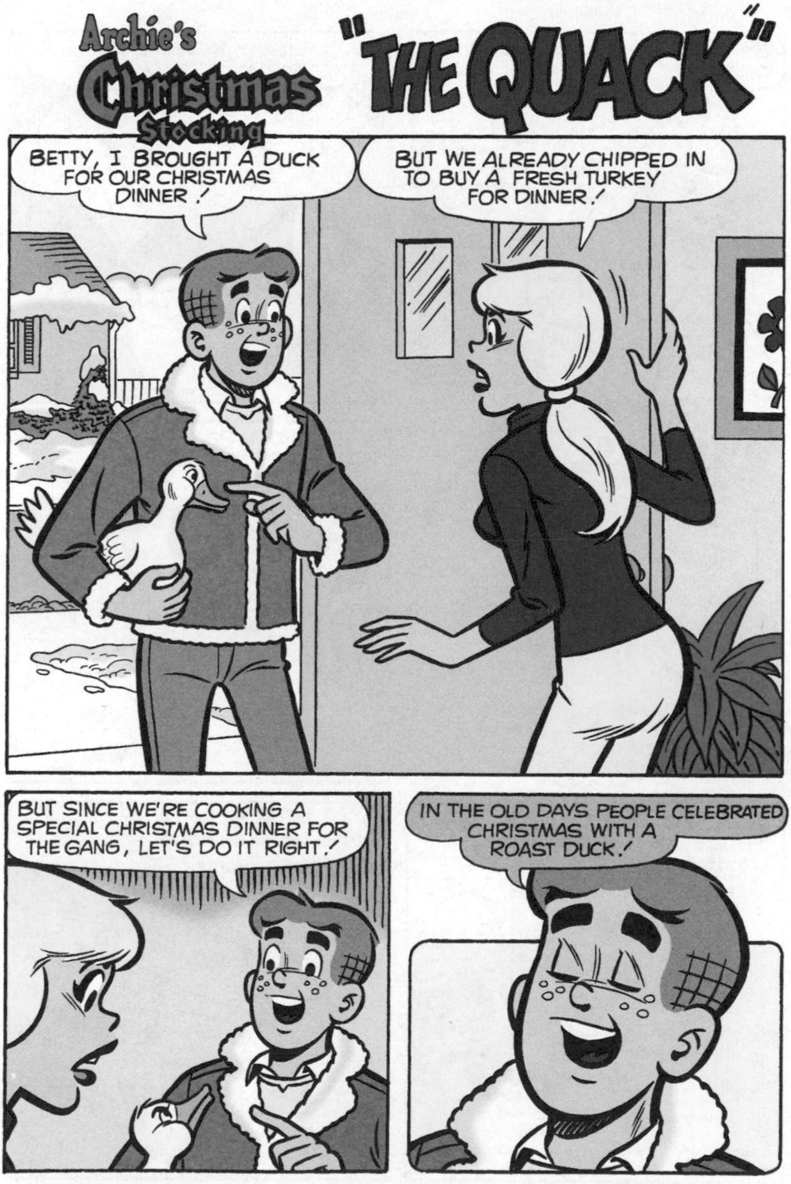
Archie's Christmas Stocking
"THE QUACK"
BETTY, I BROUGHT A DUCK FOR OUR CHRISTMAS DINNER!
BUT WE ALREADY CHIPPED IN TO BUY A FRESH TURKEY FOR DINNER!
BUT SINCE WE'RE COOKING A SPECIAL CHRISTMAS DINNER FOR THE GANG, LET'S DO IT RIGHT!
IN THE OLD DAYS PEOPLE CELEBRATED CHRISTMAS WITH A ROAST DUCK!

• From Archie Giant Series Magazine #464, December 1977 •

Dick Malmgren • Rudy Lapick • Bill Yoshida

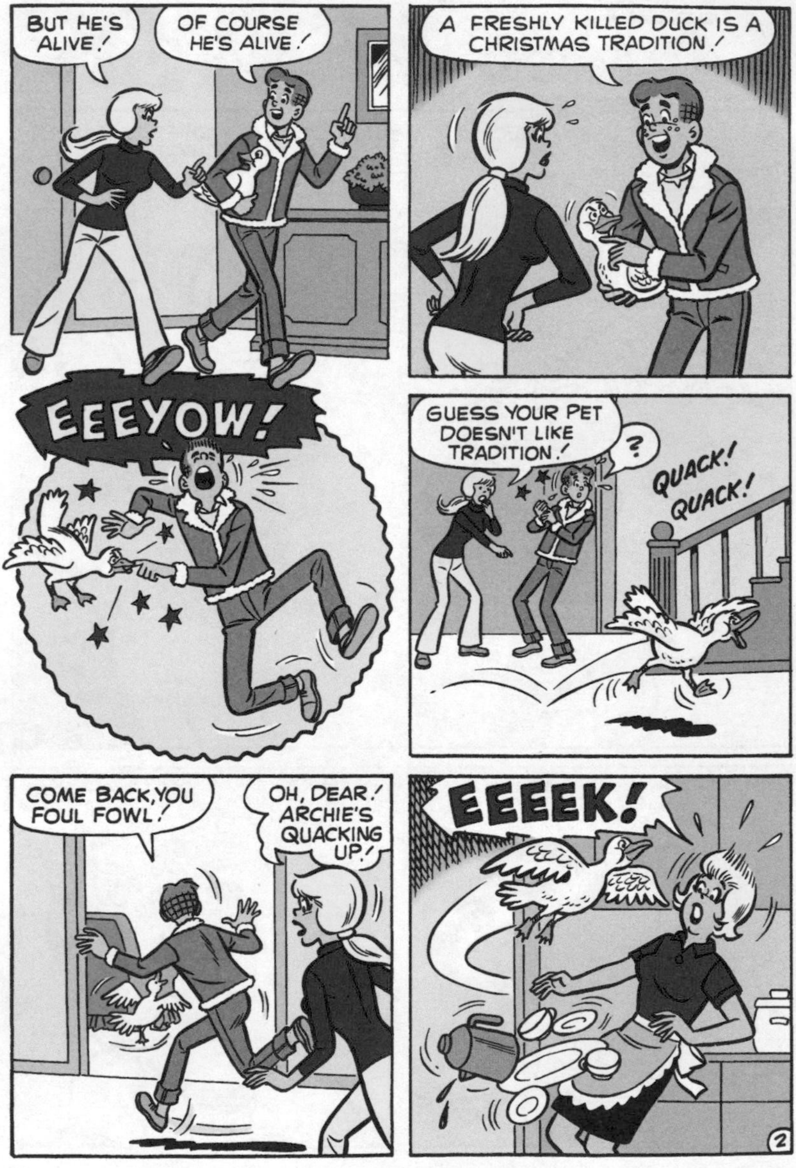
BUT HE'S ALIVE!
OF COURSE HE'S ALIVE!
A FRESHLY KILLED DUCK IS A CHRISTMAS TRADITION!
EEEYOW!
GUESS YOUR PET DOESN'T LIKE TRADITION!
?
QUACK! QUACK!
COME BACK, YOU FOUL FOWL!
OH, DEAR! ARCHIE'S QUACKING UP!
EEEEK!
2

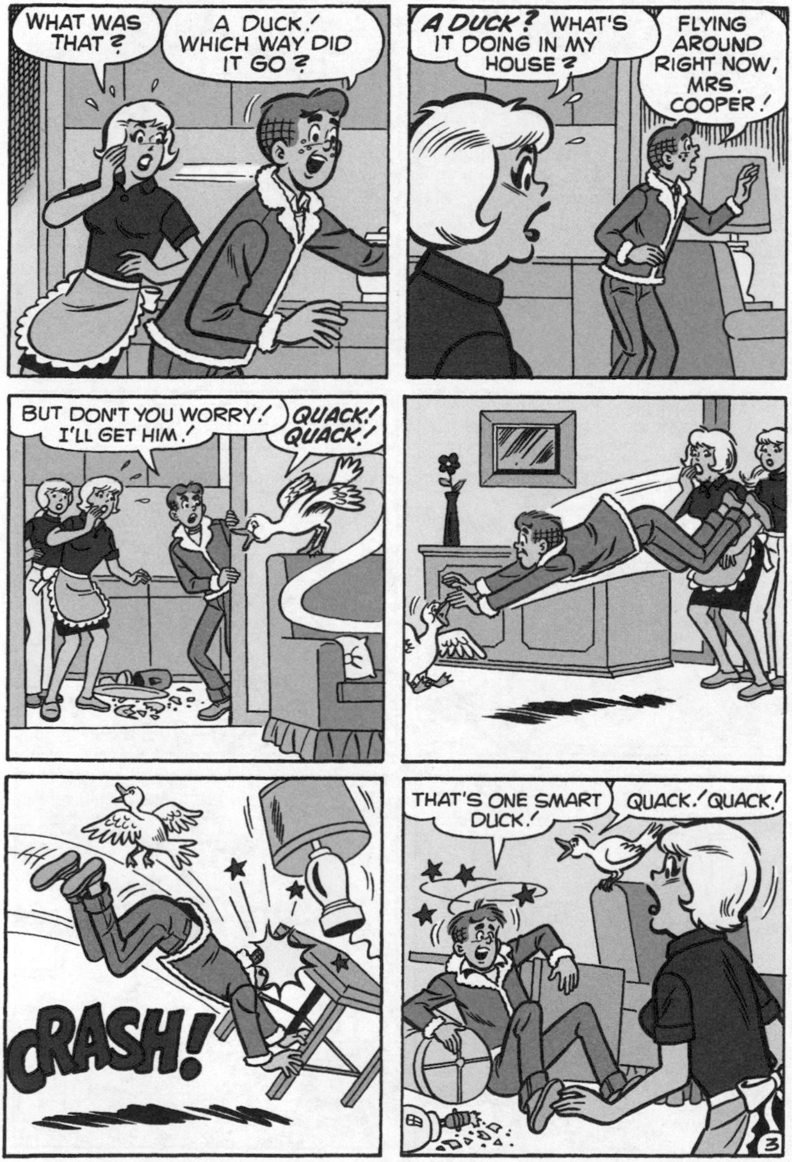
WHAT WAS THAT?
A DUCK! WHICH WAY DID IT GO?
A DUCK? WHAT'S IT DOING IN MY HOUSE?
FLYING AROUND RIGHT NOW, MRS. COOPER!
BUT DON'T YOU WORRY! I'LL GET HIM!
QUACK! QUACK!
CRASH!
THAT'S ONE SMART DUCK!
QUACK! QUACK!
3

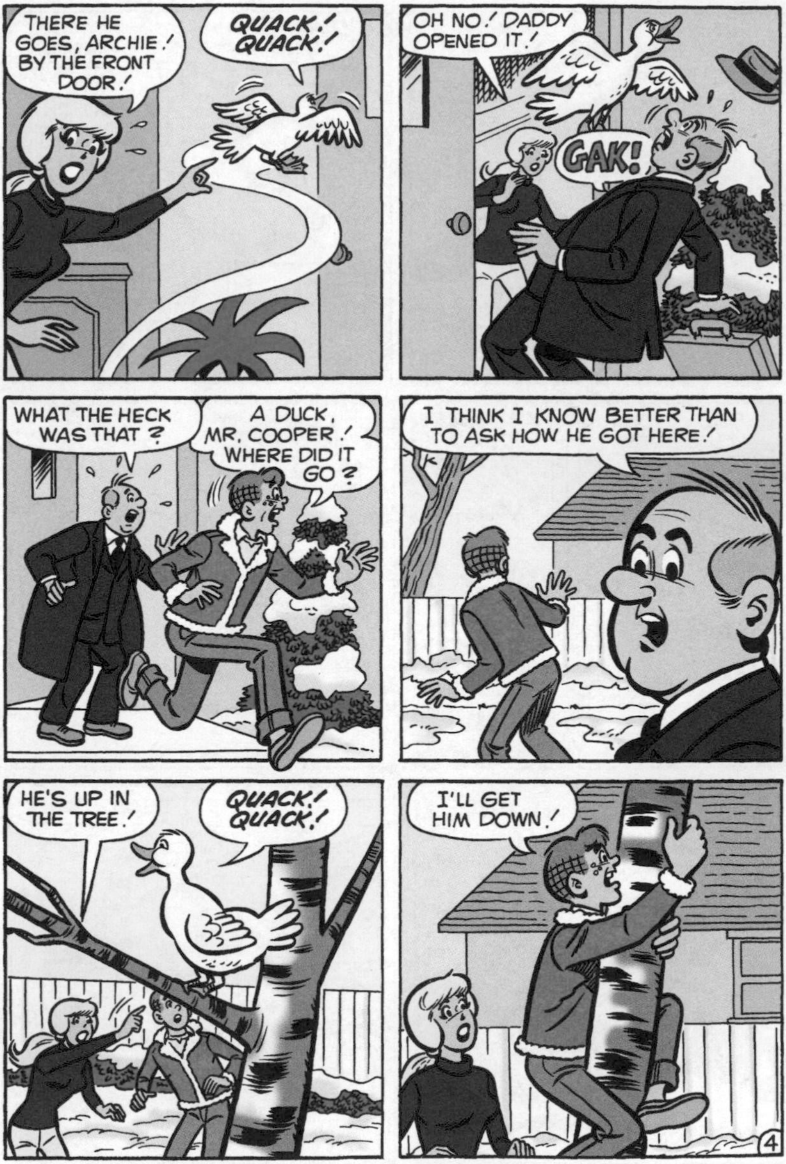
THERE HE GOES, ARCHIE.! BY THE FRONT DOOR.!
QUACK.! QUACK.!
OH NO.! DADDY OPENED IT.!
GAK!
WHAT THE HECK WAS THAT ?
A DUCK, MR. COOPER.! WHERE DID IT GO ?
I THINK I KNOW BETTER THAN TO ASK HOW HE GOT HERE.!
HE'S UP IN THE TREE.!
QUACK.! QUACK.!
I'LL GET HIM DOWN.!
4

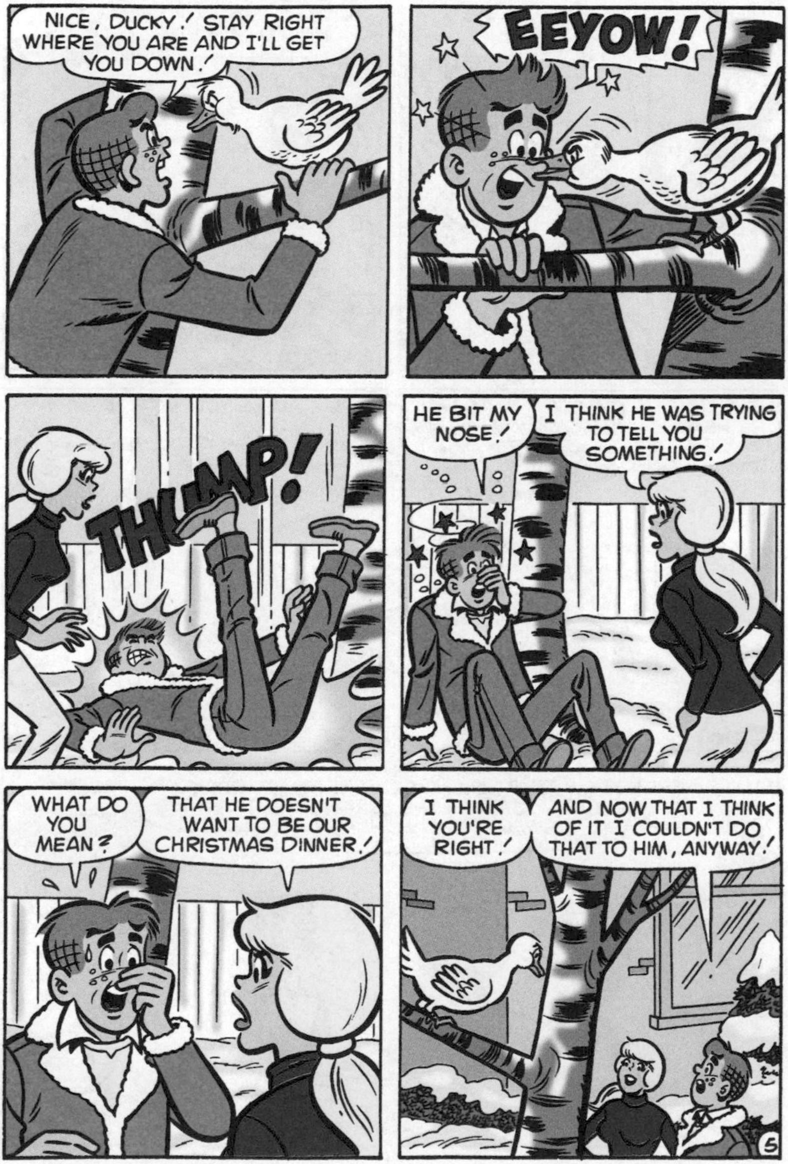
NICE, DUCKY! STAY RIGHT WHERE YOU ARE AND I'LL GET YOU DOWN!
EEYOW!
THUMP!
HE BIT MY NOSE!
I THINK HE WAS TRYING TO TELL YOU SOMETHING!
WHAT DO YOU MEAN?
THAT HE DOESN'T WANT TO BE OUR CHRISTMAS DINNER!
I THINK YOU'RE RIGHT!
AND NOW THAT I THINK OF IT I COULDN'T DO THAT TO HIM, ANYWAY!
5

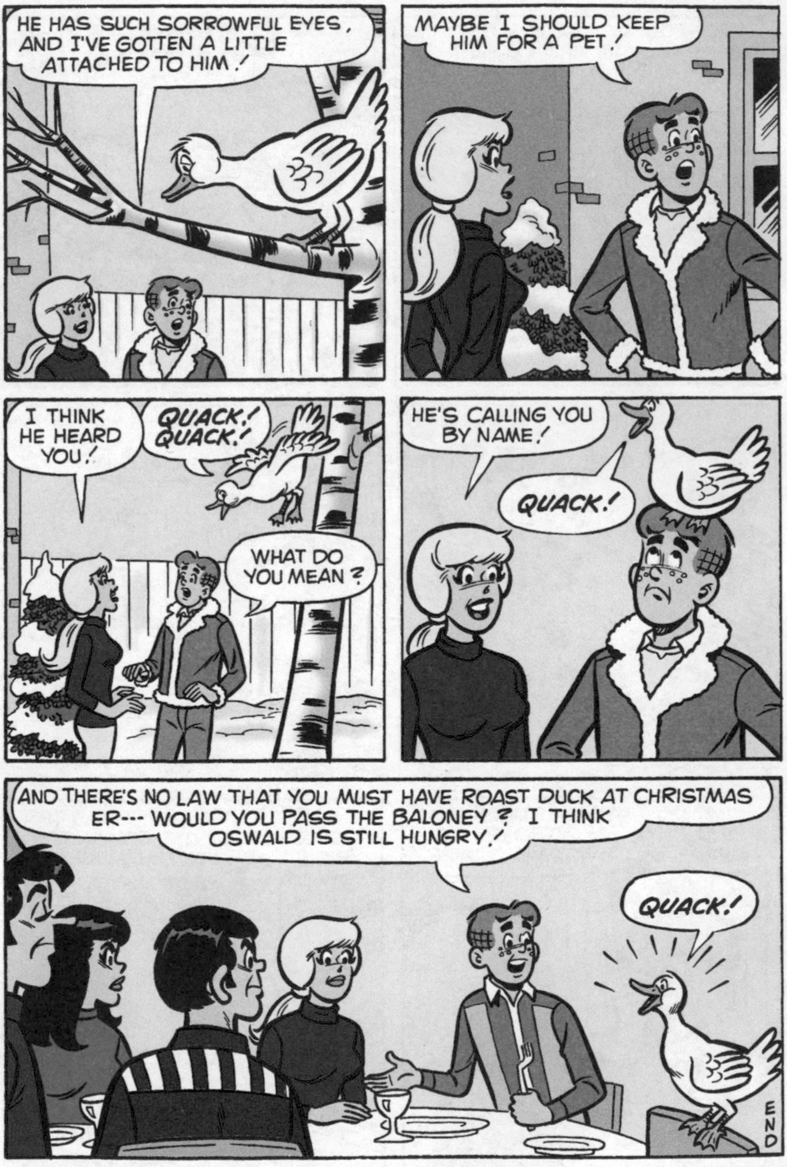
HE HAS SUCH SORROWFUL EYES, AND I'VE GOTTEN A LITTLE ATTACHED TO HIM!
MAYBE I SHOULD KEEP HIM FOR A PET!
I THINK HE HEARD YOU!
QUACK! QUACK!
WHAT DO YOU MEAN?
HE'S CALLING YOU BY NAME!
QUACK!
AND THERE'S NO LAW THAT YOU MUST HAVE ROAST DUCK AT CHRISTMAS ER--- WOULD YOU PASS THE BALONEY? I THINK OSWALD IS STILL HUNGRY!
QUACK!
END

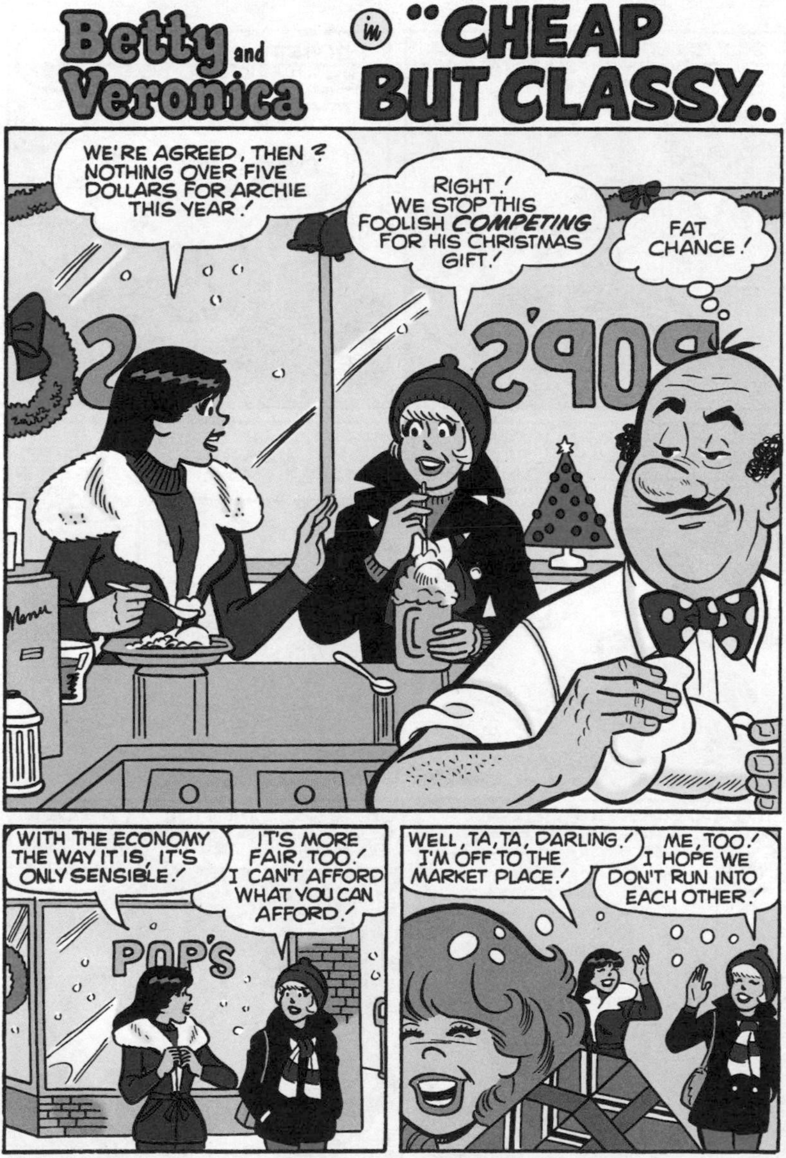
Betty and Veronica in "CHEAP BUT CLASSY.."
WE'RE AGREED, THEN? NOTHING OVER FIVE DOLLARS FOR ARCHIE THIS YEAR!
RIGHT! WE STOP THIS FOOLISH COMPETING FOR HIS CHRISTMAS GIFT!
FAT CHANCE!
POP'S
Menu
WITH THE ECONOMY THE WAY IT IS, IT'S ONLY SENSIBLE!
IT'S MORE FAIR, TOO! I CAN'T AFFORD WHAT YOU CAN AFFORD!
POP'S
WELL, TA, TA, DARLING! I'M OFF TO THE MARKET PLACE!
ME, TOO! I HOPE WE DON'T RUN INTO EACH OTHER!

• From Archie Giant Series Magazine #465, December 1977 •

Frank Doyle • Dan DeCarlo • Rudy Lapick • Bill Yoshida

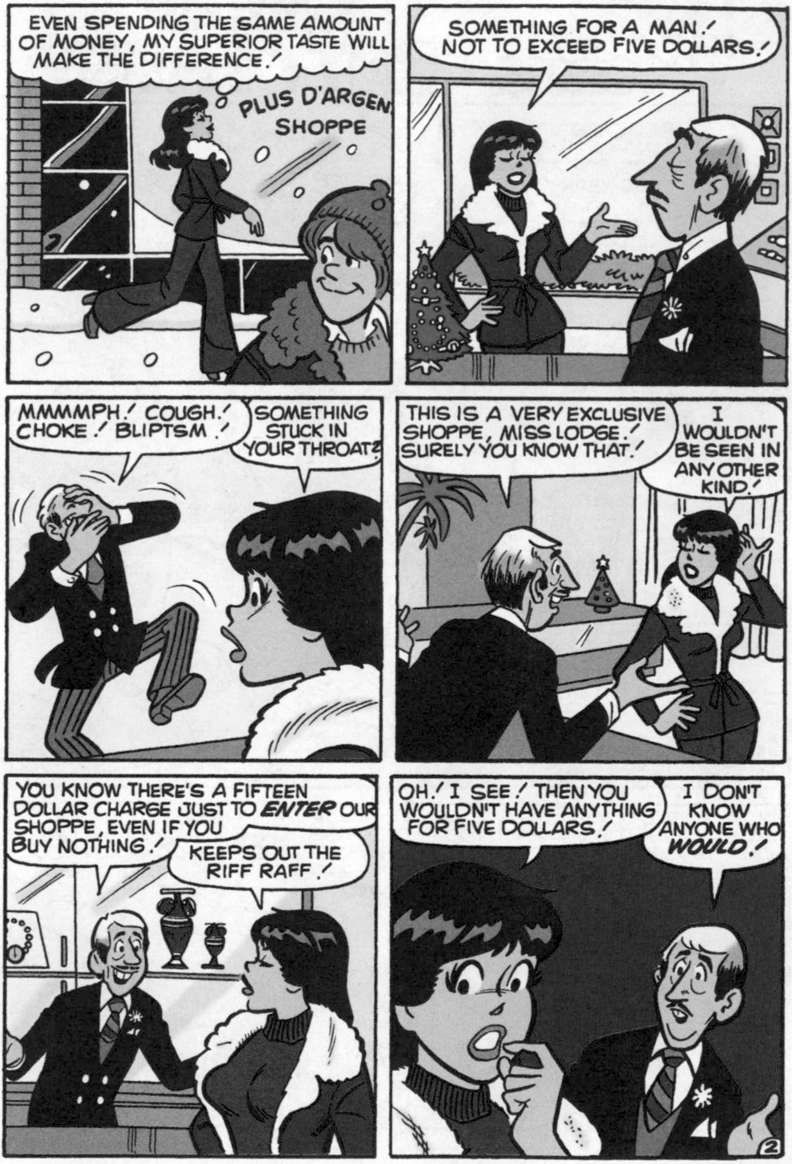
EVEN SPENDING THE SAME AMOUNT OF MONEY, MY SUPERIOR TASTE WILL MAKE THE DIFFERENCE!
PLUS D'ARGEN SHOPPE
SOMETHING FOR A MAN! NOT TO EXCEED FIVE DOLLARS!
MMMMPH! COUGH! CHOKE! BLIPTSM!
SOMETHING STUCK IN YOUR THROAT?
THIS IS A VERY EXCLUSIVE SHOPPE, MISS LODGE! SURELY YOU KNOW THAT!
I WOULDN'T BE SEEN IN ANY OTHER KIND!
YOU KNOW THERE'S A FIFTEEN DOLLAR CHARGE JUST TO ENTER OUR SHOPPE, EVEN IF YOU BUY NOTHING!
KEEPS OUT THE RIFF RAFF!
OH! I SEE! THEN YOU WOULDN'T HAVE ANYTHING FOR FIVE DOLLARS!
I DON'T KNOW ANYONE WHO WOULD!
2

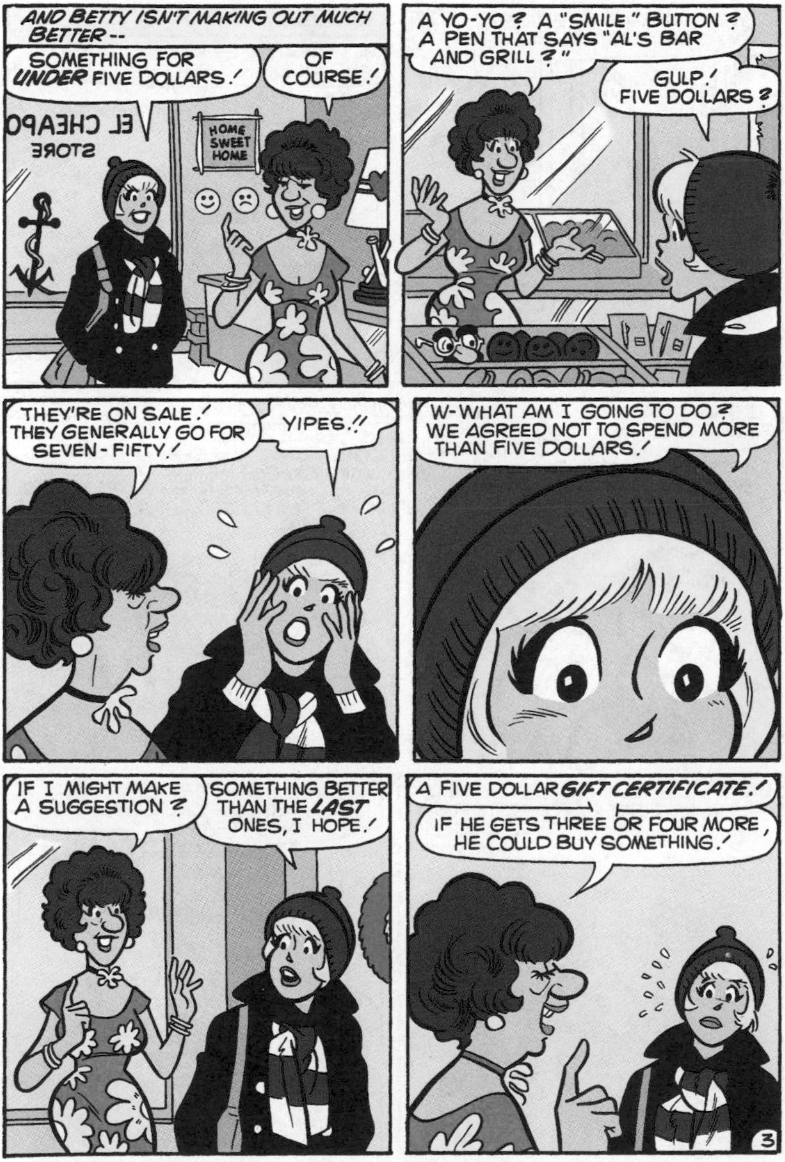
AND BETTY ISN'T MAKING OUT MUCH BETTER--
SOMETHING FOR UNDER FIVE DOLLARS!
OF COURSE!
EL CHEAPO STORE
HOME SWEET HOME
A YO-YO? A "SMILE" BUTTON? A PEN THAT SAYS "AL'S BAR AND GRILL?"
GULP! FIVE DOLLARS?
THEY'RE ON SALE! THEY GENERALLY GO FOR SEVEN-FIFTY!
YIPES!!
W-WHAT AM I GOING TO DO? WE AGREED NOT TO SPEND MORE THAN FIVE DOLLARS!
IF I MIGHT MAKE A SUGGESTION?
SOMETHING BETTER THAN THE LAST ONES, I HOPE!
A FIVE DOLLAR GIFT CERTIFICATE!
IF HE GETS THREE OR FOUR MORE, HE COULD BUY SOMETHING!
3

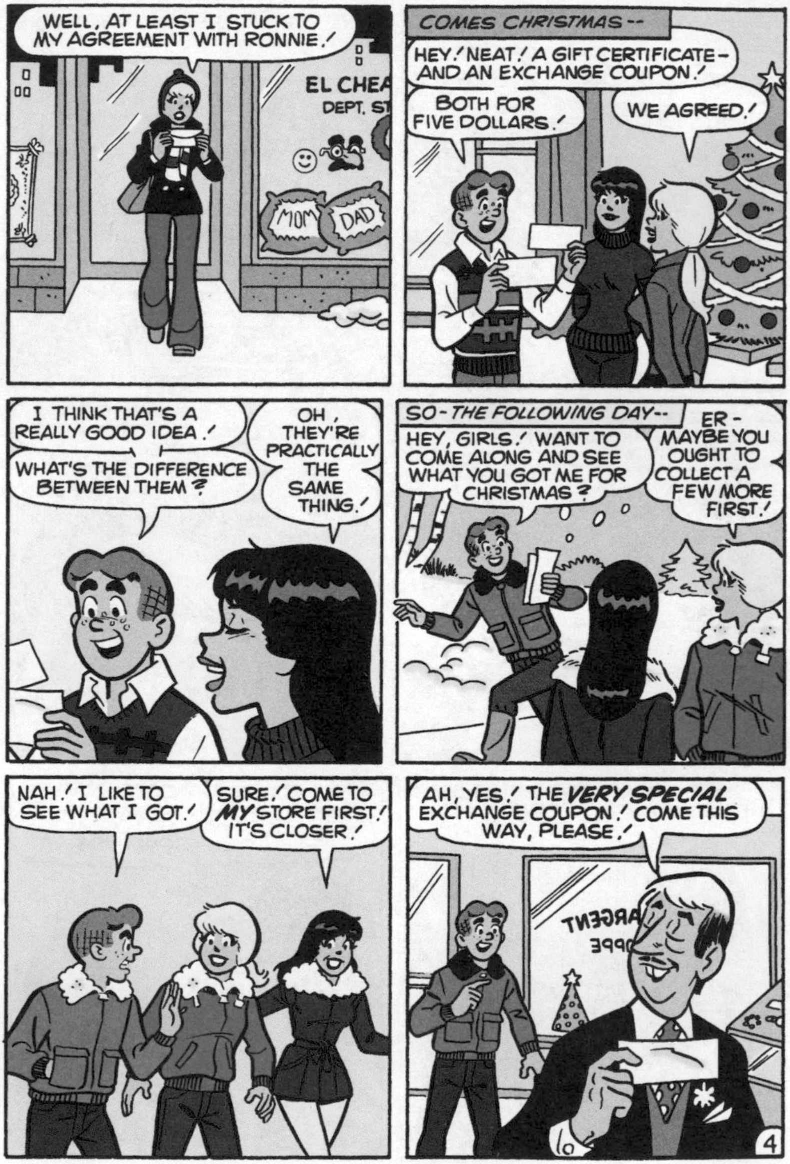
WELL, AT LEAST I STUCK TO MY AGREEMENT WITH RONNIE.!
EL CHEA
DEPT. ST
MOM
DAD
COMES CHRISTMAS --
HEY! NEAT! A GIFT CERTIFICATE-AND AN EXCHANGE COUPON!
BOTH FOR FIVE DOLLARS!
WE AGREED!
I THINK THAT'S A REALLY GOOD IDEA!
WHAT'S THE DIFFERENCE BETWEEN THEM?
OH, THEY'RE PRACTICALLY THE SAME THING!
SO-THE FOLLOWING DAY--
HEY, GIRLS! WANT TO COME ALONG AND SEE WHAT YOU GOT ME FOR CHRISTMAS?
ER-MAYBE YOU OUGHT TO COLLECT A FEW MORE FIRST!
NAH! I LIKE TO SEE WHAT I GOT!
SURE! COME TO MY STORE FIRST! IT'S CLOSER!
AH, YES! THE VERY SPECIAL EXCHANGE COUPON! COME THIS WAY, PLEASE!
4

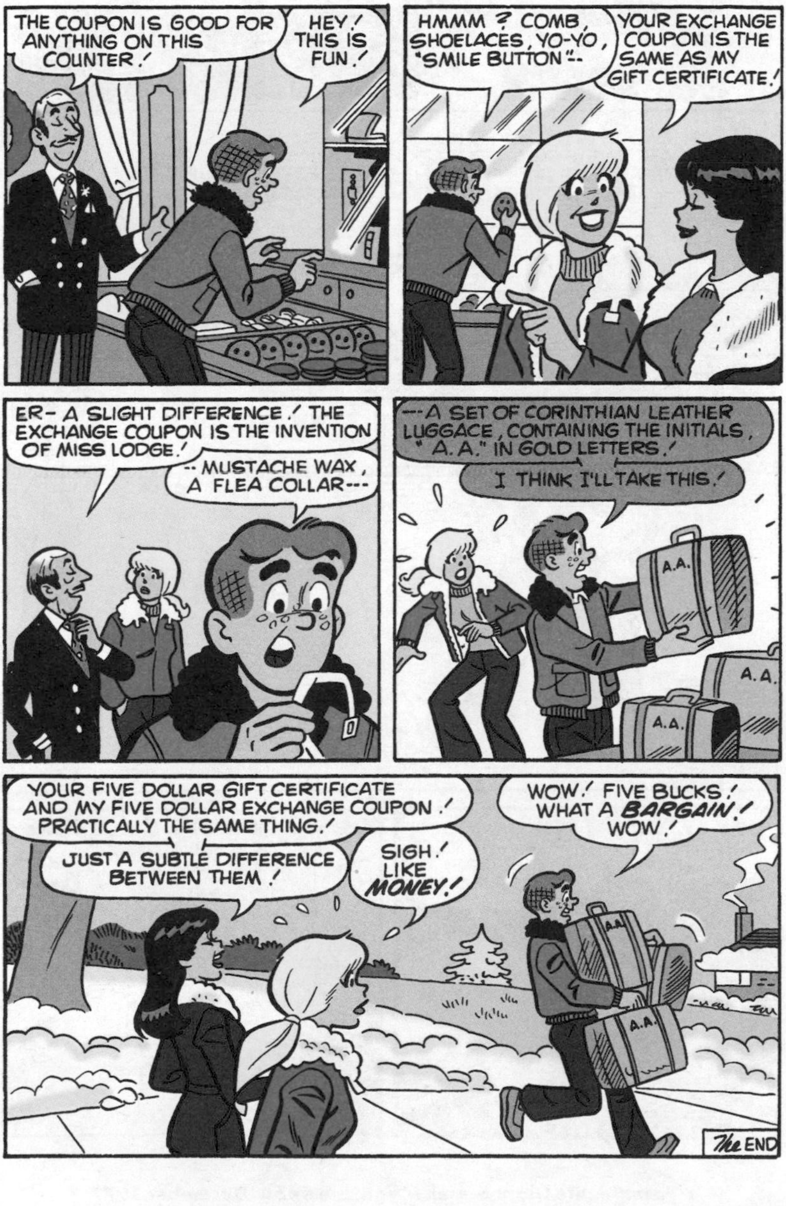
THE COUPON IS GOOD FOR ANYTHING ON THIS COUNTER!
HEY! THIS IS FUN!
HMMM? COMB, SHOELACES, YO-YO, "SMILE BUTTON"--
YOUR EXCHANGE COUPON IS THE SAME AS MY GIFT CERTIFICATE!
ER- A SLIGHT DIFFERENCE! THE EXCHANGE COUPON IS THE INVENTION OF MISS LODGE!
-- MUSTACHE WAX, A FLEA COLLAR---
---A SET OF CORINTHIAN LEATHER LUGGAGE, CONTAINING THE INITIALS, "A. A." IN GOLD LETTERS!
I THINK I'LL TAKE THIS!
A.A.
A. A.
A.A.
YOUR FIVE DOLLAR GIFT CERTIFICATE AND MY FIVE DOLLAR EXCHANGE COUPON! PRACTICALLY THE SAME THING!
JUST A SUBTLE DIFFERENCE BETWEEN THEM!
SIGH! LIKE MONEY!
WOW! FIVE BUCKS! WHAT A BARGAIN! WOW!
A.A.
The END

Betty and Veronica in "Number One"

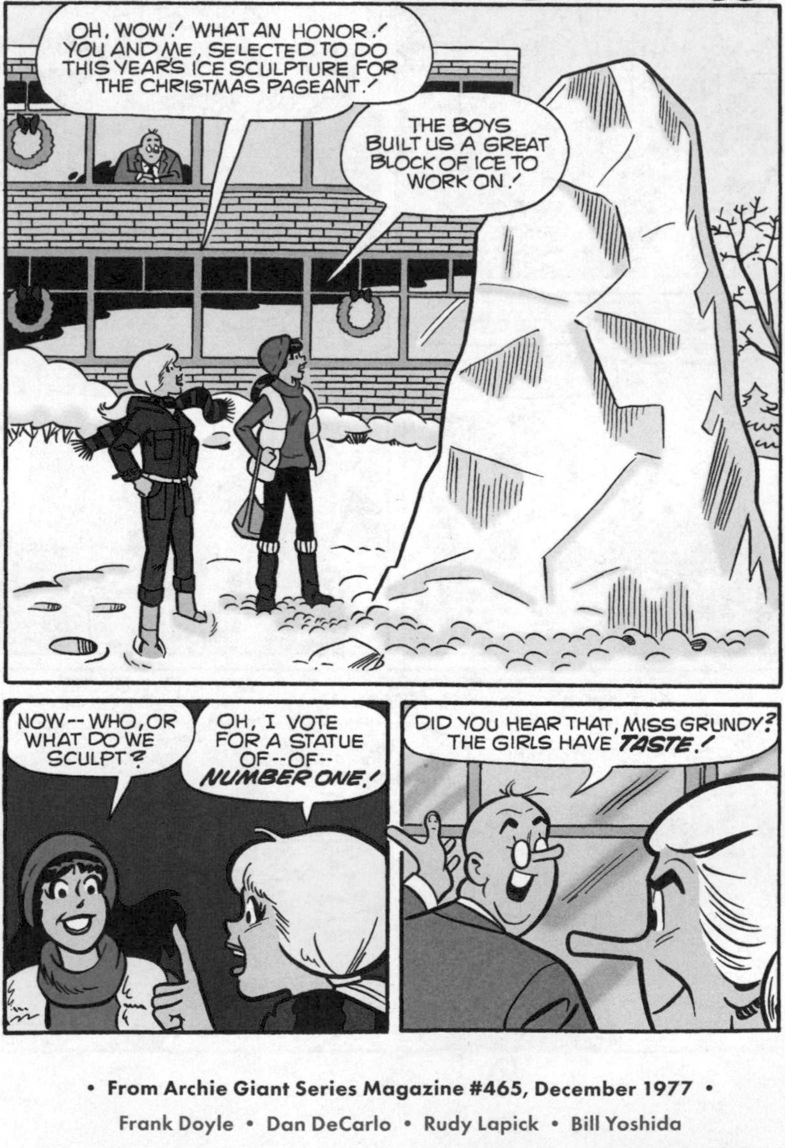
OH, WOW! WHAT AN HONOR! YOU AND ME, SELECTED TO DO THIS YEAR'S ICE SCULPTURE FOR THE CHRISTMAS PAGEANT!
THE BOYS BUILT US A GREAT BLOCK OF ICE TO WORK ON!
NOW-- WHO, OR WHAT DO WE SCULPT?
OH, I VOTE FOR A STATUE OF--OF-- NUMBER ONE!
DID YOU HEAR THAT, MISS GRUNDY? THE GIRLS HAVE TASTE!

• From Archie Giant Series Magazine #465, December 1977 •

Frank Doyle • Dan DeCarlo • Rudy Lapick • Bill Yoshida

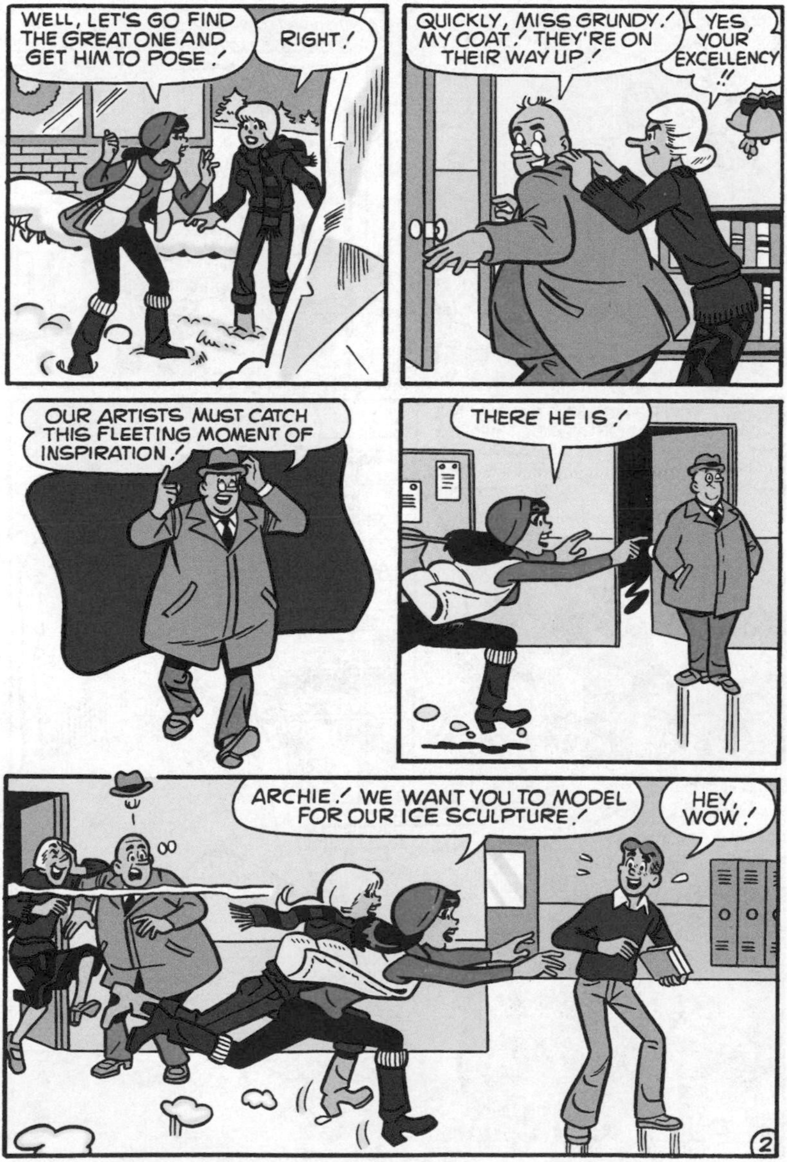
WELL, LET'S GO FIND THE GREAT ONE AND GET HIM TO POSE!
RIGHT!
QUICKLY, MISS GRUNDY! MY COAT! THEY'RE ON THEIR WAY UP!
YES, YOUR EXCELLENCY!!
OUR ARTISTS MUST CATCH THIS FLEETING MOMENT OF INSPIRATION!
THERE HE IS!
ARCHIE! WE WANT YOU TO MODEL FOR OUR ICE SCULPTURE!
HEY, WOW!
2

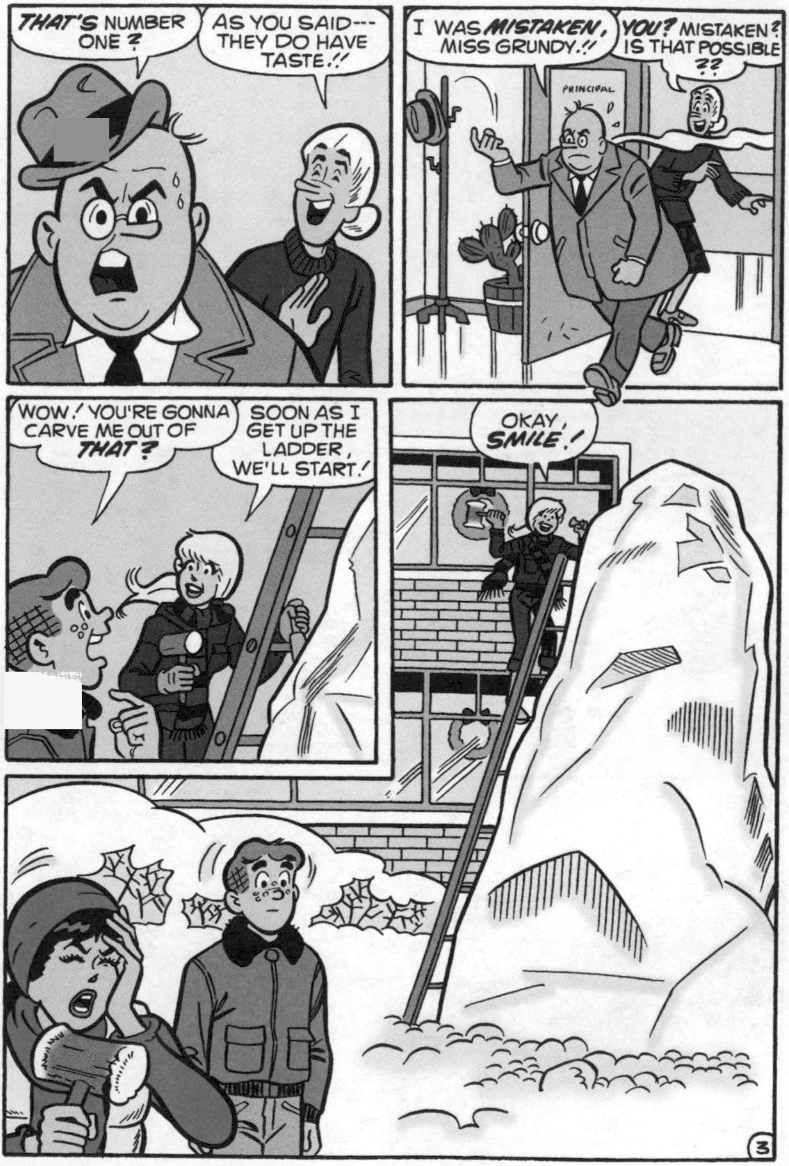
THAT'S NUMBER ONE ?
AS YOU SAID--- THEY DO HAVE TASTE.!!
I WAS MISTAKEN, MISS GRUNDY.!!
YOU? MISTAKEN? IS THAT POSSIBLE ??
PRINCIPAL
WOW.! YOU'RE GONNA CARVE ME OUT OF THAT?
SOON AS I GET UP THE LADDER, WE'LL START.!
OKAY, SMILE.!

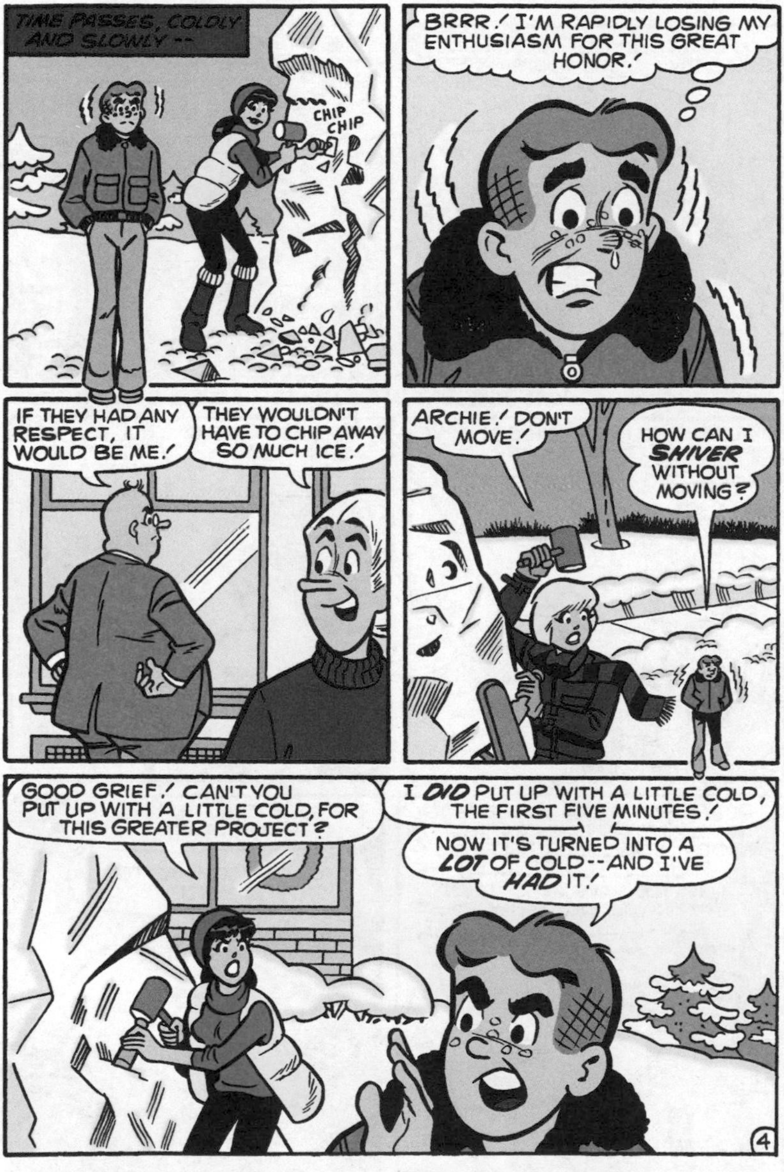
TIME PASSES, COLDLY AND SLOWLY --
CHIP CHIP
BRRR! I'M RAPIDLY LOSING MY ENTHUSIASM FOR THIS GREAT HONOR!
IF THEY HAD ANY RESPECT, IT WOULD BE ME!
THEY WOULDN'T HAVE TO CHIP AWAY SO MUCH ICE!
ARCHIE! DON'T MOVE!
HOW CAN I SHIVER WITHOUT MOVING?
GOOD GRIEF! CAN'T YOU PUT UP WITH A LITTLE COLD, FOR THIS GREATER PROJECT?
I DID PUT UP WITH A LITTLE COLD, THE FIRST FIVE MINUTES!
NOW IT'S TURNED INTO A LOT OF COLD--AND I'VE HAD IT!
4

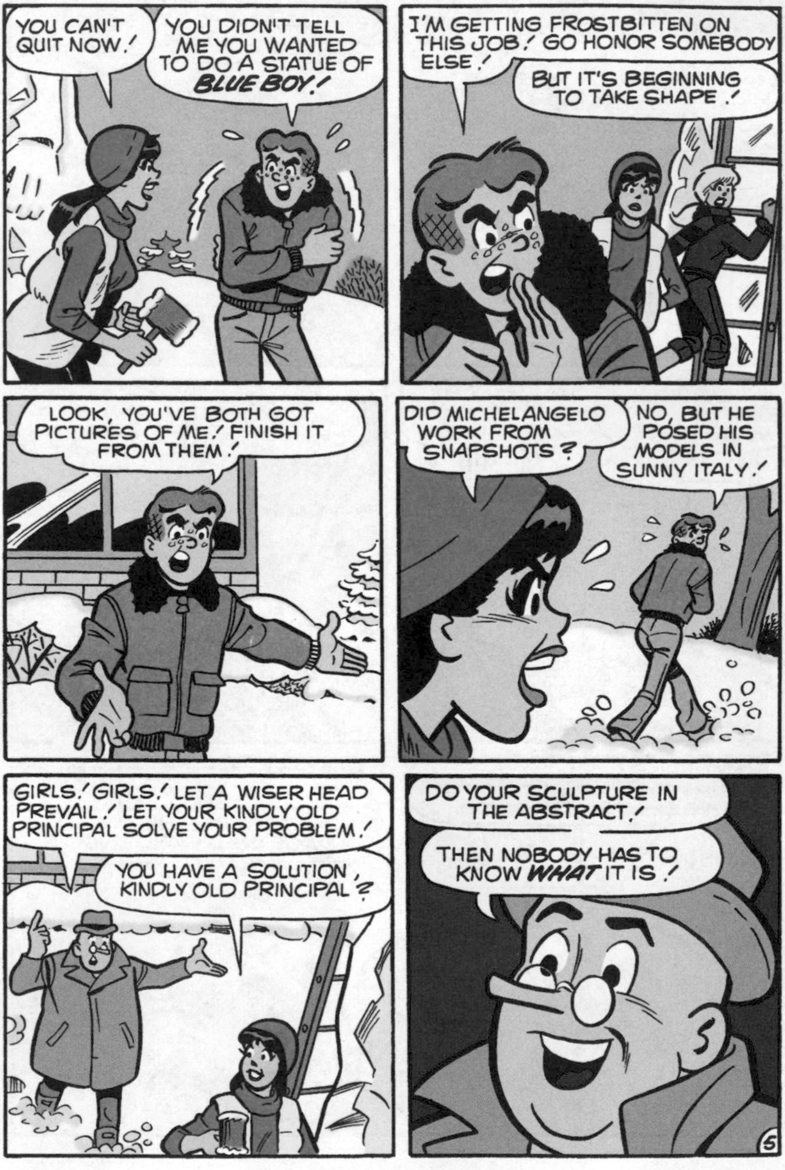
YOU CAN'T QUIT NOW.!
YOU DIDN'T TELL ME YOU WANTED TO DO A STATUE OF BLUE BOY.!
I'M GETTING FROSTBITTEN ON THIS JOB.! GO HONOR SOMEBODY ELSE.!
BUT IT'S BEGINNING TO TAKE SHAPE.!
LOOK, YOU'VE BOTH GOT PICTURES OF ME.! FINISH IT FROM THEM.!
DID MICHELANGELO WORK FROM SNAPSHOTS?
NO, BUT HE POSED HIS MODELS IN SUNNY ITALY.!
GIRLS.! GIRLS.! LET A WISER HEAD PREVAIL.! LET YOUR KINDLY OLD PRINCIPAL SOLVE YOUR PROBLEM.!
YOU HAVE A SOLUTION, KINDLY OLD PRINCIPAL?
DO YOUR SCULPTURE IN THE ABSTRACT.!
THEN NOBODY HAS TO KNOW WHAT IT IS.!
5

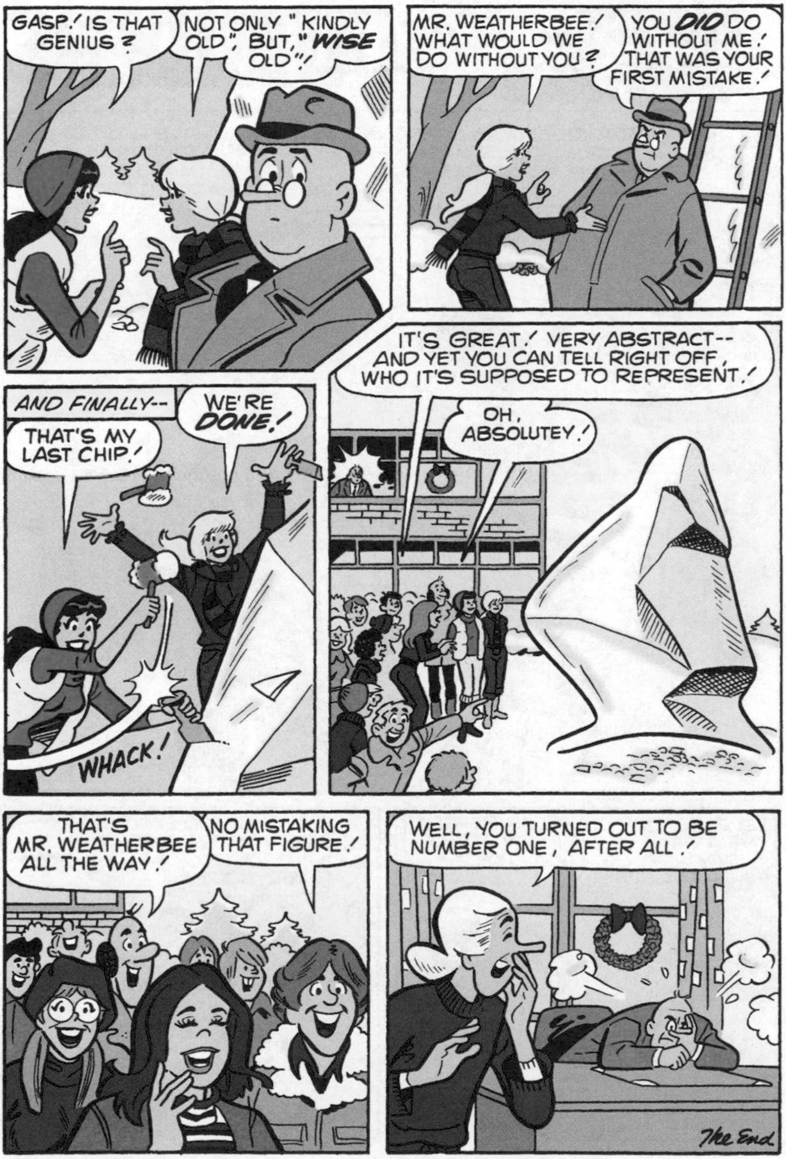
GASP! IS THAT GENIUS?
NOT ONLY "KINDLY OLD", BUT, "WISE OLD"!
MR. WEATHERBEE! WHAT WOULD WE DO WITHOUT YOU?
YOU DID DO WITHOUT ME! THAT WAS YOUR FIRST MISTAKE!
AND FINALLY--
THAT'S MY LAST CHIP!
WE'RE DONE!
WHACK!
IT'S GREAT! VERY ABSTRACT-- AND YET YOU CAN TELL RIGHT OFF, WHO IT'S SUPPOSED TO REPRESENT!
OH, ABSOLUTEY!
THAT'S MR. WEATHERBEE ALL THE WAY!
NO MISTAKING THAT FIGURE!
WELL, YOU TURNED OUT TO BE NUMBER ONE, AFTER ALL!
The End

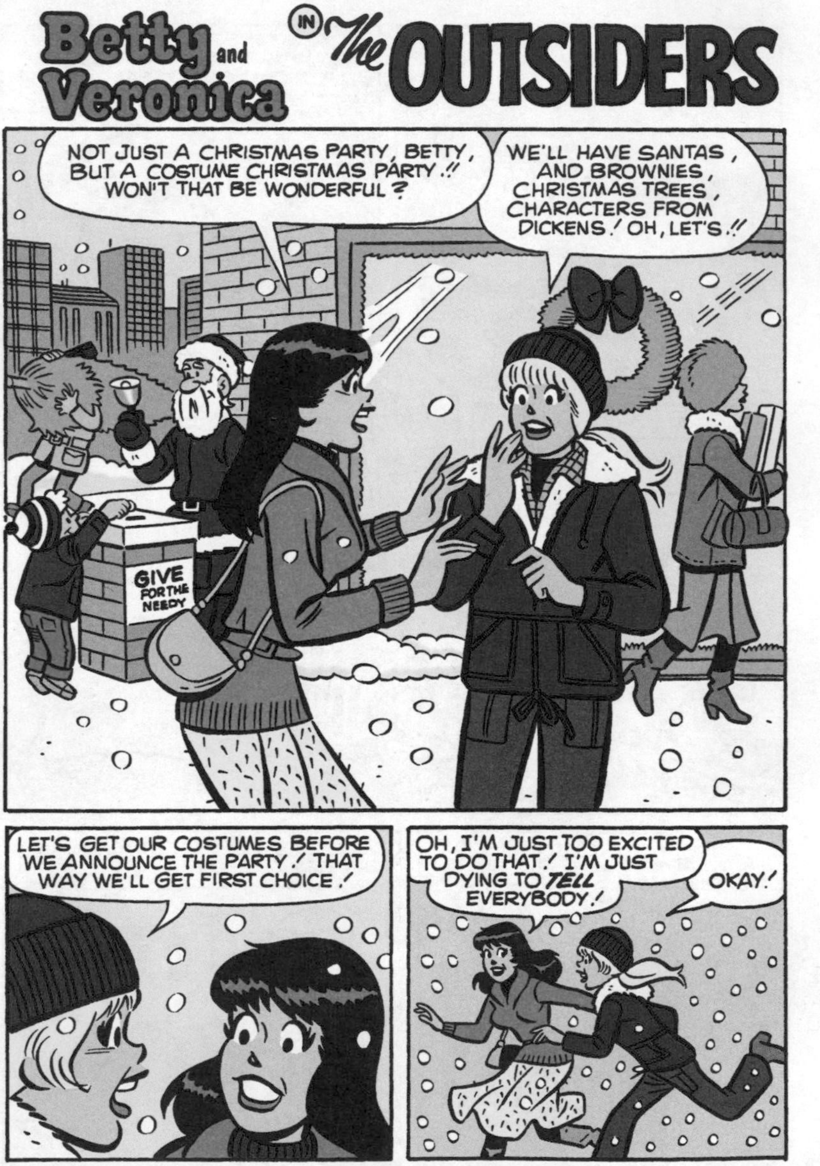
Betty and Veronica IN The OUTSIDERS
NOT JUST A CHRISTMAS PARTY, BETTY, BUT A COSTUME CHRISTMAS PARTY.!! WON'T THAT BE WONDERFUL?
WE'LL HAVE SANTAS, AND BROWNIES, CHRISTMAS TREES, CHARACTERS FROM DICKENS.! OH, LET'S.!!
GIVE FOR THE NEEDY
LET'S GET OUR COSTUMES BEFORE WE ANNOUNCE THE PARTY.! THAT WAY WE'LL GET FIRST CHOICE.!
OH, I'M JUST TOO EXCITED TO DO THAT.! I'M JUST DYING TO TELL EVERYBODY.!
OKAY.!

• From Archie Giant Series Magazine #465, December 1977 •

Frank Doyle • Dan DeCarlo • Rudy Lapick • Bill Yoshida

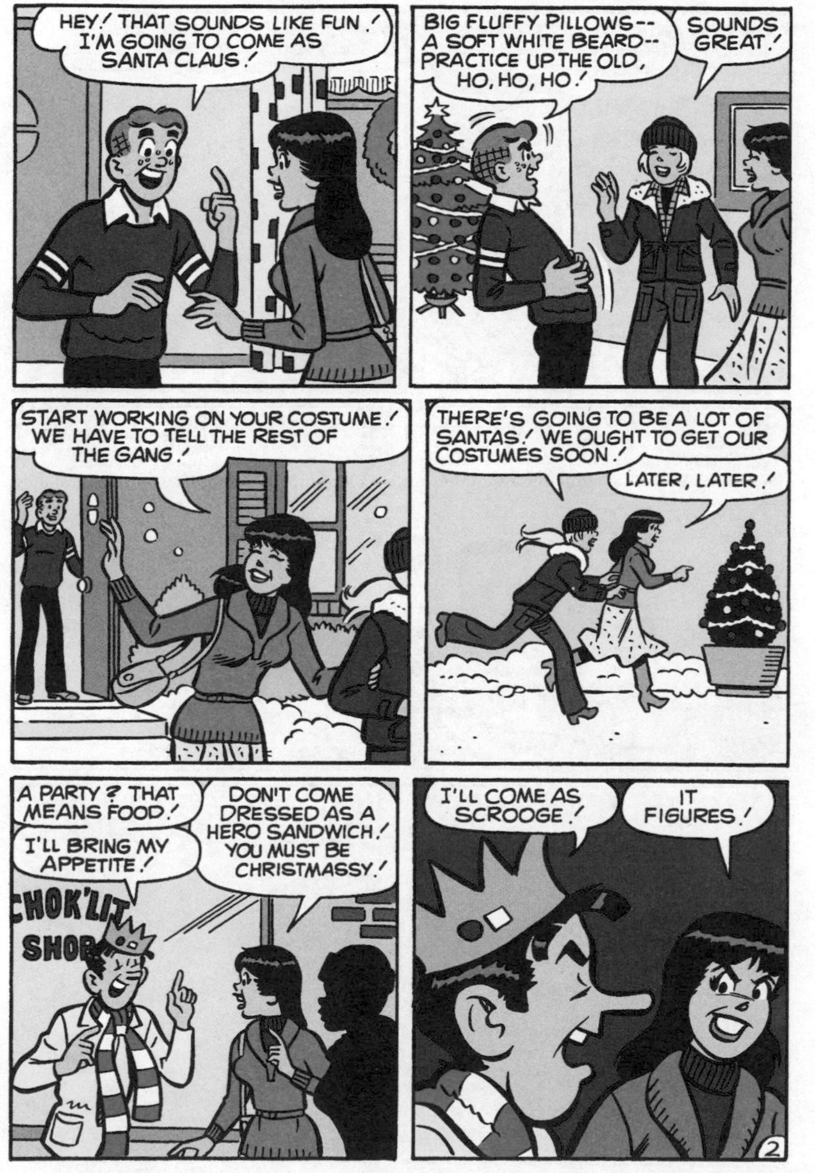
HEY! THAT SOUNDS LIKE FUN! I'M GOING TO COME AS SANTA CLAUS!
BIG FLUFFY PILLOWS-- A SOFT WHITE BEARD-- PRACTICE UP THE OLD, HO, HO, HO!
SOUNDS GREAT!
START WORKING ON YOUR COSTUME! WE HAVE TO TELL THE REST OF THE GANG!
THERE'S GOING TO BE A LOT OF SANTAS! WE OUGHT TO GET OUR COSTUMES SOON!
LATER, LATER!
CHOK'LIT SHOP
A PARTY? THAT MEANS FOOD!
I'LL BRING MY APPETITE!
DON'T COME DRESSED AS A HERO SANDWICH! YOU MUST BE CHRISTMASSY!
I'LL COME AS SCROOGE!
IT FIGURES!
2

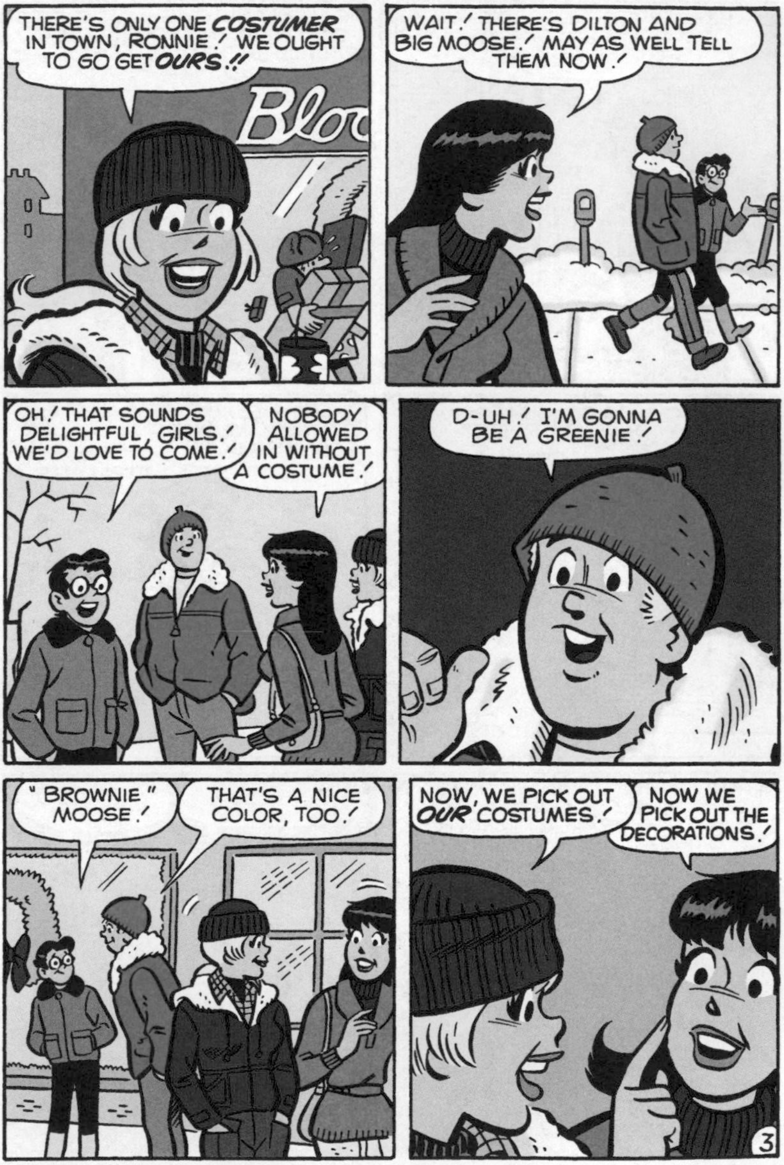
THERE'S ONLY ONE COSTUMER IN TOWN, RONNIE! WE OUGHT TO GO GET OURS!!
WAIT! THERE'S DILTON AND BIG MOOSE! MAY AS WELL TELL THEM NOW!
OH! THAT SOUNDS DELIGHTFUL, GIRLS! WE'D LOVE TO COME!
NOBODY ALLOWED IN WITHOUT A COSTUME!
D-UH! I'M GONNA BE A GREENIE!
"BROWNIE" MOOSE!
THAT'S A NICE COLOR, TOO!
NOW, WE PICK OUT OUR COSTUMES!
NOW WE PICK OUT THE DECORATIONS!
3

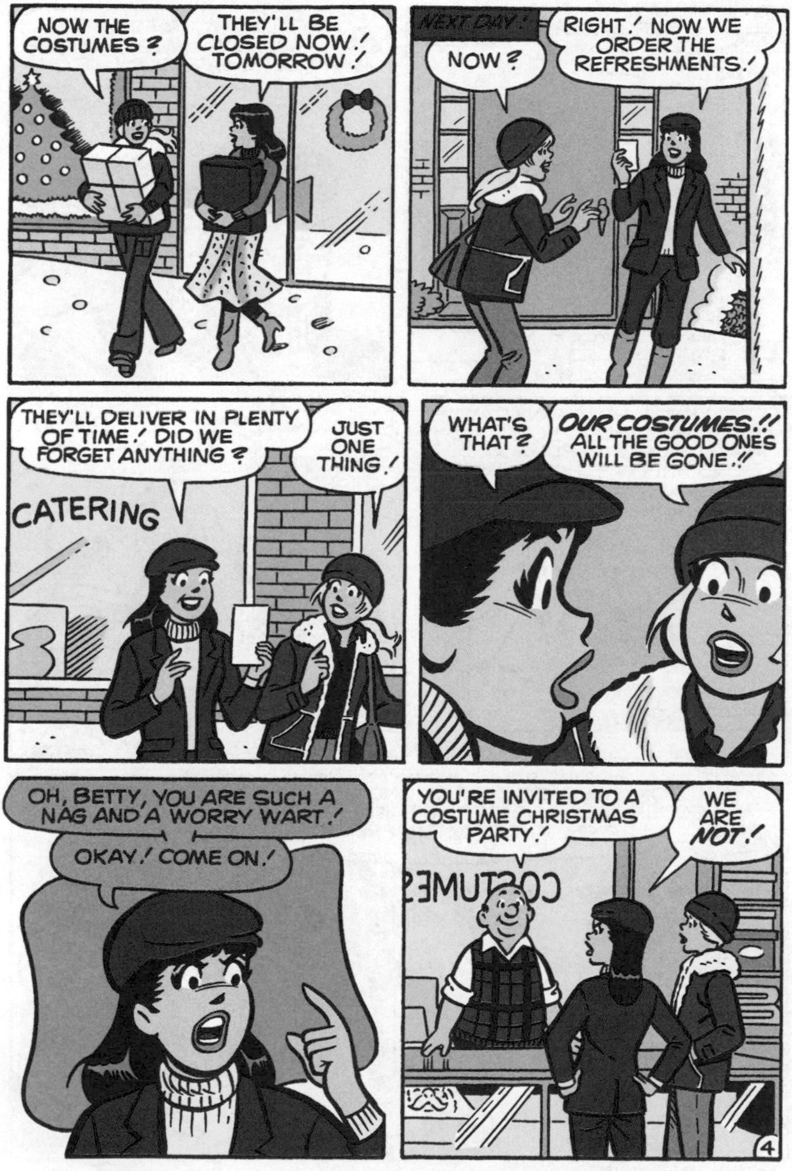
NOW THE COSTUMES ?
THEY'LL BE CLOSED NOW.! TOMORROW.!
NEXT DAY.!
NOW ?
RIGHT.! NOW WE ORDER THE REFRESHMENTS.!
THEY'LL DELIVER IN PLENTY OF TIME.! DID WE FORGET ANYTHING ?
JUST ONE THING.!
CATERING
WHAT'S THAT ?
OUR COSTUMES.!! ALL THE GOOD ONES WILL BE GONE.!!
OH, BETTY, YOU ARE SUCH A NAG AND A WORRY WART.!
OKAY.! COME ON.!
YOU'RE INVITED TO A COSTUME CHRISTMAS PARTY.!
WE ARE NOT.!
COSTUMES
4

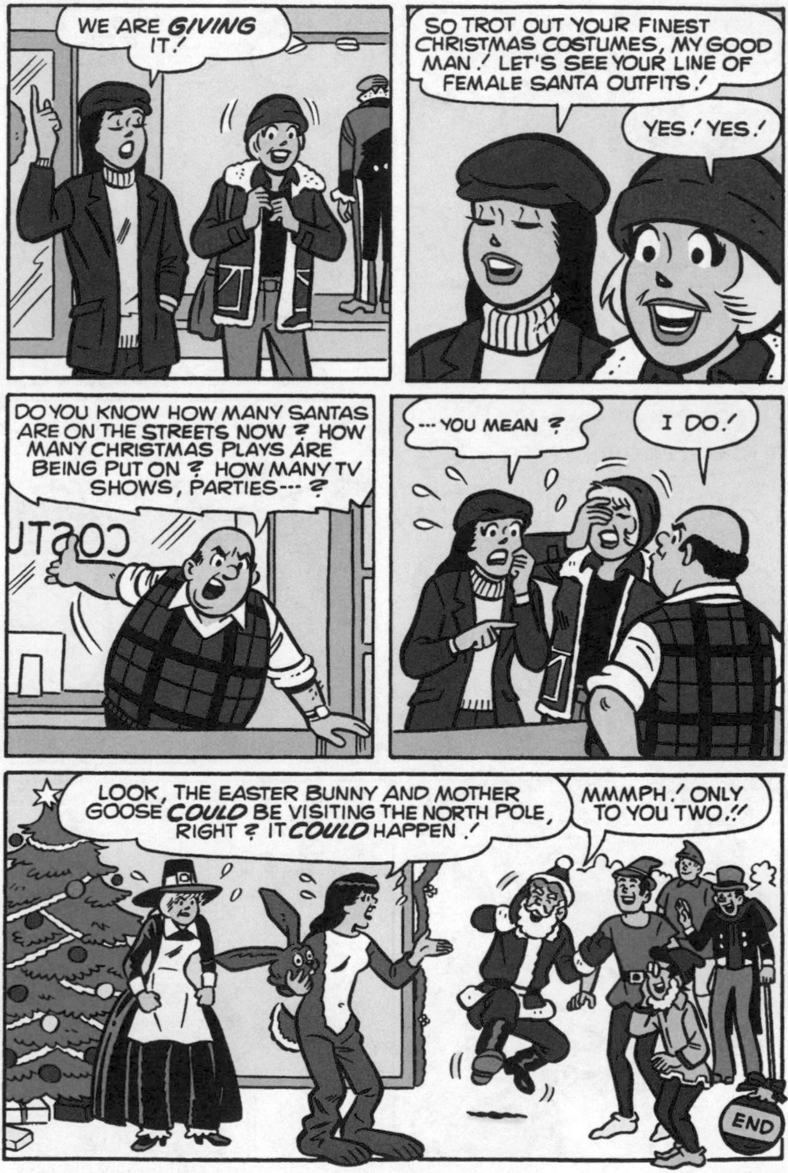
WE ARE GIVING IT!
SO TROT OUT YOUR FINEST CHRISTMAS COSTUMES, MY GOOD MAN! LET'S SEE YOUR LINE OF FEMALE SANTA OUTFITS!
YES! YES!
DO YOU KNOW HOW MANY SANTAS ARE ON THE STREETS NOW? HOW MANY CHRISTMAS PLAYS ARE BEING PUT ON? HOW MANY TV SHOWS, PARTIES---?
---YOU MEAN?
I DO!
LOOK, THE EASTER BUNNY AND MOTHER GOOSE COULD BE VISITING THE NORTH POLE, RIGHT? IT COULD HAPPEN!
MMMPH! ONLY TO YOU TWO!!
END

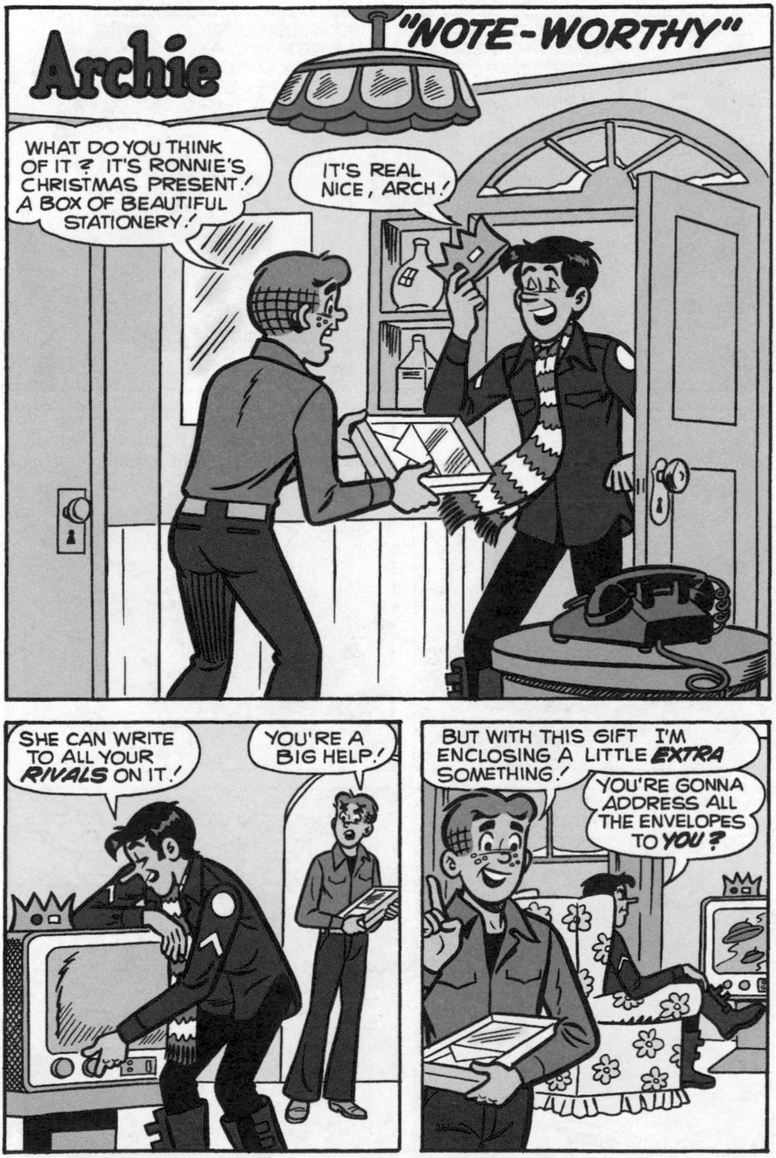
Archie
"NOTE-WORTHY"
WHAT DO YOU THINK OF IT? IT'S RONNIE'S CHRISTMAS PRESENT! A BOX OF BEAUTIFUL STATIONERY!
IT'S REAL NICE, ARCH!
SHE CAN WRITE TO ALL YOUR RIVALS ON IT!
YOU'RE A BIG HELP!
BUT WITH THIS GIFT I'M ENCLOSING A LITTLE EXTRA SOMETHING!
YOU'RE GONNA ADDRESS ALL THE ENVELOPES TO YOU?

• **From Archie Giant Series Magazine #476, December 1978** •

Frank Doyle • Bob Bolling • Rudy Lapick • Bill Yoshida

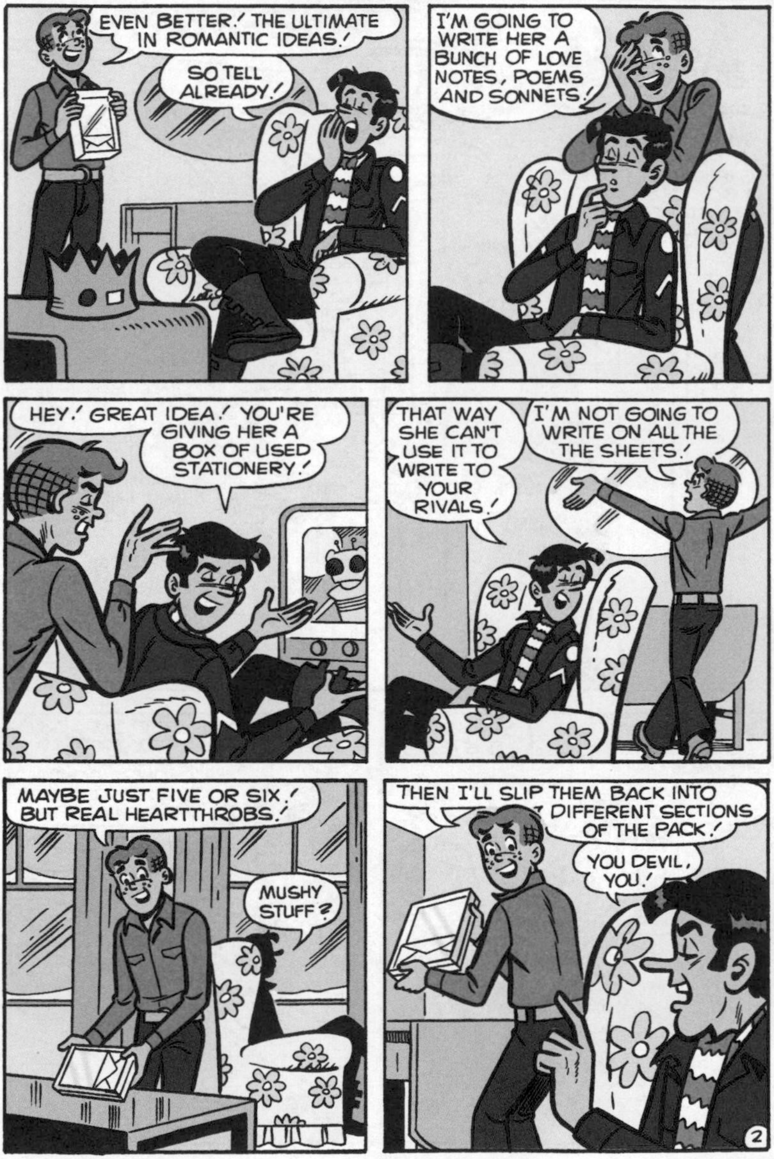
EVEN BETTER! THE ULTIMATE IN ROMANTIC IDEAS!
SO TELL ALREADY!
I'M GOING TO WRITE HER A BUNCH OF LOVE NOTES, POEMS AND SONNETS!
HEY! GREAT IDEA! YOU'RE GIVING HER A BOX OF USED STATIONERY!
I'M NOT GOING TO WRITE ON ALL THE THE SHEETS!
THAT WAY SHE CAN'T USE IT TO WRITE TO YOUR RIVALS!
MAYBE JUST FIVE OR SIX! BUT REAL HEARTTHROBS!
MUSHY STUFF?
THEN I'LL SLIP THEM BACK INTO DIFFERENT SECTIONS OF THE PACK!
YOU DEVIL, YOU!
2

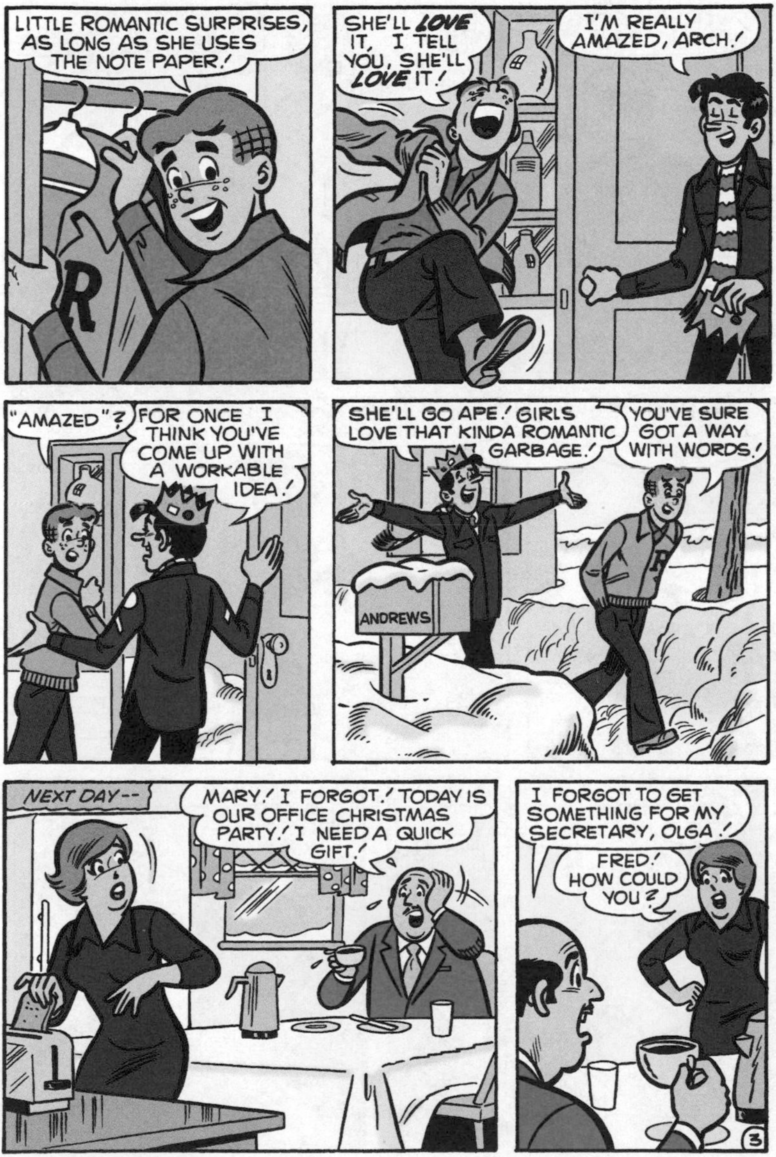
LITTLE ROMANTIC SURPRISES, AS LONG AS SHE USES THE NOTE PAPER!
SHE'LL LOVE IT, I TELL YOU, SHE'LL LOVE IT!
I'M REALLY AMAZED, ARCH!
"AMAZED"?
FOR ONCE I THINK YOU'VE COME UP WITH A WORKABLE IDEA!
SHE'LL GO APE! GIRLS LOVE THAT KINDA ROMANTIC GARBAGE!
YOU'VE SURE GOT A WAY WITH WORDS!
ANDREWS
NEXT DAY--
MARY! I FORGOT! TODAY IS OUR OFFICE CHRISTMAS PARTY! I NEED A QUICK GIFT!
I FORGOT TO GET SOMETHING FOR MY SECRETARY, OLGA!
FRED! HOW COULD YOU?
3

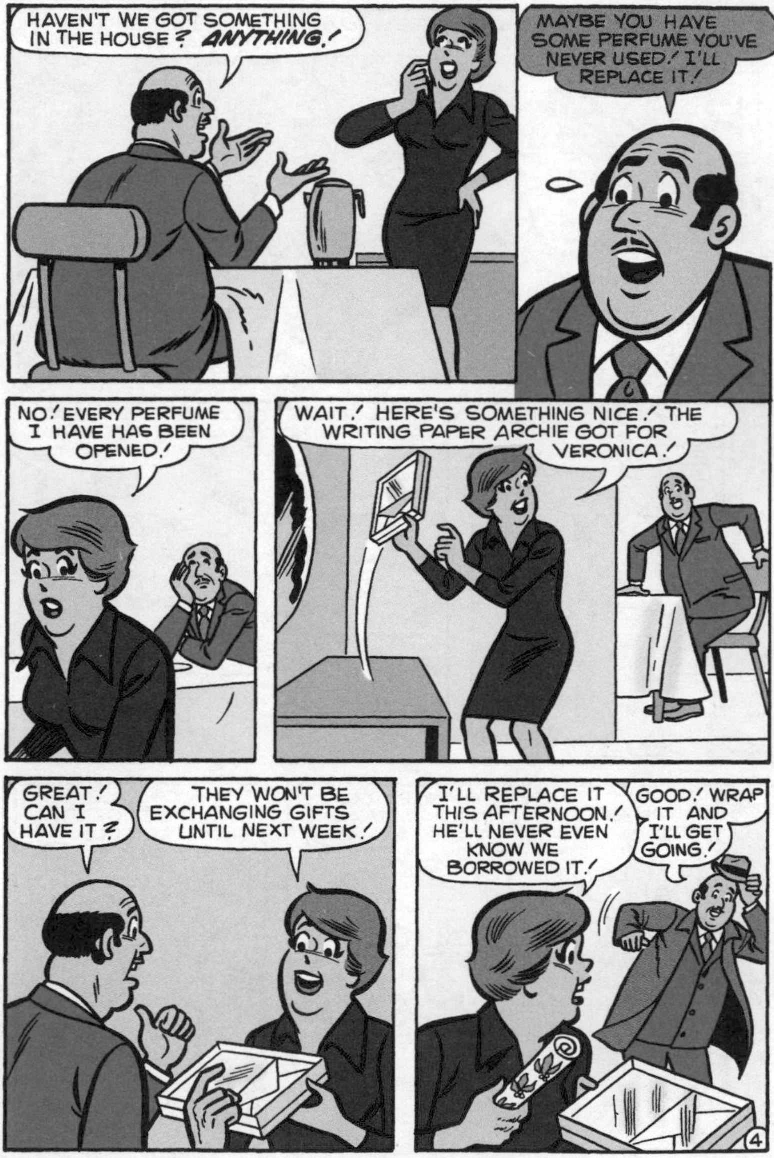
HAVEN'T WE GOT SOMETHING IN THE HOUSE? ANYTHING!
MAYBE YOU HAVE SOME PERFUME YOU'VE NEVER USED! I'LL REPLACE IT!
NO! EVERY PERFUME I HAVE HAS BEEN OPENED!
WAIT! HERE'S SOMETHING NICE! THE WRITING PAPER ARCHIE GOT FOR VERONICA!
GREAT! CAN I HAVE IT?
THEY WON'T BE EXCHANGING GIFTS UNTIL NEXT WEEK!
I'LL REPLACE IT THIS AFTERNOON! HE'LL NEVER EVEN KNOW WE BORROWED IT!
GOOD! WRAP IT AND I'LL GET GOING!
4

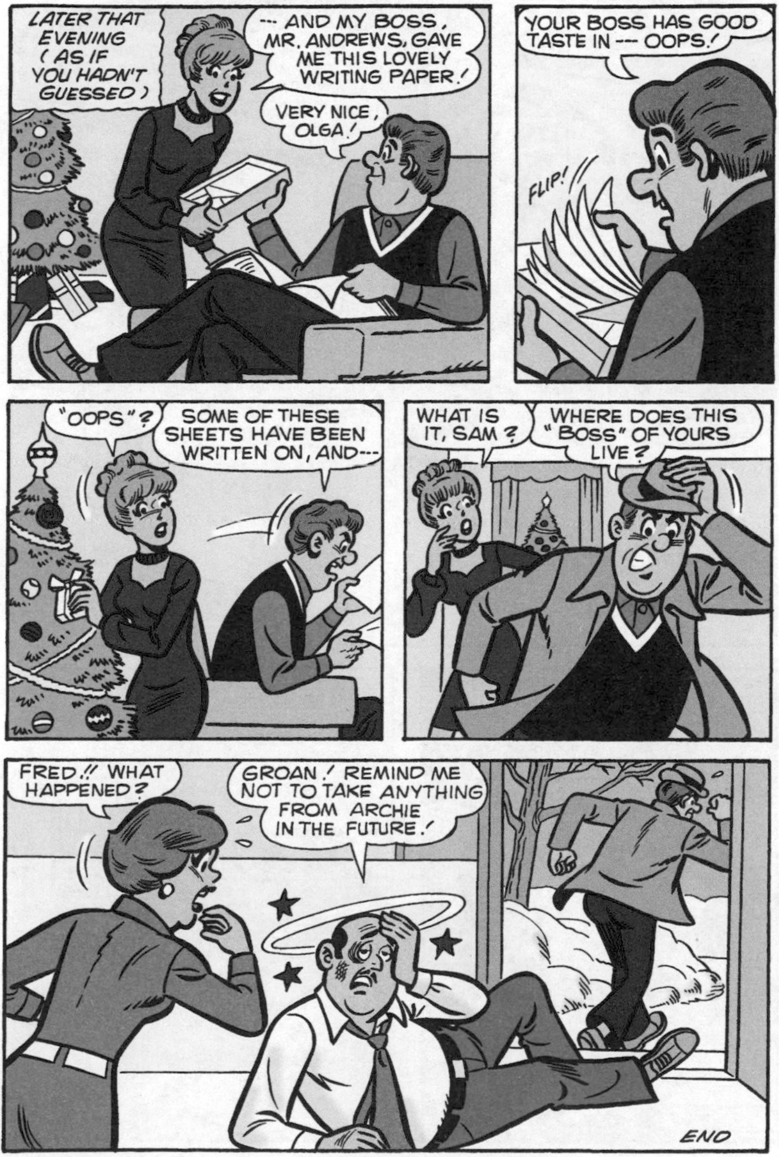
LATER THAT EVENING (AS IF YOU HADN'T GUESSED)
--- AND MY BOSS, MR. ANDREWS, GAVE ME THIS LOVELY WRITING PAPER!
VERY NICE, OLGA!
YOUR BOSS HAS GOOD TASTE IN --- OOPS!
FLIP!
"OOPS"?
SOME OF THESE SHEETS HAVE BEEN WRITTEN ON, AND---
WHAT IS IT, SAM?
WHERE DOES THIS "BOSS" OF YOURS LIVE?
FRED!! WHAT HAPPENED?
GROAN! REMIND ME NOT TO TAKE ANYTHING FROM ARCHIE IN THE FUTURE!
END

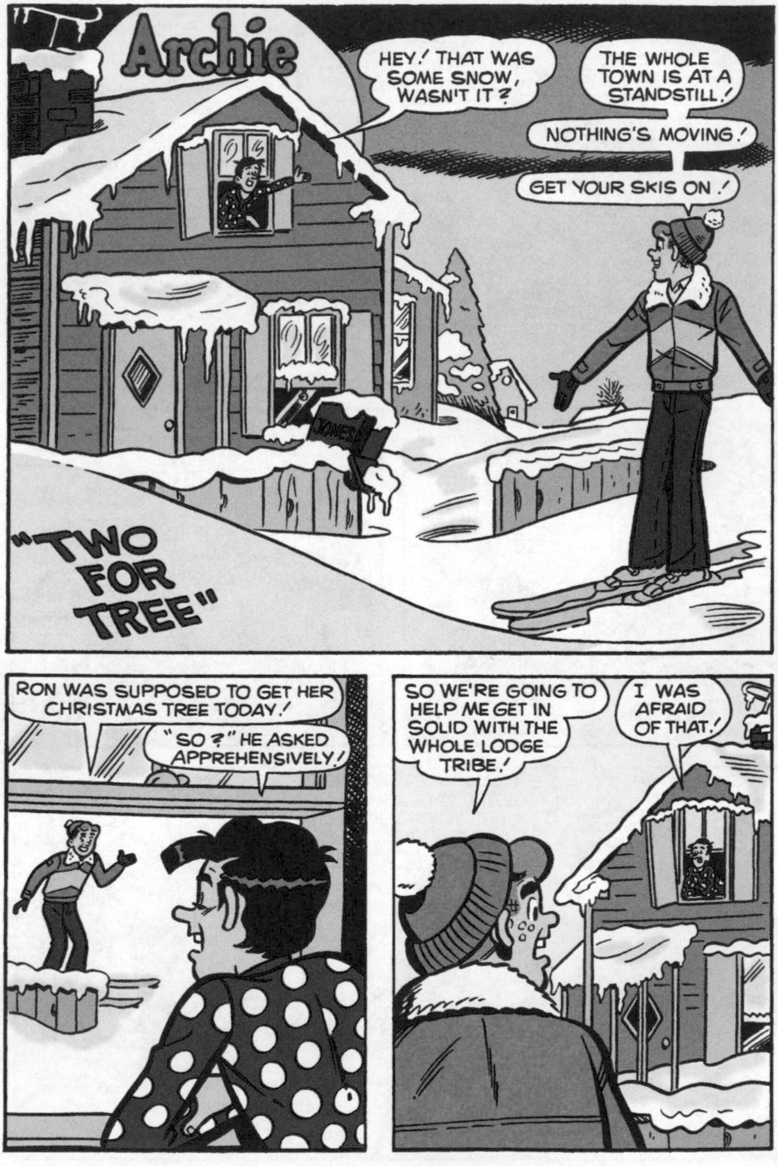
Archie
HEY! THAT WAS SOME SNOW, WASN'T IT?
THE WHOLE TOWN IS AT A STANDSTILL!
NOTHING'S MOVING!
GET YOUR SKIS ON!
JONES
"TWO FOR TREE"
RON WAS SUPPOSED TO GET HER CHRISTMAS TREE TODAY!
"SO?" HE ASKED APPREHENSIVELY!
SO WE'RE GOING TO HELP ME GET IN SOLID WITH THE WHOLE LODGE TRIBE!
I WAS AFRAID OF THAT!

• **From Archie Giant Series Magazine #476, December 1978** •

George Gladir • Bob Bolling • Rudy Lapick • Bill Yoshida

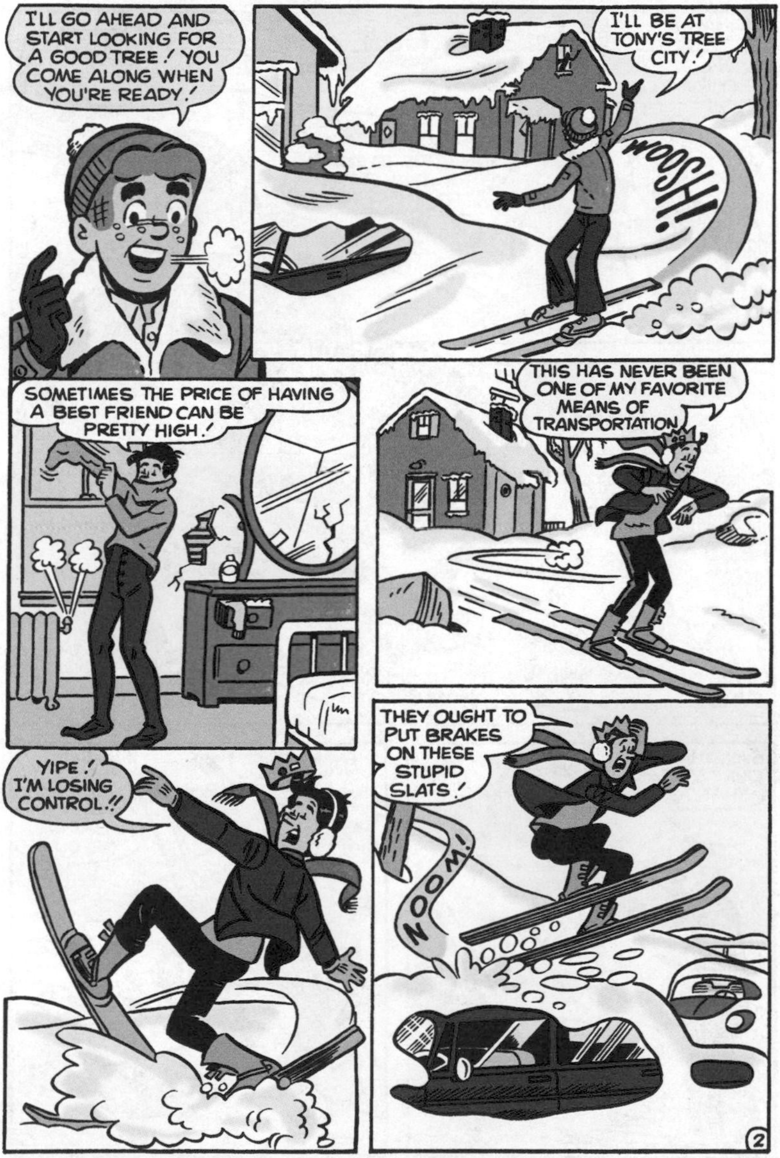
I'LL GO AHEAD AND START LOOKING FOR A GOOD TREE! YOU COME ALONG WHEN YOU'RE READY!
I'LL BE AT TONY'S TREE CITY!
WOOSH!
SOMETIMES THE PRICE OF HAVING A BEST FRIEND CAN BE PRETTY HIGH!
THIS HAS NEVER BEEN ONE OF MY FAVORITE MEANS OF TRANSPORTATION
YIPE! I'M LOSING CONTROL!!
THEY OUGHT TO PUT BRAKES ON THESE STUPID SLATS!
ZOOM!
2

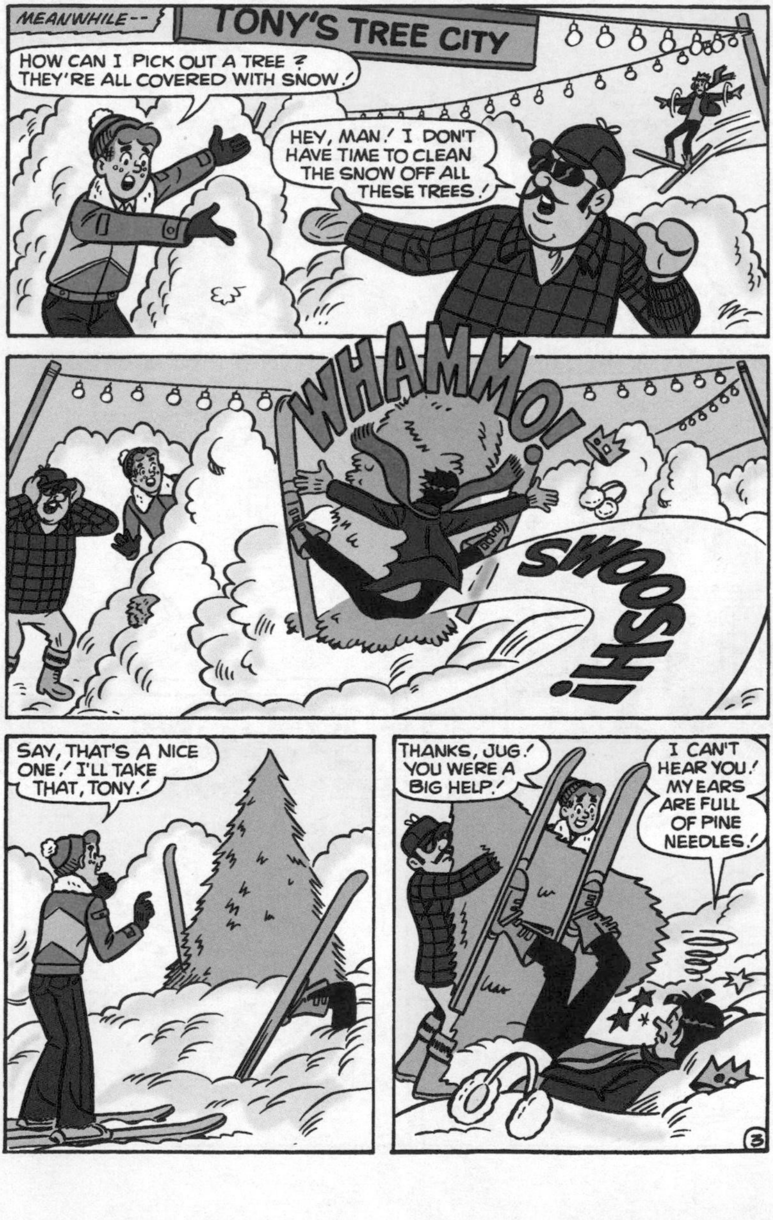
MEANWHILE--
TONY'S TREE CITY
HOW CAN I PICK OUT A TREE ? THEY'RE ALL COVERED WITH SNOW!
HEY, MAN! I DON'T HAVE TIME TO CLEAN THE SNOW OFF ALL THESE TREES!
WHAMMO!
SWOOSH!!
SAY, THAT'S A NICE ONE! I'LL TAKE THAT, TONY!
THANKS, JUG! YOU WERE A BIG HELP!
I CAN'T HEAR YOU! MY EARS ARE FULL OF PINE NEEDLES!
3

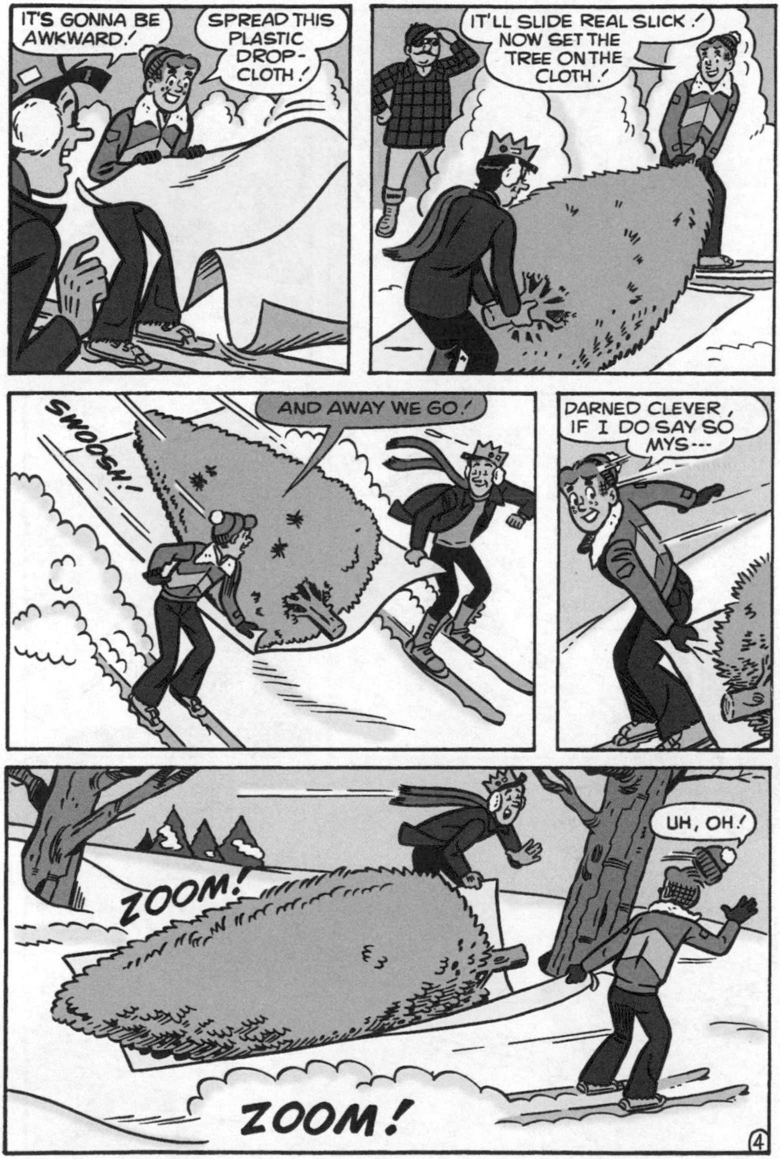
IT'S GONNA BE AWKWARD!
SPREAD THIS PLASTIC DROP-CLOTH!
IT'LL SLIDE REAL SLICK! NOW SET THE TREE ON THE CLOTH!
SWOOSH!
AND AWAY WE GO!
DARNED CLEVER, IF I DO SAY SO MYS---
UH, OH!
ZOOM!
ZOOM!
4

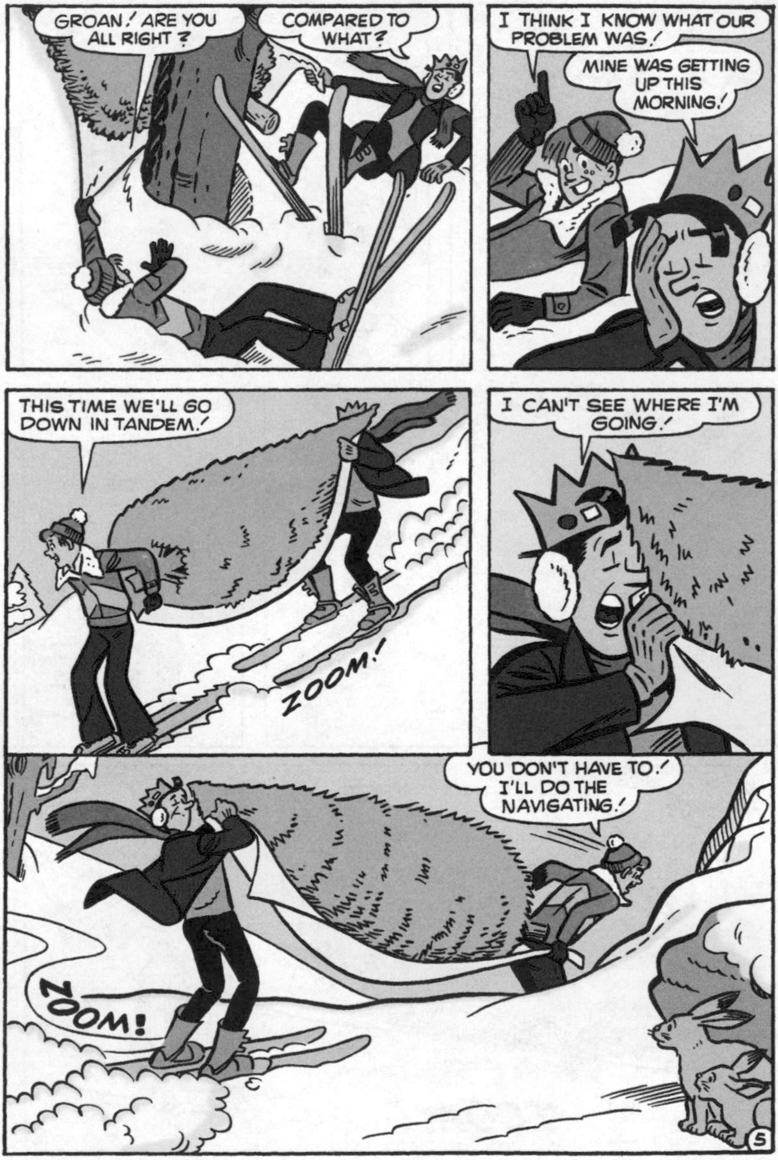
GROAN! ARE YOU ALL RIGHT?
COMPARED TO WHAT?
I THINK I KNOW WHAT OUR PROBLEM WAS!
MINE WAS GETTING UP THIS MORNING!
THIS TIME WE'LL GO DOWN IN TANDEM!
ZOOM!
I CAN'T SEE WHERE I'M GOING!
YOU DON'T HAVE TO! I'LL DO THE NAVIGATING!
ZOOM!
5

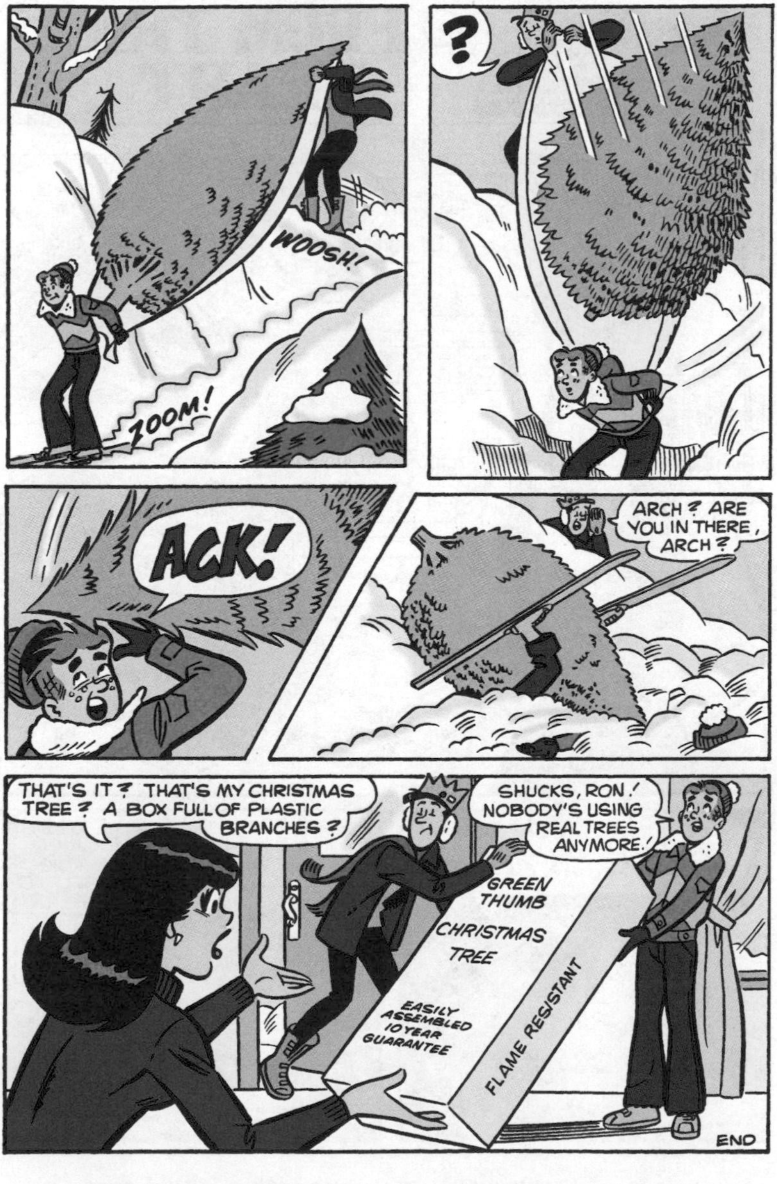
WOOSH!
ZOOM!
?
ACK!
ARCH? ARE YOU IN THERE, ARCH?
THAT'S IT? THAT'S MY CHRISTMAS TREE? A BOX FULL OF PLASTIC BRANCHES?
SHUCKS, RON! NOBODY'S USING REAL TREES ANYMORE!
GREEN THUMB
CHRISTMAS TREE
EASILY ASSEMBLED 10 YEAR GUARANTEE
FLAME RESISTANT
END

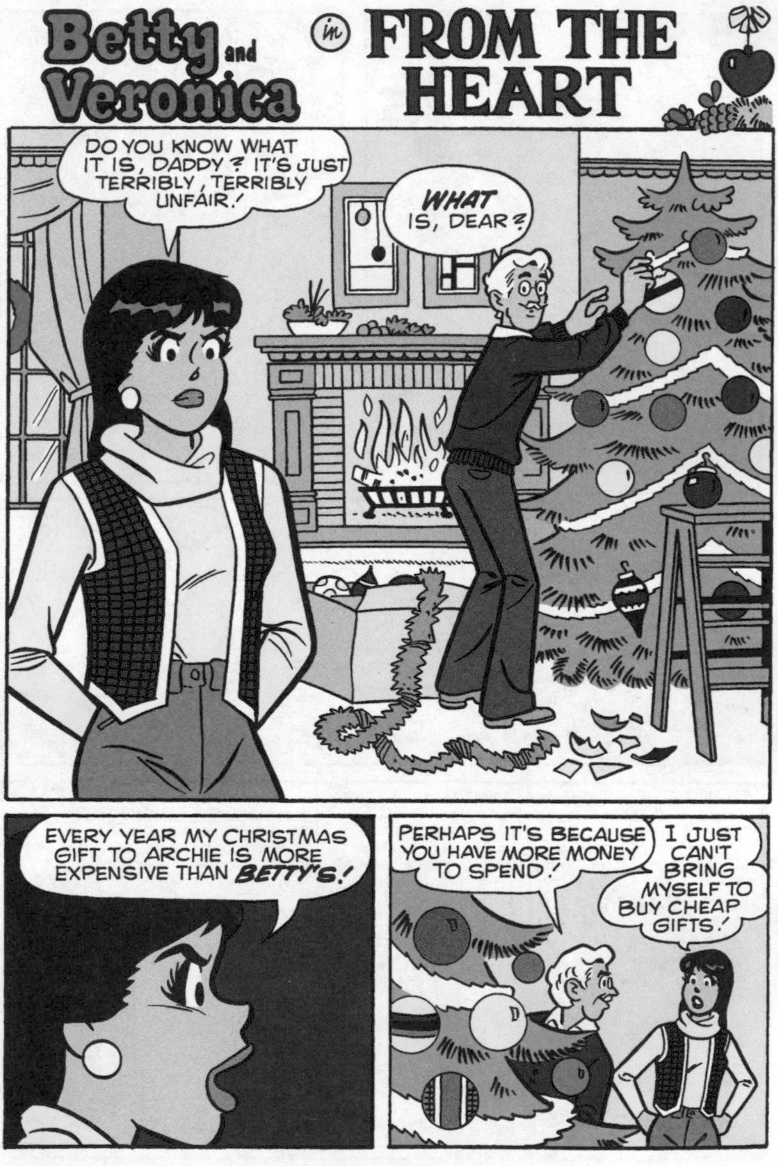
Betty and Veronica in FROM THE HEART
DO YOU KNOW WHAT IT IS, DADDY? IT'S JUST TERRIBLY, TERRIBLY UNFAIR.!
WHAT IS, DEAR?
EVERY YEAR MY CHRISTMAS GIFT TO ARCHIE IS MORE EXPENSIVE THAN BETTY'S!
PERHAPS IT'S BECAUSE YOU HAVE MORE MONEY TO SPEND.!
I JUST CAN'T BRING MYSELF TO BUY CHEAP GIFTS.!

• From Archie Giant Series Magazine #477, December 1978 •

Frank Doyle • Dan DeCarlo • Rudy Lapick • Bill Yoshida

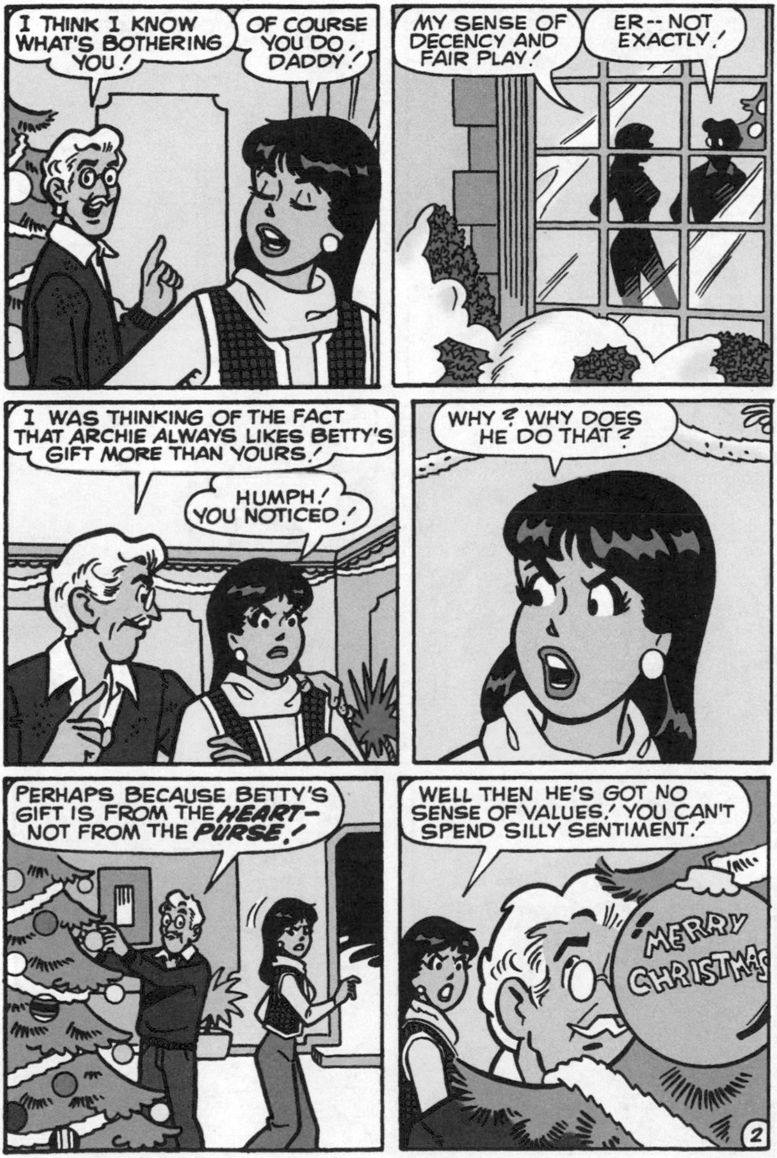
I THINK I KNOW WHAT'S BOTHERING YOU!
OF COURSE YOU DO, DADDY!
MY SENSE OF DECENCY AND FAIR PLAY!
ER-- NOT EXACTLY!
I WAS THINKING OF THE FACT THAT ARCHIE ALWAYS LIKES BETTY'S GIFT MORE THAN YOURS!
HUMPH! YOU NOTICED!
WHY? WHY DOES HE DO THAT?
PERHAPS BECAUSE BETTY'S GIFT IS FROM THE HEART-NOT FROM THE PURSE!
WELL THEN HE'S GOT NO SENSE OF VALUES! YOU CAN'T SPEND SILLY SENTIMENT!
MERRY CHRISTMAS
2

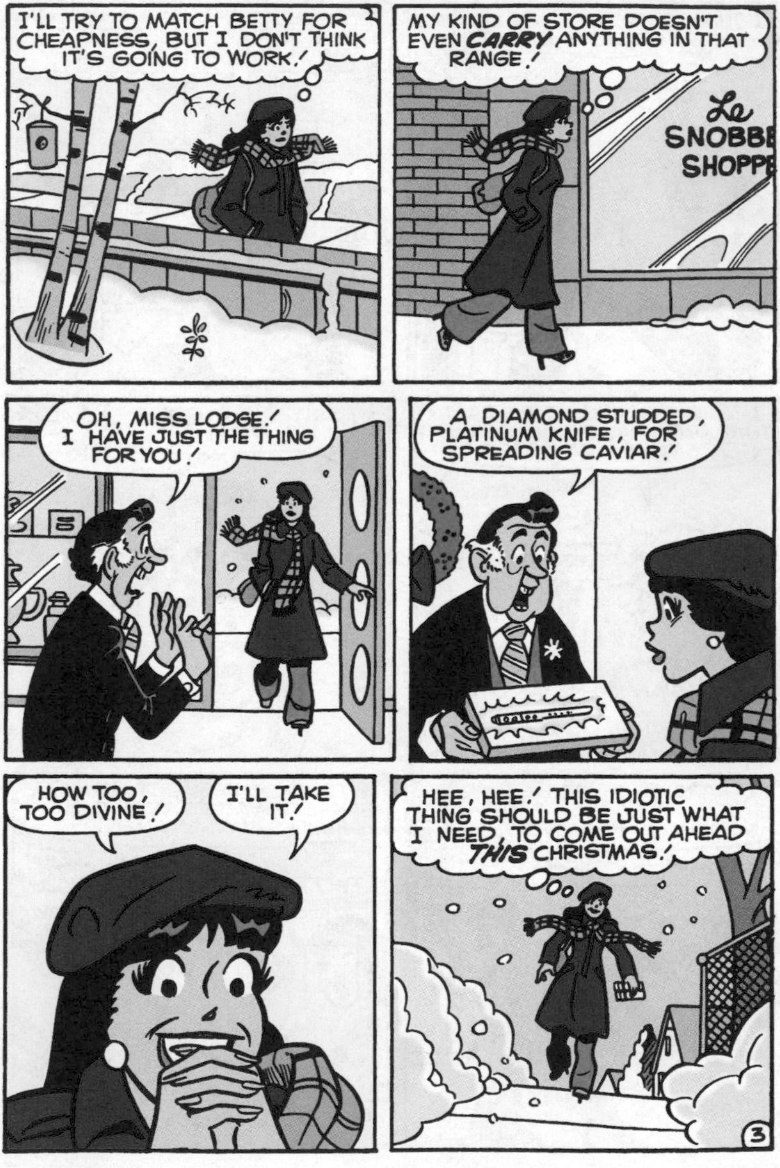
I'LL TRY TO MATCH BETTY FOR CHEAPNESS, BUT I DON'T THINK IT'S GOING TO WORK!
MY KIND OF STORE DOESN'T EVEN CARRY ANYTHING IN THAT RANGE!
Le SNOBBE SHOPPE
OH, MISS LODGE! I HAVE JUST THE THING FOR YOU!
A DIAMOND STUDDED, PLATINUM KNIFE, FOR SPREADING CAVIAR!
HOW TOO, TOO DIVINE!
I'LL TAKE IT!
HEE, HEE! THIS IDIOTIC THING SHOULD BE JUST WHAT I NEED, TO COME OUT AHEAD THIS CHRISTMAS!
3

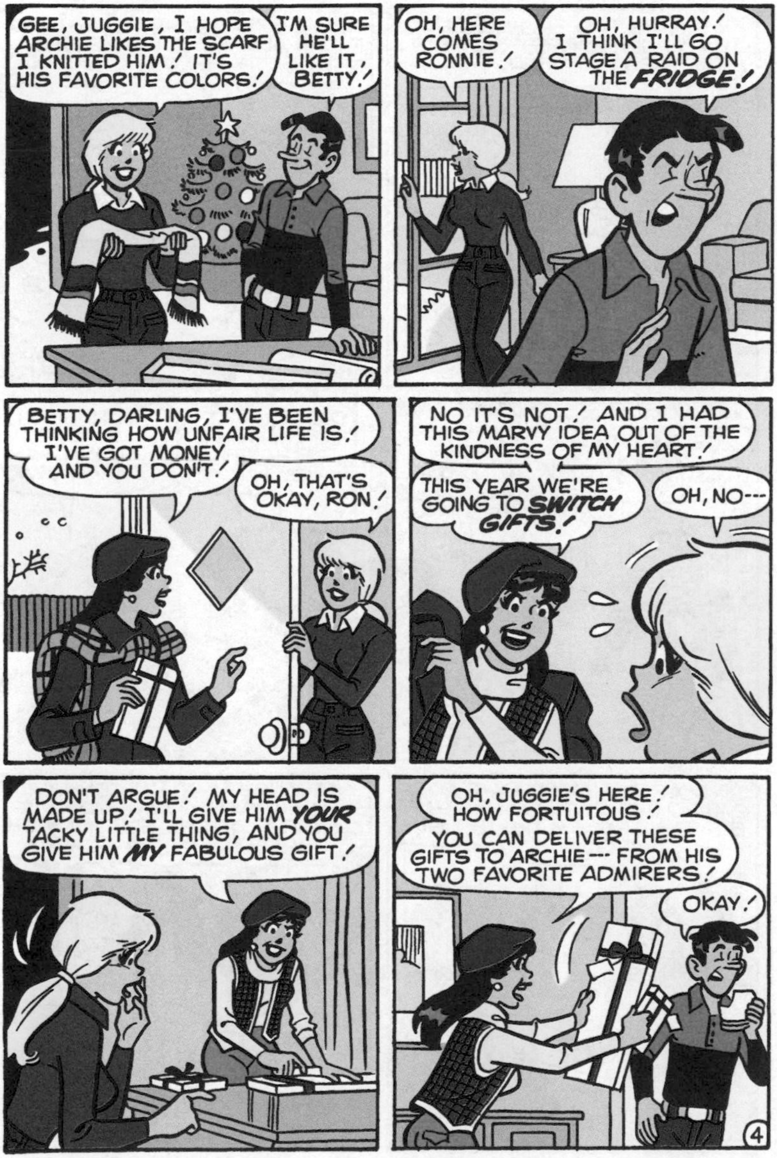
GEE, JUGGIE, I HOPE ARCHIE LIKES THE SCARF I KNITTED HIM! IT'S HIS FAVORITE COLORS!
I'M SURE HE'LL LIKE IT, BETTY!
OH, HERE COMES RONNIE!
OH, HURRAY! I THINK I'LL GO STAGE A RAID ON THE FRIDGE!
BETTY, DARLING, I'VE BEEN THINKING HOW UNFAIR LIFE IS! I'VE GOT MONEY AND YOU DON'T!
OH, THAT'S OKAY, RON!
NO IT'S NOT! AND I HAD THIS MARVY IDEA OUT OF THE KINDNESS OF MY HEART!
THIS YEAR WE'RE GOING TO SWITCH GIFTS!
OH, NO---
DON'T ARGUE! MY HEAD IS MADE UP! I'LL GIVE HIM YOUR TACKY LITTLE THING, AND YOU GIVE HIM MY FABULOUS GIFT!
OH, JUGGIE'S HERE! HOW FORTUITOUS!
YOU CAN DELIVER THESE GIFTS TO ARCHIE --- FROM HIS TWO FAVORITE ADMIRERS!
OKAY!
4

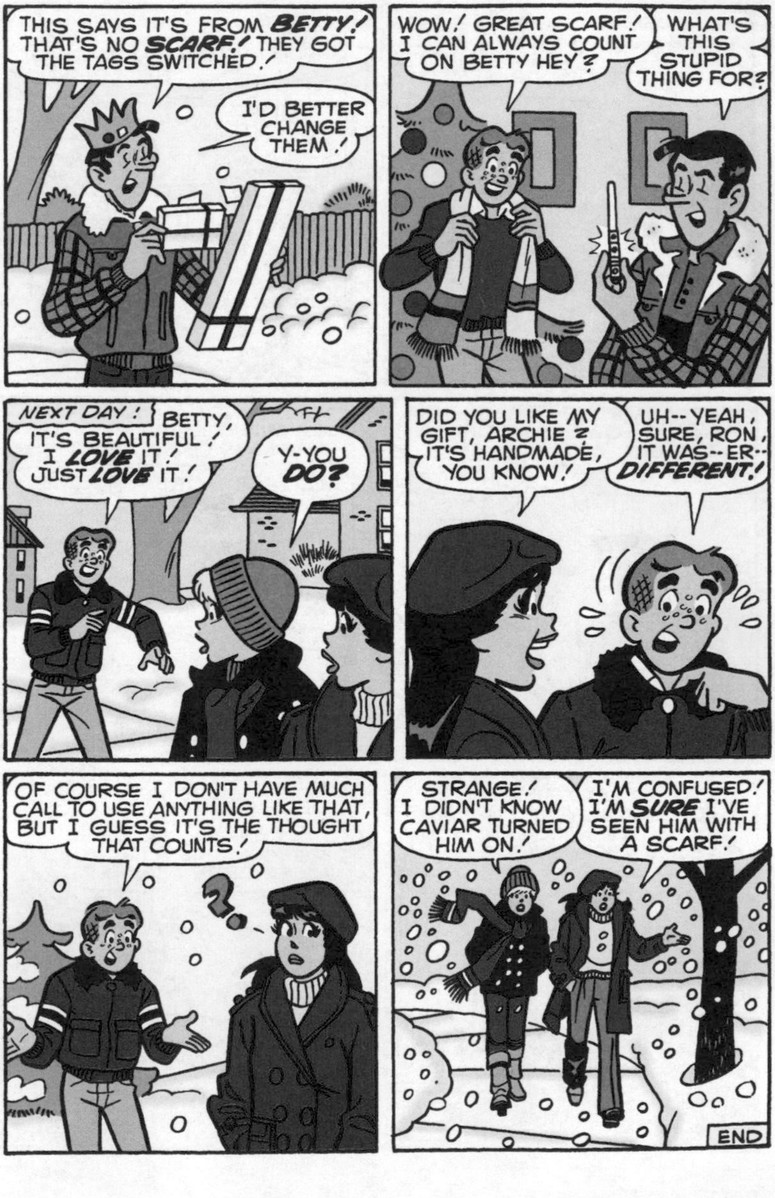
THIS SAYS IT'S FROM BETTY! THAT'S NO SCARF! THEY GOT THE TAGS SWITCHED!
I'D BETTER CHANGE THEM!
WOW! GREAT SCARF! I CAN ALWAYS COUNT ON BETTY HEY?
WHAT'S THIS STUPID THING FOR?
NEXT DAY!
BETTY, IT'S BEAUTIFUL! I LOVE IT! JUST LOVE IT!
Y-YOU DO?
DID YOU LIKE MY GIFT, ARCHIE? IT'S HANDMADE, YOU KNOW!
UH--YEAH, SURE, RON, IT WAS--ER-- DIFFERENT!
OF COURSE I DON'T HAVE MUCH CALL TO USE ANYTHING LIKE THAT, BUT I GUESS IT'S THE THOUGHT THAT COUNTS!
STRANGE! I DIDN'T KNOW CAVIAR TURNED HIM ON!
I'M CONFUSED! I'M SURE I'VE SEEN HIM WITH A SCARF!
END

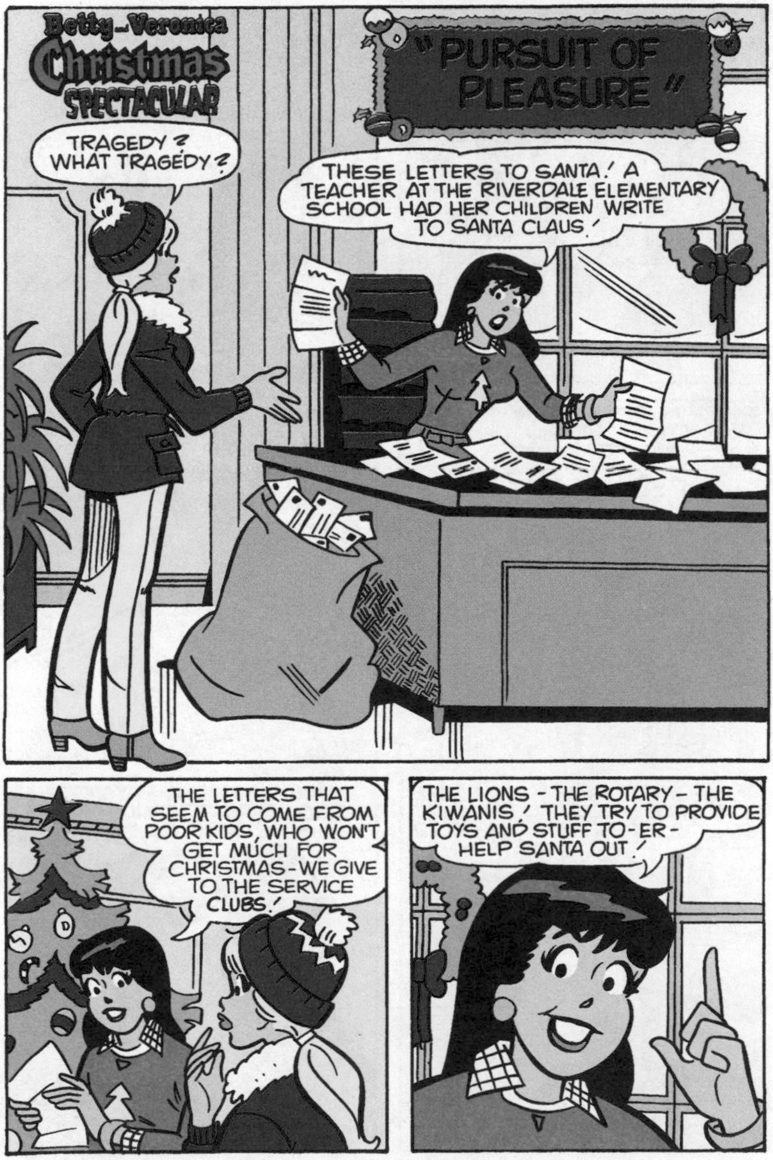
Betty and Veronica Christmas Spectacular
"PURSUIT OF PLEASURE"
TRAGEDY? WHAT TRAGEDY?
THESE LETTERS TO SANTA! A TEACHER AT THE RIVERDALE ELEMENTARY SCHOOL HAD HER CHILDREN WRITE TO SANTA CLAUS!
THE LETTERS THAT SEEM TO COME FROM POOR KIDS, WHO WON'T GET MUCH FOR CHRISTMAS - WE GIVE TO THE SERVICE CLUBS!
THE LIONS - THE ROTARY - THE KIWANIS! THEY TRY TO PROVIDE TOYS AND STUFF TO-ER- HELP SANTA OUT!

• **From Archie Giant Series Magazine #513, December 1981** •

Frank Doyle • Stan Goldberg • Jimmy DeCarlo • Bill Yoshida

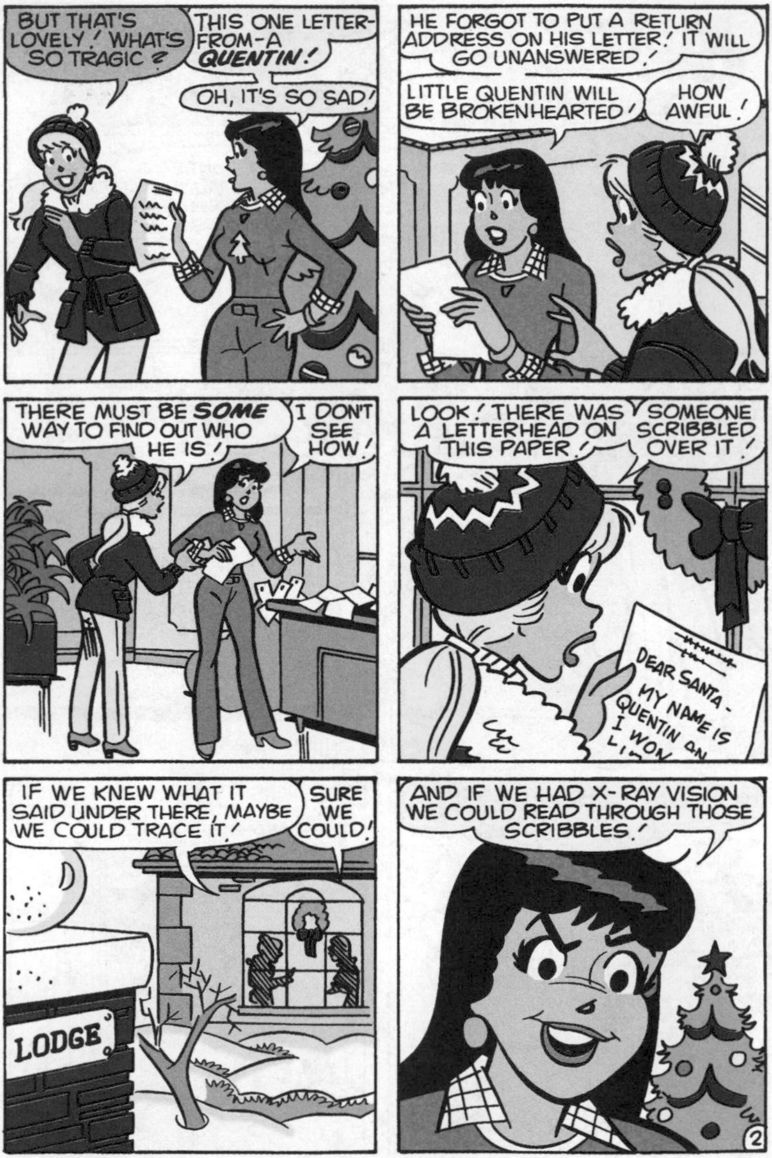
BUT THAT'S LOVELY! WHAT'S SO TRAGIC?
THIS ONE LETTER- FROM-A QUENTIN!
OH, IT'S SO SAD!
HE FORGOT TO PUT A RETURN ADDRESS ON HIS LETTER! IT WILL GO UNANSWERED!
LITTLE QUENTIN WILL BE BROKENHEARTED!
HOW AWFUL!
THERE MUST BE SOME WAY TO FIND OUT WHO HE IS!
I DON'T SEE HOW!
LOOK! THERE WAS A LETTERHEAD ON THIS PAPER!
SOMEONE SCRIBBLED OVER IT!
DEAR SANTA - MY NAME IS QUENTIN AN
IF WE KNEW WHAT IT SAID UNDER THERE, MAYBE WE COULD TRACE IT!
SURE WE COULD!
LODGE
AND IF WE HAD X-RAY VISION WE COULD READ THROUGH THOSE SCRIBBLES!
2

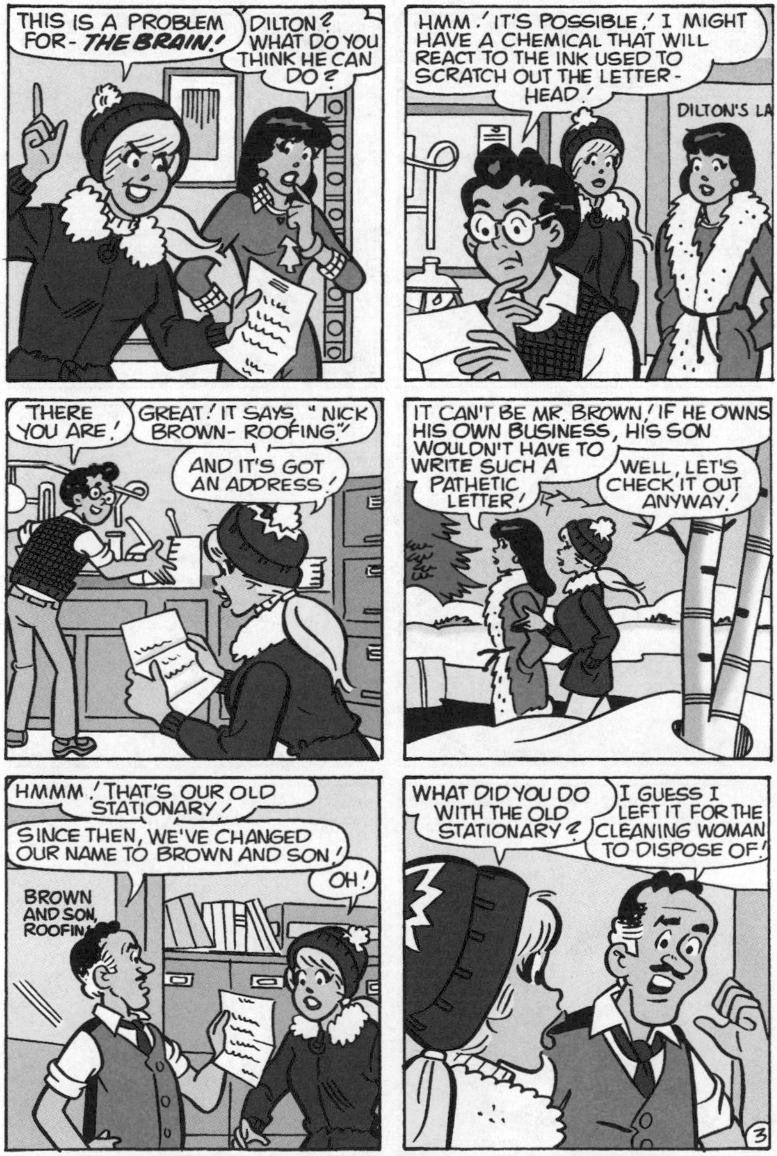
THIS IS A PROBLEM FOR- THE BRAIN!
DILTON? WHAT DO YOU THINK HE CAN DO?
HMM! IT'S POSSIBLE! I MIGHT HAVE A CHEMICAL THAT WILL REACT TO THE INK USED TO SCRATCH OUT THE LETTER-HEAD!
DILTON'S LA
THERE YOU ARE!
GREAT! IT SAYS, "NICK BROWN- ROOFING."
AND IT'S GOT AN ADDRESS!
IT CAN'T BE MR. BROWN! IF HE OWNS HIS OWN BUSINESS, HIS SON WOULDN'T HAVE TO WRITE SUCH A PATHETIC LETTER!
WELL, LET'S CHECK IT OUT ANYWAY!
HMMM! THAT'S OUR OLD STATIONARY!
SINCE THEN, WE'VE CHANGED OUR NAME TO BROWN AND SON!
OH!
BROWN AND SON, ROOFIN
WHAT DID YOU DO WITH THE OLD STATIONARY?
I GUESS I LEFT IT FOR THE CLEANING WOMAN TO DISPOSE OF!
3

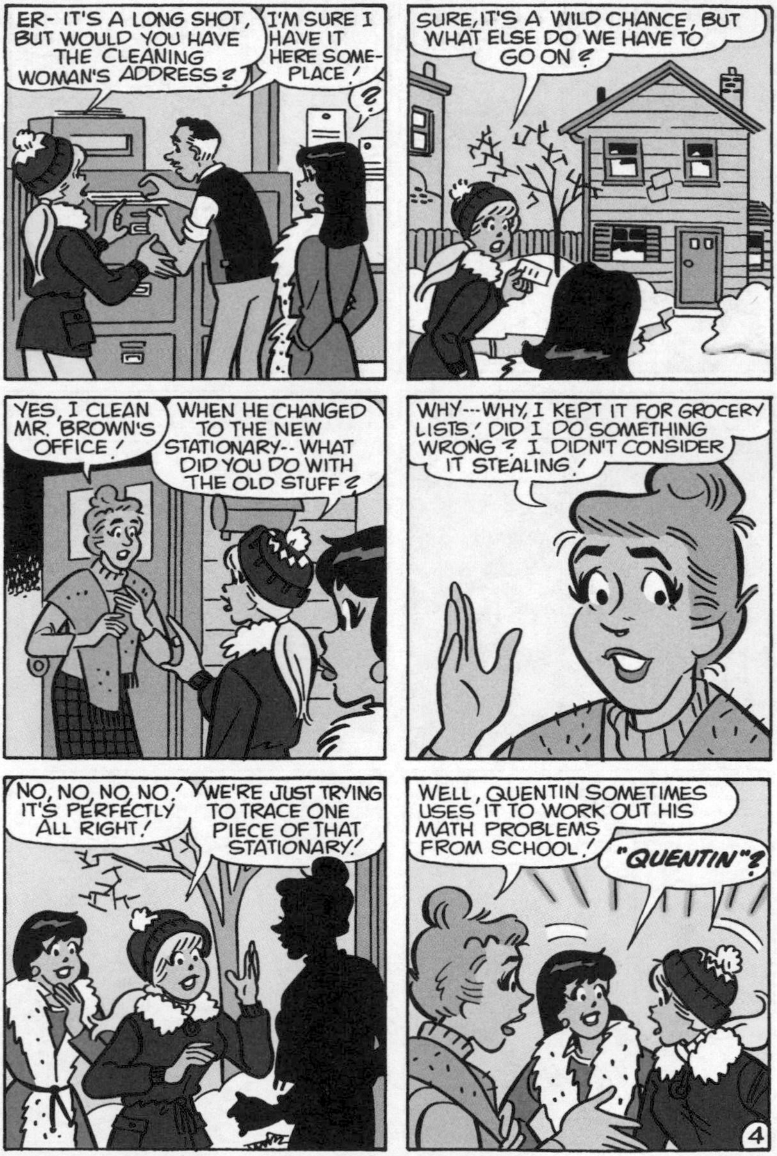
ER- IT'S A LONG SHOT, BUT WOULD YOU HAVE THE CLEANING WOMAN'S ADDRESS?
I'M SURE I HAVE IT HERE SOME-PLACE!
?
SURE, IT'S A WILD CHANCE, BUT WHAT ELSE DO WE HAVE TO GO ON?
YES, I CLEAN MR. BROWN'S OFFICE!
WHEN HE CHANGED TO THE NEW STATIONARY-- WHAT DID YOU DO WITH THE OLD STUFF?
WHY---WHY, I KEPT IT FOR GROCERY LISTS! DID I DO SOMETHING WRONG? I DIDN'T CONSIDER IT STEALING!
NO, NO, NO, NO! IT'S PERFECTLY ALL RIGHT!
WE'RE JUST TRYING TO TRACE ONE PIECE OF THAT STATIONARY!
WELL, QUENTIN SOMETIMES USES IT TO WORK OUT HIS MATH PROBLEMS FROM SCHOOL!
"QUENTIN"?
4

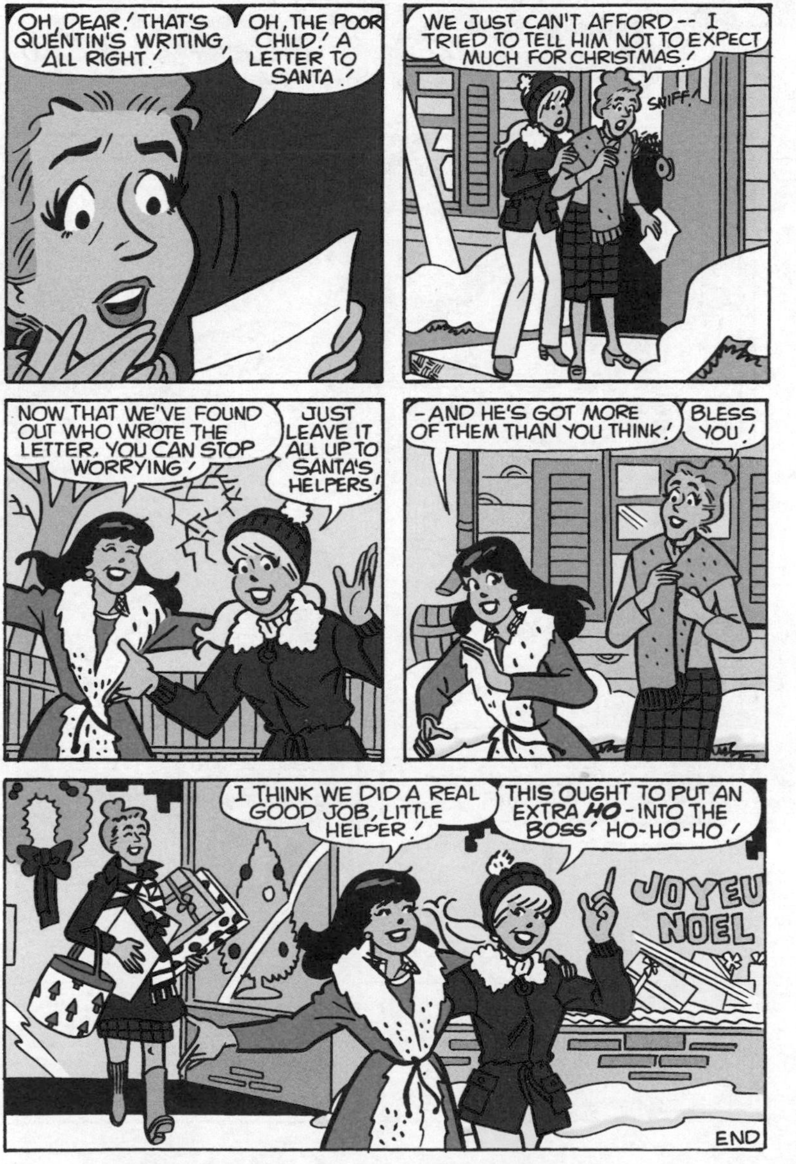
OH, DEAR! THAT'S QUENTIN'S WRITING, ALL RIGHT!
OH, THE POOR CHILD! A LETTER TO SANTA!
WE JUST CAN'T AFFORD -- I TRIED TO TELL HIM NOT TO EXPECT MUCH FOR CHRISTMAS!
SNIFF!
NOW THAT WE'VE FOUND OUT WHO WROTE THE LETTER, YOU CAN STOP WORRYING!
JUST LEAVE IT ALL UP TO SANTA'S HELPERS!
-AND HE'S GOT MORE OF THEM THAN YOU THINK!
BLESS YOU!
I THINK WE DID A REAL GOOD JOB, LITTLE HELPER!
THIS OUGHT TO PUT AN EXTRA HO - INTO THE BOSS' HO-HO-HO!
JOYEU NOEL
END

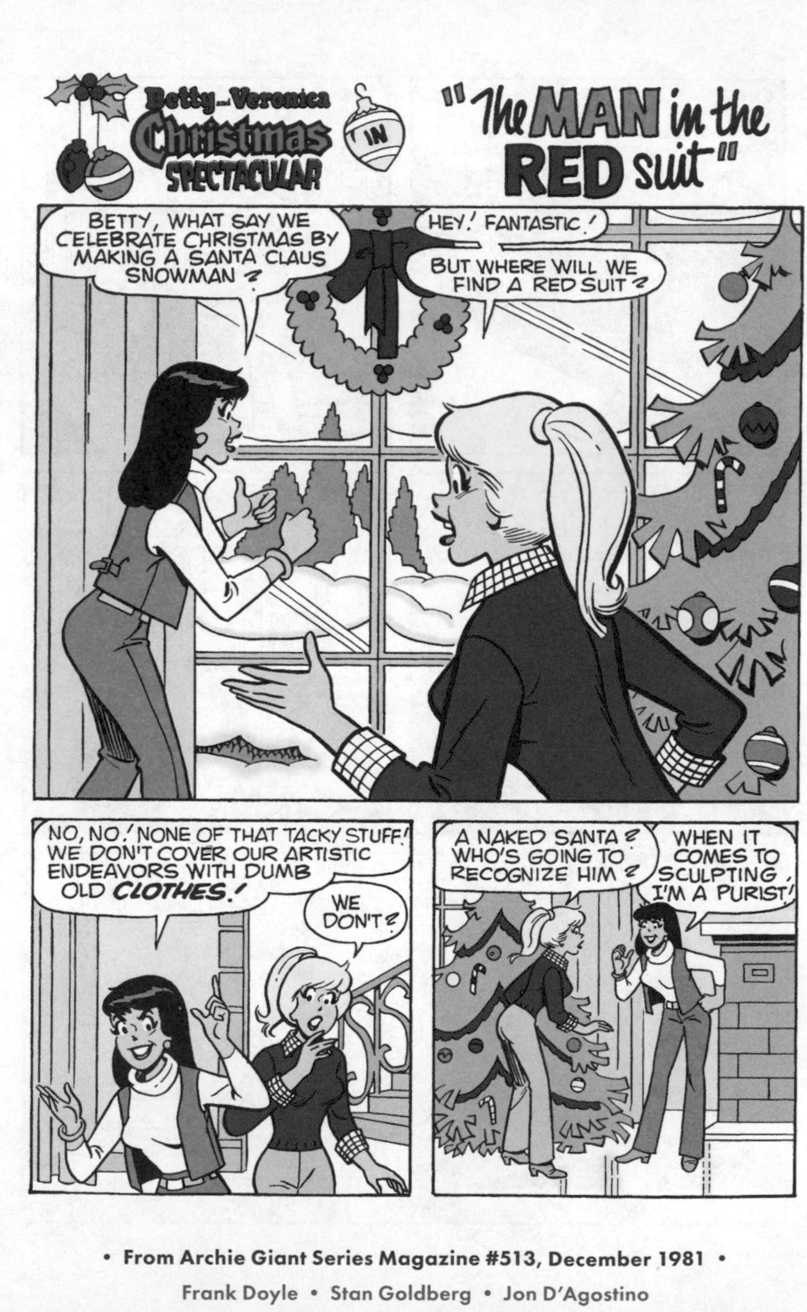
Betty and Veronica
Christmas
SPECTACULAR
IN
"The MAN in the RED suit"
BETTY, WHAT SAY WE CELEBRATE CHRISTMAS BY MAKING A SANTA CLAUS SNOWMAN?
HEY! FANTASTIC!
BUT WHERE WILL WE FIND A RED SUIT?
NO, NO! NONE OF THAT TACKY STUFF! WE DON'T COVER OUR ARTISTIC ENDEAVORS WITH DUMB OLD CLOTHES!
WE DON'T?
A NAKED SANTA? WHO'S GOING TO RECOGNIZE HIM?
WHEN IT COMES TO SCULPTING, I'M A PURIST!

• From Archie Giant Series Magazine #513, December 1981 •

Frank Doyle • Stan Goldberg • Jon D'Agostino

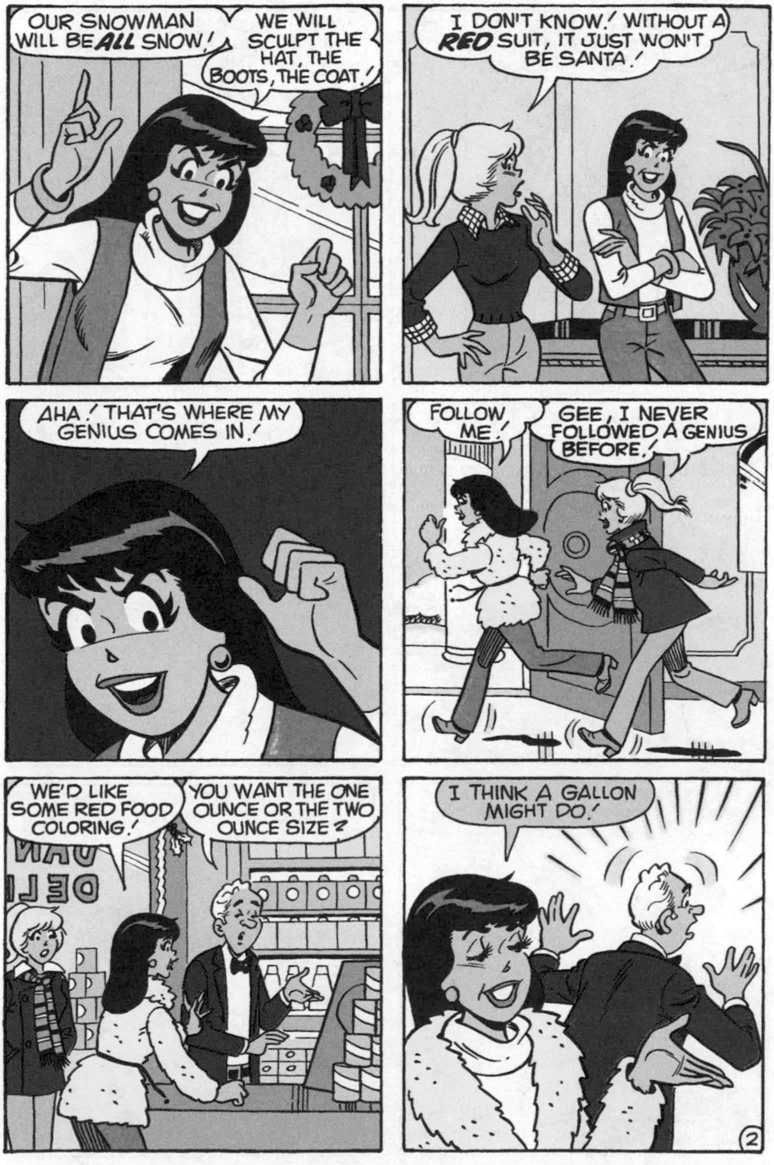
OUR SNOWMAN WILL BE ALL SNOW!
WE WILL SCULPT THE HAT, THE BOOTS, THE COAT!
I DON'T KNOW! WITHOUT A RED SUIT, IT JUST WON'T BE SANTA!
AHA! THAT'S WHERE MY GENIUS COMES IN!
FOLLOW ME!
GEE, I NEVER FOLLOWED A GENIUS BEFORE!
WE'D LIKE SOME RED FOOD COLORING!
YOU WANT THE ONE OUNCE OR THE TWO OUNCE SIZE?
DELI
I THINK A GALLON MIGHT DO!
2

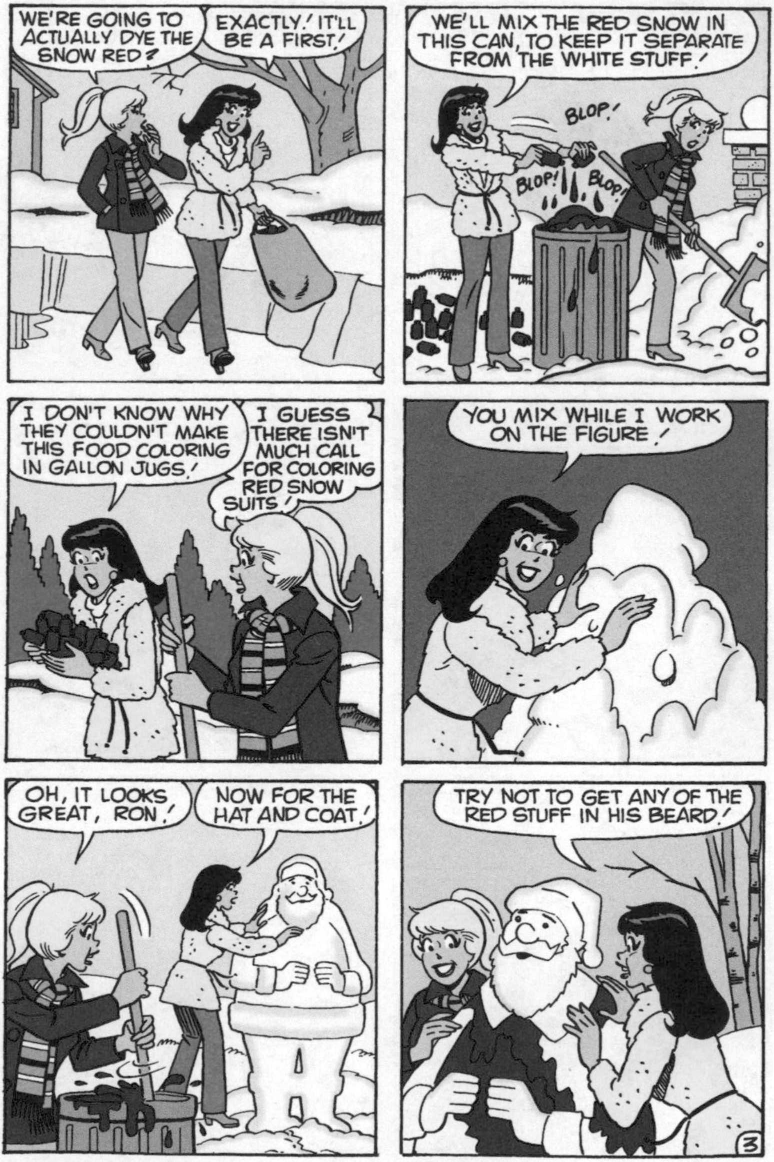
WE'RE GOING TO ACTUALLY DYE THE SNOW RED?
EXACTLY! IT'LL BE A FIRST!
WE'LL MIX THE RED SNOW IN THIS CAN, TO KEEP IT SEPARATE FROM THE WHITE STUFF!
BLOP!
BLOP!
BLOP!
I DON'T KNOW WHY THEY COULDN'T MAKE THIS FOOD COLORING IN GALLON JUGS!
I GUESS THERE ISN'T MUCH CALL FOR COLORING RED SNOW SUITS!
YOU MIX WHILE I WORK ON THE FIGURE!
OH, IT LOOKS GREAT, RON!
NOW FOR THE HAT AND COAT!
TRY NOT TO GET ANY OF THE RED STUFF IN HIS BEARD!
3

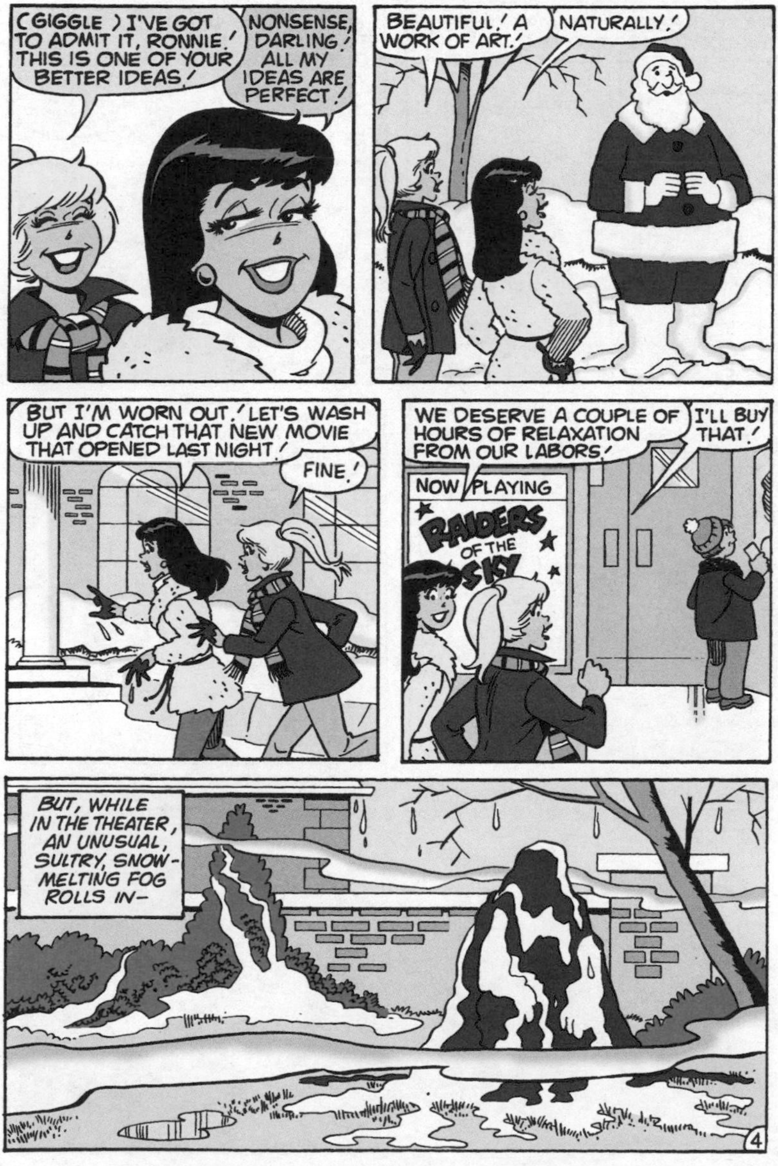
(GIGGLE) I'VE GOT TO ADMIT IT, RONNIE! THIS IS ONE OF YOUR BETTER IDEAS!
NONSENSE, DARLING! ALL MY IDEAS ARE PERFECT!
BEAUTIFUL! A WORK OF ART!
NATURALLY!
BUT I'M WORN OUT! LET'S WASH UP AND CATCH THAT NEW MOVIE THAT OPENED LAST NIGHT!
FINE!
WE DESERVE A COUPLE OF HOURS OF RELAXATION FROM OUR LABORS!
I'LL BUY THAT!
NOW PLAYING
RAIDERS OF THE SKY
BUT, WHILE IN THE THEATER, AN UNUSUAL, SULTRY, SNOW-MELTING FOG ROLLS IN—
4

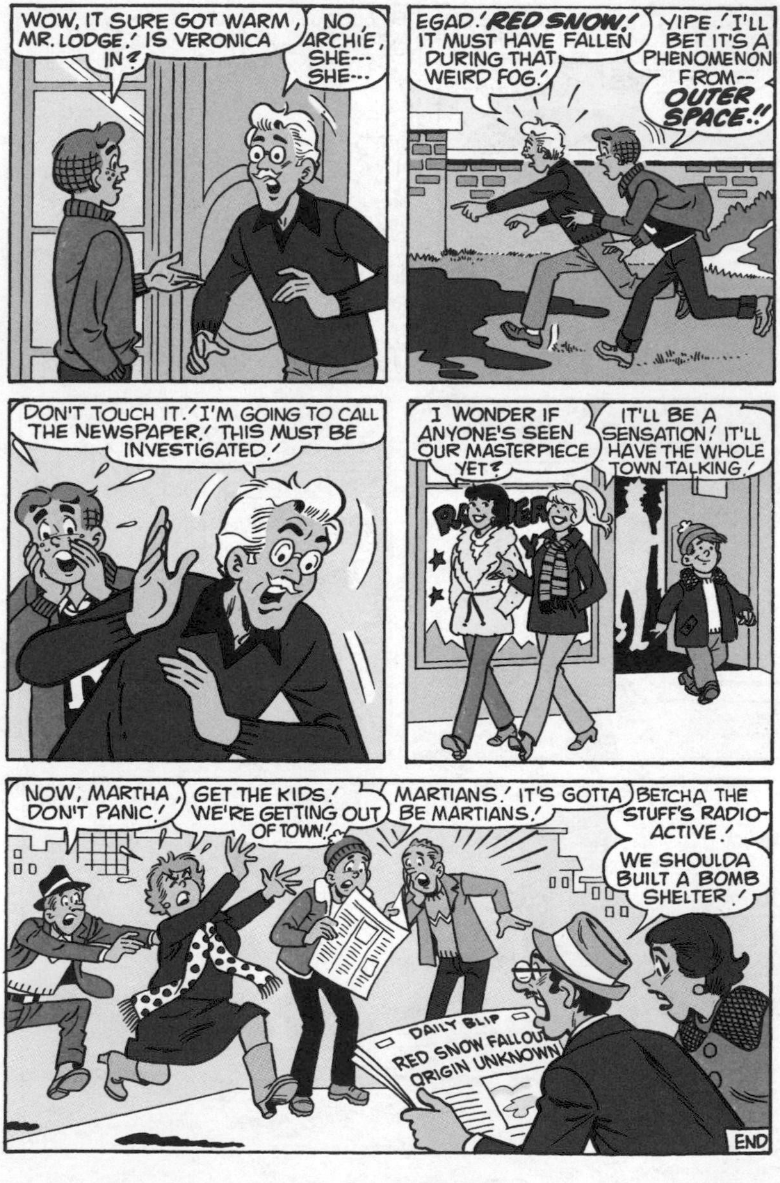
WOW, IT SURE GOT WARM, MR. LODGE! IS VERONICA IN?
NO, ARCHIE, SHE--- SHE---
EGAD! RED SNOW! IT MUST HAVE FALLEN DURING THAT WEIRD FOG!
YIPE! I'LL BET IT'S A PHENOMENON FROM-- OUTER SPACE!!
DON'T TOUCH IT! I'M GOING TO CALL THE NEWSPAPER! THIS MUST BE INVESTIGATED!
I WONDER IF ANYONE'S SEEN OUR MASTERPIECE YET?
IT'LL BE A SENSATION! IT'LL HAVE THE WHOLE TOWN TALKING!
NOW, MARTHA, DON'T PANIC!
GET THE KIDS! WE'RE GETTING OUT OF TOWN!
MARTIANS! IT'S GOTTA BE MARTIANS!
BETCHA THE STUFF'S RADIO-ACTIVE!
WE SHOULDA BUILT A BOMB SHELTER!
DAILY BLIP
RED SNOW FALLOUT ORIGIN UNKNOWN
END

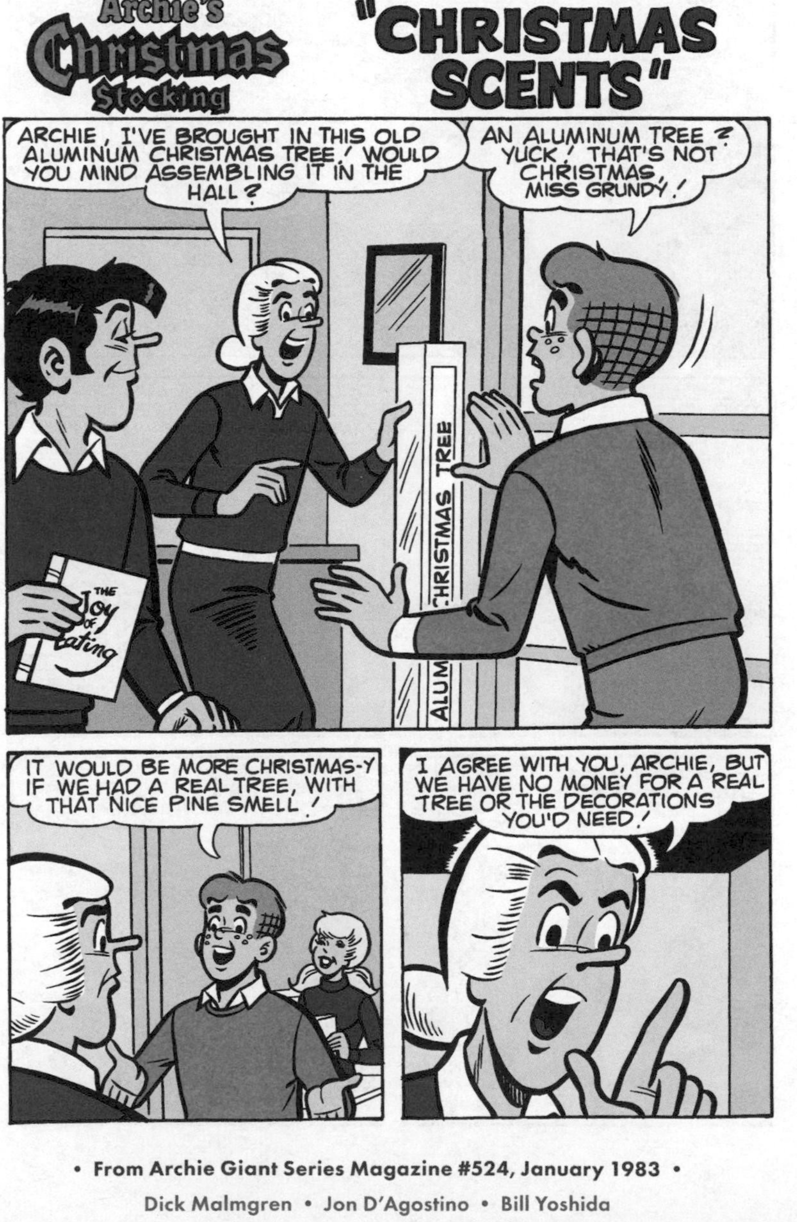
Archie's Christmas Stocking
"CHRISTMAS SCENTS"
ARCHIE, I'VE BROUGHT IN THIS OLD ALUMINUM CHRISTMAS TREE! WOULD YOU MIND ASSEMBLING IT IN THE HALL?
AN ALUMINUM TREE? YUCK! THAT'S NOT CHRISTMAS, MISS GRUNDY!
THE Joy OF Eating
ALUM CHRISTMAS TREE
IT WOULD BE MORE CHRISTMAS-Y IF WE HAD A REAL TREE, WITH THAT NICE PINE SMELL!
I AGREE WITH YOU, ARCHIE, BUT WE HAVE NO MONEY FOR A REAL TREE OR THE DECORATIONS YOU'D NEED!

• **From Archie Giant Series Magazine #524, January 1983** •

Dick Malmgren • Jon D'Agostino • Bill Yoshida

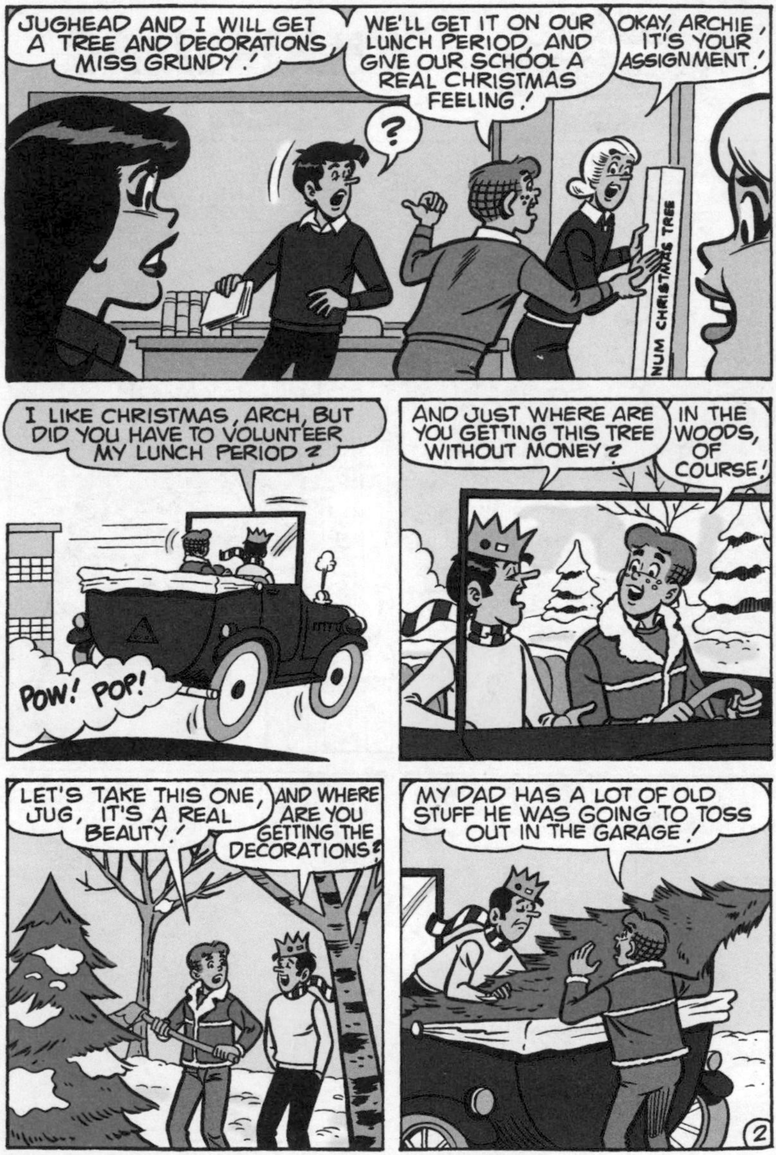
JUGHEAD AND I WILL GET A TREE AND DECORATIONS, MISS GRUNDY!
WE'LL GET IT ON OUR LUNCH PERIOD, AND GIVE OUR SCHOOL A REAL CHRISTMAS FEELING!
?
OKAY, ARCHIE, IT'S YOUR ASSIGNMENT!
NUM CHRISTMAS TREE
I LIKE CHRISTMAS, ARCH, BUT DID YOU HAVE TO VOLUNTEER MY LUNCH PERIOD?
POW! POP!
AND JUST WHERE ARE YOU GETTING THIS TREE WITHOUT MONEY?
IN THE WOODS, OF COURSE!
LET'S TAKE THIS ONE, JUG, IT'S A REAL BEAUTY!
AND WHERE ARE YOU GETTING THE DECORATIONS?
MY DAD HAS A LOT OF OLD STUFF HE WAS GOING TO TOSS OUT IN THE GARAGE!
2

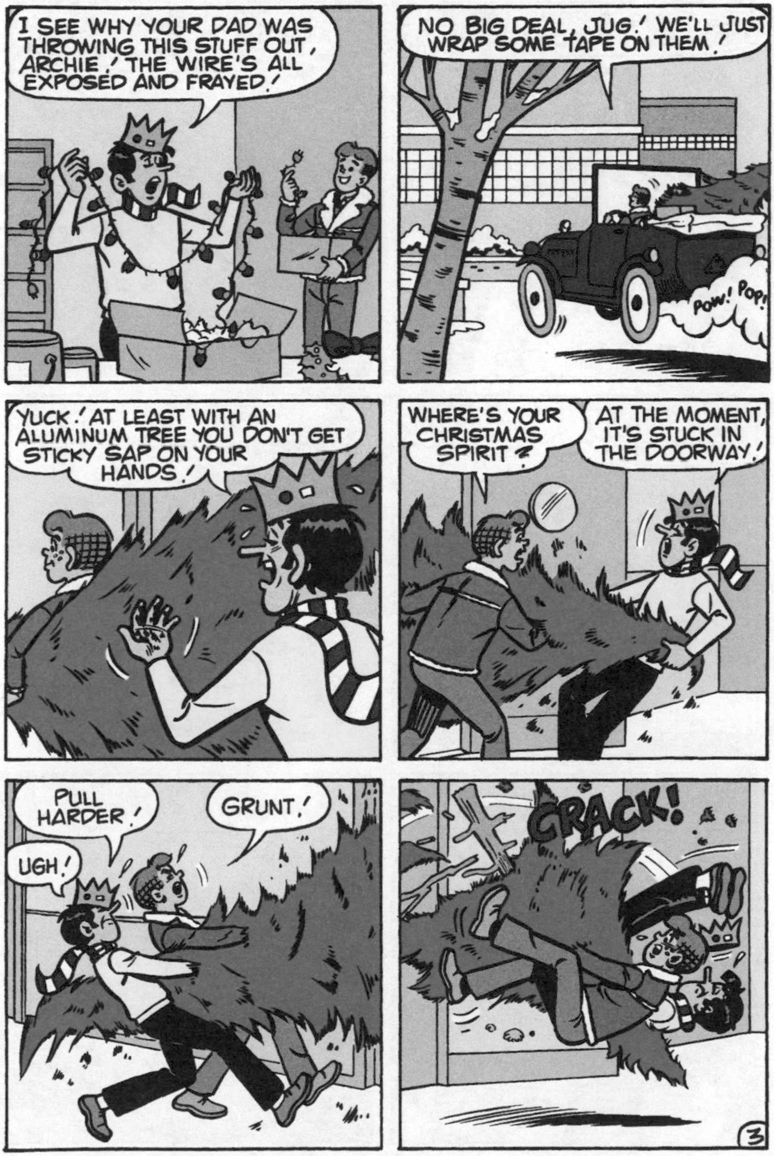
I SEE WHY YOUR DAD WAS THROWING THIS STUFF OUT, ARCHIE! THE WIRE'S ALL EXPOSED AND FRAYED!
NO BIG DEAL, JUG! WE'LL JUST WRAP SOME TAPE ON THEM!
POW! POP!
YUCK! AT LEAST WITH AN ALUMINUM TREE YOU DON'T GET STICKY SAP ON YOUR HANDS!
WHERE'S YOUR CHRISTMAS SPIRIT?
AT THE MOMENT, IT'S STUCK IN THE DOORWAY!
PULL HARDER!
GRUNT!
UGH!
CRACK!
3

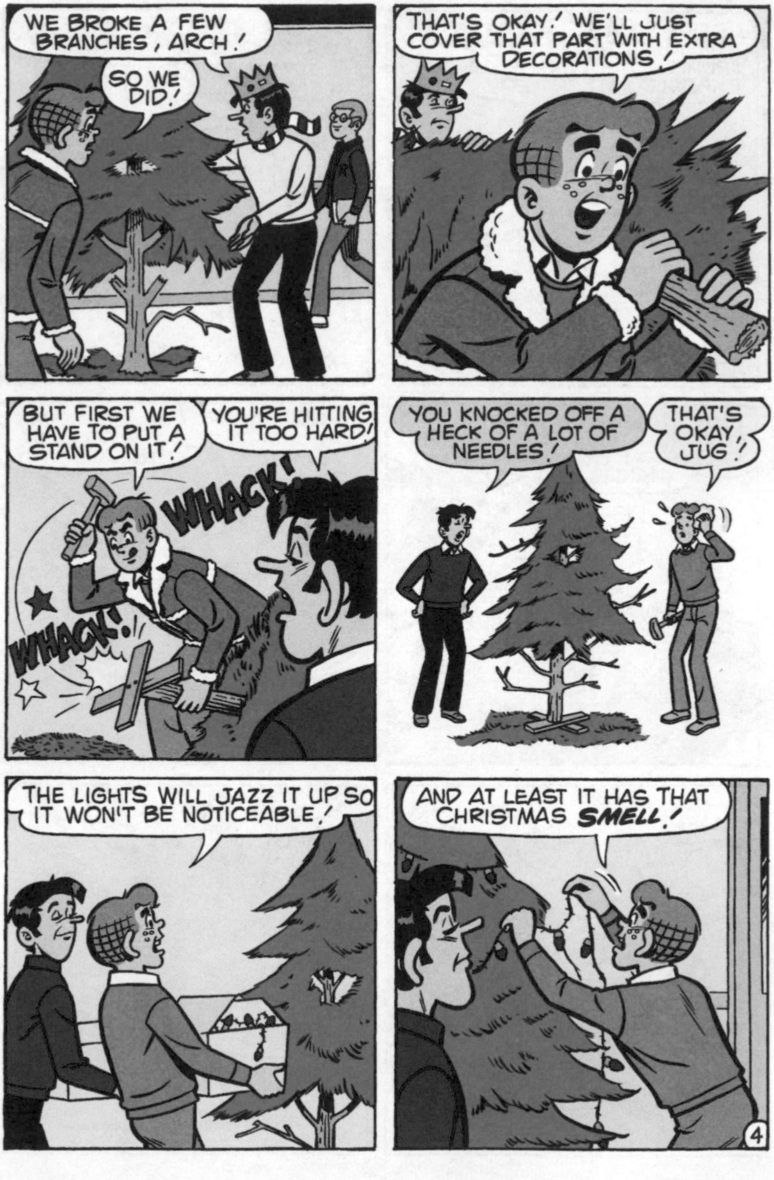
WE BROKE A FEW BRANCHES, ARCH!
SO WE DID!
THAT'S OKAY! WE'LL JUST COVER THAT PART WITH EXTRA DECORATIONS!
BUT FIRST WE HAVE TO PUT A STAND ON IT!
YOU'RE HITTING IT TOO HARD!
WHACK!
WHACK!
YOU KNOCKED OFF A HECK OF A LOT OF NEEDLES!
THAT'S OKAY, JUG!
THE LIGHTS WILL JAZZ IT UP SO IT WON'T BE NOTICEABLE!
AND AT LEAST IT HAS THAT CHRISTMAS SMELL!
4

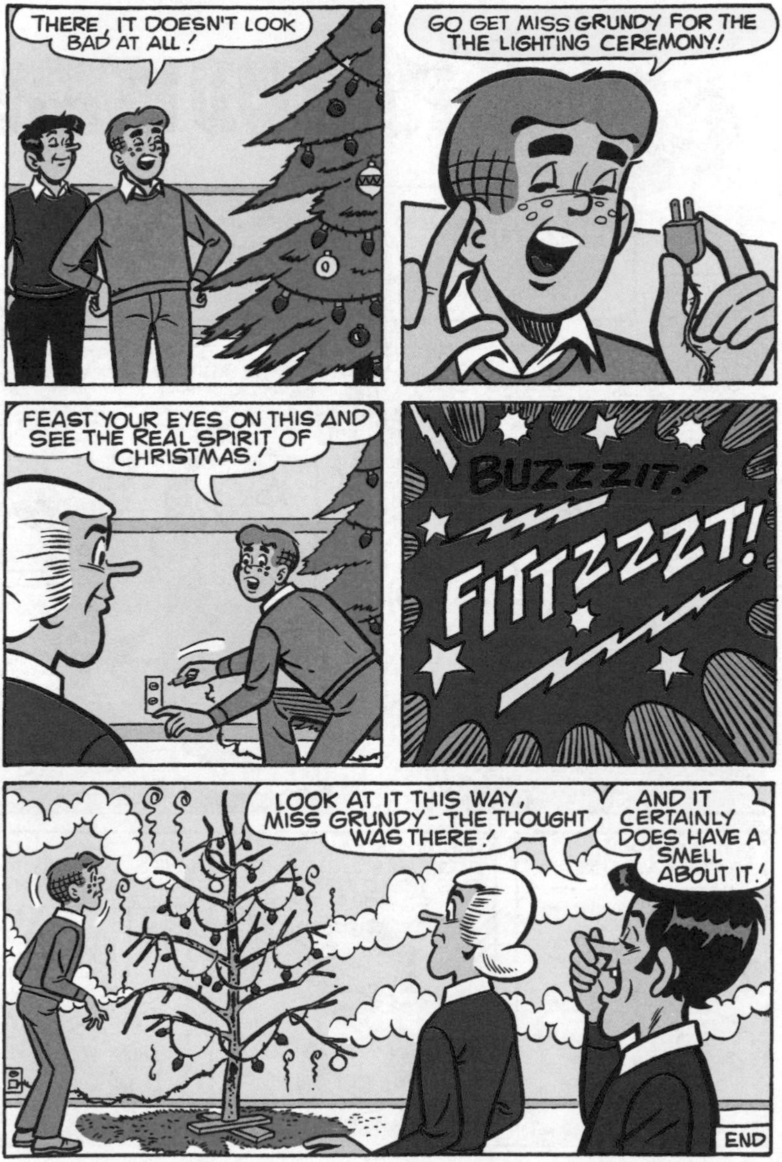
THERE, IT DOESN'T LOOK BAD AT ALL!
GO GET MISS GRUNDY FOR THE THE LIGHTING CEREMONY!
FEAST YOUR EYES ON THIS AND SEE THE REAL SPIRIT OF CHRISTMAS!
BUZZZIT!
FITTZZZZT!
LOOK AT IT THIS WAY, MISS GRUNDY - THE THOUGHT WAS THERE!
AND IT CERTAINLY DOES HAVE A SMELL ABOUT IT!
END

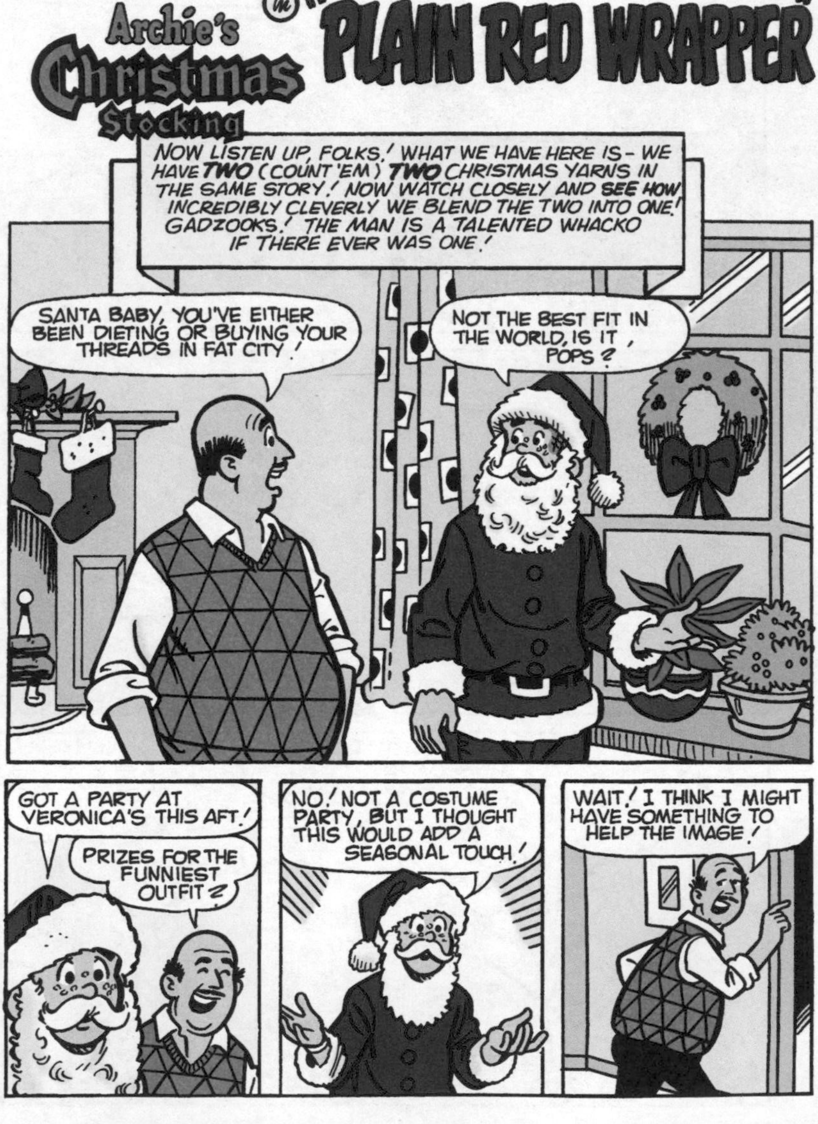
Archie's Christmas Stocking in "PLAIN RED WRAPPER"
NOW LISTEN UP, FOLKS! WHAT WE HAVE HERE IS - WE HAVE TWO (COUNT 'EM) TWO CHRISTMAS YARNS IN THE SAME STORY! NOW WATCH CLOSELY AND SEE HOW INCREDIBLY CLEVERLY WE BLEND THE TWO INTO ONE! GADZOOKS! THE MAN IS A TALENTED WHACKO IF THERE EVER WAS ONE!
SANTA BABY, YOU'VE EITHER BEEN DIETING OR BUYING YOUR THREADS IN FAT CITY!
NOT THE BEST FIT IN THE WORLD, IS IT, POPS?
GOT A PARTY AT VERONICA'S THIS AFT!
PRIZES FOR THE FUNNIEST OUTFIT?
NO! NOT A COSTUME PARTY, BUT I THOUGHT THIS WOULD ADD A SEASONAL TOUCH!
WAIT! I THINK I MIGHT HAVE SOMETHING TO HELP THE IMAGE!

• From Archie Giant Series Magazine #524, January 1983 •

Frank Doyle • Dan DeCarlo Jr. • Jimmy DeCarlo • Bill Yoshida

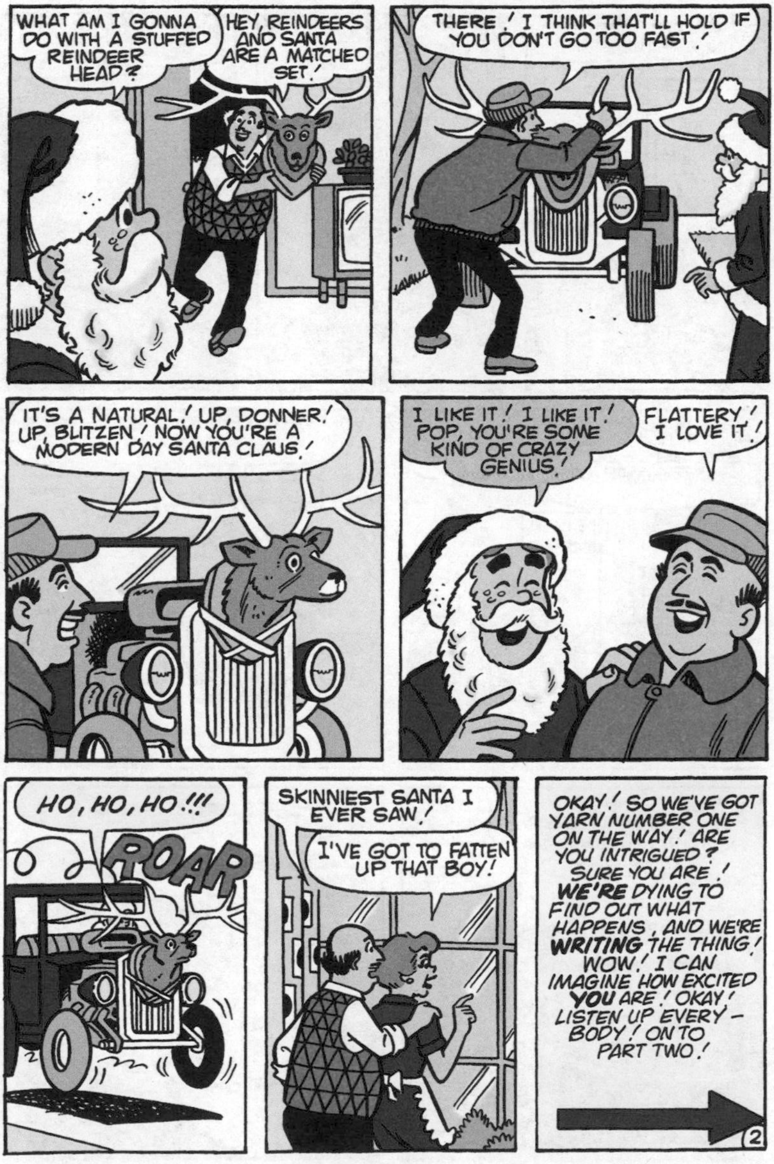
WHAT AM I GONNA DO WITH A STUFFED REINDEER HEAD?
HEY, REINDEERS AND SANTA ARE A MATCHED SET!
THERE! I THINK THAT'LL HOLD IF YOU DON'T GO TOO FAST!
IT'S A NATURAL! UP, DONNER! UP, BLITZEN! NOW YOU'RE A MODERN DAY SANTA CLAUS!
I LIKE IT! I LIKE IT! POP, YOU'RE SOME KIND OF CRAZY GENIUS!
FLATTERY! I LOVE IT!
HO, HO, HO!!!
ROAR
SKINNIEST SANTA I EVER SAW!
I'VE GOT TO FATTEN UP THAT BOY!
OKAY! SO WE'VE GOT YARN NUMBER ONE ON THE WAY! ARE YOU INTRIGUED? SURE YOU ARE! WE'RE DYING TO FIND OUT WHAT HAPPENS, AND WE'RE WRITING THE THING! WOW! I CAN IMAGINE HOW EXCITED YOU ARE! OKAY! LISTEN UP EVERY-BODY! ON TO PART TWO!
2

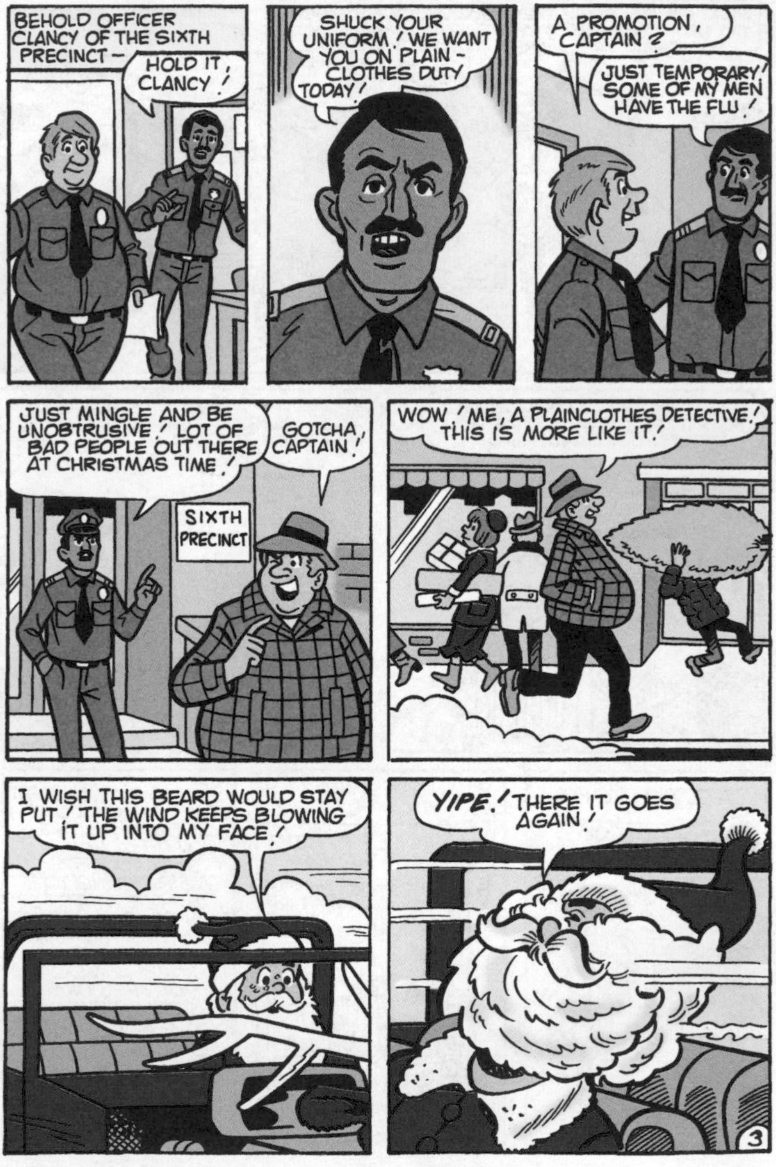
BEHOLD OFFICER CLANCY OF THE SIXTH PRECINCT –
HOLD IT, CLANCY!
SHUCK YOUR UNIFORM! WE WANT YOU ON PLAIN-CLOTHES DUTY TODAY!
A PROMOTION, CAPTAIN?
JUST TEMPORARY! SOME OF MY MEN HAVE THE FLU!
JUST MINGLE AND BE UNOBTRUSIVE! LOT OF BAD PEOPLE OUT THERE AT CHRISTMAS TIME!
GOTCHA, CAPTAIN!
SIXTH PRECINCT
WOW! ME, A PLAINCLOTHES DETECTIVE! THIS IS MORE LIKE IT!
I WISH THIS BEARD WOULD STAY PUT! THE WIND KEEPS BLOWING IT UP INTO MY FACE!
YIPE! THERE IT GOES AGAIN!
3

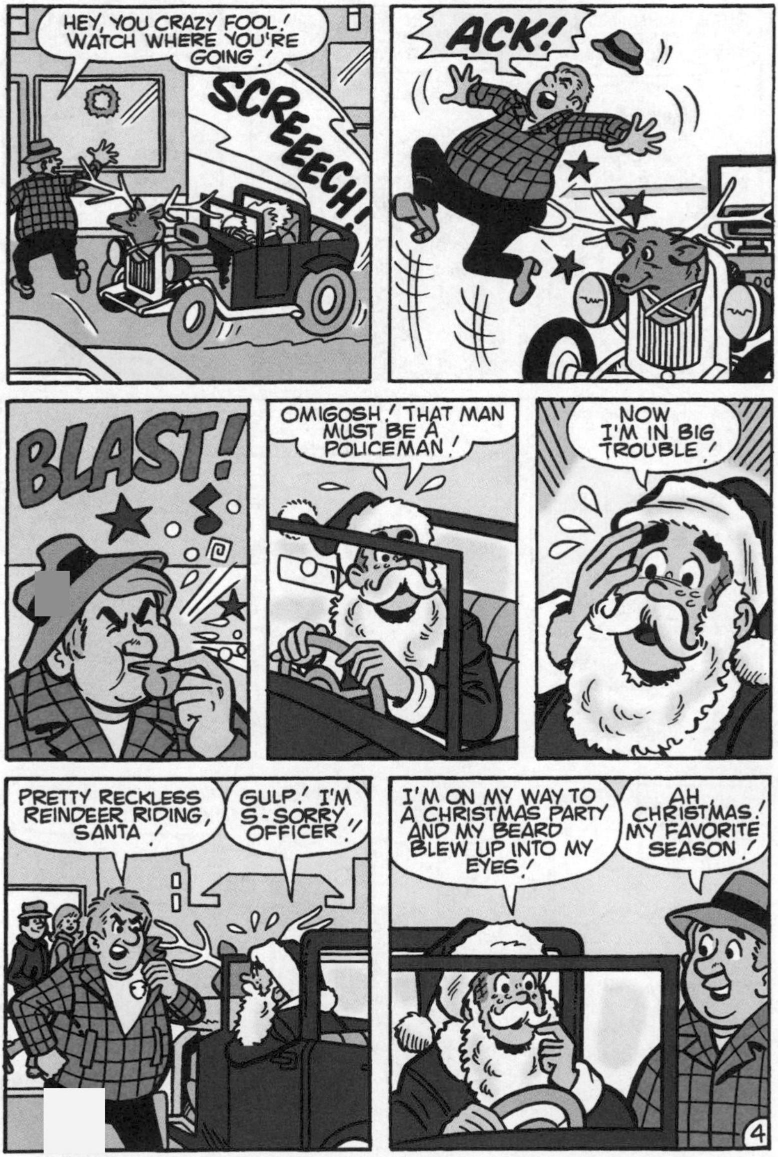
HEY, YOU CRAZY FOOL! WATCH WHERE YOU'RE GOING!
SCREEECH!
ACK!
BLAST!
OMIGOSH! THAT MAN MUST BE A POLICEMAN!
NOW I'M IN BIG TROUBLE!
PRETTY RECKLESS REINDEER RIDING, SANTA!
GULP! I'M S-SORRY OFFICER!
I'M ON MY WAY TO A CHRISTMAS PARTY AND MY BEARD BLEW UP INTO MY EYES!
AH, CHRISTMAS! MY FAVORITE SEASON!
4

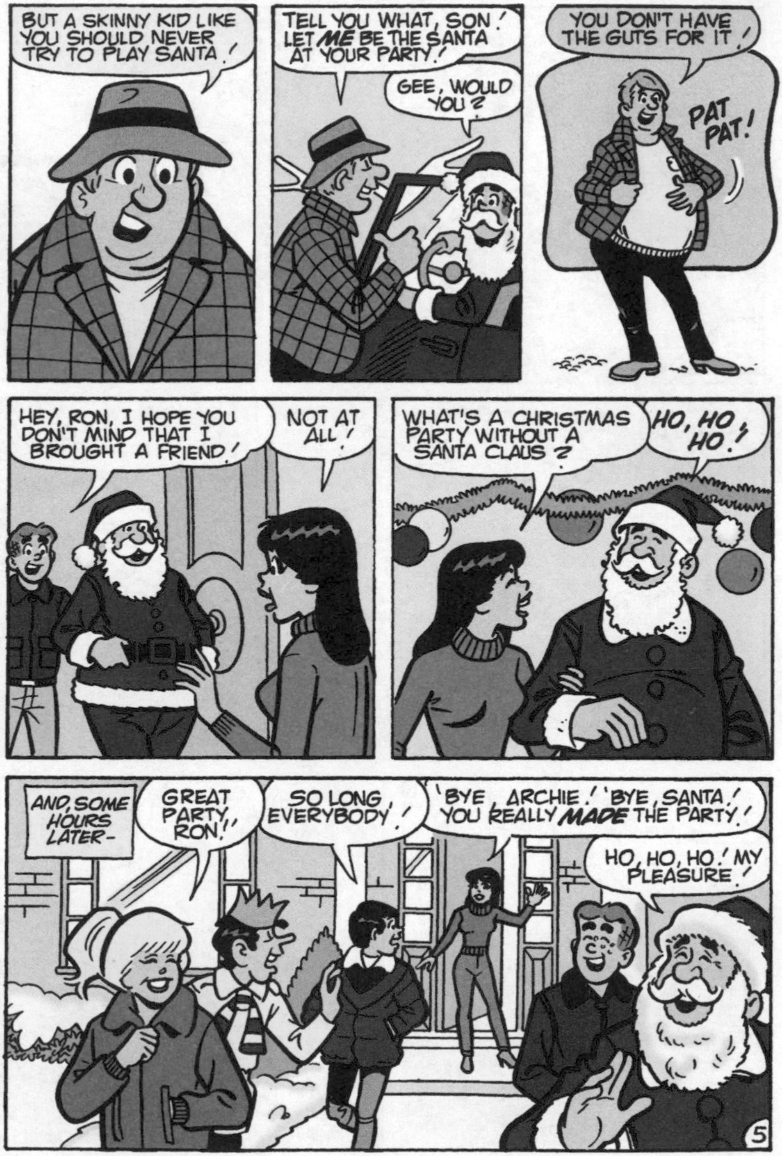
BUT A SKINNY KID LIKE YOU SHOULD NEVER TRY TO PLAY SANTA!
TELL YOU WHAT, SON! LET ME BE THE SANTA AT YOUR PARTY!
GEE, WOULD YOU?
YOU DON'T HAVE THE GUTS FOR IT!
PAT PAT!
HEY, RON, I HOPE YOU DON'T MIND THAT I BROUGHT A FRIEND!
NOT AT ALL!
WHAT'S A CHRISTMAS PARTY WITHOUT A SANTA CLAUS?
HO, HO, HO!
AND, SOME HOURS LATER-
GREAT PARTY, RON!
SO LONG EVERYBODY!
'BYE ARCHIE! 'BYE, SANTA! YOU REALLY MADE THE PARTY!
HO, HO, HO! MY PLEASURE!
5

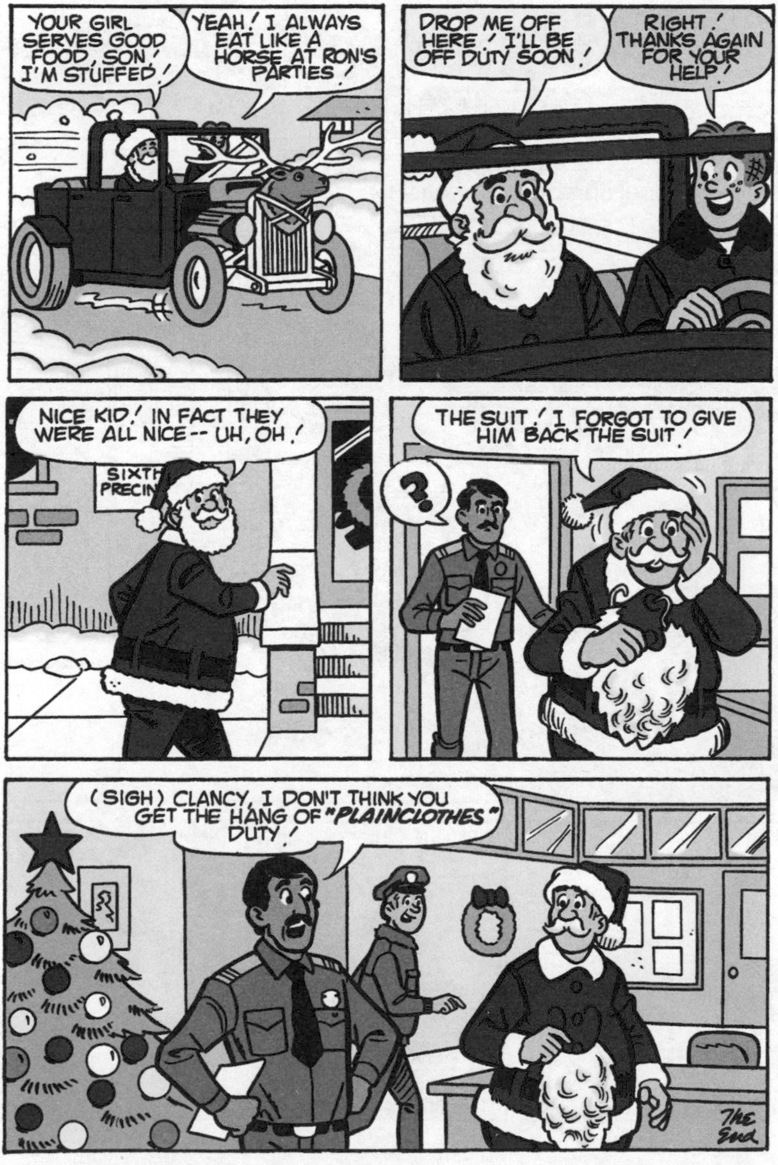
YOUR GIRL SERVES GOOD FOOD, SON! I'M STUFFED!
YEAH! I ALWAYS EAT LIKE A HORSE AT RON'S PARTIES!
DROP ME OFF HERE! I'LL BE OFF DUTY SOON!
RIGHT! THANKS AGAIN FOR YOUR HELP!
NICE KID! IN FACT THEY WERE ALL NICE -- UH, OH!
SIXTH PRECIN
THE SUIT! I FORGOT TO GIVE HIM BACK THE SUIT!
?
(SIGH) CLANCY, I DON'T THINK YOU GET THE HANG OF "PLAINCLOTHES" DUTY!
THE End

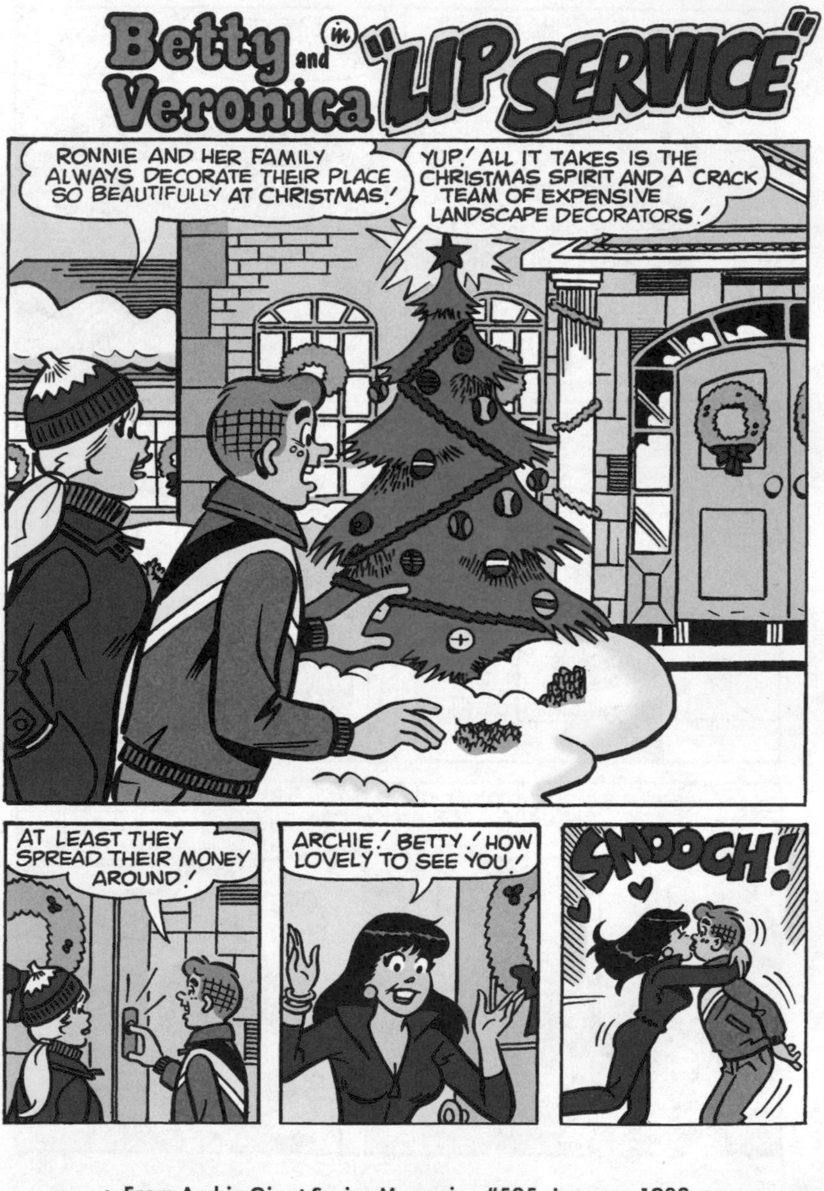
Betty and Veronica in "LIP SERVICE"
RONNIE AND HER FAMILY ALWAYS DECORATE THEIR PLACE SO BEAUTIFULLY AT CHRISTMAS!
YUP! ALL IT TAKES IS THE CHRISTMAS SPIRIT AND A CRACK TEAM OF EXPENSIVE LANDSCAPE DECORATORS!
AT LEAST THEY SPREAD THEIR MONEY AROUND!
ARCHIE! BETTY! HOW LOVELY TO SEE YOU!
SMOOCH!

• From Archie Giant Series Magazine #525, January 1983 •

Frank Doyle • Stan Goldberg • Bill Yoshida

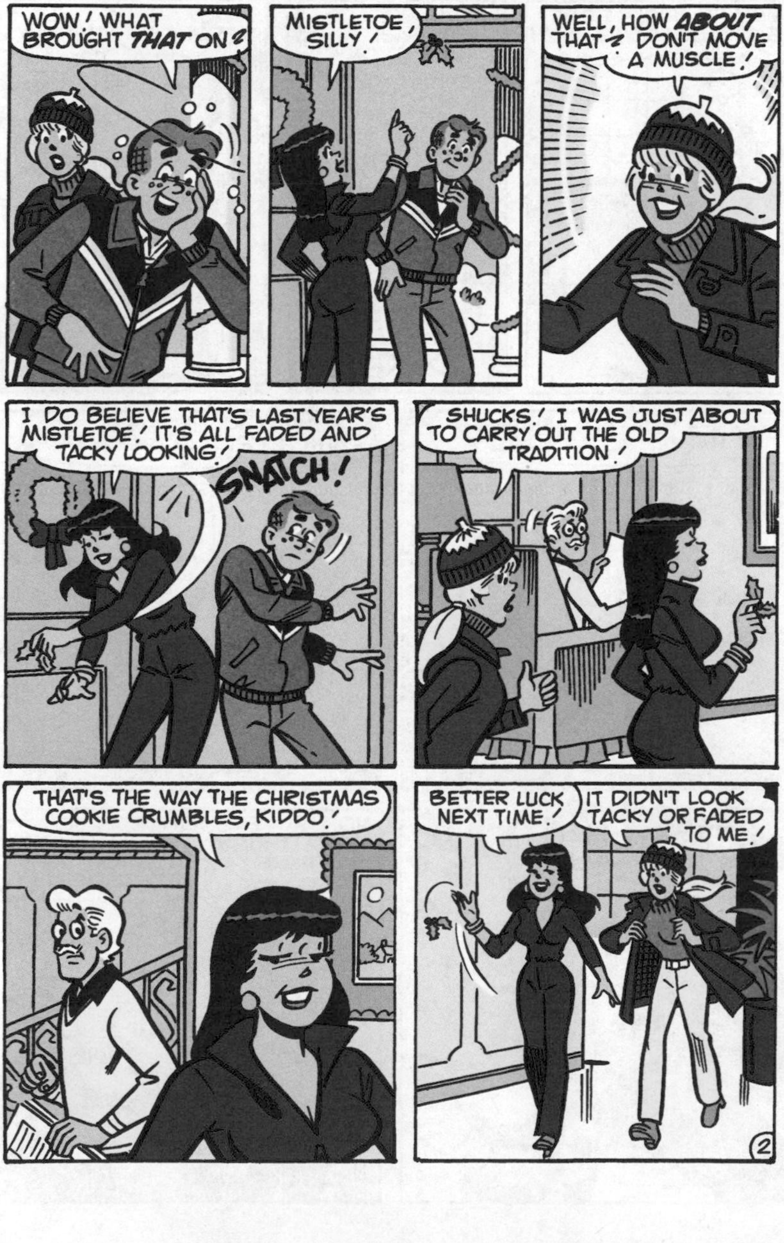
WOW! WHAT BROUGHT THAT ON?
MISTLETOE, SILLY!
WELL, HOW ABOUT THAT? DON'T MOVE A MUSCLE!
I DO BELIEVE THAT'S LAST YEAR'S MISTLETOE! IT'S ALL FADED AND TACKY LOOKING!
SNATCH!
SHUCKS! I WAS JUST ABOUT TO CARRY OUT THE OLD TRADITION!
THAT'S THE WAY THE CHRISTMAS COOKIE CRUMBLES, KIDDO!
BETTER LUCK NEXT TIME!
IT DIDN'T LOOK TACKY OR FADED TO ME!
2

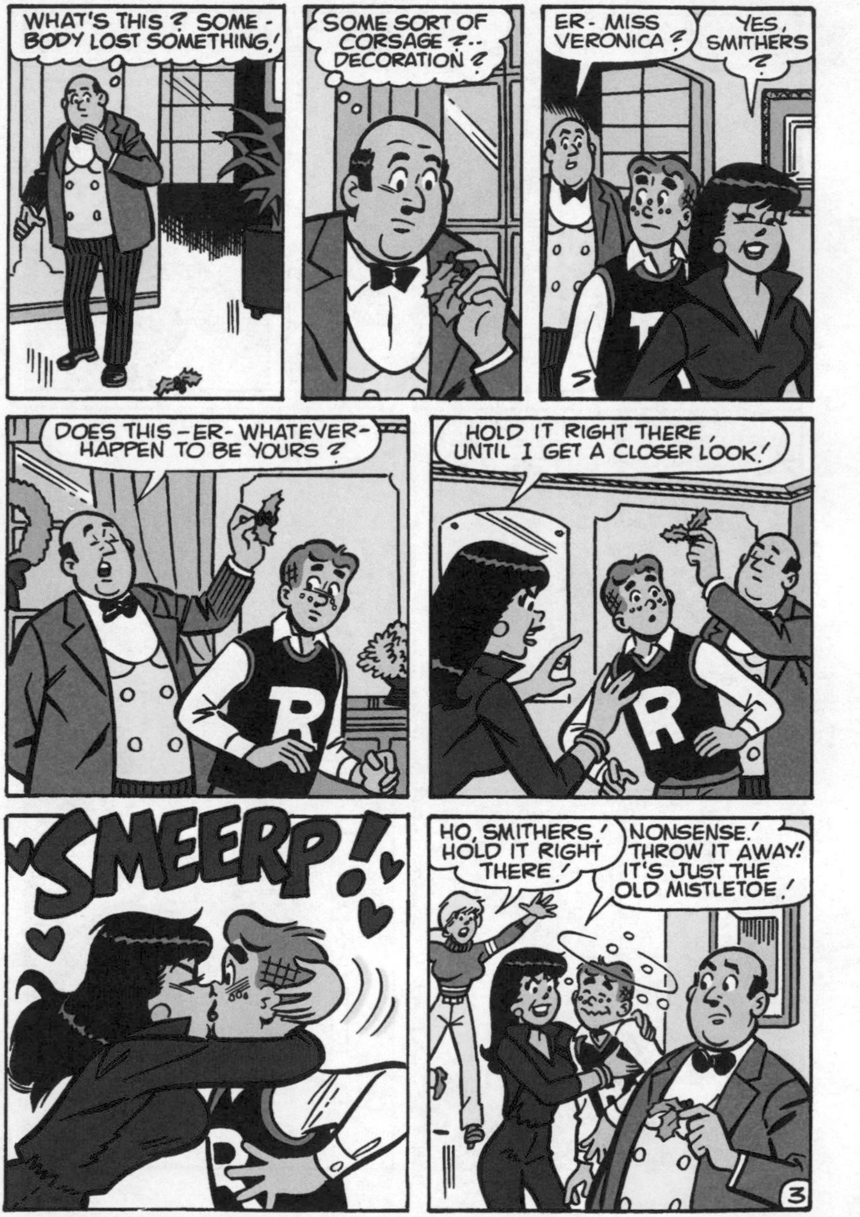
WHAT'S THIS ? SOME-BODY LOST SOMETHING!
SOME SORT OF CORSAGE ?.. DECORATION ?
ER- MISS VERONICA ?
YES, SMITHERS ?
DOES THIS -ER- WHATEVER- HAPPEN TO BE YOURS ?
HOLD IT RIGHT THERE, UNTIL I GET A CLOSER LOOK!
SMEERP!
HO, SMITHERS! HOLD IT RIGHT THERE!
NONSENSE! THROW IT AWAY! IT'S JUST THE OLD MISTLETOE!
3

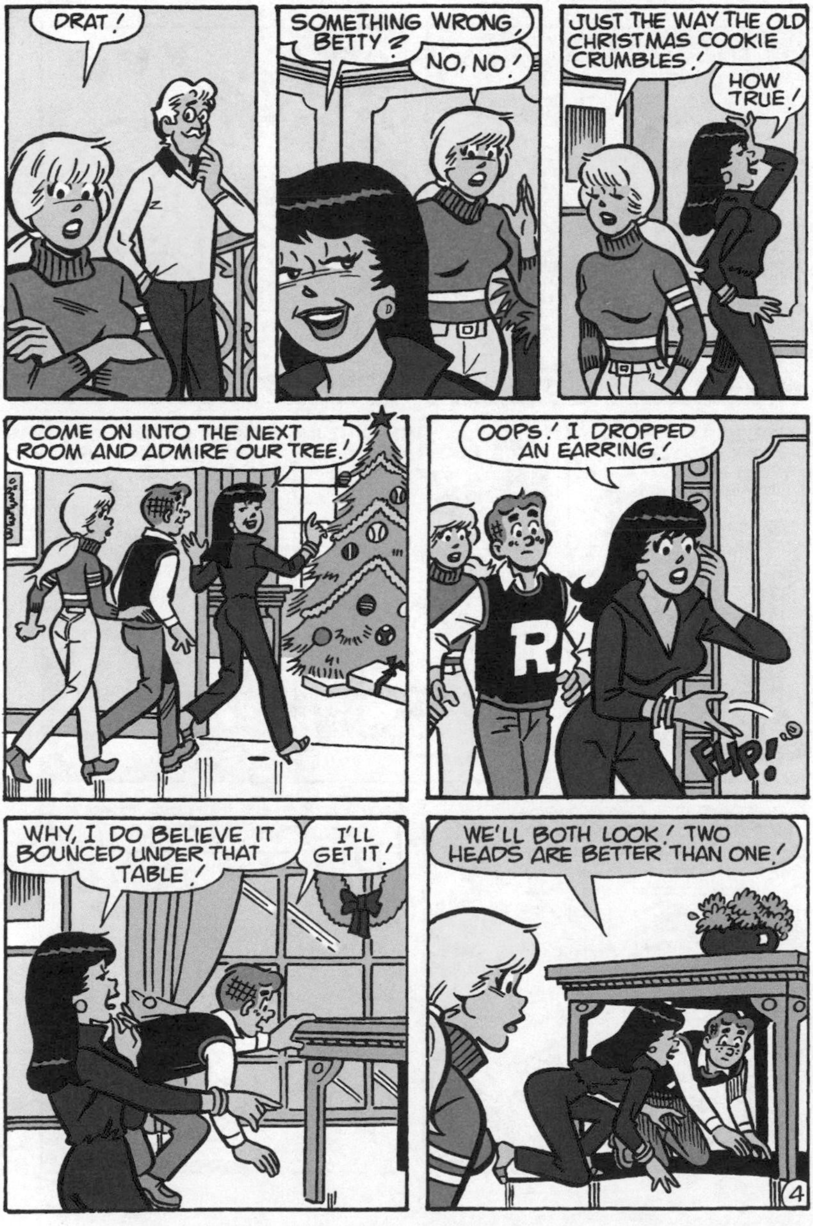
DRAT!
SOMETHING WRONG, BETTY?
NO, NO!
JUST THE WAY THE OLD CHRISTMAS COOKIE CRUMBLES!
HOW TRUE!
COME ON INTO THE NEXT ROOM AND ADMIRE OUR TREE!
OOPS! I DROPPED AN EARRING!
FLIP!
WHY, I DO BELIEVE IT BOUNCED UNDER THAT TABLE!
I'LL GET IT!
WE'LL BOTH LOOK! TWO HEADS ARE BETTER THAN ONE!
4

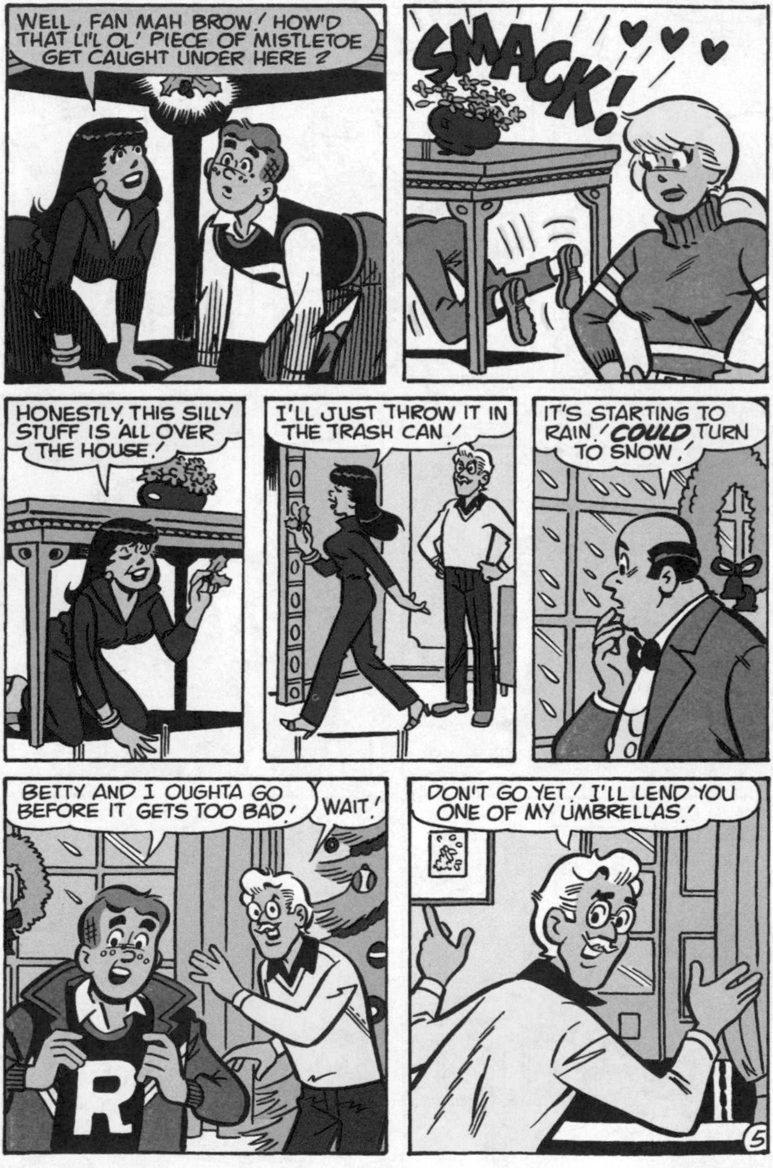
WELL, FAN MAH BROW! HOW'D THAT LI'L OL' PIECE OF MISTLETOE GET CAUGHT UNDER HERE?
SMACK!
HONESTLY, THIS SILLY STUFF IS ALL OVER THE HOUSE!
I'LL JUST THROW IT IN THE TRASH CAN!
IT'S STARTING TO RAIN! COULD TURN TO SNOW!
BETTY AND I OUGHTA GO BEFORE IT GETS TOO BAD!
WAIT!
DON'T GO YET! I'LL LEND YOU ONE OF MY UMBRELLAS!
5

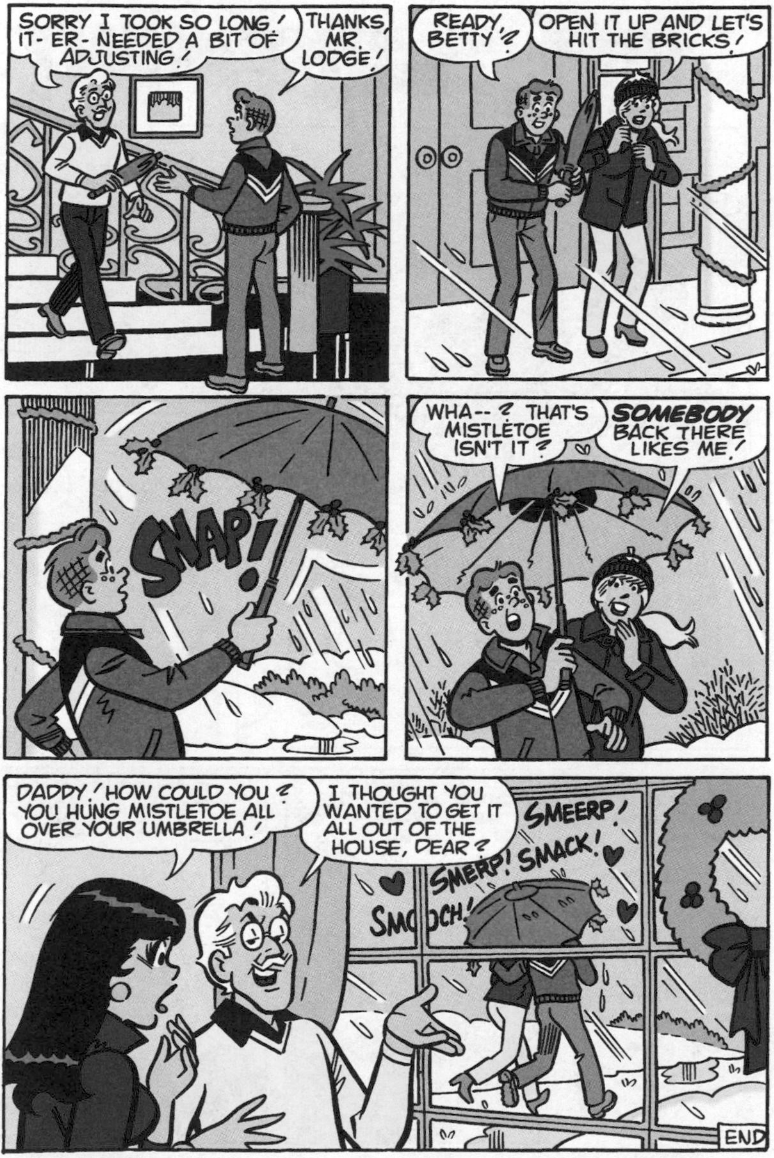
SORRY I TOOK SO LONG! IT- ER- NEEDED A BIT OF ADJUSTING!
THANKS, MR. LODGE!
READY, BETTY?
OPEN IT UP AND LET'S HIT THE BRICKS!
SNAP!
WHA--? THAT'S MISTLETOE ISN'T IT?
SOMEBODY BACK THERE LIKES ME!
DADDY! HOW COULD YOU? YOU HUNG MISTLETOE ALL OVER YOUR UMBRELLA!
I THOUGHT YOU WANTED TO GET IT ALL OUT OF THE HOUSE, DEAR?
SMEERP!
SMEERP! SMACK!
SMOOCH!
END

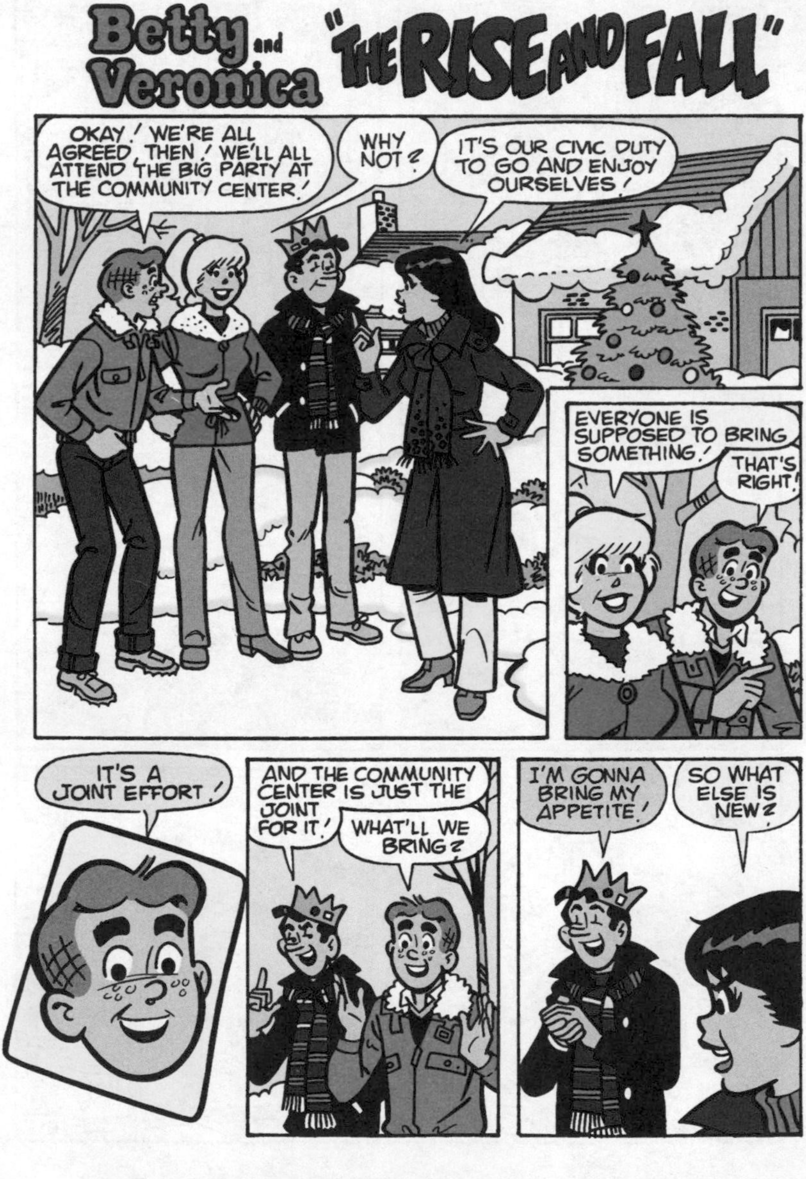
Betty and Veronica
"THE RISE AND FALL"
OKAY! WE'RE ALL AGREED, THEN! WE'LL ALL ATTEND THE BIG PARTY AT THE COMMUNITY CENTER!
WHY NOT?
IT'S OUR CIVIC DUTY TO GO AND ENJOY OURSELVES!
EVERYONE IS SUPPOSED TO BRING SOMETHING!
THAT'S RIGHT!
IT'S A JOINT EFFORT!
AND THE COMMUNITY CENTER IS JUST THE JOINT FOR IT!
WHAT'LL WE BRING?
I'M GONNA BRING MY APPETITE!
SO WHAT ELSE IS NEW?

• From Archie Giant Series Magazine #525, January 1983 •

George Gladir • Dan DeCarlo Jr. • Jimmy DeCarlo • Bill Yoshida

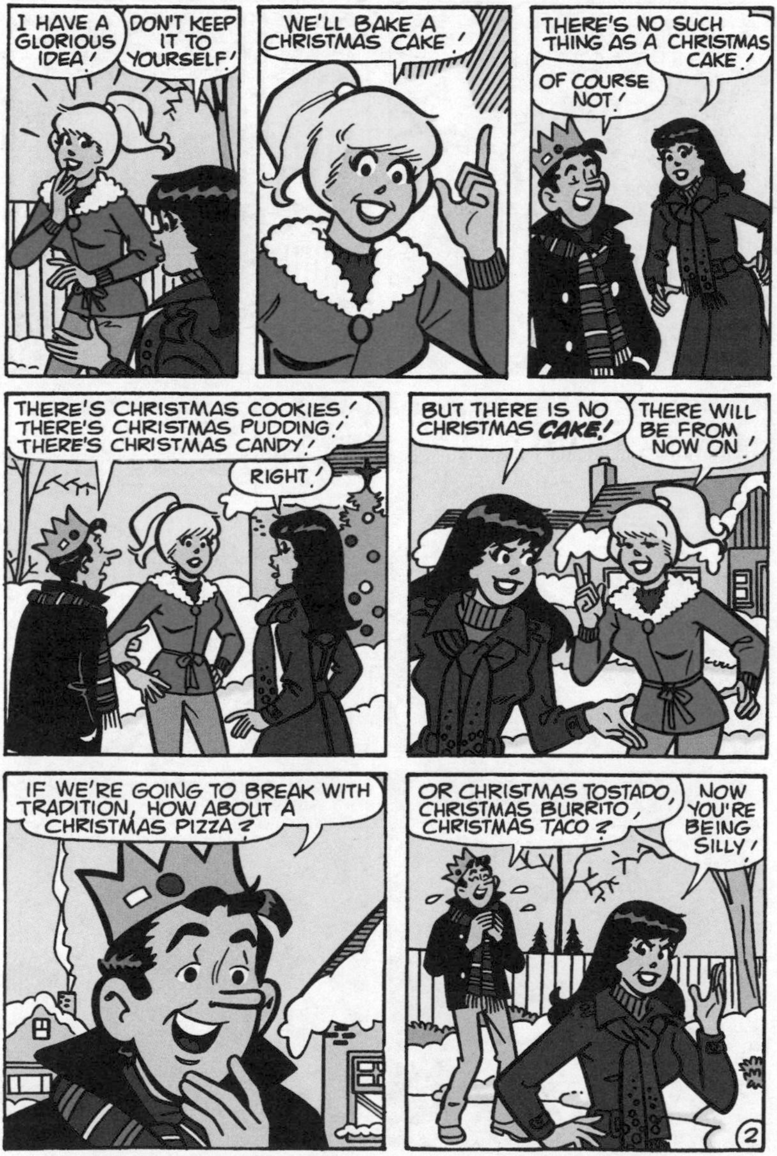
I HAVE A GLORIOUS IDEA!
DON'T KEEP IT TO YOURSELF!
WE'LL BAKE A CHRISTMAS CAKE!
THERE'S NO SUCH THING AS A CHRISTMAS CAKE!
OF COURSE NOT!
THERE'S CHRISTMAS COOKIES! THERE'S CHRISTMAS PUDDING! THERE'S CHRISTMAS CANDY!
RIGHT!
BUT THERE IS NO CHRISTMAS CAKE!
THERE WILL BE FROM NOW ON!
IF WE'RE GOING TO BREAK WITH TRADITION, HOW ABOUT A CHRISTMAS PIZZA?
OR CHRISTMAS TOSTADO, CHRISTMAS BURRITO, CHRISTMAS TACO?
NOW YOU'RE BEING SILLY!
2

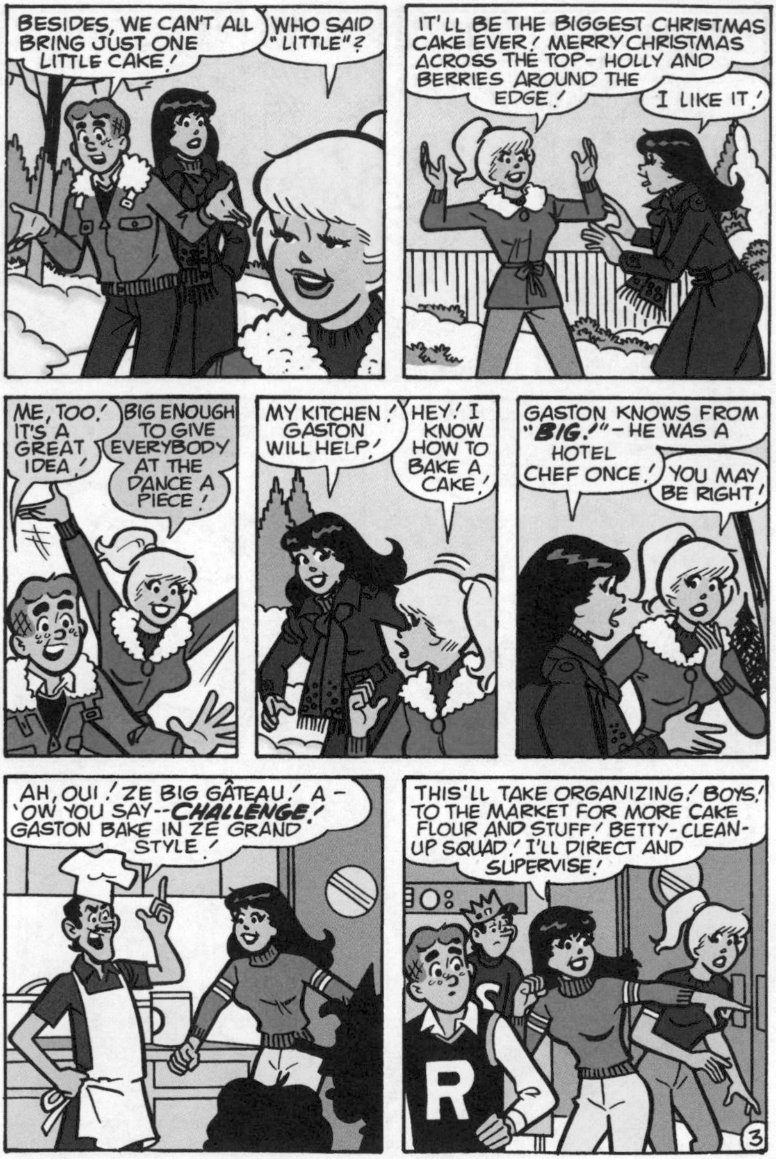
BESIDES, WE CAN'T ALL BRING JUST ONE LITTLE CAKE!
WHO SAID "LITTLE"?
IT'LL BE THE BIGGEST CHRISTMAS CAKE EVER! MERRY CHRISTMAS ACROSS THE TOP- HOLLY AND BERRIES AROUND THE EDGE!
I LIKE IT!
ME, TOO! IT'S A GREAT IDEA!
BIG ENOUGH TO GIVE EVERYBODY AT THE DANCE A PIECE!
MY KITCHEN! GASTON WILL HELP!
HEY! I KNOW HOW TO BAKE A CAKE!
GASTON KNOWS FROM "BIG!" - HE WAS A HOTEL CHEF ONCE!
YOU MAY BE RIGHT!
AH, OUI! ZE BIG GÂTEAU! A - 'OW YOU SAY--CHALLENGE! GASTON BAKE IN ZE GRAND STYLE!
THIS'LL TAKE ORGANIZING! BOYS! TO THE MARKET FOR MORE CAKE FLOUR AND STUFF! BETTY- CLEAN-UP SQUAD! I'LL DIRECT AND SUPERVISE!
3

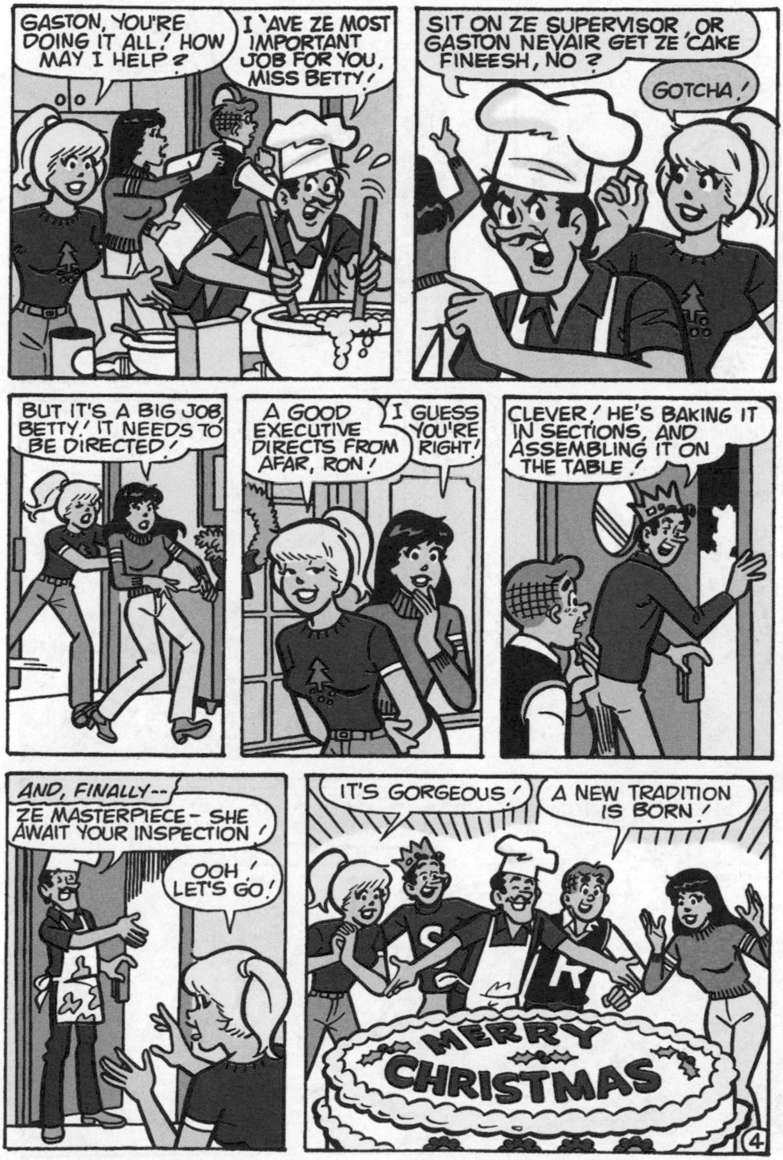
GASTON, YOU'RE DOING IT ALL! HOW MAY I HELP?
I 'AVE ZE MOST IMPORTANT JOB FOR YOU, MISS BETTY!
SIT ON ZE SUPERVISOR, OR GASTON NEVAIR GET ZE CAKE FINEESH, NO?
GOTCHA!
BUT IT'S A BIG JOB, BETTY! IT NEEDS TO BE DIRECTED!
A GOOD EXECUTIVE DIRECTS FROM AFAR, RON!
I GUESS YOU'RE RIGHT!
CLEVER! HE'S BAKING IT IN SECTIONS, AND ASSEMBLING IT ON THE TABLE!
AND, FINALLY--
ZE MASTERPIECE- SHE AWAIT YOUR INSPECTION!
OOH! LET'S GO!
IT'S GORGEOUS!
A NEW TRADITION IS BORN!
MERRY CHRISTMAS
4

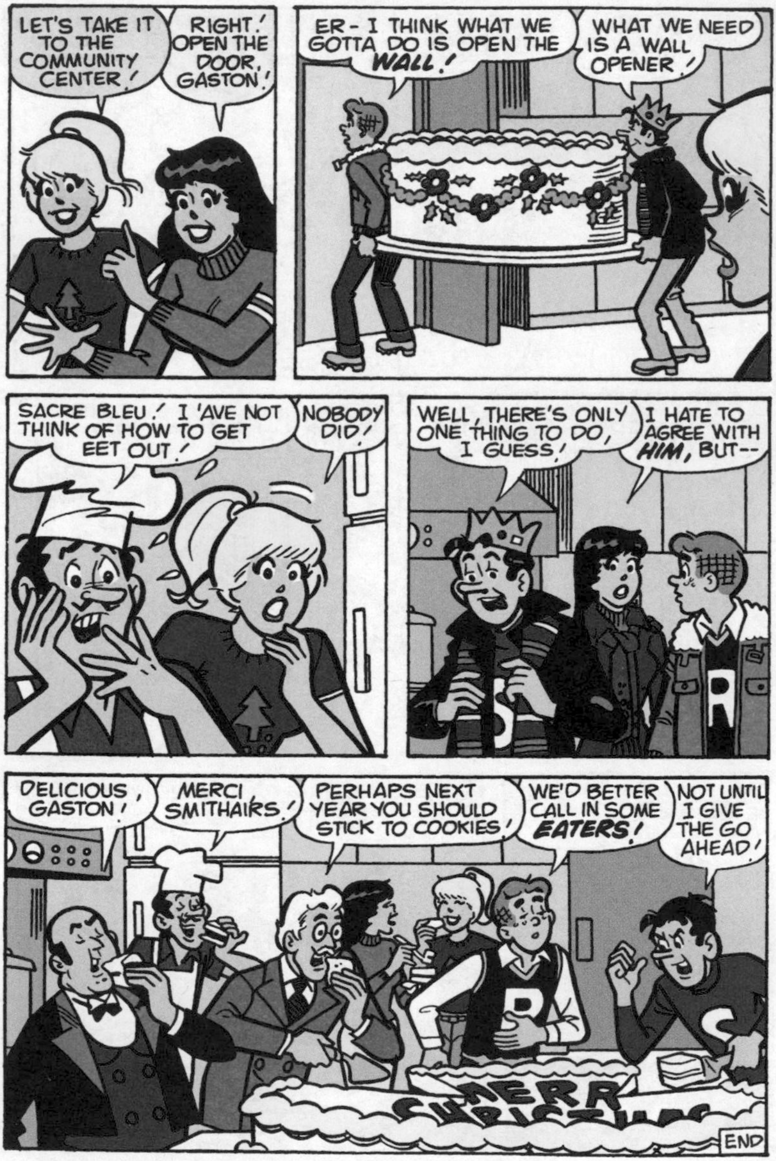
LET'S TAKE IT TO THE COMMUNITY CENTER!
RIGHT! OPEN THE DOOR, GASTON!
ER- I THINK WHAT WE GOTTA DO IS OPEN THE WALL!
WHAT WE NEED IS A WALL OPENER!
SACRE BLEU! I 'AVE NOT THINK OF HOW TO GET EET OUT!
NOBODY DID!
WELL, THERE'S ONLY ONE THING TO DO, I GUESS!
I HATE TO AGREE WITH HIM, BUT--
DELICIOUS, GASTON!
MERCI SMITHAIRS!
PERHAPS NEXT YEAR YOU SHOULD STICK TO COOKIES!
WE'D BETTER CALL IN SOME EATERS!
NOT UNTIL I GIVE THE GO AHEAD!
END

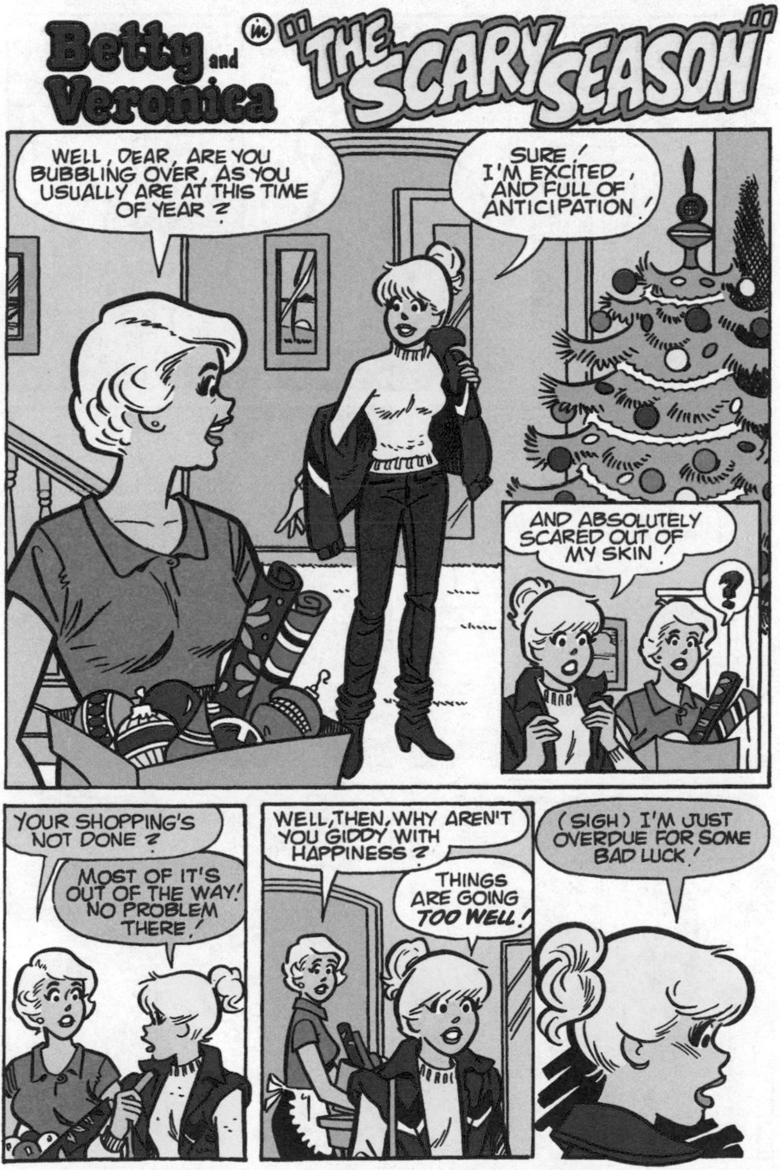
Betty and Veronica
in
"THE SCARY SEASON"
WELL, DEAR, ARE YOU BUBBLING OVER, AS YOU USUALLY ARE AT THIS TIME OF YEAR?
SURE! I'M EXCITED, AND FULL OF ANTICIPATION!
AND ABSOLUTELY SCARED OUT OF MY SKIN!
?
YOUR SHOPPING'S NOT DONE?
MOST OF IT'S OUT OF THE WAY! NO PROBLEM THERE!
WELL, THEN, WHY AREN'T YOU GIDDY WITH HAPPINESS?
THINGS ARE GOING TOO WELL!
(SIGH) I'M JUST OVERDUE FOR SOME BAD LUCK!

• **From Archie Giant Series Magazine #525, January 1983** •

Frank Doyle • Dan DeCarlo Jr. • Jimmy DeCarlo • Bill Yoshida

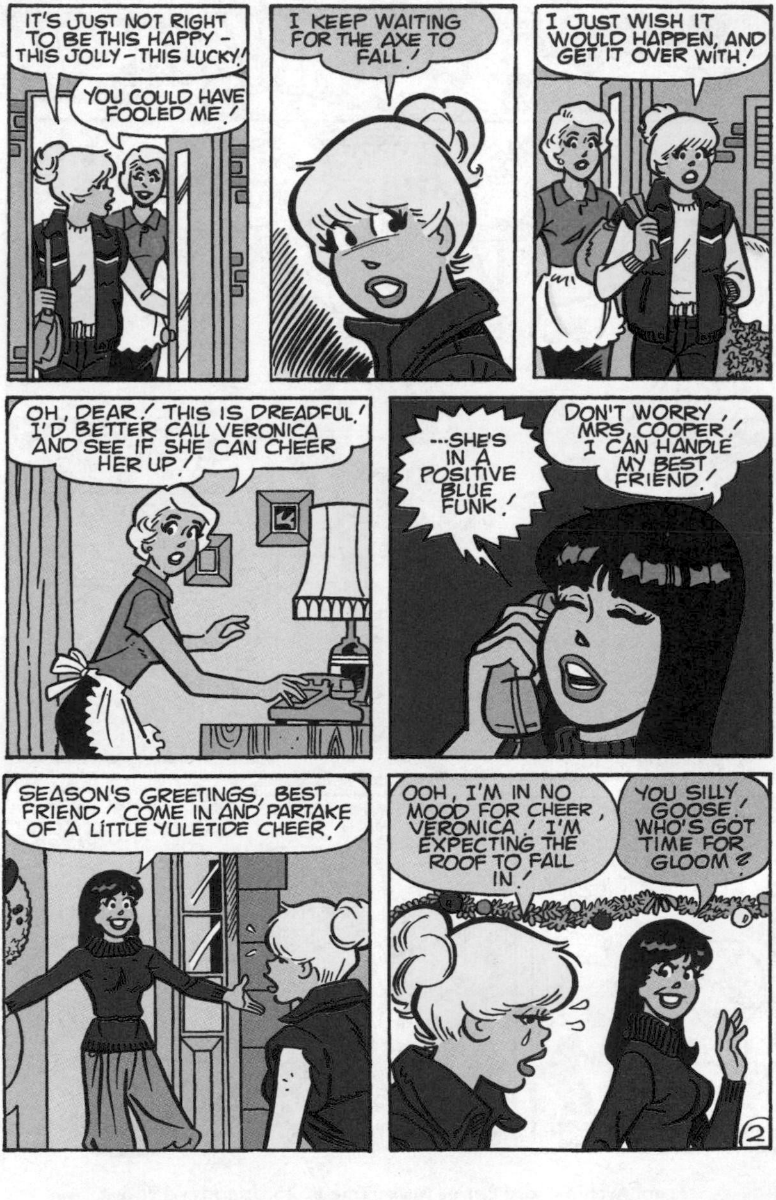
IT'S JUST NOT RIGHT TO BE THIS HAPPY - THIS JOLLY - THIS LUCKY!
YOU COULD HAVE FOOLED ME!
I KEEP WAITING FOR THE AXE TO FALL!
I JUST WISH IT WOULD HAPPEN, AND GET IT OVER WITH!
OH, DEAR! THIS IS DREADFUL! I'D BETTER CALL VERONICA AND SEE IF SHE CAN CHEER HER UP!
---SHE'S IN A POSITIVE BLUE FUNK!
DON'T WORRY, MRS. COOPER! I CAN HANDLE MY BEST FRIEND!
SEASON'S GREETINGS, BEST FRIEND! COME IN AND PARTAKE OF A LITTLE YULETIDE CHEER!
OOH, I'M IN NO MOOD FOR CHEER, VERONICA! I'M EXPECTING THE ROOF TO FALL IN!
YOU SILLY GOOSE! WHO'S GOT TIME FOR GLOOM?
2

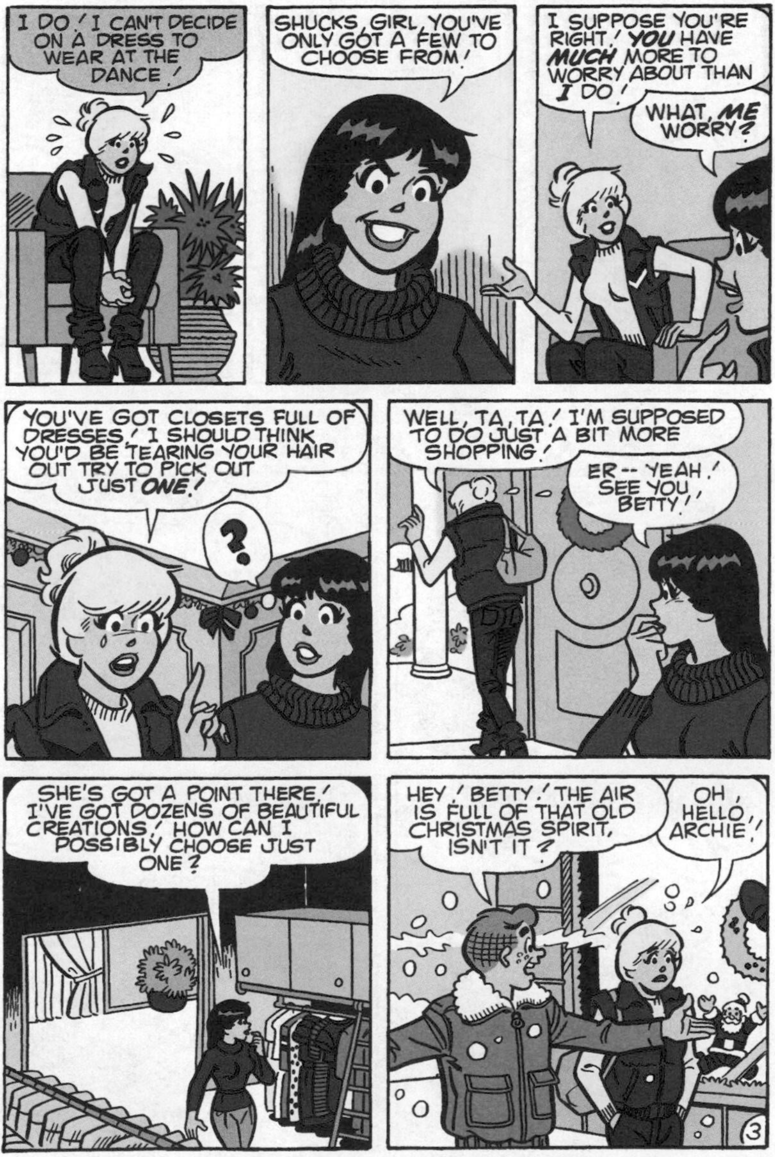
I DO! I CAN'T DECIDE ON A DRESS TO WEAR AT THE DANCE!
SHUCKS, GIRL, YOU'VE ONLY GOT A FEW TO CHOOSE FROM!
I SUPPOSE YOU'RE RIGHT! YOU HAVE MUCH MORE TO WORRY ABOUT THAN I DO!
WHAT, ME WORRY?
YOU'VE GOT CLOSETS FULL OF DRESSES! I SHOULD THINK YOU'D BE TEARING YOUR HAIR OUT TRY TO PICK OUT JUST ONE!
?
WELL, TA, TA! I'M SUPPOSED TO DO JUST A BIT MORE SHOPPING!
ER -- YEAH! SEE YOU, BETTY!!
SHE'S GOT A POINT THERE! I'VE GOT DOZENS OF BEAUTIFUL CREATIONS! HOW CAN I POSSIBLY CHOOSE JUST ONE?
HEY! BETTY! THE AIR IS FULL OF THAT OLD CHRISTMAS SPIRIT, ISN'T IT?
OH, HELLO, ARCHIE!!
3

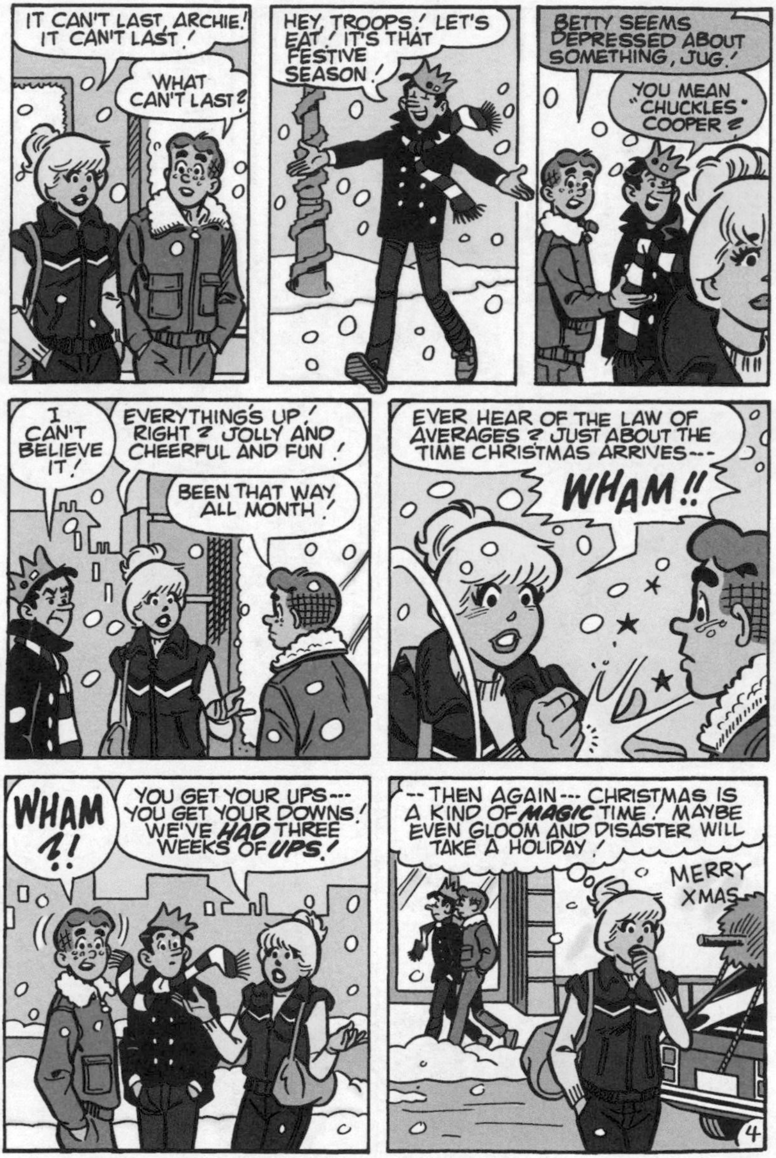
IT CAN'T LAST, ARCHIE! IT CAN'T LAST!
WHAT CAN'T LAST?
HEY, TROOPS! LET'S EAT! IT'S THAT FESTIVE SEASON!
BETTY SEEMS DEPRESSED ABOUT SOMETHING, JUG!
YOU MEAN "CHUCKLES" COOPER?
I CAN'T BELIEVE IT!
EVERYTHING'S UP! RIGHT? JOLLY AND CHEERFUL AND FUN!
BEEN THAT WAY ALL MONTH!
EVER HEAR OF THE LAW OF AVERAGES? JUST ABOUT THE TIME CHRISTMAS ARRIVES---
WHAM!!
WHAM ?!
YOU GET YOUR UPS--- YOU GET YOUR DOWNS! WE'VE HAD THREE WEEKS OF UPS!
--THEN AGAIN--- CHRISTMAS IS A KIND OF MAGIC TIME! MAYBE EVEN GLOOM AND DISASTER WILL TAKE A HOLIDAY!
MERRY XMAS
4

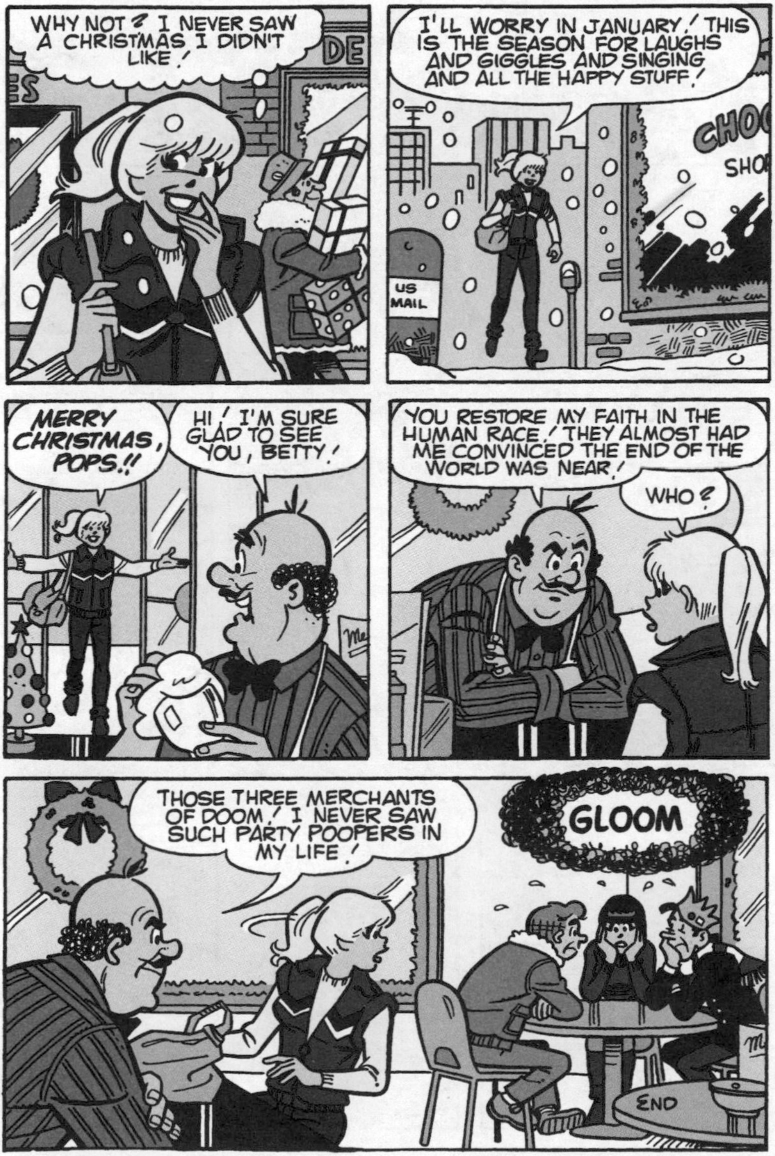
WHY NOT? I NEVER SAW A CHRISTMAS I DIDN'T LIKE!
I'LL WORRY IN JANUARY! THIS IS THE SEASON FOR LAUGHS AND GIGGLES AND SINGING AND ALL THE HAPPY STUFF!
CHOC
SHO
US MAIL
MERRY CHRISTMAS, POPS.!!
HI! I'M SURE GLAD TO SEE YOU, BETTY!
YOU RESTORE MY FAITH IN THE HUMAN RACE! THEY ALMOST HAD ME CONVINCED THE END OF THE WORLD WAS NEAR!
WHO?
THOSE THREE MERCHANTS OF DOOM! I NEVER SAW SUCH PARTY POOPERS IN MY LIFE!
GLOOM
END

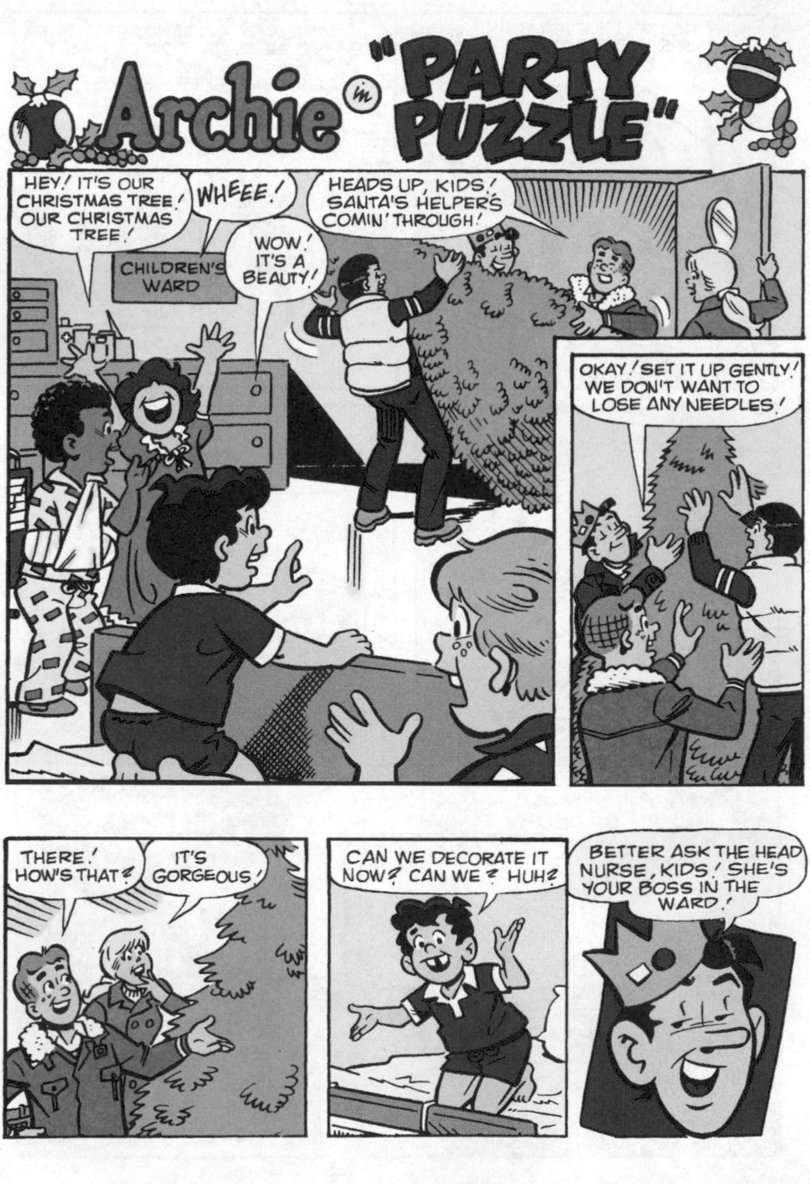
Archie in "PARTY PUZZLE"
HEY! IT'S OUR CHRISTMAS TREE! OUR CHRISTMAS TREE!
WHEEE!
HEADS UP, KIDS! SANTA'S HELPER'S COMIN' THROUGH!
WOW! IT'S A BEAUTY!
CHILDREN'S WARD
OKAY! SET IT UP GENTLY! WE DON'T WANT TO LOSE ANY NEEDLES!
THERE! HOW'S THAT?
IT'S GORGEOUS!
CAN WE DECORATE IT NOW? CAN WE? HUH?
BETTER ASK THE HEAD NURSE, KIDS! SHE'S YOUR BOSS IN THE WARD!

• **From Archie Giant Series Magazine #535, January 1984** •

Frank Doyle • Stan Goldberg • Rudy Lapick • Bill Yoshida

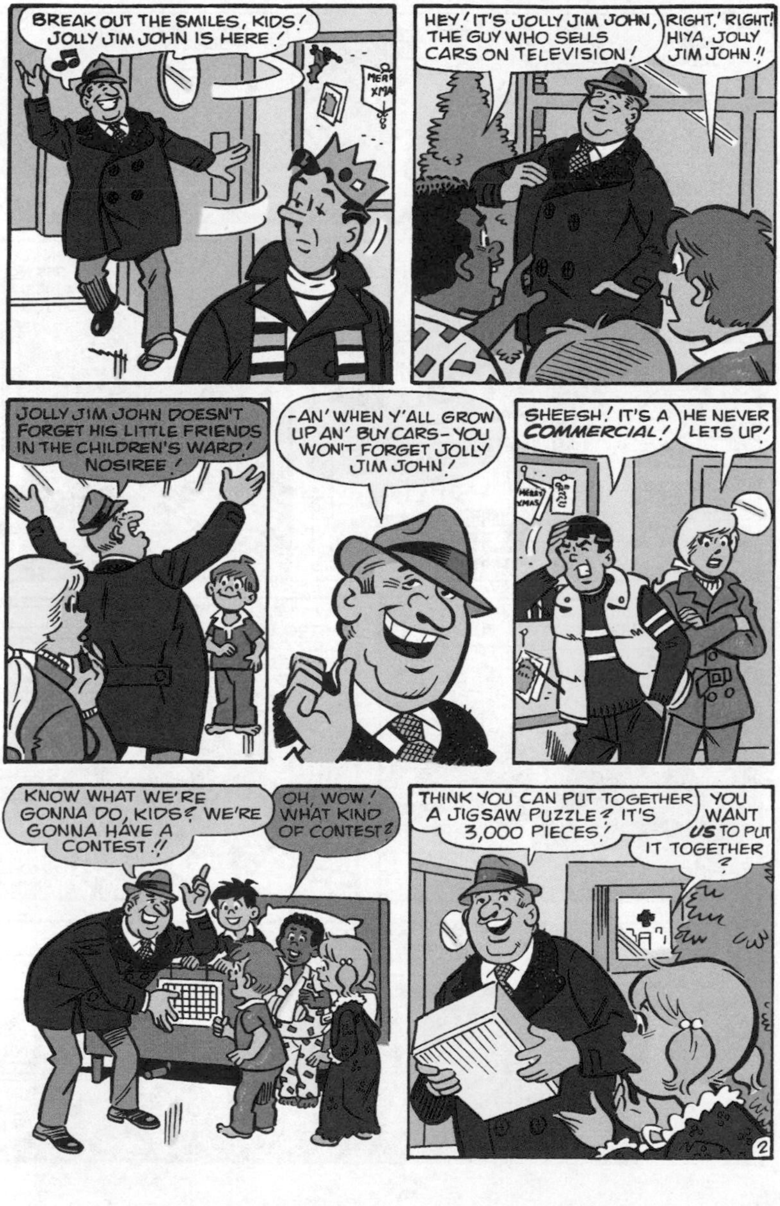
BREAK OUT THE SMILES, KIDS! JOLLY JIM JOHN IS HERE!
MERRY XMAS
HEY! IT'S JOLLY JIM JOHN, THE GUY WHO SELLS CARS ON TELEVISION!
RIGHT! RIGHT! HIYA, JOLLY JIM JOHN!!
JOLLY JIM JOHN DOESN'T FORGET HIS LITTLE FRIENDS IN THE CHILDREN'S WARD! NOSIREE!
-AN' WHEN Y'ALL GROW UP AN' BUY CARS- YOU WON'T FORGET JOLLY JIM JOHN!
SHEESH! IT'S A COMMERCIAL!
HE NEVER LETS UP!
KNOW WHAT WE'RE GONNA DO, KIDS? WE'RE GONNA HAVE A CONTEST!!
OH, WOW! WHAT KIND OF CONTEST?
THINK YOU CAN PUT TOGETHER A JIGSAW PUZZLE? IT'S 3,000 PIECES!
YOU WANT US TO PUT IT TOGETHER?
2

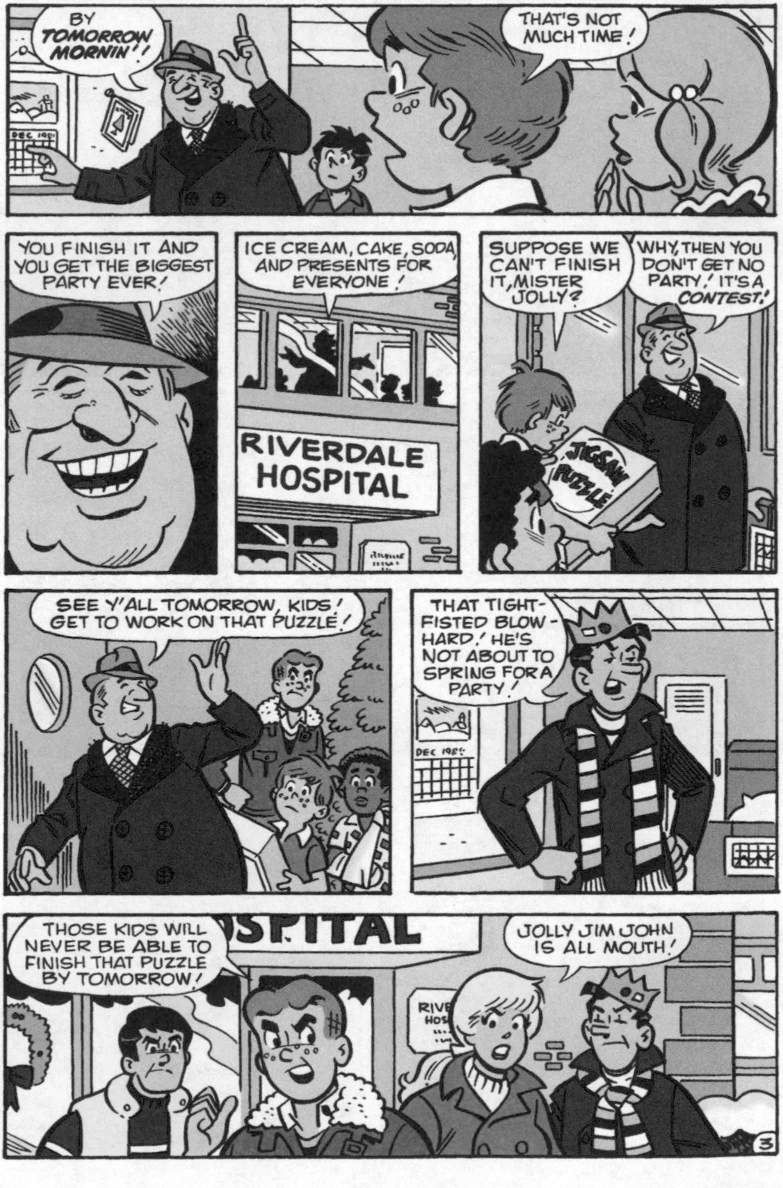
BY TOMORROW MORNIN'!
THAT'S NOT MUCH TIME!
YOU FINISH IT AND YOU GET THE BIGGEST PARTY EVER!
ICE CREAM, CAKE, SODA, AND PRESENTS FOR EVERYONE!
RIVERDALE HOSPITAL
SUPPOSE WE CAN'T FINISH IT, MISTER JOLLY?
WHY, THEN YOU DON'T GET NO PARTY! IT'S A CONTEST!
JIGSAW PUZZLE
SEE Y'ALL TOMORROW, KIDS! GET TO WORK ON THAT PUZZLE!
THAT TIGHT-FISTED BLOW-HARD! HE'S NOT ABOUT TO SPRING FOR A PARTY!
THOSE KIDS WILL NEVER BE ABLE TO FINISH THAT PUZZLE BY TOMORROW!
JOLLY JIM JOHN IS ALL MOUTH!
3

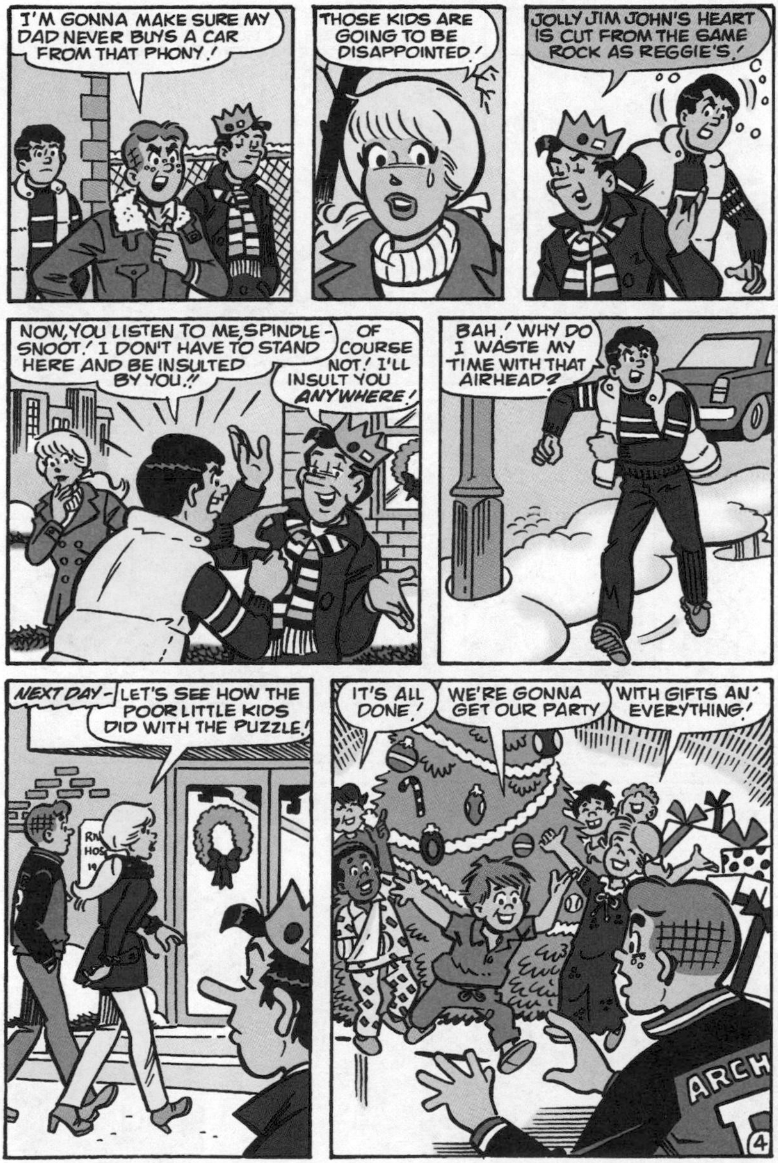
I'M GONNA MAKE SURE MY DAD NEVER BUYS A CAR FROM THAT PHONY!
THOSE KIDS ARE GOING TO BE DISAPPOINTED!
JOLLY JIM JOHN'S HEART IS CUT FROM THE SAME ROCK AS REGGIE'S!
NOW, YOU LISTEN TO ME, SPINDLE-SNOOT! I DON'T HAVE TO STAND HERE AND BE INSULTED BY YOU!!
OF COURSE NOT! I'LL INSULT YOU ANYWHERE!
BAH! WHY DO I WASTE MY TIME WITH THAT AIRHEAD?
NEXT DAY -
LET'S SEE HOW THE POOR LITTLE KIDS DID WITH THE PUZZLE!
IT'S ALL DONE!
WE'RE GONNA GET OUR PARTY
WITH GIFTS AN' EVERYTHING!
ARCH
4

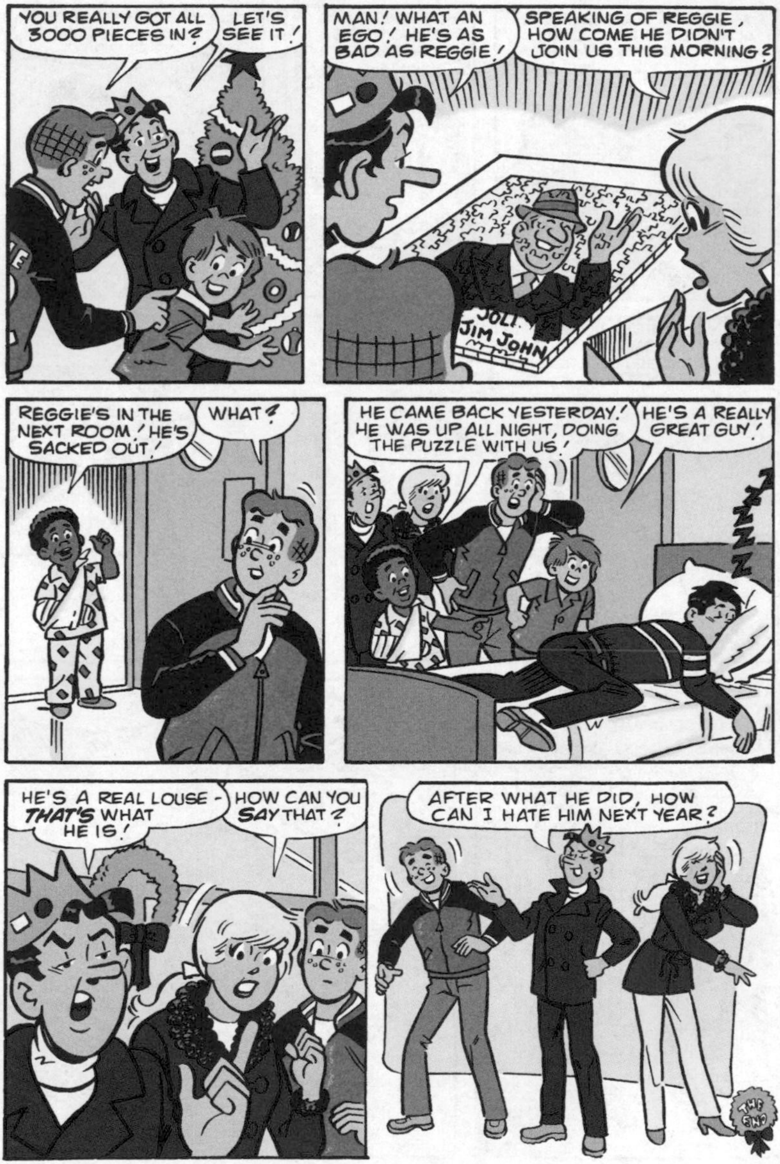
YOU REALLY GOT ALL 3000 PIECES IN?
LET'S SEE IT!
MAN! WHAT AN EGO! HE'S AS BAD AS REGGIE!
SPEAKING OF REGGIE, HOW COME HE DIDN'T JOIN US THIS MORNING?
JOLI.
JIM JOHN
REGGIE'S IN THE NEXT ROOM! HE'S SACKED OUT!
WHAT?
HE CAME BACK YESTERDAY! HE WAS UP ALL NIGHT, DOING THE PUZZLE WITH US!
HE'S A REALLY GREAT GUY!
ZZZZZ
HE'S A REAL LOUSE - THAT'S WHAT HE IS!
HOW CAN YOU SAY THAT?
AFTER WHAT HE DID, HOW CAN I HATE HIM NEXT YEAR?
THE END

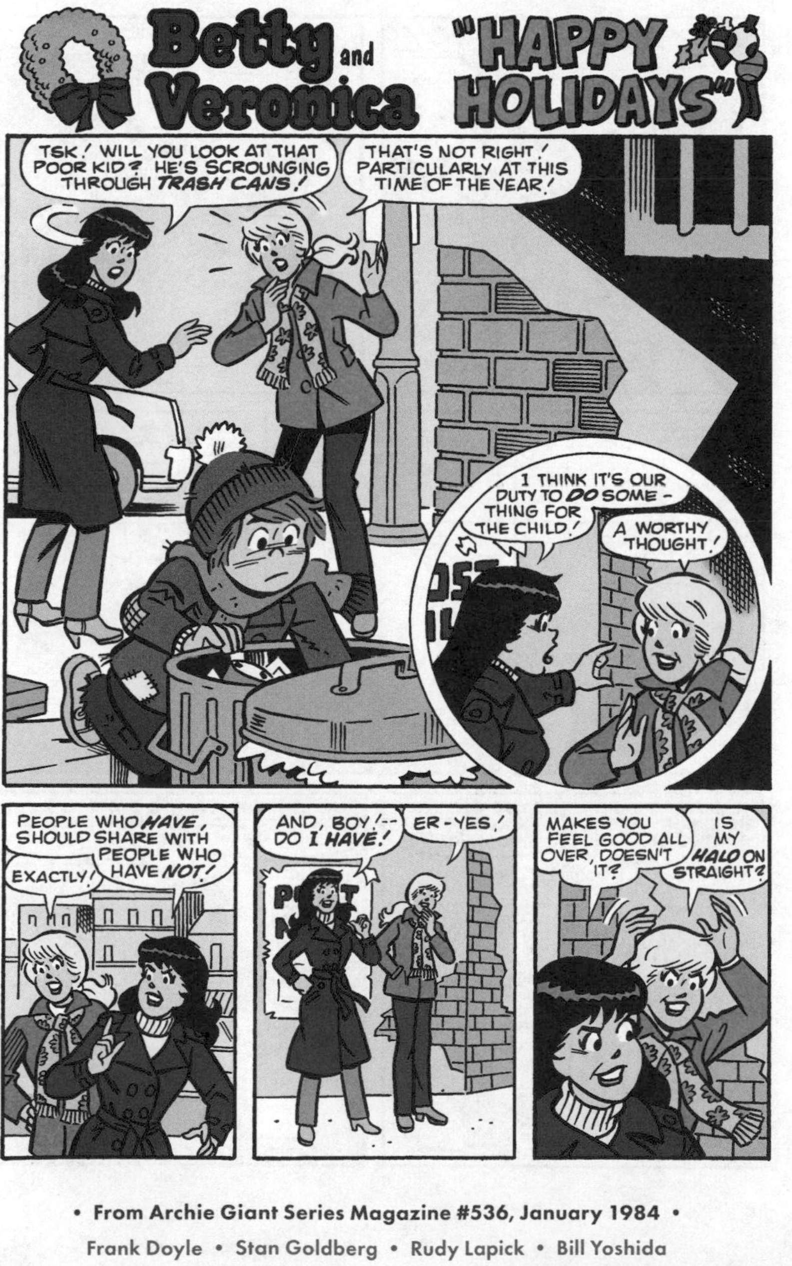
Betty and Veronica
"HAPPY HOLIDAYS"
TSK! WILL YOU LOOK AT THAT POOR KID? HE'S SCROUNGING THROUGH TRASH CANS!
THAT'S NOT RIGHT! PARTICULARLY AT THIS TIME OF THE YEAR!
I THINK IT'S OUR DUTY TO DO SOME-THING FOR THE CHILD!
A WORTHY THOUGHT!
PEOPLE WHO HAVE, SHOULD SHARE WITH PEOPLE WHO HAVE NOT!
EXACTLY!
AND, BOY!-- DO I HAVE!
ER-YES!
MAKES YOU FEEL GOOD ALL OVER, DOESN'T IT?
IS MY HALO ON STRAIGHT?

• From Archie Giant Series Magazine #536, January 1984 •

Frank Doyle • Stan Goldberg • Rudy Lapick • Bill Yoshida

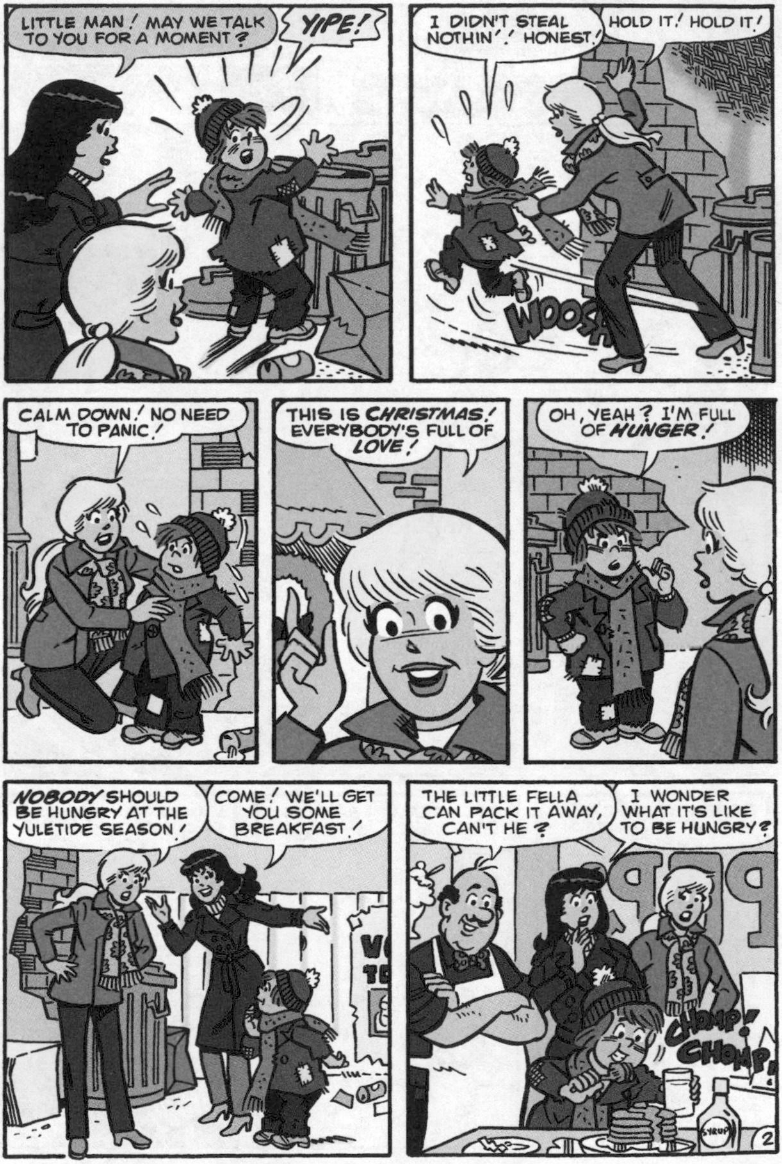
LITTLE MAN! MAY WE TALK TO YOU FOR A MOMENT?
YIPE!
I DIDN'T STEAL NOTHIN'! HONEST!
HOLD IT! HOLD IT!
WOOSH
CALM DOWN! NO NEED TO PANIC!
THIS IS CHRISTMAS! EVERYBODY'S FULL OF LOVE!
OH, YEAH? I'M FULL OF HUNGER!
NOBODY SHOULD BE HUNGRY AT THE YULETIDE SEASON!
COME! WE'LL GET YOU SOME BREAKFAST!
THE LITTLE FELLA CAN PACK IT AWAY, CAN'T HE?
I WONDER WHAT IT'S LIKE TO BE HUNGRY?
CHOMP! CHOMP!
SYRUP
2

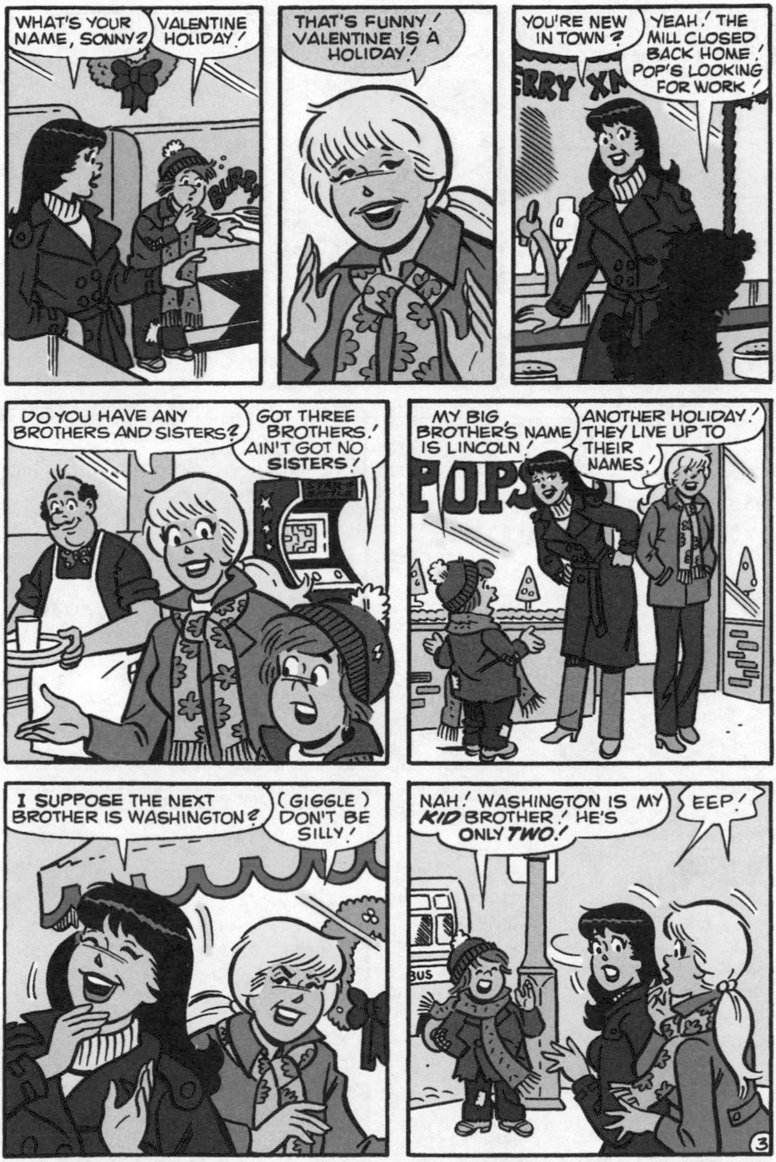
WHAT'S YOUR NAME, SONNY?
VALENTINE HOLIDAY!
BURRP
THAT'S FUNNY! VALENTINE IS A HOLIDAY!
YOU'RE NEW IN TOWN?
YEAH! THE MILL CLOSED BACK HOME! POP'S LOOKING FOR WORK!
DO YOU HAVE ANY BROTHERS AND SISTERS?
GOT THREE BROTHERS! AIN'T GOT NO SISTERS!
MY BIG BROTHER'S NAME IS LINCOLN!
ANOTHER HOLIDAY! THEY LIVE UP TO THEIR NAMES!
POPS
I SUPPOSE THE NEXT BROTHER IS WASHINGTON?
(GIGGLE) DON'T BE SILLY!
NAH! WASHINGTON IS MY KID BROTHER! HE'S ONLY TWO!
EEP!
BUS
3

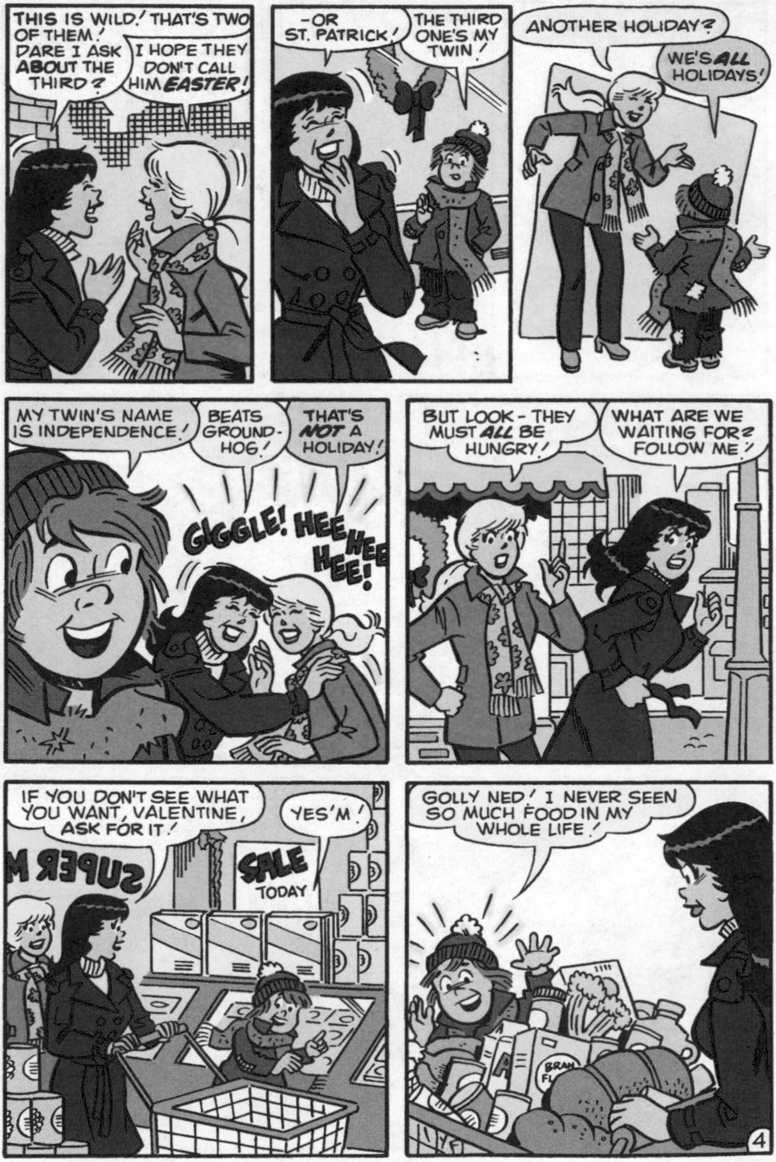
THIS IS WILD! THAT'S TWO OF THEM! DARE I ASK ABOUT THE THIRD?
I HOPE THEY DON'T CALL HIM EASTER!
-OR ST. PATRICK!
THE THIRD ONE'S MY TWIN!
ANOTHER HOLIDAY?
WE'S ALL HOLIDAYS!
MY TWIN'S NAME IS INDEPENDENCE!
BEATS GROUND-HOG!
THAT'S NOT A HOLIDAY!
GIGGLE! HEE HEE HEE!
BUT LOOK - THEY MUST ALL BE HUNGRY!
WHAT ARE WE WAITING FOR? FOLLOW ME!
IF YOU DON'T SEE WHAT YOU WANT, VALENTINE, ASK FOR IT!
YES'M!
SUPER M
SALE TODAY
GOLLY NED! I NEVER SEEN SO MUCH FOOD IN MY WHOLE LIFE!
4

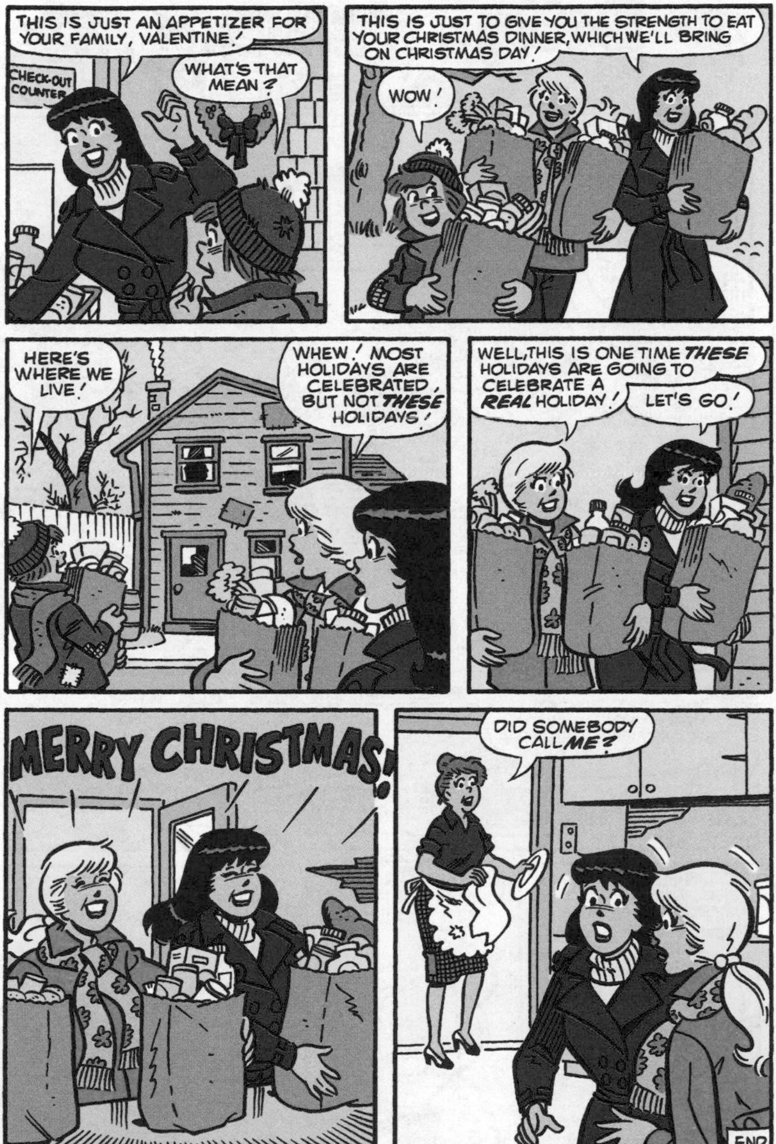
THIS IS JUST AN APPETIZER FOR YOUR FAMILY, VALENTINE!
CHECK-OUT COUNTER
WHAT'S THAT MEAN?
THIS IS JUST TO GIVE YOU THE STRENGTH TO EAT YOUR CHRISTMAS DINNER, WHICH WE'LL BRING ON CHRISTMAS DAY!
WOW!
HERE'S WHERE WE LIVE!
WHEW! MOST HOLIDAYS ARE CELEBRATED, BUT NOT *THESE* HOLIDAYS!
WELL, THIS IS ONE TIME *THESE* HOLIDAYS ARE GOING TO CELEBRATE A *REAL* HOLIDAY!
LET'S GO!
MERRY CHRISTMAS!
DID SOMEBODY CALL *ME*?
END

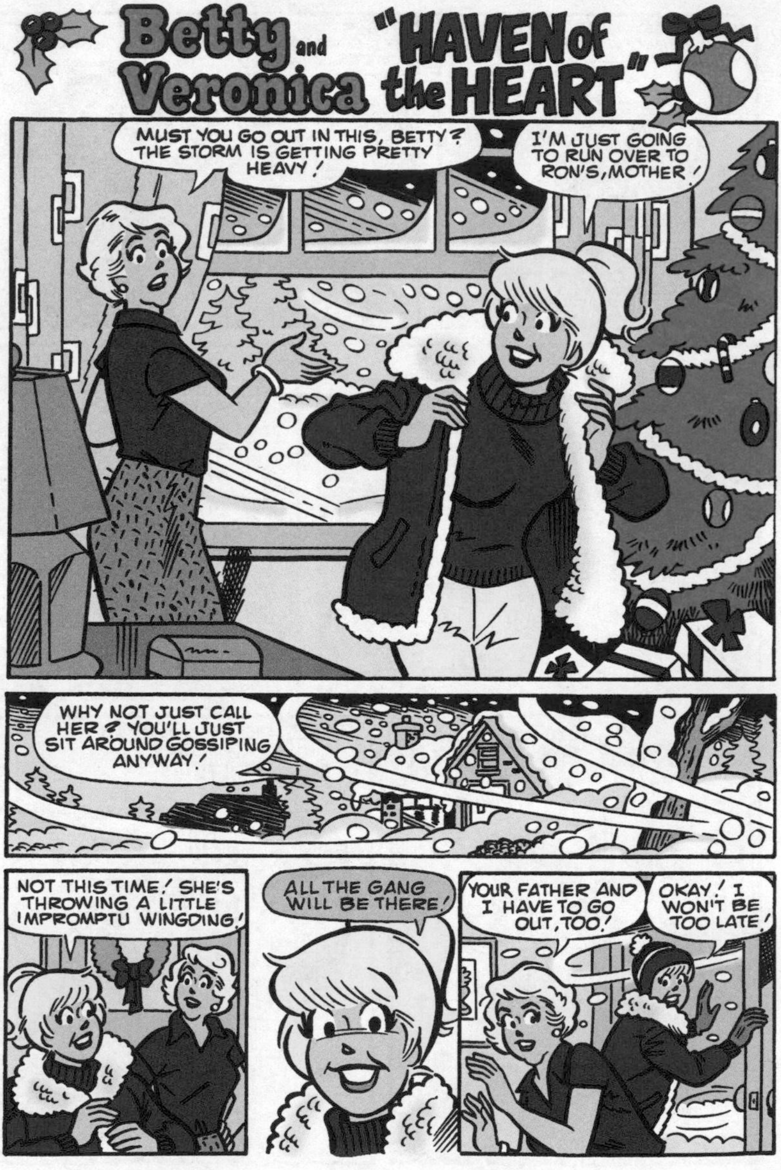
Betty and Veronica
"HAVEN of the HEART"
MUST YOU GO OUT IN THIS, BETTY? THE STORM IS GETTING PRETTY HEAVY!
I'M JUST GOING TO RUN OVER TO RON'S, MOTHER!
WHY NOT JUST CALL HER? YOU'LL JUST SIT AROUND GOSSIPING ANYWAY!
NOT THIS TIME! SHE'S THROWING A LITTLE IMPROMPTU WINGDING!
ALL THE GANG WILL BE THERE!
YOUR FATHER AND I HAVE TO GO OUT, TOO!
OKAY! I WON'T BE TOO LATE!

• **From Archie Giant Series Magazine #536, January 1984** •

Frank Doyle • Dan DeCarlo • Rudy Lapick • Bill Yoshida

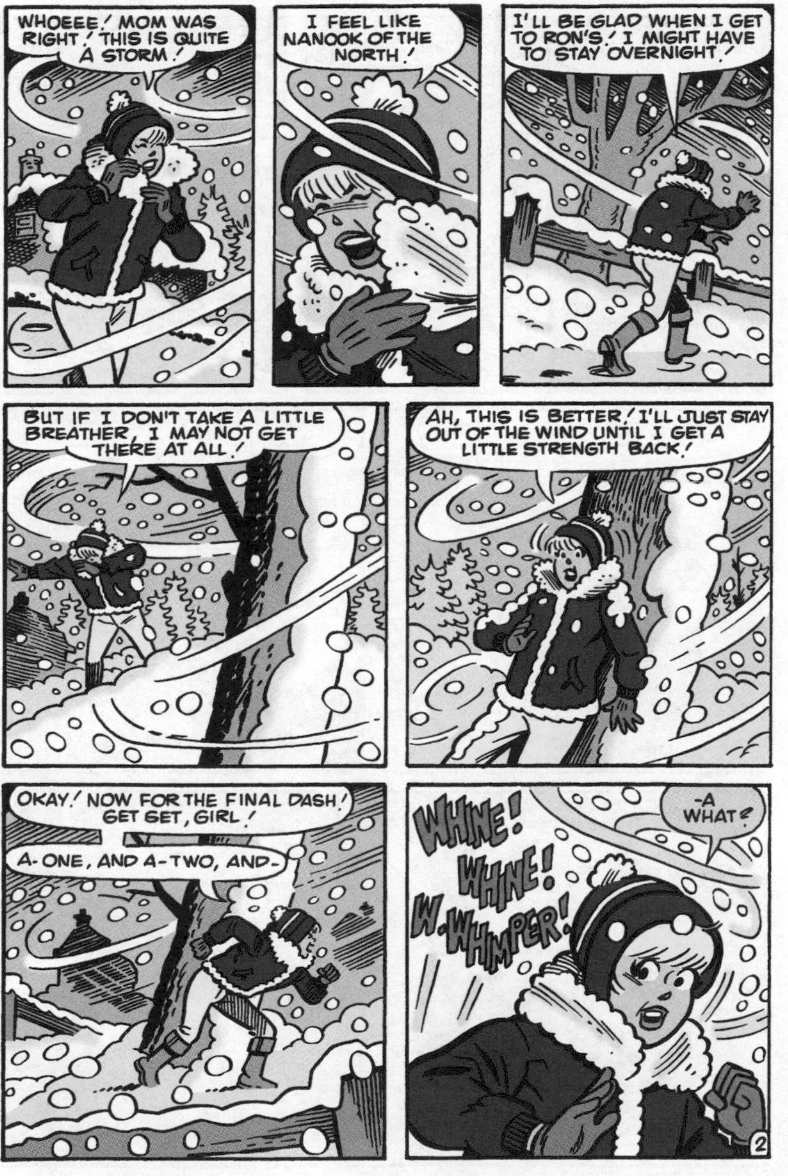
WHOEEE! MOM WAS RIGHT! THIS IS QUITE A STORM!
I FEEL LIKE NANOOK OF THE NORTH!
I'LL BE GLAD WHEN I GET TO RON'S! I MIGHT HAVE TO STAY OVERNIGHT!
BUT IF I DON'T TAKE A LITTLE BREATHER, I MAY NOT GET THERE AT ALL!
AH, THIS IS BETTER! I'LL JUST STAY OUT OF THE WIND UNTIL I GET A LITTLE STRENGTH BACK!
OKAY! NOW FOR THE FINAL DASH! GET GET, GIRL!
A-ONE, AND A-TWO, AND-
WHINE!
WHINE!
W-WHIMPER!
-A WHAT?
2

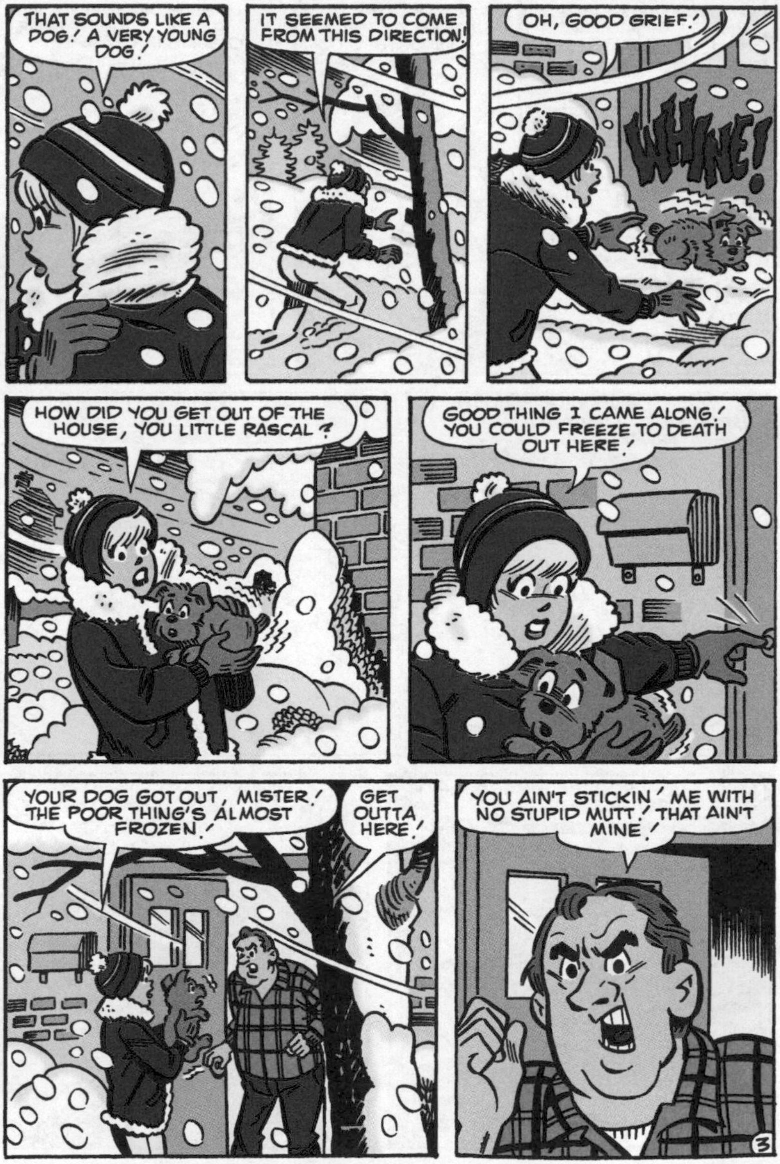
THAT SOUNDS LIKE A DOG! A VERY YOUNG DOG!
IT SEEMED TO COME FROM THIS DIRECTION!
OH, GOOD GRIEF!
WHINE!
HOW DID YOU GET OUT OF THE HOUSE, YOU LITTLE RASCAL?
GOOD THING I CAME ALONG! YOU COULD FREEZE TO DEATH OUT HERE!
YOUR DOG GOT OUT, MISTER! THE POOR THING'S ALMOST FROZEN!
GET OUTTA HERE!
YOU AIN'T STICKIN' ME WITH NO STUPID MUTT! THAT AIN'T MINE!
3

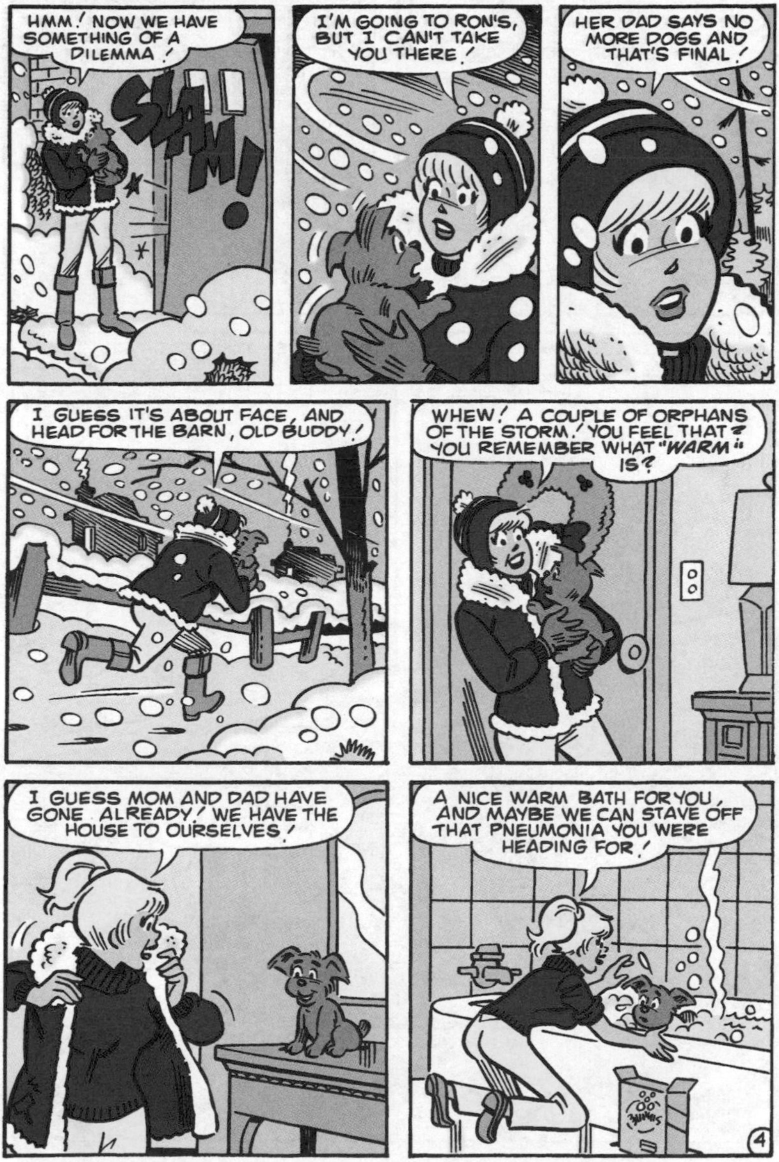
HMM! NOW WE HAVE SOMETHING OF A DILEMMA!
SLAM!
I'M GOING TO RON'S, BUT I CAN'T TAKE YOU THERE!
HER DAD SAYS NO MORE DOGS AND THAT'S FINAL!
I GUESS IT'S ABOUT FACE, AND HEAD FOR THE BARN, OLD BUDDY!
WHEW! A COUPLE OF ORPHANS OF THE STORM! YOU FEEL THAT? YOU REMEMBER WHAT "WARM" IS?
I GUESS MOM AND DAD HAVE GONE ALREADY! WE HAVE THE HOUSE TO OURSELVES!
A NICE WARM BATH FOR YOU, AND MAYBE WE CAN STAVE OFF THAT PNEUMONIA YOU WERE HEADING FOR!
4

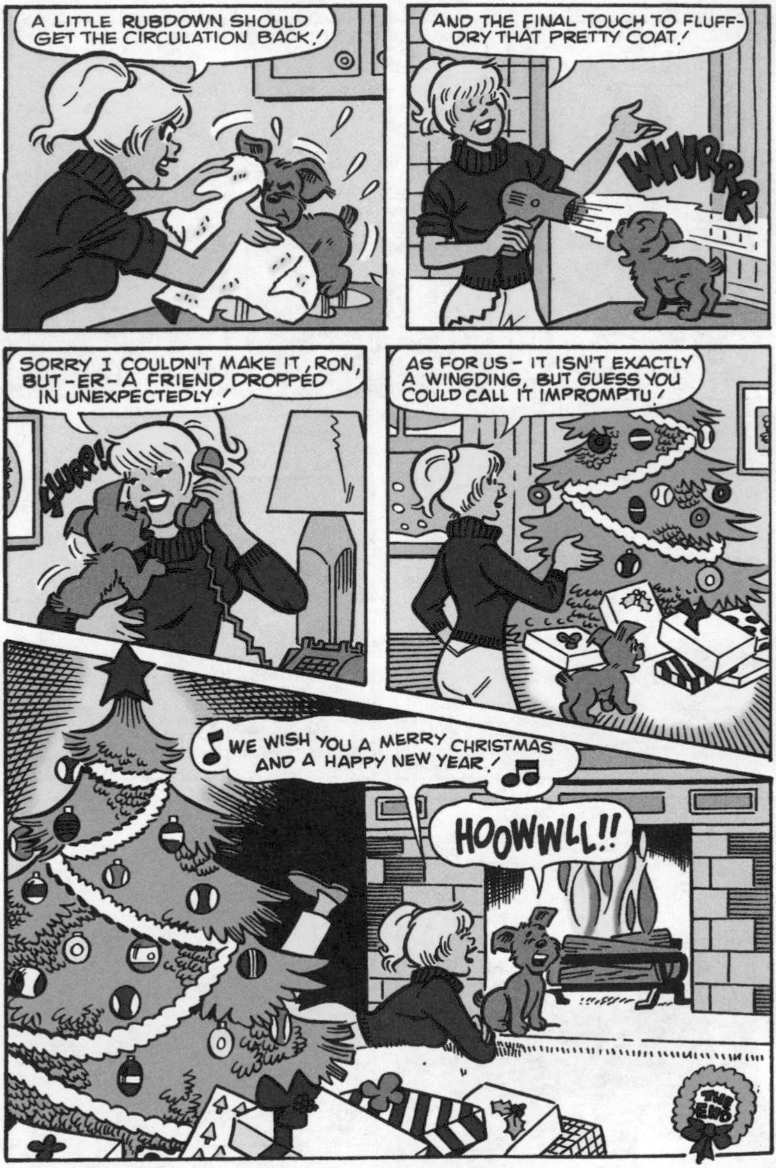

A LITTLE RUBDOWN SHOULD GET THE CIRCULATION BACK!
AND THE FINAL TOUCH TO FLUFF-DRY THAT PRETTY COAT!
WHIRRR
SORRY I COULDN'T MAKE IT, RON, BUT-ER-A FRIEND DROPPED IN UNEXPECTEDLY!
SLURP!
AS FOR US - IT ISN'T EXACTLY A WINGDING, BUT GUESS YOU COULD CALL IT IMPROMPTU!
WE WISH YOU A MERRY CHRISTMAS AND A HAPPY NEW YEAR!
HOOWWLL!!
THE END

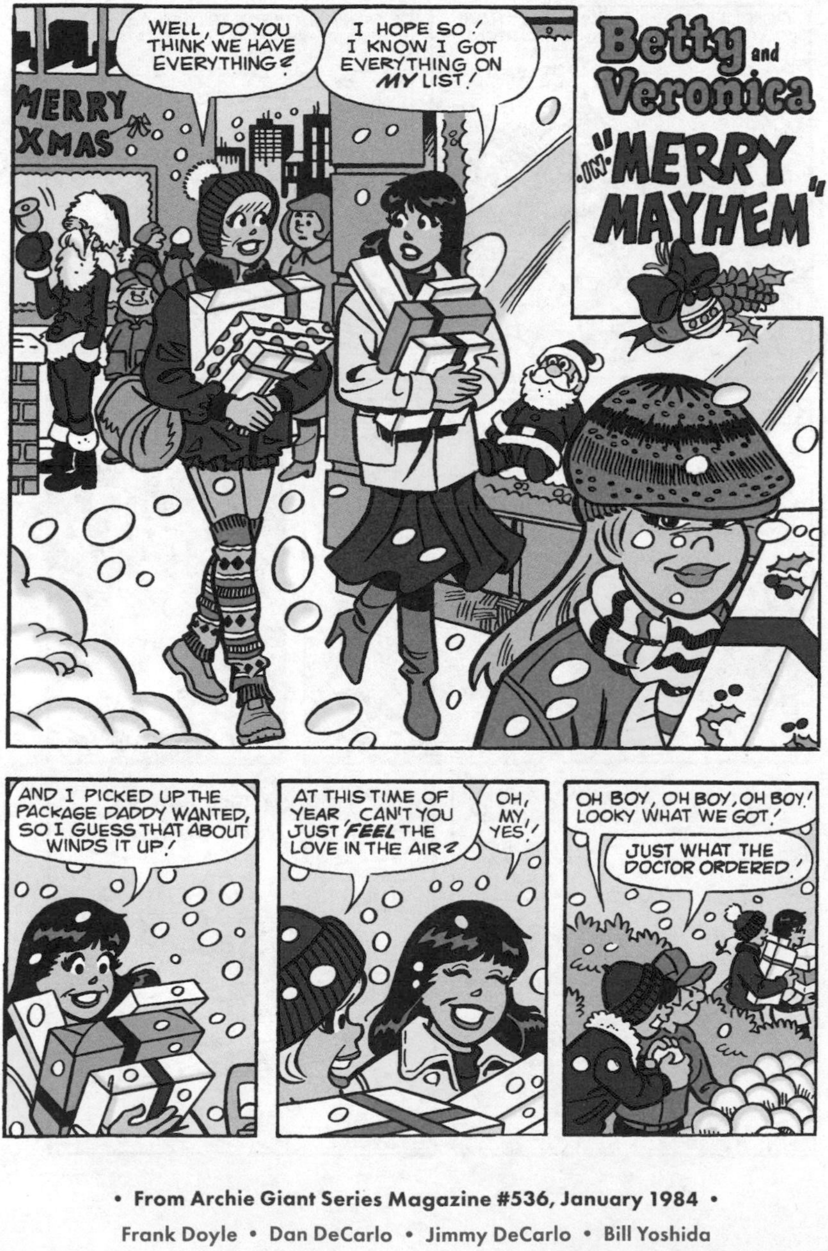
Betty and Veronica
·IN· "MERRY MAYHEM"
MERRY XMAS
WELL, DO YOU THINK WE HAVE EVERYTHING?
I HOPE SO! I KNOW I GOT EVERYTHING ON MY LIST!
AND I PICKED UP THE PACKAGE DADDY WANTED, SO I GUESS THAT ABOUT WINDS IT UP!
AT THIS TIME OF YEAR, CAN'T YOU JUST FEEL THE LOVE IN THE AIR?
OH, MY, YES!
OH BOY, OH BOY, OH BOY! LOOKY WHAT WE GOT!
JUST WHAT THE DOCTOR ORDERED!

• From Archie Giant Series Magazine #536, January 1984 •

Frank Doyle • Dan DeCarlo • Jimmy DeCarlo • Bill Yoshida

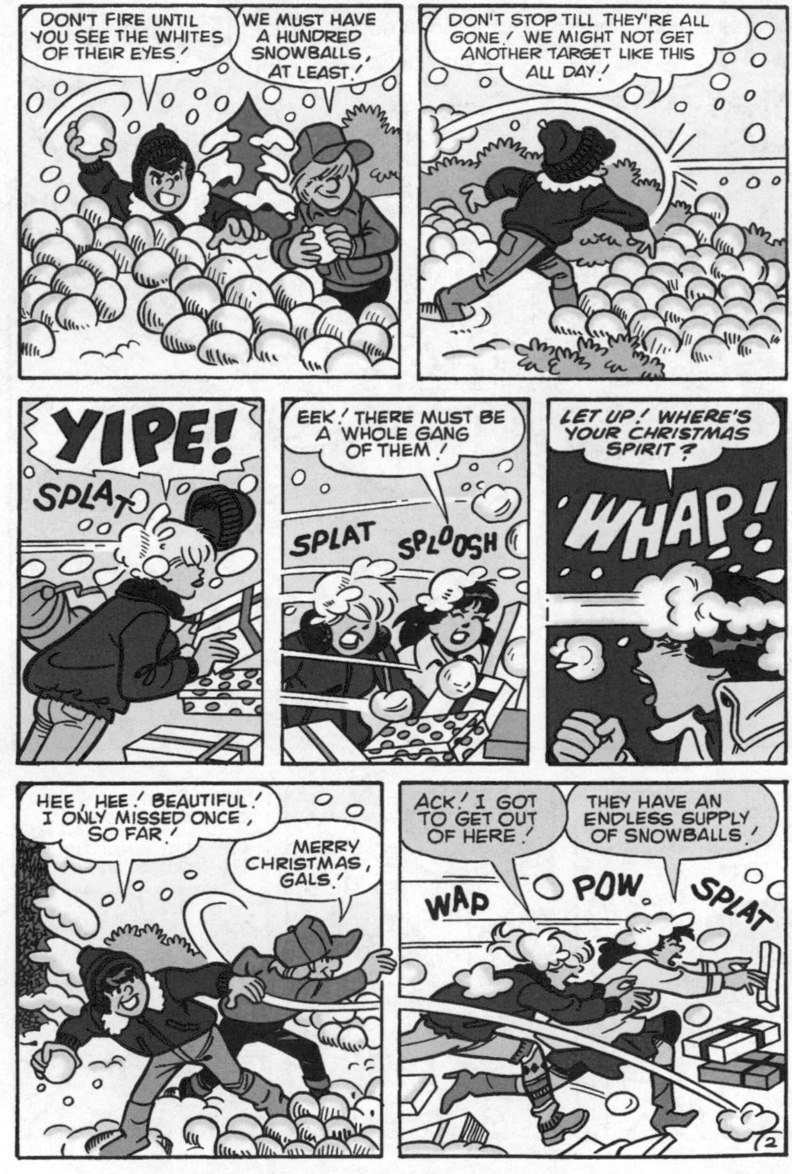
DON'T FIRE UNTIL YOU SEE THE WHITES OF THEIR EYES!
WE MUST HAVE A HUNDRED SNOWBALLS, AT LEAST!
DON'T STOP TILL THEY'RE ALL GONE! WE MIGHT NOT GET ANOTHER TARGET LIKE THIS ALL DAY!
YIPE!
SPLAT
EEK! THERE MUST BE A WHOLE GANG OF THEM!
SPLAT
SPLOOSH
LET UP! WHERE'S YOUR CHRISTMAS SPIRIT?
WHAP!
HEE, HEE! BEAUTIFUL! I ONLY MISSED ONCE, SO FAR!
MERRY CHRISTMAS, GALS!
ACK! I GOT TO GET OUT OF HERE!
THEY HAVE AN ENDLESS SUPPLY OF SNOWBALLS!
WAP
POW
SPLAT
2

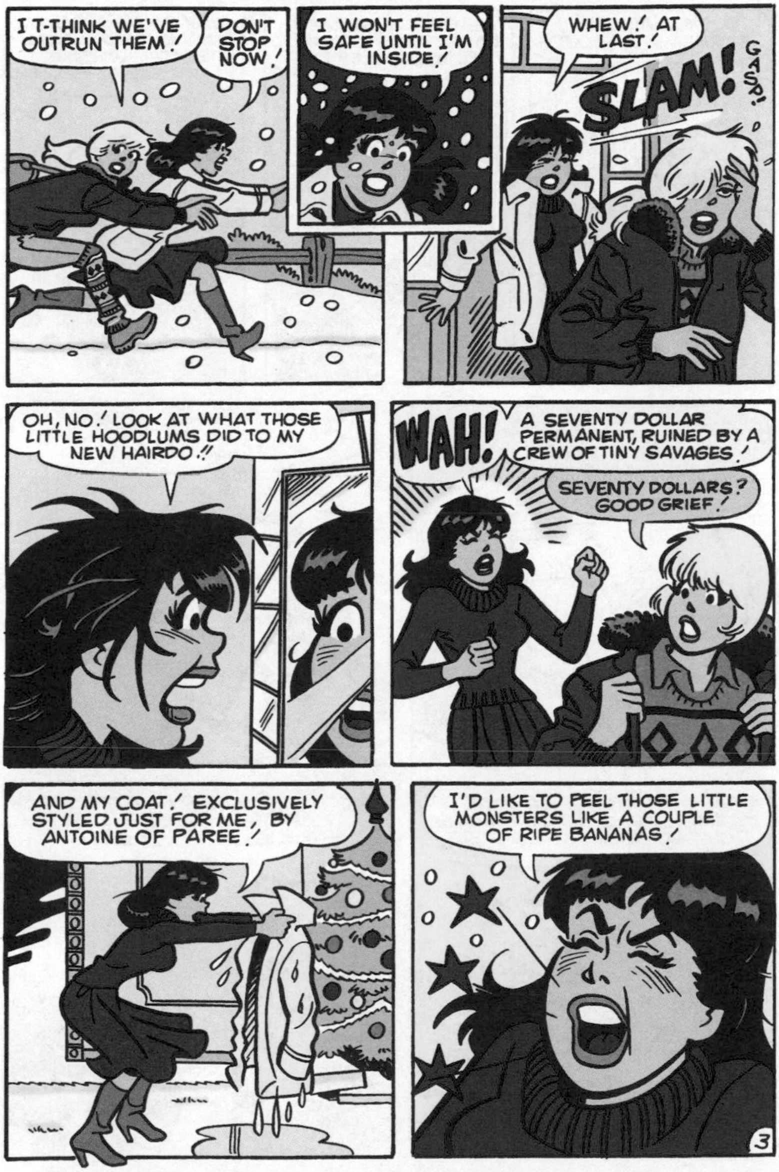
I T-THINK WE'VE OUTRUN THEM!
DON'T STOP NOW!
I WON'T FEEL SAFE UNTIL I'M INSIDE!
WHEW! AT LAST!
SLAM!
GASP!
OH, NO! LOOK AT WHAT THOSE LITTLE HOODLUMS DID TO MY NEW HAIRDO!!
WAH!
A SEVENTY DOLLAR PERMANENT, RUINED BY A CREW OF TINY SAVAGES!
SEVENTY DOLLARS? GOOD GRIEF!
AND MY COAT! EXCLUSIVELY STYLED JUST FOR ME, BY ANTOINE OF PAREE!
I'D LIKE TO PEEL THOSE LITTLE MONSTERS LIKE A COUPLE OF RIPE BANANAS!
3

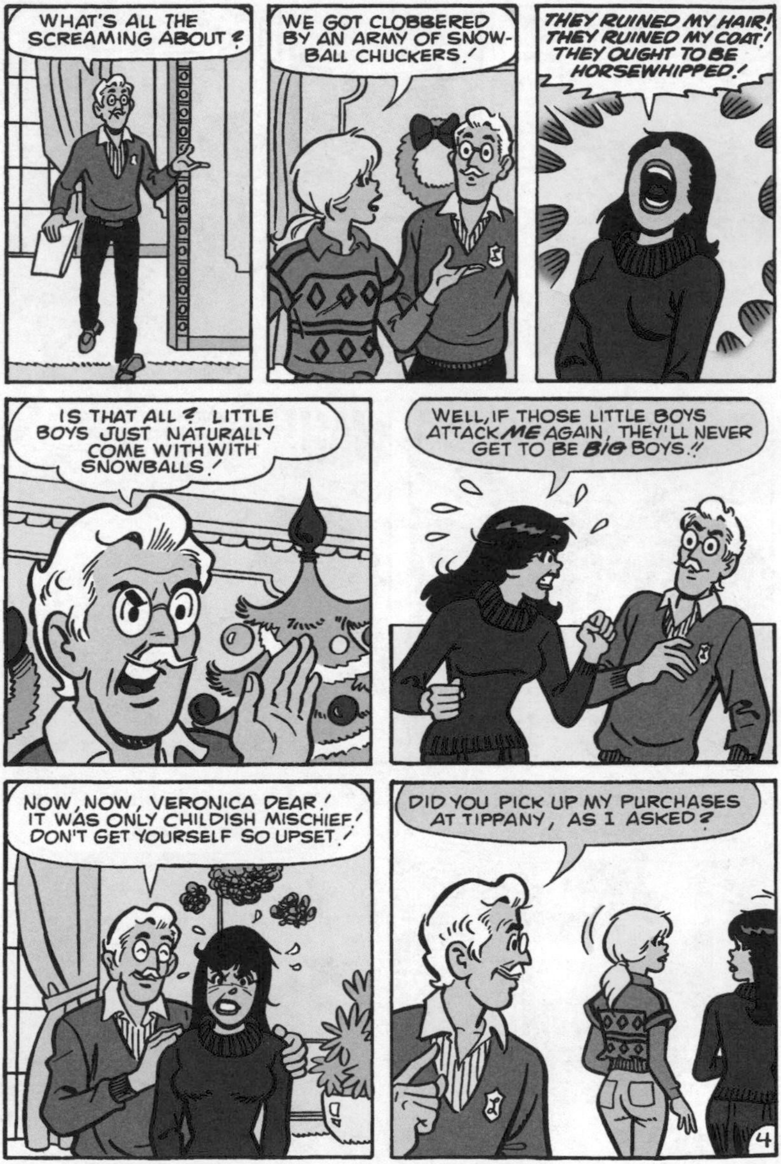
WHAT'S ALL THE SCREAMING ABOUT ?
WE GOT CLOBBERED BY AN ARMY OF SNOW-BALL CHUCKERS !
THEY RUINED MY HAIR! THEY RUINED MY COAT! THEY OUGHT TO BE HORSEWHIPPED!
IS THAT ALL ? LITTLE BOYS JUST NATURALLY COME WITH WITH SNOWBALLS !
WELL, IF THOSE LITTLE BOYS ATTACK ME AGAIN, THEY'LL NEVER GET TO BE BIG BOYS !!
NOW, NOW, VERONICA DEAR ! IT WAS ONLY CHILDISH MISCHIEF ! DON'T GET YOURSELF SO UPSET !
DID YOU PICK UP MY PURCHASES AT TIPPANY, AS I ASKED ?
4

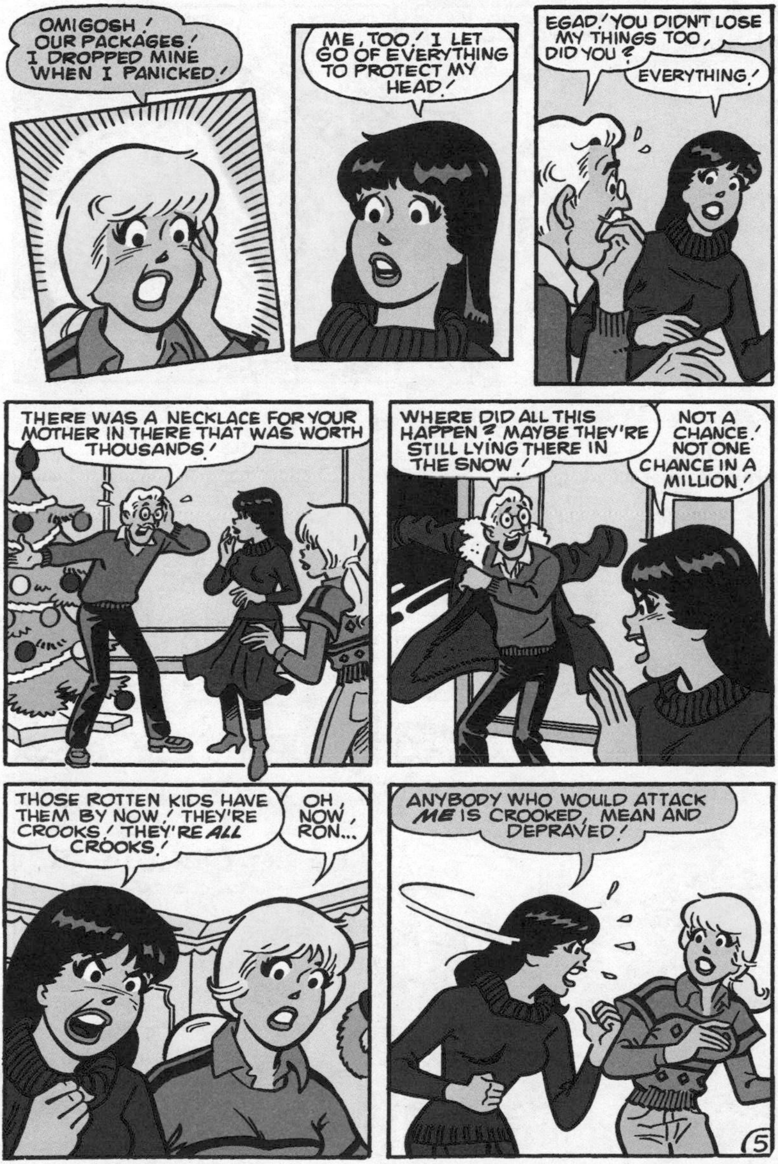
OMIGOSH! OUR PACKAGES! I DROPPED MINE WHEN I PANICKED!
ME, TOO! I LET GO OF EVERYTHING TO PROTECT MY HEAD!
EGAD! YOU DIDN'T LOSE MY THINGS TOO, DID YOU?
EVERYTHING!
THERE WAS A NECKLACE FOR YOUR MOTHER IN THERE THAT WAS WORTH THOUSANDS!
WHERE DID ALL THIS HAPPEN? MAYBE THEY'RE STILL LYING THERE IN THE SNOW!
NOT A CHANCE! NOT ONE CHANCE IN A MILLION!
THOSE ROTTEN KIDS HAVE THEM BY NOW! THEY'RE CROOKS! THEY'RE ALL CROOKS!
OH, NOW, RON...
ANYBODY WHO WOULD ATTACK ME IS CROOKED, MEAN AND DEPRAVED!
5

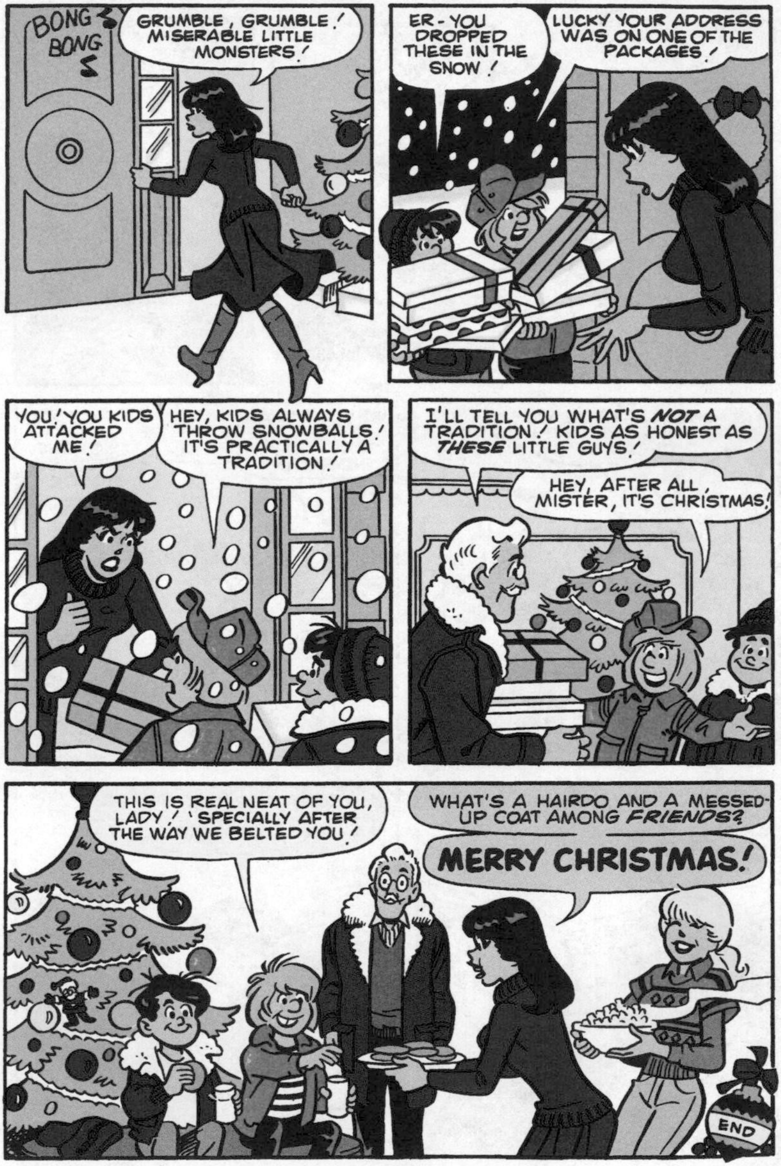
BONG BONG
GRUMBLE, GRUMBLE! MISERABLE LITTLE MONSTERS!
ER-YOU DROPPED THESE IN THE SNOW!
LUCKY YOUR ADDRESS WAS ON ONE OF THE PACKAGES!
YOU! YOU KIDS ATTACKED ME!
HEY, KIDS ALWAYS THROW SNOWBALLS! IT'S PRACTICALLY A TRADITION!
I'LL TELL YOU WHAT'S NOT A TRADITION! KIDS AS HONEST AS THESE LITTLE GUYS!
HEY, AFTER ALL, MISTER, IT'S CHRISTMAS!
THIS IS REAL NEAT OF YOU, LADY! 'SPECIALLY AFTER THE WAY WE BELTED YOU!
WHAT'S A HAIRDO AND A MESSED-UP COAT AMONG FRIENDS?
MERRY CHRISTMAS!
END

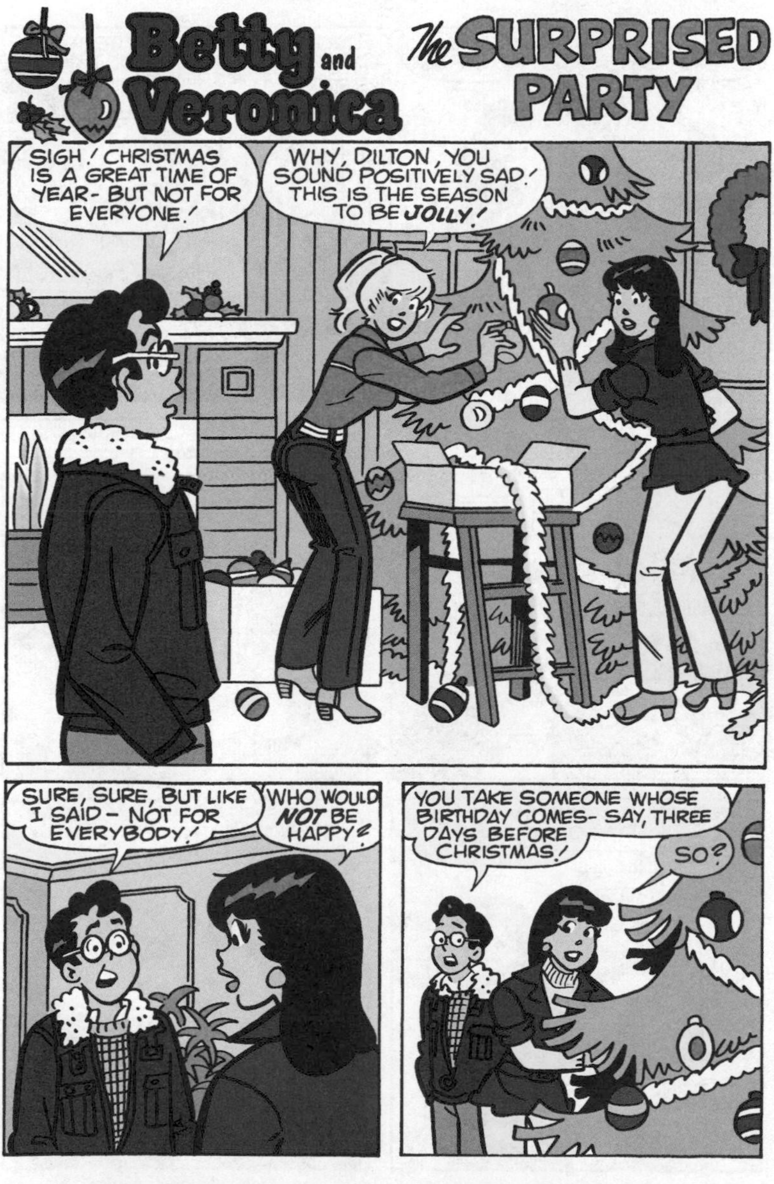
Betty and Veronica
The SURPRISED PARTY
SIGH! CHRISTMAS IS A GREAT TIME OF YEAR- BUT NOT FOR EVERYONE!
WHY, DILTON, YOU SOUND POSITIVELY SAD! THIS IS THE SEASON TO BE JOLLY!
SURE, SURE, BUT LIKE I SAID - NOT FOR EVERYBODY!
WHO WOULD NOT BE HAPPY?
YOU TAKE SOMEONE WHOSE BIRTHDAY COMES- SAY, THREE DAYS BEFORE CHRISTMAS!
SO?

• **From Archie Giant Series Magazine #536, January 1984** •

Frank Doyle • Stan Goldberg • Rudy Lapick • Bill Yoshida

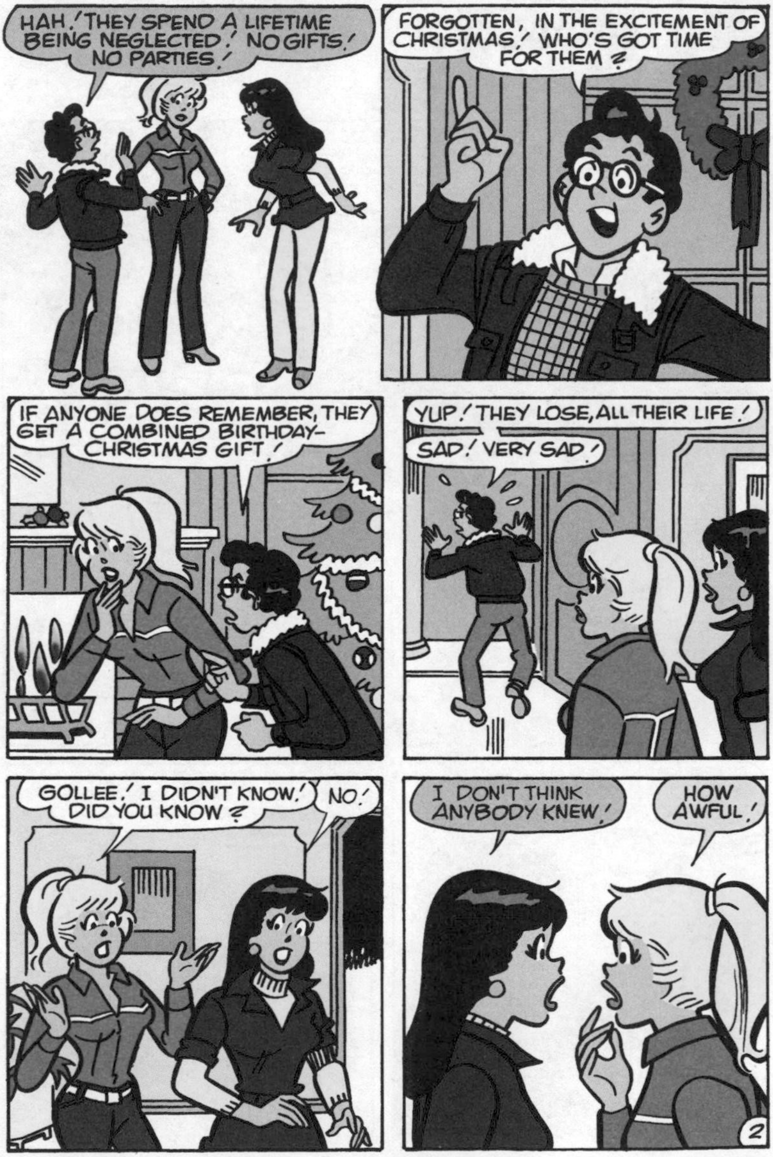
HAH! THEY SPEND A LIFETIME BEING NEGLECTED! NO GIFTS! NO PARTIES!
FORGOTTEN, IN THE EXCITEMENT OF CHRISTMAS! WHO'S GOT TIME FOR THEM ?
IF ANYONE DOES REMEMBER, THEY GET A COMBINED BIRTHDAY-CHRISTMAS GIFT!
YUP! THEY LOSE, ALL THEIR LIFE!
SAD! VERY SAD!
GOLLEE! I DIDN'T KNOW! DID YOU KNOW ?
NO!
I DON'T THINK ANYBODY KNEW!
HOW AWFUL!
2

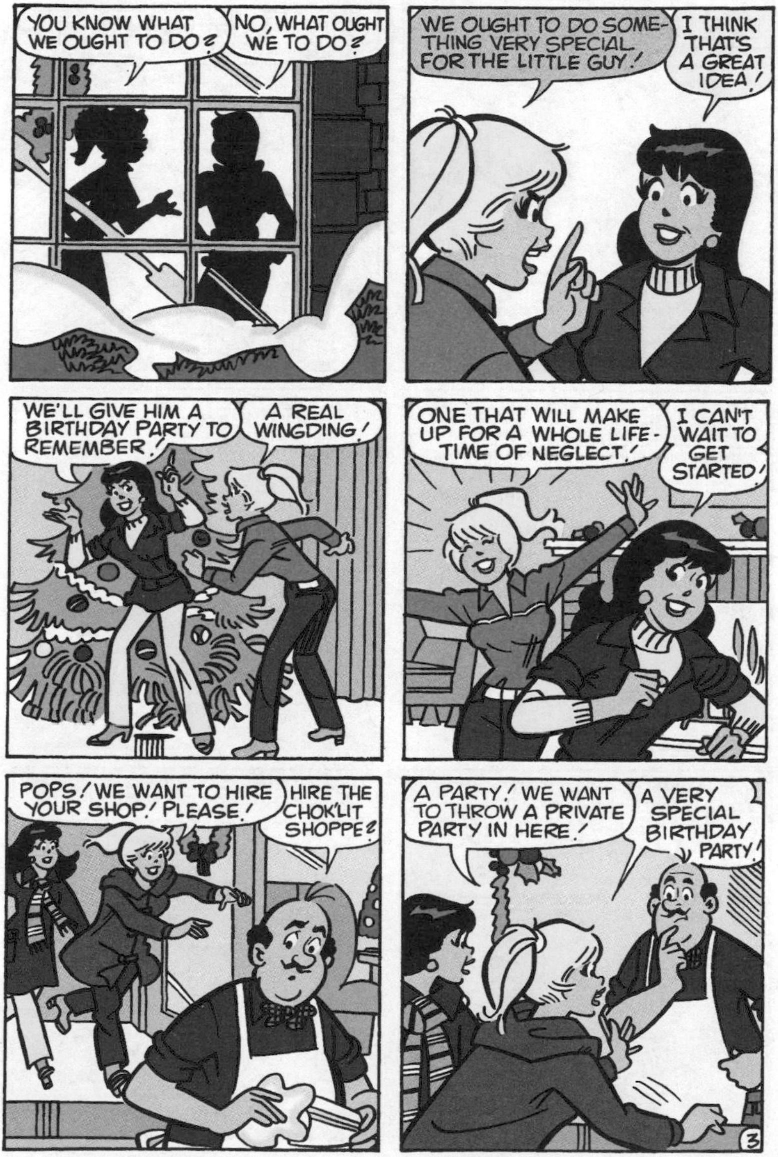
YOU KNOW WHAT WE OUGHT TO DO?
NO, WHAT OUGHT WE TO DO?
WE OUGHT TO DO SOMETHING VERY SPECIAL FOR THE LITTLE GUY!
I THINK THAT'S A GREAT IDEA!
WE'LL GIVE HIM A BIRTHDAY PARTY TO REMEMBER!
A REAL WINGDING!
ONE THAT WILL MAKE UP FOR A WHOLE LIFETIME OF NEGLECT!
I CAN'T WAIT TO GET STARTED!
POPS! WE WANT TO HIRE YOUR SHOP! PLEASE!
HIRE THE CHOK'LIT SHOPPE?
A PARTY! WE WANT TO THROW A PRIVATE PARTY IN HERE!
A VERY SPECIAL BIRTHDAY PARTY!
3

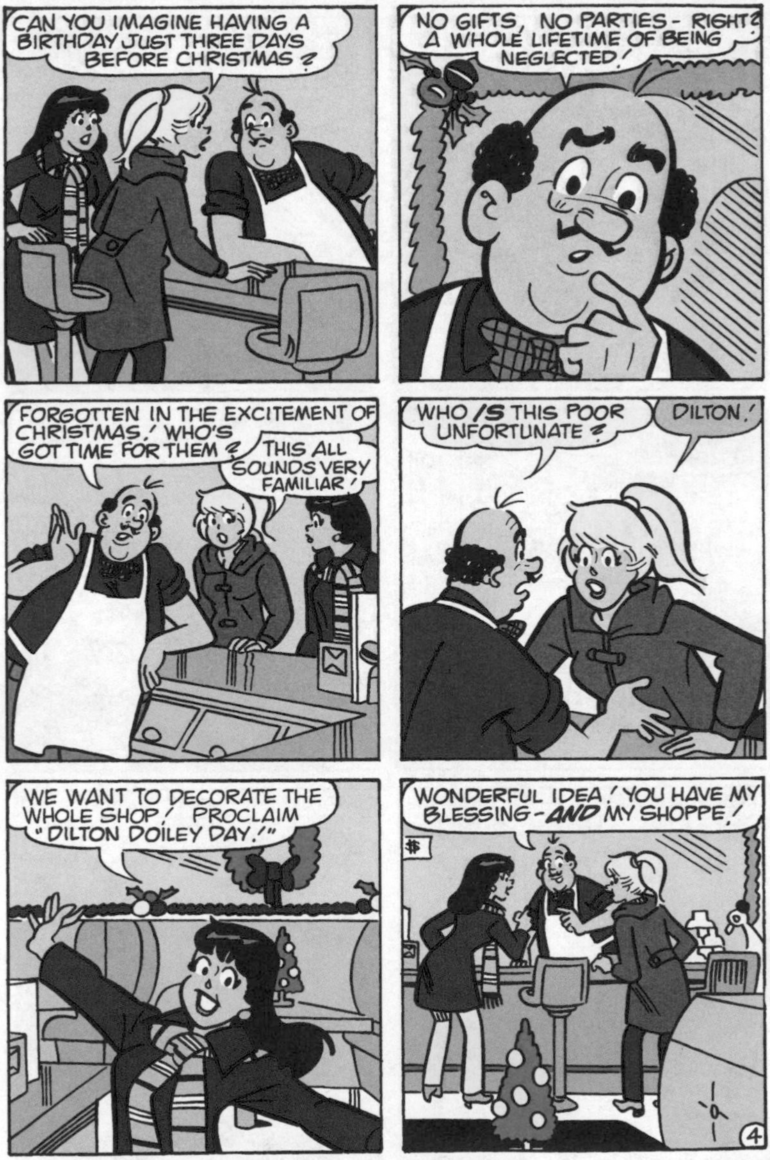
CAN YOU IMAGINE HAVING A BIRTHDAY JUST THREE DAYS BEFORE CHRISTMAS?
NO GIFTS, NO PARTIES - RIGHT? A WHOLE LIFETIME OF BEING NEGLECTED!
FORGOTTEN IN THE EXCITEMENT OF CHRISTMAS! WHO'S GOT TIME FOR THEM?
THIS ALL SOUNDS VERY FAMILIAR!
WHO IS THIS POOR UNFORTUNATE?
DILTON!
WE WANT TO DECORATE THE WHOLE SHOP! PROCLAIM "DILTON DOILEY DAY!"
WONDERFUL IDEA! YOU HAVE MY BLESSING - AND MY SHOPPE!
4

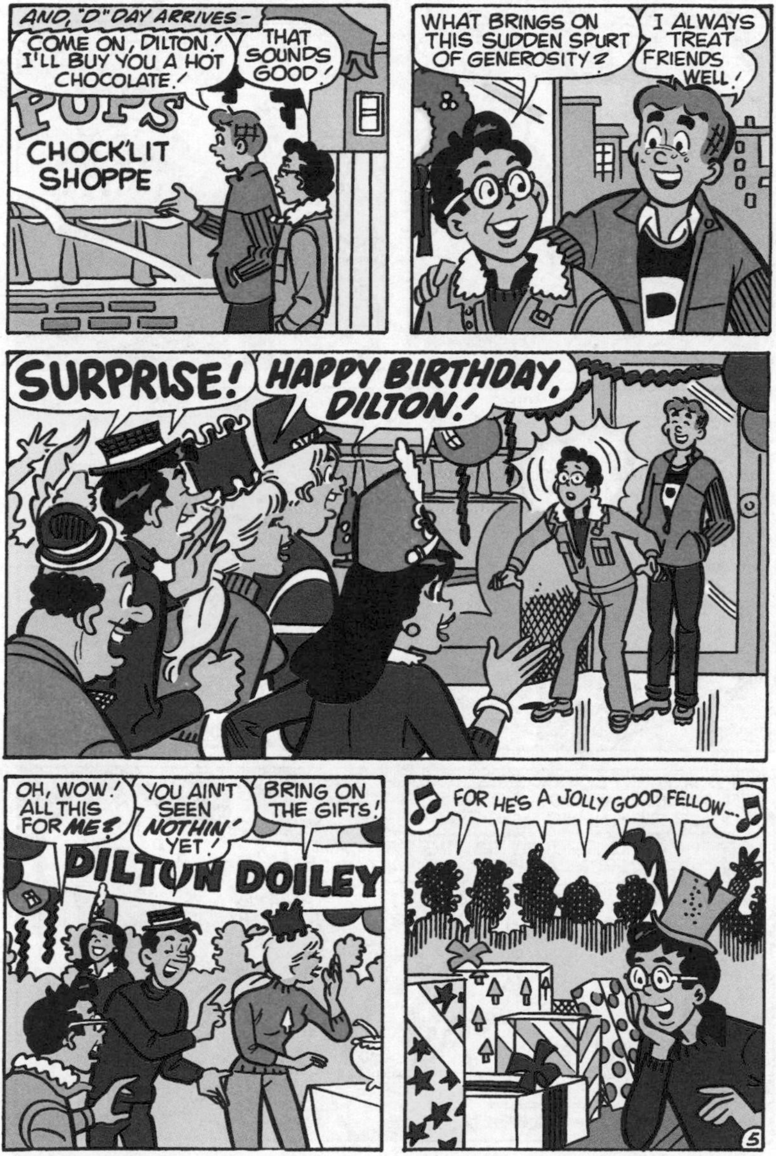
AND, "D" DAY ARRIVES -
COME ON, DILTON! I'LL BUY YOU A HOT CHOCOLATE!
THAT SOUNDS GOOD!
POP'S
CHOCK'LIT SHOPPE
WHAT BRINGS ON THIS SUDDEN SPURT OF GENEROSITY?
I ALWAYS TREAT FRIENDS WELL!
SURPRISE!
HAPPY BIRTHDAY, DILTON!
OH, WOW! ALL THIS FOR ME?
YOU AIN'T SEEN NOTHIN' YET!
BRING ON THE GIFTS!
DILTON DOILEY
FOR HE'S A JOLLY GOOD FELLOW...
5

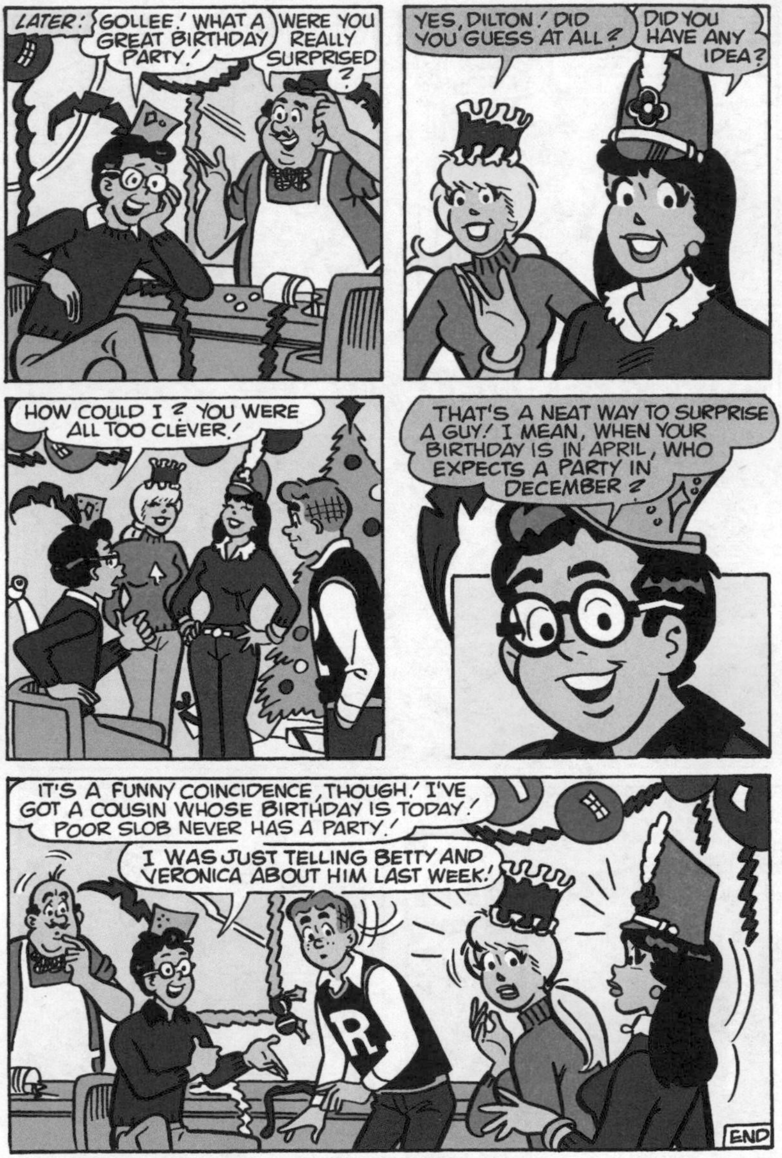
LATER:
GOLLEE! WHAT A GREAT BIRTHDAY PARTY!
WERE YOU REALLY SURPRISED?
YES, DILTON! DID YOU GUESS AT ALL?
DID YOU HAVE ANY IDEA?
HOW COULD I? YOU WERE ALL TOO CLEVER!
THAT'S A NEAT WAY TO SURPRISE A GUY! I MEAN, WHEN YOUR BIRTHDAY IS IN APRIL, WHO EXPECTS A PARTY IN DECEMBER?
IT'S A FUNNY COINCIDENCE, THOUGH! I'VE GOT A COUSIN WHOSE BIRTHDAY IS TODAY! POOR SLOB NEVER HAS A PARTY!
I WAS JUST TELLING BETTY AND VERONICA ABOUT HIM LAST WEEK!
END

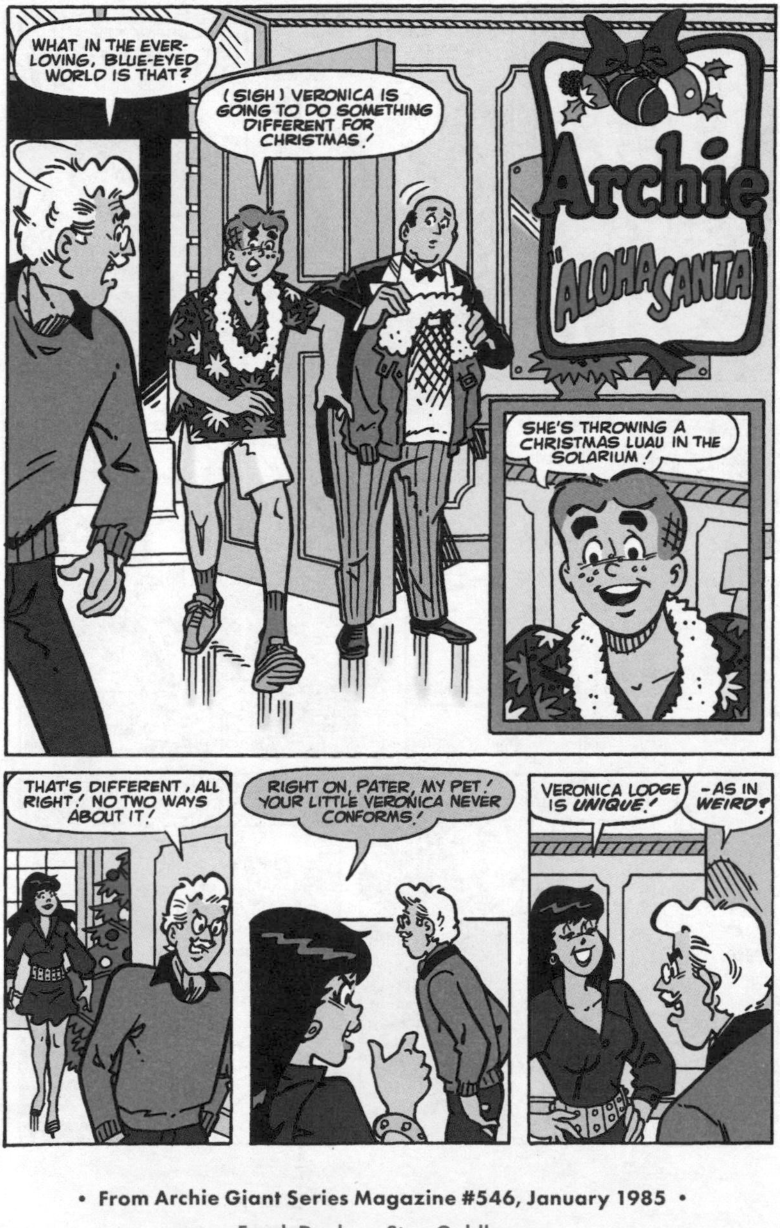
WHAT IN THE EVER-LOVING, BLUE-EYED WORLD IS THAT?
(SIGH) VERONICA IS GOING TO DO SOMETHING DIFFERENT FOR CHRISTMAS!
Archie
"ALOHA SANTA"
SHE'S THROWING A CHRISTMAS LUAU IN THE SOLARIUM!
THAT'S DIFFERENT, ALL RIGHT! NO TWO WAYS ABOUT IT!
RIGHT ON, PATER, MY PET! YOUR LITTLE VERONICA NEVER CONFORMS!
VERONICA LODGE IS UNIQUE!
-AS IN WEIRD?

• **From Archie Giant Series Magazine #546, January 1985** •

Frank Doyle • Stan Goldberg

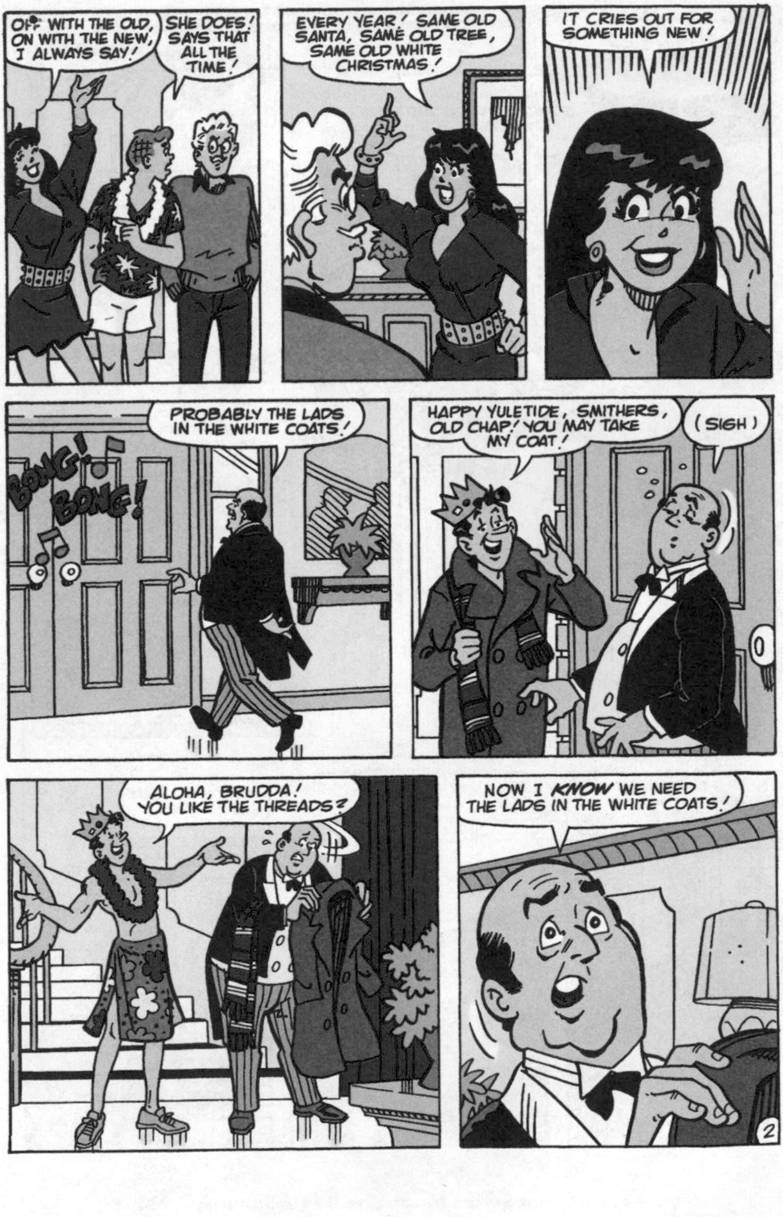
OFF WITH THE OLD, ON WITH THE NEW, I ALWAYS SAY!
SHE DOES! SAYS THAT ALL THE TIME!
EVERY YEAR! SAME OLD SANTA, SAME OLD TREE, SAME OLD WHITE CHRISTMAS!
IT CRIES OUT FOR SOMETHING NEW!
BONG! BONG!
PROBABLY THE LADS IN THE WHITE COATS!
HAPPY YULETIDE, SMITHERS, OLD CHAP! YOU MAY TAKE MY COAT!
(SIGH)
ALOHA, BRUDDA! YOU LIKE THE THREADS?
NOW I KNOW WE NEED THE LADS IN THE WHITE COATS!
2

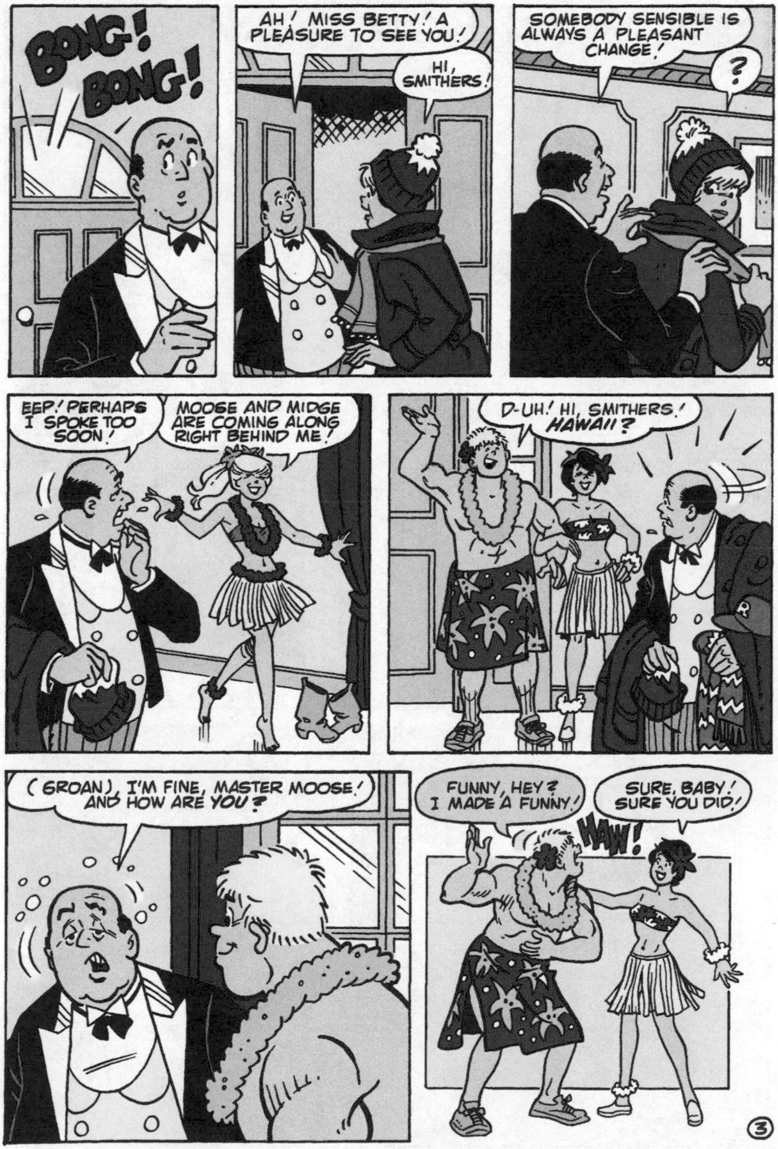
BONG! BONG!
AH! MISS BETTY! A PLEASURE TO SEE YOU!
HI, SMITHERS!
SOMEBODY SENSIBLE IS ALWAYS A PLEASANT CHANGE!
?
EEP! PERHAPS I SPOKE TOO SOON!
MOOSE AND MIDGE ARE COMING ALONG RIGHT BEHIND ME!
D-UH! HI, SMITHERS! HAWAII?
(GROAN), I'M FINE, MASTER MOOSE! AND HOW ARE YOU?
FUNNY, HEY? I MADE A FUNNY!
HAW!
SURE, BABY! SURE YOU DID!
3

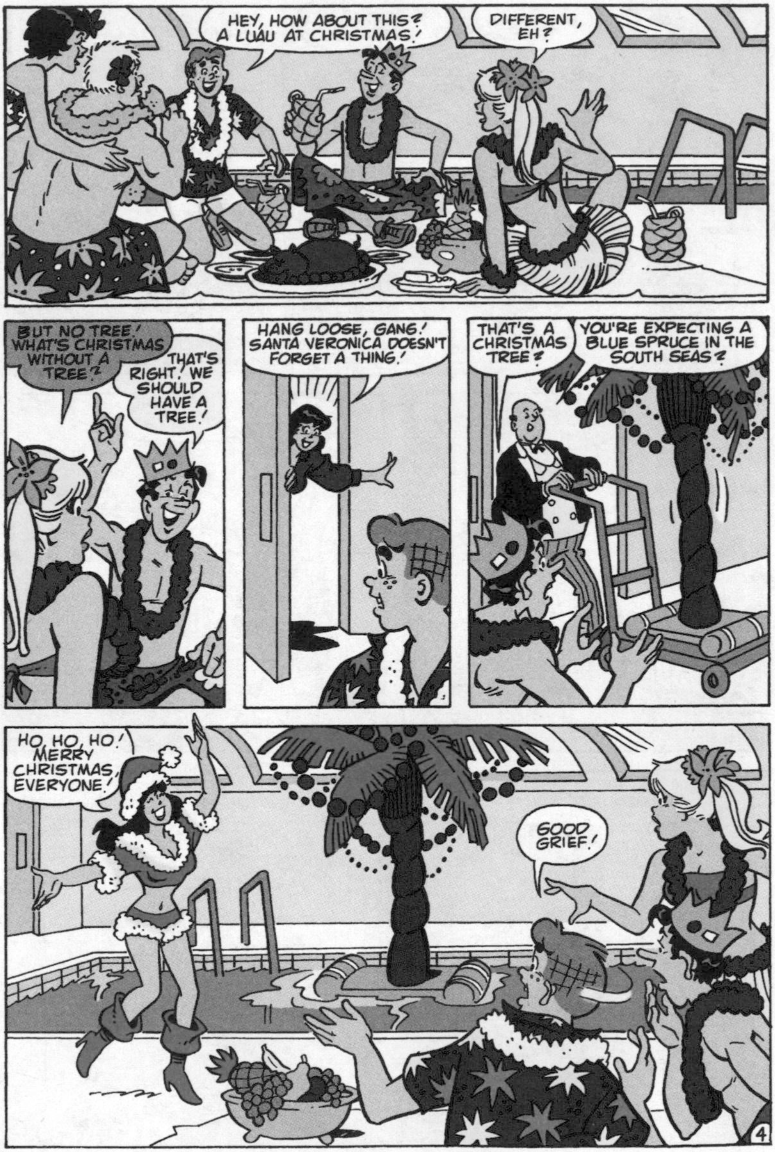
HEY, HOW ABOUT THIS? A LUAU AT CHRISTMAS!
DIFFERENT, EH?
BUT NO TREE! WHAT'S CHRISTMAS WITHOUT A TREE?
THAT'S RIGHT! WE SHOULD HAVE A TREE!
HANG LOOSE, GANG! SANTA VERONICA DOESN'T FORGET A THING!
THAT'S A CHRISTMAS TREE?
YOU'RE EXPECTING A BLUE SPRUCE IN THE SOUTH SEAS?
HO, HO, HO! MERRY CHRISTMAS, EVERYONE!
GOOD GRIEF!
4

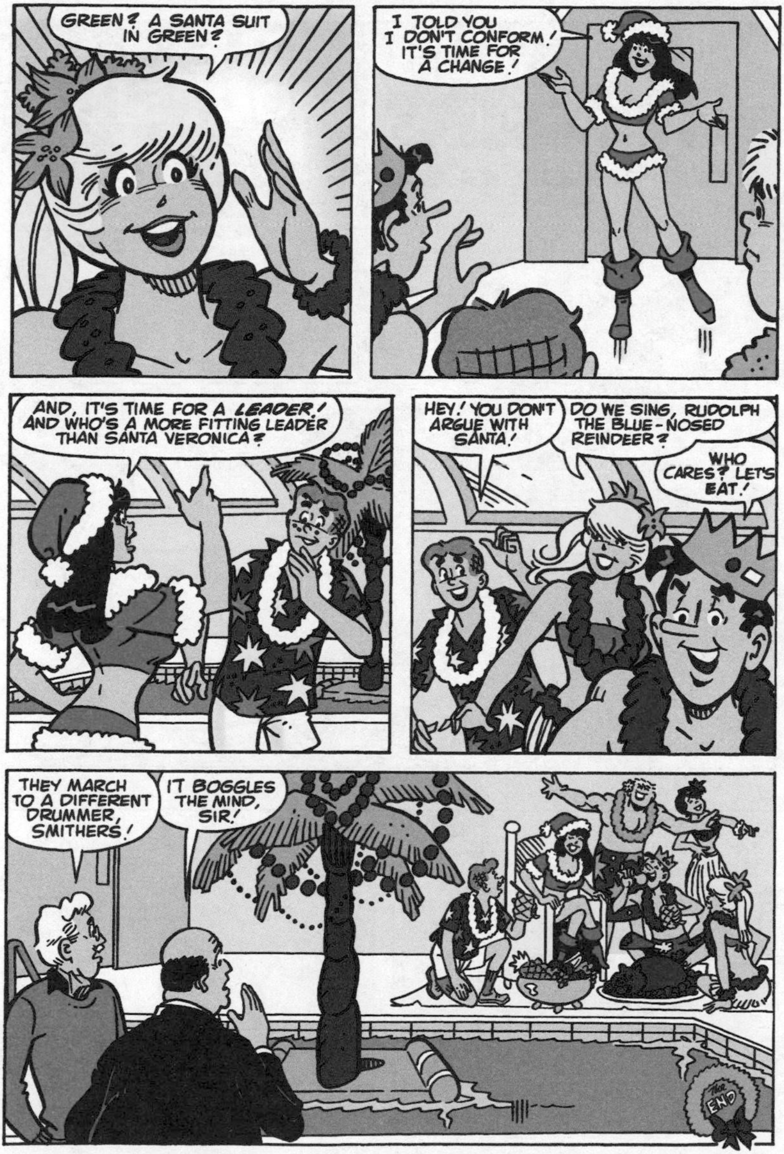
GREEN? A SANTA SUIT IN GREEN?
I TOLD YOU I DON'T CONFORM! IT'S TIME FOR A CHANGE!
AND, IT'S TIME FOR A LEADER! AND WHO'S A MORE FITTING LEADER THAN SANTA VERONICA?
HEY! YOU DON'T ARGUE WITH SANTA!
DO WE SING, RUDOLPH THE BLUE-NOSED REINDEER?
WHO CARES? LET'S EAT!
THEY MARCH TO A DIFFERENT DRUMMER, SMITHERS!
IT BOGGLES THE MIND, SIR!
The END

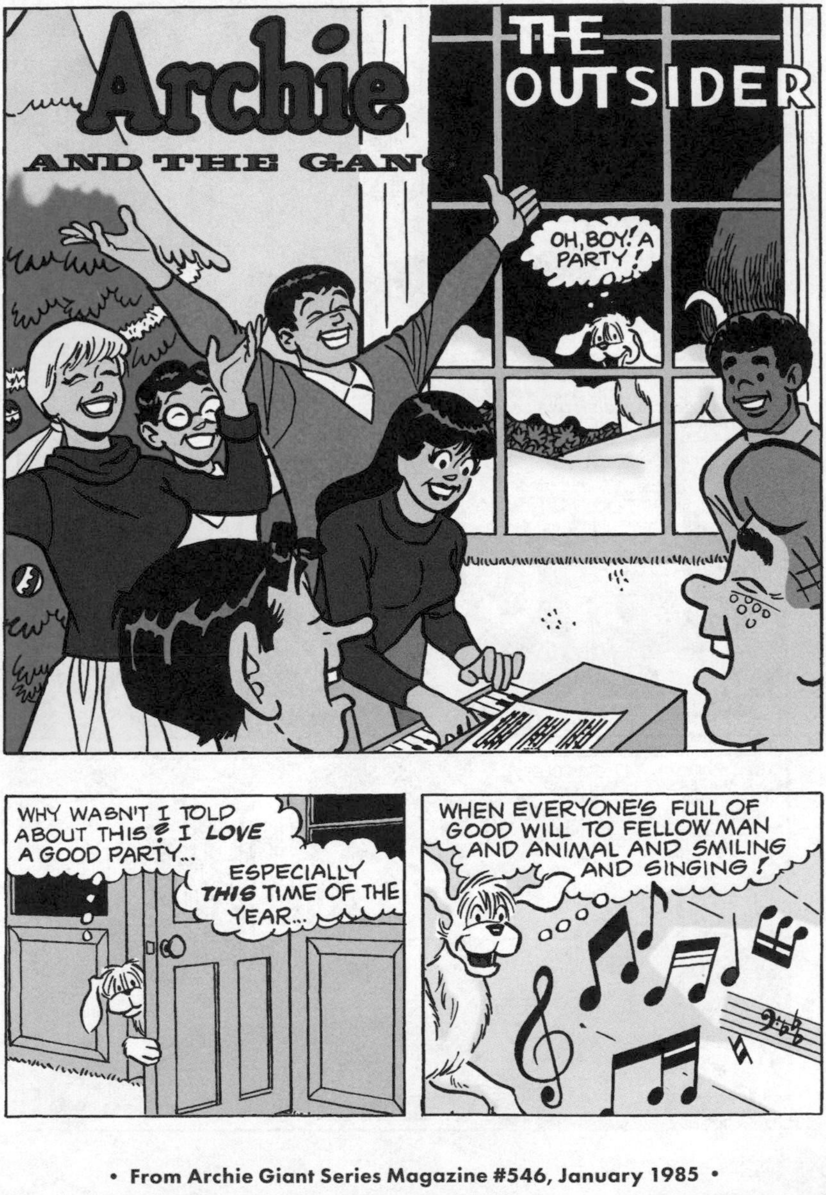
Archie
THE OUTSIDER
OH, BOY! A PARTY!
WHY WASN'T I TOLD ABOUT THIS? I *LOVE* A GOOD PARTY...
ESPECIALLY *THIS* TIME OF THE YEAR...
WHEN EVERYONE'S FULL OF GOOD WILL TO FELLOW MAN AND ANIMAL AND SMILING AND SINGING!

• From Archie Giant Series Magazine #546, January 1985 •

George Gladir • Samm Schwartz

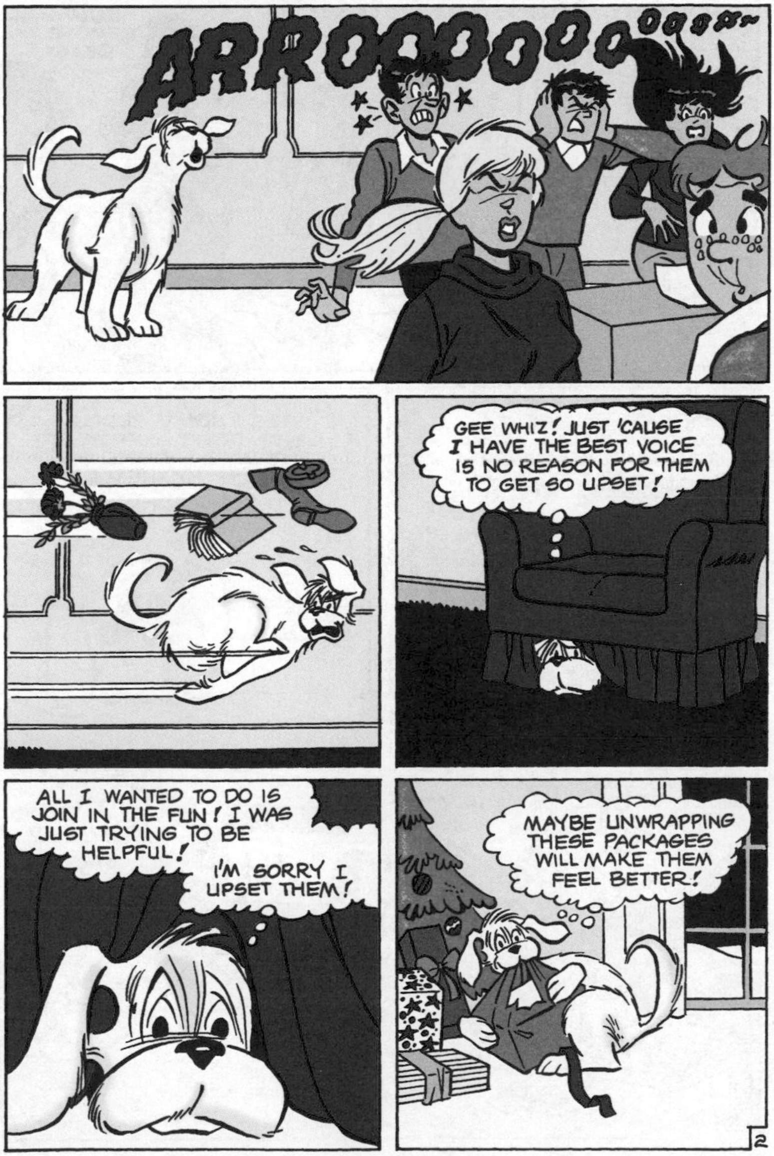
ARROOOOOOOOOOO
GEE WHIZ! JUST 'CAUSE I HAVE THE BEST VOICE IS NO REASON FOR THEM TO GET SO UPSET!
ALL I WANTED TO DO IS JOIN IN THE FUN! I WAS JUST TRYING TO BE HELPFUL!
I'M SORRY I UPSET THEM!
MAYBE UNWRAPPING THESE PACKAGES WILL MAKE THEM FEEL BETTER!
2

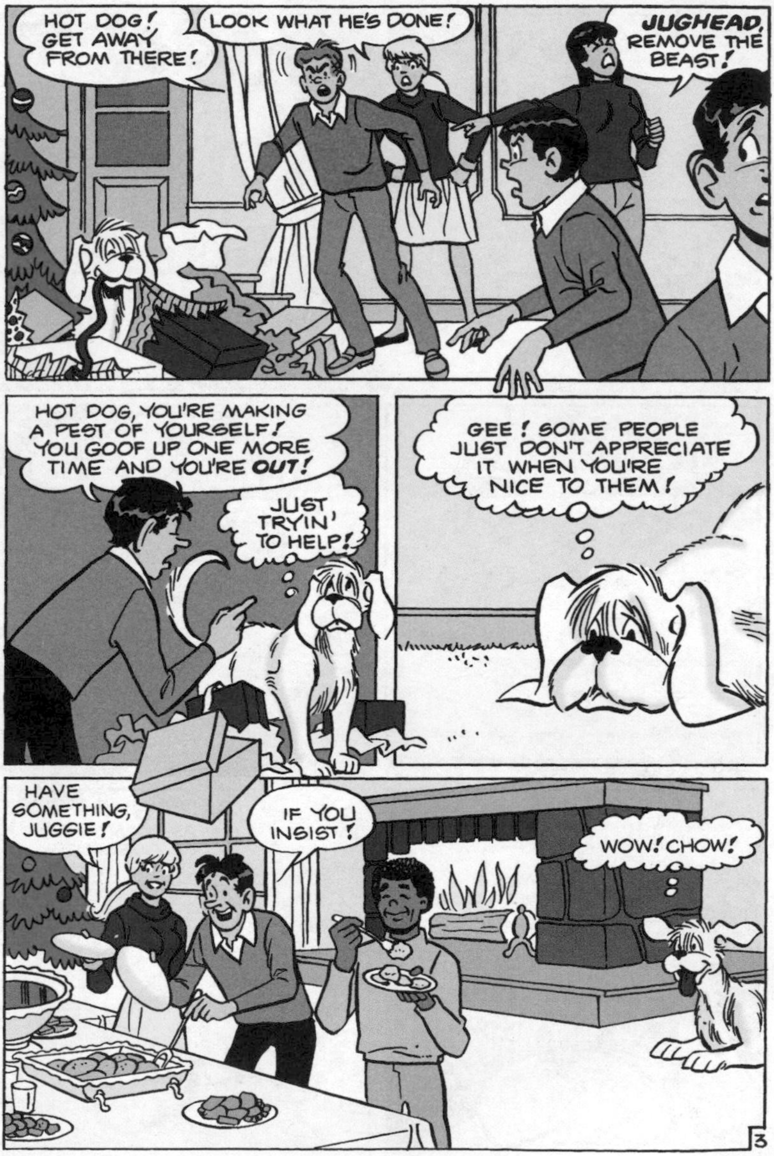
HOT DOG! GET AWAY FROM THERE!
LOOK WHAT HE'S DONE!
JUGHEAD, REMOVE THE BEAST!
HOT DOG, YOU'RE MAKING A PEST OF YOURSELF! YOU GOOF UP ONE MORE TIME AND YOU'RE OUT!
JUST TRYIN' TO HELP!
GEE! SOME PEOPLE JUST DON'T APPRECIATE IT WHEN YOU'RE NICE TO THEM!
HAVE SOMETHING, JUGGIE!
IF YOU INSIST!
WOW! CHOW!
3

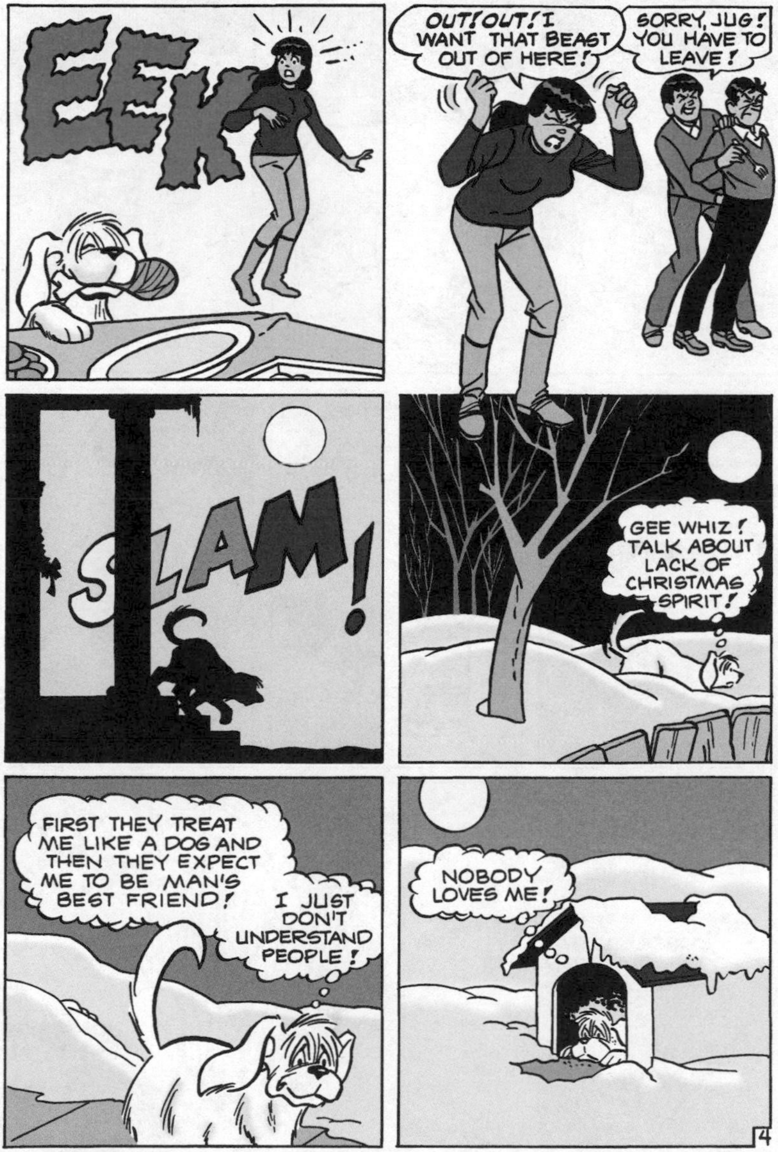
EEK
OUT! OUT! I WANT THAT BEAST OUT OF HERE!
SORRY, JUG! YOU HAVE TO LEAVE!
SLAM!
GEE WHIZ! TALK ABOUT LACK OF CHRISTMAS SPIRIT!
FIRST THEY TREAT ME LIKE A DOG AND THEN THEY EXPECT ME TO BE MAN'S BEST FRIEND!
I JUST DON'T UNDERSTAND PEOPLE!
NOBODY LOVES ME!
4

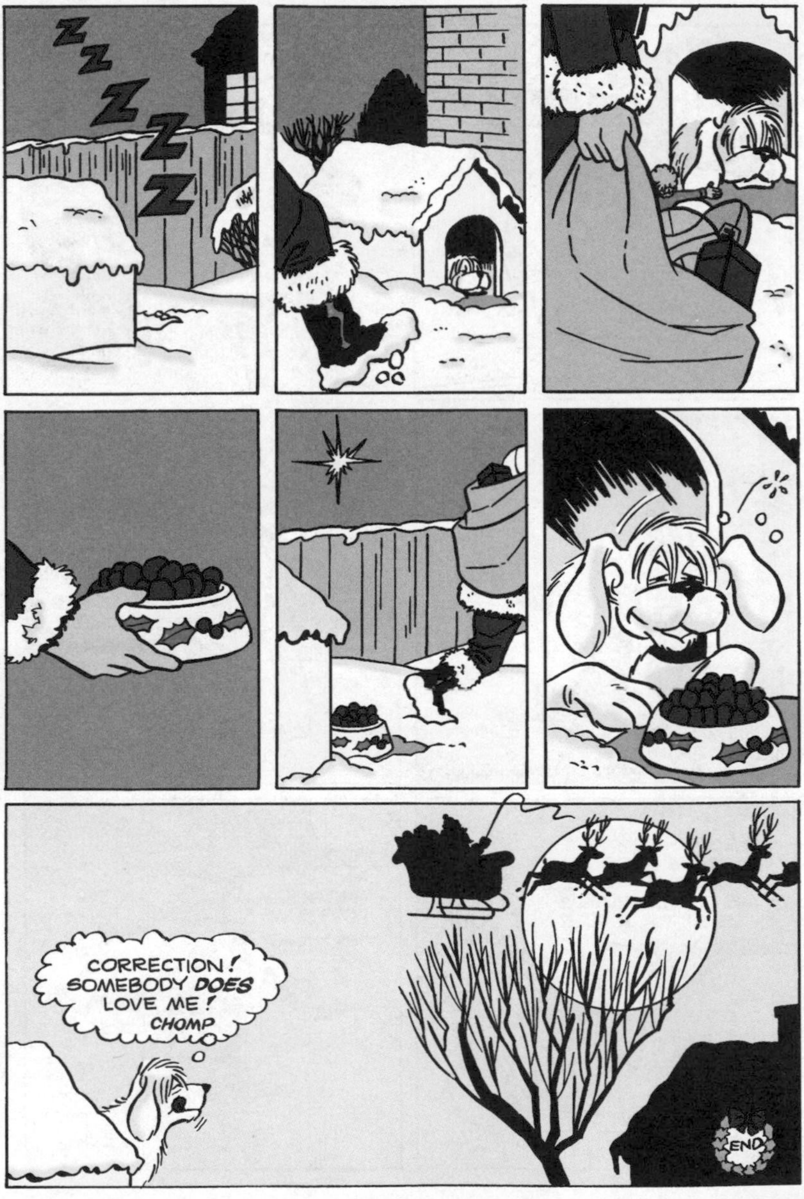
Z Z Z Z Z
CORRECTION! SOMEBODY DOES LOVE ME! CHOMP
END

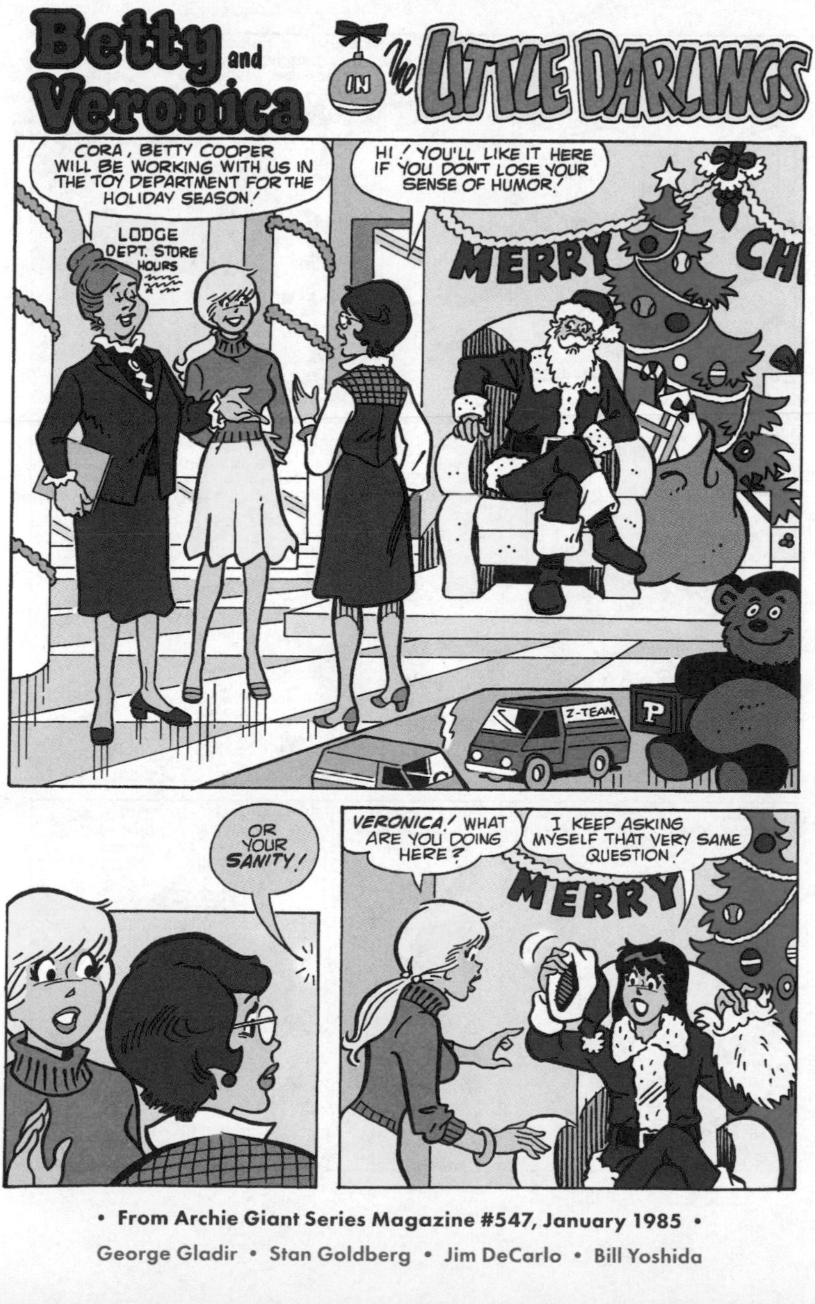
Betty and Veronica
IN
The LITTLE DARLINGS
CORA, BETTY COOPER WILL BE WORKING WITH US IN THE TOY DEPARTMENT FOR THE HOLIDAY SEASON!
HI! YOU'LL LIKE IT HERE IF YOU DON'T LOSE YOUR SENSE OF HUMOR!
LODGE DEPT. STORE HOURS
MERRY
Z-TEAM
P
OR YOUR SANITY!
VERONICA! WHAT ARE YOU DOING HERE?
I KEEP ASKING MYSELF THAT VERY SAME QUESTION!
MERRY

• **From Archie Giant Series Magazine #547, January 1985** •

George Gladir • Stan Goldberg • Jim DeCarlo • Bill Yoshida

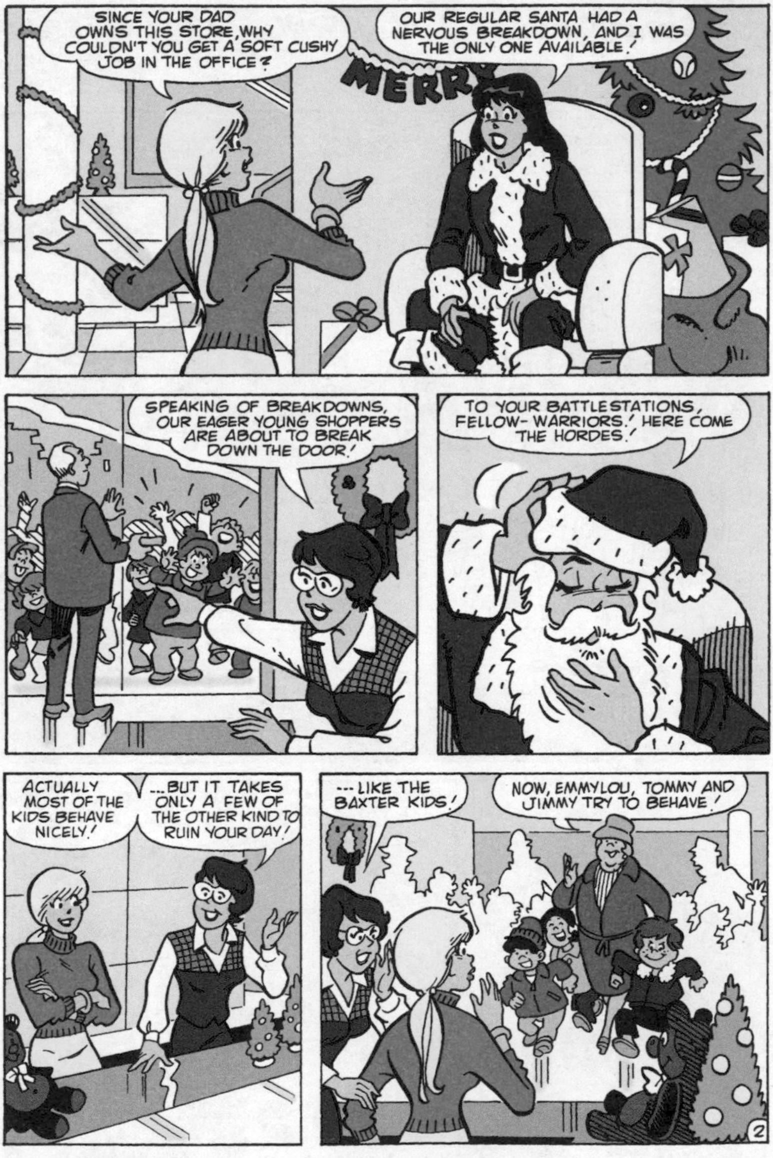
SINCE YOUR DAD OWNS THIS STORE, WHY COULDN'T YOU GET A SOFT CUSHY JOB IN THE OFFICE?
OUR REGULAR SANTA HAD A NERVOUS BREAKDOWN, AND I WAS THE ONLY ONE AVAILABLE!
MERR
SPEAKING OF BREAKDOWNS, OUR EAGER YOUNG SHOPPERS ARE ABOUT TO BREAK DOWN THE DOOR!
TO YOUR BATTLESTATIONS, FELLOW-WARRIORS! HERE COME THE HORDES!
ACTUALLY MOST OF THE KIDS BEHAVE NICELY!
...BUT IT TAKES ONLY A FEW OF THE OTHER KIND TO RUIN YOUR DAY!
---LIKE THE BAXTER KIDS!
NOW, EMMYLOU, TOMMY AND JIMMY TRY TO BEHAVE!
2

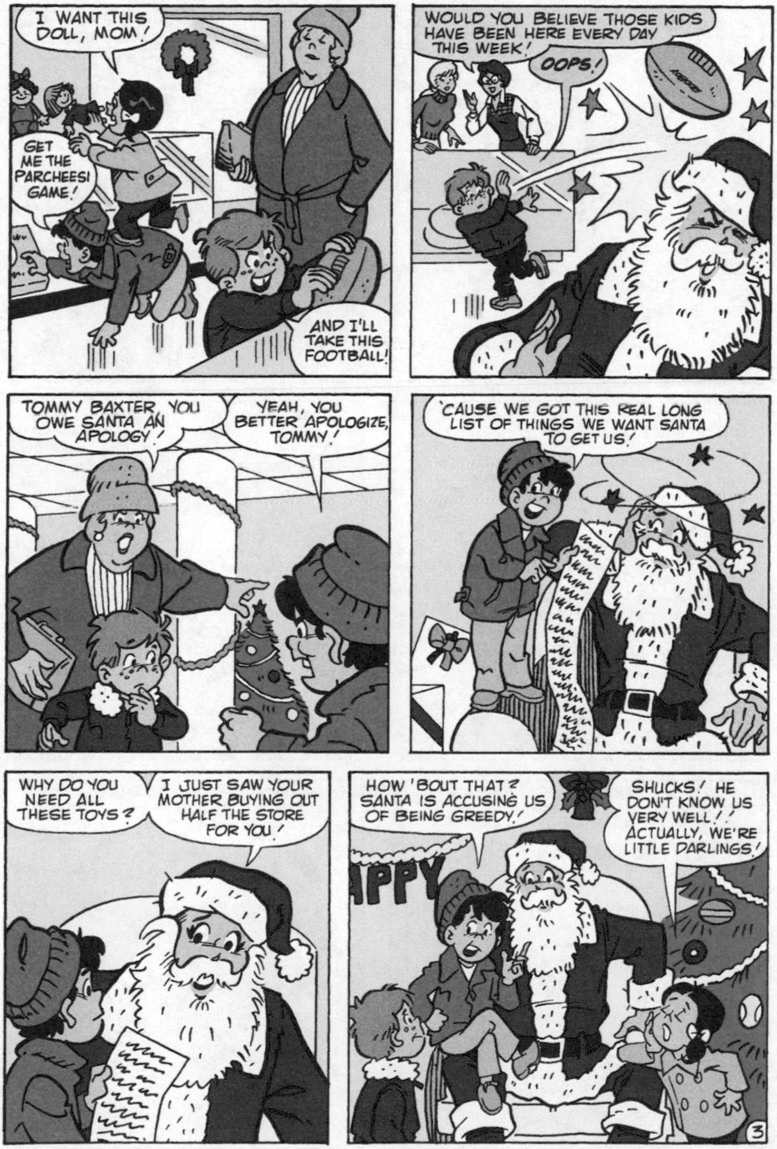
I WANT THIS DOLL, MOM!
GET ME THE PARCHEESI GAME!
AND I'LL TAKE THIS FOOTBALL!
WOULD YOU BELIEVE THOSE KIDS HAVE BEEN HERE EVERY DAY THIS WEEK!
OOPS!
TOMMY BAXTER, YOU OWE SANTA AN APOLOGY!
YEAH, YOU BETTER APOLOGIZE, TOMMY!
'CAUSE WE GOT THIS REAL LONG LIST OF THINGS WE WANT SANTA TO GET US!
WHY DO YOU NEED ALL THESE TOYS?
I JUST SAW YOUR MOTHER BUYING OUT HALF THE STORE FOR YOU!
HOW 'BOUT THAT? SANTA IS ACCUSING US OF BEING GREEDY!
SHUCKS! HE DON'T KNOW US VERY WELL!! ACTUALLY, WE'RE LITTLE DARLINGS!
3

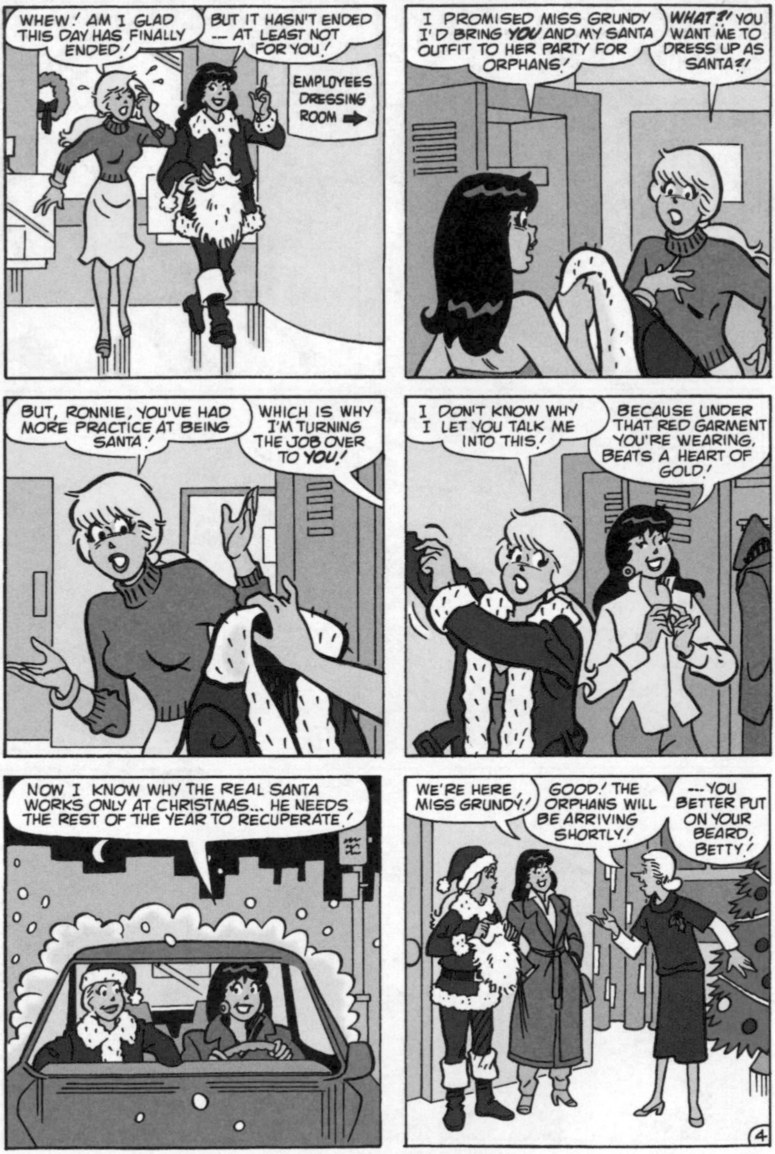
WHEW! AM I GLAD THIS DAY HAS FINALLY ENDED!
BUT IT HASN'T ENDED -- AT LEAST NOT FOR YOU!
EMPLOYEES DRESSING ROOM
I PROMISED MISS GRUNDY I'D BRING YOU AND MY SANTA OUTFIT TO HER PARTY FOR ORPHANS!
WHAT?! YOU WANT ME TO DRESS UP AS SANTA?!
BUT, RONNIE, YOU'VE HAD MORE PRACTICE AT BEING SANTA!
WHICH IS WHY I'M TURNING THE JOB OVER TO YOU!
I DON'T KNOW WHY I LET YOU TALK ME INTO THIS!
BECAUSE UNDER THAT RED GARMENT YOU'RE WEARING, BEATS A HEART OF GOLD!
NOW I KNOW WHY THE REAL SANTA WORKS ONLY AT CHRISTMAS... HE NEEDS THE REST OF THE YEAR TO RECUPERATE!
WE'RE HERE, MISS GRUNDY!
GOOD! THE ORPHANS WILL BE ARRIVING SHORTLY!
---YOU BETTER PUT ON YOUR BEARD, BETTY!
4

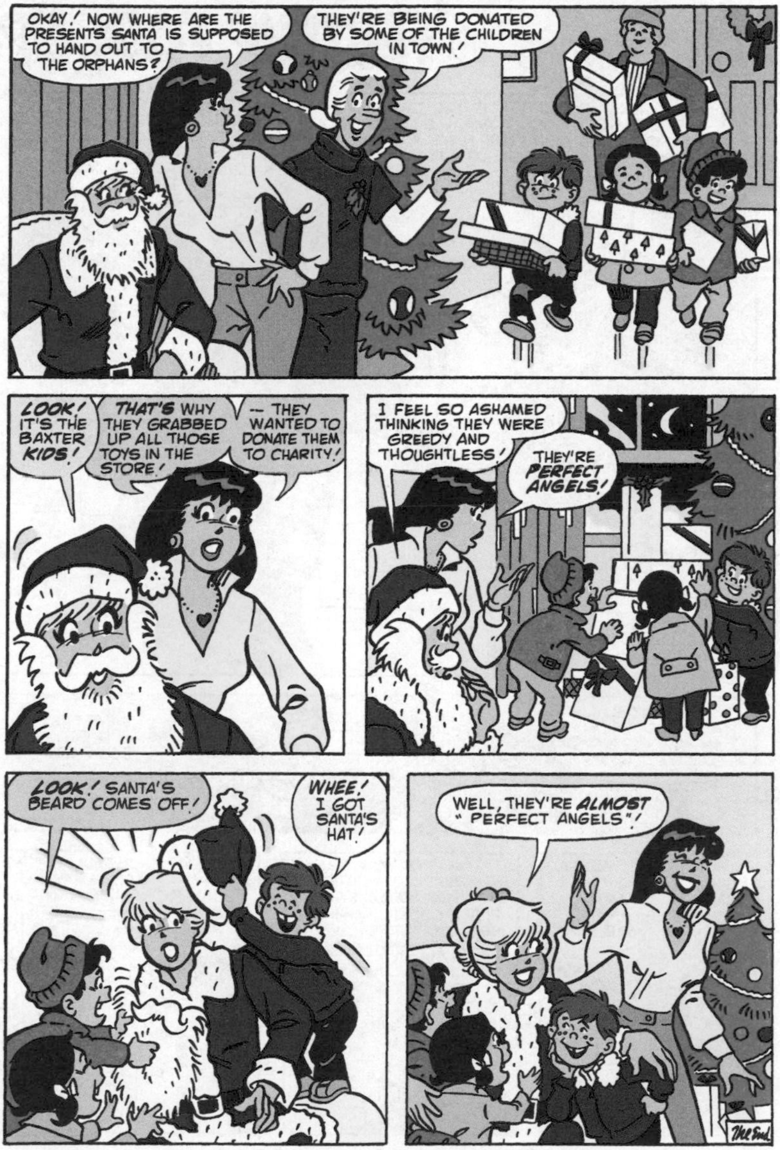
OKAY! NOW WHERE ARE THE PRESENTS SANTA IS SUPPOSED TO HAND OUT TO THE ORPHANS?
THEY'RE BEING DONATED BY SOME OF THE CHILDREN IN TOWN!
LOOK! IT'S THE BAXTER KIDS!
THAT'S WHY THEY GRABBED UP ALL THOSE TOYS IN THE STORE!
-- THEY WANTED TO DONATE THEM TO CHARITY!
I FEEL SO ASHAMED THINKING THEY WERE GREEDY AND THOUGHTLESS!
THEY'RE PERFECT ANGELS!
LOOK! SANTA'S BEARD COMES OFF!
WHEE! I GOT SANTA'S HAT!
WELL, THEY'RE ALMOST "PERFECT ANGELS"!
The End

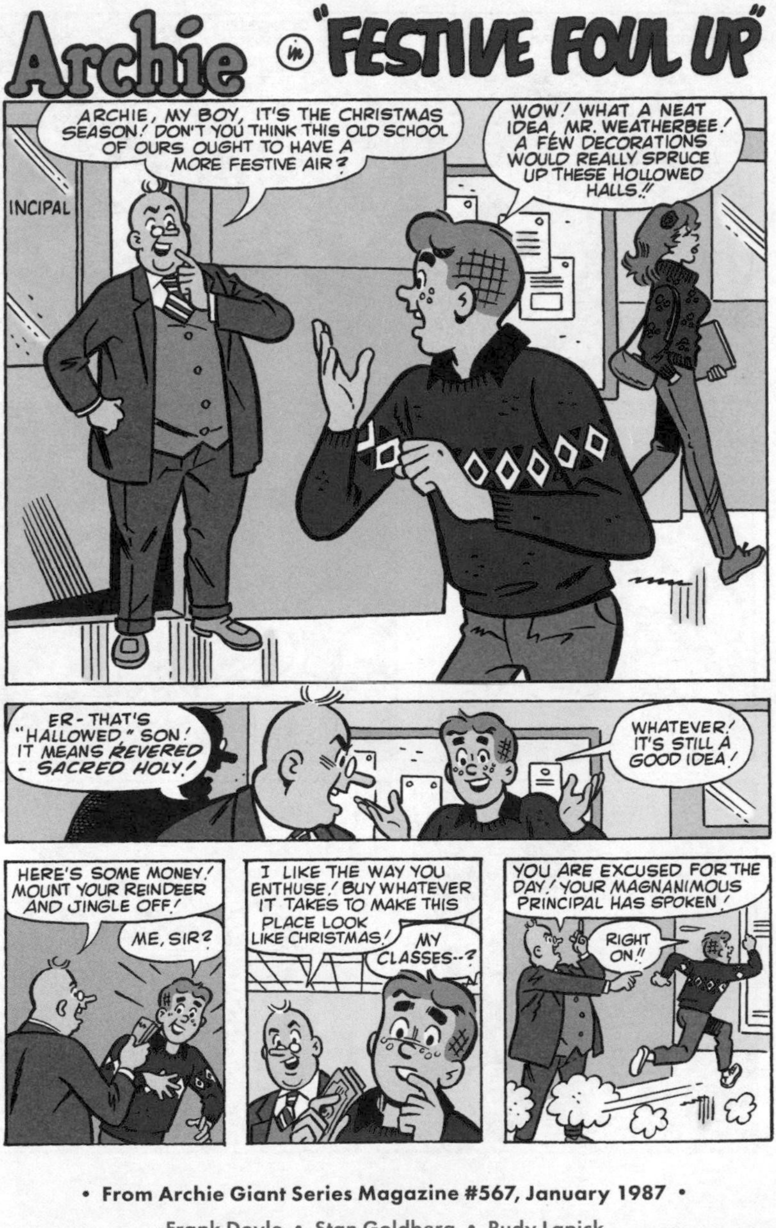
Archie in "FESTIVE FOUL UP"
ARCHIE, MY BOY, IT'S THE CHRISTMAS SEASON! DON'T YOU THINK THIS OLD SCHOOL OF OURS OUGHT TO HAVE A MORE FESTIVE AIR?
WOW! WHAT A NEAT IDEA, MR. WEATHERBEE! A FEW DECORATIONS WOULD REALLY SPRUCE UP THESE HOLLOWED HALLS!!
INCIPAL
ER-THAT'S "HALLOWED," SON! IT MEANS REVERED - SACRED HOLY!
WHATEVER! IT'S STILL A GOOD IDEA!
HERE'S SOME MONEY! MOUNT YOUR REINDEER AND JINGLE OFF!
ME, SIR?
I LIKE THE WAY YOU ENTHUSE! BUY WHATEVER IT TAKES TO MAKE THIS PLACE LOOK LIKE CHRISTMAS!
MY CLASSES--?
YOU ARE EXCUSED FOR THE DAY! YOUR MAGNANIMOUS PRINCIPAL HAS SPOKEN!
RIGHT ON!!

• From Archie Giant Series Magazine #567, January 1987 •

Frank Doyle • Stan Goldberg • Rudy Lapick

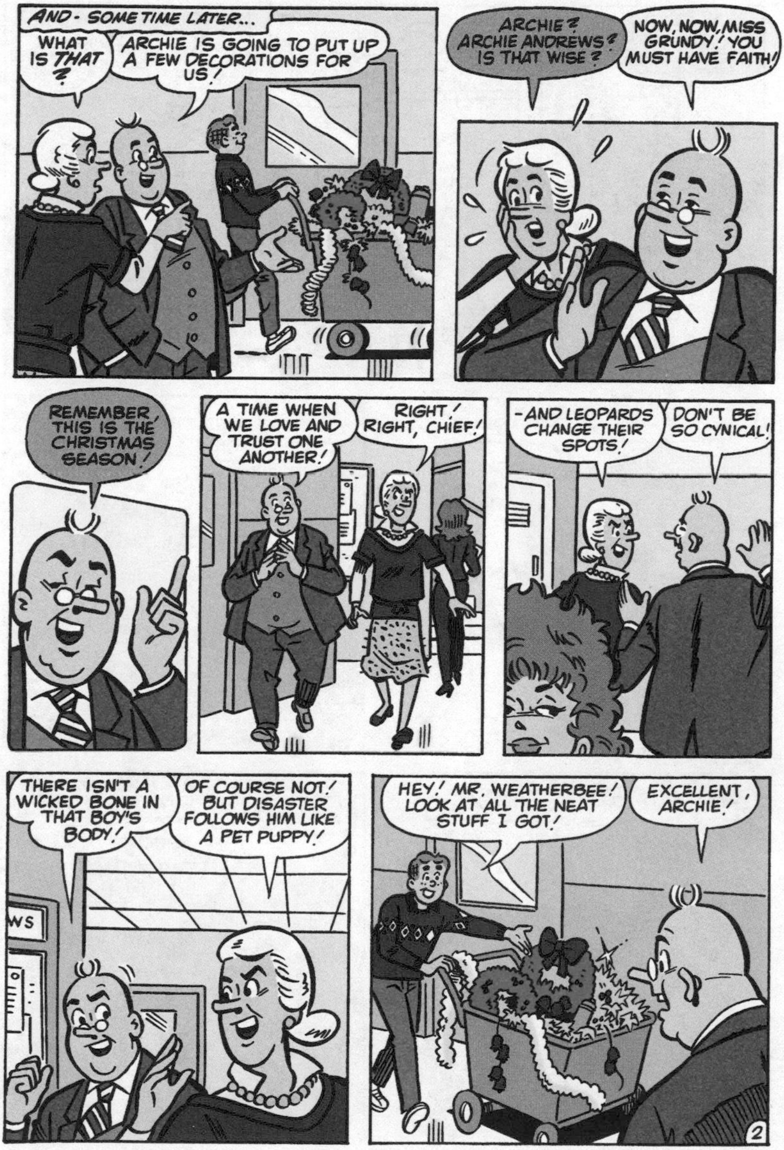
AND - SOME TIME LATER...
WHAT IS THAT ?
ARCHIE IS GOING TO PUT UP A FEW DECORATIONS FOR US!
ARCHIE? ARCHIE ANDREWS? IS THAT WISE?
NOW, NOW, MISS GRUNDY! YOU MUST HAVE FAITH!
REMEMBER, THIS IS THE CHRISTMAS SEASON!
A TIME WHEN WE LOVE AND TRUST ONE ANOTHER!
RIGHT! RIGHT, CHIEF!
-AND LEOPARDS CHANGE THEIR SPOTS!
DON'T BE SO CYNICAL!
THERE ISN'T A WICKED BONE IN THAT BOY'S BODY!
OF COURSE NOT! BUT DISASTER FOLLOWS HIM LIKE A PET PUPPY!
HEY! MR. WEATHERBEE! LOOK AT ALL THE NEAT STUFF I GOT!
EXCELLENT, ARCHIE!
2

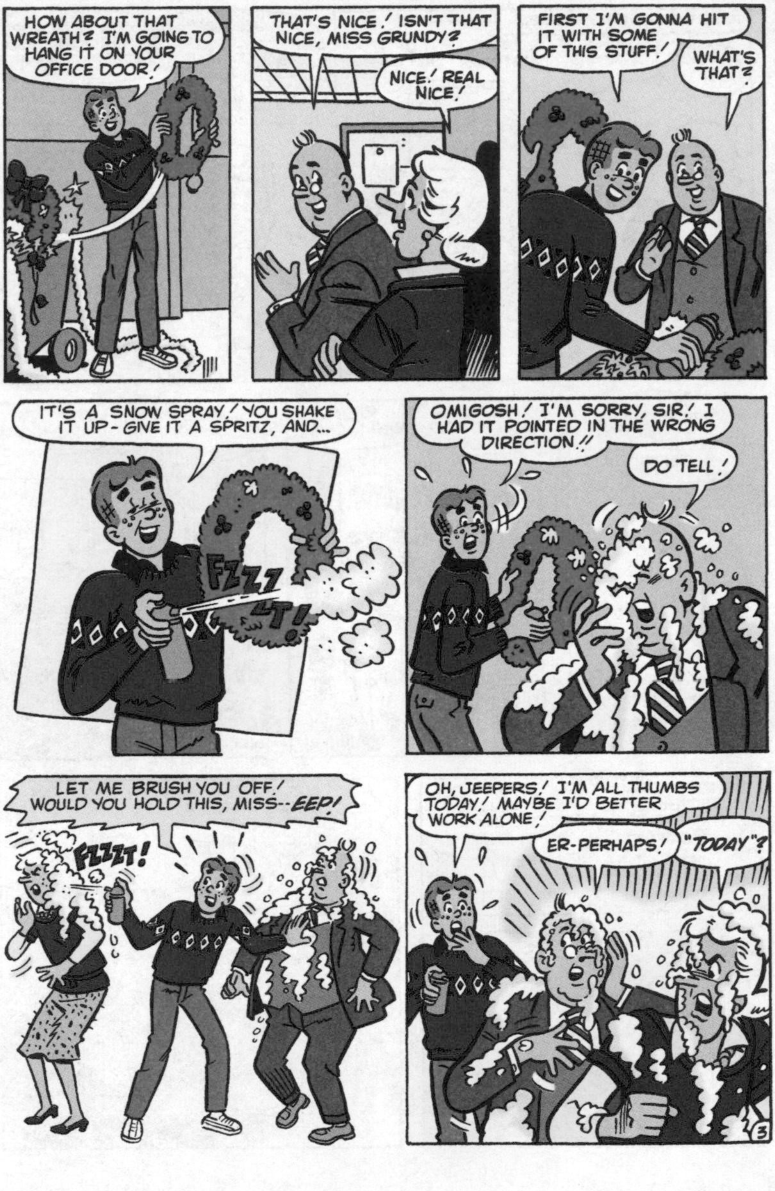
HOW ABOUT THAT WREATH? I'M GOING TO HANG IT ON YOUR OFFICE DOOR!
THAT'S NICE! ISN'T THAT NICE, MISS GRUNDY?
NICE! REAL NICE!
FIRST I'M GONNA HIT IT WITH SOME OF THIS STUFF!
WHAT'S THAT?
IT'S A SNOW SPRAY! YOU SHAKE IT UP- GIVE IT A SPRITZ, AND...
FZZZT
OMIGOSH! I'M SORRY, SIR! I HAD IT POINTED IN THE WRONG DIRECTION!!
DO TELL!
LET ME BRUSH YOU OFF! WOULD YOU HOLD THIS, MISS--EEP!
FZZZT!
OH, JEEPERS! I'M ALL THUMBS TODAY! MAYBE I'D BETTER WORK ALONE!
ER-PERHAPS!
"TODAY"?
3

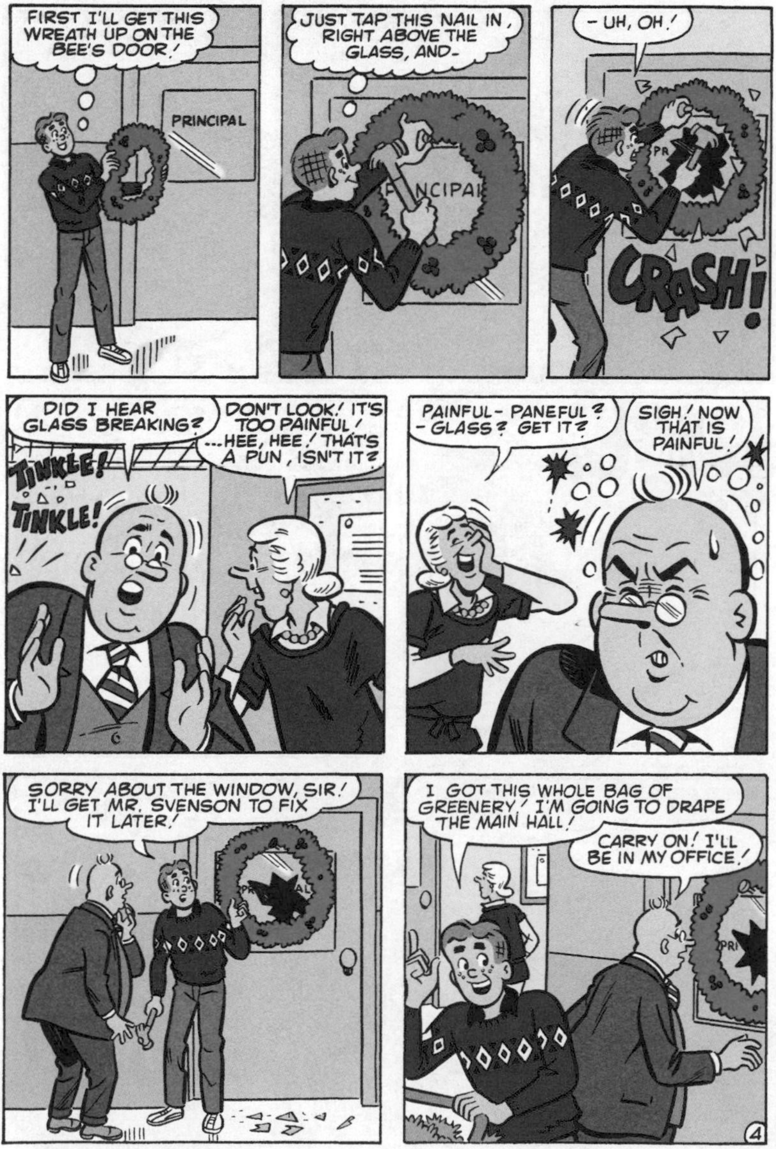
FIRST I'LL GET THIS WREATH UP ON THE BEE'S DOOR!
PRINCIPAL
JUST TAP THIS NAIL IN, RIGHT ABOVE THE GLASS, AND-
- UH, OH!
CRASH!
DID I HEAR GLASS BREAKING?
TINKLE!
TINKLE!
DON'T LOOK! IT'S TOO PAINFUL! ...HEE, HEE! THAT'S A PUN, ISN'T IT?
PAINFUL - PANEFUL? - GLASS? GET IT?
SIGH! NOW THAT IS PAINFUL!
SORRY ABOUT THE WINDOW, SIR! I'LL GET MR. SVENSON TO FIX IT LATER!
I GOT THIS WHOLE BAG OF GREENERY! I'M GOING TO DRAPE THE MAIN HALL!
CARRY ON! I'LL BE IN MY OFFICE!
4

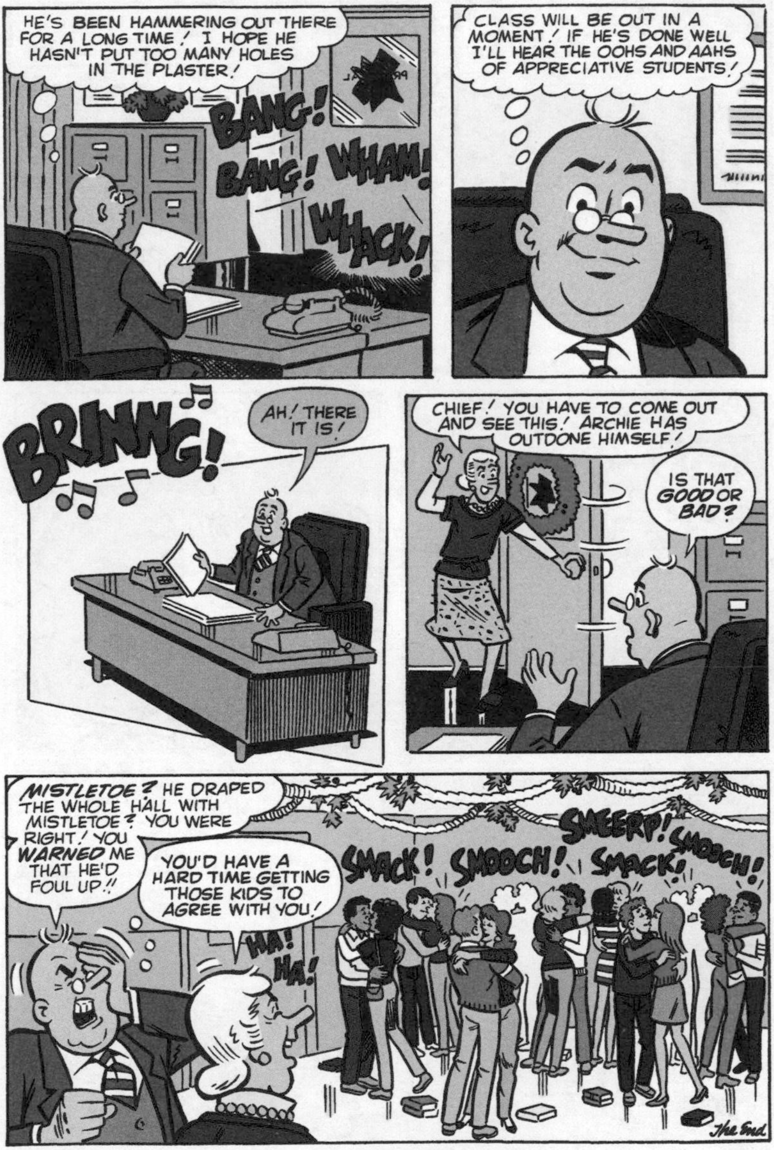
HE'S BEEN HAMMERING OUT THERE FOR A LONG TIME! I HOPE HE HASN'T PUT TOO MANY HOLES IN THE PLASTER!
BANG! BANG! WHAM! WHACK!
CLASS WILL BE OUT IN A MOMENT! IF HE'S DONE WELL I'LL HEAR THE OOHS AND AAHS OF APPRECIATIVE STUDENTS!
BRINNG!
AH! THERE IT IS!
CHIEF! YOU HAVE TO COME OUT AND SEE THIS! ARCHIE HAS OUTDONE HIMSELF!
IS THAT GOOD OR BAD?
MISTLETOE? HE DRAPED THE WHOLE HALL WITH MISTLETOE? YOU WERE RIGHT! YOU WARNED ME THAT HE'D FOUL UP!!
YOU'D HAVE A HARD TIME GETTING THOSE KIDS TO AGREE WITH YOU!
HA! HA!
SMACK! SMOOCH! SMACK! SMEERP! SMOOCH!
The End

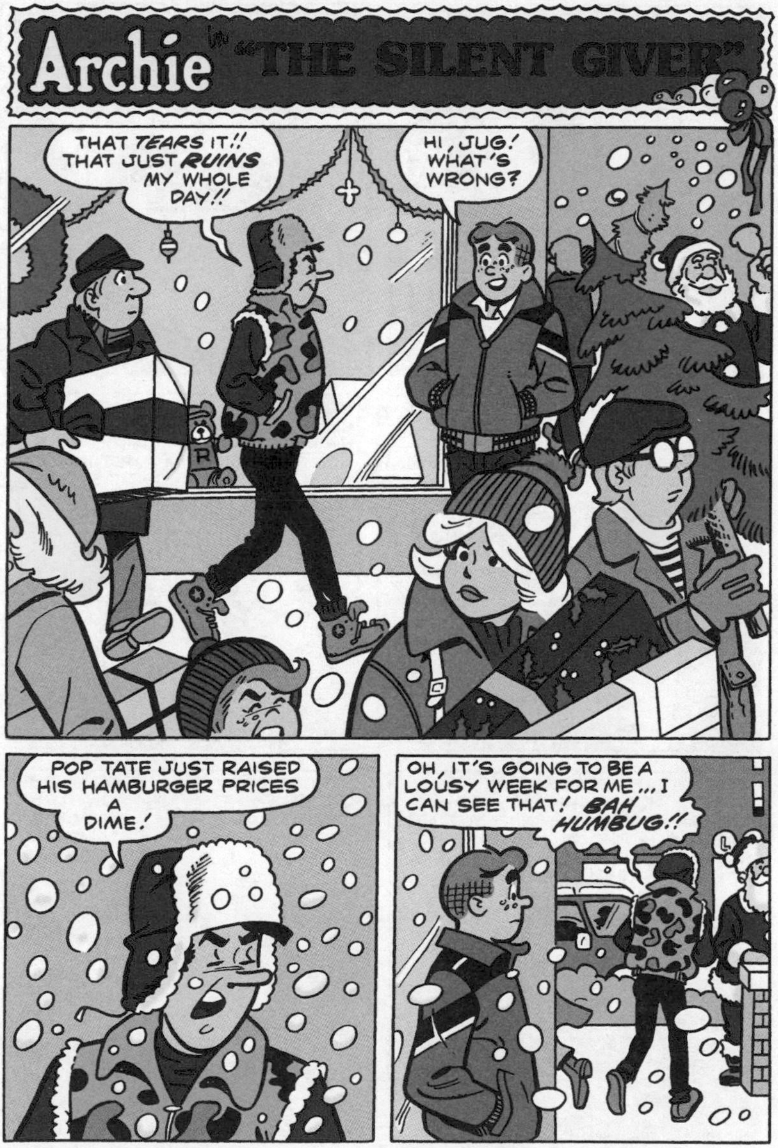
Archie in "THE SILENT GIVER"
THAT TEARS IT!! THAT JUST RUINS MY WHOLE DAY!!
HI, JUG! WHAT'S WRONG?
POP TATE JUST RAISED HIS HAMBURGER PRICES A DIME!
OH, IT'S GOING TO BE A LOUSY WEEK FOR ME... I CAN SEE THAT! BAH HUMBUG!!

• **From Archie Giant Series Magazine #567, January 1987** •

Kathleen Webb • Dan DeCarlo • Jim DeCarlo

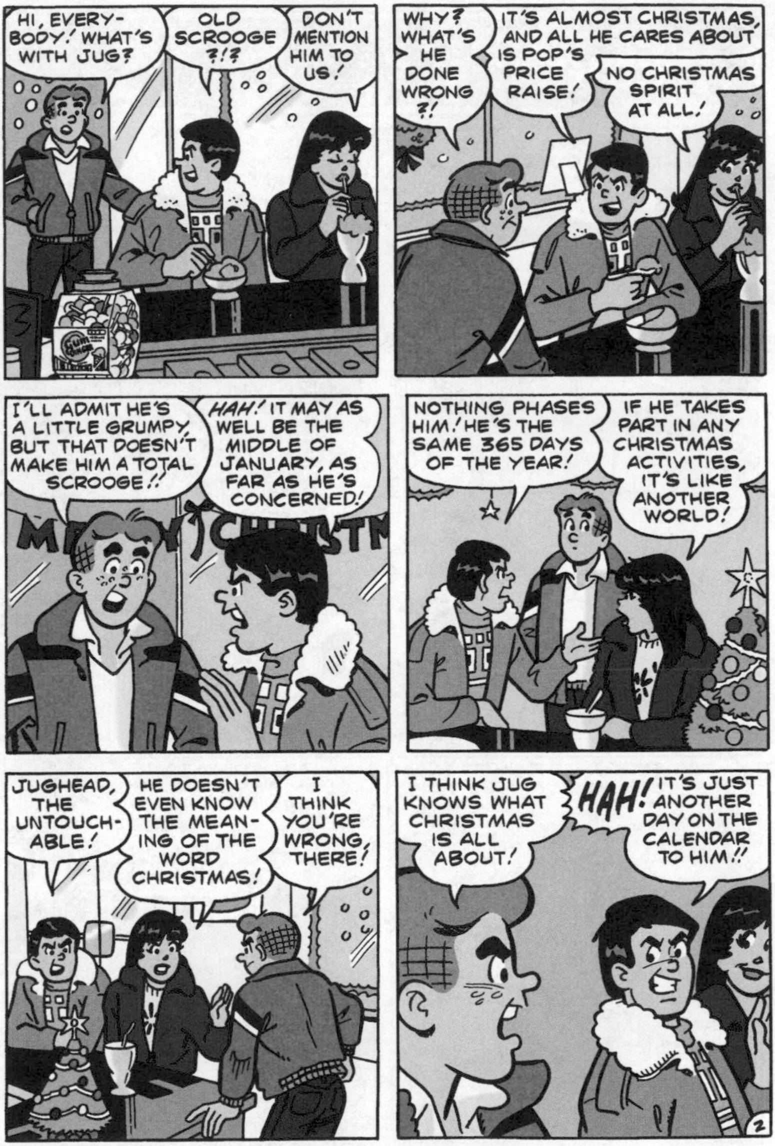
HI, EVERY-BODY! WHAT'S WITH JUG?
OLD SCROOGE ?!?
DON'T MENTION HIM TO US!
WHY? WHAT'S HE DONE WRONG ?!
IT'S ALMOST CHRISTMAS, AND ALL HE CARES ABOUT IS POP'S PRICE RAISE!
NO CHRISTMAS SPIRIT AT ALL!
I'LL ADMIT HE'S A LITTLE GRUMPY, BUT THAT DOESN'T MAKE HIM A TOTAL SCROOGE!!
HAH! IT MAY AS WELL BE THE MIDDLE OF JANUARY, AS FAR AS HE'S CONCERNED!
NOTHING PHASES HIM! HE'S THE SAME 365 DAYS OF THE YEAR!
IF HE TAKES PART IN ANY CHRISTMAS ACTIVITIES, IT'S LIKE ANOTHER WORLD!
JUGHEAD, THE UNTOUCH-ABLE!
HE DOESN'T EVEN KNOW THE MEAN-ING OF THE WORD CHRISTMAS!
I THINK YOU'RE WRONG, THERE!
I THINK JUG KNOWS WHAT CHRISTMAS IS ALL ABOUT!
HAH! IT'S JUST ANOTHER DAY ON THE CALENDAR TO HIM!!
2

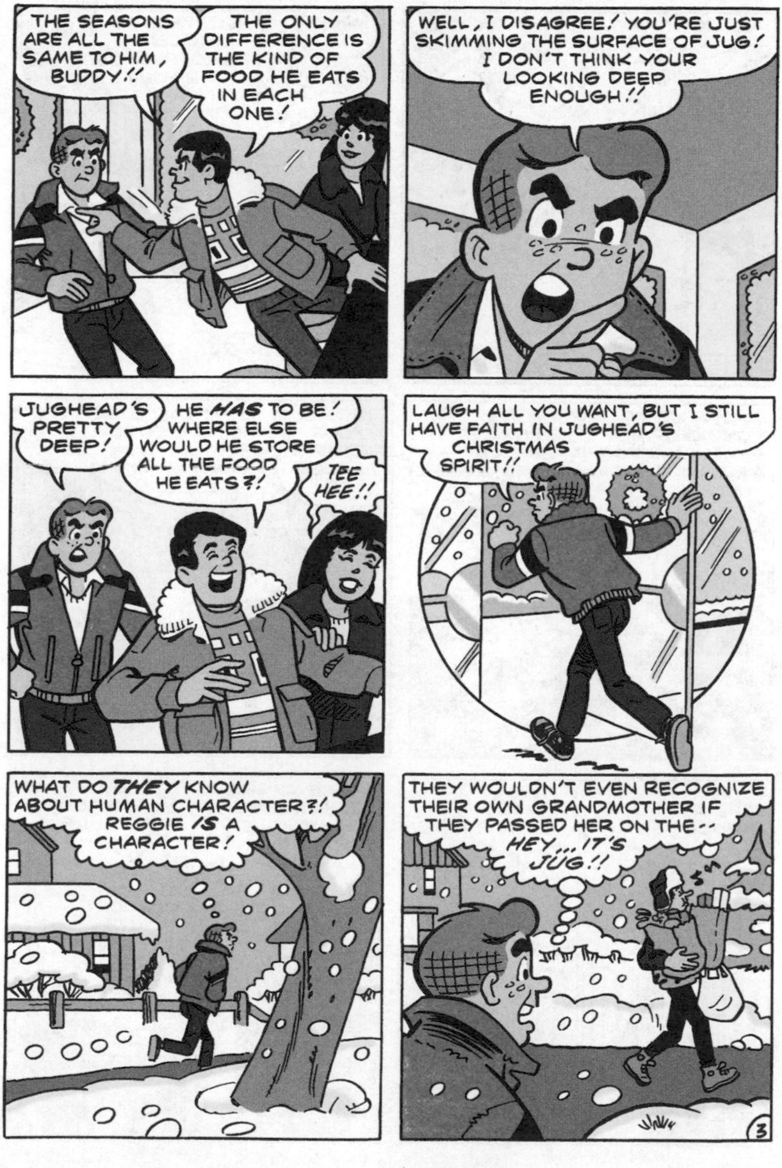
THE SEASONS ARE ALL THE SAME TO HIM, BUDDY!!
THE ONLY DIFFERENCE IS THE KIND OF FOOD HE EATS IN EACH ONE!
WELL, I DISAGREE! YOU'RE JUST SKIMMING THE SURFACE OF JUG! I DON'T THINK YOUR LOOKING DEEP ENOUGH!!
JUGHEAD'S PRETTY DEEP!
HE HAS TO BE! WHERE ELSE WOULD HE STORE ALL THE FOOD HE EATS?!
TEE HEE!!
LAUGH ALL YOU WANT, BUT I STILL HAVE FAITH IN JUGHEAD'S CHRISTMAS SPIRIT!!
WHAT DO THEY KNOW ABOUT HUMAN CHARACTER?! REGGIE IS A CHARACTER!
THEY WOULDN'T EVEN RECOGNIZE THEIR OWN GRANDMOTHER IF THEY PASSED HER ON THE-- HEY... IT'S JUG!!
3

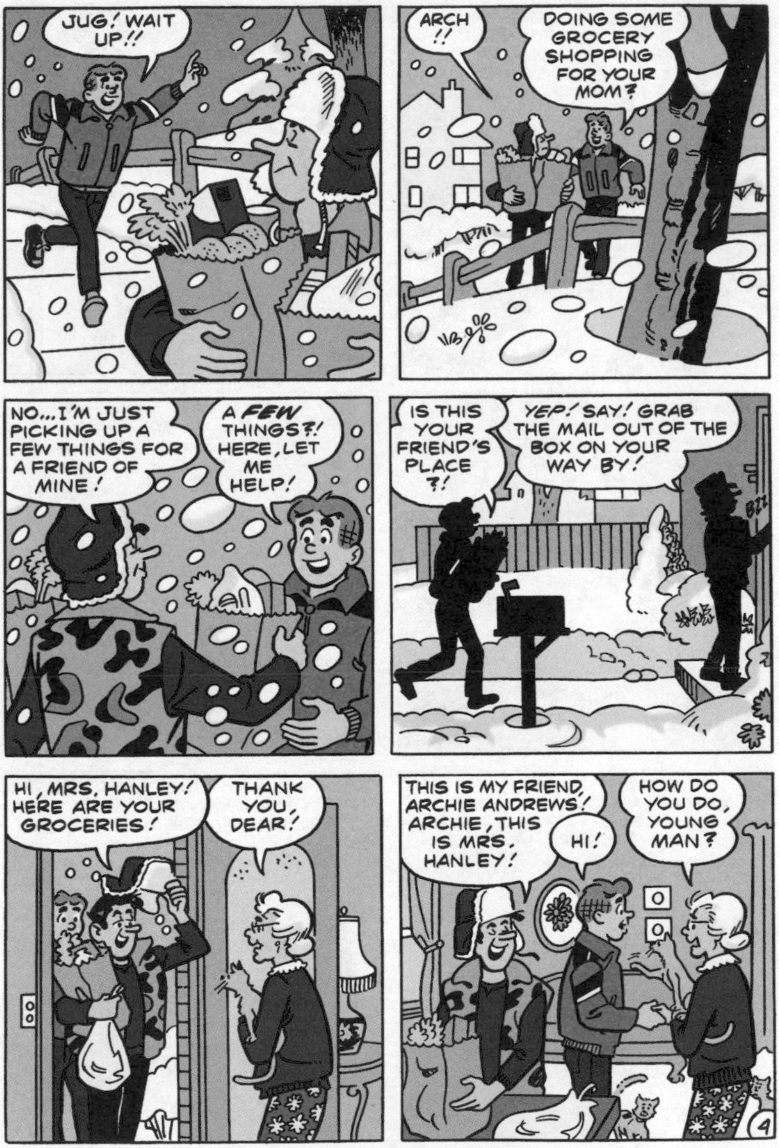
JUG! WAIT UP!!
ARCH!!
DOING SOME GROCERY SHOPPING FOR YOUR MOM?
NO... I'M JUST PICKING UP A FEW THINGS FOR A FRIEND OF MINE!
A FEW THINGS?! HERE, LET ME HELP!
IS THIS YOUR FRIEND'S PLACE?!
YEP! SAY! GRAB THE MAIL OUT OF THE BOX ON YOUR WAY BY!
BZZ
HI, MRS. HANLEY! HERE ARE YOUR GROCERIES!
THANK YOU, DEAR!
THIS IS MY FRIEND, ARCHIE ANDREWS! ARCHIE, THIS IS MRS. HANLEY!
HI!
HOW DO YOU DO, YOUNG MAN?
4

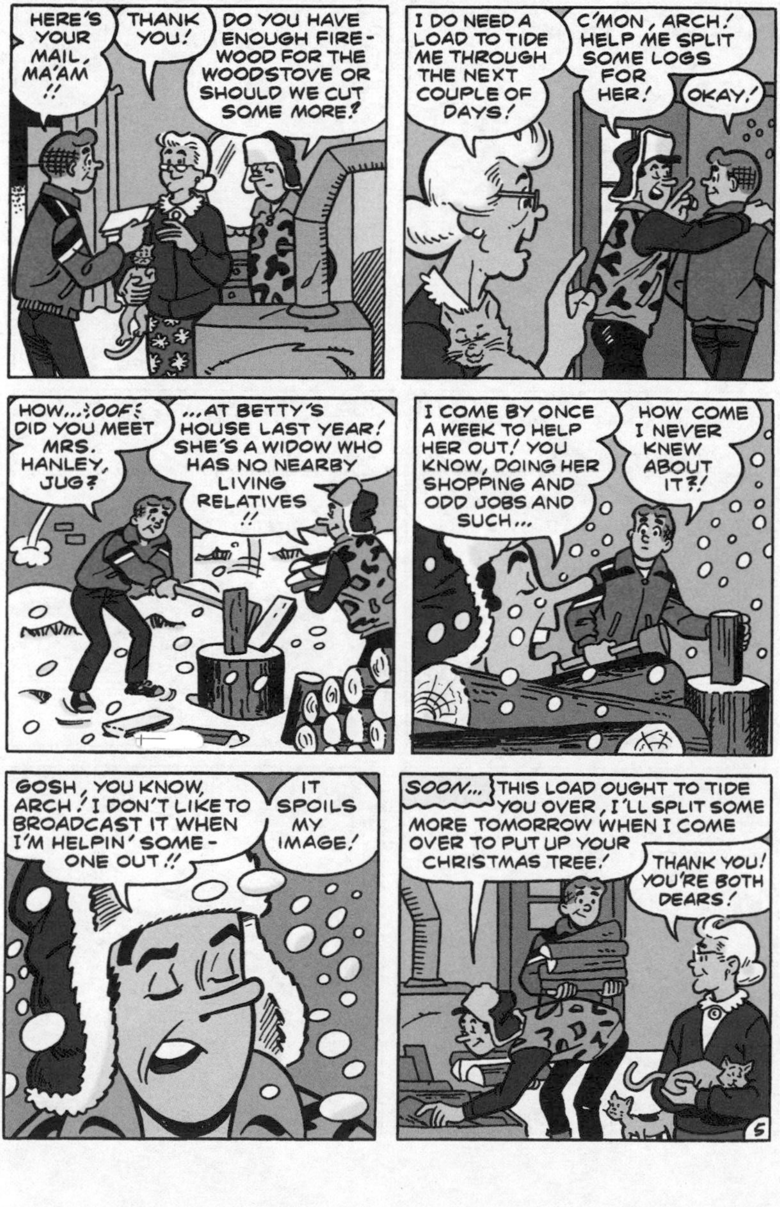
HERE'S YOUR MAIL, MA'AM !!
THANK YOU!
DO YOU HAVE ENOUGH FIRE-WOOD FOR THE WOODSTOVE OR SHOULD WE CUT SOME MORE?
I DO NEED A LOAD TO TIDE ME THROUGH THE NEXT COUPLE OF DAYS!
C'MON, ARCH! HELP ME SPLIT SOME LOGS FOR HER!
OKAY!
HOW... OOF DID YOU MEET MRS. HANLEY, JUG?
...AT BETTY'S HOUSE LAST YEAR! SHE'S A WIDOW WHO HAS NO NEARBY LIVING RELATIVES !!
I COME BY ONCE A WEEK TO HELP HER OUT! YOU KNOW, DOING HER SHOPPING AND ODD JOBS AND SUCH...
HOW COME I NEVER KNEW ABOUT IT?!
GOSH, YOU KNOW, ARCH! I DON'T LIKE TO BROADCAST IT WHEN I'M HELPIN' SOME-ONE OUT!!
IT SPOILS MY IMAGE!
SOON...
THIS LOAD OUGHT TO TIDE YOU OVER, I'LL SPLIT SOME MORE TOMORROW WHEN I COME OVER TO PUT UP YOUR CHRISTMAS TREE!
THANK YOU! YOU'RE BOTH DEARS!
5

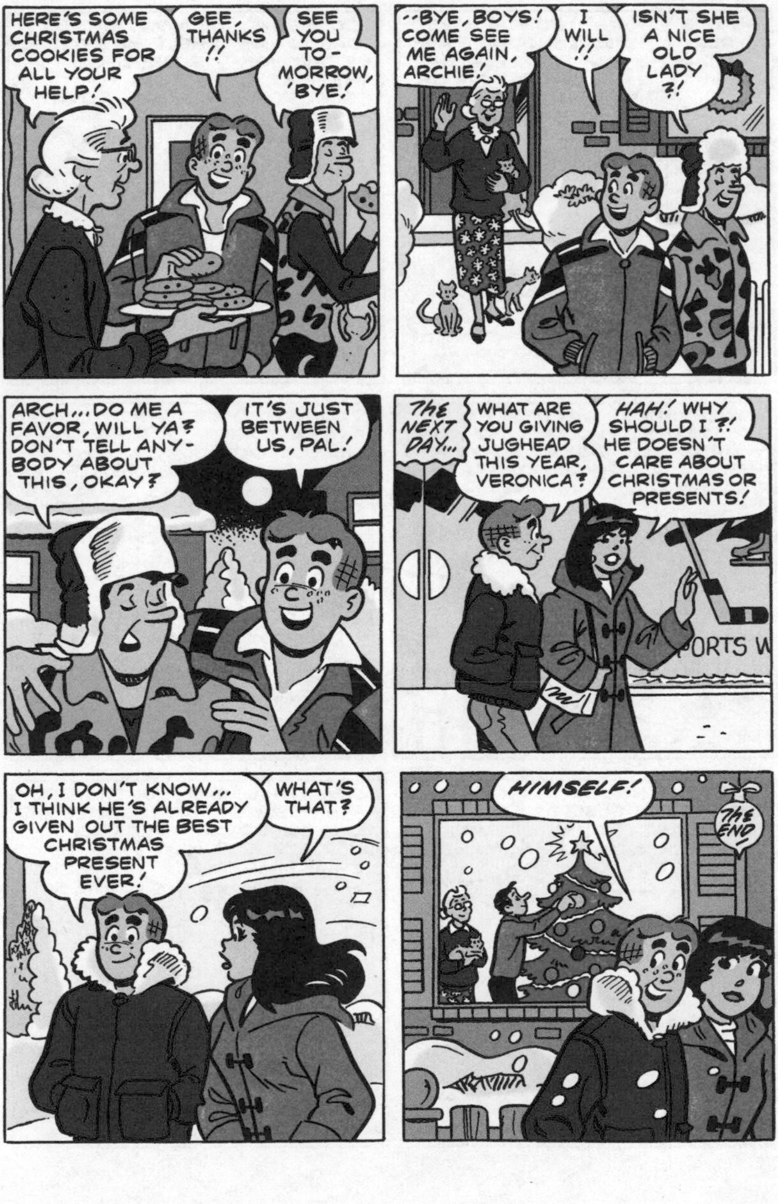
HERE'S SOME CHRISTMAS COOKIES FOR ALL YOUR HELP!
GEE, THANKS !!
SEE YOU TO-MORROW, 'BYE!
--BYE, BOYS! COME SEE ME AGAIN, ARCHIE!
I WILL !!
ISN'T SHE A NICE OLD LADY ?!
ARCH... DO ME A FAVOR, WILL YA? DON'T TELL ANY-BODY ABOUT THIS, OKAY?
IT'S JUST BETWEEN US, PAL!
THE NEXT DAY...
WHAT ARE YOU GIVING JUGHEAD THIS YEAR, VERONICA?
HAH! WHY SHOULD I ?! HE DOESN'T CARE ABOUT CHRISTMAS OR PRESENTS!
PORTS W
OH, I DON'T KNOW... I THINK HE'S ALREADY GIVEN OUT THE BEST CHRISTMAS PRESENT EVER!
WHAT'S THAT?
HIMSELF!
THE END

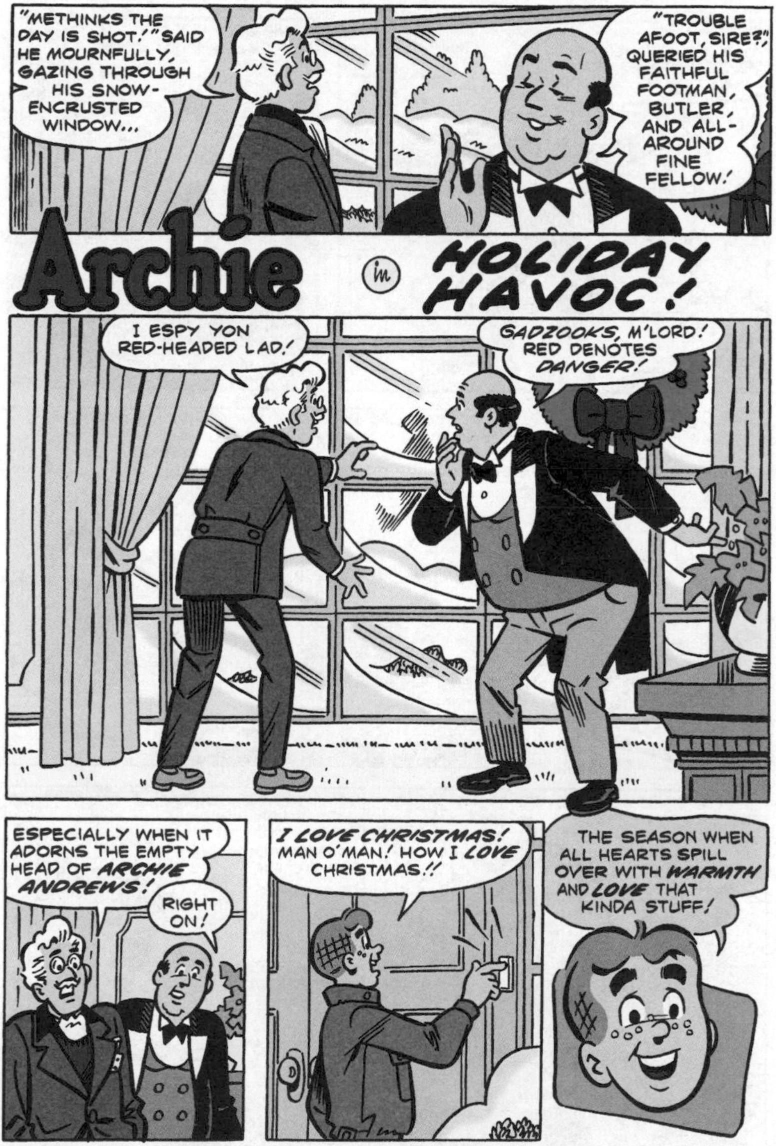
"METHINKS THE DAY IS SHOT!" SAID HE MOURNFULLY, GAZING THROUGH HIS SNOW-ENCRUSTED WINDOW...
"TROUBLE AFOOT, SIRE?" QUERIED HIS FAITHFUL FOOTMAN, BUTLER, AND ALL-AROUND FINE FELLOW!
Archie in HOLIDAY HAVOC!
I ESPY YON RED-HEADED LAD!
GADZOOKS, M'LORD! RED DENOTES DANGER!
ESPECIALLY WHEN IT ADORNS THE EMPTY HEAD OF ARCHIE ANDREWS!
RIGHT ON!
I LOVE CHRISTMAS! MAN O'MAN! HOW I LOVE CHRISTMAS!!
THE SEASON WHEN ALL HEARTS SPILL OVER WITH WARMTH AND LOVE THAT KINDA STUFF!

• From Archie Giant Series Magazine #567, January 1987 •

Frank Doyle • Stan Goldberg • Rudy Lapick

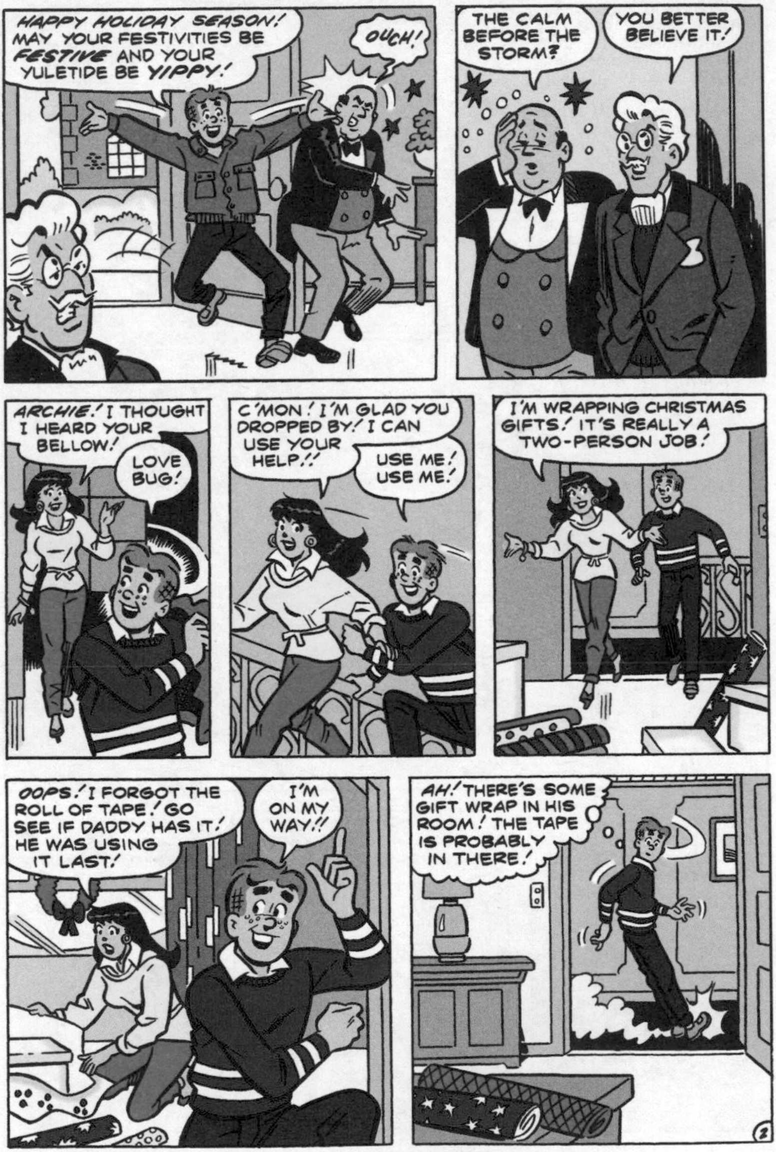
HAPPY HOLIDAY SEASON! MAY YOUR FESTIVITIES BE FESTIVE AND YOUR YULETIDE BE YIPPY!
OUCH!
THE CALM BEFORE THE STORM?
YOU BETTER BELIEVE IT!
ARCHIE! I THOUGHT I HEARD YOUR BELLOW!
LOVE BUG!
C'MON! I'M GLAD YOU DROPPED BY! I CAN USE YOUR HELP!!
USE ME! USE ME!
I'M WRAPPING CHRISTMAS GIFTS! IT'S REALLY A TWO-PERSON JOB!
OOPS! I FORGOT THE ROLL OF TAPE! GO SEE IF DADDY HAS IT! HE WAS USING IT LAST!
I'M ON MY WAY!!
AH! THERE'S SOME GIFT WRAP IN HIS ROOM! THE TAPE IS PROBABLY IN THERE!
2

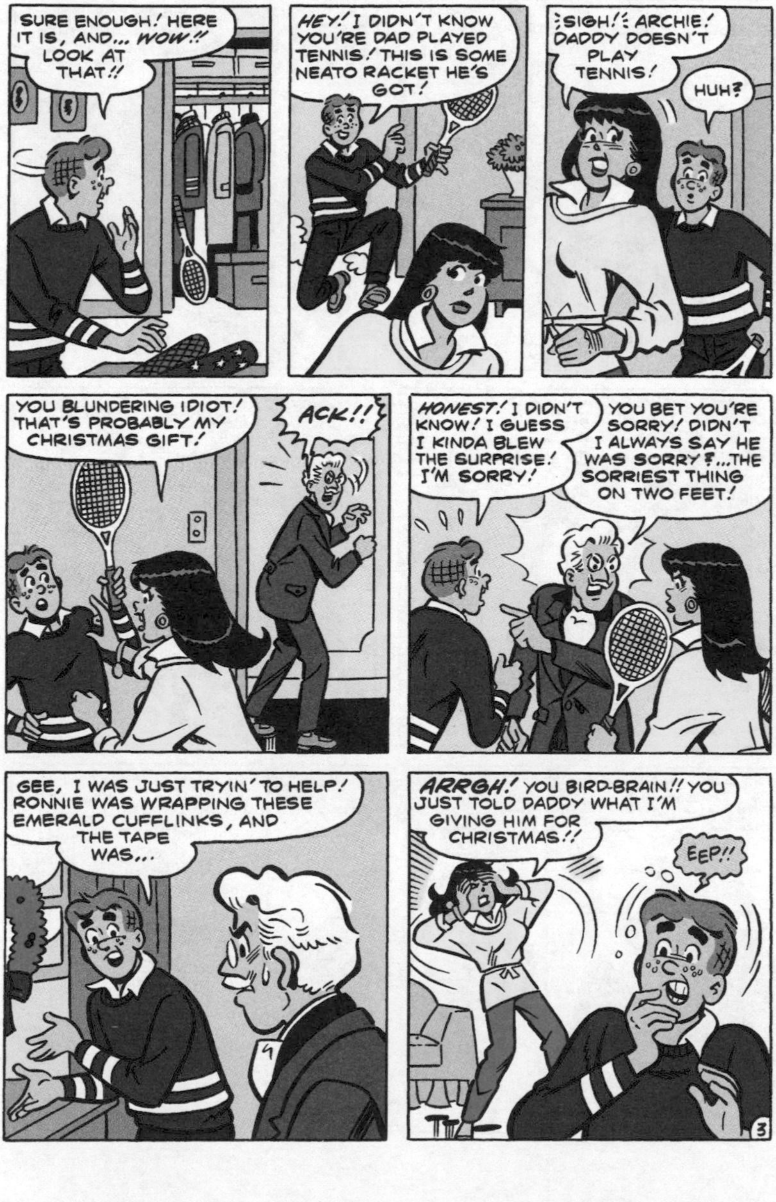
SURE ENOUGH! HERE IT IS, AND... WOW!! LOOK AT THAT!!
HEY! I DIDN'T KNOW YOU'RE DAD PLAYED TENNIS! THIS IS SOME NEATO RACKET HE'S GOT!
SIGH! ARCHIE! DADDY DOESN'T PLAY TENNIS!
HUH?
YOU BLUNDERING IDIOT! THAT'S PROBABLY MY CHRISTMAS GIFT!
ACK!!
HONEST! I DIDN'T KNOW! I GUESS I KINDA BLEW THE SURPRISE! I'M SORRY!
YOU BET YOU'RE SORRY! DIDN'T I ALWAYS SAY HE WAS SORRY?...THE SORRIEST THING ON TWO FEET!
GEE, I WAS JUST TRYIN' TO HELP! RONNIE WAS WRAPPING THESE EMERALD CUFFLINKS, AND THE TAPE WAS...
ARRGH! YOU BIRD-BRAIN!! YOU JUST TOLD DADDY WHAT I'M GIVING HIM FOR CHRISTMAS!!
EEP!!
3

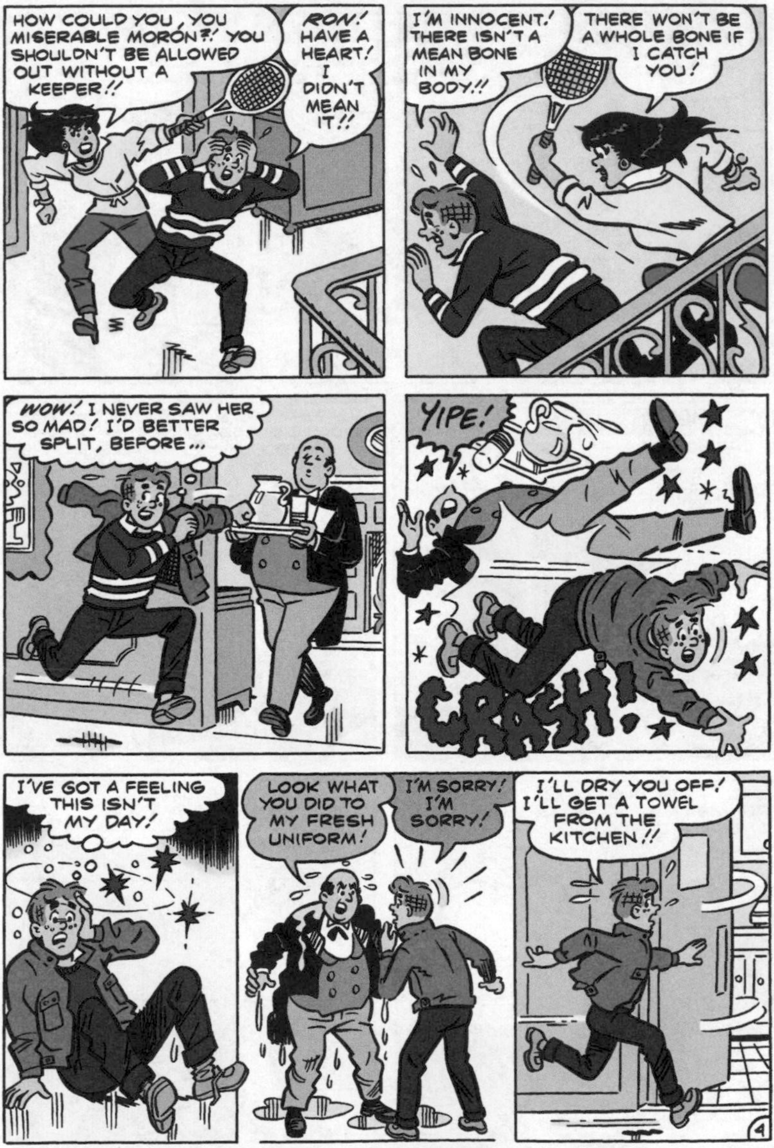
HOW COULD YOU, YOU MISERABLE MORON?! YOU SHOULDN'T BE ALLOWED OUT WITHOUT A KEEPER!!
RON! HAVE A HEART! I DIDN'T MEAN IT!!
I'M INNOCENT! THERE ISN'T A MEAN BONE IN MY BODY!!
THERE WON'T BE A WHOLE BONE IF I CATCH YOU!
WOW! I NEVER SAW HER SO MAD! I'D BETTER SPLIT, BEFORE...
YIPE!
CRASH!
I'VE GOT A FEELING THIS ISN'T MY DAY!
LOOK WHAT YOU DID TO MY FRESH UNIFORM!
I'M SORRY! I'M SORRY!
I'LL DRY YOU OFF! I'LL GET A TOWEL FROM THE KITCHEN!!
4

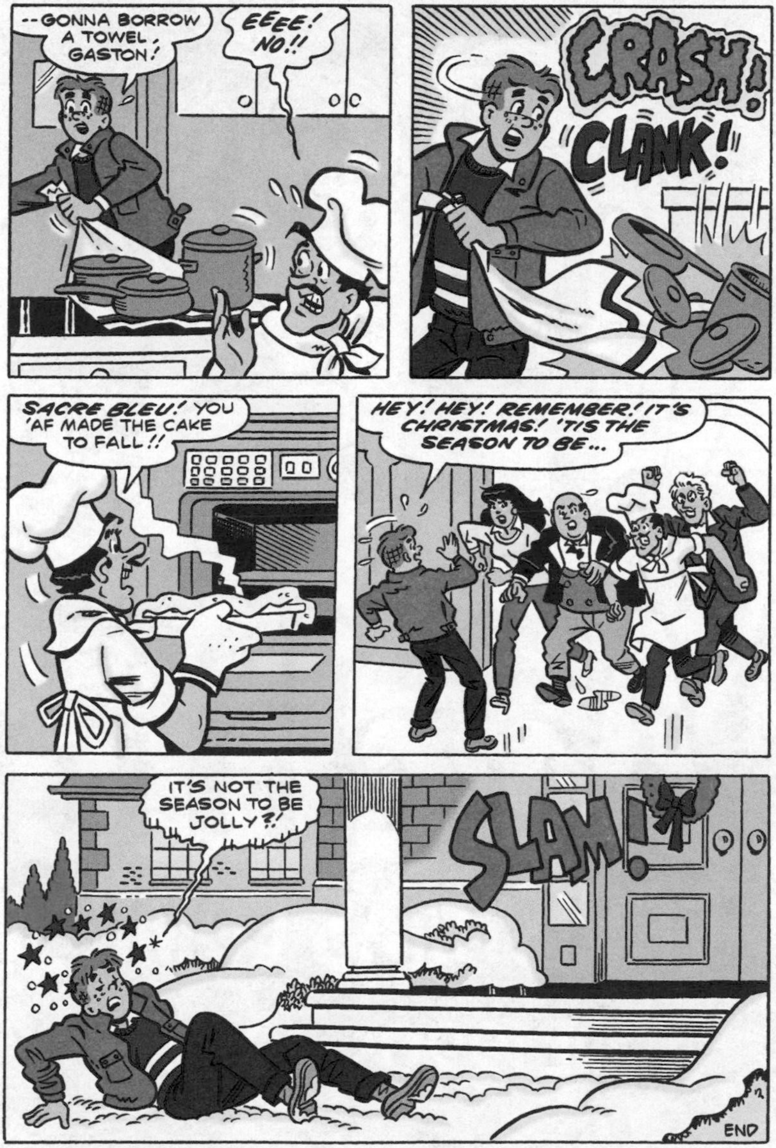
--GONNA BORROW A TOWEL, GASTON!
EEEE! NO!!
CRASH!
CLANK!
SACRE BLEU! YOU 'AF MADE THE CAKE TO FALL!!
HEY! HEY! REMEMBER! IT'S CHRISTMAS! 'TIS THE SEASON TO BE...
IT'S NOT THE SEASON TO BE JOLLY?!
SLAM!
END

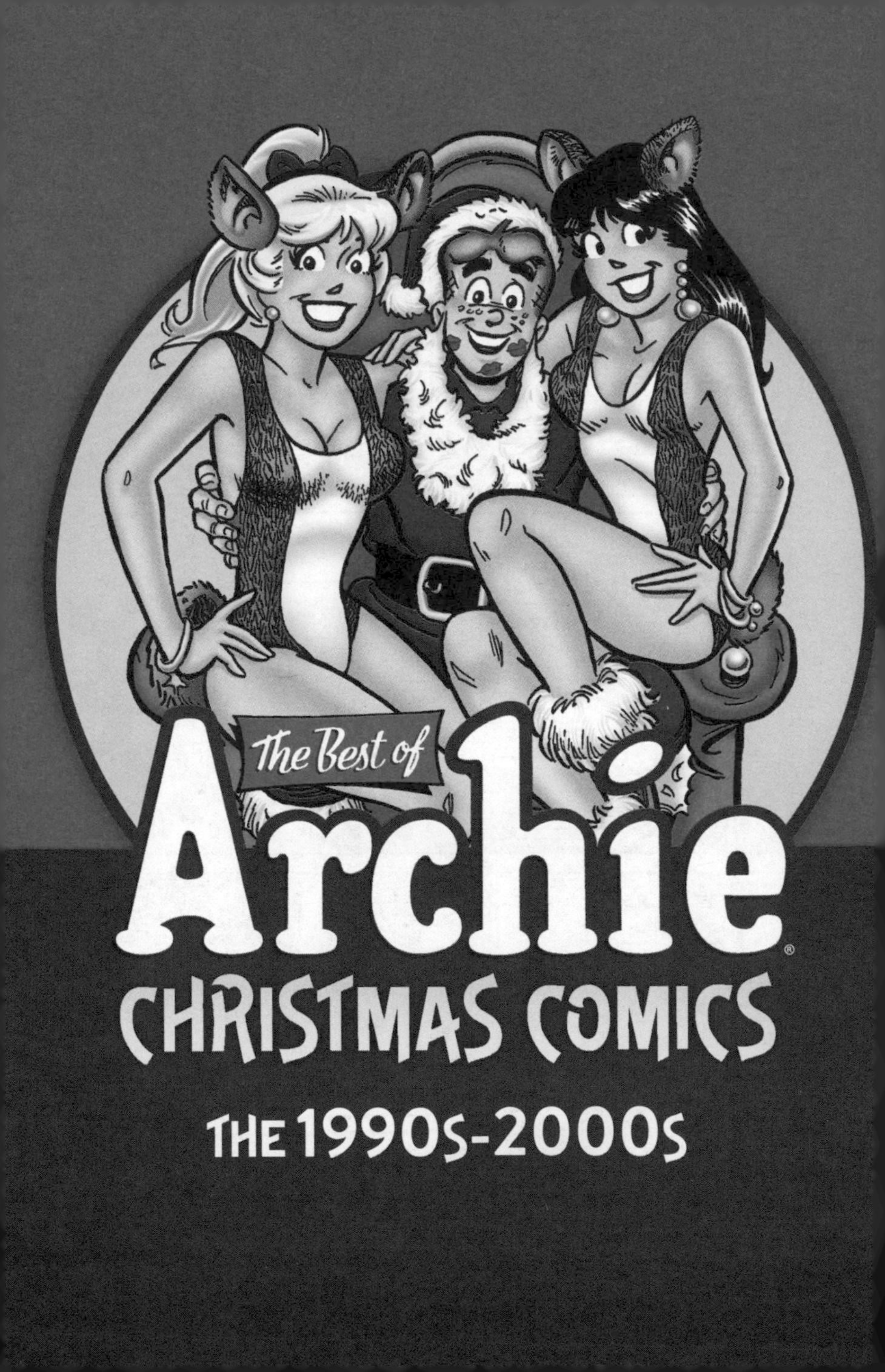

The Best of

Archie®

CHRISTMAS COMICS

THE 1990s-2000s

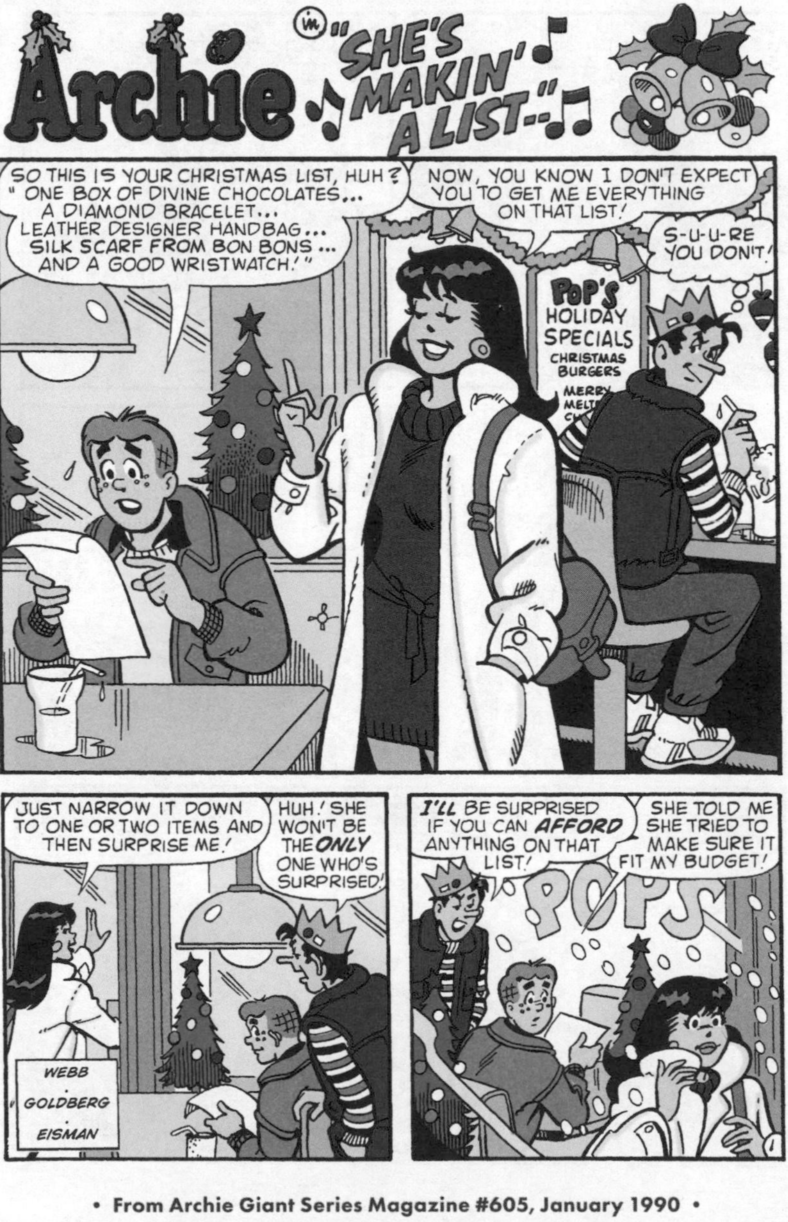
Archie in "SHE'S MAKIN' A LIST--"
SO THIS IS YOUR CHRISTMAS LIST, HUH? " ONE BOX OF DIVINE CHOCOLATES... A DIAMOND BRACELET... LEATHER DESIGNER HANDBAG... SILK SCARF FROM BON BONS... AND A GOOD WRISTWATCH!"
NOW, YOU KNOW I DON'T EXPECT YOU TO GET ME EVERYTHING ON THAT LIST!
S-U-U-RE YOU DON'T!
POP'S HOLIDAY SPECIALS CHRISTMAS BURGERS
JUST NARROW IT DOWN TO ONE OR TWO ITEMS AND THEN SURPRISE ME!
HUH! SHE WON'T BE THE ONLY ONE WHO'S SURPRISED!
WEBB · GOLDBERG · EISMAN
I'LL BE SURPRISED IF YOU CAN AFFORD ANYTHING ON THAT LIST!
SHE TOLD ME SHE TRIED TO MAKE SURE IT FIT MY BUDGET!
POP'S

• **From Archie Giant Series Magazine #605, January 1990** •

Kathleen Webb • Stan Goldberg • Hy Eisman

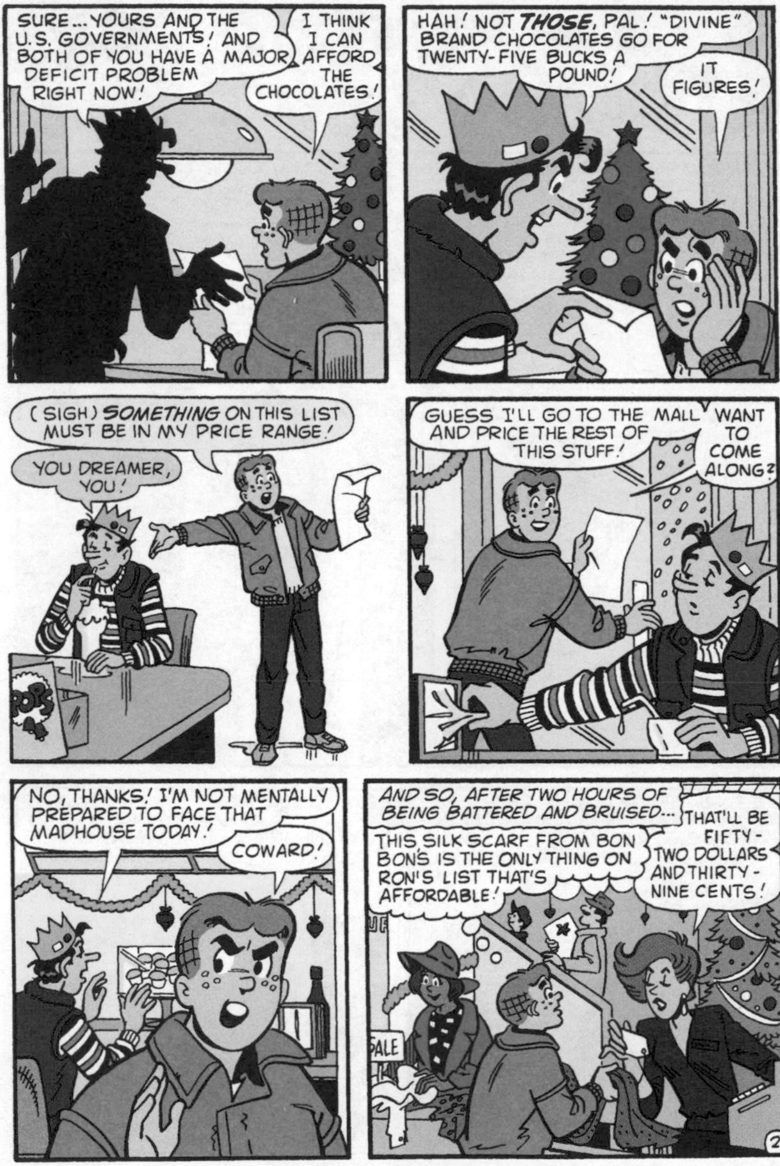
SURE... YOURS AND THE U.S. GOVERNMENT'S! AND BOTH OF YOU HAVE A MAJOR DEFICIT PROBLEM RIGHT NOW!
I THINK I CAN AFFORD THE CHOCOLATES!
HAH! NOT THOSE, PAL! "DIVINE" BRAND CHOCOLATES GO FOR TWENTY-FIVE BUCKS A POUND!
IT FIGURES!
(SIGH) SOMETHING ON THIS LIST MUST BE IN MY PRICE RANGE!
YOU DREAMER, YOU!
POPS
GUESS I'LL GO TO THE MALL AND PRICE THE REST OF THIS STUFF!
WANT TO COME ALONG?
NO, THANKS! I'M NOT MENTALLY PREPARED TO FACE THAT MADHOUSE TODAY!
COWARD!
AND SO, AFTER TWO HOURS OF BEING BATTERED AND BRUISED...
THIS SILK SCARF FROM BON BON'S IS THE ONLY THING ON RON'S LIST THAT'S AFFORDABLE!
THAT'LL BE FIFTY-TWO DOLLARS AND THIRTY-NINE CENTS!
SALE
2

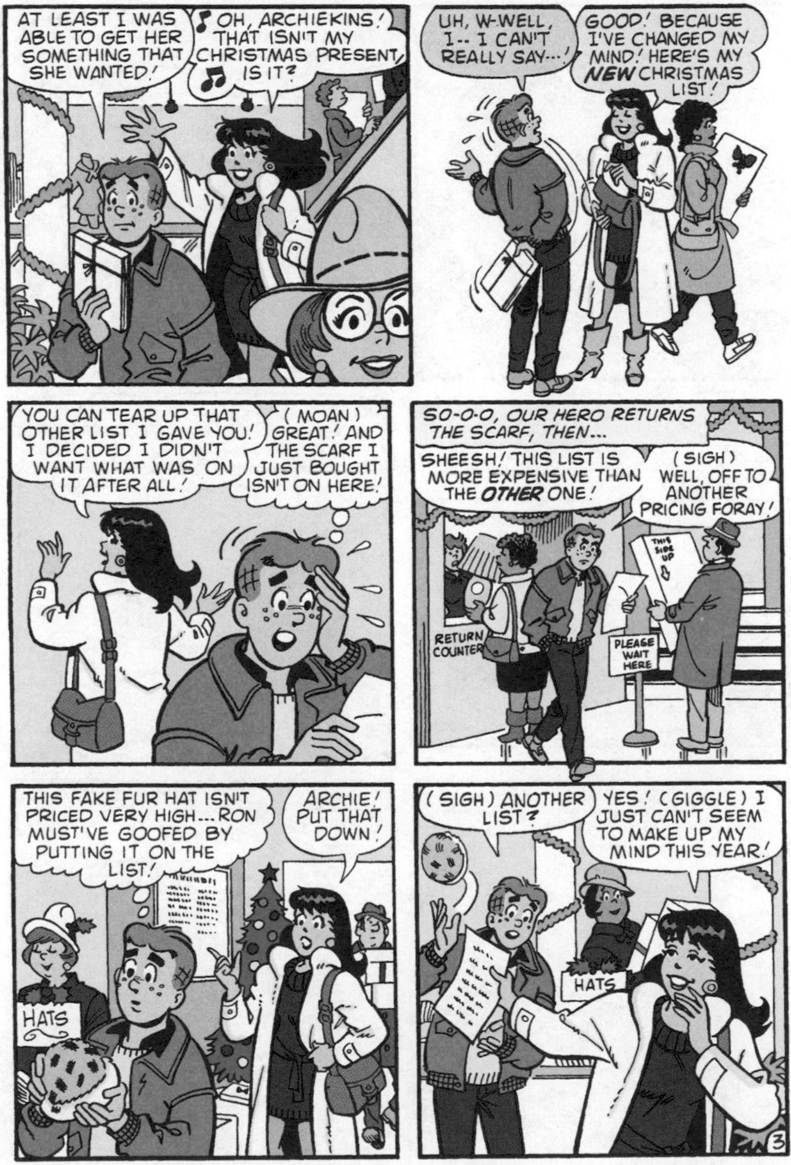
AT LEAST I WAS ABLE TO GET HER SOMETHING THAT SHE WANTED!
OH, ARCHIEKINS! THAT ISN'T MY CHRISTMAS PRESENT, IS IT?
UH, W-WELL, I-- I CAN'T REALLY SAY...!
GOOD! BECAUSE I'VE CHANGED MY MIND! HERE'S MY NEW CHRISTMAS LIST!
YOU CAN TEAR UP THAT OTHER LIST I GAVE YOU! I DECIDED I DIDN'T WANT WHAT WAS ON IT AFTER ALL!
(MOAN) GREAT! AND THE SCARF I JUST BOUGHT ISN'T ON HERE!
SO-O-O, OUR HERO RETURNS THE SCARF, THEN...
SHEESH! THIS LIST IS MORE EXPENSIVE THAN THE OTHER ONE!
(SIGH) WELL, OFF TO ANOTHER PRICING FORAY!
RETURN COUNTER
PLEASE WAIT HERE
THIS SIDE UP
THIS FAKE FUR HAT ISN'T PRICED VERY HIGH... RON MUST'VE GOOFED BY PUTTING IT ON THE LIST!
ARCHIE! PUT THAT DOWN!
HATS
(SIGH) ANOTHER LIST?
YES! (GIGGLE) I JUST CAN'T SEEM TO MAKE UP MY MIND THIS YEAR!
HATS
3

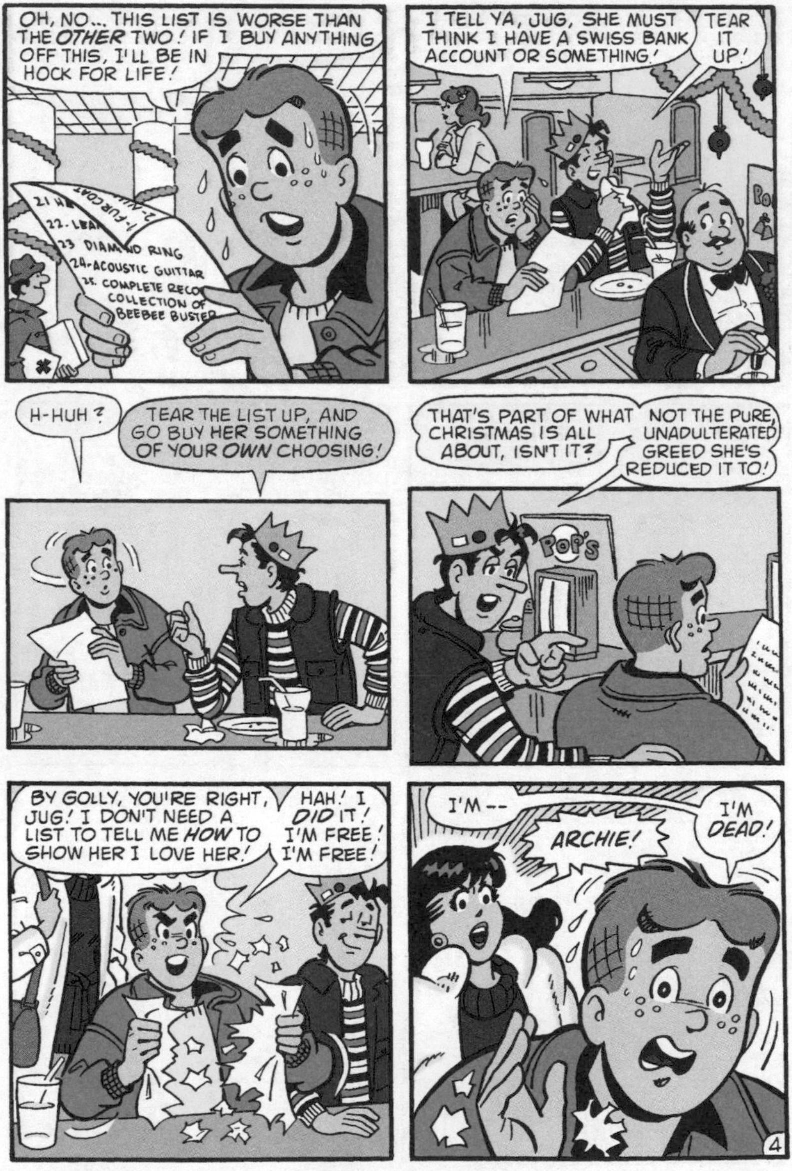
OH, NO... THIS LIST IS WORSE THAN THE OTHER TWO! IF I BUY ANYTHING OFF THIS, I'LL BE IN HOCK FOR LIFE!
1-FUR COAT
22-LEA
23 DIAMOND RING
24-ACOUSTIC GUITAR
25. COMPLETE RECO COLLECTION OF BEEBEE BUSTER
I TELL YA, JUG, SHE MUST THINK I HAVE A SWISS BANK ACCOUNT OR SOMETHING!
TEAR IT UP!
H-HUH?
TEAR THE LIST UP, AND GO BUY HER SOMETHING OF YOUR OWN CHOOSING!
THAT'S PART OF WHAT CHRISTMAS IS ALL ABOUT, ISN'T IT?
NOT THE PURE, UNADULTERATED GREED SHE'S REDUCED IT TO!
POP'S
BY GOLLY, YOU'RE RIGHT, JUG! I DON'T NEED A LIST TO TELL ME HOW TO SHOW HER I LOVE HER!
HAH! I DID IT! I'M FREE! I'M FREE!
I'M --
ARCHIE!
I'M DEAD!
4

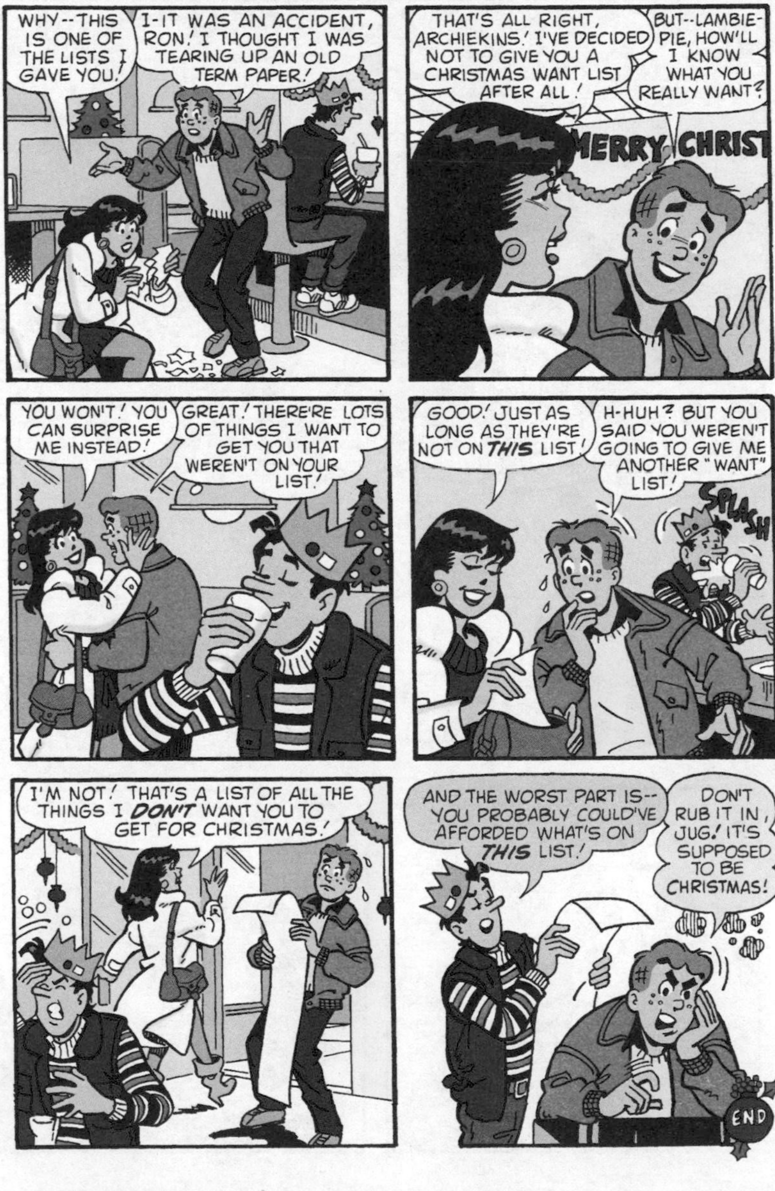
WHY--THIS IS ONE OF THE LISTS I GAVE YOU!
I-IT WAS AN ACCIDENT, RON! I THOUGHT I WAS TEARING UP AN OLD TERM PAPER!
THAT'S ALL RIGHT, ARCHIEKINS! I'VE DECIDED NOT TO GIVE YOU A CHRISTMAS WANT LIST AFTER ALL!
BUT--LAMBIE-PIE, HOW'LL I KNOW WHAT YOU REALLY WANT?
MERRY CHRIST
YOU WON'T! YOU CAN SURPRISE ME INSTEAD!
GREAT! THERE'RE LOTS OF THINGS I WANT TO GET YOU THAT WEREN'T ON YOUR LIST!
GOOD! JUST AS LONG AS THEY'RE NOT ON THIS LIST!
H-HUH? BUT YOU SAID YOU WEREN'T GOING TO GIVE ME ANOTHER "WANT" LIST!
SPLASH
I'M NOT! THAT'S A LIST OF ALL THE THINGS I DON'T WANT YOU TO GET FOR CHRISTMAS!
AND THE WORST PART IS--YOU PROBABLY COULD'VE AFFORDED WHAT'S ON THIS LIST!
DON'T RUB IT IN, JUG! IT'S SUPPOSED TO BE CHRISTMAS!
END

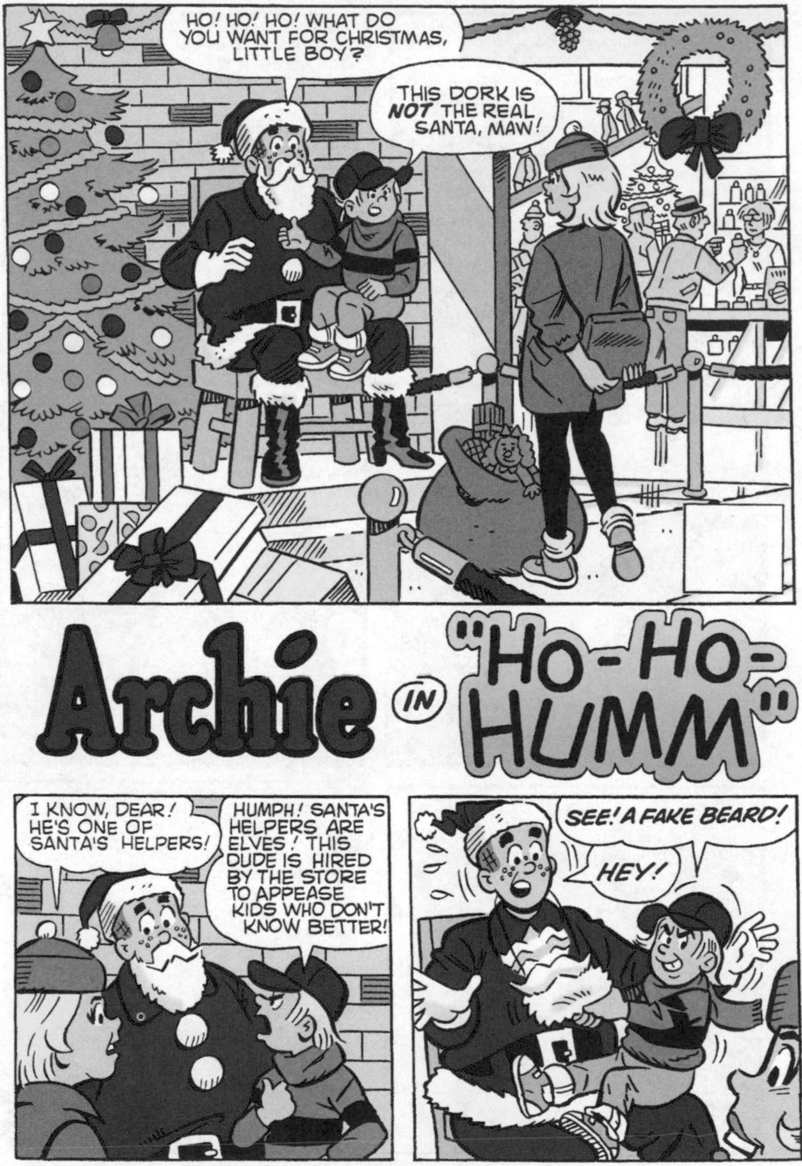
HO! HO! HO! WHAT DO YOU WANT FOR CHRISTMAS, LITTLE BOY?
THIS DORK IS NOT THE REAL SANTA, MAW!
Archie in "HO-HO-HUMM"
I KNOW, DEAR! HE'S ONE OF SANTA'S HELPERS!
HUMPH! SANTA'S HELPERS ARE ELVES! THIS DUDE IS HIRED BY THE STORE TO APPEASE KIDS WHO DON'T KNOW BETTER!
SEE! A FAKE BEARD!
HEY!

• From Archie's Holiday Fun Digest #1, February 1997 •

Hal Smith • Henry Scarpelli • Rudy Lapick

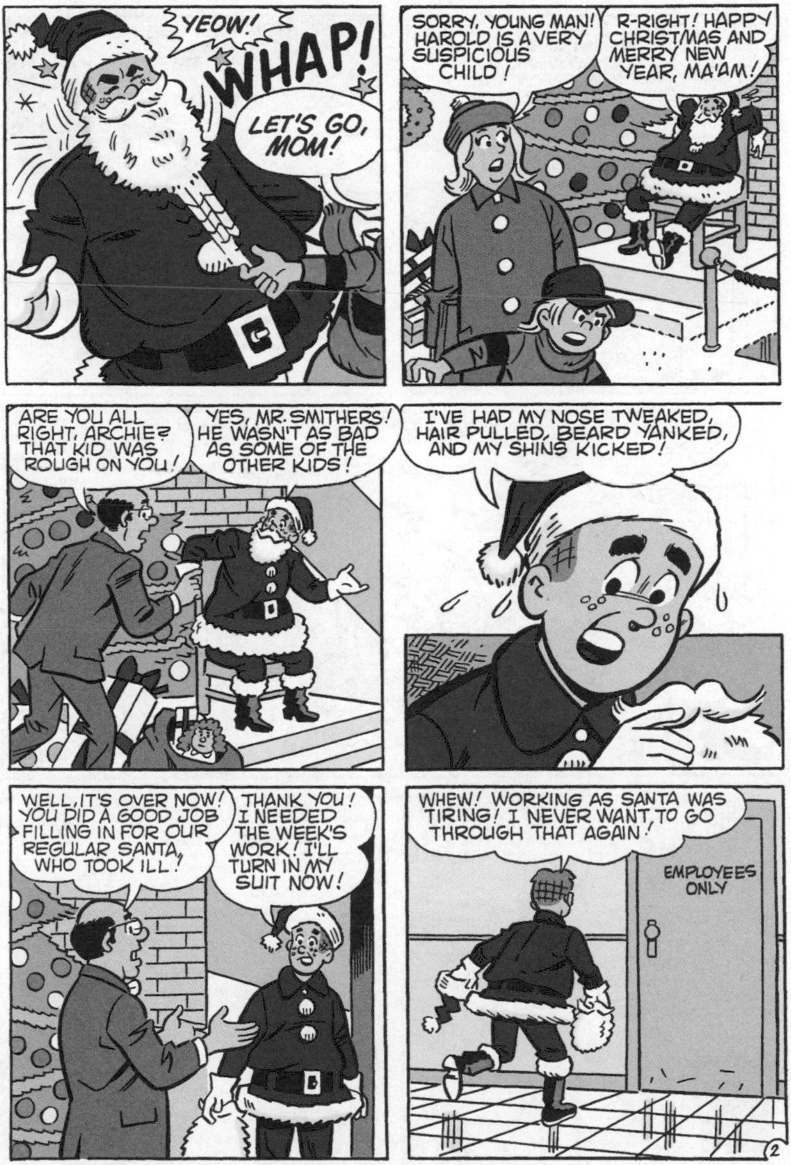
YEOW!
WHAP!
LET'S GO, MOM!
SORRY, YOUNG MAN! HAROLD IS A VERY SUSPICIOUS CHILD!
R-RIGHT! HAPPY CHRISTMAS AND MERRY NEW YEAR, MA'AM!
ARE YOU ALL RIGHT, ARCHIE? THAT KID WAS ROUGH ON YOU!
YES, MR. SMITHERS! HE WASN'T AS BAD AS SOME OF THE OTHER KIDS!
I'VE HAD MY NOSE TWEAKED, HAIR PULLED, BEARD YANKED, AND MY SHINS KICKED!
WELL, IT'S OVER NOW! YOU DID A GOOD JOB FILLING IN FOR OUR REGULAR SANTA, WHO TOOK ILL!
THANK YOU! I NEEDED THE WEEK'S WORK! I'LL TURN IN MY SUIT NOW!
WHEW! WORKING AS SANTA WAS TIRING! I NEVER WANT TO GO THROUGH THAT AGAIN!
EMPLOYEES ONLY
2

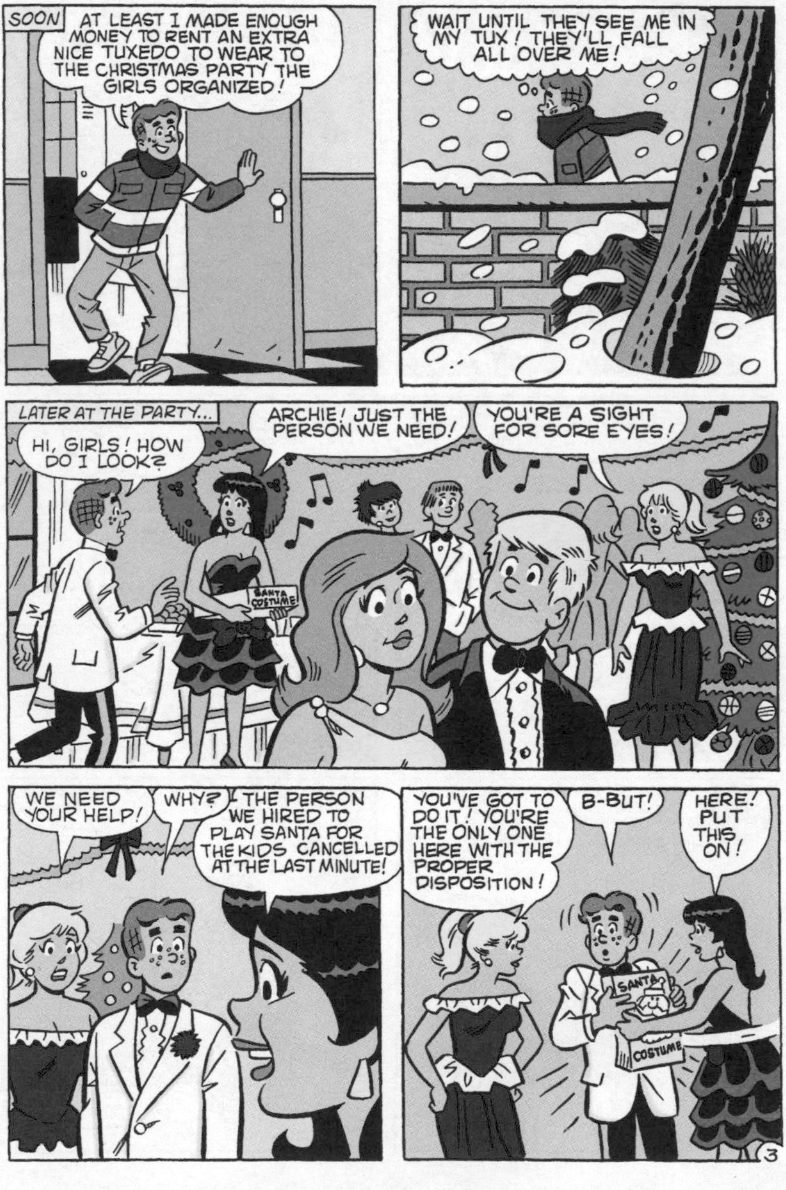
SOON
AT LEAST I MADE ENOUGH MONEY TO RENT AN EXTRA NICE TUXEDO TO WEAR TO THE CHRISTMAS PARTY THE GIRLS ORGANIZED!
WAIT UNTIL THEY SEE ME IN MY TUX! THEY'LL FALL ALL OVER ME!
LATER AT THE PARTY...
HI, GIRLS! HOW DO I LOOK?
ARCHIE! JUST THE PERSON WE NEED!
YOU'RE A SIGHT FOR SORE EYES!
SANTA COSTUME
WE NEED YOUR HELP!
WHY?
THE PERSON WE HIRED TO PLAY SANTA FOR THE KIDS CANCELLED AT THE LAST MINUTE!
YOU'VE GOT TO DO IT! YOU'RE THE ONLY ONE HERE WITH THE PROPER DISPOSITION!
B-BUT!
HERE! PUT THIS ON!
SANTA
COSTUME
3

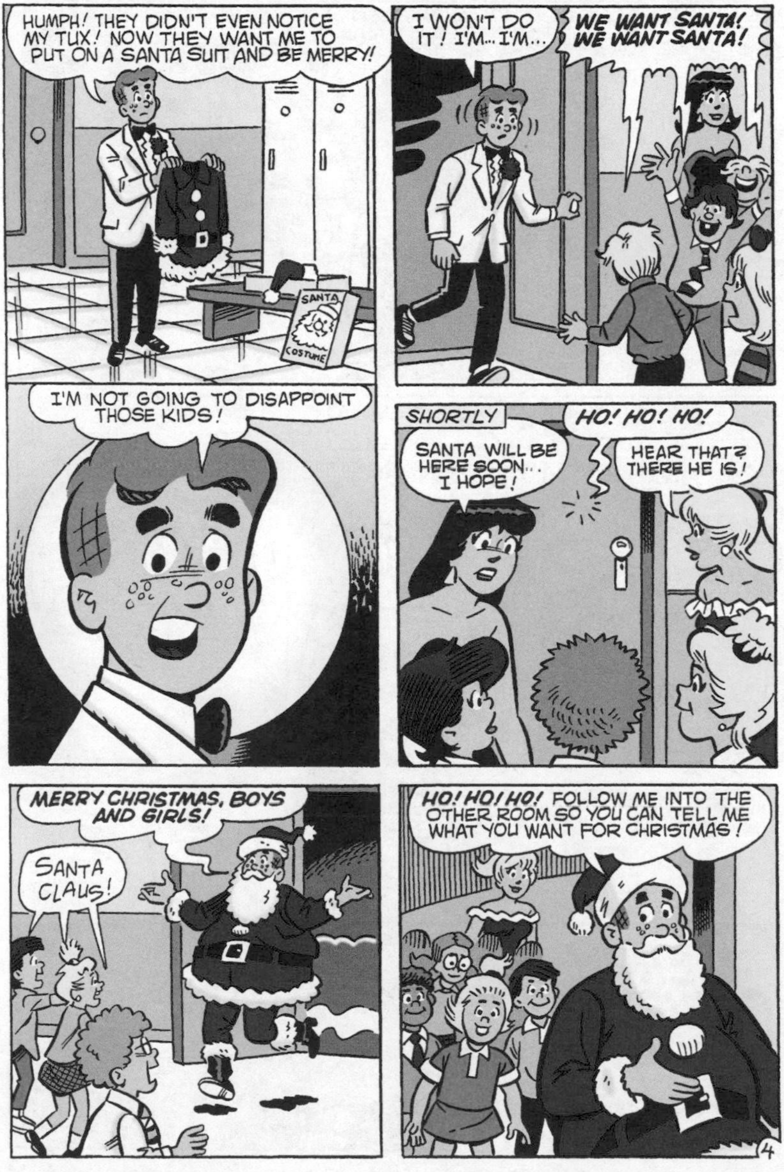
HUMPH! THEY DIDN'T EVEN NOTICE MY TUX! NOW THEY WANT ME TO PUT ON A SANTA SUIT AND BE MERRY!
SANTA COSTUME
I WON'T DO IT! I'M... I'M...
WE WANT SANTA! WE WANT SANTA!
I'M NOT GOING TO DISAPPOINT THOSE KIDS!
SHORTLY
SANTA WILL BE HERE SOON... I HOPE!
HO! HO! HO!
HEAR THAT? THERE HE IS!
MERRY CHRISTMAS, BOYS AND GIRLS!
SANTA CLAUS!
HO! HO! HO! FOLLOW ME INTO THE OTHER ROOM SO YOU CAN TELL ME WHAT YOU WANT FOR CHRISTMAS!
4

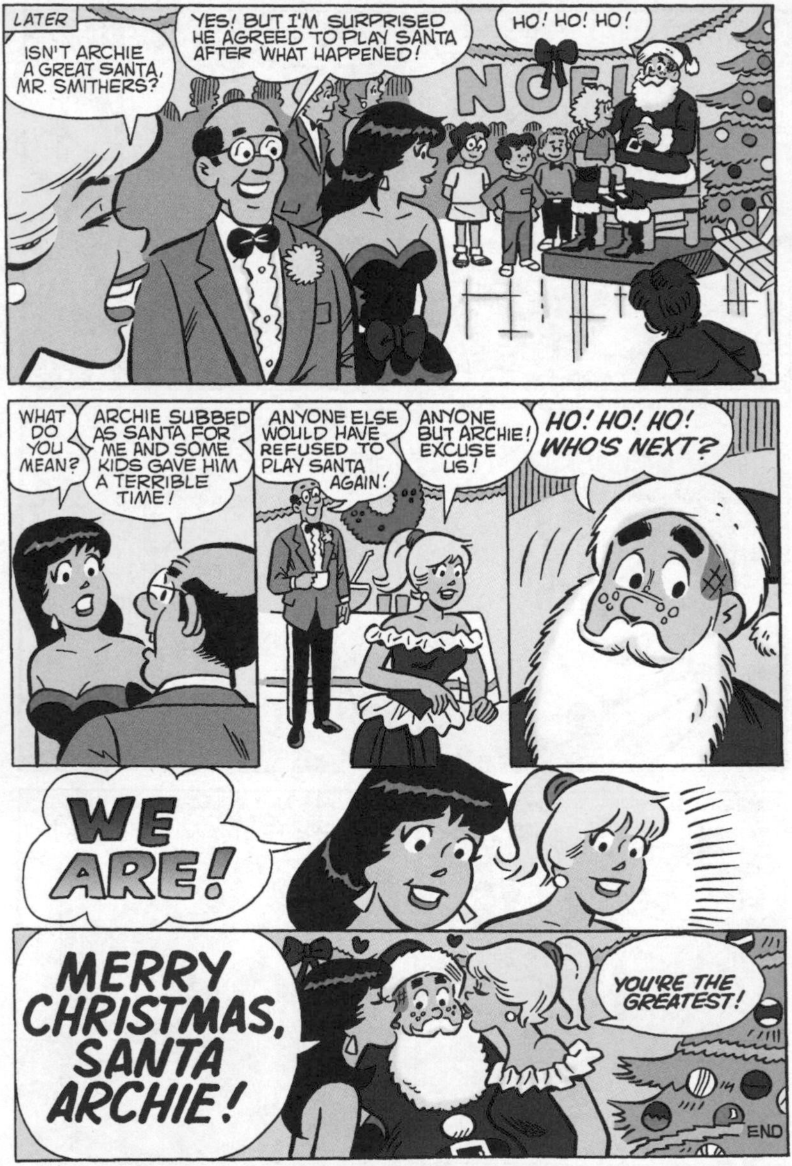
LATER
ISN'T ARCHIE A GREAT SANTA, MR. SMITHERS?
YES! BUT I'M SURPRISED HE AGREED TO PLAY SANTA AFTER WHAT HAPPENED!
HO! HO! HO!
NOEL
WHAT DO YOU MEAN?
ARCHIE SUBBED AS SANTA FOR ME AND SOME KIDS GAVE HIM A TERRIBLE TIME!
ANYONE ELSE WOULD HAVE REFUSED TO PLAY SANTA AGAIN!
ANYONE BUT ARCHIE! EXCUSE US!
HO! HO! HO! WHO'S NEXT?
WE ARE!
MERRY CHRISTMAS, SANTA ARCHIE!
YOU'RE THE GREATEST!
END

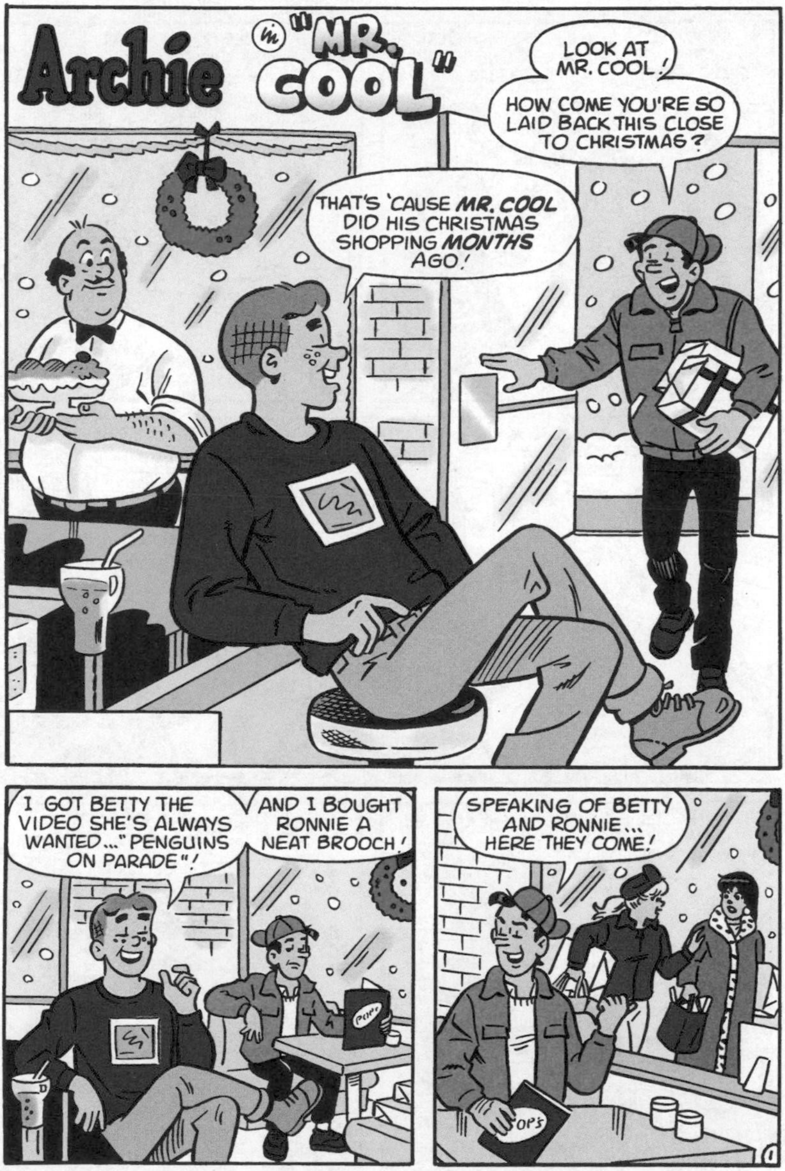
Archie in "MR. COOL"
LOOK AT MR. COOL!
HOW COME YOU'RE SO LAID BACK THIS CLOSE TO CHRISTMAS?
THAT'S 'CAUSE MR. COOL DID HIS CHRISTMAS SHOPPING MONTHS AGO!
I GOT BETTY THE VIDEO SHE'S ALWAYS WANTED..."PENGUINS ON PARADE"!
AND I BOUGHT RONNIE A NEAT BROOCH!
SPEAKING OF BETTY AND RONNIE... HERE THEY COME!

• **From Archie's Holiday Fun Digest #4, January 2000** •

George Gladir • Jeff Shultz • Rudy Lapick

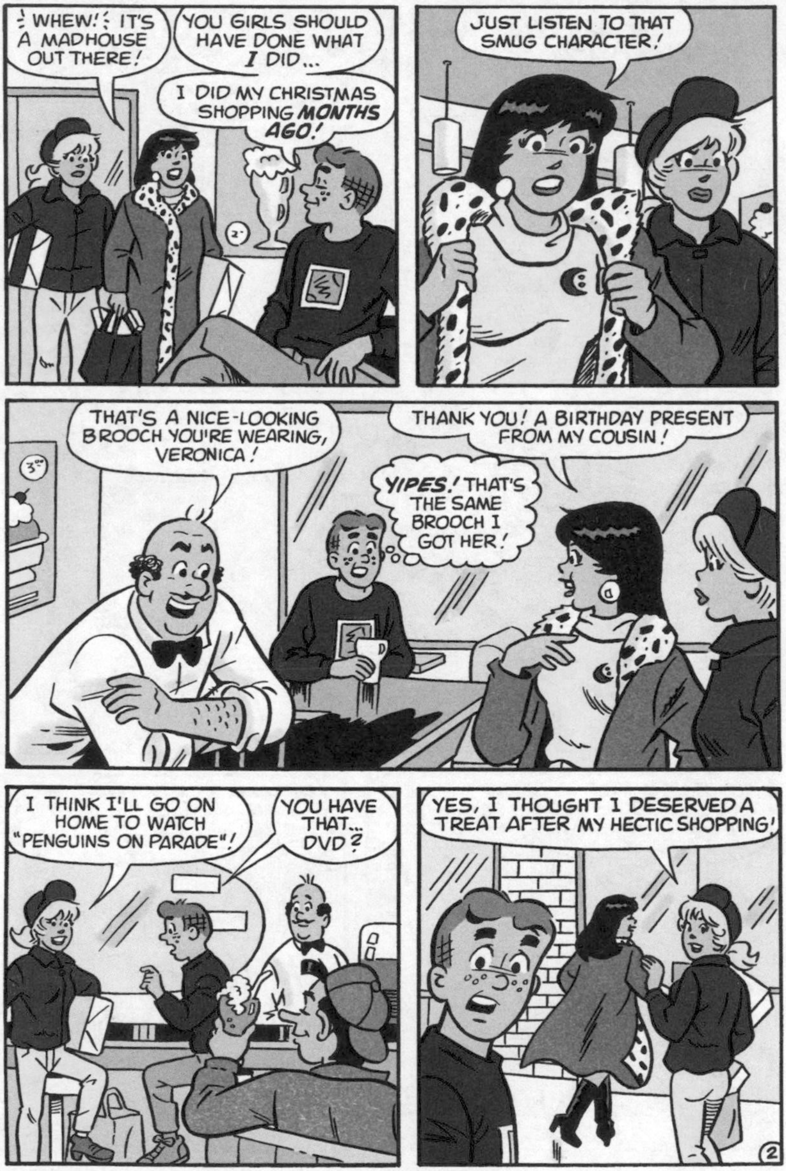
WHEW! IT'S A MADHOUSE OUT THERE!
YOU GIRLS SHOULD HAVE DONE WHAT I DID...
I DID MY CHRISTMAS SHOPPING MONTHS AGO!
JUST LISTEN TO THAT SMUG CHARACTER!
THAT'S A NICE-LOOKING BROOCH YOU'RE WEARING, VERONICA!
THANK YOU! A BIRTHDAY PRESENT FROM MY COUSIN!
YIPES! THAT'S THE SAME BROOCH I GOT HER!
I THINK I'LL GO ON HOME TO WATCH "PENGUINS ON PARADE"!
YOU HAVE THAT... DVD?
YES, I THOUGHT I DESERVED A TREAT AFTER MY HECTIC SHOPPING!
2

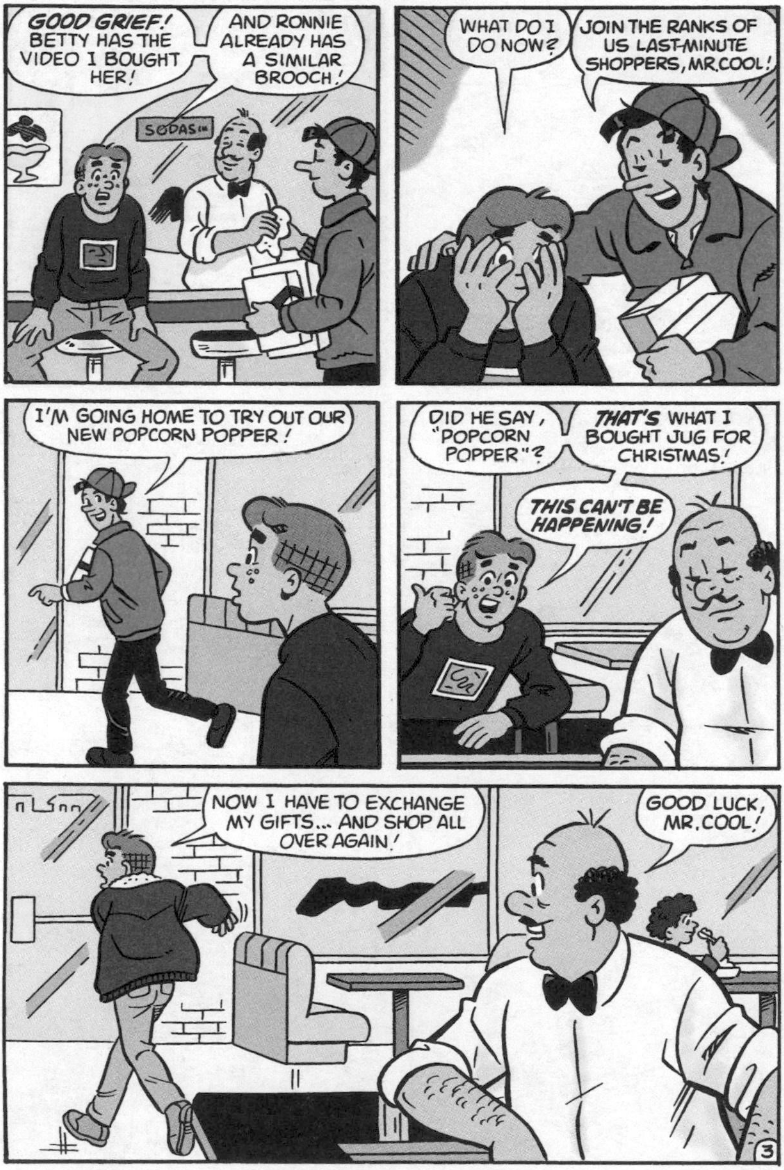
GOOD GRIEF! BETTY HAS THE VIDEO I BOUGHT HER!
AND RONNIE ALREADY HAS A SIMILAR BROOCH!
SODAS
WHAT DO I DO NOW?
JOIN THE RANKS OF US LAST-MINUTE SHOPPERS, MR. COOL!
I'M GOING HOME TO TRY OUT OUR NEW POPCORN POPPER!
DID HE SAY, "POPCORN POPPER"?
THAT'S WHAT I BOUGHT JUG FOR CHRISTMAS!
THIS CAN'T BE HAPPENING!
NOW I HAVE TO EXCHANGE MY GIFTS... AND SHOP ALL OVER AGAIN!
GOOD LUCK, MR. COOL!
3

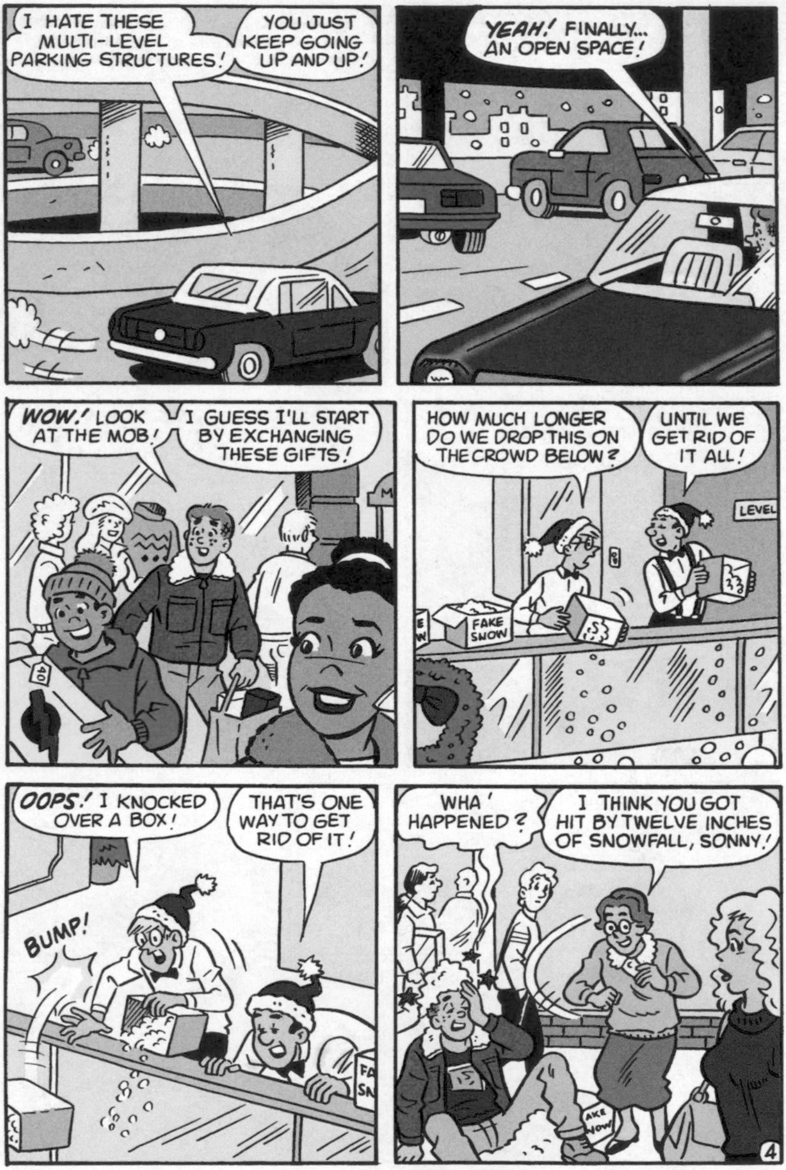
I HATE THESE MULTI-LEVEL PARKING STRUCTURES!
YOU JUST KEEP GOING UP AND UP!
YEAH! FINALLY... AN OPEN SPACE!
WOW! LOOK AT THE MOB!
I GUESS I'LL START BY EXCHANGING THESE GIFTS!
HOW MUCH LONGER DO WE DROP THIS ON THE CROWD BELOW?
UNTIL WE GET RID OF IT ALL!
LEVEL
FAKE SNOW
OOPS! I KNOCKED OVER A BOX!
THAT'S ONE WAY TO GET RID OF IT!
BUMP!
WHA' HAPPENED?
I THINK YOU GOT HIT BY TWELVE INCHES OF SNOWFALL, SONNY!
4

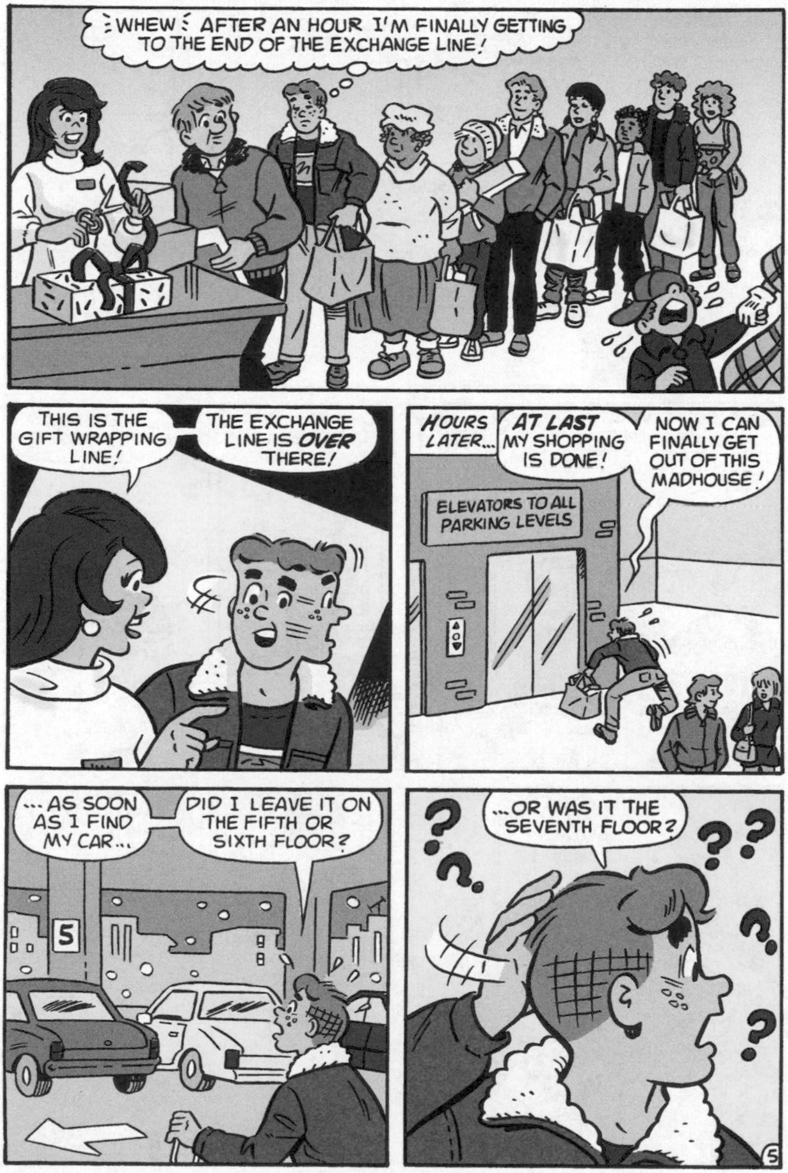
WHEW! AFTER AN HOUR I'M FINALLY GETTING TO THE END OF THE EXCHANGE LINE!
THIS IS THE GIFT WRAPPING LINE!
THE EXCHANGE LINE IS OVER THERE!
HOURS LATER...
AT LAST MY SHOPPING IS DONE!
NOW I CAN FINALLY GET OUT OF THIS MADHOUSE!
ELEVATORS TO ALL PARKING LEVELS
...AS SOON AS I FIND MY CAR...
DID I LEAVE IT ON THE FIFTH OR SIXTH FLOOR?
5
...OR WAS IT THE SEVENTH FLOOR?
5

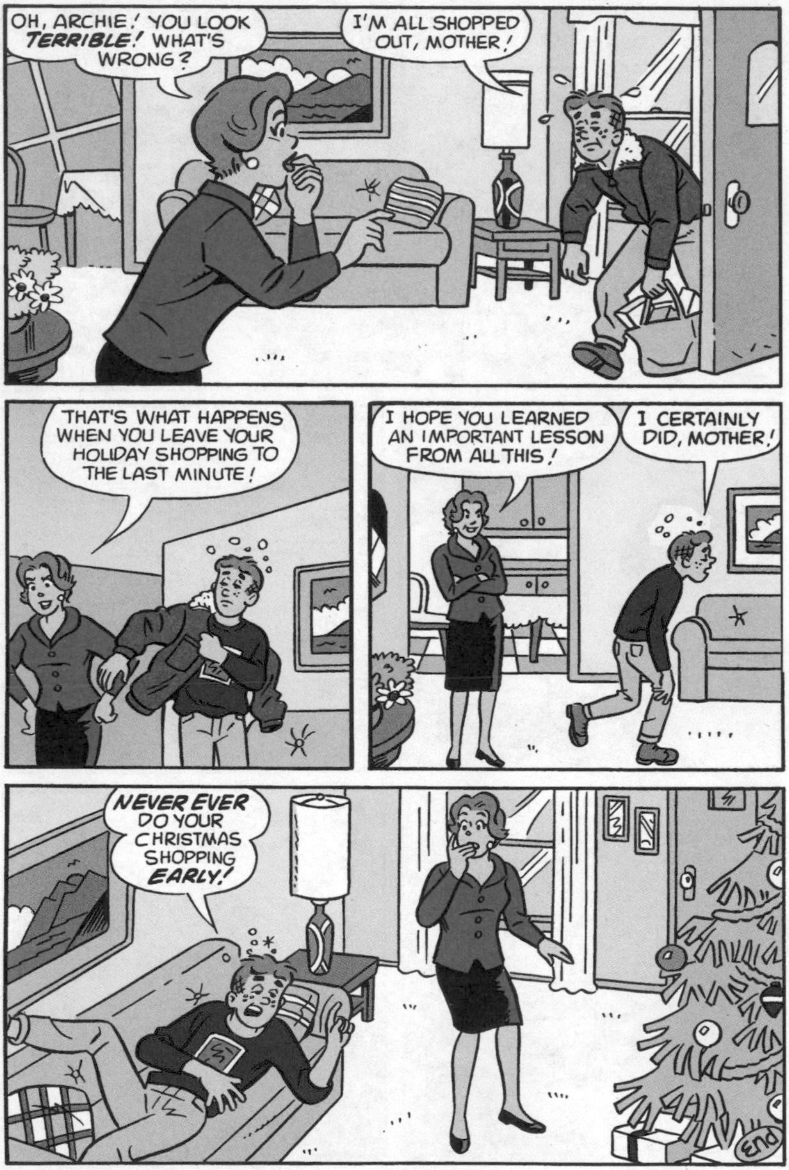
OH, ARCHIE! YOU LOOK TERRIBLE! WHAT'S WRONG?
I'M ALL SHOPPED OUT, MOTHER!
THAT'S WHAT HAPPENS WHEN YOU LEAVE YOUR HOLIDAY SHOPPING TO THE LAST MINUTE!
I HOPE YOU LEARNED AN IMPORTANT LESSON FROM ALL THIS!
I CERTAINLY DID, MOTHER!
NEVER EVER DO YOUR CHRISTMAS SHOPPING EARLY!
End

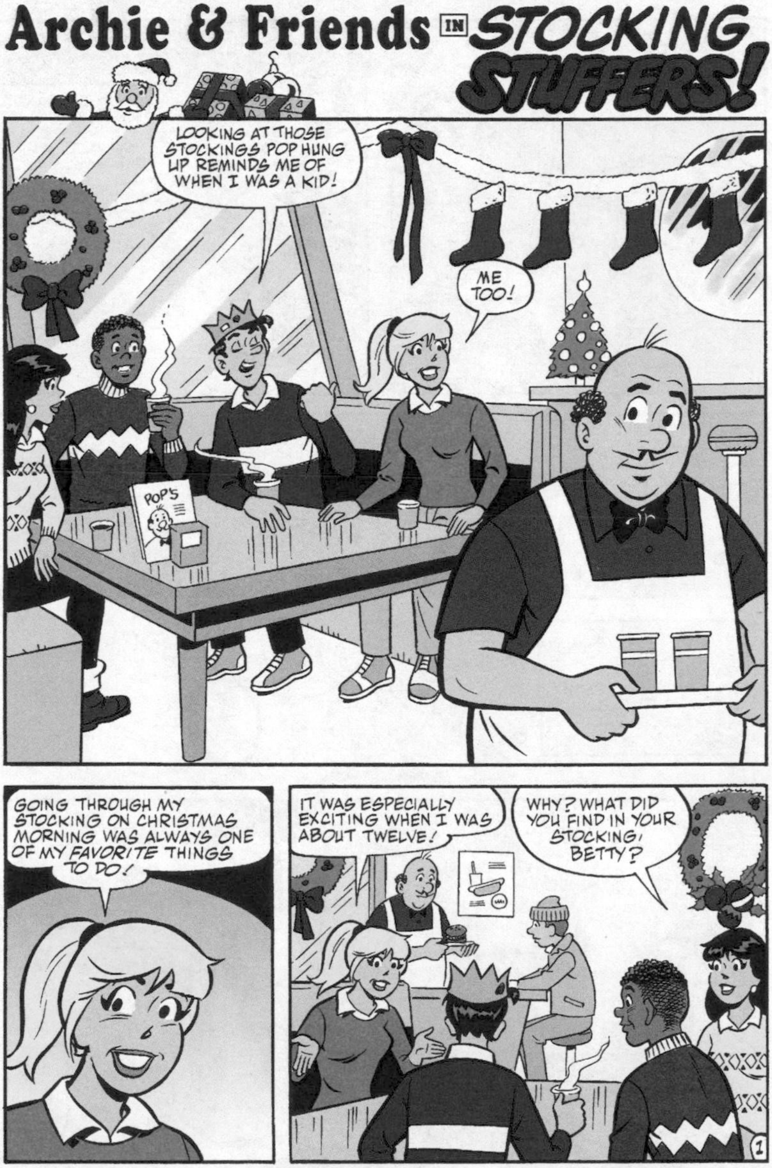
Archie & Friends IN STOCKING STUFFERS!
LOOKING AT THOSE STOCKINGS POP HUNG UP REMINDS ME OF WHEN I WAS A KID!
ME TOO!
POP'S
GOING THROUGH MY STOCKING ON CHRISTMAS MORNING WAS ALWAYS ONE OF MY FAVORITE THINGS TO DO!
IT WAS ESPECIALLY EXCITING WHEN I WAS ABOUT TWELVE!
WHY? WHAT DID YOU FIND IN YOUR STOCKING, BETTY?
1

• **From Archie's Holiday Fun Digest #11, December 2006** •

Mike Pellowski • Henry Scarpelli • Jon D'Agostino

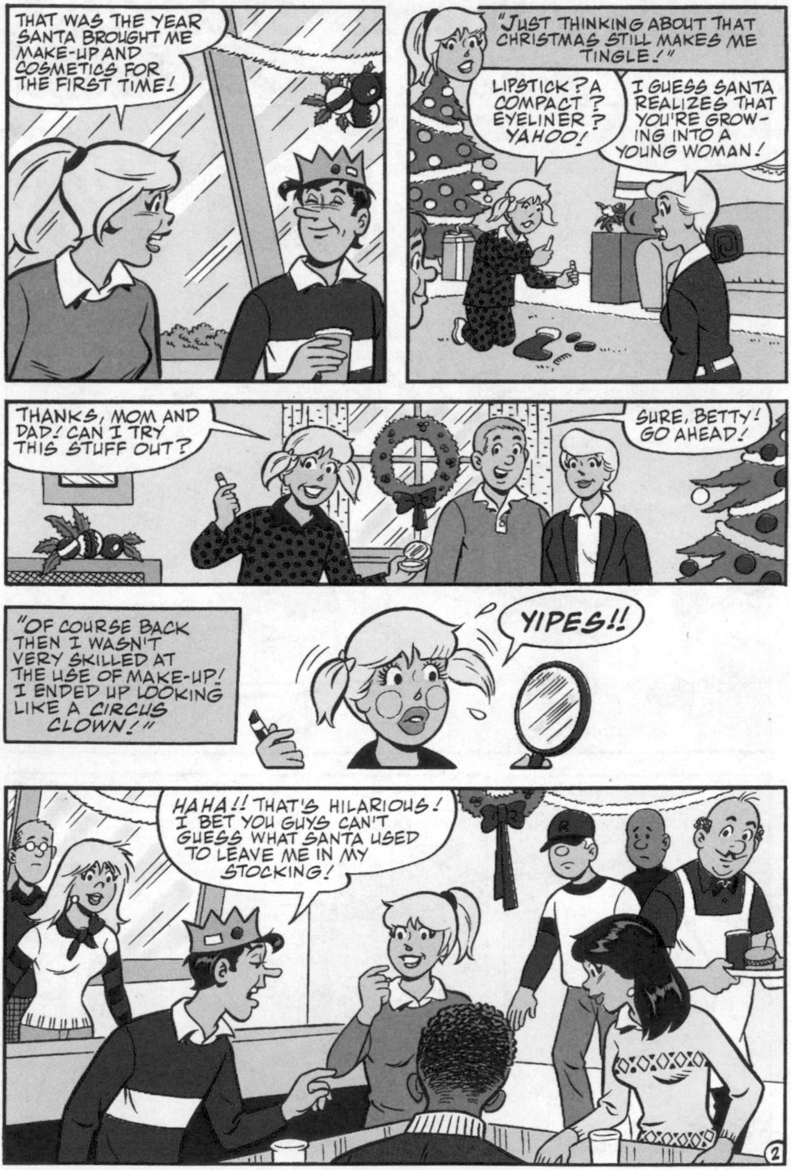
THAT WAS THE YEAR SANTA BROUGHT ME MAKE-UP AND COSMETICS FOR THE FIRST TIME!
"JUST THINKING ABOUT THAT CHRISTMAS STILL MAKES ME TINGLE!"
LIPSTICK? A COMPACT? EYELINER? YAHOO!
I GUESS SANTA REALIZES THAT YOU'RE GROWING INTO A YOUNG WOMAN!
THANKS, MOM AND DAD! CAN I TRY THIS STUFF OUT?
SURE, BETTY! GO AHEAD!
"OF COURSE BACK THEN I WASN'T VERY SKILLED AT THE USE OF MAKE-UP! I ENDED UP LOOKING LIKE A CIRCUS CLOWN!"
YIPES!!
HAHA!! THAT'S HILARIOUS! I BET YOU GUYS CAN'T GUESS WHAT SANTA USED TO LEAVE ME IN MY STOCKING!
2

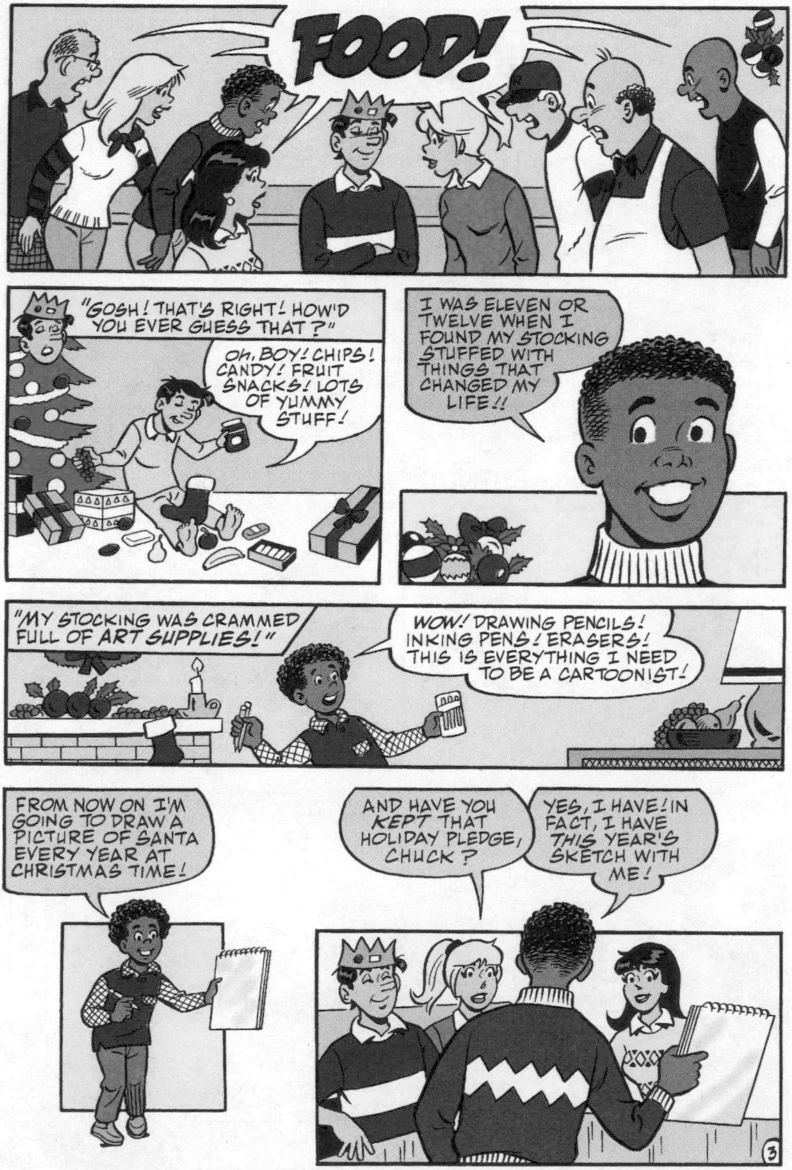
FOOD!
"GOSH! THAT'S RIGHT! HOW'D YOU EVER GUESS THAT?"
OH, BOY! CHIPS! CANDY! FRUIT SNACKS! LOTS OF YUMMY STUFF!
I WAS ELEVEN OR TWELVE WHEN I FOUND MY STOCKING STUFFED WITH THINGS THAT CHANGED MY LIFE!!
"MY STOCKING WAS CRAMMED FULL OF ART SUPPLIES!"
WOW! DRAWING PENCILS! INKING PENS! ERASERS! THIS IS EVERYTHING I NEED TO BE A CARTOONIST!
FROM NOW ON I'M GOING TO DRAW A PICTURE OF SANTA EVERY YEAR AT CHRISTMAS TIME!
AND HAVE YOU KEPT THAT HOLIDAY PLEDGE, CHUCK?
YES, I HAVE! IN FACT, I HAVE THIS YEAR'S SKETCH WITH ME!
3

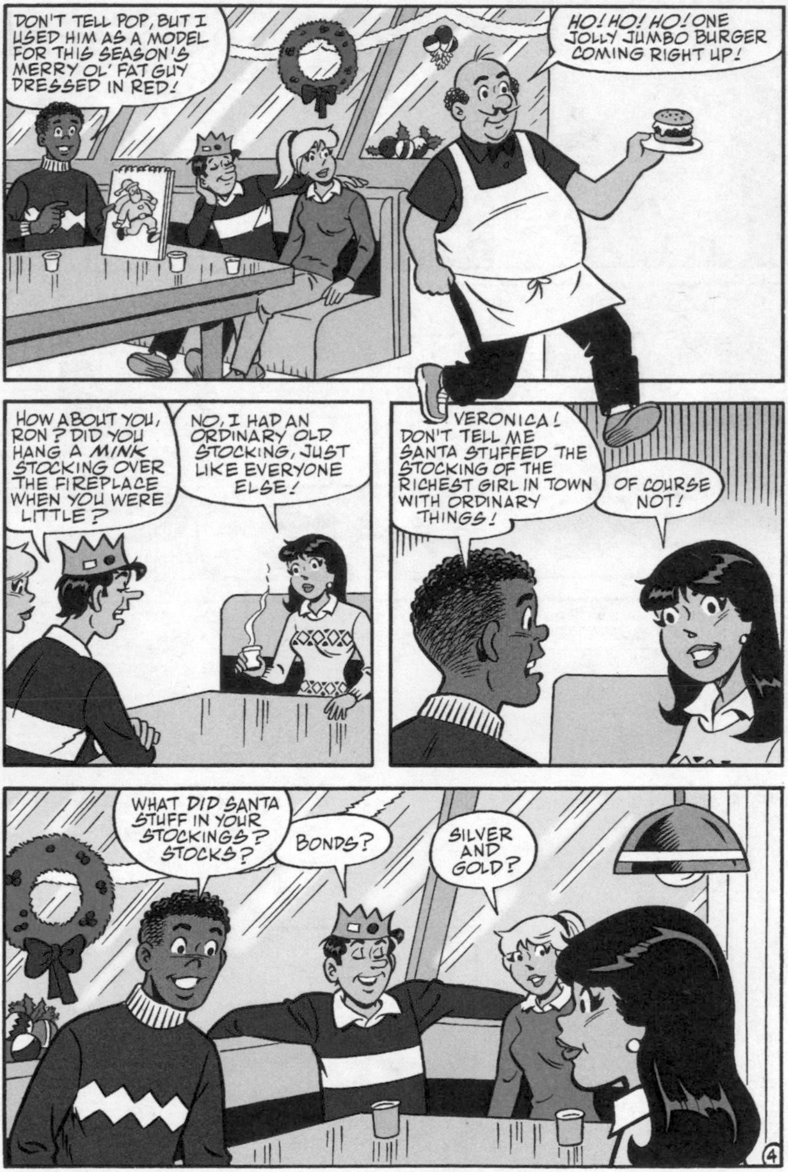
DON'T TELL POP, BUT I USED HIM AS A MODEL FOR THIS SEASON'S MERRY OL' FAT GUY DRESSED IN RED!
HO! HO! HO! ONE JOLLY JUMBO BURGER COMING RIGHT UP!
HOW ABOUT YOU, RON? DID YOU HANG A MINK STOCKING OVER THE FIREPLACE WHEN YOU WERE LITTLE?
NO, I HAD AN ORDINARY OLD STOCKING, JUST LIKE EVERYONE ELSE!
VERONICA! DON'T TELL ME SANTA STUFFED THE STOCKING OF THE RICHEST GIRL IN TOWN WITH ORDINARY THINGS!
OF COURSE NOT!
WHAT DID SANTA STUFF IN YOUR STOCKINGS? STOCKS?
BONDS?
SILVER AND GOLD?
4

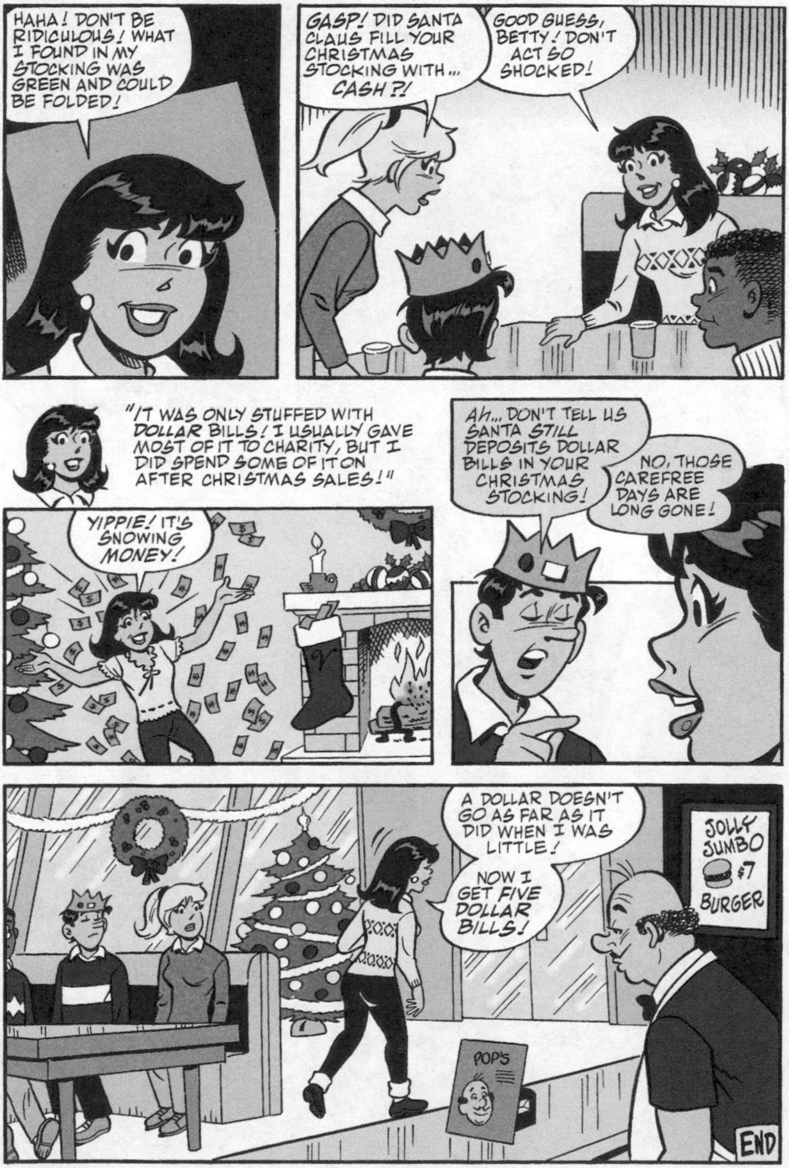
HAHA! DON'T BE RIDICULOUS! WHAT I FOUND IN MY STOCKING WAS GREEN AND COULD BE FOLDED!
GASP! DID SANTA CLAUS FILL YOUR CHRISTMAS STOCKING WITH... CASH?!
GOOD GUESS, BETTY! DON'T ACT SO SHOCKED!
"IT WAS ONLY STUFFED WITH DOLLAR BILLS! I USUALLY GAVE MOST OF IT TO CHARITY, BUT I DID SPEND SOME OF IT ON AFTER CHRISTMAS SALES!"
YIPPIE! IT'S SNOWING MONEY!
Ah... DON'T TELL US SANTA STILL DEPOSITS DOLLAR BILLS IN YOUR CHRISTMAS STOCKING!
NO, THOSE CAREFREE DAYS ARE LONG GONE!
A DOLLAR DOESN'T GO AS FAR AS IT DID WHEN I WAS LITTLE!
NOW I GET FIVE DOLLAR BILLS!
JOLLY JUMBO $7 BURGER
POP'S
END

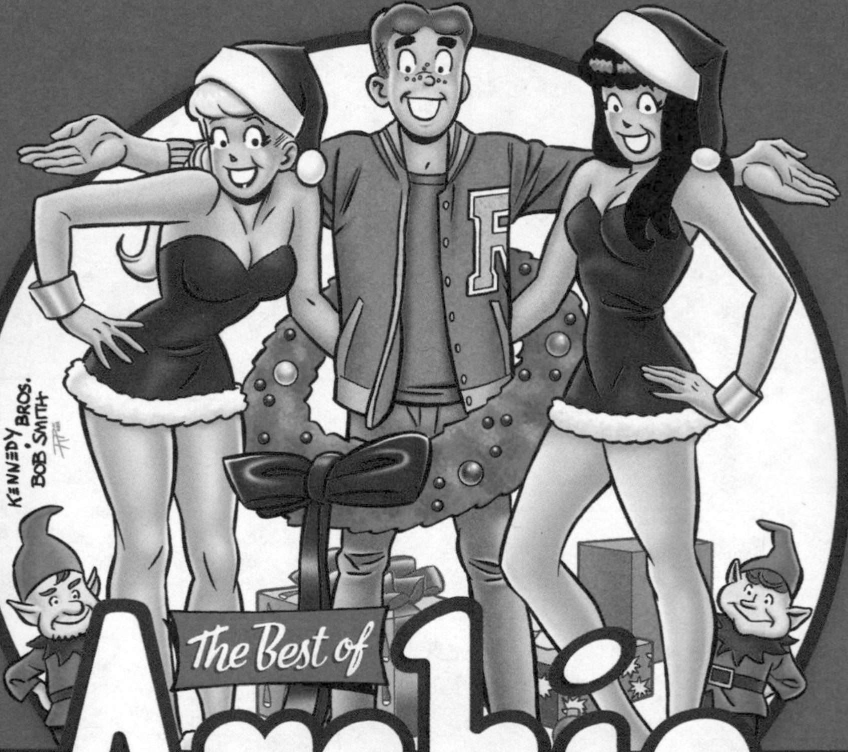

The Best of Archie® Christmas Comics

THE 2010s

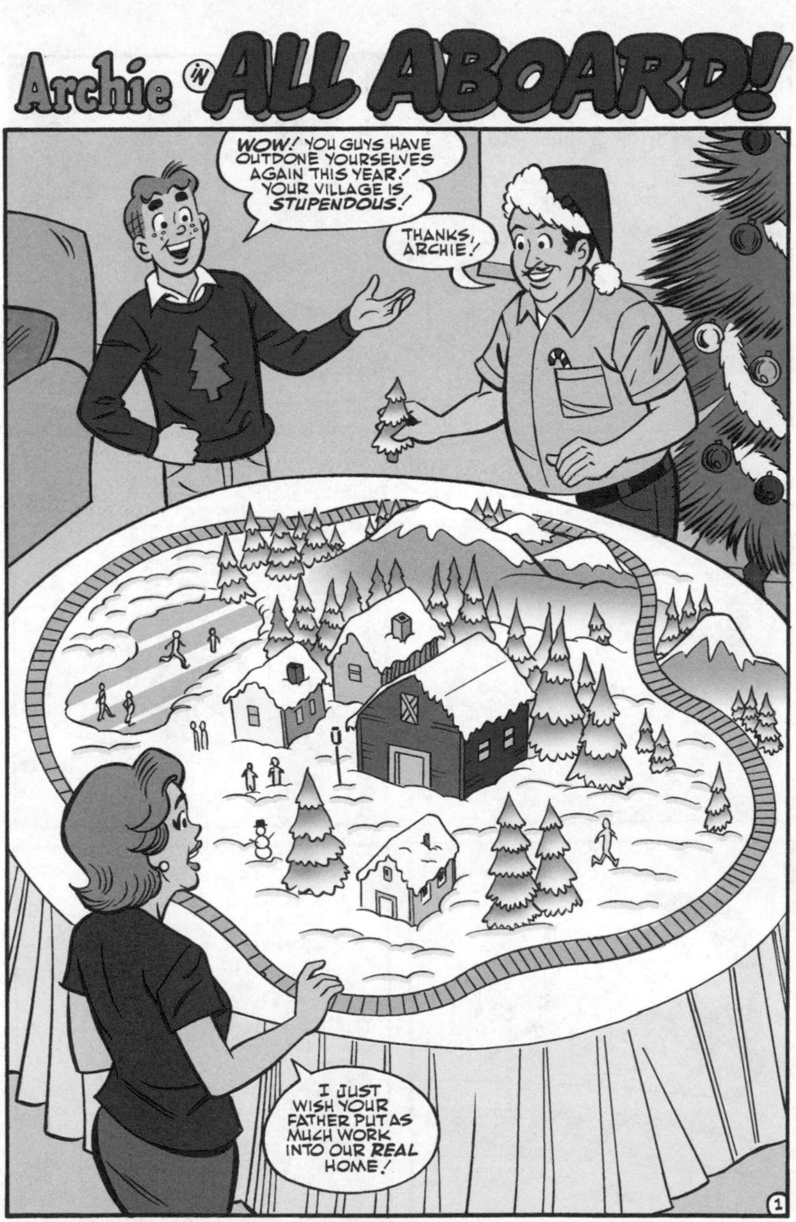
Archie in ALL ABOARD!
WOW! YOU GUYS HAVE OUTDONE YOURSELVES AGAIN THIS YEAR! YOUR VILLAGE IS STUPENDOUS!
THANKS, ARCHIE!
I JUST WISH YOUR FATHER PUT AS MUCH WORK INTO OUR REAL HOME!
1

• **From World of Archie Double Digest #73, December 2017** •

Dan Parent • Bill Galvan • Bob Smith • Glenn Whitmore • Jack Morelli

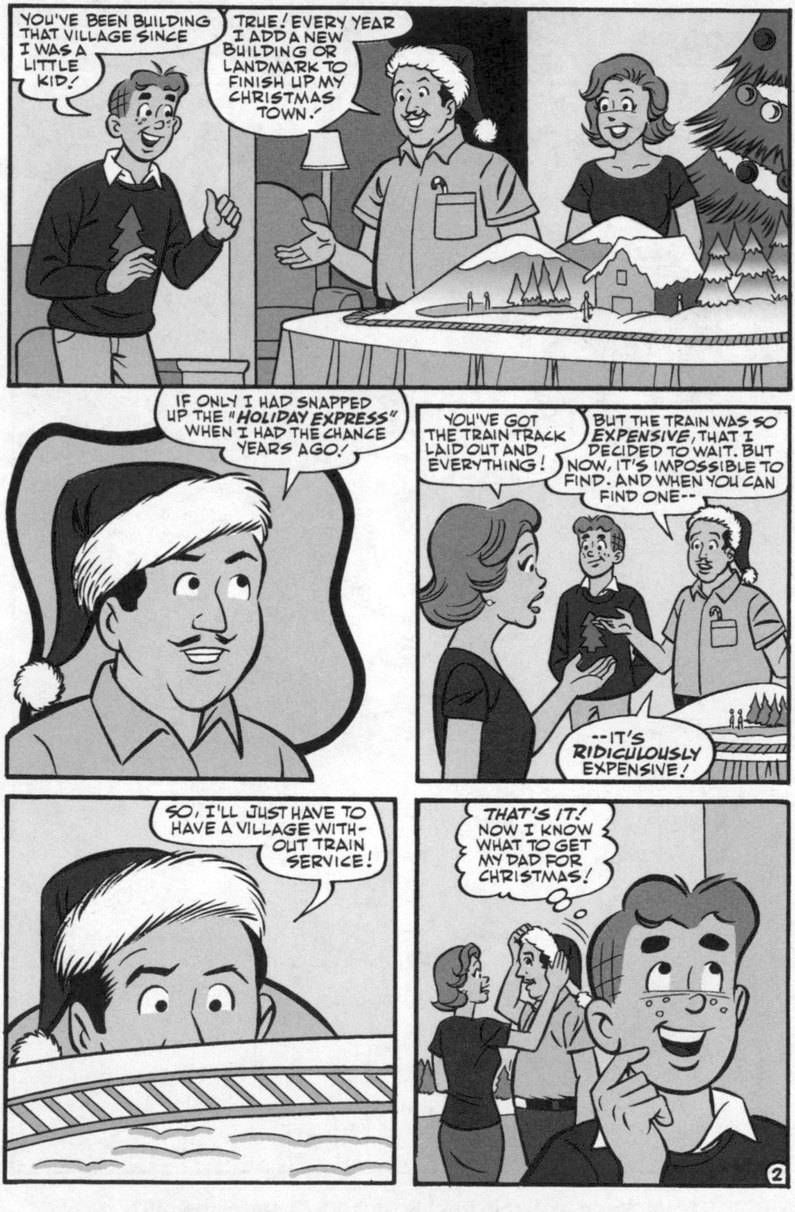
YOU'VE BEEN BUILDING THAT VILLAGE SINCE I WAS A LITTLE KID!
TRUE! EVERY YEAR I ADD A NEW BUILDING OR LANDMARK TO FINISH UP MY CHRISTMAS TOWN.!
IF ONLY I HAD SNAPPED UP THE "HOLIDAY EXPRESS" WHEN I HAD THE CHANCE YEARS AGO!
YOU'VE GOT THE TRAIN TRACK LAID OUT AND EVERYTHING!
BUT THE TRAIN WAS SO EXPENSIVE, THAT I DECIDED TO WAIT. BUT NOW, IT'S IMPOSSIBLE TO FIND. AND WHEN YOU CAN FIND ONE--
--IT'S RIDICULOUSLY EXPENSIVE!
SO, I'LL JUST HAVE TO HAVE A VILLAGE WITH-OUT TRAIN SERVICE!
THAT'S IT! NOW I KNOW WHAT TO GET MY DAD FOR CHRISTMAS!
2

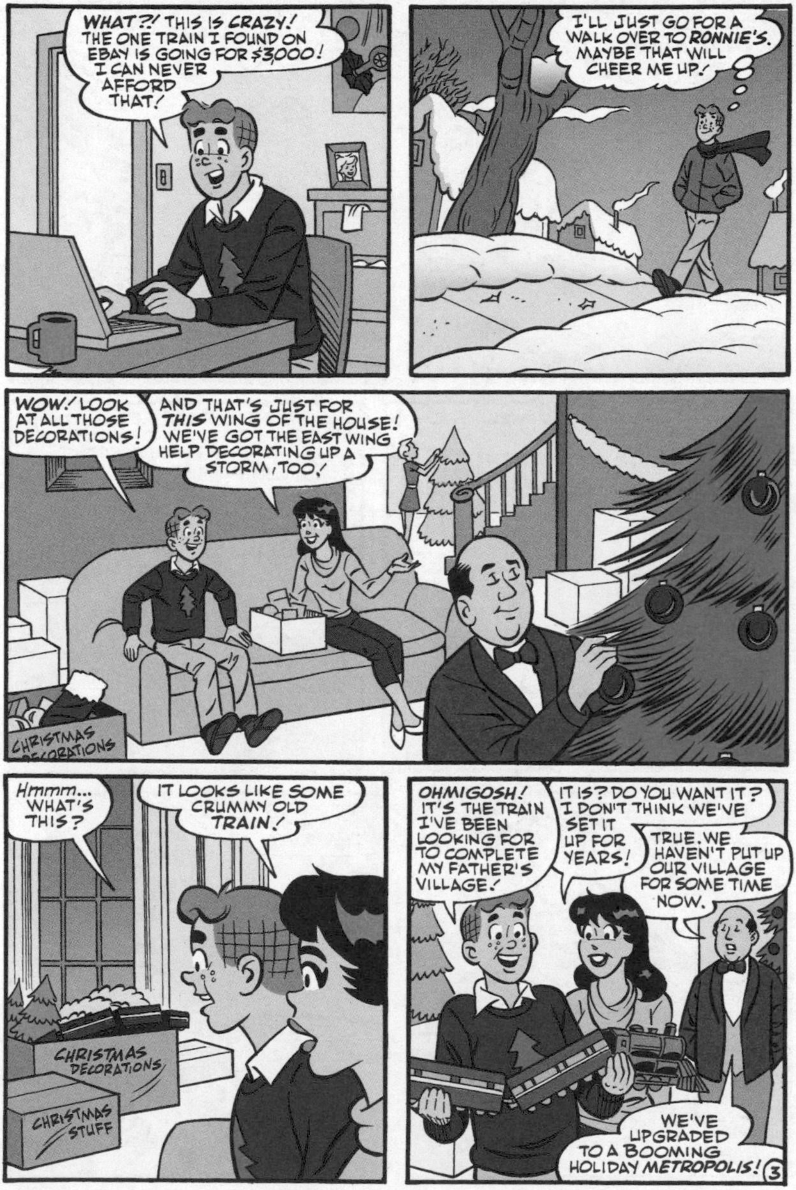
WHAT?! THIS IS CRAZY! THE ONE TRAIN I FOUND ON EBAY IS GOING FOR $3,000! I CAN NEVER AFFORD THAT!
I'LL JUST GO FOR A WALK OVER TO RONNIE'S. MAYBE THAT WILL CHEER ME UP!
WOW! LOOK AT ALL THOSE DECORATIONS!
AND THAT'S JUST FOR THIS WING OF THE HOUSE! WE'VE GOT THE EAST WING HELP DECORATING UP A STORM, TOO!
CHRISTMAS DECORATIONS
Hmmm... WHAT'S THIS?
IT LOOKS LIKE SOME CRUMMY OLD TRAIN!
CHRISTMAS DECORATIONS
CHRISTMAS STUFF
OHMIGOSH! IT'S THE TRAIN I'VE BEEN LOOKING FOR TO COMPLETE MY FATHER'S VILLAGE!
IT IS? DO YOU WANT IT? I DON'T THINK WE'VE SET IT UP FOR YEARS!
TRUE. WE HAVEN'T PUT UP OUR VILLAGE FOR SOME TIME NOW.
WE'VE UPGRADED TO A BOOMING HOLIDAY METROPOLIS!
3

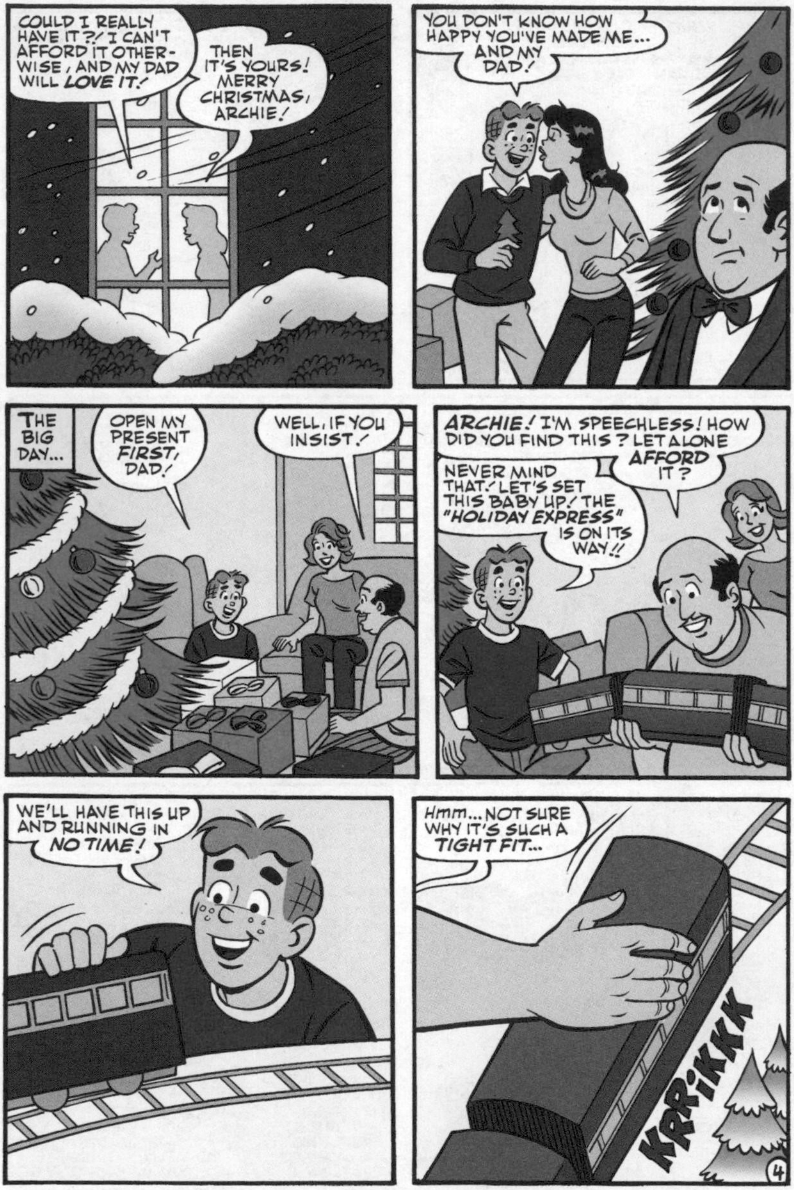
COULD I REALLY HAVE IT?! I CAN'T AFFORD IT OTHER-WISE, AND MY DAD WILL LOVE IT!
THEN IT'S YOURS! MERRY CHRISTMAS, ARCHIE!
YOU DON'T KNOW HOW HAPPY YOU'VE MADE ME... AND MY DAD!
THE BIG DAY...
OPEN MY PRESENT FIRST, DAD!
WELL, IF YOU INSIST!
ARCHIE! I'M SPEECHLESS! HOW DID YOU FIND THIS? LET ALONE AFFORD IT?
NEVER MIND THAT! LET'S SET THIS BABY UP! THE "HOLIDAY EXPRESS" IS ON ITS WAY!!
WE'LL HAVE THIS UP AND RUNNING IN NO TIME!
Hmm... NOT SURE WHY IT'S SUCH A TIGHT FIT...
KRRiKKK
4

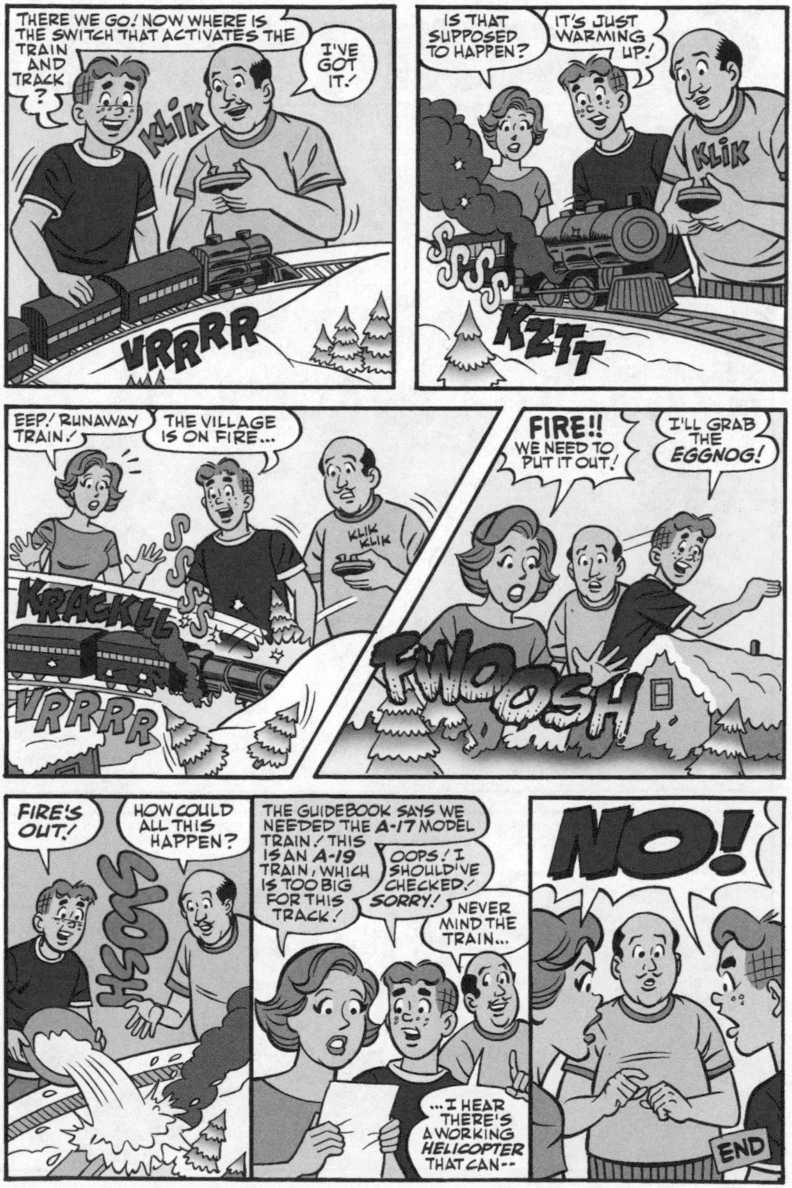
THERE WE GO! NOW WHERE IS THE SWITCH THAT ACTIVATES THE TRAIN AND TRACK?
I'VE GOT IT!
KLIK
VRRRR
IS THAT SUPPOSED TO HAPPEN?
IT'S JUST WARMING UP!
KLIK
SSSS
KZTT
EEP! RUNAWAY TRAIN!
THE VILLAGE IS ON FIRE...
KLIK KLIK
KRACKLLL
VRRRRR
FIRE!! WE NEED TO PUT IT OUT!
I'LL GRAB THE EGGNOG!
FWOOOSH
FIRE'S OUT!
HOW COULD ALL THIS HAPPEN?
SLOSH
THE GUIDEBOOK SAYS WE NEEDED THE A-17 MODEL TRAIN! THIS IS AN A-19 TRAIN, WHICH IS TOO BIG FOR THIS TRACK!
OOPS! I SHOULD'VE CHECKED! SORRY!
NEVER MIND THE TRAIN...
...I HEAR THERE'S A WORKING HELICOPTER THAT CAN--
NO!
END

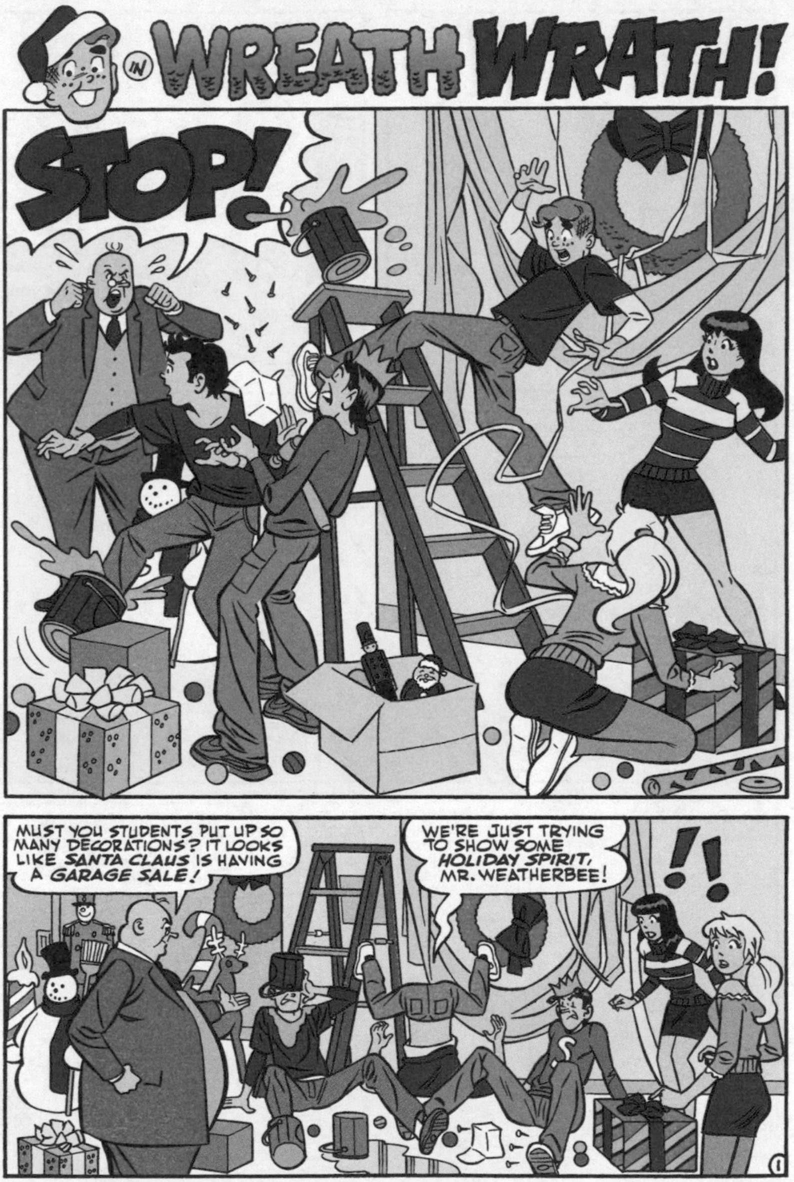
IN
WREATH WRATH!
STOP!
MUST YOU STUDENTS PUT UP SO MANY DECORATIONS? IT LOOKS LIKE SANTA CLAUS IS HAVING A GARAGE SALE!
WE'RE JUST TRYING TO SHOW SOME HOLIDAY SPIRIT, MR. WEATHERBEE!
!!
1

• **From World of Archie Double Digest #84, January 2019** •

Angelo DeCesare • Pat & Tim Kennedy • Glenn Whitmore • Bob Smith • Jack Morelli

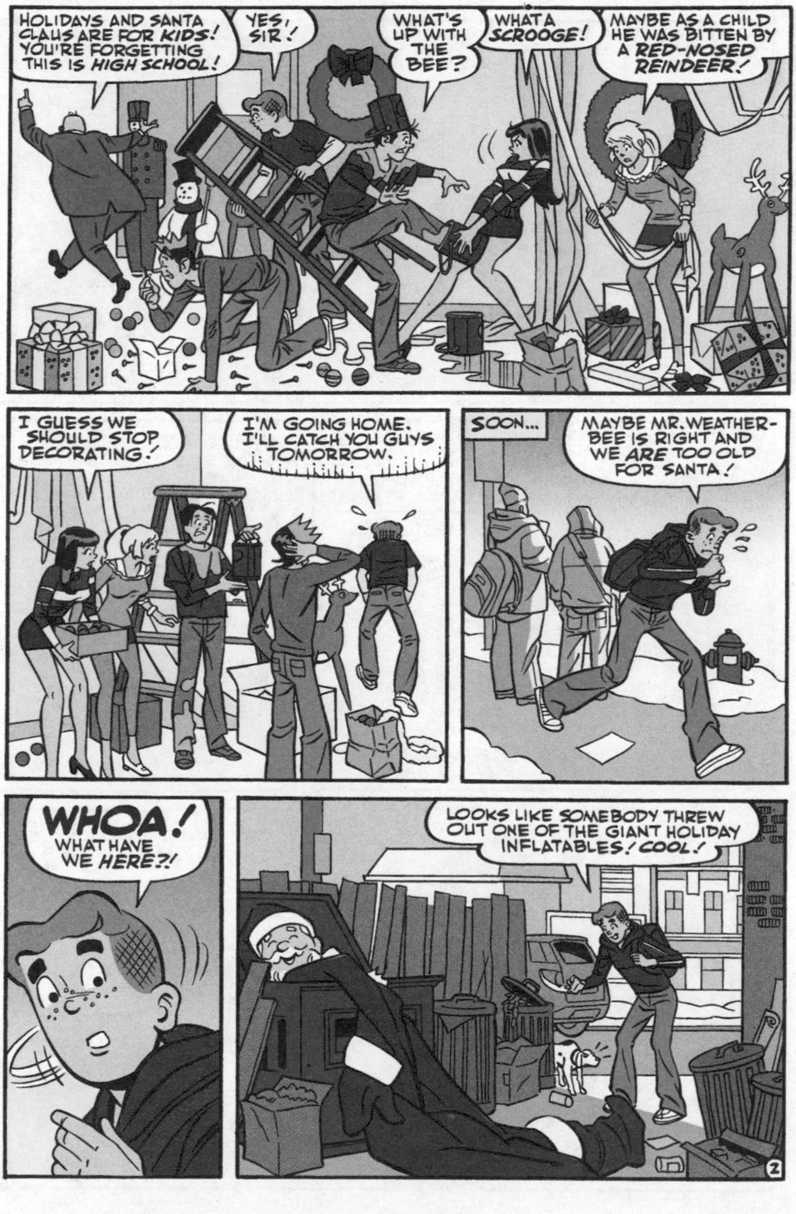
HOLIDAYS AND SANTA CLAUS ARE FOR KIDS! YOU'RE FORGETTING THIS IS HIGH SCHOOL!
YES, SIR!
WHAT'S UP WITH THE BEE?
WHAT A SCROOGE!
MAYBE AS A CHILD HE WAS BITTEN BY A RED-NOSED REINDEER!
I GUESS WE SHOULD STOP DECORATING!
I'M GOING HOME. I'LL CATCH YOU GUYS TOMORROW.
SOON...
MAYBE MR. WEATHERBEE IS RIGHT AND WE ARE TOO OLD FOR SANTA!
WHOA! WHAT HAVE WE HERE?!
LOOKS LIKE SOMEBODY THREW OUT ONE OF THE GIANT HOLIDAY INFLATABLES! COOL!
2

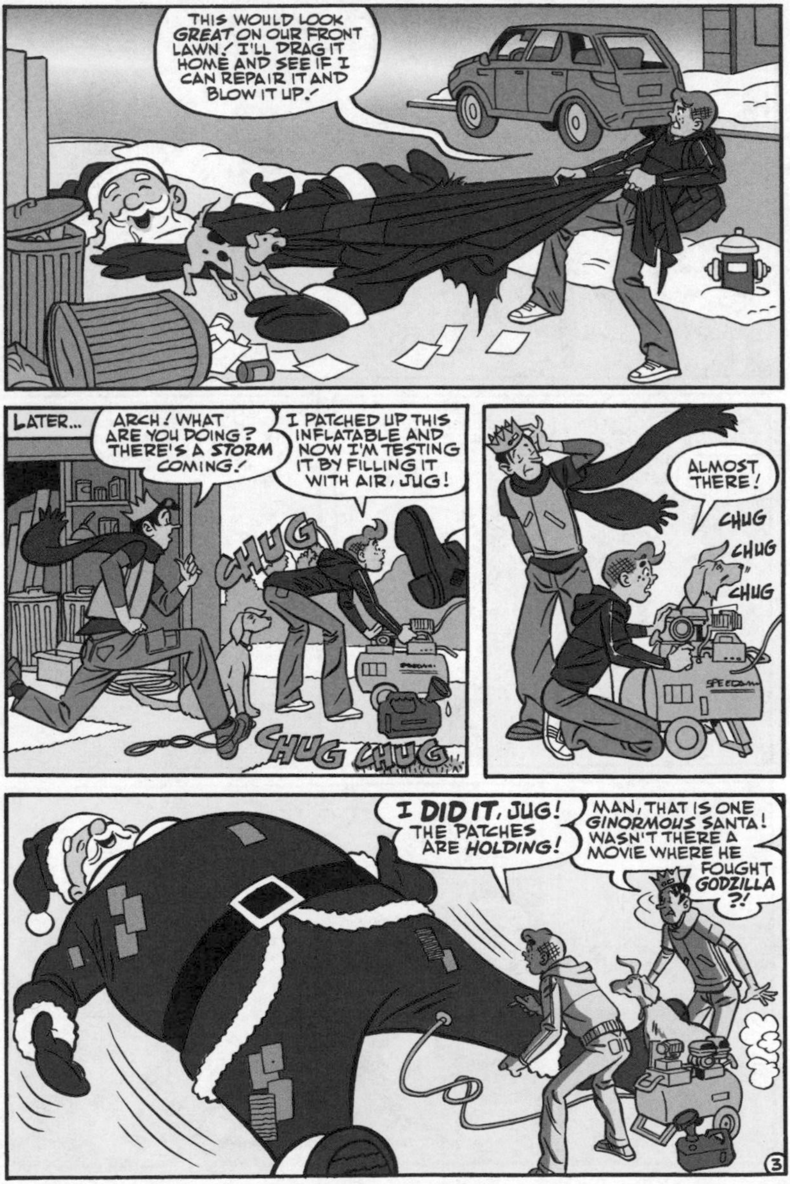
THIS WOULD LOOK GREAT ON OUR FRONT LAWN! I'LL DRAG IT HOME AND SEE IF I CAN REPAIR IT AND BLOW IT UP!
LATER...
ARCH! WHAT ARE YOU DOING? THERE'S A STORM COMING!
I PATCHED UP THIS INFLATABLE AND NOW I'M TESTING IT BY FILLING IT WITH AIR, JUG!
CHUG
CHUG CHUG
ALMOST THERE!
CHUG
CHUG
CHUG
I DID IT, JUG! THE PATCHES ARE HOLDING!
MAN, THAT IS ONE GINORMOUS SANTA! WASN'T THERE A MOVIE WHERE HE FOUGHT GODZILLA ?!
3

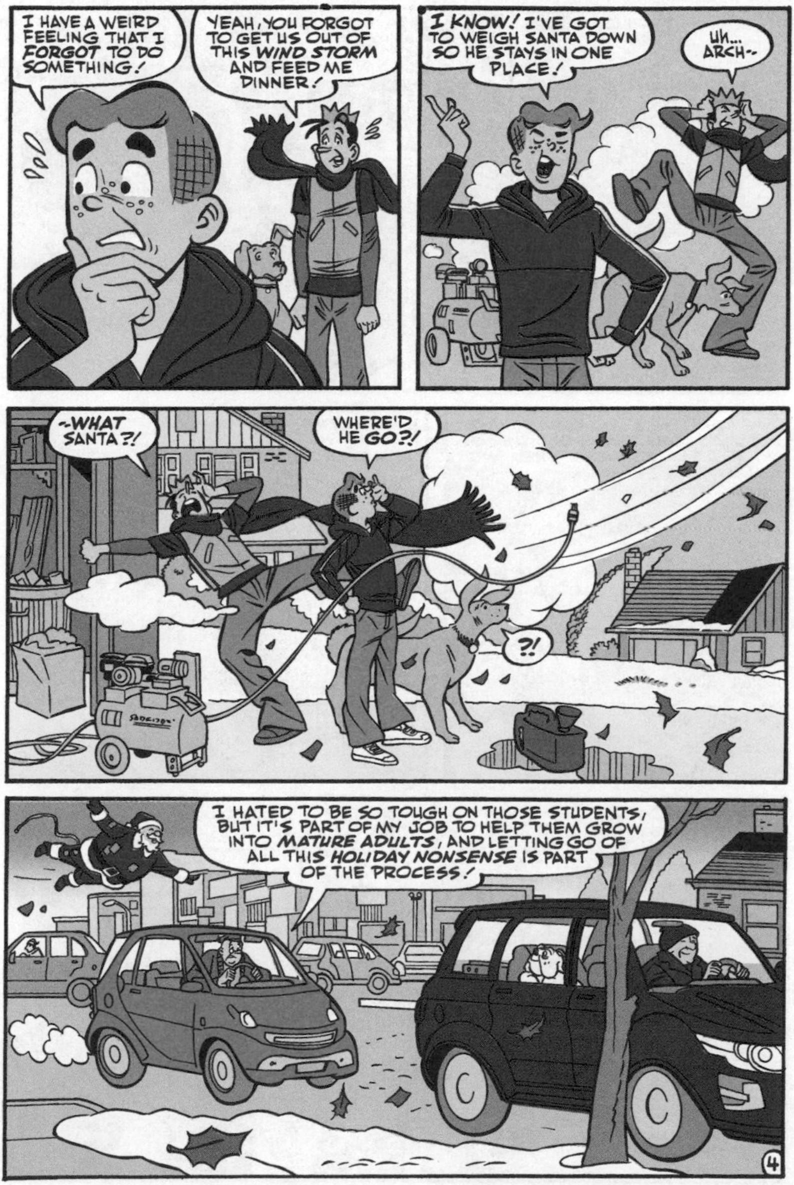
I HAVE A WEIRD FEELING THAT I FORGOT TO DO SOMETHING!
YEAH, YOU FORGOT TO GET US OUT OF THIS WIND STORM AND FEED ME DINNER!
I KNOW! I'VE GOT TO WEIGH SANTA DOWN SO HE STAYS IN ONE PLACE!
UH... ARCH--
--WHAT SANTA?!
WHERE'D HE GO?!
?!
I HATED TO BE SO TOUGH ON THOSE STUDENTS, BUT IT'S PART OF MY JOB TO HELP THEM GROW INTO MATURE ADULTS, AND LETTING GO OF ALL THIS HOLIDAY NONSENSE IS PART OF THE PROCESS!
4

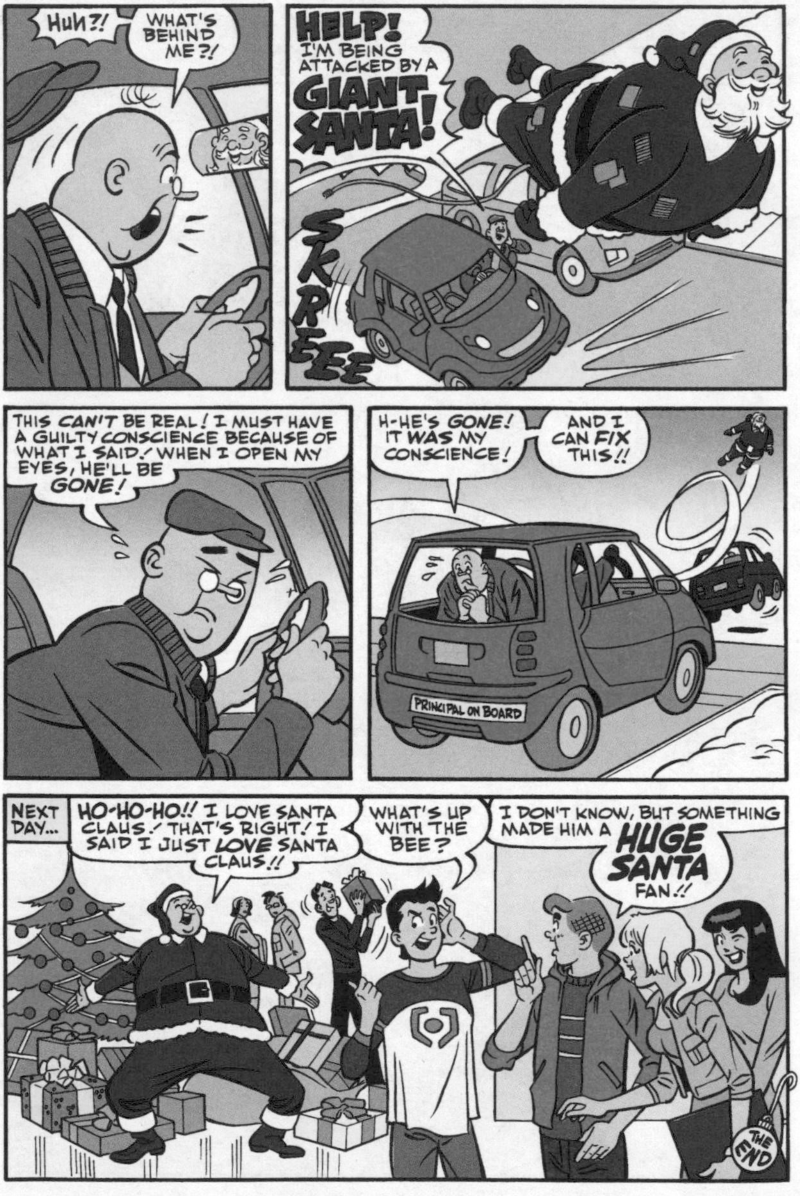
HUH?!
WHAT'S BEHIND ME?!
HELP! I'M BEING ATTACKED BY A GIANT SANTA!
SKREEEE
THIS CAN'T BE REAL! I MUST HAVE A GUILTY CONSCIENCE BECAUSE OF WHAT I SAID! WHEN I OPEN MY EYES, HE'LL BE GONE!
H-HE'S GONE! IT WAS MY CONSCIENCE!
AND I CAN FIX THIS!!
PRINCIPAL ON BOARD
NEXT DAY...
HO-HO-HO!! I LOVE SANTA CLAUS! THAT'S RIGHT! I SAID I JUST LOVE SANTA CLAUS!!
WHAT'S UP WITH THE BEE?
I DON'T KNOW, BUT SOMETHING MADE HIM A HUGE SANTA FAN!!
THE END